JUNIPER TREE BURNING

A Novel

A Novel

GOLDBERRY LONG

SIMON & SCHUSTER

NEW YORK   LONDON   TORONTO   SYDNEY   SINGAPORE

SIMON & SCHUSTER
Rockefeller Center
1230 Avenue of the Americas
New York, NY 10020

SIMON & SCHUSTER *and colophon are registered*
trademarks of Simon & Schuster, Inc.

Designed by Karolina Harris
Manufactured in the United States of America
1 3 5 7 9 10 8 6 4 2

Library of Congress Cataloging-in-Publication Data
Long, Goldberry M.
Juniper tree burning : a novel / Goldberry M. Long.
p. cm
1. *Brothers and sisters—Fiction.* 2. *Santa Fe (N.M.)—Fiction.* 3. *Seattle (Wash.)—Fiction.*
4. *Suicide victims—Fiction.* 5. *Hippies—Fiction.* I. *Title.*
PS3562.O49417 J86 2001
813'.6—dc21   00-054756
ISBN 0-7432-0203-1

Author's Note

Although it borrows its name from the University of New Mexico, the
school described in this book is entirely fictional. I am well aware that the
UNM Medical School boasts an innovative program that is superior to,
and bears no resemblance to, the program described in this book.

For Daniel Dee Long
And for Keja Love Beeson
And for Joe Dennis Long
And for Dennis Lee Long
And for Michaelle Ilona Balogh
And for my beloved
Sean Randolph Cutler.

My family. For them all.

CONTENTS

"I thought hard for us all—my only swerving—"

—William Stafford
"Traveling through the Dark"

". . . there is a might-have-been which is more true than truth, from which the dreamer, waking, says not, 'Did I but dream?' but rather says, indicts high heaven's very self with: 'Why did I wake since waking I shall never sleep again?' "

—William Faulkner
Absalom, Absalom!

PROLOGUE:
THE EDGE OF THE WORLD

I wasn't speaking to my brother, but he phoned anyway, hours before he went into the sea. I can couple this fact with what the Seattle policeman told me. The cop said Sunny called information and wrote my number on the wall of a bar. Beneath that, my brother scribbled *Juniper Tree Burning*, just to underline the point, to send it straight to me. The cop didn't say it, but I'm sure Sunny finished a drink, vodka probably, and that it was one of many. Because I know how it ended, I assume Sunny crossed the street and bought a ferry ticket and waited inside on a gray afternoon. Surely he ignored the tourists and commuters behind him, and surely he took a swig from that flask of his, and maybe he swallowed a handful of some sort of pill. He stood at the window.

Sunny Boy Blue is searching for something on the other side of the glass. He watches a man on the dock finish an apple and throw the core into the water. The gulls dive for it. The man watches them bicker and the strongest one triumph. Sunny watches the man watching. The workers dock another ferry, a touring boat painted red and white.

Sunny boards his own ferry. He stands at the front, on the lowest observation deck, and the cold wind is a tonic. Behind him, three college kids laugh and joke. One boy, the blond with a crewcut, lifts another by the collar, threatens to throw him overboard. Sunny laughs. They turn, for the first time acknowledging Sunny's presence. They like him right away; they can see he's cool, and something else, too, a Leo, or a backwards boy, in his shaggy black hair, his eyes that if they dared they'd call beautiful.

The crewcut offers a smoke, and Sunny accepts, and a friendship is easily woven out of their laughing struggles to ignite a lighter in the stiff wind of their passage. Finally, Sunny turns his back and opens his coat, and the college boy dips into this windbreak and lights four cigarettes. They smoke facing Seattle, with their backs to Bainbridge Island, their scalps and the napes of their necks freezing. They lift their collars and hunch their shoulders around their ears and no way in hell are they going inside with all the yuppies and the tourists. Sunny passes them his flask of vodka at waist level, hoping the captain, wherever he is, doesn't object, and it doesn't take long for them to get a little silly, for them to wonder if, like on the Space Needle, people really jump off the ferry. Someone says, "They should put up a net or something. A wall." The boys start jostling one another again, threatening to test out the waters with the smallest of them, and on that deck in the stiff wind, under the gray sky and before the gray island where ferns grow wild, suddenly the boy with the see-through green eyes flicks his cigarette into the water. He grins and climbs to the top rung of the railing. They are laughing, whooping. How they like their new friend! He is giving them a jaunty wave. And then, almost like falling, so that later they'll debate the point—and one of them, the boy who bent into the warm shelter of Sunny's open coat, will maintain all his life that it was an accident, a slip—Sunny is jumping. He is disappearing under the blunted prow of the ferry. He's gone.

And maybe Sunny leapt and maybe he fell. Perhaps he was reaching for help and the boys misunderstood, so they told the police Sunny waved, one last thing Sunny offered, mysterious, indecipherable. Such a simple question— Sunny's hand reaching for their own or Sunny waving—but the answer doesn't matter, because either way, he's gone, and all the answers in the world cannot undrown him.

I.

AUSPICIOUS BEGINNINGS

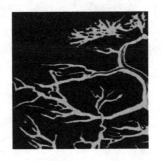

SUNNY'S WEDDING TOAST

New Year's Day, This Year, Santa Fe

BEFORE he kidnapped me from my own wedding reception, Sunny Boy Blue—that little prick, that darling Backwards Boy—he nearly skipped the Big Event altogether. He was scheduled for Christmas, but to the tune of my mother's tears, he missed his flight. Then he missed another, and it seemed that Russia was holding him back, like honey, or a fly trap. Alas, he pulled free with less than twenty-four hours to spare, time enough to wreak a little havoc, assassinate my New Year's Day, my birthday, my wedding day, all my big holidays clustered together, a gaggle of ducks waiting to be shot down by this drunken imposter flown in from Russia. By the reception dinner, I wished him dead.

Such a lovely scene, white linen tablecloths, candles, turkey and all the fixings. Any idiot with a camera knows it when he sees it: a bona fide Photo Opportunity. The Bride and Groom with their families, the Wedding Party, seven of them at the table. I, Jennie, the Bride, had no choice in this; one cannot have a Wedding Party Table without the Family of the Bride, after all. Self-educated in protocol though this Bride may be, she knows the names of things, the proper and orderly procession of ceremony and event. Her brother at her table is the price this Bride pays for normalcy.

I am the Bride and Chris is the Groom. The Happy Two, sitting like figurines at the table of honor. The room smells of the garlands of pine hung everywhere, from the vigas, around the doors, at the bases of candles on each table. Never mind her lumberjack shoulders and hulking seventy inches, this Bride, in her getup—elegant forties-era satin gown, red lipstick, hair in a French twist—she looks like a period piece. The Groom should be wearing a crisp uniform; he should be on his way to war. The photograph should be black-and-white. There should be officers making an arch of their swords, and the Happy Couple should pass beneath it. Or, at the very least, the Wedding Party should all be laughing, leaning over to exchange pleasantries, lit by candles. She has left disposable cameras on every table for the guests, and later she can study photographs of the Wedding Party Happiness in a Wedding Album.

Instead, before I could even take a bite of food, the Brother of the Bride pushed back his chair so hard it clattered to the floor. "Time for a toast," he shouted, raising the silver flask of vodka he'd been waving around since he got off the plane. The general murmur of conversation died down. People tittered nervously. What would the misbehaving brother come up with next? His curling black lashes hung low over his eyes. He looked not so much drunk as sleepy. "*Gorko! Gorko!*" he cried. "Which, for the uneducated, means Bitter! Bitter! Russians yell it at weddings to make the newlyweds kiss, to sweeten the wine. So everyone, all together now!" He didn't even wait for them; he tipped back that flask and took a long, thirsty gulp.

"*Gorko,*" the guests cried, out of embarrassment or pity or even good humor. "*Gorko!*"

Trapping me from behind, my brother wraps his arms around me, his chin on my shoulder, his cheek to mine, and I steel myself against the stink of his vodka breath, the cigarettes, the odd underlying whiff of gasoline on him, and I smile broadly. A flurry of flashes comes from the tables, and I smile, smile, smile.

At last I can pull away, and my brother catches my look. His eyes are pale green, so light they almost seem transparent. See-through eyes, I've always called them. These are my father's eyes. See, there's old Daddy, Father of the Bride, sitting at the table too, in a tux, for God's sake, a cummerbund holding in his round little belly, his wild hair pulled back, looking practically normal himself, his eyes so sad and lost they almost break me.

The Brother straightens. It seems his toast, if that's what it is, will go on. "Juniper boughs for Juniper's wedding," he says to the room, pointing his flask at the centerpiece. "In Russia, this is called *Troitsa.* Branches all over the houses, maidens' panties in the trees." He tells the guests all about Russians. He says that Russians eat lard like Americans eat peanut butter, on spoons, straight from the can. To roll a joint, they shake tobacco from a cigarette and use the paper; they'll even use a ruble. He's funny, charming, in the way loud, charismatic people are. The guests seem to be enjoying him; they laugh, listen, laugh again. The Mother of the Bride is beside herself with adoration. The new In-Laws, the Bravermans, sit straight and determinedly serene, eating with neat polite little bites.

Let him die, the Bride thinks, then takes it back, though God isn't listening anyway. God seems to have gone fishing, so the Bride prays to the God of Vodka, to the Minor Deities of Other Foreign Chemicals. Please, take him out of the picture for the night. Please, the Bride prays, I'll take drool, vomit, anything, just shut him up, silence him completely. She says, "What, exactly, is the point here?"

"The point!" the Brother announces to the room. "Juniper wants a point!" He leans over her shoulder and breathes his smoky vodka breath into her face. "Am I getting on your nerves? Am I pissing you off?"

She looks into his see-through eyes. She tells him no.

His nose touches hers. He whispers, "Liar, liar, Juniper Tree on Fire." He straightened. "The point," he said, raising his flask again. "To Juniper Tree Burning, the lovely bride!" I stared down at the boots he wore with his tuxedo, heavy black combat-issue storm troopers. He leaned around me and pointed the flask at Chris. "To her brave groom, Mr. Braverman."

"I'll drink to my bride," Chris said, raising his glass. "To the lovely Mrs. Braverman." He was smiling, playing along with the joke, only his eyes in my direction were checking on me, saying, *I'm on your side, Cinderella.*

Then Sunny looked straight at my groom. When he spoke, his voice was cold, sober, hateful. He said, "Here's hoping she doesn't leave you like she leaves everyone else."

For a beat, a second split down its middle like an atom, the room was still. Then my new husband, Mr. Prince Charming, smiled and said to the room, "Too late. She's already left me several times. She leaves me every day for work. Let's drink to her always coming back." And the crowd, relieved, laughed and drank and went back to their food, and my brother righted his chair and sat down.

S o this is what I remember of the last time I saw Sunny: his eyes, his boots. His breath. Over and over again, his voice, loud, slurred, crying, whispering, hissing: "Juniper!" As if that name were the only word he spoke. How did you sleep? Juniper! Are you hungry? Juniper Tree Burning! I think of the two days, New Year's Eve and New Year's Day, like two sides of a coin with a hole through the middle, and out of it comes pale green eyes and heavy black boots and rank vodka breath, and out of that hole Sunny Boy Blue taunts me with the name he knew I hated. I remember these various snatches of him, and I remember the fact that he kidnapped me from my own wedding reception, and I would rip out his heart if he weren't already dead. So he stole from me even the role of injured party. Once you know the guy has kicked the bucket, it's all a petty crime, isn't it? He's the winner after all, in his delightful game of Get the Bride.

The Bride, meaning me, this Ugly Chick all gussied up in the fancy dress. Nothing extraordinary about her at all, this Bride; she's commonplace, ordinary, in fact, the I-do, the Yes, the Kiss. Line her up with fifty others, their trains fanned out on the altar steps, the half-wistful, romantic gaze the photographer instructs them to hold. She's not the Bride; she's the bride. I had been waiting all my life to step into her outlines.

I have always known my rightful place in the world, which was not in New Mexico, not with my parents in a mud house without running water, and most of all, not with a name like Juniper Tree Burning. I was not meant to live like that. Even a kid knows when she's in the wrong place.

I wanted to be the bride. I wanted to fall backwards into the comfort of normalcy, like a child in the wilderness who nestles into the the snow and sleeps. I don't understand those people who want to be outside the universe of the ordinary. I was the bride, and this was enough for me. It was not snow, but a featherbed, gloriously warm and safe: it was rest.

But Sunny would not allow me to rest. He kept pulling me back into the wilderness, calling me Juniper, trying to make me be what I am not.

T H E bride and the groom stand with a knife between their palms and slice into the cake. They hook their elbows and feed each other a bite, another Wedding Album opportunity. "Juniper," calls the brother, "smash it in his face!"

The bride glares at him. A flashbulb explodes. The crowd sets off a strobe of flashes, catching not the couple's kiss but their faces, the bride's angry, the groom's startled, cake still on their fingers. Here, in the Wedding Album, it will say, *Another Moment Stolen by the Brother of the Bride*.

"I know a joke," my brother said, raising a champagne bottle. "How does it start?" The people clotted around him raised their champagne glasses, obedient sheep, and waited for the next commotion. "Let's see," he said. "In the last thirteen years, my sister—what is her name now? Oh, yes. Jennifer Braverman. It's hard to keep track, isn't it?" He lit a cigarette and used his cake plate for an ashtray. "Anyway, I've seen my sister, Jennifer Braverman, five times since I was six years old." He held up his fist and unfolded it for them, middle finger first: "When she first went off to college, at the Taos Inn, for both our high school graduations, and now. Five times. And that time at the Taos Inn doesn't really count, since she sent me away." His hand, fingers splayed, out like a traffic cop stopping a wayward motorist. He sucked hard on his cigarette. "Isn't that right, Juniper?"

"More than that," I said. I held myself at a distance—watching this woman, this bride, suck cake off the tip of her finger. She is happy. See, in the Wedding Album, you'll be able to tell: she's happy. Even as I spoke, the guests busily flashed away, recording proof of said happiness.

"Trust me," Sunny said, and took in another ravenous lungful of smoke. "It's five. Isn't this funny? I knew you wouldn't believe me." In the dim reception hall, so artfully candlelit, the cigarette glowed and faded. "So the joke goes like this: my big sister works in Taos for the summer, and I'm twelve, living in Santa Fe. All summer long, she promises to visit me but never shows up. Must be truly busy or something. So one day—I'm thirteen years old—I get up early and ride my bike seventy-nine miles, all the way from Santa Fe to Taos. Española, the canyon. Shit, you know that hill coming out of the canyon? It's August, and hot as hell. Thought I'd die. So I ride all the way to Taos, and I go straight to where she's working at the Taos Inn, and I'm standing in the lobby, thinking she'll be so impressed, so happy to see her baby brother." His cigarette glowing, fading, marking the progress of his story, his audience waiting for the happy ending. He continued on the exhale, smoke with his words: "But the joke's on me, because my sister—God bless her, always looking out for my best interests—she tells me, 'Go home.' That's the punch line, folks: go home."

My brother drank from the bottle, and when he slammed it on the table, foam rose over its lip and slid down its neck. Everyone followed his lead, draining their glasses as anyone should at the end of a toast, but their eyes were troubled, as if these were not drinks they offered but needed.

Sunny started away, finished with us, I hoped, but then he turned, slapping his head as if he'd forgotten the punch line. There were guests passing between us. He looked around them and over them and through them, and locked his see-through green eyes on me.

I thought, Now, isn't this downright exciting. Just exactly what else will he do for revenge? Beside me, Chris took my hand and squeezed it, to anchor me, or maybe to hold me back. I'm here, his fingers said, fondling my ring, stroking my palm. Right here.

"Five times," my brother said. He spouted some Russian, and then he said, "Ain't life a cocksucking bitch."

Chris, my groom, my gallant prince, whispered, his lips moving against my ear, "Right now, I'm saying exactly what you need to hear, and now you can laugh and show him he isn't winning." I smiled as if he had done his job, but I thought, Is there nothing else you can do to help me? What kind of Prince Charming are you? Over Chris's shoulder, my brother smiled back at me. I see you, his eyes said. I see right through you.

Every time I remember the way he ruined it all, meaning everything that mattered to me, I find myself sucked into the scene as if it were unfolding again, as if this time I can change its inevitable conclusion. But this is history, Jennie my dear, and so it will happen the same way every time. Even you cannot revise it. Even God.

THE BACKWARDS BOY

August 18, 1976, Arroyo al Fin, New Mexico
IN the early morning, her breath close against Jennie's cheek, Faith whispers, "Juniper. My water broke. He's coming. Get up."

Jennie doesn't want to move. Her feet love their pocket of warm air, and she's dreaming about the cottonwood hung with two hundred pots and pans. A fairy godmother brought them for the King. "It's the King of the World," she mumbles.

Faith shakes her. "My water's broken."

Jennie, floating between dreaming and waking, thinks she hears the sound of glass breaking. She wonders, how can water break? And who's coming?

JENNIE finds Faith in the kitchen, drinking tea. Faith is so hugely pregnant that only two outfits still fit, a blue-flowered dress and a pink bikini. She's wearing the bikini, and her belly has a dark line down its middle and jagged red lines on the sides. She doesn't look like a real person.

Everything seems strange, like a dream. A fine golden powder dusts the floor, and Jennie knows by its smell that it's goldenseal. Light shines through the plants in windows, like an enchanted forest. Outside in the driveway, Jennie can see the piano, a Steinway, big and black. This is the piano Faith's father sent, an inheritance. The movers left it in the driveway because it wouldn't fit through the door, and Faith put a blanket over it, as if it could get cold in the night. It feels like a million years since the piano came, but a million years is only the day before yesterday. Jennie is still trying to believe she has a mother who plays piano. That the house is cracking open. That last night, her father said terrible words to her mother.

"There's glass on the floor," Faith says.

"What happened to the goldenseal?" she asks.

"It broke," Faith says, like that's all there is to it. No cleaning up, no reason. Like it marched off the shelf and broke itself. Everything feels strange, like broken water, like dreams of kitchens growing on trees.

But also, Jennie feels ordinary, as if the world has always been this way: the pearly morning light, the haze of stove smoke, the piano outside, her mother's fingers around a cup. Maybe her mother has always been this big. Too big for Jennie to hug, always this belly between them.

Faith says, "This is how it is. I'm in labor, and your father left again."

Jennie rubs her head and feels the stubbly mess, and remembers all over again that she chopped her hair because she didn't want to give the baby *piojos*, which is Spanish for lice. She wishes for her father and it hurts her heart. She forgot to tell him this new Spanish word, *piojos*. They're supposed to be learning Spanish together.

"It's a shame it's so short. But hair grows," Faith says. "It was the right thing to do. And just in time. Today you'll stay home and watch Sunny Boy Blue come out."

"I need to go to school. We're starting division of decimals. I can't miss division. And we're learning about the Aztecs."

"You stay." Lines appear on Faith's forehead.

Jennie says, "Don't name him Sunny, Mom."

"Be quiet," Faith whispers. She closes her eyes and holds her cup tight. She breathes long and deep and says softly, "Ow. God." Finally, she opens her eyes. "Sunny Boy Blue. Stop bugging me about it."

"People will make fun of him," Jennie says.

"He'll be a Leo. He'll be a lion. A leader of men. Leos are supposed to love Aquariuses. It's God's Will, and you can't change it." Faith has been saying for days now that Clarence dreamed his name would be Sunny Boy Blue. But Jennie has also dreamed of the baby, and in her dreams, his name is different; his name is Paul, which was her grandfather's name. Why should Clarence decide the baby's name? He's not even a part of the family. Why does he get to call his dream prophecy? Why should his prophecy be the true one?

"You should know about soft spots," Faith says absently. "You should know about scarlet fever." She says that Jennie could poke her finger right into the soft spot on the top of a baby's head. She says Jennie can't kiss the baby on the lips or he'll get one of these diseases. "You get exposed to all kinds of sickness down there at school, Juniper Tree Burning."

Jennie hides behind her face. It's a good trick to have. You turn your face into a mask and then you are safe behind it, especially when your mother calls you a stupid name which is not yours and which you hate.

Faith says, "This time, I think Ray left for good." She sounds happy about it. She says, "I bet he never comes back. He's probably off screwing that Mary woman. It doesn't matter. I hope he stays away." She starts telling the same old story of Ray kidnapping her and all the signs. How she loved Clarence from the first time she met him. How Jennie doesn't know what it's like to love your husband's best friend. All the same old boring details.

Jennie doesn't really listen. She watches the baby move inside Faith's belly. A tiny foot or hand passes like a fish just beneath the skin. She sends him a message in her head: *Come out, little brother. I'll take care of you. Come out, come out.* She feels like she'll burst from waiting. Jennie says, "You should name the baby after Grandpa."

"No."

"Why not? He sent you that piano."

"Because."

"Because isn't an answer."

Faith's eyes are mean now. They say, *Don't push me. You know what happens when you push me.* Jennie thinks, Not anymore. Daddy's not here to spank me anymore. Sometimes her mother is the wicked witch. Jennie, feeding the fire, thinks about Hansel and Gretel. How they just wanted something sweet, and then the witch tried to eat them. Their mother said to their father, "Take them into the forest, and bring me back their hearts." Or was it Snow White's stepmother who said that? The kids are always sent into the forest in fairy tales. Their hearts are always proof that they're dead. But the kind woodsman is always too kind. He always kills a wolf and brings back its heart instead. And the kids always find someone in the woods who shows them the way. When her brother comes, Jennie will show him the way. They won't need woodsmen or anyone else.

Faith, staring out the window, says, "My father inherited that piano from his mother, and he gave it to my mother for a wedding present. Then my mother died of a cold, and he made me play it every day. When he didn't like my playing, he slammed the lid on my fingers."

"People don't die of colds."

"My mother did."

"You should have named me Lipa." This is her grandmother's name.

"You told us your name was Juniper."

"No I didn't. Babies don't talk."

Faith says, "You think you know so much? I was there, remember?" She goes outside to play the piano. Jennie wonders if the baby will come out right there at the piano, so that the first thing he hears is music. It seems to her it would be a good thing. But then Faith comes back, holding her belly, panting. "Go get Joy," she says. "Go now. Hurry." And Jennie runs to tell Joy that he's coming.

• • •

FAITH labors through the day and into night. Late, late in the night, in the upstairs bedroom lit only by candles, Joy kneels in front of Jennie and says, "You just sit here and watch, Juniper. Just watch and learn about being a woman."

Jennie digs her fingernails into her palms and tries to shut out the sound of Faith walking the room, the floor creaking and her soft moans. The midwife, Cassie, says, "Do you know?" all the time. She tells Faith, "Walking helps, do you know, with the pain."

Faith nods. She stops and gasps. Cassie says, "Ride it, Faith. Ride it up, and ride it down."

Jennie thinks of wild horses. Bucking broncos. Yesterday and her father giving her a ride on that Mary woman's horse, and the horse bucked them off. *Ride him*, her father said. *I'll take care of you.* The cuts on her wrists throb, and it hurts to use her hands.

The candles flicker, as if her mother's moans send winds across the room. Jennie pulls her knees to her chest. Faith lies down. On the potbellied stove, diapers boil. Cassie plasters the steaming white muslin over Faith's belly. It's hard to breathe in air so crowded with heat from the fire and the candles and four people.

Where is Jennie's father? She'd like to be with him, riding on the motorcycle with the wind so loud she can't open her eyes to see or her mouth to speak or her ears to hear. That's where her father must be. But Ray left again without saying good-bye.

Faith says, "I'm tired." She sits up, and the diapers fall off. "I have to go. I can't do this. I need to just . . . I need my piano. I need some music."

The women push Faith back and make her drink Medicine Tea. Joy dips her fingers in oil, so they're glistening, slick, and she spreads Faith's legs, and Jennie sees her mother's *down there*, her hairy, ugly, red and terrible *down there*, which she never wanted to see, not ever. Joy slips her fingers in, spreading the oil, which she says will help the baby come out.

Jennie closes her eyes because what she really wants to know is division of decimals. She knows all the easy things, the simplicity of twelve times nine, and in 1492 Columbus sailed the ocean blue, and even what "thespian" means, but what if division is trickier and she can't get it right? What if there's a quiz on the Aztecs? Twelve times eight is ninety-six.

There's blood on the sheets. Jennie feels dreamy. This isn't my mom, she wants to say. "Mom?"

Faith screams. Joy and Cassie cheer, "Good girl! That's it!"

Jennie watches (and watches like she hasn't watched anything ever before, with all of her everything, her brain her eyes her lashes her cheeks her bare

toes in the hot, hot room) the candle flame, its dance. But she can't help looking past the flame to the wrought-iron bed painted bright blue, her mother's
fist clinging to handfuls of sheet.

Joy says, "It's crowning!" and then, with terrible fear in her voice, she says,
"He's breech." They push aside diapers and oils and candles, turn on the electric lights, and Jennie can tell it's bad.

Joy kneels in front of Jennie. Jennie hates Joy, who smells like she never
washes her crotch. Plus, she has frizzy hair and too many splotchy freckles.
She is not beautiful. But when Joy touches Jennie's chopped-off hair in a gentle, sad way, Jennie almost cries. Joy says, "This is very important. We need to
stay with your mom, so you have to go down to Flaco's and call an ambulance." Joy presses a dime and a piece of paper in her hand. "Here's the number. Tell them to hurry. Tell them the baby is breech."

"Breech?"

"It's backwards. Now go. Run."

Jennie stumbles through the dark, running fast and faster, running down
the hill, running harder, the dime tight in her fist, so small, so easily lost—
running, her heart burning, on fire in her throat.

Her mother's legs were wide open and Jennie could see everything *down
there*, the blood and the hair and the way her mom was hurting, the oiled fingers sticking in and the candles, the soft light, the women whispering and her
mother moaning.

On the phone, the man says, "Tell me where you live."

Jennie begins to cry. She says, "Far away." She remembers that word,
Breech. She hears Joy's soft, urgent voice. She tries to imagine a backwards
baby; maybe the head on backwards. The sky is prickly with stars; Jennie looks
up and searches for God until she feels dizzy. She thinks of how the planet is
going so fast she can't feel it. How Columbus discovered the curve of the
earth and the way you could sail around its belly, the way Jennie has tried for
nine months to get her arms around her mother.

At last, Jennie manages to get out some kind of instructions, and she runs
back, uphill now and slower, and then suddenly, a stillness inside her as her
body finds a loping, easy rhythm, and she's running over the belly of the world
like an ant. She prays aloud, "Please, please, Heavenly Father God, please pay
attention to my mom, make her okay, not breeched," running, the sound of
her feet like an echo of her prayer, "and thank you for my baby brother, but
don't let him be backwards, Heavenly Father God"—she turns to search for
flashing lights sliding out of the darkness, curving down the highway into the
valley, but there's nothing, only the night and stars—"please God."

She runs all the way to the driveway, and when she gets there, she can't breathe, and she drops to her hands and knees and lifts her eyes toward the Milky Way, and she feels it then. The terrible turning, always there, like a giant hand moving a giant top, and she is spinning around slower and slower until one day she will fall on her side and spin off into space.

"Amen," she whispers.

When she can breathe again, she takes hold of the piano, cool and smooth and solid as God, and pulls herself standing. In the upstairs windows, the women hurry back and forth. Outside, everything is quiet summer. The river rushes down the center of the valley. Crickets and the sound of water on smooth rocks. When the ambulance comes, will it crash into the lovely piano? If she could just this one moment open it up and play something beautiful, would it make her mother feel better? When she exposes the keys, they gleam white as teeth. She doesn't dare crack the silence.

And then Faith screams. A horrible belly scream, as if blood might come out of her mouth along with the noise. Jennie runs into the house, rushes the stairs.

Joy says, "Are they coming?"

Jennie nods, but she doesn't look at Joy. For she has caught sight of Faith on the bed, her legs spread, and in the center of them a hole, like a tunnel on which Cassie has trained the lights. Down at the end of the tunnel, deep inside her mother's bloody self, Jennie sees a tiny bottom and a tiny penis, her baby brother, trapped. Jennie can only whimper, like an animal caught, and finally they send her downstairs, but even there she hears her mother calling, "Help me," calling, "Clarence? Ray?"

Jennie stands beside the stove and puts her fingers in her ears. "He's a Leo. A Leo a Leo a Leo a Leo a Leo." She listens for God to tell her how the earth turns and what it means to be breech, how water can break, how to make the music come from the piano as easy as praying, as easy as water moving over glass, over rocks, over the seaweed and the sand.

$\mathscr{B}$ROKEN WATER

New Year's Day, This Year, Santa Fe

I, too, know a joke. It also begins at my wedding reception. The lead-in takes a while, but the punch line's a doozy. There's this bride, see? She's outside on the portico with the groom, with a bottle of whiskey and several of their medical student classmates, not exactly friends, because what with courtship and schoolwork, the bride and groom have made only passing acquaintance with their classmates, invited as filler friends to swell the ranks of celebrants. The bride, especially, isn't one for friends. She has a bridesmaid out here with her, but this bridesmaid is decoration, the salt shaker for her brother's pepper, present only to make a balanced picture in the Wedding Album. Let's call her crass, or even coldhearted, this bride, arranging people like table ornaments.

The bride, shivering, splashes whiskey into everyone's plastic champagne glasses. They raise them, throw back their heads, toss down the shots. She pours again, and again they silently toast and drink with a stolid scholarly determination they can't seem to lose, poor bookish souls. She pours a third round, and they drink once more.

It has begun to snow, plump, feathery flakes. Luminarias line the long driveway, and the candlelit bags glow goldenly against the falling snow. The bride wipes her mouth, takes the bottle by the neck. "I'm going inside," she says.

"Don't you leave me," the groom says, throwing his arm over her shoulders, laughing. "You won't leave me, will you?"

They are all blinded by the explosion of a camera flash, set off by the mother of the bride. "What are you doing out here? It's freezing!" she says, floating in the bright dots of afterimage. Duck, thinks the bride, because with her mother are the brother and the father.

"This is my wife, the wildebeest," the groom says. He grins at her fondly. "A very careful operation, keeping her around."

"I'll say," one of the students calls.

"I don't think weddings are for joking like that," the mother says.

"Like you'd know about weddings," says the bride, trapped in the groom's embrace, shocked by her desperation to get out from under his arm.

"If you keep too far away, she escapes," the groom says. He looks at her, and the force of his feelings is in his eyes. His voice drops. "If you get her mad, she'll rip out your heart." He sounds as if he is praising her beauty. "And then she leaves. It's a delicate line to walk, not too far, not too close. But I'm up for the challenge."

My father said, "Guess what I saw on TV: animal sex flicks. Rhinoceroses fucking! On TV! Rhinoceroses or rhinoceri?"

"Watch it, Pops," Sunny said. "No F-words in front of Juniper's husband. Mr. Braverman here drives a *Rolls-Royce*, remember?"

"It's used," Chris said. In his way of sliding easily into the dance steps of the moment, he said, "And a fucking piece of shit."

"Rhinos," my father said. "They charge you, you're fucked. They just keep going, especially in rutting season. Nothing like a horny rhino. *Rhinoceros unicornis*. You get a wish if you see one."

"Yes, that's my bride," Chris said. And I, the bride, trapped under his arm, wondered, Just what is my groom trying to accomplish with all this babbling? "An animal worth risking your life for," he said.

"That's not the point at all," said the brother of the bride, batting his lids against the snowflakes caught in his thick lashes. He wore a Russian cap with a red star on its bill. He tilted back his flask and drank heartily, smacked his lips, stomped his combat boots, gave a shiver and a hoot. He eyed the groom with malicious intent. Taking aim. "Here's something I've been wondering: Isn't Braverman a Jewish name? Christian Braverman? Isn't that an oxymoron?"

Chris explained how his grandfather, who was Jewish, converted to Episcopalian and changed his first name to honor the occasion. Explaining, this groom sounded so reasonable, so placid. So pathetic, a voice in me whispered. Shut yer yap, I told it, but it insisted: *pathetic*.

"I get it," Sunny said. "Like my sister here."

"Stop it," I said. "Will you stop it?"

"Of course, with her, you have to ask, just what did she convert to?"

"To herself," Chris answered.

"Just shut. The fuck. Up," I said.

My mother, predictable as ever, said, "You aren't fighting with Sunny, are you?" she says. "It's your *wedding*."

"She isn't fighting," Chris said. "I've seen her fighting. This is Jennie being nice." His arm over my shoulders like a log, a deadweight. Panic surged through me, punctuated by a flash from my mother's camera. "Give me that thing," I said, and taking the whiskey bottle too, I made my two-fisted retreat, my heart racing as if I'd narrowly escaped danger. This is the joke, but now the punch line eludes me.

· · ·

A lot of people thought we jumped the gun by getting married so fast. Apparently, a wedding was proof I was a weakling, in need of a man to establish identity: "Do you really need a husband? Isn't that sort of a crutch?" And my mother asked, "Are you pregnant?" As if I were some other, imaginary daughter, the stupid one. Even Chris's mother said, quite genteelly, "You have all the time in the world."

Well, I wasn't pregnant, and I wasn't weak. So what was she thinking, this bride? I married Christian Braverman on the first day of the year, only four months after we met. New Year's Day also happens to be my birthday, the worst of 365 possibilities, in my informed opinion. People have spent New Year's Eve making reckless promises and kissing with champagne-soaked tongues, hoping this time they'll get it right. Now their heads pound and their stomachs ache. Stunned, they watch bad parades and football games, reality sitting like a fat man on their shoulders. Life marches on. Relentlessly. They have overspent, overeaten, overindulged, and now the holidays are finished and they'll keep their resolutions for maybe forty-eight hours or at best six weeks. January means winter without Christmas lights, the grind of cold with more cold still to come, and any day now, those credit card bills are due. New Year's Day is the International Day of Regrets and Despair. Oh, yes, and, by the way, happy birthday, Jennie Girl.

Well, I don't believe in the cards, or stars, or any other accident of birth. I believe in Taking Matters Into My Own Hands. My clever plan was this: I would transform My Birthday into My Wedding Day, and then My Anniversary. Never mind football, tortilla chips and bean dips, and has-been actors giving the lowdown on high school bands. January First would be a day of champagne toasts, of fragrant roses and a bouquet toss.

At first Chris resisted; he hates a big fuss. "Why not elope?" he asked. "We'll just get a bunch of toasters we don't want."

I got angry, like I can, and left for a long, sweaty run, like I do. When I got back, aching in my throat, either furious or near tears or both, I tried to explain. I told him, "I want a wedding day, a wedding album with all the stupid poses, with our hands on the cake knife, and our kids can look at it someday and say, *Look how happy they were.*" He pushed back my sweaty hair and kissed my forehead. "I want the toasters," I whispered.

He smiled. "Okay," he said. "All right. For you, toasters." As soon as he said it, that petty madwoman in me hissed, *Look at him, giving in.*

And wasn't it a silly, shameful fantasy after all? Maybe, but there I was, the betrothed, folding programs, tying ribbons, choosing tuxedos for my groom, my father, my brother. I picked the church, the food. My wedding gown, vintage satin, plain, classic, perfect. To make it even more so, I lined every seam with pearls, and as I beaded, my mind spread into a white, shimmering calm, the world reduced to one pearl at a time. I imagined my own daughter, looking at pictures of me in the dress. After January first, I'd have an album to pass on to her, and she'd grow up knowing her true place in the world.

This is what my brother stole from me. When I look at my wedding pictures, anger, my familiar friend, my birthday companion, is there as usual. Which is why I say that if my marriage is to fail, then the failure began here, on my birthday, on the International Day of Regrets and Despair.

Now I remember my punch line. It goes like this: I am my father's daughter, and my father is the King of Leaving. So, almost nine months after this fiasco of a wedding, less than the time it takes to gestate a baby or finish a school year, this bride, this Jennie—on a lark, a whim—will leave the new husband behind of her very own volition.

Not funny enough for you? Try this. I'll bet you ten bucks that no one, not even Sunny Boy Blue, would have predicted that when she leaves her husband, the bride will kidnap a girl nobody knows, little Sarah Alberhasky, and take her along for the ride. But I'm getting ahead of myself, an annoying habit. Chronology is not my strong suit.

CLUTCHING my whiskey and the camera, I squeezed through the crowded, hot reception hall, through smoke and sweat and bodies to a hallway where things were quieter, with only one girl leaning against the wall. I was no longer the bride; I was Jennie, plain and simple, Jennifer Davis, now Jennifer Braverman, furious, shaking.

The girl said, "There's a line and I'm it. Isn't this a good party? Although of course if you have to pee more than me, you can go ahead, since you're the guest of honor and everything, although I do have to pee pretty bad." The girl had amazing red hair ponytailed atop her head. She wore a pale blue dress of gossamer silk fluttering from skinny shoulder straps. The hollows of her flanks brought to mind kids in bathing suits, their sinuous, gangly grace. She was the sort of girl men want to lure into their laps, the kind who lures out the mother in me.

I said, "Jesus Christ, aren't you cold?"

Hers were large, beautiful eyes, an odd golden brown. The color of whiskey. Her brows arched high, and the wide space around her eyes made her seem slightly surprised, but also queenly, clear-eyed, grave. She said, "Crazy, aren't I? But damn, I look gorgeous, so it's worth it, right?"

She was tiny; I loomed over her. The three whiskey shots I'd just swallowed came on like a swoon, and I slumped against the wall. "I wonder what idiot let these freaks have a party."

"Like that's convincing," the red-haired girl said, grinning up at me. "If you want to go incognito, you'll have to ditch the dress first. Cool dress, by the way. It's old, right? So what's it like to be a bride?"

"Antique, not old. What are you, five feet tall?"

"Five-four, thank you very much. God, don't shrink me!" An enormous black leather bag hung over her shoulder, like a feed sack on a dragonfly.

I aimed my mother's camera at the girl. Her hair was thick, heavy, glossy-straight, an Irish setter's color, a thousand shades of gold-stained red. I considered my own hair. I thought, This here is not an equal distribution of resources. I took the picture. In my Wedding Album, I'd be upstaged by a stranger: *The Beautiful Guest.* "Damn," I said. "You have nice hair."

"I know. Isn't it awful? Hey, are you drunk? Because I am, not that I'm complaining. In case you're wondering, your mother invited me. She sells at our gallery, SARAH'S? On the plaza? Which is my name, Sarah Alberhasky, and the gallery is named for me, in case you can't tell. God I have to pee. My boyfriend, Jake? He said if I hold my pee, I'll be wearing diapers when I'm sixty, but it just seems like I have to go all the time; I'm always standing in line somewhere, waiting for the toilet? It makes life seem very interrupted, if you know what I mean; I always miss the best parts of movies, for instance, and even in the middle of sex, I have to go. Jake says it's the little girl in me, and I don't know what it is, maybe something's messed up with my organs, but even when I got raped, I remember thinking, God, I have to pee so bad."

I took a swig from my whiskey bottle and wiped my mouth with the back of my hand. "The fucker. He should be castrated."

"Well, yeah, if they could find the guy." Sarah searched through her enormous black bag. She found a cigarette and lit it, shaking her head as she exhaled. Her fingers were slender, fine-boned. Delicate, graceful hands. "Don't go all sympathetic or anything," she said. "I'm over it. In therapy they told me it was something that happened, and I can talk about it just like anything else because it's not a sccrct. So I do." She glared at the bathroom door. "Fuck. Bang on that for me, will you. Because some of us have to PEE!"

From within a woman yelled, "In a minute already! Jesus Christ."

"Jesus my ass," Sarah muttered. "I'll be an old woman in diapers if that bitch doesn't hurry." She dropped her cigarette on the tile floor and stepped on it. "Oh my God. I can't believe I just did that," she said. "It was a fresh cigarette, too." We laughed, a giddy, drunken hilarity that fed on itself. We nursed our laughter long past the joke because it felt so good, and it was only natural to go into the bathroom together, to lean against the wall and watch her pee and listen to her babble on about her weight-lifter boyfriend, Jake, who once told her, "You're beautiful." She said, "No I'm not." So he threw her over his shoulder like a sack of laundry and carried her to the mirror. He stood behind her and sandwiched her cheeks between his palms and made her say, "I am beautiful."

"I swear to God," Sarah said, lighting a cigarette. "One time he bench-pressed me." Over the tip of her cigarette, she eyed me. She blew smoke out of the corner of her mouth. "Want to hear my rape story?"

Here is the bride, sitting on a toilet with her finery drawn up to her waist, struck dumb.

"Don't be shy," Sarah said. "It's therapy for me."

It seems there was this shoe sale at Winrock Center, in Albuquerque. Sarah bought three pairs on impulse — "Even though I'm not bad that way, but I like a nice pair of shoes; is it so bad to care how I look?" — said Sarah in the bathroom with me, her arms crossed under her breasts, smoking, and those shoes were kid, so soft she even held them to her cheek, and one pair was pale ivory and one was pale blue and one pale yellow. She walked to her car with her three new pairs of shoes — "The weirdest thing: in therapy what I cried about was those shoes" — and she was thinking how she was going to wear this pair with that outfit, and the next thing she knows this man has his arm around her and there's a gun at her head and he's saying, "Get in the car."

Sarah ran water and extinguished her cigarette in the sink. She lit another. "Anyway," she said, as if she'd lost her place. "Okay. He goes, 'Get in the car,' and I start laughing. It sounded so stupid. I think he watched some movie, because everything he said sounded written, you know, like it was from a script."

I said, "Maybe he was a Method actor."

Sarah didn't laugh or even blink. Her face fell into a flat mask. In that fleeting moment of dead air, I thought of all the easily conceivable reasons why I should have known better than to say such a foolish thing to this tiny red-haired girl who had been raped. I had given myself away, an obviously graceless person in the presence of grace. I can fake it for a while, but ultimately, I always regret not the first thing I say, but the second, or the third.

Through the walls and down the hall, the music played. It was my wedding out there. People swilled booze; they danced. The moment passed. Sarah drew a lungful of smoke, exhaled, continued.

"'Get in the car,' he goes, and then you know what I say? I say, 'Why?' Isn't that the dumbest thing? Then he slams me up against the car and I guess that's when I dropped the shoes. I didn't notice. I didn't notice until he dumped me at this Texaco, and I was walking home and that's when I realized I didn't know what happened to the shoes. I never saw those shoes again. Am

I grossing you out? Boring you? I can stop. My feelings won't be hurt. Jake says I'm like a little girl. All you have to do is distract me."

"You are not boring me," I said.

"Okay. So. Back at Winrock. I get out my keys and we get in the car, him first, and he pulls me in and he goes, 'Drive.'

"'Drive?' I say. 'Where?'

"'Drive,' he says. I remember, his breath smelled like toothpaste, and his face was just shaved. He was wearing Aramis. I think he got all fixed up. I picture him in some kind of yucky hotel, you know, on Central, with a cracked mirror and a faucet that leaks, and he's brushing his teeth, slapping on that Aramis and looking in the mirror, thinking, Tonight I'll find some chick at the mall and fuck her up the ass. Make her bleed. Sorry. My therapist says being open doesn't mean I have to shock people. Anyway, I have this idea someday I'll smell some Aramis and there he'll be."

Someone was pounding on the bathroom door. "Open up in there!" my brother shouted. "I know you're in there!"

Sarah flung it open. There stood Sunny. Hands on the door frame, he leaned in, leering at Sarah. "And who is this little friend?"

She gazed back, unreadable. Then she smiled at him. "You have nice eyes."

"And you have some pretty fucking gorgeous hair."

"I know. It's my heritage," Sarah said. "Genetics."

Behind Sunny, a hulking, handsome man laughed. This, by my guess, was the weight lifter. He said, "If I got a dollar for every time I heard that." He gave Sunny a little push to the side, and he took Sarah's hand. "What have I told you about flirting with strangers?" he said, guiding her out of the bathroom.

"Brother," Sarah said, rolling her eyes. "Tio Juanito here. Good-bye, strangers!"

"You'll need this," Sunny said. He gave her a scrap of paper.

Sarah glanced at it. "What is it, your phone number?"

Sunny leered at her. "It falls on you to explain to the groom that the bride is with me," he said. "Her brother."

Jake the Weight Lifter glared, and for a moment I thought there'd be a ruckus. But Jake only said, "Off to the dance floor, little girl," and tossed Sarah, shrieking and laughing, over his shoulder, and then they were gone.

Aside from the boots, Sunny was handsome in his tuxedo, but his pupils were huge, black circles rimmed with green. What kind of drugs dilated them like that? "I have a present for you," he said. "Come and get it."

For whatever reason, I followed him outside. Which makes it my fault. I

"You prick," I said. "You arrogant, hateful prick."

"Sticks and stones," he said. "Don't forget I'm the brother of the bride. I have connections."

"You're not my brother."

"Yes I am," he said. "It's me, your brother. Remember?" He opened his silver flask and offered it to me. "Vodka?" he said.

"Unbelievable. You're no better than a rapist. This is what rapists do."

"Incest! Not my cup of vodka, Cleopatra." And the bride, she has no scathing reply, and she doesn't find an escape. Helpless, she bristles in her corner, ridiculously crinolined, petticoated, like a large, recalcitrant flower.

We finished the drive in silence. I closed my eyes and pressed my forehead to the window, and I thought, Happy birthday, baby, happy New Year's Day, happy Fourth of July and happy all the rest of the goddamn holidays too. Happy anniversary, baby. If my father had come along, he'd probably be singing that song by now. *I've got you on my mi-ind.*

didn't heed the signs; I went under my own power and climbed right into the trap—the joke, after all, was on me.

I got into my father's Chevy, another in a long line of battered trucks owned by Ray. He'd driven it all the way from Florida, and it smelled like pot and the mushy disarray of impulse, of coffee and of motor oil, and it was filled with the debris of his life, paper cups and unopened mail marked URGENT and FINAL NOTICE, humps of clay painted lipstick-red and pink, a bucket filled with tennis balls, a gas can, a hash pipe, his Medicine Box, his toolbox, two books of poetry. My father calls trucks like this bargains because their age and simple engines make them easy to fix. Which is why he has spent much of his life with bloody knuckles and greasy fingernails, swearing and punching the fender of whatever Ford or Chevy or Dodge was ruining his day. So maybe we can blame it on Ray, whose sadness always gets to me, whose truck distracted me with sorrow while Sunny started the engine, revved it, and fishtailed down the driveway.

"Where do you think you're going?" I said—too late by far—and he laughed. "Stop the truck," I said, and he laughed again. I fumbled with the door, but it wouldn't open. He laughed like a movie madman, an exaggerated, menacing hilarity, and pulled onto the road. "It doesn't open from the inside," he said. "I rigged it that way."

Scream though I did—"You asshole, you cocksucking, incredible asshole," I screamed—on he drove, laughing. I threatened violence; I said I'd kill him, but he laughed and drove on, insanely fast, careening around curves, barely pausing for stop signs. "Stoptional!" He cackled, sailing along. "Where, *where* are the cops when you need them?"

And I hated him, loathed him in fact. I was so angry I panted. Panting, I said, "You know what this means? I'll never forget this. I will never, ever forgive you for this."

He laughed. "Never say never," he said. "Even you don't know what comes next. Anyway, aren't you the one who hates clichés?"

By that time we were well outside Santa Fe, headed north. I had finished screaming. Even if I could get away, if I rolled down the window and flung myself to the onrushing pavement, if, in fact, I survived the impact, how exactly would I get back to my groom, my wedding cake, my festivities? Hitchhike? Limp along in my ruined wedding dress? What fun. What glorious fun.

Sunny said we were going to Taos. "Only seventy-nine miles," he said. "Just a bike ride away, which, as I've said, I know from personal experience. And it's just for a little while," he said, as if I were being unreasonable. "Just to give you a present, that's all."

$\mathscr{S}$ AVED

August 19, 1976, Arroyo al Fin

THE ambulance wails off into the night. Jennie crawls under the lilac bush and watches the flashing lights travel up the side of the valley before they disappear over the top, onto the mesa. She lies there and tries to kill the pictures moving in her head. Her mother's *down there*. No little girl should ever see it, so bloody and hairy, down there.

Joy and Cassie come outside; Cassie calls, "Juniper! It's okay, sweetie!" But Jennie's frozen there in the dirt, the leaves and branches poking her skin. She sees their shoes and the piano's feet. She holds her breath. Cassie says, "Poor thing."

Joy says, "She'll be fine. It's the new one I'm worried about."

Jennie remembers her mother's scream, her baby brother trapped up there, inside. She digs her fingertips into the damp earth, while Cassie and Joy get into a borrowed car and drive into the night, to town, to Jennie's family in the hospital. Jennie stays under the lilac bush and thinks about what to do. She decides that she needs to go to school. Already, she's one day behind, and who knows what comes next. There's history, Quetzalcoatl. There's division of decimals. In math, one step comes after the next, and she could miss a new step and be lost. It feels like a hole opening inside her. Like her mother's down there. She shakes her head hard, so that it aches. Get out of my head, she tells the things she's seen. I order you to leave.

Finally, she crawls out from under the bush and picks the leaves from her chopped-short hair. She brushes the dirt from her hands, elbows, and knees and goes inside. She sits at the table with Joy's coffee cup, just like her mother did with her tea yesterday morning. Jennie says to the room, "Eight times ten is eighty." The sound of it is good, firm and smart, a solid fact that seems to hang in the air before her eyes. She dips her finger in the cold coffee, and with her finger, she writes on the table: 6 x 5=30. After this, there seems to be little else; she feels hugely calmer. Her heart beats steadily and certainly, so she gets up and wads paper for a fire.

Through the east window, she watches the sun seep over the mountains.

She stayed up all night. She chops kindling, lights the fire, sets water to boil for oatmeal. She says to herself, I stayed up all night. The birds are talking outside. They live under the vigas, little sparrows who have breakfast conversations. She sits back at the table and listens to the sparrows discuss the weather, maybe Sparrow Junior who has a cough. She drinks the inch of cold coffee—today she will have to be wide awake, for math and science and all the rest. Only here they come again, the pictures of what she has seen, sneaking into her head, blood and hair and oil and light—

But look: here is her father, Ray, Daddy, her dad—zooming into the driveway on Clarence's motorcycle. Thank God it's Daddy, thank you God. Smoke fills the room. She needs to open the damper, but she wants to watch him take off his helmet and swing his leg over the side of the bike like he's getting off a horse. He looks like Wild Bill Hickock.

He comes in singing "Good-bye, Old Paint." He coughs. "Did the big bad wolf blow the house down?"

The smoke's so bad it hurts to breathe. She says, "Yep. Burned it down." She gets up and opens the damper. There he is, standing in the doorway, a funny-looking man with orange hair, light green eyes. Daddy. She throws her arms around his waist and—forget multiplication—she will never let go, never, and finally she cries, "Daddy Daddy, the baby was backwards—Daddy." He picks her up and she wraps her legs around his waist, arms around his neck, like she's a little baby again, and her nose gets wet from all her tears against his neck.

He says, "Poor Juniper. Poor Juniper Tree Burning." He whispers it; he sings it like a cowboy song: "Poor, poor, pitiful Baby Darling Girl Juniiiper," and "Poor sweetie-pie," and eventually Jennie stops crying. She lets him hold her. She keeps her eyes closed against his wet stubbly neck.

The oatmeal water bubbles and rolls, the sounds of boiling. "I can make breakfast," she says. "Oatmeal."

Ray puts her down. "With raisins?"

She sniffles. "And cinnamon."

"Boy, am I lucky today!" He lays two bowls and spoons on the table. Jennie keeps the oatmeal from boiling over. What if this were the way it always was? What if there were no Mom, no baby, nothing but Jennie and her father in the kitchen, Jennie and her father eating breakfast, talking, Jennie laughing when her father tickles her, tucks her into bed. She spoons oatmeal into his bowl, and then she leans her head on his shoulder. "I love you, Daddy."

He eats silently, his face lined with that thin-lipped look that makes him seem so sad, so lost. Her father has a face like a whale on the cover of Joy's album. The whale music sounded the way Jennie thought ghosts would sound, long moans and shrieks, as if being a whale were a very sad thing indeed, as if they felt every bad thing in the world. Jennie couldn't stand to listen to the songs of whales. She took the album and tried to shut off their voices by looking at the cover—a close-up of the whale's face, his giant nose and lined cheeks, and his tiny sad eyes. The closer she looked at those eyes, the more she understood they were a person's eyes, the saddest person in the world. Then she thought, How can something so gigantic have the eyes of the saddest person in the world? And now, watching her father eat oatmeal she has made, she sees that he, too, has an ugly face, big nose and prickly jaw, and he, too, has those small, close-set sad eyes. Only his are the color of the sea, a glowing green.

He catches her and stares back. She looks down at her oatmeal. He slaps his palm on the table so his spoon jumps in his empty bowl, and he says, "Afterbirth!" She doesn't understand, which is okay, since most of the time he doesn't make sense. She just smiles, because she wants him to know she's listening and that whatever makes him so sad, she'll try to fix it. He says, "One time, Clarence told me you're supposed to get the afterbirth and bury it." Afterbirth. She turns this word over, searching for clues. She doesn't dare ask its meaning. "We should go get it," he says. "Go see the little squirt."

He seems so all of a sudden cheerful, and she doesn't want to spoil it, but suddenly she sees the pictures all over again, her baby brother stuck up there, the blood, oil, hair, screaming, and she thinks she'll cry again. "Where were you? It hurt her bad, and you weren't even there."

How sad: how sad, his mouth turning down, his eyes looking outside for somebody, for something, for everything missing in his heart. She made him sad again. "We better go get it," he says. "Burying it will mean a long life for Baby Sunny Boy Blue."

She doesn't say, I have to go to school: I have to learn about science and math and explorers. What's important changes, she figures out in that moment, because multiplication and history mean nothing at all. She has a baby brother named Sunny Boy Blue, and only that matters. Only the weight of the helmet her father straps on her head matters; only climbing behind him, balancing with her cheek against his shoulder, arms around his waist; only the engine roaring to life, and over her shoulder, a last glimpse of Faith's piano, big and black and gleaming in the driveway. Then, on the highway, the scream of wind. Her father hollers, "Lean with me!" This is what matters: the low side-lean of the bike taking a curve, the wind and the engine a roar in her ears, blocking out sound, birds, screams, life, and afterbirth; her eyes streaming with tears—only the wind and the checkered back of his shirt, his big solid waist, and his voice drifting back to her as if from a great distance: "Lean with me! Lean!"

Soon she can tell which way to move by the way his shoulders go, by the way the muscles in his back speak to her. They are in a pocket, an envelope, an afterbirth on this bike, the wind roaring around them, parting like the sea, and then closing behind them with a splash, and in this tiny world, there's only room enough for Jennie and her father who has eyes like a whale, for his back and her cheek, and they are fearless fighters, cowboys against the world that blurs and roars around them into nothing.

Sunny's Wedding Present

My Wedding Day, This Year, Taos and Santa Fe
SUNNY took me to the Rio Grande Gorge Bridge, up in Taos. The bride and her brother, sitting in a truck out on the mesa under the stars. As fast as he drove, it still took them an hour to get to the middle of the mesa, seven miles outside Taos.

He came around and opened my door for me. I wouldn't get out. I sat with crossed arms and stared straight ahead. "Look at me," he said. I didn't. He lit a cigarette. "Come on," he said. "The sooner you cooperate, the sooner we get you back."

"You're crocked," I said. But I followed him onto the bridge. "Look down," he said. I leaned over the railing and peered into the six-hundred-foot canyon. I couldn't see far. The moon had risen and its blue light revealed the boulders and scraggly trees in the canyon. It cast our shadows on the bridge. I stood there, waiting for Sunny to finish whatever little drama he'd concocted. You can drag a bride to water, but don't expect her to ooh and ahh at the view.

"I just wanted to have you to myself," Sunny said.

"You've got me," I said. "Now let's go back."

"In Russia, hope is the last thing to die," Sunny said.

"Don't try that Russian shit on me," I said. "Save it for your mommy." The wind blew straight through my dress; the satin felt like tissue paper. He offered me his Russian army coat. When I said no, he dropped it over my shoulders. It reeked of cigarettes, vodka, pot, the rank smell of antique wool never cleaned. I stared down into the canyon's depths, to the river of darkness untouched by the moon. "Sunny," I said. "This is my *wedding day*."

Chris would be frantic by now. He would think I'd left on purpose.

"A present," Sunny said. "Put your hand in the pocket." I felt a silver flask, cool and sleek. "Take it out," he said. He flicked on his lighter so that I could see it was inscribed *JTB*, which was, of course, for Juniper Tree Burning, but I played stupid. "My middle name is Lipa. What's the T for?"

"It matches mine," he said, showing me that his flask was engraved *SBB*. "Almost like we have the same last name." He held his arms out as if to hug me, but reached into the other coat pocket and took out the dolls he'd brought back from Russia for my mother.

Once upon a time there was a boy named Sunny who came all the way from Russia to see his sister married. He came bearing gifts. For his mother, he brought the egg-shaped dolls called *Matryushkas*. The largest opened like an egg to reveal another nested inside, and then another inside that, and so on, like a set of infinite possibilities, the smallest doll opening into nothing. "That last one is the invisible doll," he said. His mother wept over the gift, because, she said, her dead Russian mother had given her the same dolls when she was little.

Then he kidnapped his sister, the bride, and stole back the Matryushkas. In the middle of the mesa, on a bridge railing, he opened each of the dolls, and lined up their halves like a family split open—the toes of their little black boots curving together, beside their upended, rosy-cheeked smiles.

From a silver flask engraved with the initials *JTB*, he poured vodka into the row of Matryushka halves. He said, "Drink with me," and his sister said no. "Come on," he said. "Drink." Again, no. A third time he asked, and a third time she said no. She didn't know him anymore. And her husband, her beloved, her groom, he was eighty miles away, thinking she'd left him on their wedding day, just as the brother foretold.

The brother drank his share, one by one tossing back the feet, the black hair, of the little Matryushkas. First, the largest, in one gulp. And the rest, their feet kicking into the air, a plump cancan line. "Come on," he said, smacking his lips. "Join the fun."

"What fun?"

So he drank her portion too, one after the other, their smiling Matryushka lips raised to his, from the biggest to the smallest. When finished, he shrugged unsteadily and said, "Your loss." He turned to go, then turned back again. "Here's a riddle," he said. "What came first, the egg or the Matryushka? I mean, Grandpa Paul or the Matryushka? Paul was shaped like an egg, an egg, remember?"

"You're drunk," I said. "Take me back."

"I promise you," Sunny said. "Somewhere beyond all this is me." He fell silent. When finally he spoke, it was the only time during the whole escapade when he sounded anything like angry or dangerous. "You listen to me," he said softly. "You're the one named Jennifer. Jennifer Braverman now. And just who the fuck is she?" But then he shrugged it off. He put the Matryushka back together.

Once upon a time there was a boy who came from Russia to see his sister married and then he kidnapped her and then they hated each other. The end.

"Wait here," Sunny said. He staggered back to the truck. I tried to make my mind blank. The wool made my bare neck itch. What was Chris doing by now? That red-haired Sarah was saying, "This is so, like, Cinderella," and Chris was wincing to hear this private joke spoken by accident. His parents, the Bravermans, were wandering around, saying, "We knew there was something fishy about her. If the shoe fits . . ." and my mother butting in, "You know, she's a Capricorn. They're all like this, barging ahead . . . when were you born?"

Sunny returned with a gas can, a bucket filled with tennis balls, and a wrapped present. He bounced a tennis ball to me, but I didn't catch it, and it sailed over the railing into the canyon. I said, "Don't expect me to lob a few with you."

"How veddy right," Sunny said. Whistling, he poured the gas over the bucket of balls, and its knife-edge stink rose in the air. "Wouldn't think of it." He handed me the present. "Open this."

Maybe Chris was calling the police while the Wedding Party became a Search Party, beating the bushes, shouting my name. I called my husband James, another joke between us. Poor James. In some part of himself, he was thinking, I knew it. She always leaves.

I dodged Sunny and made a break for the truck.

"Juniper Tree Burning," he drawled. "You get your ass back here! You can't drive a truck without keys." He jingled them, laughing. He said, "If you don't come back here, I'll jump."

He stood on the bottom rung of the guardrail, leaning over it, with his arms outstretched. It would only take a loss of balance, a good shove, for his waist to become the fulcrum, for him to fall forward into the canyon. And yes, I imagined pushing him over the edge. I imagined his wailing cry as he fell into the water. He stumbled, I'd say. He was drunk, out of control, I'd say, and I tried to catch him, but he fell right through my fingers.

"No hands," he shouted.

Yes, right. Jennie kills her brother, thereby sealing the fate of her pathetic version of holy matrimony. You think New Year's Day was bad before? Try it as the Day I Murdered My Brother.

Defeated, I rejoined him. Because no one, not even a bride kidnapped on her wedding day, not even me, is willing to watch her brother fall six hundred feet and smash into igneous rock and die. And after all, even if I hated him, he was undeniably Sunny Boy Blue, he of the see-through green eyes, my baby boy, my brother. He of the wide, curling smile, the only thing we still had in common. "Open your present," he told me, stepping off the rail. "I gave a note to your friend," he said as I tore at the wrapping. "That red-haired girl, Sarah. So don't worry. He won't go off on the honeymoon without you."

"Friend," I said. "I don't even know her."

He lit a cigarette. "Anyway," he said, "this is an old Russian tradition. Kidnap the bride on her wedding night. Get a ransom. Your new husband's rolling in the dough, am I right?"

I did not need daylight or a flashlight to recognize the gift. The book in my hand, leather bound, embossed, was the Treasured Memories, the photo album filled with our mother's childhood and, more important, our grandparents, Lipa and Paul. I stepped away from the railing because the impulse to throw the damn thing over the side was so strong I knew I'd do it. I shoved it back at him. "I don't want this," I said.

He laughed. "Yes, you do," he said.

"No," I said, and slung it like a Frisbee down the highway. He sighed. He walked to it, retrieved it, and handed it back to me. "Hold it, at least," he said.

He took a tennis ball, wet with gasoline, from the bucket. He held out his arm as if he were preparing to serve. With his other hand, he flicked on his lighter. "Now watch," he said, and he set fire to the gas-soaked ball just as he dropped it into the canyon. "Molotov tennis balls!" he shouted. A flaming synthetic comet, it lit the rocky walls all the way down, until it hit the river and went out. "Ah, pyromania," he said, sighing.

"That's right," I said. "You're the fire lover, aren't you?" And I said what I knew would hurt him most. "*You* burned our house down, you fucking drunk."

"Jesus, Junie," he said softly. He sent another flaming ball into the canyon. And another. "Couldn't resist, could you? Not Juniper Tree Burning. I knew she'd show up."

For a moment, guilt lanced my anger, but then he lobbed another ball over the side and I remembered who was the Victim here. I scrambled for a plan, which was to lie. "I'm sorry," I said. "You know it wasn't your fault. You were just a kid—" This was the truth, but I lied in the gentle way I said it. I held out my hand for his lighter. "Here. Let me try."

He lit it and held the flame near my face. His fingers reeked of gas, and I imagined him exploding in flame.

"You look like a movie star," he said almost tenderly, almost wistful, even, but this time he didn't get to me. He said, "*Gadaniye.* Once upon a time in Russia, the night before the wedding, they used to put a lighted candle in front of a mirror in a dark room. You could see the bride's future in the shadows." He traded the lighter for the Treasured Memories.

Before he could name some kind of terrible future for me or my groom, I took the lighter and touched the flame to the whole damn bucket, and the gas lit with a bang. Flaming tennis balls bounced across the bridge, rolled in the gutter, dropped off the sides of the bridge into the canyon. Sunny and I chased after them, kicking them over the edge, and I have to admit that for a moment I found them beautiful. But not pretty enough to make me forgive my brother, the kidnapping drunk.

In short order, the balls were either gone or burned out. "Take me back now," I said.

He caught my arm. "I always figured that's why you sent me home, there at the Taos Inn. Because I burned down the house."

I was freezing, shivering hard, my teeth clenched against chattering. I was cold to my core. "Take me back to my husband," I said, and my jaw ached as I said it.

He laughed, a hard little bark. "*My* husband. My *hus*band. There's a phrase. That's why you had the big fairy tale, so you could say—"

"Fairy tale," I said. "You asshole."

He spoke in Russian, then translated: "In Russia," he said, and I wondered if he knew he was repeating himself, "hope is the last thing to die. So what now? Buy yourself a house, a new Rolls, a couple of kids? Fill the family album with *your* husband? Is that the plan?"

"Exactly the plan," I said. "Now take me back so I can get started."

He was, quite suddenly, beaten. He swayed back to the truck and slumped in, half passed out, the album to his chest like a schoolbook. I shoved him over and took the keys from his hand. He said, "Here's a Russian joke. The difference between a pessimist and an optimist? The pessimist says, 'Things couldn't get worse.' The optimist says, 'Things will get worse.'"

I started the truck, and I drove us back to Santa Fe, and I didn't speak to him for that whole time. But driving those long, interminable miles back to my wedding reception, my groom, and my future, I couldn't stop it from coming back at me: my baby brother, riding his bike all the way from Santa Fe to Taos, eighty miles and thirteen years old. His eyes, his bony, sunburned shoulders, the stink of his puberty sweat.

Sunny rides his bike straight into the lobby of the Taos Inn, looking for me. I haven't lived with him for seven years. What does he want? I barely know him when I see him. Riding all that way, and coming to the restaurant. I'm working. He's thirteen years old.

J e n n i e likes waiting tables, especially at the best hotel in town, moving quietly and competently among the white linen. She wears black pants and a tuxedo shirt, the pleats crisply spray-starched. She carries a bottle of merlot, a napkin over her arm. Food is waiting, and there are drinks to serve. She has a good tip going, an old man who wears dentures and smiles as if his false teeth are his best feature.

But here she is, torn from the dining room by this sweaty kid, his bare skinny chest burned deep red. "*Hola hermana,*" the boy shouts, disturbing the tourists, who avert their eyes from the half-naked boy, not fully grown into his new bones, gangly, with big floppy hands on thin wrists. The lobby's skylight drops sunshine on him. Almost a man. Almost eighty miles. This is Sunny Boy Blue.

"This doesn't make any sense," she tells him. "I told you I'd come visit, didn't I?" She's freshly showered, and inside her barrette, her hair is damp. She has a good corkscrew in her pocket. The reservations are booked solid; it's a moneymaker Friday. She says, "You should go home, Sunny." He reeks of sweat. "You should put on your shirt."

He looks down at his T-shirt and back at her. "I came to see you," he says. "I rode my bike all the way."

"I'll come visit." She fishes her tips from her apron. "Take the bus back, okay?"

He tucks the money inside his waistband. "I can't leave my bike."

"Okay, your bike. I'll bring it down when I can. Next weekend." Her tips will be bad tonight after all. Her rhythm is shot. "I promise," she says, knowing that the dentures man is waiting for wine and flirting. "I work until midnight, and I work a double tomorrow, and I can't spend any time—"

"I get it," Sunny says, smiling, jocular even. "But I'm taking my bike."

She hugs him, holding her tuxedo shirt away from his sweaty chest. She imagines him riding through the low, flat Española valley, dodging broken glass glittering in the hot sun. His sweat dries as soon as it rises from his sizzling skin. At last, there's the canyon beside the river, cool and winding but shoulderless, with cars screaming around curves, nearly smashing into him.

When she pulls away, she meets his begging eyes, and she hates him just then, for sweating, for stinking, for needing her with his eyes. She hates imagining his bony shoulders hunching as a semi barrels past, his tires shivering in its wake.

She says, "I'll come visit," and he shrugs.

"No you won't," he says. "But that's okay." Then he leaves. It takes her an hour, a meal, an orchestration of timing, the appetizers finished and the entrees appearing like magic at the perfect moment, desserts and credit cards and the tip in her pocket—her empty pocket, because she gave everything to Sunny. That's how long it takes her to realize what Sunny didn't say. Adding up another bill, food and wine and chocolate cake, she realizes the date. *My*

God. It's his birthday today. The guilt pierces her like a sudden nausea, and for a moment she wants to leave the restaurant and hotel and run all the way to Santa Fe. But he has been gone an hour now. She's so busy. If she weren't so busy; if it weren't a Friday; if she had any hope of catching up, she would run after him. She tallies the check. She takes another order. And in the rising tide of the evening, the shame and sorrow flush out of her and she is fine.

I returned to my wedding reception to find the luminarias burned out and the parking lot mostly empty, so there I was, a tardy Cinderella showing up after midnight. My faithless groom had gone, his Rolls conspicuous even in its absence. My father sat on the portico, smoking a joint and doodling on his guitar, stoned and spacey. "Hello, Bride," he said. His eyes were very sad. He was sad in every cell of his respectable self, lit by a porch light, his puffy jacket smudging his outlines. "There she is," he crooned at me. "Miss America."

"Shut up, Dad," I said.

"I was a pissant father."

His voice turned my stomach. Where was my wild and woolly daddy, fearless cowboy on his motorcycle? "You weren't," I said. "You taught me Spanish. You sang me songs. You told me stories. You hunted venison."

"That horseshit. I ran away from home. I sold your mother's piano."

"We needed money."

"I beat you. More than once. Many times."

"I don't remember that." I would say anything to escape his confession.

"You were the best thing I ever did. I was going to be a good dad."

"I have to find that husband of mine," I said. "I have a husband now."

"I should have taken waltzing lessons for your wedding," he said. He took a deep lungful of pot, and on the exhale he began singing "Waltzing Matilda."

Like a stubborn monster, the brother of the bride staggers out of the truck. "Looky here," he drawls, bracing himself on the fender. "Isn't this a downright Hollywood moment! Daddy Burning and his Darling Juniper." He holds an imaginary camera to his face. "Smile for the album," he says. "You can do it."

"Don't you dare talk to me," the bride says. "Don't you speak to me ever again. Are you listening? Because I want to make sure you hear me when I say that we no longer speak to each other, understand?" She goes inside, the two Davis men on her tail, inescapable as always, just like her mother who sees them and cries, "Sunny! I was so *worried*," and the bride, she gives the whole lot of them the slip; she turns on a dime and hightails it back into the cold to wait for her groom, to tally her losses: no bouquet toss, no risqué removal of garter, no saucy toasts to long lusty happiness. All the ridiculous and necessary photo opportunities of weddings—what a farce.

Swearing, I punched the wall, and the pain of it took me deeper into my impotent rage. What a joke. What a horrible, horrible joke, someone like me, the Ugly Chick in her poofy dress, planning a big fancy wedding, the kind of girl who punches walls, thinking she can run through rice and drive off laughing, cans clattering, *Just Married*, the final shot at the album's end, as if the road to ordinary is so easily taken.

AND with Chris's usual impeccable timing, the Rolls pulled up to me, festooned with streamers, shoe-polished *Just Married*. Bitter, bitter, I thought. When things lie irrevocably ruined, the taste is bitter indeed, and it's not easily rinsed away; it takes more than the groom flinging himself out of his car, crying, "There you are, God, there you are." More than his hands on my cold cheeks. "There you are," he said again, his voice thick with relief. I found myself immensely irritated by the repetition. "I've been looking everywhere for you."

"That's it?" I said. "Jesus Christ, doesn't anything get a rise out of you?"

"Jennie," he said, "I'm not the villain here." But I twisted away and got into the car, slamming the door hard. My knuckles throbbed from where I had punched the wall. I dug my nails into my palms and watched Chris open the door to the hall which held those criminals and thieves and kidnappers I was forced to call my family. I imagined starting the Rolls and leaving them all behind, and it took me too long to realize I'd be leaving my groom with them.

After several minutes, he returned. "What did you do?" I asked. Please, I thought, say you hurt him. Say you shouted. Say you punched him three times hard, cracked open your knuckles on his face.

"I told him he had no right," Chris said.

"He 'had no right.' Great. Fabulous. Now I'm avenged." As these words rose up my throat and passed over my lips, I thought, I must not let this anger get the better of me, must not let loose the clumsy, graceless, destructive Billy Goat that I truly am. "My Big Knight in Shining Armor," I said.

Chris sighed. He pushed his hair out of his face, a graceful gesture which I suddenly found feminine. He started the car, and to the tune of its powerful, humming engine, he asked me, "What did you want me to say? I'd rather be with you than waste time in there."

He's right. But in the long moment that follows, and even as they drive away, tin cans clattering behind them, this bride feels her groom has failed her. She feels it on the flight to their honeymoon, and on their romantic

Caribbean beach, the stuff of fantasies and fairy tales, the montage scenes in movies.

In a bungalow beside the water, he reached for me, and I pushed away his hand. "What is it?" he whispered. "What's happening inside you?"

You have failed me, I thought, even as I said, "I'm just so tired." We lay, inches apart, until he fell into his deep, solid dreams. There, on my bridal sheets, I listened to the tide, unable to stop thinking about what I should have done: not gone to the truck with him; not stayed in the truck; thrown myself out, grabbed the wheel, hit him over the head—over and over again I went through it, as if I could change the course of events, if only I could pinpoint the moment for escaping my baby brother, that bastard, that little prick, that Backwards Boy.

Eventually, I came back to myself, crying in a bed on an island beside my husband, my Christian Braverman, my new family now. My tears were not of grief but impotent frustration. Okay, so he wanted revenge. But did he really have to steal my own wedding from me? What, *what*, exactly, was I supposed to do? It was my wedding, don't you see, my only wedding, and how could taking it from me possibly gain anything for you, Sunny Boy Blue? You will have so many more birthdays, but I had only this one wedding to ruin.

I sat up and scrubbed my eyes. I was the Weeping Newlywed, and so my brother had hijacked my honeymoon as well as my wedding. I slipped out of bed and crept from our bungalow down to the water. I ran barefoot along the scalloped edges of waves. The tide came in, endlessly striking the shore with the rhythm of breath, or footfalls, or a heartbeat. I ran and ran. The waves broke at my feet. I thought, *So this is the sound of water breaking.*

2.

TREASURED MEMORIES

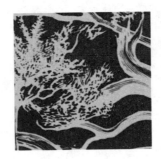

$\mathcal{T}$HE DAY THE PIANO CAME

How far back is far enough? Where is the beginning of Sunny Boy Blue jumping into the sea? Can you ever find the moment, the second, the seed? Maybe it begins with something obvious. With what my mother calls a sign. Let's say it begins with the piano, with Sunny in his mother's belly, with Juniper and Faith wearing their bikinis, pulling weeds from the sweet pea rows.

They're irrigating, and the mud sticks to the roots in clumps, which Faith says to shake off. She holds out a leaf. "This is lamb's-quarter. Try it." Juniper hesitates. Faith smiles. She chews a leaf, and says, "It tastes like watercress. We can put it in a salad." Juniper eats some and it's good, spicy, sun-warmed. Her mother knows about a lot of plants. Her mother knows their names and the places you can find them growing wild, and what kinds of illnesses they will cure. Juniper, chewing the lamb's-quarter, smiles at her mother and loves her. Faith smiles back. Juniper wants, suddenly, to throw her arms around her mother and tell her, *I love you, Mommy, my mother, my mom. I love you so much.* But Ray ran away from home weeks ago, and he still hasn't come back, and everything makes Faith mad. Juniper pulls up a big ragweed instead.

"You have to shake it off," Faith says, sitting back on her heels. "Don't leave big holes like that." Juniper waves away flies and yellow jackets, which love sweet peas. She listens to the ditchwater chuckling between the corn rows. She shakes clean the roots. The bees are everywhere this summer. They are like fairies, with the queen at home, with a secret language they speak quickly so the world can't understand.

Faith says, in a surprised, gentle way, "You're so blond." She reaches out and brushes Juniper's hair out of her eyes, tucks it behind her ear. She says softly, "I never thought I'd have a blond little girl." Everything is still and quiet and stopped. Juniper thinks, Let me stay here, where my mother loves me.

"We're opposites," Faith says, and the spell is broken.

Then, the strangest sound: a clatter and bang, so at first Juniper thinks her dad's finally home, but as it gets closer, she realizes it's too loud for the old Dodge. The noise groans and grows, climbing the steep, narrow dirt road.

Faith and Juniper look at each other. "There it is," Faith whispers, like she's telling the biggest secret in the world.

"What is it?" Juniper asks.

And then a semi truck appears and barely squeezes into their driveway and stops with a hiss, like a pressure cooker. It sits, resting, looking very strange under the cottonwood, between the house and the garden. A green and yellow van with MAYFLOWER painted on the side.

"Help me up," Faith says.

Pulling on Faith's hands, Juniper asks again, "What is it?"

"It's for me," Faith says, wiping her hands, leaving two swipes of mud on her bikini bottom. "It's my inheritance."

The driver gets out of the truck. Faith walks out of the garden toward him, Juniper hurrying behind. The man stares at Faith's belly, squints, and looks at their bare feet. He takes off his baseball cap and wipes his forehead. "Faith Chatwin, I'm looking for her."

Juniper sees her mother through this man's eyes, and she's embarrassed. Look at all the mud, the tiny pink bikini, the gigantic pregnant belly in between. She's practically naked. A naked, muddy mother.

"Davis," Faith says. "He knew it was Davis. Chatwin is my maiden name."

"I don't know anything about that. I have a delivery for Faith Chatwin." His hair is short as a soldier's.

Faith says, "Wait here," and she goes inside.

"And who are you?" the man asks Juniper. On the pocket of his green uniform, embroidered in fancy yellow curls, is the name GRAHAM. "What's your name?"

Juniper considers this. She has wanted to be Jennifer for so long. But she's afraid to lie, which is a sin against God.

"What's the matter?" Graham says. "Forget your own name?"

"I'm Jennifer," she says, and it's the first time she has changed her name out loud. Once she says it, she remembers it isn't a lie at all. It's the truth, and the other name is a lie. "Everybody calls me Jennie. I'm going to have a brother soon. His name will be John." That's the way it's supposed to be, she realizes. This is how people feel when they discover destiny, or God's Plan, or a scientific fact. They say it and they know it. From now on, in her head, she will call herself Jennie.

Faith comes panting out of the house, wearing her blue-flowered dress, thank God. She shows Graham a piece of paper. "This is my wedding certificate," she says. "See. It says Faith Chatwin and Ray Davis. We married in Seattle." Her muddy fingerprints are on the corner. "I was Faith Chatwin before."

Graham glances at the certificate. He asks Jennie, "Is this Faith Chatwin?"

Jennie says, "I think so."

"You wouldn't pull my leg, would you?"

God is giving her a chance to admit that she just lied a second ago. But she wants Graham to believe her mother, because the man's partner has opened the back of the truck, and inside, amid boxes, she spies a rocking horse, and a sofa with green flowers, and other beautiful things. "I'm not a liar," Jennie says, glimpsing a golden lamp. A box labeled BATHROOM. "I'll help," she says. "I can carry a box."

Graham laughs. "It's a piggyback order. Just this one thing," he says, pointing to a giant wooden crate in the mouth of the truck. "We can do it ourselves." He smells like French fries. He holds out a clipboard and pen for Faith to sign.

Faith wants the box in the living room. Graham and his partner look at each other. "If you want to call about fifteen friends to kick a hole in the wall, we can get it inside," Graham says. "Otherwise, we're just going to have to leave it out here."

Faith bites her lip. She smooths her dress and holds her belly. She says, "What if it rains?"

Graham shrugs. "Sorry. I don't know anything except I'm supposed to deliver this." A bee hovers near his clipboard and he bats it away.

Faith looks at Jennie. "We can take off the legs later," she says. "Ray can help us take them off, can't he?" Jennie hates that she feels she should answer, that she should pat her mother's hand.

Jennie and Faith stand by the lilac bush while Graham and his partner pull a drawbridge out of the back of the truck, then unwrap the blankets and untie the box and put it on a cart with wheels. It's hard for them to get it down the ramp.

Suddenly sharp, Faith says, "Be careful. That's a Steinway you have there."

They have to roll it around the truck, over the bumps and craters of the steep driveway. The box wants to slide off the cart. Graham pushes, his cheek close to the crate, his toes digging into the dirt. When they lower it to the ground, the box sings like a guitar strummed. It sounds like mad and afraid and joyful singing together. It sounds wonderful. Now there's the box, and the truck, sitting smack in the middle of their driveway, between the garden and the house, under the cottonwood. Jennie's heart beats fast, and her feet itch. The mud on them is drying.

Faith says, "Thank you so very much for bringing this." She follows them back to the truck, saying, "Do I have to do anything else? Am I supposed to tip you?" Something about her voice makes Jennie feel sick to her stomach. She wishes for her father. But he left mad. Faith says Ray went to get Medicine in Texas, but it doesn't matter where he is, really, just that Jennie's alone here with this box, with her mother who stands with one hand on the wood marked FRAGILE, one hand on the curve of her swollen belly.

After the truck leaves, the smell of its black exhaust stays in the air, and still Faith and Jennie stand there. They stand there for the longest time. The truck disappears down the road, and the growl of its shifting gears fades. They stand long enough for the air to clear again, for all the sounds of their silence—the ditch, the leaves moving above—to settle around them. Faith and Jennie stay, their hands on the box, until the truck has vanished, as if they are waving good-bye, as if their dearest friend were leaving for the very last time.

Faith goes into the house and returns with the hammer. She pulls off a board, nails squeaking and groaning. She lets it drop to the ground and circles the box, hammer in hand.

"What is it?"

"A present. A very big present from my daddy."

"*Your* daddy?"

"My daddy." Faith peeks around the box like she's playing. "What? Did you think I didn't have a father?" She laughs, breathless. Just moving makes her breathless these days.

Very much later, five years later, Jennie will be fourteen and she will hate—HATE—Faith. They will stand in this driveway. Faith will say, "I never made peace with my father, and then he died."

Jennie will say, "So? So? You won't trick me into feeling sorry for you."

"You were always like this," Faith will say. "You were born to be this way. Even inside me, you kicked me; you hated me."

But this is now, and Faith smiles. She says, "Juniper, do you know the Beatles? 'I Want to Hold Your Hand'—do you know that?"

"I know the Beatles."

"I didn't know them," Faith says. She braces her foot on the box and pries off a nail, grunting, stumbling back. The board clatters to the ground, nails up.

"Careful," Jennie says. "Be careful, Mom."

"I never even heard a Beatles record until I was eighteen, until Ray played one for me. I knew Bartók. You don't know Bartók."

Jennie gathers the boards and holds them to her chest, nails out.

"I played Bartók," Faith says. "My father taught me. Bartók was Hungarian, like my mother."

"Your mother was Russian."

"Yes, but first she was Hungarian. Then she was Russian."

Jennie picks up the boards, piling them safely beside the garden fence. Finally, the sides of the box fall with a crash and there it is, bundled in blankets, even its legs wrapped tight.

"It's a piano," Faith says.

"I know."

"It's mine."

"I know what a piano is," Jennie says. "I'm not stupid." She isn't mad, though.

Because look how Faith smiles, pushing back her braids and unwrapping the blankets from the piano feet, from its sides and back. She's humming a melody Jennie has never heard. "This is a beautiful piano," Faith says. "It was my grandmother's, and then it was my mother's." She strokes its top in a way that reminds Jennie of how Faith sits in the morning at the kitchen table, looking out the window at nothing at all, stroking her dress over her tummy. "We lived in a house on top of a very high hill. My grandfather built that house with his own hands. He had a Ming vase in its own special nook." The piano is dull with dust. Faith's palm leaves trails of shininess. "Now this is my piano," she says.

"What's Ming?"

"Ming is Chinese. My grandfather bought it for cheap from a Chinese man. It was a treasure."

"Where is it? Why didn't he send it?"

Faith says, "Because it wasn't mine. This is mine."

Jennie sees her own face in the gleaming black piano skin. She looks at the girl floating there and thinks, That's me. That's Jennifer whose grandpa sent a piano. She puts down the boards she's holding and touches the cool black surface. The bright sun, the dirt of the driveway, even Jennie's bare muddy feet seem to make the piano shine, like any treasure would outside in the middle of June. Around her own reflected face, sunlight winks between cottonwood leaves flickering in the breeze. A bee wanders across the shiny black like it belongs there. They will have to get the piano inside quickly. It will rain. Birds will make a nest. Spiders will weave webs and lay their eggs.

"My father taught me to play on this piano," Faith says.

"Play for me," Jennie says. She pulls on Faith's sleeve. "Play, Mom." Standing in the driveway, paper and padding and a broken box around it, the piano waits, ready. What is the bee searching for?

Faith brings a finger down on one key. "And then my mother died, and he turned mean." She sighs. "I don't remember how to play. It's been too long."

"Play. Please play." Faith is going to cry, or she is going to make the same noise the piano made when the workers put it down, a noise that contains all the sadness in the world. "Mom?" Softly, quietly. "Mom?"

Faith presses the key again. She listens, her head tilted to the side, to that one note stretching out. "That's middle C," she says. "It's out of tune, but it's middle C." The bee stops for a moment, then lifts into the air and buzzes away.

Jennie knows what to do. She touches another key. "What's this?"

Faith closes her eyes and smiles slightly. "E flat." She looks down at the keys, and then, not very fast, like she's finding her way, her fingers sneak careful and scared over the keys. "What song is that?"

Jennie smiles. "'Mary Had a Little Lamb.'" She pats Faith's arm. "Again," she says.

Faith plays another song, faster this time.

"'Twinkle Twinkle Little Star.'"

"Mozart," Faith says. "He wrote that song when he was six." She strokes her stomach. "Maybe the baby will play the piano when he's six."

"I want to play," Jennie says.

Faith zips out "Twinkle Twinkle Little Star" once more.

Jennie thinks, My mom plays piano. Never in a million years did she imagine this. "I want to learn."

With both hands, Faith plays a magical, dreamy song. Maybe, if the language of bees slowed down, it would be this music. Faith sits on the bench, leaning forward, her eyes seeing something Jennie can't. The music's spell makes Faith's skin rosy and her dress a gown of lace and pearls, makes her Faith Chatwin the queen, playing for all the bees in the world. Maybe all the bees will come to dance and dive and swarm with joy, honey falling from their mouths for Faith, their true Bee Queen.

In the middle of the song, Faith stops. She looks at Jennie. "Juniper," she whispers. "The baby is dancing inside me. He's dancing to the music." She presses Jennie's palm against the faded dress. "Feel," she says. "Do you feel him?" Her eyes are shining. "He likes Bartók. He's going to be so special."

Jennie tries her very best. She tries, but she doesn't feel anything except her mother's hard belly, the soft cotton covered with tiny flowers. She kneels down; she puts her arms around Faith and presses her face close. Finally, like the tiniest flutter of bees, she feels him against her cheek, and just for a moment she can believe anything, even that a baby is dancing.

CINDERELLA

Y o u want a love story? Have I got one for you. It begins, as they all should, with once upon a time. Once upon a time, nearly a year ago, in fact, this chick, this woman named Jennifer Davis, she lay awake on a hot August night. Though she seems so separate from me now, this woman was me. I was starting medical school the next day, and there I was, tossing and turning, sweating, thinking grandiose platitudes, like Here comes the rest of my life, and Who knows what the future may hold? What a crock. I thought I knew exactly what the future held.

I lived in a hundred-year-old adobe horse stable which had been converted to a one-room apartment. It was not as bohemian as it sounds—it had hardwood floors and a microwave—but it did retain a certain stable-ish quality, low-ceilinged, thick-walled, dark. Adobe is usually great for keeping things cool. Usually. That night last August, wallowing in rivers of sweat, I thought, I can't believe I've finally gotten from there to here. From that little girl I used to be, Juniper, lying in the dark, wide awake and six years old, listening for her father's truck, willing her father home.

Shivering, not sweating. The snow falls heavy around the house, and her father has gone to get Medicine, which is against the law, and to get a deer, which makes him a poacher, which is also against the law. He could get arrested. He could die out there on the icy roads. More than once, she rises and goes to the window, but the world is black and invisible, and she returns, shivering to her bed. If he wrecked, who would save him, keep him warm, keep him alive? *Please God*, she prays. *Please.*

At last, she hears the Dodge pull into the driveway, its brakes creaking and whining. She grabs her blanket and runs outside in her nightgown and stocking feet to find him on the back porch with the deer over his shoulders and ice clumping his beard. Drifted snow squeaks under his boots. His bad leg hurts in the cold; he's limping a little. She clutches the blanket closer. She doesn't like standing on the porch; spiders live there.

Her father hangs the deer by its hind legs from the porch vigas. She touches its wiry neck. It's still warm. Its eyes are dark and beautiful and look alive. He killed it near home, "Right on the highway," he says, smiling, a tight press of his lips. "Right in cocksucking Alfin."

"Don't say that word," she says.

"What word? Alfin?"

"You know what I mean."

"Why not?"

"I don't know," she says.

"That's not an answer," he says. He squats under the pool of yellow porch light, and with a swift flick of his knife, he slits the deer's throat. Blood pours into a coffee can. His frizzy hair turns to ringlets as the ice on it melts. When the blood stops, he slices open the deer's belly. He pulls out the blue ropes of intestines and drops them steaming into a cracked enamel bowl, and they smell like grass and dirt and summer and she will forever remember that smell, until she won't be able to distinguish the scent of the deer from the smell of her father.

He holds out a slick piece of meat. She tucks one foot behind her knee to warm it. "This is the liver," he says. It's shiny and quivers in his palm. "It stores up energy." He returns it to the bowl. "Like a woodshed." His boots are soaked, wet above the ankle. She worries his feet are frozen. He names the organs one by one, the lungs and the guts and the kidneys, and then he offers an organ which is dark, almost purple, encased in a thin opaque skin. It fits neatly in his big hand. He says, "This is the heart."

She takes it from him. She is small and needs two hands to hold it. Her father says, "It's still warm." She closes her eyes and pretends it's hot as a coal. With his knife, he slices open a vein and slips her fingers inside the heart. He says, "The blood moves from room to room. Do you feel the rooms?" She closes her eyes and feels. The heart is a house, and the blood gushes through like a flood. She imagines the deer running. Her own heart pounds. She's dizzy with the idea of blood moving inside her, even when she's standing still.

When she opens her eyes, her father is watching her face and smiling. He puts his palm on the nape of her neck, his hand heavy and warm, slightly sticky with blood. His smile touches his eyes. He takes back the heart. Her fingers are wet. He lifts his hand from the back of her neck and leaves her skin cold there. She shudders.

He says, "Get inside, you Popsicle, you."

He is her father, her daddy, her dad. She is always on his side, whether he breaks the law or not. There will come a time, years later, when she'll wonder if her father cheated when he killed the deer, if he shone a light in its eyes before he shot it. If he stood watching it jerk and thrash until it died. She'll wonder whether, in handing her the heart, he meant to teach her or to amuse himself. But even all grown up and ready to be a doctor, even doubting him, she'll remember the warmth of the heart. How she thought, her blanket slipping from her shoulders, that the meat in her hands was the beginning and the end of everything that mattered—food and life and love—and then she looked to her father's eyes, which were as pale and green as water, and his feet, cold and wet in their boots.

YEARS later, sweaty, hot, awake, I asked myself, Was that the beginning that ends here? Can you really trace a life back to the moment when all was decided? Can medicine begin with a deer's heart in a little girl's hands? And then I caught myself getting cutely philosophical, and I gave up on sleep.

I put on my running shoes and went for a run. I've always been a night runner. Yes, I know all about rapists and thieves, but let's be honest, here: I run in the dark so no one will see me run, because I've never been trained by a pro, and though I know a few things from books, and I know more than a few things about physiology, I've never had a coach with a clipboard and stopwatch to call, "What are you, playing shuffleboard?" I figure I'm a plodding, clumsy, knock-kneed sort of runner, the kind I see in the afternoons, galumphing across campus with bright red faces, their arms flapping and flailing as if they're trying to keep their balance. I run at night so no one will see me for a fool, because most people think Jennie's no fool, and it's always smart to keep up a good impression once you've got it going.

This night, though, I also ran to get to Antonio's Pool House on Central, my favorite kind of place, a Dive, frequented by mostly men, work-worn, loud with weariness that comes from lifting too much or pulling too hard or climbing too high, who know that someday they'll break out in skin cancer or cough up lung cancer or their livers will go bad, but what the hell, they got a house where the wall's rotting under the leaky bathroom sink; they got wives whose insides are falling out and a kid who sees cross-eyed, and it could just break your heart to watch the little guy stumbling around with his Coke-bottle glasses, trying to catch a ball, it could just break your heart and I'm not ashamed to say it. Everything—tar and sawdust, bloody fingers and aching backs and broken hearts—digs lines into the faces of men like that, so who can blame them for having a few, because what's better than standing at a bar with your buddies, watching a game and getting to laughing so hard you just feel it in your gut and man, sometimes you really let go, open your mouth wide and laugh and laugh. It was my father's kind of bar, and it was mine.

I arrived sweaty and breathless. I wanted to play pool, but all the tables were taken. So I put my name on the chalkboard and ordered a drink and sat at the bar, catching my breath, watching the games, sipping my whiskey.

I love to drink. Before anyone starts checking off boxes on the alcoholic's diagnostic, let me add that I don't drink to get drunk, not to chase anything away, not sadness nor some dull inescapable ache. I drink because it goes with pool. I drink because I like to lean against the wall with a stick and watch a man perform complex geometry with his eyes, and I like the way a man's hand looks when he arches his fingers for a bridge, and I especially like to take a long last drink and then set down my glass and go over to shoot some pool.

I like the men's slight smiles as I lean over the table. Their eyes are on me, and they're imagining what it would be like to lie on the table and look up at my breasts, and they imagine my hair, blond and wiry like a palomino's tail, coming loose from its clasp and tumbling over my lumberjack's shoulders, across my lips that taste like whiskey, and into their mouths. I know this every time I tie it back so they can imagine its unfastening.

I say I love to drink, but what truly I love is this: I love knowing that those men, in their denim, their twill, faded or new, ironed and rumpled and creased—that all those men will stop smiling as soon as they watch me break that tidy triangle of solids and stripes.

I can tip a cue. I know about English and follow. I can test a table for warp, and I know better than to sit on its edge; I can run the table before I buy another drink, and by that time they'll want to buy one for me, which is the whole point, the reason for my jeans and my long blond hair in a ponytail, my silver hoop earrings and my truly red lipstick. The point is not the drink, and not the men either. The point is that moment when their smiles fade and they realize they have misjudged me completely.

THERE she is, that woman who is me, on a night in August, just a blond woman sitting at a bar, sipping whiskey. This woman wears running shorts and a T-shirt; she stinks faintly of sweat. She's just settling in when her name is called, much sooner than she expected. "Jennie?" a man calls, reading her name off the chalkboard. She rises. "Jennie?"

"I heard you," she says, annoyed. She doesn't like to hear her name advertised this way. "Enough already."

The man is brown-haired and brown-eyed, tall and easy in his body. They bank their balls, and he wins the break. She leans against the jukebox and settles in to watch him. He racks the balls neatly, with an economy she likes. His jeans hang nicely from his slender hips, and his movements are measured, unhurried. He breaks in a way she admires, gently, without the loud crack of a show-off.

"Nice," she tells him. "You've got a good start."

"We'll see how it turns out," he says, chalking his cue, studying the table with a comfortable stillness.

A boy in a blue button-down and raggedy jeans sidles up to her. He props his arm on the wall and leans into her. Pale red hairs, the color of apricots, dust the backs of his hands. She lets a slow easy grin travel over her face. She takes a sip of whiskey.

He says, "What? *What?*"

She says, "You have peach fuzz on your hands."

She watches her opponent bend to shoot. At the last moment, he glances up. He says, "You're not going to let me win tonight, am I right?" She smiles at him over the Apricot Boy's shoulder.

Face it: she's not beautiful. Her eyes are small and brown, and her nose is large. Even so, she has quite a smile, one that curls up, a crescent at each corner, bracketing the grin, giving it a certain rakish mischief. She says, "You're winning so far."

"But I'm talking about the rest of the game," he says.

"So you can tell the future?" she says.

The Apricot Boy, a bit peevish, prods her shoulder. "How did you get so tall?" he says. "Fuckin' A, you're as tall as me!"

"Lumberjack genes," she says. She serves up her tired old story about her grandpa Swifty, the Lumberjack. Swifty liked to drop his hat from his perch atop a redwood, then race it down. He won if he got to the ground in time to catch his hat. And because he was so tall, he usually won. Talking, she bores herself. She can talk and think of something else. It occurs to her that the story doesn't even make sense. What, exactly, did Swifty win?

While she talks, she watches herself appear to lose. The brown-haired man is pretty good. But he only thinks he's winning.

The Apricot Boy thinks he's making another kind of progress. "So your grandpa cut down trees," he says. He looks at her shoes. "Are you a runner? I can tell a runner. Tall people always run." A table of boys begins laughing in waves, laughing so long and hard that heads turn. It's nothing. Just a table of drunken college kids, laughing.

She catches her opponent studying her. He doesn't look away, but meets her eyes head-on. "Are you concentrating?" she asks him.

"I'm focused," he says, and returns to the table.

"My grandparents are from Tucson," the Apricot Boy says.

She tells the Apricot Boy about her father's mother, Edna, raised in backwoods Oregon in the pines and quiet. One day she saw big tall Swifty Davis drive up in an old jalopy, and they fell in love. They married and became her grandparents. Edna was tall, too. Genetics, they work that way.

The brown-haired man misses his next shot.

The Apricot Boy asks what music he should choose for the jukebox. "What do you like?" he wants to know.

She finishes her drink and gets right in his face. "I don't like anything," she says, and pushes past his arm so she can go win her game. She circles the table, considering her options. The Apricot Boy watches glumly.

"Look at him," her opponent says. "You broke his heart."

"I'm not here to get picked up," she says. It's the truth. She may talk to strangers. She may tell them stories about her ancestry, but what she says only masquerades as disclosure. She's here for the pool.

"You're here to win," her opponent says. "You like to win."

She was about to make her shot. She glances up, annoyed. "Of course I do," she says. "What's your point?"

He smiles, a gentle lift of his mouth, his eyebrows raised. "No point," he says. "Just an observation."

In that moment, she likes this brown-haired, unflappable man. He is, she thinks as she kisses the ball into the pocket, serene. She likes that he doesn't seem to have made any assumptions.

And if the Apricot Boy mistook her motives, if he thought he had a real chance with her, it was his fault for assuming, just like they all shouldn't assume she doesn't know how to use a cue. Because what it comes down to is this: you haven't won until you've shot the eight ball, and even on that last shot, you can still lose the game.

F O R me, it is always about the rack, the break, the win. It's about holding back, not hitting too hard, making a great leave. About thinking three balls ahead. About geometry and physics and the clear-cut rules of them. The woman who taught me to play, my own fairy godmother, Essie Leeman, once told me that pool is like a man. You line up those balls, and with a little tap, you put them exactly where you want them to be, so gently it seems like magic, or fate, when really it's just the inevitable result of applying the right force in the right direction. No one mistreats you by accident, Essie used to say. And in pool, the balls only go where you put them. If you're good enough, the worst break in the world can be a setup for a run on the table.

Pool, like romance, isn't just about technique; it's about attitude. You have to shoot as if you can't possibly fail, with that kind of certainty. Otherwise, all the technique in the world is so much theory. For instance: I know what I look like. I'm five foot ten and strong. There's a heaviness about me, not fat but full—full breasts and hips and shoulders. I walk from my hips, something I got from my father. Men don't know what to make of me.

The Apricot Boy is imagining how he could possibly explain me to his buddies. So there's this chick, tall, walks like a man. You know what kind of chick I mean? She's got this big-ass honker and little beady eyes, and I'm thinking *dog*, and fuck if she doesn't give me this big slow smile and all of a sudden I'm thinking I want to fuck this dog. What is it about chicks like that?

It's the hair, my Apricot Boy. Being born blond is great luck—blondes have more fun, gentlemen prefer, ad nauseam. Look, my hair isn't shimmery corn silk; it's wiry, coarse, like curly hair that's been straightened. It's Howdy Doody hair. But long blond hair hypnotizes men into seeing a bombshell.

I didn't, for instance, tell the Apricot Boy how Swifty kidnapped a girl named Edna, eighteen years old and full of herself, and took her on a headlong drive up to Seattle. I didn't tell him that Swifty marched Edna onto a ferry, and as they crossed Puget Sound, he dug his logger's fingers between the cords of her neck, and he told her, *If you don't marry me I'll drown you.*

I didn't reveal any of this to the Apricot Boy or to the brown-haired man I was about to defeat. I know attraction is in what's withheld. I know that flirting is a game. The boys only go where you put them, and what you tell them is your stick. A light touch is necessary. I know about restraint, the key to tricky shots, to drinking and to men, and I know that denim is sexier than velvet, that satin is too slippery, and that whiskey is cheaper when your hair's tied back and you're good at pool.

S H E wins the first game. They play again, and once more. Finally, he lays his stick across his shoulders and hooks his arms over it. He says, "Didn't I say this would happen?"

"So you really do think you can tell the future."

He smiles and ducks his head. His bangs are long and fall in his face. There's a certain delicacy to his features, a fine-featured aristocratic bonyness, that makes him almost too pretty. It's his wide shoulders and his heavy jaw that bring him back to handsome.

He says, "There's a difference between prophecy and the obvious." She has an urge to tuck a lock behind his ear. "For instance, it's obvious you don't think much of most people."

"You're big on that observation shit," she says, once again annoyed.

"Don't get testy on me," he says. "It's not an insult."

"I didn't take it as one," she says. But she is mollified. Isn't he right, after all?

"The only kind of prophecy," he says, "is history. I mean, history is a prophecy you can make for your former self. I can look back and say to my six-year-old self, Hey kid. Watch out. One day you'll meet this woman, and she'll whomp your ass at pool."

"What good is that?"

"That's the problem," he says. "It's a paradox. Knowing the future of your past is like knowing the color of the sky. You can stand there and shout at it, but it's not going to change."

"History repeats itself," she says. "So maybe history is a kind of fortune-telling. It happened before, it'll happen again."

He pushes his hair out of his face. "You really think so?" He takes a drink, and she cannot tell if he's mocking her or genuinely asking her opinion. She likes it tremendously, not being able to tell.

She says, "I sure the hell hope not. You should see how my parents turned out."

Their conversation falls silent. They watch the pool games. She eyes him over the edge of her glass. His legs are very long. Ridiculously, she imagines him playing basketball. She sees him loping down a court, leaping into the air, his touch light, not throwing or lifting so much as guiding the ball to the hoop, his hand against the sharp blue sky and then his fingers extending to their full length, releasing. The ball rolling delicately, lazily away, like the lover's last touch before the boat pulls away from shore, and then the ball drops perfectly through the center of the net.

He's graceful like that. This containment attracts her but makes her feel large and ungainly, and also as if she's frizzy at her edges. He is fine and cleanly drawn, while she is a muddy sketch of a person. Get a grip, she orders herself. Act tall.

He catches her watching. Again, he meets her look head-on. He has the careful air of someone who studies the world, considering angles, as if life is a complicated puzzle he expects to solve.

The thought comes to her quite clearly: *It's him.* Instantly suspicious, she finishes her drink. But already, she feels a future unfolding inside her. She will have this man. She will leave without knowing his name. Calm, cool, elusive. Let him see you that way. She'll find him tomorrow night or next week, hanging around the pool tables, acting surprised to see her. If he's there, she'll have the run of him. "Time to go," she says, rising from her bar stool.

"Maybe next time I'll win," he says.

She lets her smile spread, curling, confusing. Is she ugly or not? "Don't count on it."

"I'll practice," he says. "But I know it's important to you, winning. So I won't practice too hard."

"Good-bye," she tells him firmly.

"What's this," he says. "Your Cinderella act?"

"That would require me to run home in one shoe," she says.

"Can't have that. Blisters and all."

I should be gone by now, I thought. Irritated, I found myself off balance, uncertain of how to play it. "I have to go," I said, but now I sounded tentative, or worse, petulant. Not confident at all.

"If you say so," he said.

"I have plans," I said lamely, stupidly, like a fool. Now I hate him, I thought. "Which don't involve you."

"So you're not going to tell me about your lumberjacks?" he said.

"You're starting to bug me," I said.

"Good," he said, grinning widely. "Then you'll remember me." And he rose. "I have to go, too." He started for the door, which was not at all what I wanted, though I forced myself to stay where I was, because I sure as hell wasn't going to race him for the exit.

Then he stopped and returned to me, and I was triumphant until he spoke. He said, "This is a silly game. I'll sit here and watch you leave, like you wanted. See you later, Cinderella."

"I'm taking both my shoes," I said.

He shrugged. "Alas," he said. "Off you go."

I stalked off without a word. This was no victory. It was the moment I'd planned, but he had taken its meaning out of my hands and changed it into his own. Which, running through the dark unlit streets, I found made me both angry and desperate to see him again, so I could take the meaning back.

QUETZALCOATL

THE day the piano comes from Seattle, Faith plays it through the afternoon. Jennie doesn't listen. She has to wash her hair. Tomorrow is picture day. She hauls water and lights a fire and reads a book on Aztecs which her father got from the library. In school, they're going to learn about the Aztecs, about the conquistadores who had blond hair and so were more like herself than ugly Mr. Martinez. Her hair is the one good thing about her, even though her father, who has red hair, says she must be somebody else's kid.

When she takes the warm water back outside, Faith isn't playing, just staring at the piano keys. Jennie asks, "Are your fingers tired?"

Faith looks like she might cry. She says, "Do you know what my father did? He made rules. Starting when I was five. Rule number one: *Hold on to the handrail.* He added and added to them. He had so many rules for me, he taped lists to the doors of the kitchen cupboards. I'd go for a can of soup and there they were. The night I left, I ripped them all down."

Jennie thinks, What a strange word. Cupboard. It sounds like bureau. Like settee. Exotic and ordinary at the same time. In Jennie's house, there are no cupboards. All they have are shelves made with boards and cinder blocks.

Faith glances at Jennie's bucket. "Don't do that here," she says. "This is my mother's piano."

"I'm not stupid," Jennie says. "I wasn't going to." She lugs the bucket downhill, to the end of the driveway. She uses a cup to wet her hair, and she scrubs and rinses and scrubs again, until her neck aches from bending over. Her mother's music darts and runs and jumps like some kind of animal, or like children holding hands in a circle, spinning.

FAITH gets Jennie's clothes from a box behind the Co-op, where people dump ugly things, striped green pants and purple sweaters with stains. These freebox clothes sit in one corner of Jennie's room, a heap of wrinkles and damp moldy polyester. Spiders probably live in them. When Jennie looks at the Montgomery Ward catalog, she sees what she's supposed to wear, and it's not these green-striped pants and purple stained shirt. Still, Faith brings home freebox clothes like weapons in a war against Jennie, who is winning by not wearing them. Until the day Faith found a dress in the freebox. It was brand-new, still wrapped in plastic, the ruffled collar pinned down. "Why would someone throw away a brand-new dress?" Faith said, unfolding it, holding it up to Jennie.

"Maybe a kid died," Ray said.

The dress has lace and ruffles and red strawberries printed on a white background. Jennie has been saving it to wear for picture day, which is tomorrow. She spreads it out on her bed and stands there with a towel over her hair and admires the strawberries with their tiny yellow seeds, their miniature green leaves. Wouldn't it be nice to have a Fairy Godmother to make her hair perfect with a wand? Never mind. Jennie can do it.

She rips a freebox shirt into strips for curlers, and with these, she rolls up her hair in tight knots all over her head. In the morning, she'll have ringlets. She imagines herself as Cinderella, dancing at the ball, great fat curls bouncing.

Jennie lies in bed, reading the book about the Aztecs and touching the knots in her hair. Tomorrow morning, she'll strut right into school and sit in front of the camera and smile big as can be, big as all the tomorrows in the world put together. She reads for a long time. Montezuma was the leader of the Aztecs, and he thought Cortez was Quetzalcoatl, the Plumed Serpent God who was like Jesus because he was supposed to return and save the Aztecs. But it was a case of mistaken identity. Cortez was only a man, a Spaniard. He stabbed Montezuma in the belly, which is why if you get diarrhea in Mexico it's called Montezuma's Revenge.

When an Aztec priest sacrificed someone, he lifted out the heart and held it, still beating, in his hands.

That night, the baby visits Jennie. He has blond hair and looks like her, and he sits high on a horse with feathers in his hair. He whispers that he loves her. He tells her how they'll run on the mesa between the sagebrush and swim in the Rio Grande, and his breath in her ear smells of milk. In her dream, he says, "I know all the rules, and I'll save you." In the dream, everything is perfect, and they can have anything they want.

THE next morning, Faith sits outside, playing piano, like she stayed up all night, like a Piano Meeting, Jennie thinks, lighting a fire. She puts water on for oatmeal. She takes out her rag rollers, and her hair comes out in long golden ringlets. When her hair is clean and shiny, she feels beautiful. Her hair makes her remember all beautiful women—Miss America, Rapunzel, Cinderella, and now, Cortez the Conquistador, even though he was a man. Her curls bounce on her back. At school, they call her Rubio. Go ahead, she tells them in her mind, Rubio Rubio. It sounds like red stones set in gold, like treasures. Cortez was so beautiful the Aztecs thought he was a god, and they gave him vast riches, and he conquered them all.

Jennie pours milk and honey on her oatmeal and bends close to the bowl so she won't spoil her strawberry dress. If she spins, it looks like a bell. It feels like new, like rich, like everything good and normal in the world. Like canned soup, she thinks, smiling. Like rules.

Faith sees Jennie and stops playing. "Come here," she says. "You still have mud on your legs." She spits on her fingers and rubs Jennie's calf. "It must be from weeding yesterday. With the baby, you'll have to be more sanitary. We should give you Medicine to kill any sickness inside you."

"I won't take it. I don't need it." Jennie hates Medicine. It makes her stomach hurt and her mouth taste bad.

The tinkling music follows Jennie down the road, like little mice. I'll tell you what I need, she says in her head to her mom. I should be wearing strawberry dresses every day of the week. You should be doing my hair with ribbons to match my socks. I should have cupboards, and soup in cans and cold cereal, and rules.

She nears Randall Sandoval's house. Randall's mother has decorations for every holiday of the year, and the Fourth of July decorations, big plastic flags, with smiley faces and feet, still dance across the roof. August doesn't have any holidays. If the baby comes in August, then the month will have a holiday. Jennie's heart beats faster, passing Randall's house. He has pale blue eyes and she loves him. What I need, Jennie tells Faith in her head, is holiday decorations, and a normal mother.

Jennie shakes her head to make her curls bounce.

A T Arroyo al Fin Elementary, there are rules. You aren't allowed to run under the high dark vigas. On Friday at two o'clock, there's chocolate milk, cool and thick and sweet. There's math and there's reading, and in jars on the windowsills, avocado pits pierced with toothpicks grow leaves. An E means excellent and a plus means even more so. In Arroyo al Fin Elementary, you cannot go pee unless you ask first.

There are other rules. Don't look at anyone, especially Stephanie Martinez, who has velvet dresses and long black hair she curls every night. If Stephanie catches you looking, she'll get the kids, Randall Sandoval with his beautiful blue eyes and Marcella Padilla and Tony Lucero and all the rest, to wait after school and follow you up the road, hissing, "Hey Hippie Bush, hey Forest Fire, hey Bush Bush Bush." They'll knock you to your knees and call you Hippie Girl. Even as Stephanie presses her foot into the nape of your neck, you won't say anything, and you won't cry. You'll lie with your cheek against this spinning ground and wait for them to leave.

Today, Mr. Martinez, who is not related to Stephanie, tells them that they're going to start the conquistadores unit, which Jennie already knows. He's talking about why this history is so important. He tells the class, "Your families have histories. Some of you have been here three hundred years and your land has been in your families since the king of Spain gave it to you— and the hippies took it away. Right, Cottonwood?" He calls her this, or Sagebrush, or Tree Needing Water, or Mesquite, or Chamisa. He calls her Saguaro sometimes, or Weeping Willow.

Jennie thinks up names to call him back. Fatso. Fatso with a Mole on his Cheek. Mr. Moletinez. Mr. Moletinez Fatso Face. She looks down the barrel of her pencil, which becomes a gun. She centers the point on Mr. Moletinez's forehead and sends nails across the room. One hits right between his eyes. Mr. Martinez's head explodes. Mr. Martinez is fat and breathes like he's been jogging. His voice is as loud as her own father's. He says the true owners of the land are being driven out and hippies are moving in. He tells his students they're magnificent and they have a powerful heritage, but they probably know nothing about it. He begins quizzing them on the Aztecs and Tenochtit-lán. Who was the feathered serpent? What is a floating city?

The barrel of Jennie's pencil says RANDALL'S LUMBER COMPANY. The same name as Randall Sandoval. Was he named after the pencil, or is it the other way around? Maybe his father owns the company.

Mr. Moletinez is asking her something. She stares at him, and he repeats, "What's the name of the king of the Aztecs?"

She doesn't know the answer. She knew it this morning and two seconds ago, but now she can't remember. She twirls her hair around her finger. It's so soft. The curl pulls straight and bounces, and she can stick her pencil through its middle. Everybody looks so nice. Stephanie Martinez's dress is red velvet with a lace collar. After recess they'll take pictures.

He's saying, "Aren't you listening to me? Aren't you paying attention in my class? Who was the king, and why did he die?" She makes her skin become a mask. He hates her. He hated her from the first day. She thinks, I am Quet-zalcoatl. I am a god, and now I've disappeared behind my feathered mask, and you are dead. Her classmates stare. Why can't she remember the answer?

"Because," she says softly, looking at her hands, at her pencil.

"Because?" Mr. Martinez chuckles. "What kind of answer is that?" His eyes are sharp and black and he hates her. And then he smiles. He says, "I thought you were supposed to be so smart, Weeping Willow." He turns to call on Stephanie Martinez, and then, of course, Jennie remembers.

Montezuma. He saw the conquistadores, with their blond hair and white faces and silver bodies astride horses, and he remembered the prophecy, carved in stone in the holiest of places: *One day a pale four-legged Quetzalcoatl will come from the direction of the sea.*

She remembers all this as Stephanie says Montezuma and Mr. Martinez says very good. He tells them Montezuma had never seen a horse, or a blond man, and so Montezuma thought he saw a god with pale hair and four legs. That's why he let them into his floating city, and that was how the Spaniards defeated the Aztecs.

They tricked Montezuma and killed him because he had the gold and he was powerful, and they stole his treasures and rode clanking in their metal armor to New Mexico. They searched for the Fountain of Youth and the Seven Cities of Gold, and when they saw the adobe pueblos they thought they had found them, but it was only mica flashing in the bricks, catching the sunset. So the conquistadores carved their names in the rocks and claimed the land—

Mr. Martinez stops speaking because there's a knock on the door. The students stretch their necks to see. It's pretty Nurse Gallegos in her white dress and white squeaky shoes. She calls Mr. Martinez over, and they talk softly.

Jennie hears her name. Mr. Martinez turns to her with hard flashing eyes, and these must be the eyes of Cortez when he first saw Montezuma in that great headdress, gold and turquoise and heavy with green feathers. He's smiling. He says she should go with Nurse Gallegos. Jennie stands. But she has it mixed up now. Mr. Martinez's eyes are supposed to be Montezuma's. Cortez drew his sword. Montezuma knew he had been tricked, that this yellow-haired man wasn't a god at all. The sword slid easily into Montezuma's belly. Montezuma's dying eyes: these are Mr. Martinez's eyes leveled on Jennie's. They say, *Devil. Liar. Thief.* "Juniper," he says, "the nurse needs to inspect you." Jennie follows, thinking, I know the answer. Behind her, Mr. Martinez says something in Spanish, and the class laughs. She knows now what she should have said: But he wasn't a king. He wasn't a king at all. How can I get the answer right when you don't ask the right question? He was an emperor, and his name was Montezuma.

I N her office, pretty Nurse Gallegos with her long black hair and white dress sits Jennie down and tells her, "Drop your head, please."

Jennie stares dumbly. Nurse Gallegos clucks her tongue and pushes Jennie's head forward and starts picking at Jennie's hair. Through her curls, Jennie faces the nurse's plump waist and wonders what she did wrong. Does she cheat? No. Does she swear? No. She doesn't go to church and she forgot to wash her legs, but a person can't get kicked out of school for those things, can they? "My mother plays piano," she says.

"How nice." Section by section, Nurse Gallegos works her fingernails across Jennie's scalp. She doesn't say anything about Jennie's curls. She's messing them up. But it's nice, her long fingernails scratching gently.

"My grandpa played piano, too."

"Hold still, 'hita."

The bell rings, and out of the quiet rises the scrape and chatter of children on their way to recess.

"This is a new dress," Jennie says.

Nurse Gallegos finishes. She pats Jennie's head. "You stay here, mihita."

"My mother's having a baby."

Nurse Gallegos's lips are a pale frosty pink, and they match her long fingernails. She pauses in the doorway. "Then it's a good thing I checked you. Just in time." She closes the door firmly behind her, as if to remind Jennie not to leave.

Jennie flips back her hair. Her neck aches, but she misses the nurse's fingers. Through the bumpy glass door, shapes and shadows pass, kids going to climb the monkey bars, play tag, Red Rover, Red Rover send Stephanie right over, swinging and kickball. On the wall hang pictures of Nurse Gallegos's family, older kids and a husband, and a degree.

Montezuma needed a real god. It must have been terrible to think he had found God, and then God stole everything from him, because God was only a man. Maybe he was glad to die after he realized that God was a murderer and a thief.

Jennie stares at a small spider plant on Nurse Gallegos's desk, a pencil sharpener, a bowl of candy. What did she mean, just in time? Jennie takes a red cherry drop. In the hall, Mr. Martinez and Nurse Gallegos talk in Spanish. Careful to keep the cellophane quiet, Jennie unwraps the candy and pops it in her mouth. Not cherry; cinnamon. What to do with the wrapper? Maybe they'll search her pockets like they searched her hair. She pushes it deep into the trash, below wadded papers and a Coke can.

The door opens, and Jennie jumps back from the wastebasket. Nurse Gallegos eyes her suspiciously, but her face softens and she seems almost gentle. She bends over her desk and writes a note, blocking Jennie's view with her neat plump little body. She folds it and puts it in an envelope which she writes on and licks and seals and hands to Jennie. "Tonight, take this to your mom. Don't open it." On the envelope she wrote, Mrs. Burning Davis.

Does she know? Did she hear the plastic wrapper, can she see the red on Jennie's tongue? Mr. Martinez leads Jennie to get her picture taken. She sits at a desk in front of a painting of a classroom. The photographer aims a light at her. She doesn't want to squint, but she can't help it, and anyway, her hair is ruined by Nurse Gallegos's fingernails, so the picture won't be good anyway. "Say *chile con queso*," the man says, only his accent is very bad. He says it, "Chilly cahn kweezo." She stretches out her lips and shows her teeth, but it doesn't feel like a smile at all. The flash explodes.

There are white spots floating down the hallway as Mr. Martinez leads her back to the classroom. Everyone else is at recess. She ducks past his fat belly and sits at her desk. She finger-combs her hair, trying to feel whatever it is that Nurse Gallegos felt. She can still taste cinnamon. Maybe the whole thing was a test, and now they know she steals. Maybe they're worried she'll teach the baby.

After recess the kids come in. Randall Sandoval wears a tie. Stephanie Martinez and Monica Gonzalez wear matching black shoes and white tights, and Monica's dress is blue. They're best friends. Stephanie says, "What are you staring at?"

Jennie turns away too late. Randall asks, "Where did you get your new dress, the Salvation Army?"

Monica giggles. "Your legs are dirty," she says. "Don't you ever wash?"

Stephanie's eyes narrow. "You better stop staring at me, Bush."

Mr. Martinez returns. He says that, thanks to Hippie Tree over there, they all need to stop by the nurse's office on the way to get their pictures taken. One by one, kids are taken away by Nurse Gallegos. They throw mean glances at Jennie, and their whispers hum. Jennie thinks about Tenochtitlán, where flowers hung from baskets on rafts planted with corn crops, and the priests in feathered headdresses climbed a thousand steps to the tops of temples to pray to the sun. Mr. Martinez says something in Spanish, and the class laughs.

AғтЕʀ school they block the road—Berlinda and Stephanie and Monica and Marcia and Janice and Randall Sandoval—yelling, "*Piojo! Piojo cuchina!*" She keeps her head down, her notebook pressed hard to her chest. When she tries to pass, Stephanie blocks her, dodging with Jennie's dodge, and then she grabs Jennie's long ruffled sash and pulls hard. It rips loose in her hand. "*Pobrecita*," Stephanie says. "*Qué lástima, pobrecita*, with your Salvation Army clothes." Jennie keeps her eyes down and her breath held and her face is a mask and she will not, will not cry. Her strawberry dress is ruined.

Stephanie pushes her and she falls, the rocks of the road digging into her palms. Stephanie says, "You had more of those pot parties last weekend, didn't you?" She presses her knee into Jennie's back. "Didn't you? Pot parties. Hippie. Did your mom get real stoned?"

Jennie doesn't answer. She isn't allowed to say anything about the Church. Not even that it *is* a church. Her mother always says, "What you give away, you'll get back tenfold." Jennie wonders what Stephanie will get for kicking her in the ribs.

She does not let herself think about her strawberry dress. They follow her, chanting, "Piojo Piojo Piojo." She makes her face be the empty mask. Inside, she curls tight, shaking. Help me, she wants to cry out. Please God, or Cortez, or Quetzalcoatl, Fairy Godmother. Whatever your name is, help. She begins to run, her notebook pressed to her chest, its spiral digging into her arms, and they throw rocks after her, calling, "Run, Piojo, run!"

Around the bend and up the hill, she stops and leans on her knees, her throat burning. Maybe God hates me because I don't know his name, she thinks.

Gasping, she stares at her shoes and the dust between them. If I were Quetzalcoatl, I'd make them burn in hell. Then she's afraid of her own wish and takes it back. She watches a red and black ant march past her toes. Ants can lift many times their body weight. They can find their way home by the angle of the sun. She got an A on that test, too.

She suddenly understands something so instantly, so perfectly, that it almost feels like God whispered it in her ear. Montezuma didn't need a god. He just needed to know the real names of things. He needed to look at Cortez and say, That is a Man.

She looks ahead of her, toward home. She stands up straight, looks down on Alfin, at the little houses and the buffalo grazing in the Padillas' field. Buffalo are in the same family as cows. Bovines. A blue pickup heads west, a plume of dust on its tail. The sun sets in the west. A truck moves because of the Internal Combustion Engine. She looks at the sky and she looks at the fat clouds floating away to the end of the world, as evenly spaced as corn, like God's endless rain crop. Cumulonimbus. They're filled with water. The same water that fell on Montezuma, that filled the lake where Tenochtitlán floated, that watered Adam and Eve's Garden of Paradise. The Water Cycle. Some things are true and forever like that.

It won't always be this way. Even if they laugh and call her names, she's smarter than all of them put together. They can call her Piojo and whatever else they want. She knows her real name, and inside herself she's already Jennie. She can always learn the true names of things. She knew long division before anyone else; she knows about Aztecs and the sprouting of avocados. So this is what she'll do. She'll learn. She'll learn until she can stand atop this hill and name everything she sees. Because when you know the true names of things, no one can trick you. No one can slide a sword into your belly and take all your gold.

F A I T H is sitting on the piano bench. She isn't playing; she just sits, staring. "Mom, I have a note," Jennie says.

Faith looks up, startled. "What did you do to your dress?"

"They did it."

Faith sighs. "What do you do to make them hate you?"

Jennie holds out the letter. *I hate you,* she thinks. *What do you do to make me hate you?*

"Lice," Faith says when she finishes reading.

"Lice?"

"Bugs that eat your scalp. They're called lice. I think they're in the spider family. They want me to get RID. But I'm not getting that poison."

Jennie feels little bugs, like spiders, living on her scalp.

"You can see their eggs," Faith says, plucking a hair from Jennie's head. "See?" Little white specks, clinging to the blond strand. Jennie scratches.

"Don't scratch. They like that. It makes blood for them to eat."

Jennie scratches harder; they're eating her, scurrying around, biting. "Get them off!" she cries. They are like spiders.

"Stop it!" Faith yells, trapping Jennie's hands in her own. "We'll use kerosene," she says. "They want us to use a chemical that will get into your brain and cause cancer. Kerosene will do it better." She goes inside and returns with a Mason jar of yellow, greasy liquid.

Faith makes Jennie take off her dress and put on her swimsuit and get on her hands and knees in the driveway, downslope from the piano, in the mud from washing her hair yesterday. Faith pours the kerosene over her head. It's oily and trickles down her arms and drips off the tips of her hair and runs between her feet. The fumes sting and she coughs.

"Keep your eyes closed. It can make you blind," Faith says.

Jennie worries kerosene will go straight through Faith's skin to the baby. Maybe he'll be born without eyes. She keeps her eyes open to make sure he's safe while Faith pours more kerosene. Squinting, Jennie studies the legs of the piano bench. Here: something Faith didn't think of. Hinges. The bench must open up. Maybe there's money inside, treasure, something like that. This keeps her calm while kerosene dribbles between her knuckles and between her knees and Faith scrubs hard, making Jennie sway.

"This will kill them," Faith says. "I should give you Medicine, too."

"Ow! Not so hard." It feels like she's scratching deep into Jennie's scalp, not at all like Nurse Gallegos. "You're making food for them!"

"They're dead by now," Faith says, dumping cold well water over Jennie's head. She squirts herbal shampoo and scrubs and scrubs until Jennie's hands and knees and shins are covered with mud and kerosene, and green perfumed suds. Faith rinses and soaps three times, but the oily stinging smell won't go away. Just as they're about to try a fourth time, the Dodge pulls into the driveway. Jennie knows it by the roar of its engine. Finally. Through her hair she sees her father's work boots with the hole in the toe and the red laces. She pushes her hair out of her eyes.

"It came," he says. He's talking about the piano, but for a second it almost sounds like he thinks she had the baby. Faith stands between Ray and the piano, as if she can hide it with her belly. "She's got lice," Faith says. "The school nurse sent a letter."

His thick fingertips poke around in Jennie's hair. "She smells like a gas station."

"I washed it with kerosene."

"Who told you to do that?"

"I don't know. Joy."

Jennie squints, blinks water from her eyes. "Can I get up now?"

They ignore her. Ray tries to get around Faith, but she blocks his path. He says, "When did it come?"

"If it doesn't work," Faith says, "we'll have to cut off her hair."

"No!" Jennie cries. She jumps to her feet. "I won't let you!"

"Be quiet," Ray says. He presses a piano key. The one note seems to stretch on forever, like the sound never stops—it just travels too far away for them to hear. "It's worth a lot of money. We could get a new car."

"It's mine," Faith says, slamming the lid over the keys. He snatches his hand away just in time.

Jennie says, "They're gone. I don't feel them." But she feels them.

"It got here fast," Ray says. "Who'd you fuck?"

Faith picks up the water bucket and looks like she might throw it at Ray.

He says, "That was a joke."

"It wasn't funny. Talk like that isn't funny."

He sighs. "Listen, we need this kind of money."

"It's mine."

Jennie says, "I don't feel them anymore." She goes inside and watches them from the kitchen window. Faith yelling, crying, and Ray yelling, marching around and around the piano. Jennie explores her hair. The piojos are gone. She can tell.

But that night, in bed, she scratches and scratches until she has blood under her fingernails. She smells kerosene; she dreams her father sets her hair on fire, only her father is Montezuma with a feather headdress. She wakes up, gasping. Their little legs, their little mouths chew on her, and she thrashes, tangling and snarling her hair. Piojos. Lice. Spiders.

Maybe if she could go back to sleep, she'd feel better in the morning. But lying there, she remembers the baby. Any day now, Faith says. And when the baby comes, everything has to be just right, clean and healthy.

Jennie goes to the kitchen. Some things you just have to do. Next to the stove, in a jar with a screwdriver and pens, she finds scissors.

Outside, in the muddy driveway that smells of kerosene, Jennie stands on the piano bench, her bare toes gripping its edge. She pokes the blade into her hair and closes the big scissors quickly, before she changes her mind. The hair falls, tickling her legs and back like spiderwebs, to her feet, to the ground below. She chops and cuts. She begins to cry. Be brave, she tells herself sternly, do what you have to do, and she cuts until the blades are next to her scalp and her hair is short enough, and then she is safe for the baby.

Panting, she listens to the night. She can make out her father's Dodge. The moonlight shimmers on the lice-filled mud. She can hear the river, all the way down in the valley.

It's not even an idea, really, just curiosity that makes her step off the bench and lift its lid. Inside, she finds papers, and a photo album. She takes them to her room. She turns on the light, which blinds her for a moment. She reads the golden letters on the album's leather cover. Treasured Memories. She thinks, *Montezuma*.

Here are scribbled notes in the margins of the music sheets: *Faith*, it reads, *remember . . .* and then complicated rules, instructions with words like inversion and accelerando. *When you teach Jennifer* (it says, and she tells herself, that's me: he's talking about me) *quarter notes, you'll have to cut up apples to show her,* and more: *Don't push her. Your middle name must be PATIENCE. Each child goes at his own speed, but guard against laziness.*

There are rules. Pages of them, written in different handwriting, one after the other, old yellow tape in the corners of the paper. *54. No swimming without Father. 55. No more than two tablespoons of butter a day.* The first one is written in large black letters. *Do not go down the stairs alone.* So Faith remembered this wrong.

Jennie has never seen a picture of her grandparents, and the album is filled with black-and-white photographs with fancy serrated edges. The first is of a house in a meadow with trees behind it. The caption, in flowing white handwriting on black paper, says: *The house that Grandfather built.* It looks so real,

so different from the New Mexico adobes with their flat tin roofs. Grandfather's house has a peaked roof with shingles, and a porch that stretches the
whole front of the house, and a stone chimney. It looks like something out of
Jennie's *Book of Fairy Tales.*

Lipa and Paul on their wedding day, and the horrible stairs: They stand at
the foot of stairs that go up a hill, up and up and up, probably a hundred or
even two hundred stairs. Paul, a funny little man with glasses, wears a three-
piece suit buttoned over a round little belly, a bald, round-cheeked egg of a
man. And Lipa! Lipa, tall and elegant. My grandmother! Lipa in a full skirt,
an embroidered blouse, and a crown of blond braids, Lipa laughing, bent at
the waist, but still four inches taller than Paul.

Pages of the newlyweds, and a pregnant Lipa, and then, *Lipa, with Faith
on her first day home:* Lipa sits outside on a bench, and the edges of her
cheeks and her hair—blond like mine!—glow in the sun. Behind her grow
ferns and a tree covered with pale flowers. Her smile is sleepy and joyous, but
also startled. Maybe she was staring at her baby. Paul said, *Look at me,* and
she glanced up just for a second. Beautiful Lipa.

Grandma, Jennie thinks, You don't know the future. One day, long after
you're dead, your granddaughter, me, will live with an outhouse and no running water. She will be called Piojo. Grandma, Jennie thinks, I cut off all my
hair. She touches her head, and tears rise in her eyes. Now they will call me
baldy. They will say, The tree lost her leaves. Who cut your hair, the Salvation
Army? Grandma. What do I do? She wants to hear Lipa's answer so much.
Her tears slip down her face. I'm ugly now.

Lipa, smiling gently, would say, *It will grow back, child.*

The new daddy: Paul, holding the baby in the crook of his elbow, like a
book he doesn't know how to read. And pages of the happy three, and then
Faith growing into a little girl, holding a pail, standing on a hill: *Faith and her
blueberries on Bainbridge Island.* Page after page of Faith in pigtails and shiny
shoes, swimming, sitting at a piano, blowing candles, opening Christmas presents. Jennie is very angry.

That's supposed to be my life. I should have been born in Seattle, been
raised by my grandparents in a beautiful house on a high hill. See, there is its
picture. That should have been my home. I should have learned piano so I
could sit beside my grandfather and play with him, like Faith is doing there.
My mother stole all of this from me.

Is that how Cortez felt when he saw the beautiful floating city? This is supposed to be mine? Is that how Montezuma felt when he saw Cortez? Did he
think, This is what I have been waiting for all along; this is Quetzalcoatl?

Looking at her true family history, Jennie sees the future. All of this here—

this name, Juniper, this house in Arroyo al Fin—all of this is only a case of mistaken identity, or a big lie. The truth is something else. It has another name. She will steal the truth from her mother. She'll keep it under the piled freebox clothes, her buried Treasured Memories. She'll study them in secret and learn all about her rich grandparents who played piano and lived in a place where ferns grow outside.

She'll keep Paul and Lipa's album for the baby brother who is coming. She'll tell him exactly what is his. And her middle name won't be Patience, but Lipa.

Twenty-four Hours
to Forever

Less than eight hours after I played pool, on my first morning of medical school, I found myself in the throes of disappointed expectations. I had wanted to be a doctor for a long time. A doctor was someone who knew truth, *real* truth. Chemistry, physics: how the body works. The actual interior of ourselves. Spleen, heart, liver, the electricity of potassium and sodium becoming the nerve impulses that raise your hand to your beloved's cheek.

So there I was, in the swami's courtyard. I wanted to feel wonder, but what I felt was that I was in a furniture store. Stainless steel tables cluttered the room, a body on each, and I wanted to be moved by those bodies lying under drapery and wrappings, waiting to teach me what it means to be human. But I only smelled fresh paint and formaldehyde, and I thought of half-priced sofas on the showroom floor.

I felt flat. I imagined lying on one of the tables so a student could cut into my chest to verify that my heart was actually pumping blood, because I felt—there was no other word for it—flat. Not nervous, not frightened, not thrilled or disgusted. I told myself that this cadaver on the table was once a person. This is a sad and terrible fact, I lectured myself. I tried to imagine the family who mourned this slab of meat. What was it like? There was a moment when the relatives sat bedside, around them the whir and tick of machinery. Their loved one was there, and then she was gone. The passage mattered only because there was a family to take notice. What was it like to be mourned? I could just see my father trucking in from Florida, stoned and weepy, strumming out a cowboy song, while my mother blamed it on astrology and tore out her hair in clumps. She would have a Funeral Meeting. Legions of Medicine People would come, and the pies would be whole wheat, and my mother would say a long, incoherent prayer, weeping and wailing and Heavenly Fathering about Juniper Tree Burning. Sunny would be in Timbuktu. He'd send a postcard. None of it would have anything to do with me.

No, not them. My family was not capable of the mourning I wished for myself. Nosiree Bob. If ever I've wanted anything, it's a membership in the real world of family and kids and bedtime stories, the reliable progression of the small rituals like cornflakes for breakfast and after-school piano lessons. These small melodies of life punctuated by the crescendos of big events: a sweet-sixteen birthday party, a big wedding, and yes, even my own funeral. The thing was, at that moment in the room filled with cadavers, I couldn't imagine even a husband to drop his head in his hands and cry, *She's gone.* I couldn't imagine a man who was capable of loving me that much, or, for that matter, a man I could love back.

If I care so little for people, I thought, then why be a doctor?

This was the moment of Christian Braverman's arrival. I swear he arrived at this precise instant, like an answer. Hello, Question. Hello, Answer.

"The pool shark," he said.

"The mark," I said.

This is how Jennifer Davis and Christian Braverman meet for a second time. Go ahead. Call it destiny. Or call it logical convergence: on a sweaty night before a big day, two people go out to Antonio's Pool Hall to unwind. The following day, because their names are Braverman and Davis and the ros-ters are alphabetized, they're assigned to the same cadaver. Call it God or cir-cumstance or the English alphabet. They are shaking hands, touching for the first time. Now they know names. The rest follows. It takes only another twenty-four hours to make a lifetime inevitable.

An administrator is talking now. He says the walls are freshly painted. Jen-nie, contemplating coincidence and hardly listening, leans against the wall, lifts a knee, and presses a boot print into that nice new paint. She glances at Chris, who eyes the sheet-covered body the same way he studies a pool table. Looking for the first, best move.

I was thinking, If I tell this to our children, I'll say, Three times we played pool and never said our names, but it didn't matter, because the next day—

—*There he was!* our two children will shout, tucked safely into my shelter-ing arms. I'll turn the page of our Wedding Album to his picture in a tuxedo, tall and brown-eyed, ready to solve this great big puzzling world.

The next day, I'll say, there he was. Christian Braverman. *Over a cadaver!* they'll shriek. And I will say, Over a cadaver, which means dead body, but that isn't a bad thing in this story.

The administrator went on and on about the walls. I whispered to Christian Braverman, "What does he think we'll do, play handball with livers?" Chris-tian Braverman, called Chris, pointed at my shoe pressed to the paint. I kept my position. "Aren't you observant," I said.

"Don't be embarrassed," he whispered. "Nobody saw but me."

Imagine this. What if the handsome prince, waltzing a clumsy Cinderella around the dance floor, said to her, "Don't worry; nobody can tell that you sleep in a fireplace." I stood there, faking nonchalance, dizzy with what Chris had just said. How did he see me so clearly? I hated it. I loved it. I wanted him to do it again. Then I would kill him.

T H I S is how Chris tells it:

At last, the speeches were over, and Chris was elected to make the first cut in our cadaver. He stood, scalpel poised, for a long time. He, too, was imagining his death. He thought, My parents are old. They'll die before me. He was, in other words, also feeling this odd flatness. He looked at me. I stared back without smiling, my foot pressed to the wall, my arms over my breasts. My eyes, he tells me, were indignant, as if I were thinking, How dare you become a part of my life? Once is forgivable, but twice is trespassing. He could tell I was not as mean as I looked.

I said, "The guy is dead." He flinched, startled. I said, "You won't hurt him." Demonstrating from the start my usual incapacity for niceties. Chris overlooked my words. He looked over them and through them, beyond my smile, which is like my brother's, wide, curving, my best and only beauty, and into my eyes. What he claims is this: in my eyes, he saw loneliness and grief, and it moved him. "You were afraid," he tells me.

"I was nothing," I say. "You were projecting."

"You," he says, playing along. "You times two."

We joke, but I know this next part to be true. He knew I was imagining a future for us. He, too, saw our lives laid out before us, together until the end, when one of us would mourn the other's passing.

" A N D then," I would say to my children, as I closed the Wedding Album—

"Then you fell in love!"

I'd wait, to let them know about interrupting. "Then," I'd say, after a long, squirming silence, "he gave me a ride in his golden chariot."

The first day of school and we skipped the next class, like the bad kids in a fifties sitcom. He said, "I'll carry your books for you."

I said, "You'll break your back."

"For you, anything," he said, and as always he gave me the feeling he was playing along. He took our backpacks, one slung over each shoulder. "After you, Cinderella," he said.

"So you've been searching for me?"

He grinned. "That was your plan last night, wasn't it?" and walked beside me politely, gravely.

"You're a prince," I said.

"Or a packhorse," he said.

I surveyed each car ahead, wondering which would be his, and then he stopped. I stood beside him, waiting, trying to hide my awe. He drove a 1976 Silver Shadow, which is, for those not in the know, a Rolls-Royce. I loved it, the unapologetically old-fashioned lines of the curving fenders, the two-toned paint job, the woman perched on the grill which itself looked like a metal version of some Greek temple. "It's not mine," he said, opening the driver's door. He didn't, apparently, bother to lock up.

"What," I said, "you stole it?"

"My father's. Wait here." He walked around to the passenger door.

"You're opening the door for me?"

"No," he said. "I can't allow you in. You'll melt." He left all four doors hanging open like panting mouths, and he rolled down all the windows. I thought of my brother, how I had cooled off the car for him this same way when we were kids.

Chris and I leaned against the hot fender, waiting for the worst of the superheated air to move out of the car, and we kept up the prickly bantering of the night before, a conversation like a pool game, an edgy partnership (because you need two for a game) that was also adversarial, and I was thinking, God, my God, is this him?

Chris started the whole Cinderella thing, and he probably thought I wanted a Prince Charming, but the fact is, I'm not after the kid with the Golden Chariot (though I'd never scoff at the Rolls); I'm after the knight. Not the hapless fellow who can't even keep his intended from bolting at midnight, who wanders around waving shoes at random girls, but the invincible, the perfectly certain guy on the horse, the one who comes galloping in with a map and bests the foes and sweeps me onto his horse and takes me away. This guy knows where he's going; he's got the route mapped, so that I can just rest for even the littlest while, my cheek against the horse's white mane, my eyes closed, the horse gliding through the world while I float on sleepy, safe dreams, the knight strong at my back, the horse's spine, its warm solid flesh, the beat of the hooves something like music. For once, someone else takes the reins and chooses the way. A shameful fantasy, but then what good is a fantasy if it doesn't have a hard little kernel of shame embedded deep in its heart?

I felt myself faltering. Sweating, leaning against the hot fender, I felt all at once the ways I was lacking: I'm too tall, too large, too loud, my nose too big and my eyes too small. Doubt is the enemy, but this is no pool game, and desire can lead to disaster.

Two girls, carrying books against their chests, obvious freshmen, walked past, stopped, and returned to stare at the car. One of them asked, "Is that a real Rolls-Royce?"

"No," I said. "It's a fake."

"You don't have to be a bitch," the girl said.

"You don't have to be standing here," I said.

"Bitch," she said. Off they went. I loved them for giving me a chance to regain my footing.

"You're mean," Chris said. "I'm scared of you."

Pleased, I flashed him a nice Essie grin. "So your dad just lent this to you?" I asked. "For tooling around? Hey, son, take the Rolls and get me a quart of milk? Sounds fishy to me."

He smiled. "I confess. It's mine. It's my high school graduation present." He watched a jogger trot by, goosenecking. "My parents thought it was safe, a big hunk of steel."

"You want steel, get a pickup."

"That's what I said. They said they thought a Rolls would be special, something my friends didn't have." I laughed. "Please don't laugh," he said, laughing himself. "It's no joke."

"Don't you wish they'd just given you the money?"

"That's the real joke," he said. "They got it used. It's worth five, maybe ten thousand. Minus maintenance." Among his parents' many miscalculations: the Rolls was not trustworthy. He'd taken it to the mechanic fourteen times. "And counting," he said. "Plus it gets lousy mileage." In short, he hated the car. He hated the whistles of new friends, the pedestrians in crosswalks, gaping at the goddess on his grille.

At last, we got inside. It had remarkably old-fashioned appointments, no air conditioner, no electric windows. Its luxuries were of a different sort: the glossy cherrywood dash, the dark brown leather. In the backseat, there were map-reading lights for passengers. The wide front bench seat was the size of a small couch.

I climbed over the couch, into the back. "Onward, James," I said.

"Stop it," he said. "Please."

"Poor Chris," I said, "gagging on his silver spoon. Come on back here, you sensitive man." He climbed over. I had the upper hand now, but instead of gloating, I tucked his bangs behind his ear. Reeling from the tenderness of my gesture, which I most certainly had not planned, I looked out the window. We were both sweating profusely. It's not a very good idea to sit for long inside a parked car in August in Albuquerque, New Mexico. Sweat rolled down my temple, the nape of my neck. Two teenage boys stopped, and one circled the car like he was getting ready to buy it. "See what I mean," Chris said.

"If you hate it so much, why not get rid of it?"

Chris said, "Because it's their gift to me." This, I'd learn, is his way. Chris accepts what you give him because it came from you. "My parents are old," he said. "They had me in their forties. But they were thinking, I'm guessing, that it would be"—his forehead wrinkled, giving him the look of a concentrating child; an ache came into my chest, a desire to kiss him tenderly, and it was like a fist squeezing my heart—"funky," Chris said. "They wanted to give me something that would be kitschy, unusual, hip. Don't laugh. They were thinking the Beatles, I guess. I didn't want to hurt their feelings when they were so proud of how creative they'd been. My father actually used the word 'neat,' and he wasn't talking about scotch. 'Isn't it neat?' he said. You'd have to meet my father to understand."

I closed my eyes and lifted my chin. "Kiss me, James," I said. He took his time. I waited longer than I expected. I began to get nervous, to wonder if I had said the wrong thing or misread him entirely. I wondered how I would extricate myself, how I would open my eyes and still salvage my dignity, how I would survive a semester in gross anatomy after this humiliation.

I jumped a little when at last his lips met mine. He kissed me softly, with the considerate care of a man doing an important thing for the first time. His tongue was cooler than the air around us. His hands were warm, and where we touched, the sweat followed.

It was August in Albuquerque; we were breathlessly hot. We drew back and laughed. Our hair was damp against our skin. We climbed over the seat.

The car ran not so much quietly as smoothly, a steady, even hum, a pleasing background murmur. We took the Rolls for a spin, and the people we passed stared as if it were the first car to arrive in New Mexico.

"NOW?" our someday children would cry.

"Now," I'd say. "Within twenty-four hours, we fell in love, and in four months we married, and then we lived happily ever after. The end."

They would protest, offended by my abrupt conclusion. But it would be bedtime. It would be warm pajamas with feet, kisses on foreheads. A closet cracked for light. My husband and I drawing up our covers, holding whispered conferences on the rhythm of our days.

I wish I could say it turned out like that. I want to have children, and I want to tell them how their mother and father lived happily ever after. Only things went so wrong at the wedding, and now my brother is dead, and I have run away in a beat-up old Ford truck. I doubt everything. How can I not? If I could leave Chris as easily as crossing a street, how can I predict a forever for us? How can I be sure it was anything like love?

Tonight I am driving north in this truck, away from my husband. I know nothing about the future, not even what I want it to be. I imagine going back a year to last August, to a pool hall where Jennie sits in her running shorts, sweaty, drinking whiskey. If I could walk up to her and tap her on the shoulder, what would I say? Beware, I would say. Pay attention. You don't know what you think you know. Here it comes.

Once again, I'm jumping the gun. For now, whatever we know of their future, let's just say they lived happily ever after, the bride and the groom, as long as they both did live.

ℬLAME IT ON GOD
(THE YEAR OF SIGNS)

1966–67, Seattle and New Mexico

OKAY, I confess. Before I was ever Jennifer Braverman, I was called Juniper Tree Burning, and my mother's name was Faith. My father was Ray; my brother was Sunny Boy Blue, and we all lived in a house in a valley called Arroyo al Fin.

But the story of my name begins long before Faith was anyone's mother. When she, too, was a little girl with three names: Faith Lipa Chatwin. The first is for Catholic piety; the second is after her Russian mother. The third is for her God-hating father, Paul, a piano teacher, under whose stern tutelage Faith lives, in a house on a hill in Seattle. The hill is so steep it takes 213 steps to reach their front porch.

Faith, obedient daughter, running scales with aching fingers and combing her wet hair into a tight braid. A little girl in a faraway land, where ferns grow wild and it rains all day. Her mother, Lipa, died of a cold when Faith was five, and it turned her father mean.

She hates her father. Every day after school, Faith stands at the foot of the long flight of stairs and promises herself she'll run away soon. With each step she climbs, she says, "I hate him. I hate him." She hates the endless list of rules he tapes to the insides of the kitchen cupboards. She hates him for making her practice piano, for slamming the lid down on her fingers. She hates every one of those 213 steps.

By her eighteenth birthday, she has taken to lying, to climbing out of windows and running with boys. By her nineteenth summer, she's pregnant by one of her backseat lovers, and Good Catholic Girl, she's desperate. She goes to a hippie house, to ask a friend of a friend how to get an abortion.

She knocks. A voice calls, "Open," a command or a description, and she enters a room where trash—books and newspapers, beer bottles and food scraps—lies thick on the floor. In front of the window, in a sagging easy chair, slouches a man with a leg so badly broken he smells of rot. He has painted his cast with Technicolor fish. He's playing guitar in a doodling, distracted way.

They begin with a lie. "I'm Faith," she says. "I'm supposed to watch TV." It's all she can think of, because she sees the TV in the corner. "Carrie said I could."

He begins to sing. "Good morning, little schoolgirl," he sings. "Can I go home with you?"

She asks, "Isn't Carrie here?" She carries a daisy-shaped purse. She wears plastic daisies in her hair and a daisy-printed dress she made herself. She wonders if he stinks because a part of him has already died. He's terribly ugly.

But then he smiles, a gorgeous, transforming smile, wide and lifting at the corners, bracketed by two crescents. "Carrie is sweet, but liquor is quicker," he says. His eyelids droop. He's drinking beer at ten in the morning, and he probably has any number of drugs muddling up his brain, rendering him dangerous, but she's reassured by his cast. "What happened to your leg?" She crosses her arms and longs to leave.

"Rhinoceroses," he says. "Or is it rhinoceri? What's the plural of rhinoceros?"

She smiles nervously. "Rhinoceroses," she says. "I guess."

"Guessing isn't certainty," he says. And maybe, somewhere in that trivial exchange—though she doesn't yet feel the pull of attraction for this wild-haired man who hasn't introduced himself, who sits like a king in the corner—somewhere in this exchange, she's hooked. His name is Raymond Seamus Davis. He is my father.

"Look it up," Ray says. He waves his hand in the general direction of a bookcase. Lit by afternoon sunshine, his frizzy hair glows, an orange nimbus. Her first sexual thought about him is this: I would like to cut that hair, brush it flat against his skull. "Go on," he says. "I'm a cripple here."

She fetches the dictionary, and when she finds the answer, she's frightened. Of what? That he'll send her away? "It's rhinoceroses."

He grins at her. "There you go," he says. "You were right. A sign."

Shyly, she returns his smile. How could she not? This strange-looking, ugly man has an irresistible smile. "What really happened to your leg?"

"You doubt me? You don't think I know what happened to my own leg? Were you there? Did you see it happen?" He sounds genuinely, violently angry, and she takes a step back, frightened. "I was at the circus and the rhinoceroses gored my leg. One of them was named Mildred." Ray stops his distracted guitar doodling, laying his palm over the strings. "Carrie isn't here," he says, "but you can watch TV if you fuck me first."

It's 1966. These things happen all the time. But she has taken Holy Communion wearing shiny Mary Janes. Faith, who has not yet learned to love the Beatles. What makes her say yes? Perhaps she has some vision of inevitability.

Perhaps it's his red hair in the light, or his crippled leg, his smile. "Okay," she says.

"Come here," he says.

She perches on the arm of the chair like an obedient child and, transfixed, looks for the first time into his strange eyes, close together and deep-set and the palest green she has ever seen, like bottle glass held to the light. For a moment, she thinks he'll kiss her, and in a swoon of readiness, she closes her eyes. When she opens them, he's looking at her still.

O N E day, these two people will have a daughter, and that daughter will grow into a woman who cannot tell this story without interruption. To a listener, it might seem that the daughter, who is me, is lost in thought for a moment. But in truth, the daughter is horrified and repulsed and mystified: I am the result of this ugliness. How did it happen? What of Faith, perched on the arm of his chair? Why does she say yes?

Why does a girl touch the rabid dog and think, Poor little sick thing?

And what of Ray, studying this chesty Annette Funicello look-alike, this Mouseketeer with the dictionary pressed to her breasts? Her grave brown eyes meet his, and in them he sees nothing but *Yes,* and he's afraid of what he might do with all that permission. She looks so yielding, yet also terribly breakable. She returns his stare with great solemnity and fortitude, for some unimaginable reason trusting him.

Me? He wants to ask. Really?

Without thinking, he reaches up and touches her lower lip with his finger. He traces a line down the middle of her chin, down her throat, to the first button of her dress. She doesn't flinch. Already his hand is slipping the first button through its hole, baring a white wedge of skin, and then another button, another. She sighs, but her eyes stay on his. He slides his hand inside her bra and there he finds the heavy, the warm and yielding breast. He waits for her to slap him. He thinks, *Stop me!* She gasps, a sharp intake of breath, but her eyes brim with wonder and obedience, and he feels daring, powerful.

But because this is history, the rest follows. He smiles. "I changed my mind," he says.

Run, Faith. Run breathless crying, sobbing more likely, down the stairs of that abandoned building, down the block, across the trolley tracks and to the docks where Puget Sound will finally stop you. Stand there until you stop crying. Until you realize you still have his dictionary clutched to your bosom.

• • •

T H E I R stories differ in many respects, but they both agree on that first proposal and certain events which follow. That first time, Faith is the one who
runs away. And Ray tracks her down, takes her for the abortion. Afterward, he
holds her tightly, stooping to put his arm around her; at six-four, he's a full
fourteen inches taller. He sings into her hair, "I've got shoes. You've got shoes.
When we get to heaven, we'll all have shoes." That night, he takes her out on
the Sound in a rowboat, feeds her hot toddies from a thermos, wraps her in a
blanket and sings her songs in time to the rocking of the water. He sings, "The
river is wide, I cannot get o'er. Give me a boat that can carry two, and both
shall row, my love and I." He seems to have a song for every moment of life,
and rocking in that rowboat, she imagines him singing to her through the
years, the two of them making music out of even the most painful times.

Years later, their daughter will tell herself this: I give them this night on the
Sound because there had to be something. Despite kidnappings and coer-
cion, there had to be a falling in love. There had to be a peace, a moment of
tenderness, a moment of calm. I insist on it. I will give it to them.

T H R E E months after she meets Ray, Faith hangs from her bedroom window
by her fingertips. She lets go for the last time. A year later, in the fall of 1966,
in the fifth month of Faith's second pregnancy, Ray's cast finally comes off. To
celebrate, they drop acid. They find themselves standing across the street from
the courthouse. She's afraid, because the pavement is moving and still at the
same time. Ray holds out his hand and calls, "Come on. Step off the curb. I'm
here." In this same way, he dares her into the judge's office, into marriage. He
says, "Don't be a drag, Faith. Just jump."

To celebrate, Ray takes his new wife for a picnic down by Seattle's Golden
Gardens. For a while, they sit in his Dodge, a battered, creaky relic, and watch
the boats on the water. On her knees, Faith holds a pillowcase filled with a
roasted chicken, a jug of wine, and a bag of weed. Ray smiles at her; he winks.
She smiles back. "Let's go for a drive," he says. And then, in a moment of
whimsy, or madness, or both, with only fifty-three dollars and a packet of food
stamps in his wallet, Ray restarts the truck and drives out of Seattle without
even stopping for gas.

At first Faith thinks it's fun, an adventure. They're approaching the Oregon
border when she starts to beg him to turn back, but he only laughs, teases, offers to score her a couple Quaaludes. In short, he kidnaps her.

He heads down the coast and then inland on a circuitous route, as if to be
sure no one can track them down. Faith, small and buxom, huddles against
her door, as if at any moment his long arm will unfurl like an elephant's trunk

and smash in her face. Ray—so tall, so furious and funny, of the marvelous smile and pale green eyes, his leather cowboy hat pushed down on his bushy red hair—strains over the wheel, as if over the mane of a horse, urging it forward. His hat brushes the roof. The windshield is cracked like the map of a river and all its tributaries.

Somewhere near Utah, Faith says, "What if it's cold? What if it snows?"

He stops in Wendover and trades his dead father's silver and ivory harmonica for a Coleman stove. He convinces the pawnshop man the harmonica is a hundred years old. The man throws in a sleeping bag. Ray tosses these prizes in the back of the truck. He says to Faith, "Trust me. Everything has an answer."

Faith doesn't reply. On her own, she bought herself a frail golden wire of a ring, which she presses into the skin of her marriage finger. She wears the same four-tiered skirt and gathered peasant blouse she chose for their picnic two days before. A red babushka covers her unwashed hair. She hates the way she smells; she knows her own stink by his. He wears a flannel shirt, Levi's that grow dirtier and dirtier, and it seems to her that the highway center stripe ticks off not just land but years, that they are traveling back to a time when people like the Donners spent months in the same clothes, with nothing to eat but each other. Ray has that smell, that desperate wild look about him.

She says, "How will we feed ourselves?"

Ray stops and buys them a fifty-pound bag of rice. "Winter supplies," he tells her as he heaves it into the bed of the Dodge. He tells her stories. He sings her songs about the Western Trail. "Get along little dogie," he sings, as if he knew what that was. He tells her maybe they'll go to Guadalajara, where the locals sleep in hammocks and bathe in the sea and eat avocados as big as the heads of newborns. Maybe they'll live in New Mexico and herd sheep. They'll build a house with their own hands, make adobe bricks from water and dirt. "Back to nature, the noble savage," he says. "All that shit."

She tucks her skirt under her feet, hugs her knees. "I'm cold," she says.

"That's being alive you're feeling."

He says he knows how to hunt, how to be a carpenter. She can garden, can't she? Or does she want to waste her life plunking away on a piano in Seattle?

Faith weeps silently. "I'm having a baby," she says. "What about that?"

He lifts his foot from the accelerator. Somehow, this frightens her more than if he had tromped on the brakes—this slow drift, as if Ray has forgotten where they are going. She half expects him to leave her on the high plains of Wyoming with her skirt billowing in the wind. He doesn't downshift; he doesn't steer the truck to the shoulder, and so when it loses all momentum, it bucks to a stall in the middle of the highway. They sit for a while. She bites the heel of her palm.

He gets out of the truck. The wind is hard and mean and sets Faith trembling. Ray walks to the shoulder, stands at the fence with prairie grass blowing around his legs. He has to hold on to his hat. He gets into the truck and, almost as if there's a purpose to it, he smashes his elbow into his side window, opening a neat hole in the glass. Ray whispers, "Give me this one thing, can't you?" His voice breaks. "Just this one little thing?" It's not the glass, or even his pleading. She fears he might cry, and that's enough to silence her for several hundred miles.

FAITH, when she is my mother, will love to tell this story. She'll offer it at any moment—a few seconds of history while in the garden weeding sweet peas, or in the kitchen baking bread. Faith will blame God the way she kneads bread, fiercely, breathing hard, leaning into it. I will be the little girl asking questions.

"But why did you leave?" I'll want to know. "What was so terrible about Grandpa?"

Faith, taking the bowl of dough down from its warm pantry shelf, will answer, "Don't interrupt. I wanted to be with Ray."

"But why did Daddy take you away?"

"Because Ray's stubborn," Faith will reply, punching the risen dough. "He just barges ahead, like you. He doesn't care about anything but himself."

Over the years, Faith's story will grow into an unbroken litany of her sorrows, from Lipa's death to Ray's proposition, to the kidnapping, the arrival in New Mexico, the signs that follow. The story will swallow the daughter who listens. It will say, *This is who you are.* Try as she might, grow and leave though she will, she won't escape her own inevitable, unanswerable question: *Why?*

IN northern New Mexico, Ray and Faith find a town called Ayudame Dios, named after the desperate prayers of the first explorers. *Help me God.* To them, even this name is a sign, so they stop. At a gas station, they meet gravely voiced Joy, a short, plump woman wearing a leather halter, her belly swelling over the waistband of her low-slung jeans. She looks mostly at Faith. She says, "I'm Joy; you're Faith. Clearly, we were meant to be sisters." She carries with her the smell of incense and patchouli, and she gets them high against the back wall of the gas station. "I know a place you can stay, even," she says. She deposits them miles out on the mesa, at an abandoned sheepherder's shack. Someone propped the shack's rusted tin roof against a fence, painted a bull's-eye, and shot it full of holes. "Bad aim," Ray says, sending Faith into a fit of giggles.

On this gloriously sunny day, Ray's in a great mood; with his hands and boots and a stick, he sets to digging a pit. He sings, "You ain't got a thing if you ain't got that swing." Giggling like kids, they mix up a good batch of mud, which they use to fill the bullet holes. Ray replaces the patched roof, and they have shelter.

Ray dumps the bedroll, the Coleman stove, the rice and a bag of groceries and his wife in that one room. He tells Faith to wait, to trust him, to believe he'll return. He tells her to be a brave chicken, and then he drives back to Seattle for their things.

Faith stumbles through seven days of panic. She's terrified of the sky. Too blue, she says to herself. Too big. When she glances toward heaven, she feels as if she's falling upward. How could he leave her here, alone? She thinks he won't ever come back, but then he does, his truck piled high with furniture, with books, but with nothing that is only hers.

R A Y calls their place the Little Casita on the Mesa. He says it's free, and what more does she want, and why doesn't she relax? Sometimes he picks up an odd job, building cabinets or laying roof the way his father taught him. Most of the time, though, he's off poaching deer or getting high or playing guitar in a hippie band. Faith stays home and tries to fight back the dust, to hang blankets on walls, to sweep the dirt floor and sprinkle it with water. Outside, she borders flower beds with white stones, thinking she'll plant next spring. Some days she just stands out there, trying to teach herself to look at the sky.

In Ayudame Dios, you can see fifty miles one way and a hundred another. You can see sheets of rain while the sun warms your cheeks. Ray says they can be like God, telling the future, *In an hour it will rain*, but Faith comes to understand that here, even the weather doesn't behave as it should. Clouds swerve or dry up, and rain breaks its promises, just like the baby.

In November, Faith expects a Scorpio, dark and sensual with hair the color of black feathers and eyes that know the world. She hopes it will arrive before the first snow. But the days pass, and maybe it will be a Sagittarius, a sign she knows has something to do with arrows. The snow comes. The baby doesn't. Past Thanksgiving, into Christmas, tequila and weed and roasted chicken with Joy. The snow melts. On New Year's Day, she wakes with a hangover that becomes labor, and in that room with the dirt walls and floor, Joy and Ray help Faith give birth to a squalling Capricorn who screams as soon as her head emerges, who wails when Ray catches her, who cries as Ray ties the umbilical cord in a love knot. Baby cries all that night; it seems she will never stop crying. Ray thinks it's funny. He says, "She's pissed about something. Nobody's ever going to fuck with that kid."

Joy holds Faith's head in her lap and strokes her hair back from her face. The candles flicker; Faith feels, as if on a tide, she's drifting over the rise and fall of her baby's cry. The newborn sleeps in the army trunk they're using as a cradle.

While Joy calculates Baby's chart, Faith grows woozy, sleepy, sweaty, overheated by the roaring fire. Joy pushes back her frizzy hair. Her copper bracelets clank. In her thick man's voice, she says, "Okay. This is bad. This is not good."

Alarmed, Faith watches Joy chart crabs and archers and goats. With its various colors and mathematical angles, the chart looks so mystical and precise, like nothing one could argue against.

"She's a Capricorn," Joy says. "An earth sign. Social climber, organizer, an establishment type. Stubborn." She passes her hand over Faith's sign, Aquarius. She says, "Plus, her moon's in Libra, and her rising sign is Aries, which reinforces everything. Basically, she's earth; you're water. You'll never have peace between you."

Faith nods; even in her belly, Baby moved not with the gentle, butterfly kicks she had expected, but with painful blows to her heart, her lungs, her bowels. She sees the years ahead, the fights, the misery, the punishment. All right, then. It's good to know the future.

I know Faith's future. Six months from now, Baby will climb chairs before she walks, breaking all she touches. Faith will gather the pieces of a water pitcher, and she'll tell herself it was meant to be this way. Her daughter will be filled with a hunger Faith can't ease. After she weans from the breast, Baby will suck a bottle until she's three, when Faith snatches it from her mouth and drops it down the outhouse hole. A glare will pass between Baby and her mother. Baby will stick her thumb in her mouth. She'll suck her thumb for years, the only time she seems happy, the only time she seems still. And Faith will decide, God is punishing me with this baby, for everything that came before. All the lies to my father, the backseat sex, the abortion. God has made this baby hate me.

Like all the others, Faith will tell her daughter this story to say, This is the way you always were. Always punishing me. Always making it hard.

THEY don't name her. They decide that, like her blond hair and brown eyes, the baby was born with a name; they'll come across it someday. So for now they call her Baby, and Your Daughter, and She, and It. They wait for a sign. Inside the Casita, the Capricorn daughter wails. Smoke pours from the little tin drum they use as a heater and a cookstove.

They've used the last of their firewood for a roaring fire, but it's freezing in the Casita because the first snow has melted the mud ceiling patches. The light shoots through the bullet holes, heavy with smoke. "Your daughter will never love me," Faith says. Baby's face twists like a wrung washcloth, a worrisome shade of red. She chokes on her own cries. Faith offers a breast to Baby, wincing. Chapped and sore, her nipples burn; sometimes they bleed. Baby turns her head, arches her back, nearly leaps from Faith's arms, and screams, and screams, and screams. What else can Faith do? Nothing. Or this: she puts Baby in a basket. She tucks the blankets around Baby's shoulders, under her chin. Faith puts Baby outside, on the rock-lined path, and she shuts the door against the cries. It's no colder out there, anyway. The sun will warm her up.

Ray, huddled under the covers, rolls over. "Faith has a new mothering method." Faith leans against the door and closes her eyes. "She's cold," Ray says. "We'll get firewood." He climbs out of bed, and he lifts Faith into his big arms. He says, "Of course she loves you, ye of little Faith," and kisses her forehead. Only he can drive back the chewing inside her. When he holds her like this, her feet can't reach the floor.

f o r firewood, they decide to steal trees off public land, which is illegal and means they'll have to go far from their Casita. They pick a dirt road at random. The wrong one, it turns out, because they don't come across any wood, only miles and miles of sagebrush and rolling mesa, the sharp wind blowing through cracks, the gas needle crawling toward empty.

Ray sings, "Good-bye, Old Paint. I'm leaving Cheyenne." He talks about critters. Snakes and coyotes—Wile E. types—and roadrunners, which are the New Mexico state bird, while the governor pays ranchers for every coyote hide. "What do you think of that?" he asks. Faith catches her tongue between her teeth to keep herself from screaming, or weeping.

At last they stumble upon the Rio Grande canyon. A switchback dirt road leads down the side of the cliff, and Ray takes it. He tells Faith it's probably a stagecoach road, that exhausted settlers probably coaxed their starving oxen down this path. "It's history!" he says. He swerves on purpose, and when she cries out, he laughs and calls her Little Faith. At the bottom, they cross a bridge. The road follows a smaller tributary up, out of the canyon, and Ray and Faith rise out of the canyon and stumble upon the rest of their lives.

They see a valley, its green pastures dotted with sheep, and nestled in its center, a tiny village. In the distance, the Sangre de Cristo mountains rim the world. Faith imagines sheepherders down there, getting the animals fed and watered on time; the mothers in gingham aprons calling home their children. "It's pretty," she says.

Baby sleeps at last.

They follow the road where it leads, along the river, down into the valley, past the adobe houses built at the back ends of pastures. Past trees and gardens and dogs that race after them, barking. Sheep, and in one field, buffalo, which causes Ray to start singing "Home on the Range." Faith smiles this time.

In the middle of the valley, they find a Shell station. FLACO'S, the sign above the door reads in hand-painted red. On the side of the building hang tin ads for Coca-Cola and Lucky Strikes, signs so old they make mention of the T-zone. Ray puts exactly $1.49 in the tank, and with the rest of his money, after learning from the storekeeper that the village is called Arroyo al Fin, he buys a candy bar.

In the truck, Baby howls again. Ray tells Faith, "Arroyo al Fin. Give Baby some chocolate."

"Candy makes babies crazy, and you just spent the rest of our money on it, didn't you?"

They drive alongside collapsing fences. To one Airstream trailer, someone has added an adobe lean-to. Broken cars fill yards. A dog chases them, snarling as if he could run fast enough to catch their pickup.

They take a curving road up one side of the valley and turn onto a barely passable lane gutted with ruts and pits. They see a cottonwood, a house with four windows, two upstairs, two down, like eyes, like teeth. For whatever reason, Ray stops the truck.

I T won't take so very long for Baby to grow into a nine-year-old girl, pinning diapers on the line, blowing hair from her eyes. "What was so special about this house?" this daughter will ask, because she wants it to make sense and it doesn't.

"Don't interrupt," Faith will say absently, almost to herself. She'll be gathering apricots from the ground. She'll sit back on her haunches and squint at the house. "How could anyone not love this place?" Easily, her daughter will think. Easily.

Why does Faith—child of Seattle, raised by a God-hating pianist, in a house with a contraband Ming vase—why does she love this place from the first? This will be another mystery, a great puzzle, even for the little girl who will grow up in that house.

• • •

RAY pulls into the dirt driveway and parks under the cottonwood. He shuts off the Dodge. They hear every sound, the sparrows chirping, the river, the spine of Arroyo al Fin, gurgling in its bed. Even the cars on the highway, dipping into the valley and out the other side. It seems they have never heard such merciful quiet.

They leave Baby asleep in the truck, worn out by the crying or soothed by the chocolate or calmed by the peace between her parents, and they go to look.

Behind the house, they stumble upon a round, rock-walled well. Faith tells him they could make a wish if he hadn't wasted their money on chocolate. Ray tells her it's stupid to throw pennies in your drinking water. Tucked between this well and the house, a fruit tree grows. Ray says it's an apple tree, but he's wrong. That very summer, the apricots on this tree will ripen faster than Faith can bake them, dry them, jelly them, so each time she goes to the well she'll see magpies scolding, feasting, and the smell of rotting fruit will make her gag.

The house's long, narrow acre extends sharply up a steep hill. On the adjacent land, only sagebrush and scrub trees grow, but here a haphazard orchard has sprung up, each tree different. Ray wonders who did the planting. As they blunder around, he tells Faith to imagine an owner—Reymundo, let's call him—who liked to buy fruit. He would take his cherries or pear up this steep land, and after sucking a pit clean, Reymundo would plant it, not really hoping for much and always feeling blessed when something appeared.

They find a little outbuilding which they will use as a chicken coop, where Faith will gather eggs and dodge droppings, where Ray will drag their daughter to beat her.

The house is unlocked, and they feel their way in the dark, through rooms laid out in the formation of a crucifix, with the kitchen at the feet, and what could be bedrooms at the arms and head. In its heart is a windowless room, which they will call the Middle Room. There is even a second floor. In every room, Ray finds a handprint pressed into the mud plaster. This place has a garden. It has water and many rooms. It has all they need.

For the rest of her life, Faith will point to the coincidences that led them to their home: that they took the roads they did, that they stumbled on the canyon at exactly the place where a road allowed them to cross it. That the storekeeper Ray spoke to at Flaco's had been born in the house. That they went back to the Shell station, where the man agreed to sell them the house for one hundred dollars down and fifty a month. And the biggest coincidence of all, the rarest gift: that they both agreed and loved it completely. So, you see, she will say when she tells her story, it was fate. And Faith's daughter, in her own version of the story, will offer those words as a joke: "Lucky, lucky us. God put us there."

T H E Y camp out at the house, and the following day they go into town, to Taos, for supplies. Ray waits on the plaza while Faith, carrying a blanket-wrapped, miraculously sleeping Baby, jumps at the clanging of a cowbell tied to the drugstore door. The old woman behind the counter frowns at them with undisguised revulsion. She says, "What's in that blanket?" Something in the woman's tone, some implication of disgust and the underpinning of hatred, wakes Baby and sets her wailing. Faith bounces her roughly, her face a splotchy red to match her daughter's. Faith sees what this woman sees: Baby, dirty-faced, screaming, ugly. The woman mutters something in Spanish. Then, deliberately, she crosses herself.

Faith thinks, Me? You think this of me? She turns to the rack of hair products, barrettes and headbands, hairpins and rollers. She wishes she could say, "I am not a hippie. I'm Catholic. My mother played piano." The cowbell clangs, and a woman greets the clerk, who answers in Spanish. They laugh.

Faith puts the rubber bands on the counter, and the woman says, "You can't pay for those with food stamps."

Baby screams. Faith whispers, "I need to get . . ." Then, dropping the rubber bands, she flees outside, Baby shrieking. Faith, crazy, near tears, decides she'll drop her daughter. She imagines Baby hitting the sidewalk, the thud and crunch and splash and then, silence. Blessed peace. Faith would scream over her ruined baby and then the woman behind the Rexall's counter would rush out, have pity on her, even hold Faith against her warm, girdled breast.

Her husband is talking to an Indian who wears a squash blossom bracelet, an army jacket and a blue bandanna folded and tied around his forehead. He's tall and large, with broad shoulders and a crewcut. "You hippies don't know anything," he says. The stencil on his jacket pocket reads ZAMORA. To her, it sounds like a brand name. An advertisement.

Hey, you two, with the unnamed baby. Here's your future. Clarence Zamora, a Santo Domingo Indian. Who is incidental and pivotal. Clarence who will take Faith away from Ray, a thief or a trickster, or merely a man in love. Who will one day torture Sunny Boy Blue. Who will be the locus of all blame.

"This is Clarence," Ray says. "He's telling me about cradleboards. He says we should get the baby a cradleboard." He holds up a contraption made of a pine slab and a molded leather hood and dangling laces for strapping down the baby. He has exactly what they need, and this is the first sign.

Clarence says, "That's a little howling coyote you got there."

Faith jiggles Baby. "I'm not a hippie. I'm not a pig. I keep myself clean. I just—I don't—I need a dollar." Baby arches her back, screaming. "But we don't have a dollar," Faith says, and her chin crumples and her tears spill. "You bought chocolate," she whispers.

For a moment, no one says anything. Then Clarence reaches out and thumbs away Faith's tears. "Here's a buck," he says, and like magic, the dollar is already in her palm, and he's folding her fingers around it. Her hand is very small and white inside of his. "Give me that," Ray says, and he stalks across the plaza and into the drugstore and Faith feels sorry for Beneficia, because now she's the one Ray will punish.

In the space of a conversation, their lives change direction. Clarence asks the baby's name. He has eyes as black as his hair, and a high-cheeked, smooth face. His smile is dazzling, white and larger than life. Faith can't look away. Alone with him on the plaza, she realizes: I will always remember this day. She has the sense of her life moving again, the way they moved from Washington to here. This is what her father meant when he said, "Watch out for the imaginary hand of the God that isn't there." Here, Faith thinks. Here is the hand of God again, holding out Clarence like a gift.

Clarence straps Baby onto the board, binding her hands and feet to her body. He says cradleboards calm babies, because they don't understand their arms and legs. He says the cradleboard reminds them where they end and the world begins. Baby doesn't cry. "There you go, kid," Clarence says. He doesn't say what her name should be. He isn't the sage shaman come from the hills sent by the great spirit. He's Clarence.

When he returns with rubber bands, Ray offers to buy Clarence's sturdy cradleboard for twenty-five food stamps, and the deal is struck. A station wagon pulls up, the young father leaning out the window with a Polaroid in his hand. "Listen," he calls. "We took your picture. You want it?" This will be Faith's daughter's one baby picture, a Polaroid of an infant strapped into a cradleboard. Faith wears large hoop earrings, and she has peasant's hands, cracked and stub-nailed and thick-fingered, but her face is young and the cheekbones high. She's smiling joyously, her gaze fixed on something above her, probably Clarence, although sometimes her daughter will believe it's Ray that Faith looks up to so rapturously. And Faith will say, "That was the day I met Clarence," and the fact that God saw fit to memorialize this moment is, for Faith, a sign.

CLARENCE invites them to a Meeting. They drive out to Arroyo Seco at the foot of the mountains, and bounce along a dirt road onto the mesa, and far away from other houses among the sagebrush in a clearing, they come to a tipi and a cluster of dusty cars and trucks and a small house. This is the Church.

Before they go into the tipi, Clarence tells them how to be. The sacrament of the Church is Medicine, which is an illegal drug. They do not take it to get high but because, in the Church, Medicine is God. In fact, if you take it to get high, you will get violently sick. You must hold it in your hands like the God it is. You must not waste it, or drop it, or chew it, any more than you would the Holy Host. He looks straight into her eyes, his voice low and confiding, his hands warm and gentle on her shoulders, as if to hold her to earth while he explains. Don't turn your back on the fire. Don't come between the Medicine and the fire.

Inside, she kneels and follows Clarence's rules. Clarence runs the Meeting. He announces the Meeting's Purpose, and he seems to tell people what to do without speaking. People pray, a low, constant murmuring, and then the singing begins. A man shakes a seed-filled gourd so fast it blurs, and he sings four songs in a language she can't understand while the man beside him rapidly beats a drum made of deer hide and a cast-iron kettle. The Medicine, bitter and hard to swallow, gives Faith a stomachache. The drum and the rattle pass clockwise around the tipi, and the night goes on. The fire licks the air.

When the rattle reaches Clarence, he clears his throat. And then Faith hears Clarence sing—the long vowels and sharp consonants, the fast heartbeat of the drum, the rattle, and his deep, beautiful voice, reaching inside, shaking her. She thinks, This is a man of God. She feels herself lifting, rising with the flames and sparks up to the mouth of the tipi that opens to the sky, and she is lifting and Clarence is singing and all at once she understands what God intended. She thinks, *My God. I love him.*

I N the morning, they come out of the tipi dazed but not tired. In a while, Clarence tells them, they will eat a big feast. Faith and Ray blink, rub their eyes, collect their baby from the woman who watched the children. They stumble over the mesa, among sagebrush and prickly pears and roadrunner holes. Faith wears the cradleboard on her back with sleeping Baby laced in. Faith's eyes ache. The sun and the sky are making her blind. She closes her lids and walks by hooking her finger through Ray's belt loops.

Ray stops, and Faith bumps gently into his back. Reluctantly, she opens her eyes to slits. Ray kicks a clod of dirt down an arroyo. He says, "This is our Church."

"Two days ago we were nothing, and this morning we're Indians?"

Ray laughs, but interrupts himself. The silence rushes over his interrupted laugh. Faith feels as if he has just exorcised the last of their doubts. She says, "If we join the Church, we aren't allowed to drink or smoke dope. They don't mix with Medicine. It's the Way." Already, she's learned the language: the Way, Medicine, the Church.

Ray stares at her. He walks off.

"Ray!" she yells. "Did you hear me?" She hurries after him. The sagebrush gives way to stunted trees, the kind they once wanted for firewood.

Ray stops. He turns. He says, "It will be simple. It will be good." He tells her he knew this was their Church at midnight, when the music stopped and Clarence went outside the tipi. Ray, kneeling, his kneecaps and bad leg aching, his eyes drooping, the fire hot in his face, watched the Fireman crouch before the flames, spreading the ashes into a shape that by morning would be a bird. Someone cleared his throat. Ray heard Clarence rustling through the sagebrush, and it seemed that the air was utterly silent save for Clarence moving outside, and then Clarence blew a sharp pure whistle, trilling four times. It was an eagle-bone whistle, and Ray tells Faith, "The whistle didn't come from Clarence. The whistle was the voice of God."

He tells her he thought, Here. Here I belong. He would be a good man. Not like his father, violent, hate-filled. No drink, no drugs. And not like his mother, either, bitter because her life was snatched away before she could become the educated poet she longed to be. No, Ray says, he will be a good man. He will toss his daughter in the air, laughing, and he will hold her in his lap and teach her about life, the meaning of things like roadrunners and coyotes and God. He takes Faith's hand. "Don't be so worried about things. They work out."

"I don't know what we're doing." Baby and her cradleboard make Faith's back ache. She longs to sit down, longs to sleep.

He picks up some nuts from beneath a tree. "It takes hundreds of years for one of these trees to grow five feet tall. As tall as you." He offers her one. "Try them." He cracks it open, and the meat resembles a fat grain of rice. "See, Little Faith? It's okay. You have to have some hope, I tell you."

From his outstretched palm, she accepts the nut, which tastes like wood, like damp walnut. It tastes like the smoke that scents their skin after a night in the tipi. Faith has the feeling again that she's rising, that her empty womb, lighter than air, is lifting her away from this place. She stands under the bright sun, her cheeks tingling with cold, and she realizes she can leave any time. Not suicide, not death, but a leaving is hers for the taking just by staying still, by looking to the sky and praying.

"It's good," she says.

He takes a deep breath. "You know," he says, exhaling, "we need a name."

"For what?"

"For the tree, stupid. What do you think?"

"For the tree?"

"Jesus, Faith. For the baby."

But what she wants to know is the name of this hundred-year-old tree with its rice-shaped fruit, this tree that looks more like a bush because it's so low to the ground.

"I think it's a juniper," he says.

"In the Bible, the bush was on fire and never burned up," Faith says.

"This is the same one," Ray tells her. And never mind that he's wrong on both counts, that this tree is piñon and the bush in the Bible was never named, because for once Ray has an answer that Faith believes. She loves him, too, and so this tree is a juniper, the same bush that burned and spoke to Moses.

In this moment of love and certainty, Baby starts awake. She gasps, a great indrawn breath, and, straining against the laces of her cradleboard, she lets forth a scream so fierce and filled with rage that it sounds as if someone's eating her alive. It's a sound no different from all the cries she's offered for months, but Ray and Faith know. Enlightened by a sleepless night and cloudless morning, they are ready to understand that, in a time of God, this cry can only be a sign. Out there on the mesa, dazzled by sun and bright sky, they give their daughter the name she tells them she was born for: Juniper Tree Burning. But this is not my name, and so this is not my story.

$\mathcal{T}$HE NAME GAME

A Lifelong Complaint
THIS joke, passing for a name: Juniper Tree Burning. Can we really chalk it up to a moment on the mesa? It's all so very spiritual. Can someone tell me how they kept from laughing? And what I'd like to know, what I *really* want to know, is this: which one of my parents picked the name? My mother thought that God and signs had slated us to hate each other. So maybe she decided— the beginning of our fight.

Juniper. They say it just came to them. But seriously, they spent their life in disagreement. *Tree.* Can I really believe they spontaneously burst out in stereo? *Burning.* They say I screamed to claim it for myself. Now. I ask this. If we assume the impossible—that a squalling infant chooses anything but comfort— isn't it more likely the baby's wail, translated to English, would be the loudest form of NO?

The Steinway, and the papers inside its bench, and the Treasured Memories weren't the first signs that my parents' story was not my own. For instance, as evidence of her father's evil ways, my mother told me how, after I was finally named, Grandpa Paul wrote: *Congratulations on the birth of little Jennifer. Yours sincerely, Father.* Why didn't my sign-believing mother take Paul's mistake as a sign of my true name? Maybe she was too busy with her grudge against him. Faith is the queen of grudges. His note was the last contact between them for eight years, which is exactly like forever, since he died before she forgave him.

Juniper Tree Burning. Which one of them decided?

Picture this six-year-old girl on her very first day of school, with all the construction paper and pencil sharpeners. She sits in the front row, hands twisted together, staring at Mrs. Ortiz who has curly black hair and smells of perfume and hair spray. "I just had a baby," Mrs. Ortiz tells them, "and that's why I'm a kind of *gordita*." The class laughs, because *gordita* means fat and Mrs. Ortiz is so skinny, and Juniper likes Mrs. Ortiz, who's funny and nice. Juniper already knows how to read. She thinks, I will tell the teacher how I read a whole thick book of fairy tales, the real ones where Cinderella's sisters cut off their toes and get their eyes poked out. Mrs. Ortiz will say, How smart you are! And then she will love me.

Mrs. Ortiz calls out their names with a cozy roll of her tongue. Patricia Arellano. Here. Alexander Cordova. Here. Mrs. Ortiz pauses. She looks up, then back at the paper in her hands. She smiles merrily. She says, "Jennifer? Jennifer . . . Davis?" A sign! How else could Mrs. Ortiz know her true name, the one her grandfather gave her? Hope surges inside the little girl. God and Mrs. Ortiz are taking care of her. "Here," she says.

But Mrs. Ortiz, reading her paper, makes a pretend shocked face, hands on cheeks, eyebrows high. "*Dios mio,*" she says. "Your eyes trick you, *qué no?* Juniper? Juniper Tree Burning Davis? When you see what doesn't make sense?" She clucks her tongue. "*Qué lástima, mihita.* What a crazy name you have." And now the kids are laughing and now she knows what it costs to have a name like hers: for the rest of her life, she'll always be sliding lower in her desk. Through second grade, third, fourth, Miss Maestas, Mr. Padilla, Mr. Martinez, there is always a teacher, laughing with the students. They are always calling her Juniper. Or Cottonwood. Chokecherry Bush. Piñon. There are so many trees in the world.

Juniper Tree Burning. How she hates that name! In Safeway, her mom pulls out food stamps to pay, and everyone stares. Juniper hightails it to the ice cream aisle, where she reads the cartons: tin roof and rocky road and spumoni. Faith yells, "Juniper Tree Burning!" Mud pie. Orange dream. Who is that crazy woman, shrieking funny stuff? "Juniper! You come when I call!" It's punishment, hearing that name out loud in the frozen food section at Safeway. It lets everyone know: this girl is not a member of the real world.

HERE'S a hoot of a joke: one teacher thought it would be hilarious to make me learn all about juniper trees, and I had to write a report on what my brilliant parents named me for: a stunted, twisted bush, an excuse for a tree that barely grows five feet tall, a low-rent shrub that lives at the margins, the slums of the world of flora, in rocky deserts where no self-respecting Sequoia would ever set up residence. Poor juniper, always desperate for water, bending and deforming in the wind. Good for cleaning chimneys and flavoring gin, lousy for campfires; it burns too hot and throws off sparks, and you could burn down a forest that way. Why, I wonder, didn't my parents, believers in signs, do just a little research? The reasons for a different name are written in the library.

You want to talk about signs? Here's a sign. How many people really have a fairy godmother? I had Esther Leeman, Essie to her friends, who took me under her wing and into her house when I was fourteen, though I was a child raised by my parents, as close to being raised by wolves as a girl can get. I moved into her house and she called me Jennie, and like magic, like waving her wand, she transformed me into a citizen of the world. If that isn't a sign that I am finally living my true life, with my real name, then I don't know what is.

But I do not believe in signs. I don't believe in fate. I believe in self-determination, in renovation, not religion. I belong to the Church of Reality, and our commandments are simple: See what you have. Know where you're going. Do what you must. What my mother calls signs, I call careless mistakes, a thoughtless careening toward disaster, with a wailing, terrified infant bouncing behind, screaming, *No! No, no, no!*

Rest easy, baby girl. A name is not destiny. There are so many ways to correct mistakes.

To change your name, use another for seven years. Or go to city hall, and for a fee you can be anything.

To change your name, you can marry and enlist in a man's family. This was my mother's strategy, and my own, to some extent. Needless to say, this strategy works only for certain members of the population.

To change your name, use your history. The Pecan-grower's Daughter. The Lumberjack's Son. The Piano-player's Granddaughter.

To change your name, become someone's beloved. Honey Pie. Sweet Cheeks. Cinderella and Lipishka—my personal examples.

To change your name, engage in psychic phenomena coupled with a hot line to the Deity. According to my mother, I changed my name when I was only two months old. Beware, however: the name achieved by this method may be less than satisfactory. Especially if you were only screaming and have not yet grasped the intricacies of language.

To change your name, do something. Acquire a degree. Then you can be Doctor. Get a job: Sir, Senator, President, Waitress, Esteemed Councilwoman. Officer. Get a disease—they'll call you the Cirrhotic Liver in Room 53. Be born with a condition: the Boy in the Plastic Bubble, or the Girl with Easily Bruising Skin. Do something stupid, bad, or sick. The Boston Strangler. The Girl Who Ran Away from Home. Be the victim of any of these. The Fool Who Married the Runaway—my husband's new name.

Sunny Boy Blue kept his name, my baby brother, my baby boy. But to me, he was also the Backwards Boy, a name he achieved simply by being born. He was the Boy with the See-through Green Eyes. He was Sunny. He is the Brother I had, the Brother Who Drowned.

My name is Jennie. My name is not Juniper Tree Burning, or Juniper, or even June. I am not that name. I am something else entirely. Do not call me

Juniper. My mother still tries. On the morning of my wedding day, she said, "Juniper, give me the bread."

I sighed and picked up the bread. "Mother," I said, "my name is Jennie." She shrinks when I speak to her this way. I am like my father, and Faith is still, completely and forever, my mother, mistaking me for Juniper.

It's all right, though. I can make Faith disappear before my eyes. I am Jennifer, and nothing my mother calls me will change that fact. It amazes me, when I look down and see that my fingers have dug deep into the loaf, that I'm up to my knuckles in bread.

ALONG CAME A SPIDER

I would not be able to tell my kids about the rest of the twenty-four hours. Chris was looking for an apartment, and he had collected keys, and we made the rounds. First, to a hot, carpeted place, where we kissed against the wall in front of the sliding glass doors, the afternoon sun beating in on us, and then we were naked, and then we were on the floor, and afterward he had raw spots on his knees, and I had a wound in the small of my back. Oh, it's loads of fun, going at it in a strange place, skin sliding on skin like it's oiled. We finished and dressed and moved on, to a crummy little shack behind a larger house, a dark furnished place with an impossible bed, so soft we could hardly gain purchase, and the sink was beside the bed, and the curtains were green calico, so the hot light coming through them was like being underwater. Through the window we could hear children playing, and this time we were less frantic, slowly, quietly taking ourselves there, and there, and there. The third apartment was in one of those motel-like complexes with people passing outside the living room window, and in that place we went to the cool linoleum floor in the bathroom, giggling at ourselves, sore and tired, and then we took a cold shower and drank water from our cupped palms. I could not say where the three apartments were in the city; dazed, hot, stinking, we drove from one to the next in a strange frenzy of fucking, not really apartment hunting at all. It was so hot. Maybe that's why the owners or realtors or whoever just gave him the keys. I never asked. It felt inevitable, that we would have these various places to consummate our romance, months of courtship crammed into three hours, all the learning, the talking, translated into the mingling of fluids all over the city.

We bought burgers and went to his hotel to feed his cat, a mean little thing with a stub of a tail whose name was Bob. We ate, and then we took off all our clothes and lay down, too exhausted for sex, the curtains drawn, the air conditioner blowing. I said, "We should be studying." We were like guilty, misbehaving kids. I thought, So here we are, fucked to exhaustion. "The young lovers, naked in the afternoon," I said. "All we need is a busybody neighbor with rollers in her hair."

Chris said, in an old-biddy voice, "They were always humping over there."
He drew a finger up my thigh, over my pelvic bone, and I shivered. His cat
held sentry on the bedside table, its yellow eyes narrowed with cool hatred.
"It's really quite shocking," Chris said. "I hear them all the time."

W E went back out into the blasted afternoon heat, and this time we took the
cat. We stopped at a little adobe house, with two windows on either side of the
entry, with a dirt yard and one tree and a straight sidewalk up to the stoop.
The wooden door had a window the size of a piece of paper, with bars over it,
as if miniature burglars were expected. "The truth is," Chris said, killing the
engine, "I already saw this one, and I'm pretty sure I'll take it."

"So what was all the house hunting?"

"Come on now, Cinderella. Isn't it obvious?" He poked his soda straw into
Bob's crate, and Bob batted it irritably, unamused. "I had to get you on neutral
ground," he said. "Off the playing field. Out of the dance hall."

"Into the bedroom," I said. I got out of the car. A low adobe wall encircled
the dirt yard. I went up the sidewalk to the front door, trying to decide what I
was: angry? flattered? I sat on the stoop. My inner thighs ached in the pleasantly bruised way of afternoon sex. He walked toward me, and I thought, Are
you my Knight?

The Knight sits on the step beside Cinderella. She meets his sidelong look.
His brown hair is streaked with gold, and his brown eyes are shot with gold,
and the tips of his lashes are blond. She thinks of Midas. He has a face that
can seem perfectly still without being dangerous; no anger or sadness sits in
the corners of his mouth or between his eyes. His face is simply in repose. Perhaps, she thinks, it's his irises. They are overly large; they give him an artifi-
cially innocent, bushy-tailed look. He smiles. "You're pouting," he says,
smiling. They have been smiling, it seems, all day. Her cheeks ache. She pulls
her mouth into a frown, but, disobedient, irrepressible, her lips stretch back
into that silly grin. She smiles partly because she feels ridiculous, seeing herself through the eyes of a pink-rollered busybody. Partly, she smiles because
she is a young lover, sitting on a stoop in the hot afternoon. "Let's go inside,"
she says.

They fuck again, on the living room carpet, gingerly now, raw and painful
in their skin, and their caution makes them so tender it shouldn't be called
fucking anymore. Afterward, they lie on their backs and look up at the vigas,
stained nearly black. The room is cool and dark, and in its shadows, the afternoon seems endless; the movement of the sun hardly matters.

"Okay," he says. "Tell me."

"Tell you what?"

"Something important. Enough of this libido; it's time for secrets."

The vigas are tree trunks, peeled and cured and laid across adobe walls, but tree trunks nonetheless. A car passes. A gentle murmuring shoosh of rubber on hot pavement wafts through the wide window they've opened. The window offers little air. Their sweat pools and beads and drips and gives them the sour smell of just-finished sex.

Between the vigas, she sees a spiderweb. In the corner, where the ceiling meets the wall, another, with a fat spider in its center. At the edge of the fireplace mantel; in the doorway, in the corner by the heater. Fear shoots through her, pure and irresistible, obliterating anything else.

"I'm afraid of spiders," she whispers, and at this, this precisely, terribly wrong moment, he says it, his lips against her hair.

"I love you," he says gently, calmly, with astonishing certainty.

But the spiders are crawling on her; she feels them, and rising, she beats her clothes before pulling them on because there could be spiders in her pants, in her boots, and the spiders *are* there, here, everywhere, crawling through her hair, scurrying down her back—this woman grew up in a house infested with black widows, those bitches waiting to inject venom that causes symptoms like heroin withdrawal, and this woman, this young lover, she once had a black widow fall out of her hair; she once had one crawl down her arm—and this Jennie, now dressed, is no lover in the afternoon; she's a madwoman, slapping herself, running out the door, standing on the sidewalk in the hot sun.

Across the street two girls are playing. She feels crawling at the nape of her neck; she slaps, rakes nails through skin and hair, and anyone watching, the girls across the street, for example would wonder, Do I have to help her? But they don't, because Chris has seized her hands and pulled her to his chest. He murmurs, "Hey now, hey love, hey, it's okay," but it is not okay and and she thinks, Don't give me avowals of love; go kill the spiders. I can still feel them crawling on me. His arms trap her and she hears again his declaration of love and there's a monster living inside Jennie, and it hisses, *He is weak.* He will need you, will pull and pluck, and you'll slog forward through life with this heavy deadweight hanging around your neck. She twists free of his arms. She takes a step backwards, toward the gate. She says, "I wish you hadn't said that."

"I meant it," he says.

He is gentle and sweet but he's weak. "That's . . ." she says, and she's afraid of this monster who always says exactly the wrong thing and she must get away from him, and the spiders, and this mad day which should have been one of somber study because she really wants to be a doctor and *he is weak*—"That's kind of pathetic," she whispers, and anger spreads in her, hissing and spitting, a hot oil that obliterates shame or fear.

Standing in the hot sun, all the golden parts of him alight in sun, he smiles, and gently, as to a cornered animal, a feral cat, say, or a stranded dog, he says, "There's nothing pathetic about knowing what you want."

But who is this man, anyway? Just who the hell does he think he is? The monster inside is named anger and has spread to fill her, and it lies just under her skin and she opens the gate and prays to herself or God or whoever decides such things: Please don't let me say something terrible. "I'm really sorry," she says, astonished that she is still whispering and not yelling, "but I have to go now," and then she's the Ugly Chick, running down the street in the blazing afternoon heat in her cowboy boots and jeans.

Five o'clock rush hour is a bad time for running—heat and car exhaust—but she runs, her sweat evaporating as soon as it hits the air, her shoulders dry, hot, sunburning; her legs, already fucked into soreness, chafing against the seams of her Levi's; her ponytail switching across her shoulders; and she is dizzy but safe, out here in the open. The thing about spiders: they can hide. They can hide anywhere, tiny and malevolent, in your shoes, your bra, in gloves and purses, in the box of condoms on your bedside table. Any moment can be shattered by these dangerous sneaks. You reach into the closet for your favorite jacket, and a brown recluse ruins your life. You can avoid them carefully and still there is danger lurking in the smallest most intimate corners of your life, a black widow in your underwear drawer, her body like a fat bullet, her long spindly legs, a red hourglass on her belly, evil decoration as if to say, *Your days are short. Your hours are numbered.*

Running, she pushes past businessmen unlocking their cars, old women making it to the corner market, and she's so grateful to be moving with nothing over her head but sky, because in the open air, it's that much harder for them to find you, meaning spiders, meaning anyone, and God, it's hot out here, and why did he have to ruin everything with one little sentence? Take me back to an hour ago; it was so wonderful, an hour ago. Hypnotize me backwards.

Then she's cold. She stops. She's cold and dizzy and sick. I've gone too far, she thinks. Good. I have put that much distance between us.

But here he is in the Rolls, pulling up alongside her. "That was a lousy thing to do," he says.

The Ugly Chick leans over her knees, still panting. "Do you know the difference between heat stroke and heat exhaustion?"

"Why did you leave?" Chris asks. "Because you're afraid?"

"I think I have to cool off," she says. "I think I need water." Will she faint? Will it come to that?

"Get in the car," he says.

She straightens and glares at him. "No." She waits for him to say the thing that will undo this mess, but he says nothing. She leans into the car. She meets his gold-shot irises, his gold-tipped eyelashes, and she thinks, He is weak. The spell is broken. I am myself again; I am the Ugly Chick. And he is weak. "Leave me alone," I said.

"There's no reason to be ashamed," he said. "Everyone's afraid of something."

"Go away," I said. "You're a freak."

He starts the car. "Okay," he says. "Maybe you aren't up to this." Just like that, the Rolls-Royce majestically sails off, a mirage shimmering over the hot pavement. She thinks, So easily? You give up so easily?

O N the way home I drank from a hose in a stranger's yard because I really was starting to worry about how I was stumbling along. I drank greedily, letting it spill down my front, and then I used it like a shower, soaking myself from head to toe, so I had to limp home in wet denim, which made for more chafing, more blistering. I was like an old woman by the time I got to my door. A limping, arthritic, disappointed old woman: I expected him to be sitting on my stoop. He doesn't know where you live, I told myself. You fool.

I peeled off my wet clothes, examined my various wounds, my blistered heels, my thighs marked by his pelvic bones, the rug burn in the small of my back. I thought of kissing against the wall and went dizzy with desire. I showered. My body stung and burned and ached.

I dressed in running shorts and shoes and shirt and tried to put on an Essie attitude: You're well rid of him, that needy, desperate boy—but I couldn't stop thinking of how he said it, softly, gently, not desperate but quietly certain: "I love you."

I could not stay in my home, trapped inside four walls when a door was right there. I set off walking because I was too sore to run. Even the soles of my feet hurt. A low-rider passed, and slowed, and offered me a ride. "Go away," I said. I walked on. Then my body knew what my mind did not and broke into a run, too impatient for coddling blisters and bruises. It was my body that steered toward Antonio's, and my body that fluttered in fear when I pushed open the door, then went weak with relief at the sight of Chris sitting at the bar, my backpack at his feet.

I sat on the stool beside him. He had a whiskey waiting for me, an impressive move. "You're a cocky one," I said, trying to catch my breath so I wouldn't sound like I had hurried there. But I couldn't help my panting. Panting, I ordered water. "So sure I'd come?"

"I have your backpack," Chris said.

"We've set off our medical careers on the wrong foot," I said. "We've made some mistakes. But I'm a Capricorn. Capricorns just barge ahead." I had no idea how the sentence, my mother's sentence, had escaped my mouth. Faith had always believed the Capricorn in me had cursed her. I exorcised my mother by drinking an entire glass of water.

"Sometimes it's not a mistake to take the leap, the plunge, the hill," Chris said. "Anyway, I don't believe in stars, in signs."

"I don't either." Bizarrely, I felt like a liar.

We sipped our whiskeys. Then we spoke at the same time. I said, "Did you bring my slipper?" And he said, "I'm sorry I scared you."

We smiled. He said, "I should have put it this way: I *feel* like falling in love with you."

I closed my eyes, a swoon of relief. "Isn't this a Hallmark moment," I said. He was quiet. I glanced at him, and I couldn't seem to take a breath. "Christian Braverman," I said. "I feel like loving you too." I wasn't entirely sure what I meant. But God, Jesus Christ, Holy Ghost, what a wonderful story it would make. Such a thing to tell the grandkids. Love at first sight, fate, destiny, happily ever after. All that shit, as my father would say.

Chris reached out and lightly traced the line of my jaw. "There it is," he said. "The look."

"Shut up," I said, laughing, batting his hand away. "Don't try that touching-the-face shit with me." But I was laughing because I should, joking because it was the place for a joke. Now it was his turn.

He said, "If I shut up, will you tell me all about the lumberjack?"

"That crap," I said. "I have a better one. My grandmother Lipa came from Russia, and she was my grandfather's student—" Hook them fast, reel them in. Cha-cha-cha.

"There you go again," he said. "Performing." Irritated, I finished my drink in a swallow. How did he read my mind like that?

"Hey now," he said, his hand on my shoulder. "I swear, you're like milk on the stove. One degree too hot and you boil over."

"My grandfather," I began, but I was shaking a box with one stone inside. I could hear the meaningless rattle in my voice.

Chris, watching me with a bemused smile, prompted, "The lumberjack."

"The other one," I said. "The piano teacher." Lipa, my Russian grandmother, and Paul my grandfather, her piano teacher, and he pressed violets between the pages of her music books, and as I spoke, a wave of sadness caught me by surprise. I crossed my legs, squeezing my bruises together, welcoming the low throb, an artifact of earlier in the day, when I had no doubts inside me. Now, glad though I was to find Chris here, I was also suspicious.

This man, this Chris. Was he the sort who always gave in? If I shoved him, would he push back, or would he always bend, sway, accept? Would he ever draw the line? He did, I reminded myself. He rode off in his chariot and left you panting on the sidewalk. Remember? I clung to this evidence of strength so I could stay there with him.

The door opened, letting in a slice of sunlight, then closed, and we were back in the black-walled universe of Antonio's Pool Hall. The Apricot Boy had arrived. "The lumberjack lady!" he said, sitting beside me.

"Jennie was just telling me about her grandfather," Chris said.

"I already heard that one," the Apricot Boy said, pleased to be in the know. "He was a lumberjack."

I gave him a wide Jennie smile. "Aren't you my new best friend."

"Wouldn't mind if I was," the boy said.

How much easier it is to tell the story to this boy with his easily readable features. To explain how, from the moment he met her, my other grandfather intensely, completely loved his wife—a nauseatingly sweet, perfect sort of love—or so I liked to say. So the story went. Love like that is a lie, I decided, even as I rattled off my grandparents' story, truth embellished into a baroque gargoyle of itself, every word a step away from the lover and toward the admirer, until a string of words had put miles between Chris and me. I am a liar, I thought as I spoke. I am not to be trusted.

So trust this, Jennie: destiny, fate, a cadaver, this Chris. Something besides your own foolish eyes. Trust your body knowing what your mind does not. Trust a moment ago, or else just pretend you believe in love at first sight.

I gazed into the Apricot Boy's eyes, and he looked back, unsuspecting and ready, smiling, smiling, smiling. "But then," I said, "Lipa died of a cold, and Paul hated God for the rest of his life."

"No way," the Apricot Boy said. "You made that up. I never heard of dying of a cold. You take two aspirin, call the doctor, right?"

Chris drained his glass and gave me a wicked, slyly mocking glance. "Let's shoot some pool, CindyLou," he said. "We know the ending to that one."

And so the day finished where it started. The three of us played Cutthroat. It's a mean game, aiming to sink your two opponents' balls before they sink all of yours. "Are you on tonight?" I asked the Apricot Boy.

"I'm on!" he said. He reminded me of a puppy, poor thing.

"I'm off," I said, exchanging a look with Chris. He smiled. Less than twenty-four hours, and already we had an unspoken language. "I'm off, too," Chris said. And then, without discussion, we toyed with the poor Apricot Boy. We played the fools, Chris and I, sinking each other's balls until I had only one left and Chris had none. The Apricot Boy grinned, ecstatic, triumphant, sure of his win. That was when I cleared Mr. Apricot's balls neatly, quickly, and finished the game.

"Fuck!" Mr. Apricot cried. "Fuck, I almost had it! Fuck!"

We stayed until midnight, Chris and I. A perfect circle, twenty-four hours of the clock, and inside the circle was a meeting, a reunion, a first kiss and first fight and first reconciliation, and at the end of the day we stepped out of the circle and into the parking lot, into his golden chariot waiting for us in the shadows. He noticed my limping and in the Rolls he took off my shoes, peeled off my socks, and held my blistered, battered feet in the palms of his hands. "Cinderella," he said tenderly, teasing, "we must get you some decent shoes." And then we painfully fucked, or gingerly made love, or both, until it was past midnight and into the rest of our lives.

TRUE FAMILY HISTORY

SUNNY'S birthday is tomorrow, so Jennie is making him a Lady Baltimore cake, and though she only has whole wheat flour and honey, she'll make it as delicious as she can. Faith doesn't believe in sugar. Only brown foods are good: rice, bread, corn tortillas, oatmeal. Brewer's yeast is good for getting vitamin B, but if you add too much you'll get a rash. To get a complete protein you have to eat beans and rice together. Don't eat too much cheese or you'll get mucusy. Don't eat fruits and vegetables in the same meal. But most especially, don't eat anything made with white sugar or flour. Pixie Stix are poisonous, their dyes cancer-causing. Bit-O-Honey will yank out your teeth. Ice cream will clog your sinuses, soda pop will disrupt your breathing, and doughnuts will coat your intestines and stay there for seven years.

Cakes from honey aren't as good as sugar cakes. But Sunny has to have a birthday cake, Jennie tells herself, getting out the brown flour and golden-brown honey. Cakes shouldn't be made from brown things, but even some of the eggs have brown shells, which Faith says are healthier.

Jennie tells Sunny all the words that mean delicious. Tasty. Scrumptious. She can't think of more. Yummy. Yumdillyicious.

While the woodstove heats up, Jennie separates the eggs. "I'm hot," Sunny says. You have to be careful not to get yolk in the white, or they won't stiffen up. Faith taught her this. On special occasions, like Meetings, Faith makes sweets. So she's a hypocrite, Jennie thinks, pleased to know the right word.

"Too bad," she says. "Today we're hot, if you want cake."

"I want to go swimming." It's August and it never rains and Faith can't take them to the river because Ray took the car to town.

"For the millionth time," Jennie says, "we can't go swimming today."

"But it's my birthday."

"Tomorrow's your birthday. Anyway, do you think they care?"

Outside in the garden, in the lettuce and sweet peas and carrots, Faith is crying. She had a fight with Ray last night, and he drove away and didn't come back. Faith will probably forget Sunny's birthday.

"I want to break an egg," Sunny says.

Jennie cracks another egg and separates it. A Lady Baltimore takes six eggs, and if Faith finds out, she might get mad. If she gets mad, Jennie will say, Who feeds the chickens? Me, that's who. Anyway, it's Sunny's birthday. Jennie cracks the third egg. It's your son's birthday, she'll say. Can't he have a birthday cake on his birthday? That will work on Faith, except she might say Jennie's poisoning Sunny.

"I want to!" Sunny says.

Jennie cracks the fourth egg. Outside, Faith stretches her back and wipes her eyes. She looks out over the valley toward the highway, like she's going to see Ray on his way home. Maybe he'll run away for good this time. Jennie cracks the fifth egg.

"PAY ATTENTION!" Sunny shouts. "IT'S MY BIRTHDAY!"

"Fine," Jennie says. "You don't have to shout." She gives him the sixth egg, and very carefully, he hits it against the rim of the bowl. He is so careful that the egg doesn't break open. "You need to hit it harder," she tells him. So of course he smashes it, and shells and yolk get into the egg whites, so now they won't whip right. "You dummy," she says. "You ruined it."

"I didn't!"

She's ready to be mad at him, only his little face is so sad, so worried, and it's almost his birthday. She scoops out the yolk and the whites are just fine, so she says, "You're right. I'm sorry."

"Will it still be good? Will it still be delicious?"

"Of course it will," she says. "This is a Sunny Boy Blue birthday cake." She decides to make the cake apricot. They go outside by the well, to the tree. The apricots are perfect, so sweet and sunshine-warm. She stirs them into the batter and saves some for them to eat. She sends Sunny to the chicken coop for another egg. The cake will be delicious. Jennie, putting it in the oven, remembers Hansel and Gretel. A house made of candy. That's the best part of that story. If she could give Sunny a house made of candy, it would make him so happy, because he has the sweetest tooth in the world. Of course, there's the wicked witch, but look what happened to her. Into the oven with you, Witch!

While they wait for the cake, they'll tell stories. Jennie gets the Treasured Memories album from its hiding place in the bedroom. It's a horrible hot August and the air outside has a sour, salty smell to it, of heat, or of browning and cracking.

Usually, they go far away from Faith, to the concrete culvert that runs under the highway. But today they have to be nearby to get the cake out of the oven. So they climb the hill behind the chicken coop, near the compost pile. There, sprouted from seeds thrown out with watermelon rinds and eggshells and coffee grounds, a whole crop of sunflowers has grown tall and healthy with heads the size of Ray's hands. Their stalks droop under the weight, and around their bases, enormous ragweed bushes grow. Inside this stand of sunflowers and ragweed, Jennie and Sunny have trampled a clearing. The sunflowers look down on them like guards.

Their rooster, Mister, is afraid of the chickens. He hides in the bushes, waiting for them to leave. Mister has almost no feathers. His wives have pecked them all off. Sunny chases the chickens away and feeds Mister some apricots. "I love Mister," Sunny says. He feels sorry for anything that doesn't have a fair chance. Mister gulps down the apricots, then catches a leaping grasshopper neatly in his beak.

Sunny sits in Jennie's lap, and she spreads Treasured Memories across their knees. They eat apricots. The bright green grasshoppers leap on Treasured Memories, then spring away when Jennie turns a page. One lands in Jennie's hair, and one on Sunny's cheek. The chickens come to catch grasshoppers.

Once upon a time, long ago and far away, at practically the Edge of the World, there was a place called Seattle, where rain fell soft and quiet and the ferns grew wild. In this place, on a hill so steep it took two hundred and thirteen steps to get to its top, a little man named Paul Chatwin lived alone, in a house his father had built with his own two hands. The house had secret nooks and crannies, with an attic and a basement and a high pointed roof, and it was filled with special things, like a Ming vase.

At the Edge of the World, it was never too hot and never too cold and never too dry. It rained every single day, so everyone had green grass, and you could go out into the forests and pick blueberries or giant bouquets of violets. There were always bees, and they never stung. It was always cloudy, but that suited Paul just fine, because he was a rainy sort of fellow. He was short and round as an egg, and he had a round little face.

Paul taught children to play on his mother's piano. When new students came huffing and puffing up the horrible stairs, Paul would ask, "How many steps?" The students would pant, and clutching music in their sweaty fists, they'd say—

"Two hundred and thirteen!" Sunny shouts. "Two hundred and thirteen!" Mister squawks and scurries away. Jennie turns the page. "Don't interrupt," she says. But she doesn't mean it. Interrupting is part of the story. When Jennie is older, old enough to be in a bar playing pool, she'll say, "My grandfather was a piano teacher," and she'll hear Sunny's five-year-old voice, listening out loud: "Two hundred and thirteen!" She'll tell Lipa's story, racking the balls, lining up a shot, but what she'll feel is her cheek against Sunny's warm black hair, and she'll glimpse his see-through green eyes shining at his big sister, who's telling him where he came from and where he belongs.

"Two hundred and thirteen!" Paul's students would cry.

Paul loved his students, and he loved the piano that sat in the middle of a long room which faced Mount Rainier. Big and black and shiny, it was like a friend Paul had known forever. He knew all of its quirks and all of its tempers. Sometimes he imagined that in the middle of the night it sang songs to itself, very softly so no one could hear. When he didn't like how he played, he pretended the Steinway was mad at him. "You bad old piece of wood," he'd whisper. "What did I ever do to you?"

Every once in a while the rain stopped and the clouds cleared, and then Paul stood on his porch and looked at Mount Rainier, far-off and pale and perfect, and he'd make his wish. It was a special kind of wish. He didn't know exactly how to say it, so he would just whisper, "Two hundred thirteen," and though he knew it didn't make sense, he believed that God and Mount Rainier were sure to understand. What Paul didn't know was that he was wishing for love.

The ditchwater gurgles over rocks, and trucks hum on the highway in the distance. A bad feeling comes over Jennie, a sadness in her heart that says things are going to change, and soon. It feels like rain is coming. Thunderheads are rising over the Sangre de Cristos.

"Junie?" Sunny whispers. "Tell it?"

Jennie turns to the picture of Paul in his flannel suit, his tall bride beside him. "Now," she says, "now comes the happiest part of the story."

It happened that down in the city there lived a maiden who had come from a very faraway place called Russia, which is like no place you've ever gone.

"What does Russian sound like?"

"Like nothing you've ever heard," she says.

The bad feeling is making her grumpy. She takes a deep breath. Sunny sighs. The grasshoppers hop, and Mister comes back to eat them.

And then, one day, the maiden knocked on Paul's door. She wore a blouse embroidered with violets, and as she stood there, a hummingbird darted up to investigate the flowers on the back of her shirt. She wore a small gold cross on a chain around her neck. She wore her blond hair in two braids fastened on top of her head like a crown. She spoke with a strange accent that made her sound like she was about to burst out singing. She talked very quickly, as if she had practiced. Paul soon learned that this was her way. Lipa was the kind of person who charged ahead, like she was born knowing what to do. She believed in things: in God, in herself, in cookies and cakes and doughnuts, in hot delicious white bread with lots of butter melting on it.

She held a book of music against her chest, and her cheeks were pink as she explained that she was Lipa, fresh from Russia. That she had been very poor since she came here, without her parents and with little else. Over there, her fa-

ther had enough money to pay for her lessons. She played piano and learned English over there. But one day her father died, and her mother bundled her up and kissed her on the cheeks and pressed money between her palms and put her on a boat to a better life. Here in Seattle, she said, she scrubbed floors, and at night she lay in bed and tried to see the keyboard on the backs of her eyelids but of course that wasn't the same. So now, after reading of his lessons in the newspaper, she wondered if Paul would trade with her. She wondered if he would let her, for instance, clean his kitchen in return for a little help with Bartók. That is how she put it exactly: "A little help with Bartók."

Paul stood with his hand on the doorknob, amazed by her. He asked her how many steps she had climbed, and she said, "Two hundred thirteen." Paul stared, speechless. "I counted," she said. "It's good to count, a way to make easier climbing." Then she said—

"I clean very well, and I play a little bit better than that."

"And then—"

"And then he loved her."

"And then he loved her."

One day, Lipa was washing dishes. There was a window over the sink, and the sunshine made her glow around the edges. Paul sat at the table, pretending to read, but really watching her through his eyelashes. She was humming a Russian song as she worked. All at once, she leaned forward until water wet her short sleeves. She looked out the window, and Paul saw that she was watching bees on the violets in the windowbox. "Isn't it wonderful?" she said. "We love the flowers, and the bees make honey, and then we eat honey which is like eating the flowers. It makes me want to compliment God for making things so tidy."

At that moment, he knew he loved her more than anything in the world. So he made up a song. "Marry me," he sang. "Marry me, marry me, Oh please Lipa, marry me?"

W H E N Jennie gets to the part about Lipa dying, Sunny wants her to live, like he always does. "A happy ending," he yells. "Happy happy happy! It's my birthday!" Mister crows and the grasshoppers leap and Sunny yells and they don't hear Faith until the sunflowers part and there she is. "I was calling you," she says, and then she stops and stares at Treasured Memories, lying across Sunny's knees, open to the picture of her, Faith, with a pail of blueberries and shiny black shoes. Faith's eyes are terrible, her voice low and dangerous. "That's mine." The grasshoppers leap frantically. Mister darts into the weeds. "That's mine," she says, and again, "That's mine."

Sunny says, "Mom?"

Jennie says, "Mom—"

"Shut up!" Faith says, snatching the album. "Shut up! This is *mine!*"

"Mommy," Sunny says. "I'm sorry."

"You *thief.* I could kill you," Faith says, crying, Treasured Memories pressed to her chest. "You let me think he didn't send me anything. You stole from me. You're exactly like your father." She means Jennie. Never Sunny. "I wish you were dead," she whispers, and then she leaves. The sunflowers close behind her. Everything is the same but different. "Mom," Sunny calls. "Mom?" He asks Jennie, "What will she do?" Jennie, leading him down the hill, admits to herself that she's afraid. But in they go to the hot kitchen, where Faith stands at the stove, roasting chiles. It's so hot. The sweat trickles down her temples; her hair clings to her neck. Jennie whispers, "Mom?" The sweet baking cake smell mixing with the smell of burned chile skin.

Faith looks at them. Her eyes fill, and without a sound, her tears rise over her eyelids and slip down her cheeks.

"Mommy?" Sunny says. "Don't be sad?"

"You don't think," Faith tells Jennie. "You just barge ahead. That was my gift from my father, and you're not touching it again." She lifts the stove lid and stirs the fire, and Jennie understands. Faith burned the Treasured Memories.

Jennie takes Sunny's hand. "Come on," she says. "We're leaving now."

"You come back here," Faith yells. "I'll tell your father about this!"

Jennie pulls Sunny along, through the garden. But at the sweet peas she comes to a stop. Sunny tugs her fingers. "Junie?" he says. "Junie, what did she do with the pictures?"

She stares at the peas. She knows she sees them, but still, she feels blind. "She burned them," she says.

"Don't cry," he whispers. "Junie, don't cry?"

She blinks and swipes at her eyes. "I'm not crying," she says. She leads Sunny back to the empty kitchen. She checks the cake, but it's not done yet. I am the thief, she thinks, and she finds Faith's purse on the counter and takes a five-dollar bill out of Faith's wallet. It's the only money in it, and Faith will know, but Jennie doesn't even care.

At Flaco's, they buy chocolate and lemon drops and Bit-O-Honey and Pixie Stix. Forbidden sugar. The candy is his day-before-his-birthday present. Sunny doesn't complain. He doesn't cry. He never does. Jennie takes him to the culvert. Inside the big concrete tunnel, they can stand straight up. Their voices stretch and grow hollow. When a car passes over them, the whole world rumbles and shakes. Outside, the sunlight is blinding, and the weeds at the ends of the culvert are dead. Her eyes aren't used to the dark; Sunny is a shadow.

He sits between her legs and they press their bare soles against the cool ce-
ment. The cars rumble like monsters. Sunny's a big boy; he can walk all the
way down to Flaco's and back up the hill and he isn't afraid of the cars. "We're
Hansel and Gretel hiding in a cave," she tells him. He's almost five. Tomorrow, he'll be five.

She tells him the story without the pictures, and it's just as good, and true,
because it's history. She remembers it just fine.

After they married, Paul and Lipa had a baby and they named her Faith.
From the start, Faith never stopped crying. She woke them up in the middle of
the night with her screaming. She cried all day long. She chewed Lipa's nipples
when she nursed. Lipa went to her priest, who said that Faith was like a baby
possessed, which means that there were demons inside her. It was fate. She was
born to hate her mother.

"I don't like this part. She was a nice baby."

"No, she wasn't. Will you be quiet and listen? Or should I stop?"

"I'll listen," Sunny says. She feels sad, too, hearing his sad voice, and she
thinks, That album was ours. They were our Treasured Memories.

Faith grew into a little girl, black-haired like her mother and short like her fa-
ther. She was very difficult and hated playing piano. Once she hid when it was
time for her lesson. Paul and Lipa searched in the woods at the edge of the
meadow; they searched the two hundred and thirteen stairs; they called and
called. Lipa cried. Paul got angry. It began to rain, but they couldn't go inside
because they couldn't find Faith. She was hiding under a bush. She could hear
her parents calling her name, but she stayed there. When they finally found her,
Lipa and Paul were soaking wet.

That night, Lipa came down with a cold. She got sicker and sicker, and she
had a fever like she had never had before; she yelled in her sleep and Paul sat up
all night, giving her sips of water. Finally, he fell asleep, too, his head back
against the wall. And in the early morning, he woke up, and she was dead. And
so it was Faith's fault she died of a cold. Because it was Faith who kept her out
in the rain.

"This isn't how you tell it," Sunny says. "This is wrong!"

At the end of the culvert, the world is a circle of light that's hot as a fireplace. He says, "I want to go see Mom!"

She eats another square of chocolate and wraps up her candy again. She's
saving some to surprise Sunny later. It's going to be a long walk back home.
She's very sleepy. She wants to stretch out right here, in the culvert, and take
a nap. She closes her eyes and sees it so clearly, the house with its pointy roof,
the sun shining through the window, the gleaming wooden floors. All that water, stretching to meet the sky at the Edge of the World, the green ferns.

Sunny asks, "Do you think she's still mad?"

"We'll be good," Jennie says. "Okay? And don't say anything for a while, okay? Be very quiet."

"Okay." Sunny nods, so serious that Jennie feels like crying. She kneels in front of him and gives him a piece of her chocolate, then licks his cheek with her big wet sloppy tongue. "Cow kiss," she says. Sunny gulps her chocolate with his cheeks bulging out, and she tries to give him more cow kisses until he sprays chocolate in a gobby mess and they laugh and laugh. Their laughter travels in long hollow spirals until it bounces outside and gets mixed up with the hot bright world, with the semis and their mother and all the rest.

THEY have a couple of years left together, Sunny and Jennie. And over those years she'll tell it again and again, a family history half invented, based on stolen photographs: their only inheritance. And over and over, Sunny will ask for a happy ending. "I hate this story!" he'll cry. "It never has a happy ending!"

Hush, Sunny. This is history, irrefutable and absolute. You cannot change what happened, but you must learn from it, because memories may be treasures but they are also warnings, and directions so we know which way to go. Hush. There really is a house our grandfather built. It's standing there, on the Highest Hill at the Edge of the World, waiting for us to come and claim it as our home. So you see, there is a happy ending for you after all. We just haven't gotten to it yet.

WHIRLWIND

Last Fall, Albuquerque

THE perfume of our four-month courtship was formaldehyde, and our song was "Deck the Halls." Fa la la la la. By October, Christmas carols were blaring away, and in my memory they're the soundtrack as we peel apart the layers of the human body. In early November, Chris and I executed a transverse section of a female. Let's call it what it is. We used a two-handled saw on her waist, like lumberjacks, and separated her body into upper and lower halves. When we finished, we could see a cross section of spine and the body cavity, the tops of the pelvis bones.

Our partner—Guapo, we called him, because he was so pretty—shouldered the legs like a rifle. "Deck the Halls" blared over the speakers. 'Tis the season. Watching Guapo carry her legs, I noticed the cadaver's toenails were painted a frosty pink. Think of it. Once those upended legs were attached to a girl on a couch, a phone tucked to her ear, tufts of cotton between her toes as she painted her nails and gossiped with her best friend. I told Chris, "Now she's a pair of stiff legs."

"Or a legless stiff," he said. The humor of our courtship was mostly tasteless jokes, and we made them recklessly, laughing with hysterical gusto. From gross anatomy, I learned there's no soul lurking somewhere in the body cavity. It's all just flesh. When you steep it in formaldehyde, the flesh turns varying shades of gray. Yellow-gray, brown-gray. The green-gray thumb of the gallbladder. It all reeks of preservative.

We'd forget we smelled like that, too, until, riding on an elevator or shopping for vegetables, we would see a nose wrinkle, eyes narrow. In Safeway, a woman fingering beets turned away from us with an expression of bewildered disgust, as if she knew we were up to something unsavory, even if she didn't know what it was.

"We're undertakers," I told her. "You can smell it, can't you?"

She smiled politely. We're just buying avocados, I wanted to yell at her. For guacamole, dammit! And besides, we're in love!

Chris put his arm around me. "Don't be frightened," he told the grocery shopper. "Everyone dies." The woman, shocked, tried to push past. "And everyone falls in love," he said, moving out of her way. "I'm in love, here." The woman glanced over her shoulder, something almost like envy underlining her confusion, and scurried off to the dairy section.

Maybe it wasn't the formaldehyde that got her. Maybe it was the underlying reek of coitus, because we kept it up, two rutting goats, in stairwells and bathrooms, in his car outside Antonio's. We were studying in the library, and I put down my pen. One look between us, and next we were in a storage closet that smelled faintly of mold, giggling, admonishing each other to hush. "O Come, All Ye Faithful," I whispered, touching him in all the right places. "Joyful and triumphant," he sang, shuddering. Even then, I knew that there was a certain hysteria in me as I egged it on, this outrageous fucking in dark corners, as if I wanted it as evidence later: Look there. See that? We were in love. Love, love, love.

In Safeway, fondling avocados, Chris whispered to me, "Now I can make it official. I love you."

"Stop saying that," I said.

"I'll say it as much as I want." Then, gleefully, while selecting produce, he began explaining the progression of his love. My walk, he said, sniffing the overripe flesh of a tomato, was the first thing he loved about me. He saw this chick walk into the pool hall, all panting, sweaty, and this chick goes straight to the chalkboard, her back straight, her stride cocky. She stood near him. She was in running clothes; she smelled faintly of sweat.

"So you're saying I stank up the place."

"I'm saying you were strong." He chose onions; he chose garlic. "The third thing I loved," he said, bagging cilantro, "was the way you made that first shot. I knew you were the kind of woman who scares most men."

"Insulted again, thank you very much."

"But I was in love," he said, thrusting his nose into the bag, "from the moment I saw you at the bar, stinky and breathing hard. Ah, cilantro. Perfume of the gods."

"Please," I said. "You make love sound like a recipe for salsa."

"I saw you write your name on the chalkboard. So I looked for a woman's name and called it out."

"James," I said, "you cheater. You pumpkin eater."

He bumped me gently with the cart. "I skipped the second thing. The second thing was the look in your eyes when I saw you talking to that kid, talking and talking, but you had this little smile that said, *I know a joke, and I'm not telling.*"

"Enough with this mush, already," I said. "We need some hamburger."

"Then," he said, "there you were the next morning. So the footprint on the wall was the fourth thing."

"Third," I said, thoroughly annoyed. I walked ahead, and he followed me with the cart's wheels clacking like a gossipy woman.

"This is my love story," he said. "I keep count. Third is how you play pool, and four is the footprint."

I sped up, heading for the meat. "You tell it out of order."

"Just keeping my Ellie on her toes," he said.

"Stop it," I said, maybe a little too loudly. An emaciated, string-armed woman choosing skinless boneless breasts glanced over at us.

"Wait," Chris said gently, quietly. "Think, Jennie. I'm telling you I love you."

"So finish," I said. I reached for the hamburger, pushed my fingers into the flesh. I hated Chris. I don't know why I hated him so intensely, but I did; I wanted to throw the meat at him, or rip open the plastic and do some sort of damage. Ground round. Ninety-eight percent lean fuselage. "Then shut up."

Chris sighed. We had ourselves a little staring match, and he spoke quite deliberately, like a kid on a playground going for a win. "There you were, foot against the wall, looking like you were thinking, What nerve, showing up in my life again. Does he think this is funny? But under all that prickly Jennie Goat Gruff was fear, or, rather, hunger, a ferocious hunger—"

"What did you say?"

"And I thought, Somewhere in there, this woman needs me—"

"Did you just call me a goat?"

"And that was the fourth thing, the footprint, giving you away, because when you saw what you'd done, you had this flash across your face, like, I'm starving. Give me something to eat—"

That was it. I said, "You don't know me. You don't know me at all, or you would have shut your fucking mouth at the avocados." And I left. I trotted past the cleaning supplies and out the door of Safeway and he didn't come after me and I ran home and he didn't show up and I waited but he didn't call and there was No Fucking Way I was calling him, so here's the Ugly Chick, running past his house but not going inside, just on her way to Antonio's to shoot pool instead of memorizing the bones of the foot, all so she won't be at home to wait for his call, and this Ugly Chick, feeling uglier and uglier, will never admit that she's the fool and regrets herself. One eye on the door, she loses her games, and she'll never admit that she wants more than anything in the whole black world for this Christian Braverman to come through the door and offer her a bowl of guacamole. She plays until closing but he doesn't arrive.

In the morning, though. On her front step, the Prince has left one shoe. Gorgeous, from the twenties, alligator skin dyed dark red, the size of a child's foot. A Betty Boop shoe, so dainty her hand won't fit inside. No note at all. But she knows what he means. I'm here, the shoe says. Still looking for you.

THAT night, he showed up with a grocery bag and a speech. He said he'd gone to the library. But he also said, "You *are* a billy goat, you know; you eat your way through anything and head-butt anyone who gets in your way. A guy could get hurt with all the head-butting. But I'm stubborn, too. You won't get rid of me just by throwing a tantrum. I'll just go away, catch up on all the studying I skip with you, come back when you've cooled down."

I stood in my one-room stable, chewing on that cud, wondering if the anger would rise in me again. But it didn't. He took me by the shoulders and looked me in the eye and said, "Fair enough?"

"Fair enough," I said, and swallowed.

Then he made me guacamole. He's a genius with spices and garlic and a chef's knife. What a thing to see, Chris chopping onions. I stood behind him with my chin on his shoulder and watched him blaze through an onion like nobody's business. He wanted to be a surgeon, to operate on fetuses, in fact. Yet the knife was so close to his fingers, and the fumes made tears leak from my eyes. Under my chin, the muscles of his back worked in time to the blade. "The way I see it, that prince guy had it all wrong," he said. "He looked at the shoes instead of the woman. I've picked the woman. I figure I'll just keep bringing you shoes until I find the one that fits."

"Try again," I said blithely, as if untouched. But watching him magnificently wield the knife, dicing tomatoes, onions, garlic, cilantro, and I had to lean against the counter, because this pure, intense love swept over me like a release of breath. I thought, Is this a swoon? Over onions?

He left for a study group after he finished. Alone, I sat on my front step with the bowl in my lap, and I ate the guacamole with a spoon, and I licked the bowl clean.

HE tortured me by calling me Cinderella. Jennie-ella. Billy-ella. Ellie. Cindy. Sin. If I got mad about something, he'd tell me quietly, an observation, "You're being a goat." He'd disappear into the library for a day or two. But I'd always find another shoe on my stoop, a sort of reverse Cinderella, and I'd know he'd come back.

He brought me a shoe barrette, a chocolate shoe which I ate in two gulps.

"Quit with the shoes, already," I told him, but in truth I loved the playfulness of a glossy riding boot made for a Canadian Mountie the size of Paul Bunyan. "I know you love it," Mr. Swami said, reading my mind yet again. He brought me a wooden cobbler's last, with the customer's name burned in the side: Aureliano Sanchez. "This is a man's foot," I said.

"Worth a try," he said.

He brought me a moccasin beaded by hand, a baby shoe and a down-stuffed shoe for an Iditarod sled dog. "Now I'm a dog," I said. "It's warm," he said. A shoe horn and a shoe tree, and even a shoe painting. "Shoes," I said. "You have a fetish."

"It's so hard to find a good fit."

"You fit me," I said. I reached for him. "Let me show you how you fit me." Because in sex it all became so much simpler, a pure exchange, and I wouldn't call it desperation so much as acceleration—at times I saw us coupling in the center of a tornado, cadavers and textbooks and shoes flying wildly around us as we fornicated, oblivious to the howling of the wind.

F O R Thanksgiving, we drove the Rolls up the eastern back of the Sangre de Cristos, off to Denver and the big parental introduction. The drive is long and mostly boring—there are towns along the way, but all you see from the interstate are green signs and broad, high plains. Chris drove, and I read to him from textbooks. There was much joking, laughing, fondling of knees.

We did eighty. The Rolls felt like a gliding upper-crust men's club, minus cigars and nicely aged whiskey. We passed drivers who gawked at the millionaires. I gawked back at them, but Chris kept his hands on the wheel and his eyes straight ahead. He was a careful driver.

Alongside the highway, hawks perched on every three or four posts like soldiers. Once, driving on the highway, my mother saw a dead red-tailed hawk and screeched to a stop. She leapt out of the car, and while she plucked its wings and tail feathers for a Meeting Fan, the putrid smell of carcass oozed into the car. We drove away with all the windows down, but we couldn't get rid of the stink. Where were we driving? I have no clue, but to this day I can call up the smell we carried with us. I remember thinking the hawk was punishing us for stealing his feathers. I did not tell Christian Braverman about any of that.

W E passed the sign announcing Las Vegas. I've often wondered what it was like for the non-native, the passers-through seeing the sign as a magical transportation to Nevada without the long, boring drive. But there is no city of electric lights and slot machines in New Mexico; we only have an off-ramp. Tucked away from the interstate, our Las Vegas doesn't even seem to have buildings, so it's like a cruel hoax.

Then it came to me. "I think I lived there once."

"Did you?" Chris said. He drove with his long fingers curled lightly, casually, around the wheel. "When was that?"

"I can't remember," I said slowly. But even as I said it, I did remember. I was young, really young. How old? Four? My father was starting college, to be a teacher. My mother and I went with him. We lived in a normal house. It had wooden floors. I was afraid of the shower; the water raining on my face made me think I was drowning. We stayed a month, but something, probably money, sent us back to Alfin. My father didn't return to college for years, until he had left us and moved to Florida.

The memory of that month had returned to me complete, like a stone appearing whole in my palm. We drove past a sign for Storey Lake. "We went there," I said. I remembered gray, choppy water, the rocky beach. "I don't know how I forgot this," I said.

Chris said, "We all forget things."

"Aren't you the wise one." I decided it was best to keep my mouth shut. We passed miles of fence, miles of telephone wire. I fumed, sure that Chris was making all sorts of false assumptions about repressed memories, probably thinking I'd been molested by the Las Vegas ice cream man.

But Chris had other things on his mind. He directed me to look in the glove compartment, where I found a long, flat box wrapped in glossy paper. "Open it," he said, so nervously that, to tease him, I unwrapped the paper with meticulous care and lifted the lid ever so slowly. There was a pair of red gloves inside. They were kid, and long, made to bunch at the wrists. Marvelous, soft baby animal leather. I stroked my arm, my cheek, my lips with them. "Baby goat gloves," I said. "I've never owned anything so perfect." By his smile, I realized I was letting something slip. "Does this mean you're giving up shoes?"

"Put them on," he said. "See if they fit like gloves."

I drew them on, and inside the third finger of the left hand, there was a ring. It was fastened in somehow, so it slid neatly down my finger.

He said, "I had the wrong idea with the foot. It was the hand I wanted. Your hand, Jennifer Lipa, your beautiful, pool-sharking, fist-wielding lover's hand." Here he was, jumping the gun once again, saying, "Jennifer Lipa, marry me, please won't you marry me?" Stealing my grandfather's lines, sneaking the ring on my finger before I could say no.

This was perfect, a romantic declaration, the asking of my hand with just the right words. So why were my fists clenched so tightly that the ring threat-ened to break through the soft red leather? I was afraid of myself, of the Ugly Chick who must always guard against the second thing she says. "You're every woman's dream," I said, trying to keep it light, cheerful. "Our Chris, Prince of Jumping the Gun."

Chris stared at the road ahead. He gave me enough time to regret both of the sentences that had sprung from my mouth. Time to tally every one of the words. Exactly eleven mistakes.

When at last he spoke, his voice was exceedingly calm, his own version of anger, tightly controlled, strangled. "Don't you dare make a joke out of this," he said. "Don't you dare. This is real life. You can say no. You can put those gloves back in the box and forget all about this. But I won't let you make a joke out of it."

I had done it again. Sadness welled up in me, but I couldn't see what to do, or to say, to salvage this moment. I laid the gloves back in the box. I re-wrapped the paper I'd so carefully removed. I returned the package to the glovebox. I folded my arms and stared out the window, as if I'd rewound time, erased the whole incident. Any moment now, he'd turn to me and say, "I can't stand this anymore, your huffing and puffing. The house has blown down."

He took the Raton exit and pulled into a gas station. He killed the engine and turned to me. "I love you," he said. "Remember that."

Stunned, I didn't answer. Had his thoughts been this far from my assump-tions? I was so glad to be wrong, to be surprised by him. Astonishing, wonder-ful Chris. But I could not answer yes. I could not speak at all, and we drove the rest of the way to Denver in silence.

WE arrived in the late afternoon and drank coffee with his parents in the kitchen. The three Bravermans, mother, father, son, sat around a table tucked into a bay window, chatting. The tall and the handsome, sitting in a circle, comparing notes on this old friend and that old family member, while through the window I watched the snow falling on the garden. I knew I should speak. His parents probably found me rude, or worse, irritatingly boring.

They were old, Chris's parents. On the backs of her hands, his mother's blue veins trembled with her pulse. Her hair was gray rinsed blond, and her eyebrows were thick, black. I fell in love with the creases in Mr. Braverman's pants; I had never known anyone with such crisp straight lines down each leg. Like his son, Mr. Braverman was tall enough to play basketball. A ridiculous idea, a basketball in the elegant hands of this man whose legs, in finely tai-lored pants, stretched before him Astaire-like, crossed at the calves, this man who had been a vice president for an oil company in the Middle East. This was a man who had given his son a Rolls-Royce and called it neat.

We drank coffee from dainty cups with garlands of orange flowers on their rims. On the domed ceiling, painted cupids floated in fresco clouds, their bows drawn. I gaped at the whorls of blue and white, the fat winged babies above me, at the translucent edge of the cup in my hand. I wondered if the ceiling was something Mrs. Braverman had commissioned, if she'd celebrated its completion by making love with her husband on that oak floor. I asked her about it. "Does it make you feel romantic?"

She smiled. "It *is* romantic, isn't it?" And over her shoulder, Chris met my look, and I was relieved. I had not spoken to him, but at least I had spoken.

A ƒ т е ʀ the parents went to bed, Chris and I sat at the kitchen table, drinking whiskey like I had never tasted, mellow, smooth, older than me.

The snow still fell. We had turned off the lights so we could watch the wet, clumpy flakes drop past the windows. In the summer, Chris informed me, the garden was tangled with roses. "My dad likes you," he said. "He says you're tall." Despite myself, I smiled. Chris said, "I have a few things to say to you." I got up and stood at the counter. "Just listen," he said. "Don't bolt."

"I'm still here." Such an effort it cost me to speak.

"First of all, I'm sorry I ambushed you earlier. Maybe I didn't want to give you a chance to say no. Because you have this play in your head, and I'm not sure, I mean . . ." He paused, took a drink. "I just think you need to be surprised sometimes," he said. "You like that I surprise you, that things don't always go your way."

"You make me sound like a brat."

"No. I make you sound like someone who's so busy running the show that she doesn't realize there's no show here. I see *you*, Jennie. I see past the show and into your frightened little girl heart and I love *you*, not the big face you put on to scare everybody. I just want to say, Rest here for a while."

"So you have me all figured out."

"Jennie, come sit down. Come sit down by me." But I got only as far as the table. I stood with crossed arms, and I feared I might cry. He was so wrong. I was no frightened girl; whatever lurked inside me wasn't as harmless as that. "I'm so tired of this," I said. I intended nastiness, but I spoke in a weary, weary voice I hardly recognized.

He said, "I know you are. I'm just saying, Come sit by me. Rest a while. Be yourself. Let down your guard."

I couldn't move. The snow fell, endlessly falling without seeming to land.

"I know all about faces," he said. "My family patented faces. Look, I'll tell you something about faces, if you'll sit down beside me."

Quietly, insistently, he told me a story. He said that when he was six years old, he found his mother weeping, a keening, childlike cry, and he was so young he thought she was sick when in fact she was drunk. She staggered and swayed into the walls, and methodically, she took money from her apron pockets and crumpled it and lit it on fire with a silver lighter while his father ran behind her, grabbing the money and slapping out the flames. And all the while, Mrs. Braverman cried, "Look at my brave man! *Mister* Braverman!"

The next morning, Chris found his father drinking coffee, his mother flipping pancakes. "There you are!" his mother said. It felt like the cheerful brightness of Christmas morning. He waited for some explanation. His father read the paper, and his mother had made pancakes in the shape of smiley faces, the way he liked them. She told Chris that he could decide to be happy or sad, but he needed to remember that the world likes a happy face, that it wasn't smart to run around showing all your feelings like she had yesterday. Then she smiled and asked if he wanted strawberry or regular syrup. And that was the end of that.

"The end?" I asked. I was still trying to believe that Mrs. Braverman, so coiffed and polite, could be the drunken madwoman Chris described, and here he was ending the story. "What do you mean, the end?"

"I mean, it was like I had imagined it, because we never mentioned it again. And the only reason I knew it was real was because I saved a half-burned fifty-dollar bill. And I never told anyone about it until you." He took out his wallet and laid the burned money on the table like he was raising the ante. He said, "There it is. Evidence. Proof."

I still couldn't bring myself to sit down. For a time we were still, sipping our drinks, watching the moonlight, the falling snow. I asked, "What did he do to make her so mad?"

He shrugged. "Probably something small. I think she just had to get out from behind the happy pancake face for once in her life."

I wondered why he'd never considered something larger. A mistress, probably, or something even messier. Was the mistress a hooker? Did Mr. Braverman pay for his teenage-hooker lover's abortion? "There's a reason to stay inside the smiley face. She could have burned your house down."

"Jennie," Chris said. He laid the red box on the table, as if I'd never opened it. He said, "I want to let you know, there are gloves in this box, which I thought would be clever, the opposite of shoes. They're nice gloves, but just so there's no mistake, I should tell you I took a needle and thread and with two tiny stitches, I sewed a ring inside the third finger of the left hand, and just so there is no confusion or surprise, and just so everything is aboveboard, I want to make it perfectly clear that this is my misguided attempt to ask you, Jennifer Davis, to marry me, Jump-the-Gun Christian Braverman, who knows he loves you."

I couldn't answer just then. How did this man, this Christian Braverman with his surgeon's fingers do it? He opened me up with a scalpel of words, his voice operating on my cold unbeating heart. He knew just what I needed to hear.

I sat. I laid my hands palms down on the table. I did not take up the box.

Chris put his hands palm down, like mine. He said, "Do you know what I'd like? I would like to hear something you've never told anyone before."

The quiet was so complete that I imagined, if I listened hard enough, I could hear the falling snow outside. I said, "My father and mother got married on a dare—"

"Not something you've made into *Something*."

I stared at my hands. Why was it so hard to reach for the red box? Why couldn't I just find a memory and make a gift of it to him, so that he could see I had a capacity for honesty and uncalculated revelation? I cast around inside myself, but I found only the usual set pieces, lumberjacks and piano players, kidnappings and thievery. All of it tidied by tellings and retellings. I spoke in desperation. "Remember how I said I lived in Las Vegas?"

"When you were little."

"My dad was in college there."

He waited. I felt the pressure of his silent, patient waiting, which was exactly like the snow falling. Soft, but accumulating branch-breaking force.

"There was a neighbor girl. She had a pink banana-seat bicycle. I must have been three or four. She seemed all grown up. She painted my fingernails pink."

He smiled. I stared at my hands, and at the box. I realized I wanted to open the box. "She said it would make me stop sucking my thumb."

"Did it work?"

"Yes," I said, which wasn't a lie, but an answer to a different question. I meant, Yes, I will put on these gloves. Yes, I will marry you. "Yes," I said, and reached for the box. "I've never told anyone about that," I said.

"Thank you," he said.

I pulled on the gloves slowly, the ring sliding over my knuckle. "They fit like gloves," I said softly, tamping them into the valleys between my fingers. "What did you do, trace my hand while I slept?" I heard myself make a joke. God, I thought, stop me from ruining this.

He turned his hands over, palm up, infinitely more vulnerable and welcoming. "Your hand is the same size as mine," he said.

I ran a red leather fingertip up the inside of his arm. "Soft," I whispered. He nodded. "You should probably know," I told him, "I'm not to be trusted. I'm not very nice."

He smiled. He said, "The fifth thing I loved about you was when you got mad and called me pathetic. You ran off, and I stood there, thinking, I'm going to marry that bitch."

With my red leather fingers, I traced the arc of his cheekbones, which are high and Slavic; he closed his eyes for me and I stroked his lids, which are more Asian than Caucasian—his great-grandfather was Lithuanian. I stroked his temples, his forehead. "Tickles," he whispered. I moved those red fingers, which were mine but also not mine, over the crown of his skull, and I ached in the center of my body, just above the diaphragm and and below the sternum, an ache which I could call hollow or hunger or lust or love. I stood and touched the little-boy nape of his neck with those red leather fingers. I drew his cheek to my belly. Here, I thought. This much is true.

He lifted my sweater, and against my bare belly his cheek was bristly and his lips were as soft as my gloves. He pulled me closer, tightly to his face, and for a while we stayed like that, his head cupped in my gloved hands, my belly meeting his breath, under a domed painting of heaven, with the snow falling softly outside over the tangled bones of roses. And then we made love on the kitchen floor, quietly, so carefully and slowly that I could almost call it snow. The tile warmed beneath me, and it seemed to yield, just as the domed ceiling seemed to rise, higher and wider in the blue light of the moon glinting off the snow, and somewhere above us, his parents slept.

Afterward, we lay prone on the tiled floor, softly laughing at what we had done, trying to keep our noise to ourselves. I thought, I believe in this. Trust snow, trust red gloves. Chris. I was sure I loved you then, with the secret of our kitchen transgression between us, with those beautiful red gloves on my hands. Yes, I said to him. Yes.

3.

INCURABLE AILMENTS

$\mathcal{T}$HE FIREPLACE

1975–76, Arroyo al Fin

OR. Maybe the piano isn't far enough back. Maybe the beginning is simpler, humbler, with my father's honest, misguided attempt to make something useful. With the fireplace, a simple construction of adobe. Who knew it would lead to so many disasters?

Begin, then, with a cold night, with Juniper, eight years old and doing double-digit addition homework at the kitchen table, half listening to Ray play his guitar in the Middle Room. She jumps when he yells.

"It's too goddamn cold in here!" Which is strange, since it hasn't snowed yet, even though it's November. He yells, "Too goddamn cold and too goddamn dark!" Juniper shivers. She remembers his wet boots, the deer he slaughtered in front of her, winters ago.

"Ray!" Faith yells back. "Don't say that word."

He comes into the kitchen. "What word?"

Faith sighs. "Oh Ray." It's what she always says: Oh Ray.

He says, "My fingers won't work, it's so goddamn cold in there." He rummages through the coffee can that holds everything, silverware, scissors, chopsticks, a screwdriver. "You know what I'm going to do? I'm going to build us a fireplace. Don't we have any pens? Because what's a house without a fireplace? A house without a fireplace, that's what."

Juniper wants to know how you build a fireplace. He draws a picture on a grocery bag. "This is a floor plan of our house," he says. It looks like a cross, or Jesus on the cross. She thinks, I sleep in Jesus's head. The kitchen is in his feet. And his heart is in the Middle Room, and it will be on fire. So she's glad Ray is making the fireplace. Her mother always says, Open your Heart to Jesus. "Daddy?" she asks. "Do you know how to make a fireplace?" Then she's worried. Will he be mad at her for asking?

He only waggles his eyebrows. "That's what libraries are for." Faith sweeping, stirring up dust, says, "You know what's going to happen? He'll burn us down. Or else he'll make the roof leak. Once your father patched a roof with mud. Guess how long that lasted?"

Now Ray's mad. "I'll tell *you* what's going to happen," he says. "I'm going to build this cocksucking fireplace the right way, and the only fire will be where it's supposed to be." He slams the screen door hard and drives away.

He comes back late with a pile of books about adobes. He's always getting library books Juniper doesn't understand. About art, about jazz. He says, "There's a world of geniuses out there, kiddo. Louis Armstrong is the Black Beethoven. Dizzy Gillespie, John Coltrane." He's always wanting her to remember names, like these people are his best friends. He believes in books more than God.

I N the morning, Juniper finds him digging a hole behind the house, between the woodpile and the well. He throws his shirt at her. He has splotchy freckles and white, white skin. His hair is frizzy and almost orange and sticks out all over the place. His bones stick out too. But he's strong. Juniper sits on his shirt and watches him dig. "You'll catch cold," she says, but she's not really worried. It will be Christmas soon, but the sun is warm on her face.

He says, "Guess what? Reymundo's having a baby."

"A *baby*?"

Ray laughs. In goes the shovel. Out flies the dirt. "What, you thought he built this big old house for the hell of it?"

She doesn't say anything. With Ray, you can say the wrong thing and he'll stop, or never start. You have to be still, and careful. Especially when he's about to tell a Reymundo story. If she pushes, he gets mad.

On the wall of each room of their house, there's a palm print pressed into the adobe. Ray says these hands belonged to a man named Reymundo. Ray can learn each room's history by fitting his hand inside Reymundo's handprint and closing his eyes. Then he tells the stories to Juniper. Juniper would rather hear fairy tales, but Reymundo is like a fairy tale, sort of.

As he digs, Ray tells how one morning over breakfast, Reymundo's wife told him they were having a baby. Reymundo's eyes filled with tears, he was so happy. That very day, Reymundo began making vigas for a new baby room, and while he worked, he dreamed of the son he already loved.

"*Hijo de mi corazón*," Ray says to Juniper. "*Digame.*"

"*Hijo de mi corazón*," she says. They're learning Spanish together. Ray has been studying it for nine years, which he says is because he's a lazy sonofabitch, but Juniper knows it takes a long time to learn a language.

Ray digs until dark. Juniper sits listening to his breath, his singing, the scrape of the shovel, the sling of the dirt onto the growing pile, until Ray tells her to go inside. Later, he gets Clarence for a Drum, which is when they sing Meeting Songs without a Meeting.

. . .

RAY. My father, my daddy, my dad. He played drums and guitar, and I know he loved jazz, which as far as I know is about theme and variation, and he loved the blues, which is something like a sad relative of jazz. I know that Ray liked to make up guitar songs, and when he finished, he'd gently lay his palm on the strings, as if it were a sleeping baby's back.

On the Meeting Drum, he used a long smooth stick blackened with coal, and he was red-faced, thin-lipped, his fierce concentration something like anger as he hit the drum at hundreds of beats per minute. The Drum was a cast-iron bowl filled with water and topped with a the hide of a deer he killed himself, gutted and skinned, the hide he'd salted and worked between his hands and tied to the cast-iron bowl to make a drum. The water danced on the taut leather as my father, holding the stick lightly, loosely, the way you hold a pool cue, beat the pulsing rhythm for Clarence, who sang the regular, chanting Indian words whose meaning even Clarence didn't know: the opposite of jazz, the beats repeating on and on through the Meeting night. Despite his dedicated Drumming, I don't know if my father believed in God. I know he loved jazz, and the blues, and I know he loved Clarence. Sometimes I think that's all I know.

JUNIPER lies in bed. The drumming is like the heartbeat of the house. She remembers the deer heart. Would Reymundo be happy that his house has a heartbeat? In Spanish, Reymundo means King of the World, and he was, not because he was rich, but because he was never cheated or sick or downhearted. Nothing bad ever happened to him. Ray says that Reymundo was the happiest man who ever lived, and the happiest man rules the world.

Ray says that before there was ever a Juniper Tree Burning or a Ray or a Faith, the Indians lived here, and then the Spanish came. One day, at the foot of the mountains called Sangre de Cristo which means Blood of Christ, the Spanish explorers found a small river. They followed it down from the mountains, through canyons that opened into valleys and then closed again into canyons, like beads on a string of water—and just before the river emptied into the Rio Grande, they found one final, wide valley, and they named it Arroyo al Fin which means Valley at the End. Now the tourists and Anglos call it Alfin, which rhymes with Ralph-in.

The settlers built their homes on the banks of Rio al Fin, beside pastures of rich soil, under the shade of cottonwood groves. The crazy Fresquezes, however, settled up on the valley side, and everyone laughed at them for building so far from the good pastures. But after the first winter, the Rio al Fin began to rise, and soon the settlers' houses were swept away, all except for the house of the lucky, lucky Fresquezes.

Then the settlers had trouble digging wells, except for the Fresquezes, who had a spring on their land. Over the generations, nobody could grow a single fruit tree, but Reymundo Fresquez, the great-great-grandson of the first Fresquez, dropped fruit seeds and they sprouted. When Reymundo fell in love with the prettiest girl in the world, she loved him back, and they married.

Clarence and Ray drum Juniper to sleep, and she dreams of Reymundo's son, who will be the next happiest man in the world.

BESIDE the hole, boards are nailed together like tic-tac-toes. These are forms, Ray says. Clarence brought them. Ray says it's time to make dirt. "You can't make dirt," Juniper says.

"You can make it better," Ray says. First they lay the screen across the hole and shovel on the dirt. By lunchtime, they have a pile of sifted soil down in the hole. She jumps in and her legs sink into the soft, cool dirt. Without rocks, dirt feels clean. So it is better.

At lunchtime, Faith's mad. She bangs the stove lid. She doesn't look at them. Ray says, "Little Faith. We can have marshmallow roasts. Hot dog cook-outs. We can do it on a bearskin rug." Faith's lips sneak up at the corners. "That gets her every time," Ray tells Juniper. "She's on our side now."

"Marshmallows are poison," Faith says. "And we don't have a bearskin."

"I'll hunt us up one," he says, and now Faith really smiles, and he lifts her off the ground so her feet dangle and he kisses her. Juniper goes outside, back into the cool soft clean earth.

AFTER lunch, they dump bucket after bucket of water into the hole, and then Ray jumps in. "Come on in!" he shouts. "The mud's fine!" They stomp around with mud up to their knees, singing about getting people's hearts, and then about fires in the belly, about light shining through and "I've got shoes, you got shoes, when we get to heaven we'll all wear shoes."

Ray adds straw and more water. He adds sand. Juniper stomps and stomps. The mud sucks when she pulls out her foot, a kissing, popping noise, and splorshes when she plunges her foot back in. The pieces of straw prick her feet in a nice way. Ray sings "Good-bye, Old Paint," and she tries to guess the part of the song when he'll shout, just like a cowboy, "Yee-haw!" But he changes it every time, and she's always surprised.

The sunset's blazing by the time they put the mud into the forms. Juniper helps scoop mud into a bucket which Ray carries up a ladder. They slop it into the forms until the sun has been gone a long time, and down in the hole, Juniper's cold, her teeth chattering. "Just wait," her father says. "One day we'll go inside and sit around the fire when we get a little chilly."

They make bricks for days. The bricks dry on the outside first, and then they come out of the forms but have more drying to do. Curing, it's called, which sounds strange, as if the bricks have a cold. Ray makes up a song: "Them bricks, them bricks, them sick bricks."

While the bricks are still soft enough, Ray presses his hand into the mud. "You too," he tells Juniper. She smiles. She can't stop herself from smiling. Next to her father's handprint, she presses her palm into the warm mud, which is soft like cake but solid.

RAY climbs up on the roof. Juniper and Faith sit inside, upstairs, on the bed. They're supposed to help. The bed frame is metal, with fancy curlicues. Wrought iron, it's called. Ray painted it bright blue. Faith tells Juniper— again—that this bed came all the way from Seattle, that Ray forgot everything that mattered to her and brought only furniture, and books. "He never thinks about anyone but himself," she says. Over their heads Ray moves, creaking and squeaking. "I can't stand this," Faith says, and stomps downstairs.

Her parents' bedroom, Juniper realizes, is right over the heart of the house—Jesus's heart, the best place. In a while, her father's saw pokes down between the vigas. The insulation is dirt, so it shrieks as he pushes his saw back and forth, back and forth. A circle of wood falls to the floor in a shower of dust and clod, opening a circle of sunlight in the ceiling. Here is her Daddy, looking down, smiling. He says, "Hey, little schoolgirl, clean up down there, will you?"

Juniper goes to the kitchen for a bucket or a bag and finds Faith banging around in the pantry. "I'm not stupid," Faith says. "Roofs can leak." Faith glares at Juniper. "Did he get dirt all over everything?" Juniper says no, so they won't fight, so the fireplace won't leak, so there will be warmth and light in the middle of their house, which is a cross, which is a heart, which is under where her parents sleep. She hurries upstairs with a broom as if she's the one who got dirt over everything. Faith clangs her pots.

The sun coming down from the roof is like a stovepipe of light making a sun on the wooden floor. Juniper looks up at the circle of blue sky. Her father's face appears. "Pretty far-out, don't you think?" he says. "I'm coming down." His face vanishes.

Ray arrives to cut a hole in the floor, which is the Middle Room's ceiling. With a pencil, he traces the circle of sunlight on the floor, and again the dirt insulation screams. The wooden ceiling falls in a shower of dirt. Faith yells, "Ray! You're making a mess!"

Juniper stands at the edge and looks into the Middle Room. It's a way of seeing she never knew about. Is this how God sees things, like spying on people through a hole in the floor of His house? This new way of seeing makes her have a different memory of everything that ever happened in the Middle Room.

That's when she sees the black widow dangling right in front of her face, its long legs busily working down its spider rope, a mad spider who was living in the roof before someone cut a hole in its house and made it mad, and Juniper can't move because if she doesn't move the spider won't notice her and then she screams and runs, beating herself, and she won't go upstairs for a long, long time, until she can hardly remember why she's so afraid of that room.

IN the kitchen, Faith and Joy are having coffee. "It's just a spider," Faith says.

"A black widow's a big deal," Joy says. She says she knows a lady who got bit by one and now she has nerve damage and she can't walk normally. Juniper feels spiders scuttling over her skin, and she slaps her body, her hair, while Joy and Faith talk about the right way to build a fireplace and how Ray's doing it wrong.

Faith makes Juniper go clean up the mess in the Middle Room. There's light in there now. A beam of sun comes down and makes a circle on the floor. Juniper sweeps, and Ray shovels dirt into a wheelbarrow. When Joy tries to tell him how to make a fireplace, he just looks at her like she's the smallest bug he's ever seen, and Juniper almost feels sorry for her.

In the Middle Room, Juniper lies on the floor with her face in the circle of sun. Through the ceiling, through upstairs, through the roof, she sees a circle of perfectly blue sky. It's like God is reaching down from heaven. Plus, she can see any spiders coming.

Her mother's feet come up beside her. "What if it snows?" she asks Juniper. "It's wintertime, you know."

"It's okay, Mom," Juniper says, because the circle of sky makes her feel safe. "It's going to be okay."

RAY takes Juniper to get a Christmas tree. You're supposed to have a permit, but he says, "Screw permits. Cocksuckers." They drive up the Ski Valley road, then park. They climb the side of the mountain, searching for a good tree. Ray carries his saw over his shoulder. She looks for a perfect triangle tree. They will put it in the living room. She'll hang a stocking over the fireplace. It will be a real Christmas. When they get home, Ray nails two boards in a cross on the tree trunk, so it will stand up. They put it in the Middle Room.

They don't have the Christmas Meeting. They have a hole in their roof, after all. Faith is mad, but what can she do? For Christmas, Ray gives Juniper a book of fairy tales. It's thick and old and it's a grown-up book. "Ray," Faith says. "That's too old for her."

"No it's not," Juniper says, flipping through the pages. It's all words. "I can read it."

"She's a big girl," Ray says. In the back, Juniper sees the library pocket with the library card in it, and she closes the book fast, before Faith can see.

THEY save the Christmas tree to be their first firewood. It's dry and dead. All the needles have fallen off. It looks very sad, sitting naked on the woodpile. Three days after Christmas, it finally snows, just a little. Juniper wakes up and finds a circle of snow on the Middle Room floor. She isn't worried. Her father will finish the fireplace soon. Faith says, "You see? He doesn't think ahead."

They have to wait a few more days for the bricks to dry, but God's on their side. The sun comes out on Juniper's birthday. Ray gives her another book, about the circulatory system. It's for kids, but Juniper likes it as much as the fairy-tale book because the pictures are interesting. Plus, there's no library card in the back. Plus, Ray starts building the fireplace on her birthday. It's called a kiva fireplace. It looks like a face, with curved cheeks and a round mouth. He puts their handprint brick over the fireplace mouth.

Ray builds up and up, and higher and higher the chimney goes until one day it reaches the ceiling, and the Middle Room is dark again.

"What if it burns the vigas?" Faith asks.

"Little Faith," he says, "with you, it's always something."

He leaves for town, and in two hours he's back with a shiny stovepipe. He carries it upstairs and shoves it down the chimney. "Should have done this first," he says, grunting because it's a tight squeeze. "Improvising," he tells Juniper. "You see an opening and you fill it." He puts a collar of metal around the upstairs floor and then stretches the pipe to the roof. He builds an adobe chimney around the pipe, and he leaves a hole for a woodstove heater in the upstairs bedroom.

Juniper puts her head inside the fireplace and looks up. Through the metal tube, she can still see the sky, but it's not the same. It doesn't feel like the light's reaching down; rather, the chimney is like a periscope, and she's stealing a peek. The inside of the fireplace smells like the wet mud. There won't ever be spiders inside the chimney. If they ever go in, they'll burn up. This makes her happy.

N o w they plaster. Faith helps. They're careful to let the handprints show through the white plaster, which dries their hands terribly. At night, they rub Faith's herbal lotion into their skin. It smells like leaves. Faith is best at plastering; hers is smooth and pretty.

"You're a plaster Picasso," Ray says. "I'm a Jackson Pollock plaster man." Juniper knows both those names. They're in a library book about art. She wants to tell him she remembered, but she can't figure out how to say it. Ray asks Faith, "Who taught you how to be so good at plastering?"

"Joy taught me," Faith says.

"Lucky me," Ray says. "There's hidden talent all over this town." Behind Faith's back, Juniper makes a face. She hates Joy. Ray sees and winks.

Faith waters down some plaster in a bucket until it looks like milk. She dips a piece of sheepskin into this and rubs the fur over the plaster until the surface is perfectly smooth. It looks as if the fireplace wasn't made at all, as if one day it just appeared, whole and seamless. As if Reymundo made it a hundred years ago to keep his new baby warm.

When the plaster dries, they paint it white. Faith is good at painting, too. It doesn't take long, with all three of them working. It smells good, clean and fresh. Ray paints Faith's butt. "Oh Ray!" And they are laughing.

The fireplace takes two weeks, and the weather holds, as if God is waiting on them. When it's finally finished, Ray brings a little potbellied stove home in the back of the truck, and he installs this upstairs. That night, he chops up the Christmas tree.

Ray lights a tiny fire in the fireplace. He says they need to keep it burning for a week, to make the adobe strong. It's chilly outside. "Perfect fireplace weather," he says.

The three of them sit in the Middle Room on the floor in front of the fireplace. They feed the Christmas tree into the fire until it's gone. Ray goes to the woodpile and returns with fat snowflakes in his hair. "It's snowing for real now," he says. "A sign. God approves of our fireplace."

"Maybe so," Faith says softly. "Do you really think so?" She smiles up at him. The three of them sit on the floor. They are alone together. Ray gets his guitar and sings "Good-bye, Old Paint." Then he plays without it being a song, just a nice sound that is a part of the room, like the snap of the burning wood. It's snowing outside, but it's so warm in the Middle Room. Ray puts down his guitar and Faith curls inside his arm. They watch the reflections the fire makes on the walls, moving and light and moving and dark, and for a long time they sit and don't say anything at all. This is the best night ever.

Ray says, "Faith. Reymundo's having a baby. Any day now."

"Ray," Faith says, *please* and *thank you* in her voice, so she sounds as if she's praying. "Really?"

"It will make our lives perfect," he says.

She sighs. He kisses her. He whispers something. Juniper watches the fire. Her parents make sucking and popping noises, but she listens to the fire instead. It's hissing. The snow made the wood wet, and you can't build a good fire with wet wood. Behind her, Ray and Faith scramble to their feet and stumble up the stairs, giggling. Juniper gets her new books and reads Cinderella, Snow White, Sleeping Beauty. The fairy tales are different in this book. In this Cinderella, the stepsisters chop off their toes and heels to fit in the shoe, and instead of a fairy godmother, birds help Cinderella. She never thought Cinderella could be told more than one way. In the end, the birds pluck out the stepsisters' eyes.

Juniper puts down her book and watches the fire. The handprints, one big and one little, change colors in the firelight. She remembers the deer's heart in her hand, all its little rooms. She watches the fire turn to coals before she thinks to feed it. Later, Faith will tell her that this was the night they made Sunny Boy Blue.

$\mathcal{E}$ V E R A F T E R

New Year's Eve, Last Year, Santa Fe

H E R E are three tall people, tromping through the snow-covered Santa Fe foothills. A young man, brown-haired and slim. An old man, tall but sagging, his frizzy gray hair sprouting from the hem of a woolen cap, a swell of a belly on his skinny frame. A young woman, her wiry blond hair hanging down her back. Though it's morning, the light is weak, like twilight. Snow clouds hang low and white, and already a few tentative flakes have wafted to the snowy ground.

This is the bride and this is the groom and this is the father of the bride. Today is the last day of the year, the last day of betrothal. Today is the end of one life. Tomorrow is a new year, a birthday, a wedding, the beginning of the rest of my life, thinks this bride, this Jennie, this former me. Tomorrow is the beginning of happily ever after. Does she really believe such nonsense? Maybe she does.

Each of the three carries a saw. They spread apart, not talking, at times glancing nervously around before they grasp a tree branch and saw quickly, the snow on the upper branches shaking down on them. They do not fell trees. They take only branches, like offerings. They are not supposed to be here. They have no permit, so they're stealing the decorations for the wedding. They'll wire them into garlands and hang them like bunting.

The air is so cold and still that the sounds they make—their feet in the snow, the rustling of pine needles, the scrape of the saw and crack of a branch—seem dangerously loud. They work as quickly as they can, the woman pointing out acceptable branches. Anyone watching might take them for misguided lumberjacks.

As they fill their arms, the smell of pine grows stronger around them, and the black pitch stains their gloves. They peer around armfuls of branches; some boughs are laden with powdery blue berries. Some smell of cedar. The snow begins to fall in earnest now, plump flakes that quickly coat their hair and then melt, so that the old man's hair turns to ringlets. "Let's get out of here," the woman says, and they start back.

Here, parked beside the road, standing out against the fresh snow, is a chalk-blue pickup truck, battered and ancient. In the bed of the truck is a heap of sand, bought yesterday for the luminarias. "Stealing branches, buying dirt," the old man says. Everything he says sounds like a riddle without a useful answer.

The bride sets up the camera on the hood of the truck, and the three of them stand with branches in their arms waiting for the flash to go off. The old man tilts his face to the sky. He opens his mouth and sticks out his tongue to catch the snowflakes. The young man and woman join him, smiling, the pine growing heavier in their arms, and the snowflakes gather and melt, gather and melt. The timer finishes, and the shutter clicks open and closed. This is my family, the bride tells herself, feeling the chill on her sweaty neck. She hurries to climb in the truck. Look at them carefully. They are as near to happiness as they will be for a long, long time.

CANDLES flicker in every window of her mother's house. The walls are hung with bright Mexican bowls painted with roosters and turquoise stripes, framed pictures of the Virgin Mary, Buddha, and on the counter, a statue of a half-elephant, half-human Hindu god. The flickering candlelight makes the bride think of Mary and Joseph and their donkey.

The father and his son sit face-to-face. The father plays guitar while his son peels apples. The groom, also peeling apples, holds up a ribbon of green skin. The mother is frosting the wedding cake. They pass a joint between them. The groom declines with a smile, a polite shake of his head, and the bride is relieved. The mother puts down her knife and takes a picture of the three men.

Later, after they eat, after the father has gone off to his cheap hotel, the bride and the groom stack blankets on the mother's living room floor. This will be their last unmarried bed. Their feet are at the fireplace hearth; their heads are under the boughs of the Christmas tree. It's a small, cold room. The brother comes in and takes their picture. "Your last night in sin!" he says.

The betrothed lie, waiting for sleep, listening to the steady stream of talk between the mother and her son in the kitchen. Loud with him, soft with her. Back and forth. He wants to live in Russia forever, he says. But it's so cold, she says. That's what gloves are for, he says. And borscht, he says.

"God," the bride whispers, "I wish they'd shut up."

And from the kitchen come the smells of ginger, nutmeg, cinnamon. The brother's voice, spinning his stories of Russia. "Say something Russian," their mother demands, and the brother chants. It's a Russian proverb, he says, and translates: "If you want to go to war, think once; if you want to go to sea, think twice; if you want to get married, think three times."

The groom pulls the blanket off their faces. "Why are you so angry?" The colored lights blink in a stately rhythm.

She looks up through the branches to the ornaments glistening in the light. "James," she says, "you don't know me."

He sits upright, leaning back on one hand. "Yes I do," he says. "I'm marrying you." He's pale and gangly, a boy with hair falling into his eyes.

"Maybe that's a mistake," she says.

"Come on," he says. "You don't mean that."

"Don't you tell me what I do or don't mean, Sparky."

"All right," he says. "I'll wait for you to explain."

She doesn't. For a time she lies with open eyes, watching the color of the sofa legs change from gold to red to blue and back again, until she sleeps.

T H E bride starts awake to a loud noise. The fire has died, and she's cold. The noise came from her mother's greenhouse. She goes to investigate. Before her eyes have time to adjust, the door swings open again, and her mother is there, in a heavy flannel nightgown, saying, "I heard something."

Through the glass above them, the moon shines, full and bright. They understand that they both woke to the sound of accumulated snow sliding off the slanted glass roof and crashing to the ground.

The greenhouse is heady with the smell of flowers, the purr of the heater. All around them are beds of flowers, with special light fixtures hanging over them. In the dark, the blue moonlight glinting off them, these extinguished lamps look like hovering guardians.

The bride takes a deep, long breath. "Isn't it wonderful?" the mother says. The moon tinges the shadows blue. The mother, small in her white flannel nightgown, looks like a young girl. Only her hands betray her as old, the tips of her fingers, deeply cracked from polishing silver jewelry, her fingernails stubby and black, her palms thickly callused. Somewhere in the room, water drips. The mother says, "I wish I'd had a Meeting for you, to bless your marriage." She doesn't expect an answer, and the bride doesn't give one.

The mother uses these flowers—orchids and nasturtiums, miniature roses and columbines and many others—in her version of the lost wax method. She chooses a perfect flower and dips it in wax. Through years of experiment, she has perfected her methods, so the flower doesn't wilt, the wax quickly cools. Then she lays the flower in a bed of plaster, and when this mold has hardened, she pours silver or sometimes gold in through a tiny hole in its top, and when the plaster falls open, inside is the beginning of a lapel pin, a barrette, earrings, the center of a bracelet. In one custom order, a tiny golden forget-me-not became the setting for a ring.

"I pray for you all the time," the mother says.

The daughter walks from flower bed to flower bed. There are chambers, some hotter, some colder, with heavy plastic drapes between them. The mother follows, tenderly touching a plant here, a flower there. She calls to her daughter. "Wait here," she says. She leaves the greenhouse and returns with a gift. Inside the wrapping paper is a perfectly formed silver juniper twig. The daughter lets her mother pin it to her nightshirt.

"Juniper," the mother says.

"Listen to me," the daughter says softly. "That is not my name." Anyone watching, say a stranger peering through the glass greenhouse walls, might wonder why the daughter speaks so fiercely, whispering but with such anger in her face that she might as well be shouting. The stranger might pound on the window. Hey, he might call. What does it matter? What's in a name? The daughter leans closer. She says, "If you ever want me to come into your house again, don't call me that name one more time."

The mother takes a step back and raises her hands in front of her face, as if she fears her daughter will strike her. "All I ever wanted," the mother says, "was to make a beautiful thing."

The daughter looks at her mother for a long time, considering the things she might say. Perhaps it's the moon, or the middle of the night, or maybe it's because she's half dreaming, but some sort of magic eases away her anger and she sees only her mother's fear, and grief, and longing, and for a brief moment she's pierced with love. So she says nothing.

THIS bride, this Jennie, this me, she leaves her mother in the greenhouse and returns to the bed beneath the Christmas tree. She removes the juniper pin and lays it beside the other presents. Shivering, she pulls the blanket over her shoulder and curls into her groom. She can't hear him breathe, and she puts her palm on his back, on his chilly skin. In the moment it takes for his ribs to expand, she thinks, He's dead. I knew it. Too good to be true.

But he's alive. He is alive, turning to her, embracing her. They kiss. The lights shine through her eyelids, and his tongue is clean and wet and cool against her own, his hands familiar and safe, and everywhere they touch, chest to chest and thigh to thigh, they're warm, and everywhere their flesh doesn't meet the air chills them. She pulls the blankets over their heads and takes him into her body. They rock gently, the way the lights don't blink so much as wash from one color to another, and the air is pine-scented and so very cold, everything silent and deeply still, the only sound their breath. She hides her face in the hollow between his jaw and shoulder and his arms tighten around her and in this cold stillness a wave of such gratitude sweeps through her that she feels she might weep.

She lifts her head.

There. Past the boughs of the tree, there, standing in the doorway, her brother is watching.

She doesn't know that this is the last time she'll make love to her groom wholeheartedly, that in the following months she'll curl away from him and hope he'll just leave her alone, not ask for anything at all. Each time his voice comes softly across the universe of sheet between them, asking, *What,* asking, *Tell me,* she'll curl tighter and tighter into a hard little ball, and she will hate him.

At this moment, she knows only that despite her brother, she will not stop her lovemaking. She drops her head back into the heat and breathlessness of the blankets, because she's past stopping and because she wants to be there alone with her groom under the pine branches, moving together, their bodies warm where they join, each face cradled against the neck of the other, pulses against cheeks, and this is all she wants and all she is and all that there can be, so she makes herself believe her brother is not watching. When they finish, they let their heads out from under the blanket. Her brother is gone. The Christmas lights shine down on them, taking their course of flashing color again and again through the night. Outside on the street, cars pass occasionally, their headlights sliding across the wall, lighting the living room in brief washes, like searchlights asking, Over here? Is it here?

THE DAY THE WORLD
CRACKED OPEN

August 1976, Arroyo al Fin

THIS is a story rife with liars and counterfeiters, with shreds of information passing for the truth. Consider this: I remember a flurry of disasters just before Sunny's birth. The piano, the crack, the piojos. And fights. Many of those. Only, Sunny was born August 18, and I find myself confused. I had to be in school. How could so much happen so early in the school year? The more I consider what I've always known, the less certain I become.

But I am my father's daughter, both of us quick to anger, both of us thieves. Together, my father and I stole everything Faith inherited from Paul. So it's easy for me to imagine how it was for Ray, this man unable to look at his wife's enormous belly for longer than a moment. Faith reminds him of Humpty-Dumpty. It makes him afraid to see something so much like an egg, the unbroken surface apparently safe, yet fragile, and inside, worse yet, the yolk. He thinks perhaps Faith sees this fear in him. For months now, she has alternately tugged on his arm or turned away, eyes cast on some distant thing. And Juniper. Her wariness offends him, as does the sucking need in the way she says that name: *Daddy*. And the piano, worth, in his mind, oceans of money, sitting like a taunt in the driveway.

I remember we were irrigating. I remember I had already cut my hair, and I had the album, the rules, the music. I remember my father, carrying his shovel on his shoulder, and his hair, bright as an orange marigold and just as frizzy, bobbing along with his footsteps.

JENNIE and Ray are following the ditch up the hill. Ray limps a little, the way he always does when he gets mad. Jennie scrambles behind him, worried what he might do to the Water Thief. Somebody has stolen their water. Today is their turn, but in the middle of irrigating the corn, the flow slowed to a trickle and then just stopped. Ray is furious. He holds his shovel like he's trying to choke it. If he finds the Water Thief, he says, he'll pound that cocksucker into hamburger meat.

Faith didn't even notice the water. She was too busy playing piano. Even this high on the hill, the tinkling music follows them. The music feels different to Jennie, now that she has the Treasured Memories and the rules; when Faith plays, it sounds like it's saying, "Thief. You thief. La la."

Just the same, Jennie's glad she stole them. Children need pictures, and rules. Jennie decides to make her own list of rules, for her brother who's coming. She might not even be sorry she cut off all her hair for him.

"Make a fist," Ray tells Jennie. She does, but he laughs. "That's no fist," he says. "You'll break your thumb like that." He shows her how to make a fist and how to throw a punch. "Now you're a tough girl," he says.

On they go. After a while, she realizes she has kept the fist, and she shakes out her hand. Ray, ahead, keeps his fist tight, like they might find the Water Thief behind the next tree.

She usually likes to walk the ditch with Ray. She feels like a girl in a fairy tale, wandering the woods. Her father is the poor woodsman, and she is his daughter, who will one day go out into the world under some enchanted spell.

Her job is to clear the ditch of junk that dams up water while Ray shovels dirt to make the sides stronger. Her hands get muddy and scratched by tumbleweeds and goatheads, but she has collected beautiful things: a faded plastic daisy; a piece of cup painted with a foot dancing among roses; a penny so old it's green. She keeps them lined up like soldiers on her windowsill. When she looks at them, she imagines they're fairy-tale leftovers. The cup belonged to Cinderella, for instance. Or no, the cup belonged to Lipa. It was the one cup she could drink from in Russia. The plastic daisy was the only flower she was allowed to have.

Ray isn't talking anymore. It would be better if he kept on talking about the Water Thief's puny mind and his paltry concept of decency and fair play and his *puta madre*. But he just climbs, fiercely, silently, his long legs eating up the hillside, his fist big and tight. Jennie falls behind. She walks in the middle of the ditch, looking for a treasure, which is exactly what she finds in the wet sand and pebbles: a tiny skull, maybe a prairie dog's. She holds it gently, wondering if it was a baby when it died. Her mother will be having a baby any day now. This makes her worried about things like baby prairie dog skulls, and what killed them.

When the baby is old enough, she'll take him for walks up here. She'll teach him how to speak Spanish. She'll give him the penny she found. She sees him so clearly, pinching the penny between his stubby fingers. My brother, she thinks. Faith says the baby will be a boy, and Jennie believes her because there are signs, like how high Faith's belly is, for instance. Jennie and her brother will be the children in a fairy tale, Hansel and Gretel in the woods, only Jennie's baby brother won't need to be afraid, because she will never do something stupid like leaving a trail of food for the animals to eat. In her head, she adds Hansel and Gretel to the list. But is that a rule?

Jennie doesn't see the water until it reaches her feet and rolls past. She runs after Ray, the skull cradled in her palm, knocking lightly against her curled fingers. "Now it's okay," she says, panting, when she catches him. "It must have been some weeds, right, Daddy?"

Ray grunts. He stabs his shovel into the ground and leans against it and stares down into Arroyo al Fin. Finally, he says, "Did I tell you about the time Reymundo decided to get a family photograph taken? They didn't call them pictures back then. They called them *fotografías*."

Jennie rolls the skull in her shirt, waiting. She tries to remember the Spanish word for bones. With her shirt rolled up, her belly button shows. Her father tied her belly button when she was born.

Reymundo was having a hard time with the sheep, Ray says. It was too hot for the furry little suckers. At the end of a long hot day in June, Reymundo came into the kitchen where his wife flipped tortillas on the stove. He embraced her from behind, cupping her breasts—

"I think this is the wrong story," Jennie says. She strokes the fragile bones of the prairie dog's cheek. "I don't think you're supposed to tell me this." Sometimes Ray forgets he's talking to his daughter, and she has to remind him. "Tell the part about how he planted trees. Tell that part." Lipa and Paul would never tell the wrong stories. When her brother comes, Jennie won't either. She adds that to her list. But it, too, doesn't seem like a rule.

Ray stares at the mountains in the distance. He stares a long time. "Dad?" she says. "Tell that part?" He shakes his head and walks off, the shovel on his shoulder. He doesn't like it when she meddles in his story. Meddle. That's a word he taught her. She wonders if he knows how to say it in Spanish. She starts after him.

THEY follow their ditch all the way to the *acequia madre*, which means mother ditch. Jennie likes that name. It makes her think of the Old Woman in the Shoe, and her children, the little ditches, running around her skirts and trailing from her fingertips. The mother ditch is as wide as a driveway and very deep. Kids have to stay away from its edge. This is what she'll teach her baby brother. She will be a big mother ditch, but also she will keep him away from the mother ditch. Thinking about this, she confuses herself. So she doesn't put anything on the list.

"Juniper," Ray says, "stay away from the water. We can't be having Juniper stew." He winks at her.

This is the mysterious part, what makes him get over the mad. She doesn't understand it yet.

The problem is, now she wants to touch the water. To put her hand in the fast current, to feel it stream over her fingers. If she gets too close, she won't be able to stop herself. So she stands back, behind Ray.

Ray needs to shovel some mud so their fair share of water will go down their little ditch. While he works, he tells her more about Reymundo. "After the baby came," he says, "Reymundo was happy for three years. Because he said the baby was the *hijo de mi corazón. Digame.*"

Jennie almost asks why he's leaving out three whole years. She stops herself just in time. "*Hijo de mi corazón,*" she says.

Ray finishes closing their ditch gate. "Say Reymundo."

"Reymundo." She holds the skull up. She can see sunlight through it.

"Rrrrrrrrrrrrrrrrr," he says. "Reymundo. Try it again."

"Rrrrrrrrrrrrrrrrr," she says, and then—who can say how—her fingers fumble and the skull rolls into the water. It bobs, moves away. She scrabbles after it, reaching toward the current.

"GodDAMMIT," her father roars, "get away from the fucking water!"

She jumps, eyes blind with tears. "I didn't do anything," she whispers. "Don't yell at me."

"Don't do anything bad and I won't."

She doesn't cry, though she feels like he just peeled away her skin. "Yes you will," she says, because she doesn't really understand, not yet. She runs away, crosses a field and climbs a fence and crosses another field. She sits under a tree and leans back on her hands and looks straight up at the sky until she's lost in all that big beautiful blue. Her baby brother will be named Paul. He'll ask about the sky, and she'll explain it to him.

JENNIE decides she won't speak to Ray. This will be his punishment. When she gets back, Ray sits in the kitchen, drinking coffee and studying his muddy boots. Faith sits beside him, her arms propped on her belly, staring out the window at the piano. Nine months pregnant. She looks like she could explode. Ray tells her, "You look like an egg. Better not fart or you'll pop."

"That's not funny," Faith says. Jennie hides behind her own face and walks by them without saying a word. They start fighting. The piano could get them money, and they need money, Ray says. No, Faith says. No, no, no.

Lying on her bed, listening to them fight, Jennie stares at the ceiling. She hates her father for disappearing inside himself. She hates Reymundo. She hates this house that Reymundo built, the musty adobe smell, the feeling of being underground, buried. Lipa and Paul's house doesn't have bugs. Bugs love adobe. Crawly silverfish plant millions of eggs, and they hatch, and on rainy days, they scrabble down the walls. Children of the earth slither in under the doors. The ceiling is the worst, because latillas crisscross the vigas, making nooks and crannies where spiders live. Silverfish and children of the earth are ugly, but they can't kill you like spiders can. Spiders can rot holes in your skin or make you scream in agony. Thinking of them makes Jennie's heart beat faster. She could die in this house her father loves so much. And what about the baby?

She practices her fist. She practices punching air. It feels good, like she could really hurt something if there were something to hurt.

She stares at the wall. On the other side of this wall is the fireplace she helped her father build. In the winter, she rolls against the wall and the fire heats the plaster so it's like hugging a person, like the house is alive. Staring at the wall, she sees it: up in the corner, a crack in the plaster, and she follows it up with her eyes. What if she were as small as a bee? This crack would be like a path, growing into an arroyo, and then a canyon, and then the world would be splitting in half—"Dad!" she calls. "Daddy!" Because high in the corner, up by the vigas, the house is cracked open in a zigzag. She can see the bricks and spaces between them; she can see the vigas in the Middle Room, and any minute, the roof and all its spiders could come tumbling down around her head, burying her alive, eating up her bones. "Daddy," she cries, "Daddy, Daddy, Daddy!"

And as my father's daughter, I know he imagined rain, the house collapsing in a gush of water, and Juniper's skull bobbing among the melting adobe bricks, the bones of her head as fragile and transparent as oiled paper. He imagined waking in the middle of the night with the house cracked open like an egg. The stars. His family exposed, the naked, quivering yolk.

JENNIE, careful, quiet, watches her father study the crack. This is a time to say the right thing. In the Middle Room, they find where the water leaked around the fireplace chimney and began melting the adobes. Ray stares at it, his hands on his hips. "Hooray," he says. "Isn't this just swell. Just cocksucking peachy." He squats and looks down the length of the room. "The floor is tilted," he says. "Why didn't you tell me about this?"

"No sé," Jennie says, huddled against the wall, out of his reach. "Daddy," she says. "Can you fix it?"

Faith says, "Can't we just fill in the hole?"

"No," Ray says. "Don't be stupid."

"I was just saying—"

"You were just saying something stupid. The walls are sinking back into the ground. They're melting. One night the house will be a pile of dirt."

Faith says, "I know what you're thinking, but you can't."

"Yes I can," Ray says.

"It's not for you to decide."

Ray opens his mouth, then closes it. He goes to the Middle Room, and they follow him like worried ducklings. The crack is on this side, too, up by the fireplace. He paces, returns to the crack, and then slowly, almost carefully, punches the wall, saying, "Fuck." Saying, "Fuck fuck fuck," softly, fiercely, as he punches, until his hand is bleeding and Jennie knows it because blood appears at the base of the crack. "Daddy," she whispers, but he goes on softly chanting, "Fuckfuckfuck." "Daddy?" she cries, and Faith says, "Ray, you're scaring us, Ray?"

He turns, fist raised, and Faith throws up her hands and Jennie pushes herself between them, grabs his arm, cries, "You're bleeding, Daddy!" and she hangs on tight, babbling—"It's not so bad," beginning to cry, "it's okay, see?"—and suddenly he roars at her, "How many *fucking* times do I have to tell you to keep your *cocksucking* hands away from things?"

For a second they are all frozen. She looks up from where she has fallen and she says, "I knew you would do it again." This is not the thing to say; this was exactly the wrong thing, because his voice is deadly quiet: "I've had enough of this," and he's dragging her up the hill and she is crying, "No Daddy no, please, Daddy," as he drags her to the chicken coop, because this is what he does when she says exactly the wrong thing.

But all grown up, I understand too well how this dam in him trembles and bursts, how anger rushes over despair like water over mud—he grabs his daughter's wrist, his head filled with the roar of a burst dam, a flash flood, and he drags her out of the house. She stumbles and cries, *Daddy Daddy Daddy*—that unfair name when he is only one man, and even when he tries to do something right and good and true, the world outsmarts him—he drags her to the chicken coop, where the hens scatter, and there, with the white shit the straw the eggs, he yanks down Juniper's pants and pulls off his belt and he cannot hear the sound of her voice crying out as if she calls across an arroyo gushing with floodwaters: *Daddy. Please please no please Daddy.* He cannot hear as he brings down the belt on her bare flesh, again and again and again.

· · ·

HE leaves her in the chicken coop and she falls on her hands and knees and sobs and the snot from her nose and her tears fall onto the straw which is covered with chicken shit. Shit, she thinks. Shit. Shit. It helps, to think that word. Shit. The chickens won't come into the coop. They're walking around outside, complaining. But Mister, the rooster, comes in and comes close. She stares at him, his golden eyes, and that's when she notices she has stopped crying. She wipes her face and stands. Her breath comes in shudders.

She goes down by the well and climbs the apricot tree. The branches aren't wide or strong, and she has to hold on tight. The black rough bark hurts her hands and her feet. The apricots are ripe, golden with smudges of red. They are warm and sweet. Soon they'll start rotting and the bees will come. Her eyelids hurt from crying. She wishes the bees would sting her father to death, starting with his eyes. They would sting him, but not to death. She would be a Bee Princess, disguised as Cinderella-Juniper, and the bees would be her thousand fairy godmothers, and they would hum her true name, *Jennifer, Jennifer*, and they'd grab hold of her shirt and fly her to a bee castle in the air to marry the Bee Prince.

Then her dad would really be sorry. Please come home, he'd cry. I miss you so. She picks another apricot and slowly presses it with her tongue until it bursts, and the warm sweet juice floods her mouth. Faith is playing piano; the music floats around the side of the house and reaches Jennie like a secret. She spits out the pit. She takes a long, hiccuping breath. The problem is, she can't go away until her baby brother comes. Then the bees will take him, too. He will eat honey instead of milk. Anyway, she will never let anyone hurt him. She doesn't need to add that to the list—it's the first thing she put there.

Ray finds her in the tree. He calls, "Here, kitty kitty kitty."

"Daddy." She won't look at him. "You shouldn't have done that."

"I know," he says. "I'm your daddy, your father, your dad, and I'm a boob. I'm a very bad dad. Don't be mad at your old bad dad or he'll be a very very sad lad, that cad."

The fairy godmother bees take her in their tiny hands and lift her into the sky. The piano music is the magic sound of their two thousand busy wings.

He clears his throat and says, "Do you want to hear about Reymundo?"

She thinks, I'm listening to the piano and not to you, Daddy.

"I love our house," he says. He sounds so sad. If her father cried, what would she do? He holds out his arms. She can't move. She closes her eyes. She feels herself flying away. She makes a fist. You have to stay, she reminds herself. Your brother is coming.

Ray tells her about his own dad, her grandfather, a lumberjack named Timothy though everyone called him Swifty. He was a treetopper, which meant he shimmied up the trunks to cut off the tips of the tallest pines. Before he came down, he'd drop his hat, then race it to the ground. Timothy Davis, Swifty, a daredevil logger man. At twenty-two he goes to his foreman's house in the Oregon woods.

Mad as she is, Jennie will remember this story, pour it out in bars, offer it in a shot glass, neat: *My grandfather was a lumberjack.* The foreman's daughter, Edna, meets Swifty on the porch with a hand on her hip. She is not a beauty. She's as tall as Swifty, with orange hair frizzing around her face and great splotchy freckles, with a manly nose and tiny, pale green eyes, but something about the challenge in her carriage, in her lush figure and square shoulders, makes Swifty ask her to the movies. She smiles a wide, sly grin with a crescent at each lifting corner, and says yes. But her Holy Roller daddy says they have to be engaged first.

Swifty, besotted, brings Edna a tiny garnet on a gold band. For her part, Edna just wants to see a movie and has no special interest in marriage. She aspires to Seattle, where she'll wear smart hats and work in an office, alphabetizing files. She'll paint her nails red and read a thousand books, and she might write a poem or two.

Logging is dangerous: snapped cables, wayward hooks, tumbling logs, the everyday visitations of death. To ease this hard life, lumberjacks have booze, and women, and fighting about women. Edna finds these things intensely boring, and one day she returns Swifty's little garnet. She says, "This is for the woman stupid enough to marry you. I'm going to Seattle."

At that moment, Swifty feels a terrible rage which makes him single-minded and irrevocable; he throws Edna into his truck, as if she were nothing but a saw or a broom. He aims the truck north and presses hard on the pedal. "You want to go to Seattle so bad," he says, "I'll take you there." The following morning, they arrive, and he forces Edna onto a ferry. Out on Puget Sound, he stands with her at the prow and grips her neck and says, "If you won't marry me, I'll drown you." Seasick, trembling, Edna promises, though she tells herself that she can always leave, even as she recites the marriage vows. Soon enough, she discovers leaving isn't so easy, and so they stay together until the end of their lives.

J E N N I E , up in a tree—like my grandpa, she thinks—can't help herself. "But why?" she asks. "Why would they stay together?"

Ray looks away, past the garden and past the mountains, all the way to the edge of the world, like he sees Swifty and Edna there. "Because," he says, "love and hate are exactly the same. And leaving feels worse than staying. All you can do is try to get the other person to make you leave."

"That doesn't make any sense," she says. "I think they loved each other. That's why they stayed."

He laughs, making her feel silly and a little ashamed. "Edna and Swifty were never about sense, or love," Ray says. "But you go on thinking that way, if it makes you feel better."

Now she's mad again. "I don't want to hear about this," she says, looking away.

Ray sighs a long, sad sigh. "The ditch is flooding," he says. "I have to go fix it." He walks away, the shovel peeking over his shoulder like the face of a person he's carrying, like a small boy. She listens to her mother's piano, which is the foreign language of an enchanted prince, wandering the world in search of the Bee Princess. The prince is her brother.

Ray's gone a long time. He returns with wet boots and a muddy shovel. He looks up at her, and she looks down at him. He says, "I'm going to town to find some books about fixing cracks." He puts down the shovel, and a few seconds later she hears him trying to start the Dodge. She hears him swearing, opening the hood, fiddling around. Then the Dodge roars to life, and he drives away.

RAY. My father, my daddy, my dad. Raymond Seamus Davis, whose mother made his name rhyme so it would be a poem. Clarence was right—he always said that Ray wanted to be better than he was. Ray was always scheming to learn Spanish, studying up on stories about poets, painters, good men. Ray, a self-taught man with a bad teacher. Why is it so much easier to forgive him than anyone else?

Here's what I'm asking: where did Ray go, after he tried to coax me down from the apricot tree, on that afternoon when our life fell down a crack in a wall? And here's what I know for sure: he went to the Harwood Library—he came home with the books on adobes, after all. And given what came at the end of the day, I can surmise that after his research, Ray, not wanting to go home to his Humpty-Dumpty wife and his pissed-off kid, walks to La Cocina for a beer.

Inside, he sits down next to a woman with long blond ringlets and a gauze skirt. Ray thinks, Huh. He puts his books on the bar, so she can know he's not any bozo, and he orders. He doesn't say hello, because any fool knows eagerness gets a man the old cold shoulder. After a while, smiling slightly, the woman introduces herself, pointing to his stack of books. Her name is Mary Lively, and one of the books has her name on its spine. Maybe it's just that way in Taos, where adobe is common and drinking at La Cocina is, too, so you're likely to discover the author of an adobe repair book sitting beside you.

But Ray thinks, This woman was sent by God to save my ass. Because he has some of Faith's belief in signs.

Mary buys old adobes in Santa Fe, remodels them, and sells them for huge profits. He's shamed by her riches, her golden bracelets, the bells sewn into the hem of her skirt. He thinks, She shall have music wherever she goes. He tells her about his house, confesses about the fireplace. Mary has laugh lines around her eyes, which make her look permanently amused. When he asks if repairs will be expensive, she smiles, and he flushes and asks how much she thinks a Steinway might be worth. Mary pulls back her hair and knots it in a effortless gesture. "Not enough, probably," she says. Ray orders more beer, more salt, more lime.

I know one more fact: Clarence stole Sunny's name from my father. I know this not because Ray told me, but because years later I found evidence on my father's bookshelf, a history of the blues with underlined passages about Sonny Boy Williamson. So here's what I think. After my father discovered Mary, he went to Clarence for a certain kind of permission, or advice, or policing.

Clarence didn't drink alcohol. He always said that everybody expects an Indian to be a boozer, so why should he? He didn't like mountains or nature, either. He never went to the river. He said everybody expects an Indian to be a nature lover, so why should he? He said, "I don't know nothing about no woods." And then he laughed, because even his bad grammar was a poke at expectations.

He kept sodas for himself, and beer on hand for Ray, and they always sat outside in the sunshine, drinking. So I see Ray and Clarence, slouched on weather-beaten chairs, not talking, just drinking in the sun. Ray slugs down his beer fast. He crumples his empty and starts a pile next to his chair. "What's your hurry, Lone Ranger?" Clarence says. They always joked about that. Clarence said Tonto was the real hero, putting up with the Lone Ranger's shit, his shenanigans always getting them into trouble.

Clarence gets another soda, another beer. They drink and watch the motionless, sun-stained valley. This is one of many things Ray likes about Clarence. They could sit here all night, and it would be fine.

Eventually, Ray tells Clarence about the house, and about Mary. "Fuck," Ray says. "It's her hair, I think. Long, curly, blond. Or something." He shakes his head. "She's just something."

Clarence drinks his soda. He says, mildly, like he doesn't have any point to make or bone to pick, "What name you giving that baby? Or are you two going to wait around like you did on the last one?" This is his way of reminding

Ray about family. It's also another of Clarence's graces. He can give a guy a little lesson without getting too preachy. Like he's supposed to, Ray thinks about the baby, his family in general. They let the silence take over. Their conversations always have this lazy rhythm, sentences oiled or watered before delivery.

Ray is a little afraid of Clarence, who is better and more beautiful than himself. Clarence, who understands the value of stillness. This is the kind of shit Ray would never say out loud to anyone, especially not to Clarence. Out loud, he says, This is my brother, Meeting Way.

Ray starts telling Clarence about Sonny Boy Williamson, a Chicago bluesman who was beaten to death outside a club, and then later, another guy starts calling himself Sonny Boy Williamson and says he's the real one, that the first man was a fraud. The first Sonny Boy's songs were like funny poems, and he was a bighearted, generous guy, and everybody loved him, and the second Sonny Boy Williamson was sarcastic and wild and original, more sly and mean than Sonny Boy number one, and number two said that number one, the one everybody loved, the poet, was a fake. A thief. So which one do you like better? The answer is, you like them both. "I'm thinking they're two sides of the same man," Ray says. "Maybe number one didn't get his head smashed. Maybe he just wanted a chance to be mean; maybe he was sick of everybody loving him. Maybe the two guys were duking it out in him, and the second one finally won." He says he wants to name the boy after Sonny Boy Williamson. Like Faith and everyone else, he believes the signs: it's a guaranteed boy. And Clarence, listening, cannot possibly know that the name is Sonny, not Sunny, and of course Sunny's name also becomes a mistake. Did Ray add the Blue? Did Clarence? Sunny Boy Blue, come blow your horn. Was the name my father's attempt to honor everything a boy could be inside?

"Sunny Boy," Clarence says.

"Only Blue," Ray says. "Sonny Boy Blue, to get a little blues, a little sky, in there. Sounds like a song to me."

Clarence drinks. "What does She say?" This is how they talk about Faith, when they do. She is She. And Ray tells him that Faith won't have it, that she won't listen to anything he says about the baby because she has decided it's hers, that he gets Juniper and she gets this one, and he hasn't even mentioned it to her (or has he? Either way, she never gave him credit). And Ray, talking about this, looks so sad and lost and hopeless that Clarence, like anyone who loves Ray, like Juniper or even Faith, rises to rescue this man from his own despair. "I'll tell her," Clarence offers. "I can get her to like it." So the bargain is struck, and Ray, who despairs of ever being a good man, believes Clarence can give what Ray cannot offer. Clarence should be the man to raise Sonny Boy, Ray thinks, a new and better father, Meeting Way.

And a new husband for Faith. Ray knows he fails her again and again. It's as if she perched on the arm of his chair, that first afternoon they met, and she never left. *Yes*, she always says, following him into anything clinging, weeping, worrying, yes, yes, yes, but terrified all the same. In his failure to calm her, he knows himself for a weakling, which is so unbearable he flees. Yet he can't abandon her. In that, he would feel weakest of all. But if he left her with Clarence, it would be something besides abandonment, wouldn't it?

Am I making excuses for my father? Am I trying to salvage grace from his leaving? Even if the answer is yes, I still believe I'm right. It was my father's most generous act, his attempt to leave us with Clarence when Sunny was born. As usual, it was a misguided, flawed attempt, a swipe at getting it right that turned out as badly as cracking fireplaces—Clarence eventually left her alone, after all—but it was a try nonetheless.

Clarence asks about the crack, and Ray clears his throat, suddenly nervous. He tells Clarence he wants to sell the piano. Ray braces himself, marshals his arguments, but Clarence doesn't speak. Ray finishes his beer, crumples the can. "I don't know what else to do," Ray says softly, to himself, or God, or Clarence.

"You have to do something," Clarence says, and he sounds equally ashamed, equally plaintive. To Ray, it sounds like Clarence is mourning his brother's dilemma. Ray can't quite believe it's real, this Meeting Way brotherhood, that Clarence could be his brother. He can't even look at Clarence, he loves the man so much. So he glances wildly around the yard, latching on to Clarence's Yamaha, black and built to go fifty miles on a gallon of gas. Ray admires it, and Clarence knows he does. Meeting Way, what you admire is given to you. So Clarence tells him to take it. Take it for the afternoon, for the evening, for as long as he likes. "I'll take it into town, to meet that Mary woman," Ray says.

Which is as good an explanation as I can devise for why Clarence showed up in my father's Dodge and named my brother, while my father arrived afterward on a motorcycle, a strange woman following him in her VW convertible.

Ray, my father, my daddy, my dad. You think you understand Clarence. Soon, Clarence will help you load the piano into the back of the Dodge. The two of you will tie it down, take it to Santa Fe, but even then, you'll return to Faith and your children. It will take five more years for you to leave, for Clarence, your brother, Meeting Way, to lie down beside your wife, and your children will be his children, and your house will be his house, Meeting Way.

And because he admires them, you'll let him take all these things from you. But the two of you won't speak again after that.

If I am searching for a culprit, then I choose Clarence, who was a thief himself. Or is it too easy to blame him? What of my father? What of Faith? I am led, inevitably, to the question, What of myself? I was also a thief. But I was only a child. That is my alibi.

FAITH and Jennie have to take over the irrigation, which makes Faith mad. "I'm nine months pregnant," she tells Jennie. "Pregnant women aren't supposed to do this kind of thing." Faith says she should expect this from him by now. She says when she was pregnant with Jennie, he left her for seven days alone on the mesa with a bag of rice and a roof with bullet holes in it. Her nose is sunburned. She's wearing her pink bikini, and her belly sticks out like a mountain in between little fields of pink. She says only two outfits fit her: the bikini and a faded, flowered sundress. Actually, Jennie knows she has other outfits, but Faith likes to make everybody feel sorry for her.

In the garden, Faith bends over the muddy rows, and Jennie stares at the sunburned valley between Faith's swollen breasts, her mountain stomach. Her legs marbled with blue veins. Her jiggling thighs. Her muddy feet, her soles, thick as leather, mud ground into her cracked heels. Jennie's embarrassed. How can this dirty person play the piano?

Faith hacks at the mud. "I shouldn't have to do this," she says. "My feet are like balloons."

Then the Dodge pulls into the driveway, which confuses Jennie, because she's still mad, only she's so happy to see it. But Ray isn't driving. It's Clarence. What happened to her daddy? What if she didn't say anything nice and now he's dead? What about her baby brother?

Faith doesn't think about that. She sees Clarence, and she's happy as can be. She says, "I knew he'd come. He always knows when I need him." She runs to him with arms wide, and he folds himself around her, his long arms, his chin on her head. Jennie picks up the shovel, which Faith dropped in the mud. You can ruin a tool, leaving it in the mud like that. Faith never thinks about the important things. Jennie takes the shovel to Faith so she can realize her mistake.

Jennie stands there with the shovel, like a soldier, glaring at Clarence. "Why do you have my daddy's truck?"

"He's got my motorcycle," Clarence says. "We traded for the day."

This is a terrifying fact. Jennie tries not to think of Ray smashing into a telephone pole, rolling down a cliff, turning over and over, cartwheeling to the bottom, exploding. Or else driving and driving, all the way to the edge of the country, to the ocean, to Seattle. Which would be worse, having him dead or having him gone, somewhere in the world where she can't find him?

Clarence puts his palm on Faith's belly. He says, "That's a sunny boy you have in there. I dreamt it—"

"He moved!" Faith says.

"He knows his own name," Clarence says. "Sunny Boy Blue."

"Sunny Boy Blue," Faith whispers.

"That's the dumbest name I ever heard," Jennie says. "You should name him Paul."

"You be quiet," Faith says. "You don't know what you're talking about. Clarence had a dream."

Jennie wants to hit her mother with the shovel. How can she be so dumb? "Where have you been, Sunny Boy, Sunny Boy? Where have you been, charming Sunny?"

Clarence grins, his big white teeth flashing between his coppery cheeks. "Sunny day, everything's A-OK," he says. "Don't worry. He'll be charming. He'll be A-OK." He winks at Jennie. "She just wants to take care of her baby brother," he explains to Faith.

Suddenly, Jennie loves Clarence, who understands, who's on her side, who's her uncle, Meeting Way. He's nicer than her father. He'd be a better daddy. Then she feels so guilty she might cry. "I'm mad at my daddy," she tells Clarence, blurting it out, surprising herself.

Clarence presses his lips together and nods thoughtfully. He looks like he's about to say something important when Faith says, "Come sit down. I'll play piano for you. Juniper, go check the ditch."

Jennie thinks, Fine. I'll do what you're too lazy to do. She takes the muddy shovel to the garden and hacks at the ditch, redirecting water. A child shouldn't have to run around like this. A child is only a child. I'm just a kid, she thinks, glaring at Clarence and Faith talking in the yard. When her baby brother comes, Jennie promises herself, she'll make sure he doesn't ever have to do any grown-up work. She'll make sure he plays all day. And she won't let them give him such a stupid name. The problem with fairy tales is that mothers are always giving stupid names to their kids, like Snow White or Cinderella or Juniper. Nobody protected Jennie, but now she's around to speak up for her brother. She's getting a little worried about her list. It's so long. She'll need to write it down soon.

Faith plays the piano for Clarence. He sits beside her, listening, with his hands on his knees, not tense, not relaxed. More like ready. Strong, tall like a king of the world, watching Faith's hands. Meeting Way, he's Ray's brother. He shouldn't be sitting there next to Faith. He works construction. He could

smash a baby's head like a beer can. He should go build a house or something. Jennie forgets how she liked him a minute ago. He's trying to take Ray's
place and that isn't right even if Faith loves him, and probably he gave Ray
the motorcycle so he would drive off a cliff or something. Jennie, hacking at
the mud, gets so mad she doesn't think about what's the right or wrong thing
to say. She marches over to them and stands with one hand on the shovel and
one hand on her hip and she says, "Are you in love?"

Faith stops. She says, "You watch your mouth."

But Clarence isn't mad. "Why do you ask that question?" He's just paying
attention, thinking.

"Where's my dad?"

Clarence keeps his hands on his knees, resting there, and he looks at her,
his face calm and ready. "I'll tell you something about your daddy," he says.
"He always wants to be a better man. He has a fistfight inside him, and he's always hoping the good guy wins."

"Like an enchanted prince," Jennie says. "Like the woodsman."

Clarence says, "You have to understand that about him. You have to believe in the good guy, try to help him along."

Jennie says, "If you see him, you should tell him to come home."

Clarence throws back his head, his thick black hair shining, and holds his
belly and laughs and laughs; he fills the air with his laughter, like Old King
Cole, the merry old soul. She isn't mad and she doesn't hate him. She smiles
a little herself. And that is her best memory of Clarence.

CLARENCE is gone, and Faith and Jennie are up on the hill when the motorcycle pulls in the driveway. Relieved, Jennie can't breathe for a moment.
"It's Daddy," she says.

Faith leans on her hoe and sighs. "Finally," she says. Only behind the
Dodge, a red car pulls in, a convertible VW Bug with a beautiful woman in it,
whose tight blond ringlets make Jennie think of Rapunzel.

"Sonofabitch," Faith whispers. "That sonofabitch." She begins running
down the hill, weaving in and out of fruit trees, and Jennie runs behind her,
calling, "Mom? Mom?" Because Faith is nine months pregnant and her feet
are like balloons and there's a baby inside her and what if she falls? Ray and
the beautiful woman, talking, laughing, stand by the piano. The beautiful
woman opens its lid. Faith, huffing, gasps, "Don't. You. Touch. My. Piano."

They all stand in the driveway. Ray has his eyes on Faith, who has her eyes
on the woman. "This is Mary Lively," he says, and tells the story of how they
met. "Destiny," he says, watching Faith. "A sign. She'll help us."

Faith, gasping, tells Mary, "He can't pay you with my inheritance."

"Fine with me," Mary says. "I don't know what the deal is yet."

Jennie pictures her father hopping into Mary's VW, all shiny and red with its top down. He'll leap in like a bank robber jumping on a horse, and then Mary will jump in behind him. Off they'll go, waving their hats in the air.

"I mean it," Faith says. "What's mine is mine. It's my *mother's* piano."

Mary sits on the hood of her Bug and braces her bare feet on the bumper. She has little strings of bells around her ankles, and they tinkle softly. She wears a loose blouse that slips from her shoulder, a shawl around her hips, a skirt with gold threads woven through it. She's rich. Maybe she's a fairy godmother. Mary says, "Three dimes and a nickel says you're Juniper Tree Burning." She speaks with a heavy, slow drawl. She must be from Texas.

Jennie draws in the dirt with her big toe. Mary smells like flowers. Roses. Lilacs. Smells are important. Faith stinks of sweat. Jennie sees her mother through Mary's eyes, Faith's huge belly between two little scraps of pink bikini. Her skin has terrible red marks on it, like it's ripping, and her belly button sticks out like some kind of disease.

"It's a real pretty name," Mary says.

"We can't afford to fix the house," Faith says, still breathing hard. "We don't have money like that." Why can't she breathe like a normal person? What is it doing to the baby?

Ray says, "Maybe the house will oblige us and fix itself. Then we can have piano concerts. Invite the local intelligentsia. Serve tea."

"I'm not selling it."

Mary hops off the car, and the bells jingle. "Why don't we all go take ourselves a look before y'all start fussing about selling this and that." She leads them inside to the Middle Room. She gets on her knees and looks up into the chimney. She leads them outside again, around to the back of the house, a little parade. Follow-the-leader, Jennie thinks, is a stupid game. Mary squats and looks at the foundation. Ray gets her the ladder, and she climbs to the roof. She calls down, like God. "Y'all got yourselves a big problem here."

"It's not that bad," Faith says. "It's a good house."

Mary smiles at Faith. "How much did y'all pay for this place?"

Faith hugs her belly. "Does how much it cost make it a good house?"

"More like a good deal or a bad one," Mary says, starting down the ladder. Ray tells her how much they paid and she says, her feet on the ground, "I bet y'all thought that was a big ol' bargain, too." She links arms with him and starts for the driveway. "You have a problem worth more than all those fifty-dollar payments put together."

"Oh God," Faith says. "Oh God." The way she says it makes Jennie feel like she's choking on candy.

"I'm sorry, but it's just true," Mary says.

Jennie says, "Will it take long to fix it? Because the baby's coming soon. Any day now."

"When's it due? Are y'all using a midwife?" Jennie wishes Mary would stop saying y'all.

"Maybe we can get credit," Faith says. She shifts from foot to foot, and Jennie remembers her swollen feet. "I have to sit down," she says.

"Poor little thing," Mary says. "Y'all can sit in my car."

She opens the door and Faith sits on the white seat. "Look at you in there," Mary says. "You look just great, like you're fixin' to head to the beach in your itty-bitty pink bikini."

Looking great in a red Bug must make Faith happier. She says, "I'm using a midwife. My first baby was a bad birth, hard, and Ray caught Juniper, but she was a month late, a Capricorn." Her hand rests on the swell of her belly. "This one will be good," she says. "I know that's how God wants it. He'll be a Leo."

Mary says, "Leos are good people."

"I know," Faith says. "He'll be musical. He'll be a leader." She reaches out to feel Mary's skirt. "This is so beautiful," she says softly. Mary laughs again. Why does she laugh so much? Jennie wonders if it's because she's happy, or if she just thinks they're stupid.

"You go on and have it," Mary says, and in front of them all, she takes it off and hands it to Faith. Her blouse hangs over her butt, and she ties the shawl around her hips again. "What are y'all looking at?" she says, laughing. "It's not like I'm buck naked. Faith here has less on than me."

As soon as Mary leaves, Ray zips off on Clarence's motorcycle. Faith looks like she might cry. She takes the skirt upstairs, and Jennie wishes she were brave enough to sneak up there and try it on herself. Faith, with her big pregnant belly, can't wear it anyway.

At night, Jennie lies in bed, waiting for Ray to come home. She tries to figure out what to add to her list about today. But she doesn't know what to call it. *I won't*, it starts, but she can't finish the sentence. Later, much later in the night, Jennie still hasn't heard the Dodge pull into the driveway. How will she know if it's her father or Clarence? Then she remembers Ray's boots. She will know her father by the sound of his boots on the kitchen floor. When she hears his boots, she'll finally sleep.

INTERIOR DECORATION

Spring and Summer, This Year, Albuquerque

I believe anything can be made beautiful with time and effort and good old-fashioned ingenuity, that bank account of the poor. You don't need bags of money. You just need a sense of what you want and enough smarts to figure out how to approximate it, given what you have, even if all you have is a library card and sixty-three bucks. I made our newlywed house into my home. I made it beautiful with a belt sander and some seedlings. I painted the walls fabulous colors: a pale, silvery gray for the bedroom, mustard yellow in the living room, green in the bathroom, with bright pink towels and framed prints of flowers (cut from an old calendar, each month a reproduction of a Victorian seed packet). I caulked the bathtub. I ripped up the living room carpet, sanded the wood floor, and varnished it—nothing I had done before, but I learned with a book. My studies, how they suffered; my half-decent grades came from a great memory and late nights, which, as an added bonus, kept me out of the marriage bed.

Chris watched me the way he watched the cat stalk imaginary prey: amused, but respectful of the inexplicable obsessions of another species. I got so sick of Chris accepting who I was. I wanted him to yell at me for who I wasn't.

Like a dutiful wife, I displayed the Cinderella shoes he'd given me on a bookshelf in our bedroom: one Canadian Mountie boot, one Betty Boop heel, and so on. I hated them. Whimsical had become silly. In the closet, I had a basketful of their mates which he had saved. Our relationship was split in two like that: the first half lovely, romantic, whirlwind, the hope and possibility of one shoe. The second half, the steady, dull reality of two shoes, a pair, a closed circle. One shoe is a mystery hanging on a telephone wire alongside a highway. Two is simply the attire of day-to-day living.

I remember the months by the rooms I painted: the bedroom in January. The bathroom in March. In April, I moved our couch to the hall, so we had to climb over it to get to the bathroom, the bedroom, or the kitchen. The bookcase, lamp, and coffee table huddled in the center of the room, swathed in sheets. I was on a ladder to get at the ceiling, and from that view he was quite handsome, with his straight brown hair falling into his eyes, his high cheekbones, his wide mouth. He wanted me to come to bed; I was determined to finish.

"Cindy," he said, "it's just a rental. We'll be gone soon."

"Yes, but we're here now," I told him.

By then it had been two months since we'd had sex. To my horror, I found he revolted me. What had been a lanky body became bony, frail, white, flawed, and monstrously unappealing. What had been containment became timidity. Whywhywhy? I can't explain the vagaries of attraction. I know only that in bed, if he tried to touch me, I'd pull away, even though I wanted to love him. I wanted to curl into him and make sweaty, terrific love in the middle of the night. I wanted what we had for an afternoon in August, which I'll call certainty.

I argued with myself, up on the ladder in the living room. Look here, Jennie Girl, that's your husband in there. The deal is, you promised to say yes. But as soon as I thought yes, the no rose inside me, fierce, adamant. I washed my brushes and resolved to give him what he wanted. I got into bed naked. But when his hand climbed over my shoulder, tentative, needy, and I felt his bony hips touch mine, I pulled away, revolted, angry at him for being weak, for tolerating what I dished out.

I wish I could say that once I finished painting, all became swell in the newlywed household. Alas, the school year ended, and I had a summer job, and a garden to tend. I'd get home from work around seven, change my clothes, and spend the remaining daylight digging, dumping in peat moss and manure, making a garden. In the backyard I planted corn and sweet peas and lettuce, and in the front yard I scattered cosmo seeds which grew into a tangled mass of lacy leaves and delicate, bright pink blossoms with their optimistic yellow centers, their eight petals, so much like a little girl's drawing under the vocabulary word "flower." And after I gardened, I ran, long runs that lasted well past ten or eleven. When Chris asked why I ran, I found myself speaking in slogans that sounded like passages from exercise books. I said, "It relaxes me, relieves stress." I said, "Endorphins." I said, "Health is best preserved, rarely regained." He drove me to clichés, and I hate clichés.

On the rare occasions when I felt peaceful, I wouldn't run. Once or twice I even drifted into a nap. Once I woke to him kneeling beside me, watching. He said, "It's so good to see you relax."

"What," I said, "now you're calling me uptight?" I was so angry I had to go for a run. He couldn't win. But why did he have to watch me as if I were keeping secrets? Chris and that horrible cat, the bobtailed Bob, who followed me from room to room, staring with his yellow eyes.

I came home one evening to find a package from the Little Prick. I knew what it was without opening it. Treasured Memories, the photo album, neatly wrapped and addressed to Juniper Tree Burning. Inside, a postcard, too, with onion-topped Russian buildings on one side and a message on the other, maddeningly written in Russian. "Why is he writing me?" I said. "We don't speak. I told him, we don't speak."

"You need to let go of this, Jennie," said my brilliant husband. "You should be touched, that he sent that album." Here's Jennie, fists at the ready, fixing to sock her husband, to kick his cat across the room. This is why people with guns shoot family members.

"How can you say that? How can you say that, when it was your wedding he ruined? Don't you care?"

"You're being ridiculous," he said.

"Ridiculous," I said. "Do you ever get mad? Do you ever fight back? You're so calm you don't even exist; you're nothing but a face, with all your speeches about faces—" and I knew I was picking a fight, hoping he'd either show me a little gumption for God's sake, scare me, make me afraid, or else go away, disappear into the library like before.

"Stop it," he said gently, sweetly even. "Don't."

I left the room because I was afraid of what I might say or do, even if he didn't have the good sense to be afraid of me himself.

I stood in our backyard, watering the sweet peas. That fucking prick, sending me Treasured Memories when he'd ruined my own wedding album. Either he didn't know what he'd done or he'd sent the album to rub it in. Either way, I hated the prick. I hated him for making me a petulant child over something as trivial as snapshots. I hated him for ruining everything with one turn of a key.

If only I'd refused to go out to the truck with Sunny. If I'd jumped out when he first started the engine. If. But I hadn't done anything. And neither had Chris. Why weren't there sixteen police cars, lights flashing, waiting for me? Why wasn't my mother huddled under a blanket, shivering, her tear-wet face glistening in the red and blue cop lights? A SWAT team, a helicopter. Or simply Chris's fist in my brother's face. Something, anything strong. "There you are," he had said. If only he'd been angry. And there I was, if only-ing myself crazy. Inside the house, my husband lay in wait. What's wrong, he always wanted to know. Tell me. We'll fix it. You, I wanted to say, you, sitting over there on the couch with your neat stacks of notes and your wrinkled brow and your cat curled in your lap: you. I began weeding in dirt softened and muddy.

The screen door slammed, a warning: here comes the husband. I yanked weeds, crabgrass and goatheads, ragweed, and I saw I'd pulled up a sweet pea. Now Chris knelt behind me and lifted my hair and kissed my neck. I shrugged him off and parted the soil so I could put back the plant. Chris knelt in front of me. He took my face in his hands and kissed me, and I let him. I could hear the gurgling hose, the neighbor girls playing, traffic, sirens, airplanes overhead as he kissed me. Chris pulled back. "Where are you?" he asked. "Where is my Cinderella?"

"I'm right here," I said.

He kissed me again, leaning forward, toppling me and cradling me as he nestled us into the sweet peas. I tried to lie still in his arms. He raised my shirt and cupped my breast. The softened, muddy soil beneath me, the tender scent of crushed sweet peas. He pressed his knee between my legs, and suddenly I had to say no, and I shoved him away and then I was standing, muddy, in the ruins of my flower bed. "Look what you did," I cried. "Goddammit, look what you did."

He stood. "I won't be treated like this. I'm your husband."

"'I'm your husband,'" I said in a fey voice. "Don't think I've forgotten it." The soil had saturated; water rose around my feet. The sky, livid with sunset, blazed behind Chris, who paced the length of the backyard and returned. "You are such a mess," he said. "You can be so unbelievably cruel, and you don't even know why."

I went straight for my running clothes, my muddy footprints marking the floor. I nearly made my escape, but Chris waylaid me at the front door. He said, "Jennie, listen to me. The wedding is over." He opened his arm to take in the golden living room walls. "*This* is what we have, and it's good."

"Please," I said. "Just don't talk to me. Just let me out of here."

"We have to talk about this," he said.

"Don't you understand? It's ruined. He ruined it. We have nothing, because he left us with nothing." I pushed past him. He called after me, "You don't have to run, Jennie." But I was already on the road, into the city, running a long, random course through the dark and often dangerous streets off Central.

The truth is, I did have to run. The choice wasn't mine. Chris couldn't possibly understand—my calm, quiet husband whose natural state is *still*—what it's like to feel a sort of rolling inside, like a car on a hill whose emergency brake has failed, and at first the rolling is slow, but it gathers speed; it propels me from my chair and from room to room, until I have to leave; I have to get out and then I'm running, running, running, trying my best to get lost, because I've always wondered what it would be like to look around and realize I've no idea where I am, or where I came from, and now I'll just have to wander for a while.

Still muddy, still caught up in anger, I ran, and I remembered my mother's face, when we returned from the bridge. How she scurried to him, crying, "I was so worried!" as if I had perpetrated the crime. Her baby, her Sunny Boy

Blue, her darling child. The day she found us with my grandfather's photo album, the joke was once again on me, because Faith didn't burn it; she only tucked it away and saved it for Sunny. She bided her time, and when I left home young, escaping or driven out at fifteen, Faith finally had her life perfectly rearranged, the ultimate interior decoration: fresh husband, one less child, no more ugly Ray and Juniper cluttering up the place, and then Faith let Sunny in on the secret. In fact, she made a Christmas present of the Treasured Memories, their special story, shared together in front of the fireplace without pesky Jennie to steal anything from them.

And there she is, Jennie, fifteen and sleeping in her Fairy Godmother Essie's house, dreaming about Prince Charming holding her in his arms and kissing the top of her head, only his fingers are a spider, something—she sits up, gasping, slapping it away, but it's only Sunny, breathless, barely able to speak. "Juniper—everything's—burning." Is he joking about her name? And he came through her window again; it's wide open, which really makes her mad, and then, with the light on, she sees he's clutching the album to his chest, and she hates him at the exact second when he says, "Junie. You have to come home—the house is on fire—Junie."

So again in the middle of the night it's left to her to rescue everybody, and God, I wish they had just burned up in the fire, a thought like a slap which she takes back, do you hear me God? I take it back. She kisses Sunny, hugs him, and Sunny, who never cries, is crying, saying, "I wanted to burn up the album and I used the blowtorch to start the fire and I didn't burn the album, I burned the house down—"

Jennie calls the firemen, then steals Essie's keys from the silver tray on the mahogany table by the door. Across the valley, their burning house lights the sky pink, like sunrise in the middle of the night.

Driving Essie's Cadillac, Jennie repeats the fact of the burning house carefully to herself, but she doesn't believe it, even when they get to the fire. She says to herself, I am sitting in this car, in the middle of the road, watching the house burn, but it feels like watching a play, like pretend. Sunny, sobbing, holds on to his mother's waist like he's trying to keep her from flying away. Faith, arms hanging, won't hug Sunny back. There's Clarence, leaning against the white car, his arms folded over his chest.

Jennie explains to herself, like telling a child about the play, We are waiting for the firemen to save our house, but we live too far away, and the house has already burned too much. And the child in her answers, Why? She can't seem to move. She tells herself, The adobes won't burn, because they're made of dirt, but wood always burns—Why? and the vigas are tree trunks, so inside, the ceiling is on fire, and that's why the flames lick out the windows like that, like tongues. The fire growls and moans and roars, a loud, living thing. It isn't alive, she tells herself.

For the third time in Sunny's life, Jennie searches the dark valley for the lights that say rescue is coming. Clarence walks over to her. "There's a lot of bracelets in there," he says. "A lot of silver." Why is he talking to her? She gets out of the car to escape him, to go to her real family. "Mom?" Only the fire is too loud, and Jennie shouts: "MOM?" Faith turns, but her eyes are empty and she doesn't answer. *You are my mother, Mommy, Mom*—she wants to cry against her mother's breasts and hear her mother say, *Sh sh sh hush, child, hush*, patting her head, *hush. Everything will be fine.* "Mom?"

The house answers for Faith. Its tin roof groans and shrieks as it twists in the tremendous heat and then it collapses, sparks and flames shooting into the sky, catching the lowest branches of the cottonwood. Now the tree is burning, too. Sunny, running toward the house, slings the photo album at the fire, but he's too weak to throw it far enough; the album drops to the ground, its black pages open, fluttering in the fire's wind. "It's my fault!" Sunny screams. "My fault!"

"It's not your fault," Jennie yells back.

"Me," he shouts, "it was me!"

Jennie gives herself instructions: that is your brother over there, and you need to help him, but now you can't, because your mother is coming at you, screaming, "It was you—it was always you—" Get away, Jennie, back up, because your mother wants to hit you, and who ever thought a fire would be so loud? Your brother following, yelling, "I started it, it's mine!" Hurry Jennie; get to the safety of the car.

Faith screams everything Jennie ruined: Faith's life, Faith's family, and now this fire, which Sunny made for Jennie, so he could burn the photo album, so Jennie would love him again. "It was you," Faith cries, "you did it, *you*—you don't think about anyone—and you ruined it, you ruined it all, you and your father and I knew it would turn out like this, and I wish you were dead I wish you had never lived—" Her voice breaks into a sob, the noise she made the night Sunny was born, that howl rising from deep in her belly, only this time her son joins her. "It's my fault, mine," wails Sunny, arms around his mother's waist, shouting for all he's worth.

Jennie. You can't save them. They're too much for you. You're only one person and there's not enough in you left over for them—I can't I can't—she gets in the car and starts the engine. A voice in her head whispers, *Save yourself.* Whispers, *This you can do.* Sunny calls, "JunieJunieJunie!" She turns the car around. Sunny grabs the door handle, but she keeps the car moving and he has to let go. "Don't leave me," he screams, but she cannot hear or she makes herself believe she can't, and she makes herself not look in the rearview mirror because he's running down the middle of the road, and behind him the cottonwood, all its branches flaming into the sky, as if reaching up to send a message to God.

Okay, she tells herself, drive to Essie's. Now put the keys back. You shouldn't steal Essie's car. Don't do that again. But after that she doesn't know what to do. She stands in the yard, under the sky prickly with stars like the night Sunny was born. Across the valley, the sky glows. She sees the fire engines wailing down the highway, their lights flashing.

She turns her back, but she knows the glow in the sky is still there, and the temptation to look is worse than seeing it. She has to get farther away. There. She has a command for herself: go where you can't see the glow in the sky. *Run.*

She obeys. She runs fast, faster, faster. The road rises steeply up the back end of Arroyo al Fin, and she takes this horrible hill as fast as she can, saying out loud to the slap of her feet, "I can't. I can't, I can't," until she isn't talking about her family but whether she can reach the top of the hill, and the effort hurts in every cell of herself, in her knees and her throat and her lungs, but the pain is good, wonderful, and she says out loud to the beat of her footfalls, "I. Am. Not. Ju. ni. per. Tree. Burn. ing. I. Am. Jen. ni. fer. Li. pa. Da. vis," until she can't speak because she needs her breath to get up the hill. I can't, she thinks, can't can't can't, but she runs on because she is strong and stubborn and can go anywhere with her own two legs. It's what she has. It's the one thing she knows she can do, and she is not sobbing, she's only fighting for breath, and now she's at the top; she has conquered the hill, but she doesn't even think *I can*; the pain has wiped her mind clean, and she runs on, only her body, only the pain, and she knows only that her name is Jennie and she's running, and she feels as if she always has been and always will be running, as if there are only those two things in the world: I am Jennie, who runs.

If that was the beginning, then this is the end: now I am Jennifer Braverman, running away from my husband, and I am running so hard I'm hurting myself, and my breath comes in sobs and how I hate the little prick my beautiful Backwards Boy has become—on I run until I can think of nothing but my ragged throat, my aching knees, my blistering feet—I push on despite exhaustion and screaming muscles, because this is why I run, husband of mine, because in the management of pain I can forget everything.

$\mathcal{I}$N CHIMAYO

August 17, 1976, New Mexico

IN the morning it's like Mary and yesterday never happened. Except Ray's home, and the Dodge sits in the driveway with the piano, and the crack is still there. Ray says he's taking them to Mary's. "I'm due," Faith says. "What if I go into labor?" Jennie, worried about the baby, doesn't want to go, but she doesn't want to stay. So she's glad when Ray decides for her.

But the Dodge won't start. "No spark," Ray says. "No big deal. Just a little cleaning is all." He gets out of the truck, lifts the hood. She hopes he's right, because if it doesn't start, he'll yell and punch the fender and get bloody and she'll have to try to disappear.

It starts. Ray and Jennie drive in silence all the way through town and into the canyon. She gets so used to the quiet that when he speaks it makes her jump. He says, "Do you know where we're going?"

"South," she says, and he chuckles. It's a good thing, to make Ray laugh. A hard thing. But she regrets speaking. She still hates him for spanking her yesterday. Maybe she hates him forever. Maybe she'll never talk to him again. That was the last time. South, she says in her mind. That's all. The end.

"Guess what?" Ray says. "Mary wrote a book about fixing adobe houses."

"She talks like a Texan," Jennie says.

"She's from Houston. Nothing wrong with that."

They pass a sign. Watch for falling rocks. A picture of a rock hitting a car. "Did you see that?" Ray asks. "One time I heard about a whole bus full of people that got smashed. You be the rock lookout and let me know if one's coming." She doesn't answer. Old bills, poems, books cover the floor. She sits down there and tidies everything into neat stacks.

"In school, do you speak Spanish?"

"I don't know."

"*No sé. Dígame.*"

Furious with herself for speaking, she raps the edge of a stack of papers against the floor. You're my dad and you should know what I do in school when I'm nine years old.

He says, "Are you punishing me?"

"I don't know."

Jennie watches the canyon slide by, its rocks, high and beautiful, jagged, sometimes pink, sometimes black with green and yellow splotches on them, which are lichen. The canyon rocks look like the castles of gnomes. When the baby comes, she'll tell him stories about the gnomes, who are the real Seven Dwarfs from Snow White. The gnomes throw the rocks down on people they don't like. That's what she'll tell her brother. She makes a message to herself to remember. She still hasn't written down her list. Which makes her think about her hidden Treasured Memories, and she's worried Faith might find it.

Ray starts a Reymundo story. He says that one day, a photographer came to take Reymundo's family picture. And the photographer came behind Reymundo's wife with his white, white hands, and his arms encircled her and he spread his palms over the gentle swell of her belly. Reymundo should have been back from the sheep by now, but he stayed away, because he hated the photographer and his camera. She willed her husband home. She loved her husband.

"That doesn't make any sense," Jennie says.

"People can want opposite things simultaneously," he says. "At the same time."

"I don't like this story anymore," Jennie says. "Stop telling this story. Reymundo is supposed to be King of the World."

"Okay," Ray says. "All right. Can't have the little genius pissed at me."

Now her father is telling her a story about his mom and dad. At first it's a good story, but it gets scarier and scarier, and Ray's face looks so terrible and sad that she's afraid to interrupt because she knows that look and if she says anything at all he'll stop the truck and take off his belt and then she will be sorry, and even though she tries, she can't stop her ears from listening.

EDNA and Swifty spend their lives torturing each other with cheating and screaming and beating and, worst of all, inconsolable weeping. By the time he's a teenager, Edna and Swifty's only child, Ray, has become an expert at hiding. He runs cross-country and track and hides out at practice, which makes Swifty happy, and he hides out in his room reading books, which makes Edna happy. In the summers, he works on a lumber crew, lying about his age, building his workingman muscles, and he uses this money to buy a motorcycle so he can go on long drives up into Canada. In these clever ways, he keeps clear of the daily cruelty.

He wants to leave, but what will he do? Where will he go? What will happen to Edna and Swifty? So he hangs on, reading in his room, teaching himself guitar, biding his time, saving his money. Finally, he graduates. He has won a scholarship with the Northeastern Washington University track team. He has only the summer to survive.

That summer, Edna runs off with a drain salesman; Swifty tracks her down and drags her home by the hair. Ray, hearing them, puts his finger in his book and walks down the hall. They haven't even bothered to close the bedroom door. A line of poetry from his book rings in Ray's head, like a bell tolling: "Margaret, are you grieving? Margaret, are you grieving?"

Swifty holds a gun and a bullet. He says to Edna, "I'm going to shoot myself first, in the gut, so you know I'm dying." He pauses, looks her in the eye, and drops the bullet in the chamber.

Margaret, Ray thinks, are you grieving?

Swifty holds up another, and he says just as quietly, "And then I'm going to shoot you in the cunt so you can think about what your whoring got you." Edna doesn't flinch. She sits calmly on the edge of the neatly made bed with her hands folded in her lap and gazes impassively at him. He loads the bullet, selects another, shows it to her. "And by then," he says, dropping it into the chamber, "you'll be begging for a hole in your heart." They don't seem to notice Ray. For a moment, because he is his mother's son, he considers simply taking his finger out of his book and continuing to read where he left off.

But the other part of him, the big-fisted lumberjack Ray, crosses the room and punches his father so brutally that Swifty stumbles against the bureau, and Ray punches his father again, and again, and again, until Swifty's nose breaks and he falls to the floor.

Ray picks up the gun and empties the bullets into his palm. His knuckles are bloody from the force of his punches. Three bullets, Ray thinks stupidly. One for each of us. At a distance he hears the sound of his father beginning to cry, and from this same dim place, he watches his father crawl to his mother's feet and climb her sturdy calves and lay his cheek against her thigh. "Eddie," he whimpers. "Eddie. Eddie." Edna looks down at him for a moment, and then she begins stroking his hair, whispering, "Never mind. Don't never you mind anymore."

Ray goes outside, the book in one hand, the bullets in the other. He shoves the book in his back pocket. Maybe Swifty's finally gone too far, and his mother will tell him to fuck off, the great big No. As he stands in the rain outside his father's house, the last words of the poem come to him, like an answer to the riddle: "It is Margaret you mourn for."

Ray gets on his motorcycle and drives away, into the rain which is like mist, driving as fast as he can. He won't go back, he promises himself. He goes faster still, and faster again, his knuckles frozen tight over the throttle and clutch, his teeth chattering against the wind. The book digs into his flesh. And then Ray thinks nothing at all, because he has emptied and stalled out his mind, and he's opened the throttle and is flying as fast as he can, still holding the bullets, the three of them between his palm and the brake, which maybe explains the accident. A semi roars up behind him and Ray lays down the bike, and the chain saws into his leg, cheating him of Northeastern Washington University and track and poetry and any possibility of escape.

The doctors set Ray's leg and send him back to his parents. Thirteen days later, he starts awake in the night, nauseated by his own smell, by the pain. I'm rotting, he thinks. His father tells him of course it hurts; it's a goddamn broken leg. By the time Ray takes himself to the emergency room, his flesh lies open to the bone; he'll wear a cast for two and a half years. He doesn't go home. He goes to the Public Market, hobbled on crutches. He doodles tunes on his guitar until a couple of hippies strike up a conversation with him, and they invite him to stay with them. It's the sixties, after all, and such things are common, including the sudden acquisition of a family in an afternoon. He shares the place with twelve other people. They steal electricity from a main line; they drink water from jugs they fill at a gas station. They have a stolen television, enthroned on a milk crate, shared with anyone who asks. The weed they smoke; the booze they drink! It's paradise in hell, and one day an Annette Funicello Mouseketeer shows up in hell, a girl with teased black hair and a purse shaped like a daisy to match her daisy-printed dress: Faith, stammering, round-eyed, with enormous breasts, but a good girl, and Ray tells her, "You can watch TV if you fuck me first." She blinks, and then according to them both, she says yes. And then he tells her he changed his mind.

Jennie can't stand this confusing story. Yes equals no, and love equals hate. She wants happily ever after. She wants something better than those awful words. She wants Lipa and Paul. Ray says, "The point is this. Your mother brings out my father in me."

At my wedding, I asked my father, "Why do you hate her so much?," and Ray replied, "I don't hate her. There isn't a word to describe how I feel about your mother." Call me a monster, but I knew exactly what he meant because I felt the same. I think that the story of Edna and Swifty was the closest my father ever got to explaining himself. What passed for a reason. The longing for poetry and goodness, written in his rhyming name by his mother. The capacity for beatings he held in his massive, beefy fists, the same hands as his father's. The confusion of loving and hating, leaving and arriving, leaving and arriving, like the ocean, the tide, the waves.

. . .

"STOP telling me this," Jennie says. She climbs back on the seat and stares out the window.

"This is your history," Ray says. "Don't you want to know where you came from?"

The glass feels good on the tip of her nose. She watches Española go by slowly, the low-riders creeping along, and then they turn toward the mountains. They pass aspens, which in late September will turn a delicate, glimmering yellow, their leaves flickering the sun. "This is the way to the Santuario de Chimayo," Ray says. He tells her about the shrine, how its dirt floor is said to heal the sick. "People make pilgrimages to get dirt," he says. "Maybe we should make a pilgrimage for some dirt to heal the crack in the house."

"That's stupid," she says. She rolls down the window so the wind makes it harder to hear him.

"Put up that window," Ray says. She slumps back against the seat, and then he puts his hand on top of her head. "You're a smart cookie, you are." His eyes. She sees her father's sad eyes, and there's no way to be mad. She pats down her hair where he messed it. How can she ever stay mad at him when his eyes look like that? And suddenly she knows, with more certainty than she has ever known anything, that he will never be as good as he wants to be. He'll never be the woodsman in the forest who saves the children. That is why he is so sad.

The road curves through trees and hills, and they find the dirt drive that leads to the beautiful house perched high in the foothills, among the piñons and junipers. "*Aquí estamos*," Ray says, killing the engine, pulling the emergency brake. "*Estamos aquí.*"

Mary's house has whitewashed adobe walls hung with paintings of the *Virgen de Guadalupe*. She has wood carvings of saints in little *nichos* on her walls. She wears another skirt with bells in the hem and no shoes. Her toenails are dark red. Mary touches Jennie's hair. "What gorgeous hair. It's just a big shame you had to cut it off. We could be sisters. I could be your mama."

"That doesn't make sense. My hair's straight and yours is curly."

Ray says, "Your mom has black hair. That makes even less sense."

"Maybe she's one of those changelings." Mary lifts Jennie's chin, inspects her face. "Are y'all human or changeling?"

Jennie ducks away. "I am not."

"You don't even know what a changeling is," Ray says.

"Yes I do," Jennie says, confused. She loves Mary's house and she hates them both. She wishes Mary would decide that Jennie really is her daughter,

and Jennie could live here. But that would make her a traitor. She worries
about her mom. Is the baby being born right now?

They sit outside on the patio. The hills drop steeply away from the patio
wall, and Jennie pretends she's in a tower, like Rapunzel, the prince climbing
up and down her braid. Or else she's in Lipa and Paul's house, on the Highest
Hill.

Mary feeds them hot dogs and potato chips. Jennie wishes she could give
up her whole family to live with this woman in her house on the hill; she
wishes her father would stop laughing so loud. Ray tells the story of the tin
roof and the Casita on the Mesa. Jennie wishes she couldn't see Mary's pink
nipple through the armhole of her blouse. Seeing it, Jennie feels ashamed,
and she remembers her baby brother, and she's disgusted that she thought
about leaving him behind.

Across her knees, Mary opens a tablet and begins drawing a solution to the
crack. Far across the valley, a thunderstorm gathers, and Mary smiles with a
white flash, like the lightning across the valley. "God's light show," Mary says.
Jennie eats three hot dogs in white buns and she eats great handfuls of chips.
She hopes for dessert, but Mary doesn't bring any. So Jennie says, "I like ice
cream."

Mary laughs. "Do you, now? Do y'all like strawberry?"

Ray answers. "She likes anything sweet." The way he says it, staring at
Mary, makes Jennie feel sick. Anyway, she likes chocolate. Jennie counts the
time between the lightning and the thunder in thousands. The storm is closer.

Even though Jennie is mad, when Mary brings strawberry, she eats heaping
spoonfuls, the cold sweet slipping down her throat.

Mary says, "You just slow on down, Christopher Robin."

"We'll have to call you Piglet," Ray says.

Jennie is finished. She dips her finger into the puddle at the bottom of her
bowl. She wants seconds. She says, "I wish I wasn't done."

"If y'all want something, ask for it," Mary says. "Don't hint. Hinting is just
plain pathetic."

Jennie's shame roars louder than thunder, brighter than lightning. Mary
and Ray are talking, but Jennie can't hear. She won't cry. She will vanish behind her own face. She stares at her sneakers with their muddy laces, the cold
bowl cupped in her hands. She wishes she hadn't eaten any of that stupid
woman's ice cream, that stupid woman who talks like a Texan; she wishes she
had stayed home with her mother who needs to sit down, who has a baby inside her—Jennie could have helped make bread—and then she has already
thrown the bowl against the wall and it has already shattered, pieces of the
white china skittering across the patio.

Her father stands. His face is huge and terrible. His fists are made. He takes off his belt and the thunder and lightning are closer and he will beat her and she backs away; she says, "No Daddy, no Daddy please no," and his face is hard and mean and she backs into the wall, her hands behind her, and he—

Mary says, "Ray, come on now. It's just a bowl. It doesn't matter. Let's go ride my horse." Her forehead is high and clear and curls fringe her hairline. She is beautiful. Mary says, "His name is Ralph."

Ray laughs. He looks at the belt in his hands. He says, "Good idea. Because if I stand here like this any longer, my pants will fall down."

"Y'all should come with us," Mary tells Jennie. But Jennie can only stare at her shoes. The storm's wind stirs the bells on Mary's hem and they ring with a high, delicate music.

ALONE on the patio, Jennie watches the storm. The clouds have covered the sky and blocked out the light and the wind is blowing hard. Maybe lightning will strike her in the head. Then she will die. Her dad, crying, will kneel beside her and whisper, "I made a mistake."

She pulls her chair into the kitchen and stands on it before the open freezer and gulps down huge spoonfuls of strawberry ice cream straight from the carton until an arrow shoots through her eye. She tosses the carton back, slams the freezer door, returns the chair. From the patio she watches her father on a black horse, circling the driveway. Mary is nowhere. She'll never fix their house. Maybe she's walking back to look for Jennie, to tell her what a brat she is and how she should learn to behave. I broke it, Jennie thinks suddenly. She returns to the patio and looks for every sliver of bowl she can find, on her knees to reach the white pieces behind the potted flowers, shining like eggshells in the shadows. Lightning cracks so close the thunder is right there with it, which means a person could die, like her father, high on a horse, high in the air, just the right height for the lightning to find and kill, and this scares her so much she has to go find him.

Ray sits high on the big black horse. The storm spits lightning, booms thunder. "Ride him," Ray says. "I'll take care of you." Jennie looks up into Ray's sad eyes and reaches for him. The wind blusters and barks and kicks up sand. It will rain soon. He leans over and scoops her up. She almost slips free, dangling inside his one arm, her belly brushing the warm side of the horse. Ray juggles her, trying to get a better grip so he can swing her in front of him on the saddle, but then the lightning cracks, a loud electric explosion, and the horse bolts and Jennie's legs flap and bang the horse's side as Ralph sweats and snorts and gallops over rocks and sand and the rain begins, wet fat drops and he'll never stop they'll die and why doesn't her dad pull her up or let her go and *Where is Mary?* And then they're flying through the air, Jennie still in her father's arms, and he hits back-first on the rocky riverbed, and she lands on his belly, and even then Ray holds her tight. Rain splatters Jennie's face and drops in her mouth as she cries, "I'm sorry, Daddy, I'm sorry!" Mary's running toward them, screaming Jennie's name, but then Jennie hears better, and it's *"Ralphie! Ralphie! Ralphie!"*

In the kitchen, Mary dabs at Jennie's wounds with a hot washcloth. Outside, Ray limps from one end of the patio to the other, getting soaked by rain. His frizzy hair hangs in wet ringlets close to his skull. When he fell, he cut his back, and his wet, bloody shirt makes sadness spread like a sore in Jennie's chest, like the crack in her bedroom wall.

Mary says, "You poor little girl. Poor Juniper." She dabs hydrogen peroxide into the cuts on Jennie's palms, her wrists, and up her arms. "Y'all must have tried to break your fall with your hands," she says, which doesn't make sense to Jennie, since she landed inside her father's arms. But she says nothing.

In the Dodge, Jennie stretches out, lying with her head on her father's leg. The truck bucks and sways. She doesn't look. She feels her father's thighs tense as he shifts and brakes and accelerates. And then Ray whispers, "Are you asleep?"

She asks, "Are you in love with Mary? Are we going to live with her?"

He laughs, but it sounds almost like a cry, a short, high, gasping laugh. "Kiddo, this is no fairy tale. Nobody gets to live happily ever after."

"But you said—"

"No," he says, ferocious, the Swifty Ray, and she closes her eyes and feels his thighs tense and shift, tense and shift, as he takes the steep curves down from Mary's house. "A woman like that doesn't want an old loser like your pissant dad."

She stays very still. Very quiet. She wonders, Does a fairy tale have an opposite? If so, it would have terrible words in it, like the ones in the story of Grandpa Swifty, and hate instead of love, and blood.

Jennie sleeps. She wakes once because the truck has broken down, and doors are slamming, and red lights circle through the cab. Her father carries her to a police car, and they drive, the radio crackling quietly. She sleeps. Her cheek against her father's thigh, the purr of the police car surrounding her with something like silence, she sleeps, and in her dreams, her dad's arrested for killing Reymundo's baby, which is Faith's baby, who is Sunny Boy Blue.

Then she's stumbling to the house and standing in the kitchen. Her mother is asking Ray, "What happened to the truck? Why did the cops bring you? Did you do something wrong?" Mom, Jennie thinks, be quiet, don't bother him, but she can't talk and she's too tired to do anything but watch.

Ray, bent into the refrigerator, says, "Don't we have any meat?"

"Were you with that woman?" Faith pokes the cookstove coals like she wants to kill something.

He laughs. "Jesus, Faith. You think you're in a fucking movie. This isn't *Gone With the Wind*. You need new lines, already."

"Did you have sex with her?"

Ray sits down and takes his stash bag from his pocket. "With who? Vivian Leigh?"

"This isn't a joke!" She slams down the stove lid and takes a shuddering breath. "With that woman. With that *Mary*."

"Oh. *That* Mary." He sifts the pot; he fills the paper and rolls the joint, licks its edge and twists its end. "If you want to know the truth, I fucked *that* Mary in the stables." He lights his joint and speaks while holding the smoke, so his voice sounds tight, like a strangled man. "Next to the horses, a roll in the hay." The smoke, whooshing out of him: "What a ride, if you'll excuse the pun."

Jennie, stupid with sleep, swaying on her feet, thinks, No. Thinks, That is not the truth, no, Mom, it's not true. Don't listen. But how can she call her dad a liar? What would he do if she did? He is her daddy, and her mother's tears fall, and everything is the wrong thing to do. "No," Jennie whispers. "Mom, no."

I am Jennie, tall with lumberjack's shoulders, and I will not stay inside that moment, will not listen as my father goes on, talking of cocks and cunts and coming, while Faith shrinks smaller and smaller into a shocked and controllable silence. I think he hates himself for inflicting this cruelty on Faith, biting her lip, her eyes shiny with tears. She whispers, "I'm having a baby. *Your* baby." Faith, whose voice says: *Thief. Fornicator. You there.* How does he work, this hungry man, my father, my daddy, my dad? Does he love his wife with her long braids and quivering face? He doesn't know. He loses himself, just as I do now, when I use words like a slap.

I know this ugly truth: I could have called him a liar and saved her then. But I was afraid, a sleepy little coward. I let him torture Faith.

"Flexible lady, that *Mary*," Ray says. "She lifted her legs over her head. She came five times."

Jennie whispers, "Daddy, I need to go to bed."

He says, "She couldn't believe the size of my cock. *I* couldn't believe how far she swallowed it." Ray offers Faith the joint. "Want some?"

"God," Faith whispers. "My God, I'm all alone in this world."

Jennie, swaying, her wrist throbbing, thinks, But I'm here. The baby's here. Don't forget us. But Jennie doesn't count, since she went to Mary's. She doesn't count, since she can't call her father a liar. I am so tired, she thinks. She wonders what Lipa would do. But Lipa and Paul would never be here.

Ray stares at the end of his joint. "We can't even afford meat. You'd rather starve to death before you sell your precious piano."

Faith takes a package of hamburger from the refrigerator and cries, "You want meat? Here's your meat!" The meat thuds against his back, where his blood still shows through his shirt, and Jennie doesn't know whether to be worried about him or Faith, sobbing, her face in her hands.

Ray sighs, and when he speaks, he sounds as tired as Jennie. "Go to bed." Jennie does; she goes to bed. She hears her mother climb the stairs. She hears the front door slam as her father leaves. Now, she tells herself. Go make things better for your mother. Tell her the truth, and then she'll never let Ray come back and your baby brother won't see fighting and hear bad words. But Jennie wants to run after him, yelling *Daddy, Daddy, take me with you.*

My daddy. You make Faith cry, and then you leave, limping off down the road, despite the pain in your leg, thinking about anything besides this valley with these stars over your head, this black velvet sky, this cracked-open house with your family—a baby is coming. But you can't think about Sunny Boy Blue; the terror and guilt are too much. So you think about Clarence's motorcycle and your hands on the throttle, the clutch. How great it would be to drive as far as you can, say to Florida, to live in the Keys, watch the sunsets down there, like Hemingway and the rest of them. You don't think about Sunny Boy Blue, soon to be born. You walk the seven miles to Valdez, to Clarence and his motorcycle, and the pain of your leg is part of the good escape.

Jennie wants to go to her mother but then she's asleep, dreaming. Jennie dreams about Reymundo and his son, dancing under the apricot blossoms where the bees don't sting them. She dreams about Reymundo's wife in the kitchen, calling them to supper. The lilacs are blooming; the sheep graze in the fields. Reymundo is King of the World.

In her dream, Jennie realizes that Reymundo is Sunny Boy Blue, all grown up. Her brother is happy; he has everything he needs. He's the King of the World, and nothing bad ever happens to him. She dreams it's true. And in the morning, Faith's water has broken.

BRUISES

Spring and Summer, This Year, Albuquerque and Santa Fe

W E all have our set pieces, our made-for-TV memories. We tell them and tell them until they lose all meaning, like pictures we haul out to show our new friends. This is Dad; this is Mom; this is me. You say, *My father beat me when I was a child, with a belt, by the way,* and after a while it's like your astrological sign, a by-product of living, masquerading as revelation. They aren't lies; they happened. Only you don't really feel anything when you tell them, and you know exactly the result you will get. *My mother came after me with a knife.* Gasp! Horror! You poor, poor thing!

Essie taught me this. Esther Leeman, my fairy godmother, who taught me to smile in a sly, knowing way, to make even my flaws seem like trophies. Yeah, that's right, I'm tall. She taught me how to say this right. She also taught me how to fold towels in thirds, and to wear vintage clothes because you can't get good tailoring these days, which is how you put it if anyone asks, or you say, I save a bundle on clothes—it's all in the presentation, *how* you say it, how you smile, the slow, easy grin simultaneously splitting your face open and hiding everything.

Consider this. I spent the last two years of high school in New Hampshire, at the John Paul Robinson School for Girls, JPR, Essie's own alma mater. Full scholarship, room and board, tuition. I got in by hawking my sordid past, making it seem tragic and lovely, and painting big, idealistic plans for the future:

The most important thing anyone can give anything is a name. God, whose prerogative it was, let Adam name everything in the world. My parents, as was their prerogative, gave me a name: Juniper Tree Burning. This name was based on misinformation and superstition, a result of their backgrounds, their lack of education. They have always claimed I named myself.

A ballsy beginning. I swallowed my pride, used up the currency: how my parents were descended from a widowed piano player and a lumberjack, how they were hippies who believed in signs, in magical healing and burning bushes and the like. I told about getting lice. I told about my brother getting sick and my parents trying to heal him with prayer. I told about my science projects, about wanting to be a doctor. I said, I want to know the real names of things. I want to know history, and art, and science. I said, I am just the sort of student you need. A complicated life, a passion for education. In this way I formulated my clever disguise as Jennie, the normal girl who knows exactly what she wants.

I had perfected my disguise by the time I applied to a small liberal arts college in New Hampshire. Oh, how they loved it. "We are pleased to invite you to join . . ." On my financial aid forms, they wanted to know about my father. I wrote *Whereabouts Unknown*. I figured if they knew about him, they'd think he should pay something, and God knew, he wasn't going to cough it up, as if he could.

Off I went to my education, on a full scholarship for more annual cash than my mother had earned in her lifetime, to a place where the dorms were nicer than my childhood home. All part of the plan, my life unfolding nicely, step-by-step to happily ever after.

My college adviser, a seashell of a woman in her gray wool twinset, fingered her pearls and told me, "You're so *lucky* to have such a rich family history." *Lucky lucky me*. She must have seen something on my face; she hurried on. "I know it must have been difficult, but listen to an old woman. Someday you'll understand how lucky you are."

What shit, I wanted to tell the lady. What do you know, lucky you, with your ordinary life, your happy childhood, Christmas mornings, the dull unfolding of your days. Your bologna sandwiches, Easter candy, flushing toilets.

There were problems. This avant-garde little liberal arts college was full of pot-smoking, coke-tooting versions of my parents, the only difference being the heaps of cash in their budding-nonconformist bank accounts. I was too normal for them, and too poor besides. This is my Essie way of telling why I left. In truth, I left because of Sunny.

Sunny was suffering at the hands of Clarence and Faith. No surprise there. My baby boy, he witnessed things. I can only guess, having seen the start of it, my mother flung across the room. Apparently, it went downhill from there. One day, Sunny stood in the middle of the road outside his school, and when a car approached he stared straight at it and the car nearly squished him flat. A teacher saw. The teacher called social services, who called my father in Florida. "He didn't move an inch," they told Ray. "Like an inch would matter," my father told me. In any case, the important part was this: the car was driven by Clarence, who swerved only at the very last moment. Later, thinking more clearly, I knew the story was not as simple as the teacher told it. Clarence was not insane. He was not a monster. But I gave him this credit much, much later.

So I lured Sunny to New Hampshire, and Ray whisked Sunny Boy Blue off to Florida. Silly me. Believing my own disguise, deluded by the fantasy of a normal father, I mistook myself for a normal sister saving her normal brother. Did I really think he was safer with Ray?

After my father and Sunny left, I got a summons from Seashell Woman. "We need to ask a few questions of you ," she said gently. She had my application file in front of her, and I suddenly knew what I should have known from the start. She said, "I understand your father visited you recently."

Caught. I didn't think of clever excuses; I panicked. "I have to go," I said. "I have a test." Mrs. Seashell made a short murmuring sound: "Hmm," she said. She asked, "When, exactly, did you locate him?," and my panic blossomed into anger, blessedly righteous, unafraid: "Are you calling me a liar? I can't imagine why you'd want a liar at your fabulous fucking school." And then, before she could be indignant, or worse, before she humored me, I left her office.

I didn't go back after my freshman year. I spent a summer and a semester waitressing in Taos. On rare occasions, I visited my mother in Santa Fe, and I started noticing this shop on the Santa Fe Plaza called Las Novias, an ordinary bridal shop with an antique dress in the window. I saw possibilities. I must be frank: I saw dollar signs. By the time I started at UNM with a full scholarship, I had a plan.

Look at her, my younger self, proposal typed up, complete statistics, market projections, inventory costs. Isn't she cute, in her vintage suits she got from Essie Leeman, the Fairy Godmother?

I told the owner, Look, the best thing you've got going is location—smack-dab on the historic Santa Fe Plaza, but you're not using it. Make me the manager, and I'll set up the place to cash in on the tourists' idea of the quaint old-fashioned out west. Take one bridal shop. Decorate it like Miss Kitty's brothel, with red velvet and gold fringe. If you have an embroidered tapestry of a maiden seducing a unicorn, hang it over the dressing room door. Layer Oriental carpets on the floor. Just for the hell of it, use an antique spittoon as a candy dish. Fill the racks with hundred-year-old wedding gowns, the kind Miss Kitty would have worn if she hadn't been a whore no man would marry. Make up stories of brides who wore those rotting dresses, gunslinger fables for girls, and tell these fables to the rich tourists, then gouge the suckers for every penny you can get. Believe it or not, a bride will pay for the privilege of saying her dress was worn by Wild Bill Hickock's niece. You'd think it would be morbid, but instead, it's History.

I worked there through the four years of my BA, saving money for medical school, I told myself, and yes, I saved, but I confess I also fell in love with making heaps of money. Call me avaricious and I'll confess: a beefy bank account is a fine lover indeed. I lived in Albuquerque, where the rent is cheap, and set up a carpool for commuting; I didn't even have to buy a car. After I graduated, I spent another year full-time at Las Novias. Why didn't I go straight on to medical school? Let's call it setting up a shot. Sometimes, watching me play, you can't understand where I'm headed until I win the game.

Sarah, the little red-haired girl, had her stories, too. I should have known by the cheerful way she rattled off her rape the first time we met. I should have known there was more to her, but she was awfully convincing. And here I am, getting ahead of myself again.

WHEN you get down to it, my gift is this: I know potential when I see it and I can remodel anything. Since August, my big renovation had been myself: the Budding Doctor, the Young Lover, the Newlywed, the Woman with a Big Future.

Yet I remained the same. The summer after my first year of medical school would be the last freedom I, or any medical student, would have for a long time. What was I doing with it? In my infinitely heartless wisdom, I went back to managing Las Novias—a pretty embarrassing job for the learned. I should have been researching, studying up, or volunteering, like my dearest husband, helping the sick little bald kids at the children's hospital back in Albuquerque. But the med student trousseau is a pricey set of goods, what with stethoscope and sphygmomanometer and the like, and as I've said, I made a killing at Las Novias. I decided to explain myself with the brazen approach, What are you doing this summer? Raking in the dough. You?

And I drove there in a Rolls-Royce. Never mind that I bought a tank of gas every few days; I loved that drive. I knew every curve and hill of those fifty-nine miles between Albuquerque and Santa Fe. Doing eighty, gliding north on glass. In a Rolls. It was the best part of every day, moving farther and farther away from my brand-new marriage and the husband who went with it.

One day in June, I was on my knees in Las Novias, inspecting a newly arrived dress, a silver and gold beaded flapper's gown that glimmered in the sun, and okay, it was beautiful—the train was shaped like a peacock's tail, each panel an intricately beaded feather—but on my knees beside it, I hated the woman who spent months on end beading, pricking her fingers, holding them away from the precious silk until her blood clotted. I hated the debutante bride who ate bonbons and dreamed of walking down the aisle all ashimmer, her guests whispering, *She's the bee's knees; she's some bird.* I decided to call the bride Clotilde. Clotilde, who married a banker who lost his fortune in the crash and they sold everything except her Paris original wedding finery—he wouldn't let her part with it. A tragic tale, yes, but they were married for sixty years and they died on the same day, Clotilde first, his little peacock. They say he saw the body and lay down for a nap and fifteen minutes later he was dead. I sat back on my heels. Or maybe it would be better for Clotilde to die before the wedding, and the dress arrived after her death, all the way from Paris. Her groom would be named something stupid and upper-crust like Herman.

The bell rang, and in walked Sarah Alberhasky, the little red-haired girl from my wedding. She paused just inside the door, hands on her hips, surveying things as if she were considering buying the place. I suddenly thought of the Princess and the Pea. Ninety-nine mattresses wouldn't be soft enough for this girl. I stood. We eyed each other for a moment too long. "Hello," I said. "What can I do for you?"

The Pea Princess said, "How much is that dress in the window?" Questions, I'd find, came out of her like demands, as if she had a right to everything, including answers. She was chewing gum. She blew an enormous bubble and drew it back into her mouth with an efficient snap. She wore a ridiculous, southwesty outfit: a three-tiered orange velvet skirt, a concha belt with hand-size links, a white tuxedo shirt, and knee-high beaded moccasins. She caught my eye and pirouetted. "This is my sucky uniform," she said. "For work? Don't you think since the gallery's named after me I should get to pick what I wear? Hello?" It was her hair that mesmerized. Long, glossy, straight. Amazing red, shimmering gold in the morning sunlight, shining like a demand: adore me. Russet. Auburn. Titian. They invent words for hair like that. "Did you hear what I just said? How much is that dress in the window? That sounds like that song about the dog, doesn't it?"

I said, "It's not for sale."

"I just got engaged—see my ring?" She waved her hand. At least a carat twirled on her skinny finger.

I said, "Now here's a guy pissing on his territory."

She didn't miss a beat. "Like that makes you sound so tough. Anyway, Jake doesn't want me to wear an old dress even though I tried to explain there's a difference between old and antique." She spit her gum in her palm and examined it like something she'd found in her meal. "How embarrassing. Chewing gum makes me look like Quasimodo, but it keeps me from smoking and I have an oral fixation. Do you have trash?" She walked around the store and found the wastebasket under my desk. "I'm trying to quit smoking for my boyfriend—fiancé, God I love saying that, fiancé, fiancé—even though I know it won't work, and it's making me such a bitch, but Jake, that's my fiancé, says he'll buy my dress if I quit. Anyway, I saw you through the window and thought I'd come in. Are you pretending you don't recognize me?" She continued to wander the store, fingers trailing along the back of the settee, stroking the unicorn and his maiden, the dresses in their garment bags. She led with the tips of her slender, busy fingers, like a blind girl taking a tour of the room. It was classic. The red-haired Pea Princess surveys the realm. Meanwhile, the Ugly Chick watches, her mouth hanging open.

"I recognize you," says the Ugly Chick.

"So what about the dress?"

"Still not for sale."

"Not? Then why's it in the window? To torture me?"

"Not you in particular."

She stared. She pulled a cigarette pack out of her bag and tapped its end against my desk. "That's supposed to be sarcasm, I guess."

I said, "It's the dress that gave the owner the whole idea for the shop. It was Governor Bent's daughter's dress. You can't smoke in here."

"Can't you at least let me try it on? I won't tell."

"Governor Bent? The one who got massacred in the Indian uprising?"

"So she got massacred, too? Cool. Is there blood on the dress?" She took out a lighter. It was a nice lighter, the silver kind that opens and closes with an audible click. She opened it and squinted at the flame, as if lining up her rifle sights. "Don't worry, I won't light it," she said. "I'm just testing myself. What about the governor's daughter?"

"She was in love with an Indian." I gave her the whole story about Matilda, the recalcitrant daughter running barefoot to meet her Indian lover, until she gets caught and forced into betrothal with a young lieutenant in her father's army. The dress comes from New York in tissue paper, shiny and white and smelling of the lavender seeds spilling from its folds, and Matilda bursts into tears and doesn't stop crying until the uprising, when she flees north to find her sweetie, where she's slaughtered along with all the other settlers.

Blood and guts and true love. It's a great story. I should know, since I made it up. I don't even know if Governor Bent had a daughter. I do know the dress is old, and my boss wanted to keep it in the window; she's sentimental about the thing. I had to make up a story to keep the brides from wanting it.

"But we're friends," Sarah said. "You can trust me."

"Really."

"Remember? At your wedding? Your mom sells her stuff at my mom's gallery? I bet I was a pain that night. I was all drunk. Jake says I'm the most obnoxious drunk on the planet. He says brides don't want to hear about rapes on their wedding day. But you were pretty cool. You didn't go all feminist on me. It's in December. *My* wedding, I mean. Like yours. What did your brother take you away for, anyway? So can I try on my dress or what?"

There she was, gazing up at Matilda's dress, a circa-1890 gown of moiré taffeta. The tight sleeves ended in long satin cuffs, twenty tiny satin buttons apiece. Across the breast of the high-necked bodice, satin orange blossoms punctuated a complicated latticework of lace and velvet cord. Princess seams ran from the shoulders, over the nipples, to just below the belly button, where they met in a precise point. The dress had three skirts: a moiré underskirt gathered full in the back. Over the moiré, a heavy satin skirt, edged in orange blossoms, opened in front like a curtain. The top skirt, made of velvet, swooped back into a bustle fastened with a bouquet of still more orange blossoms, and dropping from the bustle were five tiers of satin festooned with orange blossoms, pleated taffeta, and edgings of lace and fringe. A dress smacking of hysteria. In its day it might have been called shockingly overdone, but for our newly affianced Sarah, it could only be called amazing. And no story was going to dissuade this girl.

I offered her Clotilde's dress, spread on the carpet. She said, "I'm getting married, not going to the Academy Awards." Of course. Sarah needed fluffy, happy love-story dresses from pre-1880, when they were especially bowed and swagged and blossomed. I steered her to the settee. I led her through my album, Polaroids of each dress on a mannequin, labeled with the original bride's name.

I showed her Agnes, and Esther, and Camilla. I told her their stories. She fiddled with everything, the buttons in the tufts of the settee, the mints in the spittoon. I thought, This girl will never feel the fool. She has always been the prettiest, the richest, the most wanted, so what's a little klutziness? Now she was twirling her cigarette like a baton through her fingers. Smiling rakishly, she threw her arm around me. "You made those stories up, didn't you?"

"Aren't you the clever girl."

"I've wanted that dress so long. Even before we were engaged, I wanted that dress. Every day on my way to the gallery, I walk by and I think, There's my dress. And when Jake proposed last week, the first thing I thought was how the shoes from when I got raped would have gone perfect with that dress. And then when I saw you today, I remembered how you work here and I thought, This is a sign." She eyed me over the tip of her unlit cigarette and blew imaginary smoke out of the corner of her mouth.

I convinced her to try on a different dress, better made, better preserved. Anise's dress. Anise who lived to eighty-three and wrote secret journals in her spare time, which were published posthumously to great acclaim. Usually, I go into the dressing room with the brides—there are stays and lacing and buttons and yards of antique lace to contend with—but I let Sarah go in alone, at her insistence. A moment later she called for me, laughing, crying, "Help!

Help, I'm trapped!" I found her tangled in the gown's multiple skirts, the netting and the taffeta and the satin and the embroidered train. I could see we had to start from scratch. I whisked it off.

And stopped.

Here is Jennie, horrified. Not, not laughing, because there before her in a crinoline and a merry widow stands a redhead with skin so fragile her veins show like a map, and on that white skin are bruises. Everywhere, bruises, climbing her ribs, crawling her chest, circling her waist. The vague shadow prints of fingers, of hands.

Sarah lifted her chin and glared. She said, "Gorgeous, isn't it?"

"Did the rapist do that?"

She rolled her eyes. "God. Get a clue. No. That was two years ago, you dork. I have a skin condition."

"That's an explanation? It's worse than 'I ran into a door.'"

"Oh, thank you very much, Doctor Jennie. All I'm saying is I bruise really easy. I can't explain it any better than that right now. So will you please put the fucking dress on me?"

I dropped the gown over Sarah's upraised arms and smoothed it over the crinoline and snapped the train so it settled like a bedspread. I fastened the buttons. Sarah watched me in the mirror, a haughty, nonchalant Pea Princess. I said, "Nobody would guess you just got the shit beat out of you." For a moment, that flat, expressionless mask came over her features.

I said, "He hit you, didn't he?"

She met my eyes in the mirror, and hers filled with tears which I watched spill over her lashes and travel down her cheeks. "We had a fight," she whispered.

"So he hit you?"

She didn't answer. She cried. She cried while I unbuttoned her, opening the satin to a row of bruises, and she cried as she dressed in her own clothes. "I love him," she wailed. She told me she had sensitive skin. She said she loved him some more. Abruptly, she stopped. She sighed, wiped her eyes. "Sorry about that," she said. "If I'm not peeing, I'm blubbering, I swear to God. It's my Latin heritage; it makes me passionate. 'You're such a little girl,' Jake always says." She gave herself a last inspection. "Thank God for waterproof mascara," she said. She smiled brightly at me and slung her big bag over her shoulder. "Off to work I go."

"Just like that."

"Oh, so now I'm supposed to give up my life because you think it would be better for me to break down and bawl my eyes out all day on your sofa? No thank you, Mrs. Jennie, or Dr. Jennie, or whatever your name is." She paused and took a deep breath. "See how you got me all worked up?" Grinning, she patted my arm. "You're all worried about nothing. Just remember, I'm fine. And I'm going to work now."

So there is Jennie, standing in the middle of her shop, trying to understand what has happened in front of her eyes. She feels as if she were driving along the highway and caught a glimpse of what looked like a crime in progress. But did you see what you thought you saw? You need to get to work. Maybe it was just somebody having rough sex or horsing around. In your heart you know, but it's so much easier to keep driving, even though all day long, you're thinking, I should have stopped. God help me, I should have done something about it.

DRIVING home that night, I started to think about the house of my childhood. The man who built it had pressed his handprint into one adobe brick in each room, like a signature. I thought of this, and a sharp nostalgia, a kind of grief, shot through me. When I got home, I sat for a long time on the front stoop, looking at my cosmos, watching the girls across the street play. Chris came out and sat beside me. He handed me a drink.

"What do you see?" he asked.

I shrugged. "I don't really feel like talking," I said.

Across the street, the girls shouted and laughed. Once I had caught them stealing cosmos from the front yard. They stood there with bouquets clutched in their little fists like I was the Wicked Witch preparing to eat them. The younger one said, "We didn't," as if saying it could make the flowers vanish from her hand. The elder tried a different strategy: "They're for our mom," she said.

"That's stealing," I told them. I meant to go on, to say they could have some any time. But I had gotten off on the wrong foot with those girls; they thought I was mean, and they ran away before I could tell them it was okay.

Beside me, Chris sighed. I glanced at him. "What?" I said sharply.

"Nothing," he said.

I felt like I might hit him. Frightened, I went inside, to the bedroom to change into my running clothes. But when I opened the closet, I saw a can of leftover paint, and for a reason I cannot fully articulate, I squeezed into the tight, dark space and closed the door. I opened the can. I dipped my hand in the living room's golden yellow and pressed it to the wall. I crouched next to the basket of shoes, the other halves of the Cinderella slippers Chris had used to court me. I began to cry. It was the first time in as long as I could remember that I had cried.

I sat in the closet for a long time with my hand covered in paint, feeling the latex tighten around my skin as it dried, like a glove, and I cried. I cried for Treasured Memories, tucked against the closet wall behind the basket of shoes, and for my grandparents who loved each other. I cried because the common cold killed true love. I cried for my marriage, probably over before it began, and for Sarah and her bruises. I wanted to tell her, *There's always a moment when you think, My God, I love him.* There's always that perfect, still, golden moment when even the dust in the light is beautiful. You look into his eyes and he looks into yours, and like a message from God, you know the future. That second fools you. You lie in the sweaty sheets and you think, Yes. Yes, exactly, yes. That's the moment you assign the thing a label. Love. Ah, but Sarah, Sarah of the long red hair, soon, the next day or month or year, one of you thinks, no. I was mistaken. Which moment is false, the yes or the no? Sarah, believe the bruises. They are evidence. They are undeniable truth, like fire, or tears, or anything else you cannot mitigate with clever wording and a cocky attitude, like the newborn Sunny Boy Blue, my little Backwards Boy, whose head fit into the palm of my hand when I was nine years old, getting a bucket of water for my mother.

And I am her, Jennie, a child on her way to the well. Jennie stops to listen. Sunny Boy Blue is sleeping in the house. She doesn't hear him crying. He never cries. Sometimes in the middle of the night, she jolts awake and hurries to find him lying still as death, and she thinks of all the ways he could die, especially by black widows which can easily kill babies, and he lies so silent she puts her palm on his back, then holds him close to see if he's breathing. Some nights, she takes him to her bed, and then she's afraid she'll crush him if she falls asleep, so she stares against the dark and worries. Faith writes bad checks, and Jennie worries the cops will come, and they'll find Medicine which is illegal, and they'll handcuff their mother and take her away. They need wood for the coming winter; they could freeze to death. Her father has been gone for two months. Who will haul the wood if Ray never comes back? Their house has a crack straight through a wall. Will it collapse? Will they starve?

Jennie reminds herself where she is and runs to get the water, the steel bucket banging her leg. Today the sky is blue as a teacup, and she wants to get swallowed up in all that big beautiful blue. The shovel has been sitting under the apricot tree for too long. If Ray hadn't run away from home twice this summer, the shovel wouldn't have rusted in the rain for all these months.

She ducks under the apricot branches hanging low with their ripe fruit. Bees are eating. Their buzz sounds like a song, for Sunny the baby and Jennie the big sister, for woodpiles and apricots and blue sky, for summer and the start of school that's coming. Jennie stands under the tree and breathes the smell of ripe apricots. She imagines herself a bee princess. She will stand under this apricot tree with arms outstretched and flowers will burst into bloom and drop petals on her, and the bees will notice her and crawl up her arms and across her eyelids, not stinging, into her mouth where they'll drop honey and say, Bless you, bless you little Jennie, bless you. I am a bee princess, she tells herself. I can taste the smell of the apricot flowers.

Her mother calls, "Juniper! Where's the water?" Faith is washing diapers in the driveway. All morning she's been grouchy, and if Jennie's not careful, her mother will make her do it instead.

Jennie stands at the round rock wall and drops a bucket on a rope into the well, careful not to let it down too fast, which would make it bang on the rocks and get holes, or land upright on the water and take forever to sink. After it fills, she pulls it up, her arms starting to ache. The rope burns her hands and the water sloshes, and she heaves the bucket over the side and pours it in the kitchen bucket, careful not to spill on herself.

She leaves the water to heat on the wood cookstove and goes out to the washtubs, where Faith is lifting wet diapers high, so the sparkling sheets of water fall off the muslin. Faith's black hair escapes her braids in wisps. She drops a diaper and lifts again. She says, "Don't ever have babies, Juniper. You'll be up to your elbows in sewage."

Jennie helps, wringing out the clean diapers. There are many more; Faith likes to have lots of clean diapers all the time, so Sunny won't get a rash. Jennie goes to check on the heating water, and inside she stands very still, listening. Sunny is so quiet. They put his crib in the Middle Room, where it's coolest and closest to the kitchen. She has to check on him, lying so still, his little butt scooted into the air, his cheek pressed into the blanket.

Heavy in her arms, he smells of pee and powder, baby smell. She presses her nose to the pink newness of his neck. She isn't allowed to kiss him. "You'll infect him," her mother always says. "He'll get sick, a cold, the flu, and then . . ." Jennie knows what then. *He could die.* That's enough for Jennie, who kisses his arms, his fingers and his toes, but never his lips. She'd do anything to keep him safe.

She puts her palm over the top of his head. Her mother told her about the delicate growth of Sunny's brain and skull beneath his pulsing soft spot. The heat comes through that dent like fire inside his head. Jennie feels in herself the terrible power to press through his scalp and stir his brain like coals, messing up all the magic that's her baby brother. Sometimes she's afraid, like she'll do something when she isn't watching herself. "I love you," she whispers. "I love you."

She brings him outside, singing, "Sunny Boy Blue, come blow your horn.

The sheep's in the meadow, the cow's in the corn." She walks between the rows of white muslin, and the wet diapers cling to her eyelids and plaster her face like a mask.

Her mom takes the wrung-out diapers and snaps them unwrinkled. Snap, and then the squeak of old clothespins. The diapers flapping, the hum of bees. In Jennie's arms, Sunny breathes deeply, and his body relaxes into sleep. She weaves in and out of the diapers. In these rows, certain things disappear—like where her father was when Sunny was born, and where her father might be right now, and why he ran away. All the world is the clean, pure blue sky and bleached curtains of white, and Sunny sighing off to sleep and the bees singing in celebration of apricots and the smell of summer.

Her mother is crying, softly, quietly, but Jennie can always tell. Jennie wants to stay in the blue and white. She'll pretend Faith isn't even there, and she doesn't hear the sniffling in between the snap of diapers and the flap of wet cloth. But Faith won't let her. Her voice comes through the white curtains. "I'm alone," she says. "He didn't come, and I'm all alone here."

Jennie squeezes Sunny tight, and he wakes, whimpers. "Don't say that. I'm here. Sunny's here." He makes little noises, like he's holding in his cries, which is as bad as he ever gets.

Her mother whispers, "I'm in the dark. I have nothing left. My husband ran off; my house is cracking open. I don't even have my piano. If it weren't for you kids, Juniper, I'd kill myself."

Jennie presses a cool, wet diaper over her eyes and nose and Sunny's face. If she were a good person, she would tell Faith about the things she has hidden under the freebox clothes in her room. But she doesn't. Through the white muslin, the light shines special as church light. The damp cloth soothes her cheeks.

"I don't think he really loves me," Faith says. He, Jennie knows, is Clarence, but it could be Ray, or just as easily Sunny. Parting the diapers, Jennie finds her mother. "Yes he does," she says, holding Sunny out to Faith. "Here. Take him." Faith claims him, kisses his fingers, his eyelids. She carries him inside, the screen door banging behind her.

Now that he's gone, Jennie's arms are light as petals. She is the Bee Princess. Her bees dive and buzz in the sweet apricots. The Bee Princess unsnaps diapers. She hangs them to dry, her arms tiring from the bend, the lift and snap, the heavy weight.

And then, her arms raised to pin a diaper in place, she sees it, unmistakable, black, shiny, wicked: a black widow, crawling down her arm, toward her face, and for a moment she cannot move and she watches, mesmerized, seeing her arm, the blue sky, the white diaper, and the black, black spider making its slow way toward her face. "Mom?" she whispers. And then she begins to scream and to flail her arms and by the time Faith comes out of the house the diapers lie on the ground, dusty and ruined.

And Jennie's all grown up now, sitting in a closet, crying over doomed love, over photo albums and bruises, Jennie, with her yellow hand in a dusty closet, a spider haven, she realizes, and the fear cuts through sorrow so fast that she doesn't even know she's screaming, thrashing, and her husband comes running to ask questions she can't answer, and give comfort she doesn't want, and she is all alone even when he's there.

CULPRITS

W H O killed Sunny Boy Blue? Where should the search begin? One generation ago? Two? My grandmother Lipa died of a cold when my mother was five. Shall I call that the beginning? My grandfather Swifty threatened to kill my grandmother. How's that for a villain?

No. If there has to be an autopsy of the sordid past, let's blame the parents. Aren't they the primary suspects, anyway? As the eyewitness, I'll testify to that. My mother may have been naive, but she certainly wasn't innocent—she was pregnant once before me, after all. So I'm the counterfeit eldest. And now, with Sunny dead, I am the false youngest. And my father, the fake adulterer, and Clarence, the fraudulent oracle, the false healer. But Sunny, he was True Blue. Was there ever anything false about him? Not as far as I know, which isn't far, according to Sunny.

But I digress. Let's begin, then, with a mystery: how did Faith travel from the land of Steinways and Ming vases to the Siberia of food stamps and hauling water from a well? Her only attempt to explain herself comes down to one sentence: her mother died of a cold, and it turned her father mean. Only I call this easy alibi into question.

L E T ' s get the sequence right. The piano. The crack. The Mary, *that* Mary. Ray says terrible things to Faith, then sends her to bed without her supper. He walks all the way to Valdez. And then her broken water, and a contraction starting. Now? she thinks. God, now?

Faith sits in the kitchen, looking out at the piano, black, sleek in the dawn. She should have put a blanket over it, that instrument of torture. As a child, Faith sat practicing with aching, stumbling fingers, what she feared more than her father's rage was the way he'd say something like, "Even your mother would say an elephant could do better."

She hated the piano, a kind of monster, large and horrible. Once she crawled under it and, with a paring knife, gouged a wound in its belly. *God-*

damn, she carved. A word that shot through her like adrenaline, shocking, dangerous, a word she would never speak aloud, the opposite of music, a curse against the terrible monster.

Even so, Faith, holding her contracting belly, longs for music, because it's so tangled with her mother. If she could only play a little Bartók, she might remember the sound of her mother's voice.

Faith drops her face into her hands, which have forgotten Bartók. They've forgotten the fine feel of silk, of makeup smoothed on by fingertips. These hands, red and ugly, know the white, bony shoulders of her husband and the stretched skin of her pregnant belly. They know the rope of the well. From the first time she met Ray, they have known terrible words.

She takes a blanket outside. Another pain comes. She leans against the piano, clutching the blanket, waiting for it to pass. Are they already so close together?

She remembers herself at five, Little Girl Faith, crying in the bathtub after that rain-soaked blueberry afternoon. Paul is angry. Lipa sits on the edge of the tub, explaining that Faith must understand her father, must see the little boy he used to be.

Faith studies her mother's blond braids, listens to her mother's lilting voice. Lipa says that when he was a boy, little Paul's father was never home. All week, he left for work before the sun rose, and came home after Paul had gone to bed. From Friday night to Sunday afternoon, Paul's father camped out on the Highest Hill building this very house. The only time little Paul saw his father was in the bathtub, every Sunday evening. Lipa says Faith should imagine that lonely little boy getting himself all muddied up, just so he could have a half-hour bath with his daddy. "Just picture it in your head," she says, lathering Faith's long dark hair. She blows bubbles from her fingertips and smiles. "Try to see," she says, "that he wasn't so lucky as you."

Faith sees her father clutching her wrists, slamming her hands again and again into the keys, yelling, "It's simple! Practice! Play!"

"I don't like him," she says, sliding under the water, then coming up gasping. "I don't like him at all."

Lipa tells Faith how she fell in love with Paul, even though he was grumpy. Then he fell in love back, and love is the hand of God and it saves us all. "The black keys were like a mustache," Lipa says, "and those white keys, how they grinned!"

"I hate him," Faith says.

Lipa sighs. "Poor baby. No, you don't. I could die of a broken heart to hear you talk like that."

Faith begins to cry, because she does love him; he is her daddy, her papa, her jolly wee father who is shorter than her mama and wears glasses like little round O's. She decides to copy her mother. When she feels like she hates her father, she'll remember Lipa, sitting on the edge of the tub, her golden hair and the soft yellow light and her white skin and red cheeks, smiling, saying, "God meant your father to be a happy man, but your father forgot this, so I had to remind him." She'll remember her mother and try to be like her, so she can make her papa happy.

That night, Lipa comes down with a cold, and soon, she dies.

f A I T H spreads the blanket over the piano. At the woodpile, she balances a log on the chopping block and hoists the ax over her head, her belly pushing her off balance. Then a contraction comes and she drops the ax. Has Ray ever said the word love? Has he ever praised Faith's beauty, or has he ever held her and whispered with his lips against her hair? How could he say those things to her last night? How could he say all the things he ever said to her?

Balancing the wood, bringing down the ax, she stops crying and gets furious. Over and over, she thinks, *He has no right.* She leans into the chopping, panting, fierce. The effort seems to lessen the pain. He has no right. The words fit with the rhythm of her chopping. Ugly words, from the very start. You can watch TV if you fuck me first.

Faith. I am your daughter and I've heard that story all my life but in truth I've never really believed you would have said yes to Ray's first vulgar proposition. I know it's history, but how can I trace the progression from that first moment to Faith, chopping wood, in labor, abandoned? Why can't I sort it out? It's not a complicated puzzle. She loved Ray and she loved his best friend, Clarence. Even a child could understand the end of that equation. And I was there. I smelled the Mayflower van's diesel, and I saw the moving box sitting in the driveway, waiting to be opened. FRAGILE. I remember how she stared. I knew even then what that piano meant to her.

Awkwardly, Faith carries two buckets full of water inside, her belly disrupting her balance. She makes a fire. She collects goldenseal and chamomile, for a Labor Tea. And the contractions come. "God Jesus," she whispers, not a curse, but a prayer. "Jesus."

She thinks, He has no right to leave me alone, after all the years I didn't leave him, all those years I never once dared to love Clarence out loud. He has no right. She imagines her husband and that Mary, his long fingers in her ringlets. *She came five times,* Ray said. *She couldn't believe the size of my cock.*

Faith stands in her kitchen, and she whispers, "He has no right!" She throws the jar of goldenseal and it explodes against the wall, glass flying, the fine powder sifting through the air, catching the sunlight. The word she carved under the piano is nothing compared to what Ray said last night. She whispers, "He has no right." A contraction waxes and wanes. She drops the chamomile into the rolling, bubbling water.

Juniper finally gets out of bed, and Faith sends her for Joy, and then, alone in her kitchen, Faith has an idea. Outside, Faith uncovers the piano. A contraction. When the pain has passed, she opens the bench, her heart beating faster. Faith. I should have known you'd look; even a nine-year-old should have known, and you'd long to find your entire past there, Lipa with her blond braids and pansies embroidered on her blouse, Paul with his round glasses, blueberries, chocolate cake, miniskirts and hair spray and shiny patent-leather Mary Janes. But the bench is empty. Nothing. No message, no letter, no gift from her father. Nothing to say, You are my daughter, and I love you despite everything. And I am so sorry, Faith, my mother, my mom, that I stole his one act of contrition from you.

Her tears spill again. After Lipa died, she played music over and over until she thought she'd drown in the notes, trying to conjure her mother by thinking of the keys as a man with a mustache. Her father and the piano lid closing on her fingers, and then her husband, Ray, and then Clarence with his hand on her belly, and Oh God, my God, who takes everything away in the end.

Back in the kitchen, Faith swallows Medicine, and then she feels better. Stronger. She sweeps the floor. She prays, Heavenly Father God, please, I've paid my debt. Let this baby be mine. I have a right. And God answers with a sign. How else to explain that, exactly now, Clarence arrives?

He stands beside the stove, studying her, this little woman dusted in gold. What do you think, Clarence? What do you love about her? Is it her desperate need for your love? Does she pull you up to some finer and better version of yourself? I know he loves her, though he doesn't kiss her. He won't kiss her for a long time, for over five years, until his best friend has left this house for good. For now, he simply lays his palm over the curve of her swollen belly, and the baby trembles, rolls closer to his hand. They both smile. Clarence says, "How's our Sunny Boy?"

"He's coming," Faith whispers. She sways toward this long-fingered brown hand, hot and gentle. Her kicking, dancing baby speaks for her. She looks up and falls into Clarence's dark eyes. This man's soul is as large as the sky. Clarence is saying he has to go. He's saying he'll be back. And Faith is thinking, A new baby, and Clarence. I have a right to this. And God agrees.

Well, yes, your eyewitness wasn't there for that one. But I'm guessing he might have made a guest appearance while I was running for help. Why not? If nothing else, I'm sure he showed up in her mind, the morning star, the evidence of hope and possibility.

I know this: my mother called for both Ray and Clarence during Sunny's birth. Maybe, because she needed someone, anyone, the two men became interchangeable. They aren't so different, Ray and Clarence. Both of them weaker than their hearts. No wonder she called for them both again and again through her difficult backwards labor. And no wonder that in the end they both left her alone.

But neither man is there, and so Faith tries to find focus on the piano sent by her father, on the memory of music, and not on the pain widening and deepening inside her. She floats on the pain like oil on water. She doesn't long for Clarence. She doesn't wonder where her husband has gone because she knows he has gone to Mary with her golden hair and her VW Bug with the top down. It doesn't worry Faith. For she has become oil spread thin over a great sea of pain.

Rescue

WAS Sarah my friend? Well, she was something to me, though not what I'd call a friend. A curiosity, perhaps. No, more than that. I worried about her. She fascinated me. Pretty and tiny and, most beguiling, fearless, a result of always getting what she wanted, I thought. Except, of course, for Jake, and those bruises, which drew me in and kept me from hating her.

She worked on the plaza, too, at her mother's gallery, SARAH'S, and she visited me nearly every day, cheerfully obstinate. "Just thought I'd stop by," she'd say, "see how my dress is doing. Are you annoyed yet? Admit it; you're tempted to let me try it on, aren't you?" She pursued me. She reminded me of all the girls at John Paul Robinson, that boarding school for the nicely refined — they all developed crushes on me, exotic in my vintage Essie clothes and red lipstick, teaching them to play pool in the basement. But none of the JPR girls were friends. They were acolytes, fans. Sarah, in her relentless pursuit, wanted more from me. She wanted my history, my opinions, my self. Flattered and, I admit, delighted, I took her up on her invitations for lunch, for coffee, for drinks, for dinner after work. She became my little friend, the puppy who led me away from home.

We usually ate lunch at the Plaza Café, which is a real diner with a counter and walls tiled in broken dinner plates. Fifty years old or so; just my sort of place. I ordered huevos rancheros; she ordered a hamburger and a mound of fries. Like toothpaste to a toothbrush, she squirted a line of ketchup down a fry and popped it in her mouth. She announced, "My favorite meal is French fries and a Diet Coke. I have this theory that regular Coke thickens inside you, like a plate sitting around covered in maple syrup? Jake says that's unscientific, but regular Coke makes me feel like my tonsils are stuck together. Anyway, like I told you before, I have an oral fixation, so I'm always putting something into my mouth. Lollipops, gum, cigarettes, Coke. Good thing I drink Diet or I'd be a fat cow. I guess there's some kind of sexual innuendo in all that, too." She took off her moccasin and scraped nail polish off her toes. She rearranged the salt shakers and fidgeted with the silverware and traced the edge of the table. She fondled her straw, fiddled with my purse, with her enormous black bag, twiddled an unlit cigarette, flicked her lighter on and off.

I watched the tidy movements of her nimble fingers, and I understood that, beyond the chatter and makeup, Sarah could always believe she knew everything. I envied her that, because she wasn't a dumb and spoiled child, as I had first thought. She stood on the firmer ground of arrogance, or maybe something more innocent, call it faith. She glanced at me, smiled. "And posole. Liking posole is in my genes."

"I thought you were Irish."

"Everybody thinks Irish people are the only ones allowed to have red hair. I'm like, hello? My last name's Alberhasky, not O'Haskimannon? I'm Spanish, like I told you before."

"Alberhasky's not Spanish."

"No, Dr. Know-it-all. Martinez is Spanish. I'm adopted, and my real name was Martinez, not that Alberhasky's not my real name. Anyway, Jake's last name is Martinez, too. So it's like going back to myself, marrying him? Wouldn't it be weird if he turned out to be my brother, not that he will since we're genetically totally different. Including that he's about twice as tall and strong as me. Did you notice his muscles?"

I said, "I've noticed the impact they have on your skin."

She said, "Did you know lots of Spanish people have blond hair, and red hair? My hair's red because I'm a true Spanish . . . *rojizo*, or something like that. *Rubio.*"

"*Rubio* means blond."

"And you know that because you're so fluent. And I'm so impressed. God. Where's that waitress? I'd do anything for another Diet Coke. Either that or I'm lighting up a cigarette and we'll see how much they like it. If Jake were here, they'd be running around, worried he'd kick somebody's ass."

I tucked my hair behind my ears and considered what I might say. "Wait," Sarah said. "Stop right there." She leaned over the table and turned my head to the right and the left. "You," she said, "have the tiniest ears I have ever seen. They're adorable." Without missing a beat, she moved on, ketchuping another fry, popping it in her mouth.

SARAH was the baby of a woman who showed up at Lovelace Hospital already in labor, calling herself Maria Martinez, which in New Mexico is the equivalent of saying her name was Jane Smith. Still, all through the labor she cursed the Martinezes: *puta madre* Martinez, *chingadero* Martinez, *pinche* Martinez. After her labor, she ran away in her nightgown, leaving her dress and her shoes behind.

Meanwhile, Helen and Wells Alberhasky were down south in Las Cruces, living on Alberhasky Farms, the biggest pecan orchard outside of Georgia. On a typical summer day, 105 degrees if you were lucky, you could drive through the Alberhasky trees and the air cooled off. That's how big it was.

One day, Wells was drinking coffee, watching Helen clean the oven. While the sulfur smell filled the room, Wells suddenly heard something banging around inside his chest. "He wrote me a journal," Sarah said, "where he explained everything. He wrote, *Dear Sarah, one day I was sitting in the kitchen and your mama was cleaning the oven and I suddenly heard something banging around inside my chest and I realized it was my heart and I needed something to love and that something was you.*"

So Wells told his wife, Helen, "Let's get us a baby."

Helen said, "I'm too old for that." She meant she was too old to have a little kid running around on her beautiful new white carpet. Sarah's mother was an ugly woman, and everyone said so. She had little eyes and a little nose and little mouth, all squished together in the middle of her face like they were afraid of her big ears. She spent her time decorating and cleaning her house, so she could feel beautiful by association. Wells wasn't gorgeous, either. He was tall and bony and scary-looking, with a thick head of white hair. He looked like Ichabod Crane, but he was nice, even to his wife, and everyone loved him. He was the best thing that had ever happened to Helen, and the real reason she didn't want a baby is that she wanted to keep Wells to herself.

"We'll adopt us one," Wells said, and Helen started to cry.

It was easy for them to adopt red-haired orphan Baby Martinez from Albuquerque, since they were rich and upstanding citizens. They brought the baby home and named her Sarah. Wells spoiled her. He bought her beautiful dresses and let her eat French fries for breakfast. But the best thing about her father was that he loved to play. They irrigated the orchards by flooding them, and the water mirrored the trees and the sky. Sarah loved riding on her father's shoulders and splashing around in the orchard, especially when he stood perfectly still. "Be very very quiet," he'd whisper. "Look very very carefully." The dirt settled and reflections formed, and her father whispered, "Do you see the little girl who lives in the trees and the sky?"

"No," she'd say, but she did. She saw herself, sitting on her daddy's shoulders.

When Sarah was five, Wells took her to play under the trees, where it was cooler. "We were playing tag, and I was it," Sarah told me at the Plaza Café. "I still remember. We ran and ran and ran." All of a sudden, her father stopped and leaned against a tree and looked down at Sarah and he smiled a sad smile and he said, "My heart." Then he fell down and lay there with his eyes open like he was looking for something. Sarah laid beside him in the muddy irrigation water. She saw branches and leaves and the sky. She said, "I don't see! I don't like this game!" Who knows how long it took her to figure she should run for help?

The medics drove the ambulance screaming through the endless trees, and they almost ran over Wells, lying in the middle of the trees, the water settled into a mirror around him. When they found him, Helen told Sarah, "You killed him."

Sarah had finished her fries, but I just stared at my huevos. "That bitch," I said. I listened to the diner's clinks and shouts and gurgling conversation, because I could not think what else to say. I wasn't even sure what her story made me feel. I wavered somewhere between compassion and suspicion. Clearly, Sarah wanted me to see her as the poor little orphan girl, but it was the Pea Princess who sat beside me, waiting for my tears.

Sarah shrugged. "Don't get all weepy on me. I'm fine now, see? Anyway, I'm not looking for your sympathy or anything. I just like to talk about myself. Jake says I'm like a Vegas showgirl. Give her a stage. I told him Vegas show-girls don't give speeches, but he said that was beside the point."

Despite myself, I smiled. I thought, There will come a time when she can get me to do anything she wants.

ONE day in July, I was in the display window, dusting off Matilda's dress, when I spotted Sarah on the plaza with her boyfriend. That's him, I thought, the bastard. They were fighting. He said something. She replied. He took her by the shoulders. He shook her, let go. She began a desperate pleading, her face crumpled and ugly. I stood in the window holding the veil, watching this big boy of a man with his face set in a statue's stare. Sarah tugged his sleeve. I felt something like pity and something like revulsion, nearly the feeling I had for Chris those days. Mostly, I hated this unfair match. No, I whispered. Meaning, no, Sarah, don't clutch and pull and beg. Turn away. Just walk away. But she clutched and begged, until he unpeeled her fingers and said something that sent Sarah to her knees.

People had stopped to watch the show. A pretty girl on her knees with arms outstretched. A big bad boy walking away. The girl's mouth open in a wail that makes him return. Will he give in? Will he pick her up and make everything better? He's reaching for her. All the gawky boys on skateboards drop their de-termined nonchalance; all the Indians gaze past their silver wares; the tourists hide behind their cameras.

He yanks her to her feet, and her head falls back. He shakes her the way a parent might a recalcitrant child, then walks off, leaving her stranded by the flagpole in the middle of the plaza with all the strangers staring.

She stood, watching him leave long after he had gone. No one helped. So I went to her.

"Sarah," I said. "I'm here."

She looked at me and she wasn't crying. "Is that for me?"

I still held Matilda's veil. "Not for any wedding with that dickhead." She smiled wanly. "Jake the Jerk," I said. I wanted to produce another zinger, but all I could think of was the old standby. "That cocksucker."

I led her into Las Novias and sat her on the velvet settee and gave her some water. She sobbed against my chest. "He was so *mean*," she wailed. "Why was he so *mean*?" She wouldn't say what it was about. She couldn't tell me anything I didn't know anyway. She may have been twenty-three, but she was a baby with a baby's idea of love, and that caricature of a man was just the sort to use love as bait for his harpoon. I have heard that drowning victims fight the lifeguard and sometimes even take their rescuers down with them. These thoughts pushed me to catch her by surprise, although primary in my mind was a gorgeous picture of the asshole coming home to the empty, lonely existence he deserved. I said, "We're moving you out right now."

"Now?" she said, her voice filled with hope and terror.

I wrote a sign that said FAMILY EMERGENCY and locked up the store and led Sarah to the Rolls, because if I didn't help her, I was sure to do something terrible to the next person I saw. My certainty seemed to comfort her, and she walked beside me, brightly, tinnily babbling about Jake, good riddance, about what she would do next, plenty of fish and all that. When she saw the car, she said, "Holy cow, look at you, in a Rolls and everything."

Sarah and Jake lived on Canyon Road, behind a gallery. It took only two minutes to drive there, and she kept up a stream of words until I parked. Then she burst into tears, and cried continually—sometimes quietly, like rain, sometimes violently, like thunder—the entire time we were there, in the house filled with this asshole's toys: two bikes, a kayak, a canoe, paddles, two sets of skis, a weight-lifting bench and the appropriate dumbbells, a surfboard. "He lived in California for a while," Sarah explained, weeping. He was, apparently, a river guide, a ski instructor, a personal trainer. "A professional playmate," I said, loading on as much dismissive contempt as I could muster.

I took the drill-sergeant approach, leading Sarah around, pointing at things, saying, "Is this yours? Is this?" and throwing her belongings into trash bags from the kitchen, little Jennie storm trooper coming to the rescue, as if I'd been trained in this at some battered women's boot camp. Barking orders, I ignored her crying, while inside I felt broken, desperate, as if by saving her I was keeping myself on this side of sanity, or at least the law. She had shoes everywhere, sneakers, high heels, chunky boots and cowboy boots and hiking boots, buckled things and sparkly mules and bright pink espadrilles, all of them tiny, adorable, and I entertained her with stories of Chris and all the Cinderella shoes, though to me the memories felt as distant as childhood, as imaginary as a fairy tale. This, a bruised child, an urgent escape, was real.

Sarah followed me listlessly, weeping, dragging her trash bag, and when she stopped, gazing mournfully at a racing bike, I said, "I don't have forever here, Sarah, so unless that piece of shit's yours, let's just get a move on." What drove me truly insane was this: how little belonged to her, as if she weren't a person, but merely another surfboard propped against the wall.

In the bedroom, an enormous number of plants hung randomly from the skylit ceiling, some of them so annoyingly bushy and overgrown, on such long ropes, that I had to part vines to get through. He seemed to have a penchant for smelly plants, and as I made my way, the heady smell of herbs rose from their leaves—basil, oregano, mint. The bedroom walls were painted navy blue, to match the curtains, the bedding on the massive walnut bed. I had a sudden and terrible vision of the two of them naked, his hands around her waist, squeezing hard. I said, "What's this, his imitation of a sex jungle?"

Sarah, weeping, whispered, "He loves plants. He takes such good, good care—" She broke into sobbing, and I pulled a blue pillowcase off a pillow and gave it to her. "Blow," I said.

"Great care of the plants, I mean, you should see him, mixing up his special fertilizers and spray, spraying them with his little spray bottle, and there's twenty-five, one for every, every, year of his life, and my year is lav— lav— lavender—"

"You sound like a song," I said lightly, but she only sobbed harder, a keening, desperate grief. She stood in the middle of the room, her face pressed into the pillowcase, her little shoulders heaving and shaking.

How I hated him. Every offense that had ever come into my life had been distilled into one pure loathing for this hideous boy with his muscles and his toys and his fists, and I yanked a plant from the ceiling and threw it against the wall, so it exploded in a deeply satisfying hail of dirt and leaves and pottery, covering the blue bed with filth. Sarah screamed, and I took her by the shoulders. "Listen to me," I said. "You deserve someone who would never hurt you." I longed to kill every one of them, like killing him twenty-five times over (this man I'd never met but knew so intimately by the autobiography he left on Sarah's skin), and Sarah, hysterical, screamed while I threw another at the wall, the basil, a pesto smell rising from the bed. "Juniper Tree Burning," Sarah screamed.

I stopped in my tracks. "What did you say? Don't you say that to me."

A standoff: glaring, she said, "Then you stop killing those plants."

So I did, in a manner of speaking. I took them all. I crammed them into the trunk of the Rolls, not bothering to be careful with their leaves, in fact deliberately crushing as much as I could without sending her into further fits, and the rich smell—geranium and mint and lemon verbena, rosemary, lavender—rose from the trunk, and their oils were on my fingers, so I felt stained by him, like the murderer I wanted to be that crazy morning, while Sarah stood by, not helping but watching, as I went back and forth with all his precious years.

I drove to her mother's house, a big remodeled adobe behind an adobe wall on Agua Fria Street. Very swanky. Sarah said we had to leave the plants on the porch. "My mother will kill me," she said.

"Fine with me," I said.

"So she can kill me but Jake can't?"

"The plants," I said. "Let them stay outside. Maybe they'll get killed in some freak hailstorm."

Her mother, Helen Alberhasky, defined house-proud. In her bathroom, Helen had a dish of expensive soaps shaped like sea anemones and sea horses and starfish. They matched her wallpaper and her shower curtains. "In this house, everything's coordinated," Sarah said. "You aren't allowed to use those." She showed me where to find the cheap deodorant soap under the sink. I wasn't allowed to use the plush towels, either. There was a ratty Kmart special on a hook under the sink. In the kitchen, copper pots hung from the ceiling. These, of course, were never used. Sarah showed me the cheap pots in the cupboards. All this made me think of Essie, the first rich woman I'd ever known, my fairy godmother. Essie would have sniffed and said, How gauche. How nouveau riche. Essie with her effortless chic, her French words and her British slang. Her bloody pretensions, hanging nicely on her slender, aging ballerina shoulders. Poor Helen Alberhasky; all her efforts toward beauty only looked like the desperate scrabblings of a plain-Jane.

The weirdest was Helen's fruit, a centerpiece bowl of perfect green apples, kumquats, and pomegranates. "She buys color-coordinated fruit," Sarah said. "She polishes them, arranges them in a bowl, and they sit around on the counter until they get ripe and ugly, and that's when they go in the fridge and you're allowed to eat them." To prove it, she showed me the crisper drawer of overripe fruit and offered me a shriveled brown pomegranate.

SARAH vanished for three days. I peeked in the gallery window, but she wasn't working. I left messages but she didn't return my calls. I thought about driving by her mother's, but I wasn't ready to go that far. Then one morning, she was waiting in the Las Novias doorway when I got to work. "There you are," I said. "I thought he killed you."

She held out a cup of coffee and a bag of doughnuts. "I need to tell you something," she said.

I felt queasy. "You're back in his loving arms."

"I just need to tell you something."

We went to sit on the benches in the middle of the plaza. She was smiling a lot and flinging her blazing hair around. She had on her orange velvet skirt and tuxedo shirt uniform. "Don't look so serious," she said. "You're such a serious person."

"So?" I said, annoyed. "Tell me something." The tourists were starting to appear with their cameras and pointing fingers. How I hate the sweet pandering face of the Santa Fe Plaza—the low adobe buildings, the portals dripping with chile *ristras*, the Indians sitting on lawn chairs beside blankets spread with a picnic of silver squash blossoms, concha belts, strands of turquoise beads, and the tourists. If I were one of them, I'd see the buildings, with their flat roofs and exposed vigas, as strangely foreign, weirdly graceful, like a woman lifting her skirt and squatting to pee. But I only work here. I looked at my watch. I was late. "I can't wait forever."

She lit a cigarette and let the smoke out in a long sigh. "I hope they figure out how to fix lungs before I get cancer." She watched the skateboarders hop curbs and otherwise risk their necks. She said, "My mom got arrested after my dad died."

"Sarah. I need to get to work."

"Just listen. For once in your life. I'm trying to explain."

Explain, indeed. That she had moved the plants back, and the shoes, and the clothes, and now she was back in the house herself, sleeping under a new basil plant, under the lavender, the occasional purple blossom wafting down on her black-and-blue skin, and maybe I wanted a reason. So I sat.

"After Daddy died, after his funeral," Sarah said, smoking, "I looked in the mirror and I said to myself, 'I killed him,' and I put my hands around my neck and I squeezed as hard as I could, because I thought, If I squeeze hard enough, maybe I'll kill myself too."

"Sarah," I said. "Sarah."

"Shut up," she said. "Will you please just listen please? On my first day of school, my mom was making breakfast, and she was putting on her apron—I remember this so clear, like a movie—and she yanked her apron strings really tight, deep into her, and she scrambled the eggs like she was killing them, and I knew then and there that she was imagining killing me, and I told her I wasn't hungry. But she made me eat all the eggs. So at school, I had a horrible stomachache, and I sat there, thinking how I had killed my dad and no wonder my mom hated me, and I just leaned over and barfed up all the eggs. Every day I sat in my desk thinking about my mom and dad, and every day I barfed, until my teacher, Mrs. Lucero, started to worry about me, which makes sense I guess, and next she spotted these bruises all over me, and Mrs. Lucero, who had a mole on her eyelid, asked me, 'Does your mommy hurt you? Is she mean?' I remember I just stared at Mrs. Lucero's mole and wondered if it made it hard to blink. Finally I said, 'My mom hates me,' and it was the truth; it wasn't like I was *trying* to get my mom in trouble or anything. Only the next day my mom was in jail and I was in foster care, and I mean, talk about overreacting, I swear to God. I have this theory that people don't really care if they're right or not—as long as they believe they're right, it's okay.

"Of course, nobody could prove my mom beat me, because she didn't, and I told them over and over that never in my whole life had my mom hit me, but that wasn't what convinced them. The thing was, the bruises were still around even though my mom wasn't. So the doctors decided it was a skin condition, because of my dad's death, and they said it would go away, but they were wrong about that one, I can tell you that. So my mom couldn't stand everybody whispering about her, because even if she was ugly, she didn't want people *noticing*. So she sold Alberhasky Farms, and we moved to Santa Fe, and she started a gallery, naming it after me like some big gesture, but every time I look at the SARAH's sign I know she's saying, *You bitch, this is all your fault*. Don't get me wrong, she spoiled me rotten because she was afraid she'd get blamed for my bruises, which made me perfectly happy, I mean who wouldn't want to get French fries for breakfast?"

"So what about Jake?"

"What about Jake what about Jake what about Jake," she said. "Please. You sound like a parrot." She fiddled with her coffee cup. She lit another cigarette and drew in a deep lungful of smoke. "I'll give you a cracker if you'll shut up."

I took a sip of coffee, and it was terrible. Did I really want a bit part in this week's episode of How the Sarah Turns? Not hardly. I stood and dumped my coffee.

Sarah drew her knees to her chest. Her eyes filled, and the tears spilled nicely down her cheeks. "I just always wanted someone to love me," she whispered.

I tossed the cup in the trash. I watched one of the teenagers ride his skateboard on a park bench. I spoke coldly. "Do you really think I'm this stupid?"

"But I just *explained* everything. Don't you understand? I love him."

"Love," I said. "Let me tell you about love. Either you love more or you love less, and the one who loves more ends up fucked. And you, pretty Sarah, are the one who is fucked. He comes to you all weepy and sorry, and you hop into bed and you let him put his dick in you, and then you gaze into each other's eyes and you think, My god, I love him, and he loves me, he really does, but in the morning, his eyes are as hard and dead as the headboard."

"You don't understand," Sarah whispered, wiping her eyes.

"Whatever you say," I said. "I just wish you'd leave me out of it. Because frankly, it's a little too much work for me."

I left before she could say anything. I walked across the plaza to my shop. I opened the store and dusted and managed to avoid looking out the window. For the rest of the summer, I caught glimpses of her unmistakable hair, and once or twice I saw Jake swagger across the plaza, but I didn't speak to her until after I got the phone call and learned that my brother had died. "Almost certainly drowned," the policeman said, as if he were hedging his bets, as if that softened the blow.

Leaving Cheyenne

August 19, 1976, Arroyo al Fin

H ᴇ ʀ father comes the morning of Sunny's birth, and they get on his motorcycle and she thinks she is saved, as he shouts in the wind, "Lean with me!
Lean!"

But they lean the wrong way. They lean toward Valdez, and then lean
down into the valley, lean into Clarence's driveway. Ray stops the motorcycle
and she says, her voice muffled through her helmet, "Why are we here? This
isn't the hospital." The Dodge sits in the driveway, and for a moment she's
confused, caught up in trying to trace the lines of history that put the Dodge
in this place.

"Advice," Ray says. Clarence comes out, ducking to get through his low
doorway. Clarence's house is too short for him or Ray, who's telling Jennie to
go sit in the truck. In the truck, she can't hear anything. She takes off her helmet, but she still can't hear anything. She watches them talking, Clarence
nodding, listening, Ray looking off to the mountains and talking, talking, talking, pacing, talking.

Was it Clarence's idea? Who suggested, and who decided? Let's say that
Ray rails about her stubborn attachment to that piano. "What about the
house?" he says, pacing Clarence's yard. "She has flesh-and-blood children
right in front of her." What Ray doesn't say matters: *And a husband. Right in
front of her.* Clarence doesn't say it, either. They let the omission hang there,
saying everything.

One of them says, "We could just take it anyway."

One of them says, "We could." She loved them both. Does it matter who
said it first? What really matters is that they both decide. Both of them.

Jennie rolls down the window. She hears Ray say, "About an hour."

"You're sure about this?" Clarence says.

Ray shrugs and glances back at Jennie. "She won't listen to me," he says,
and Jennie thinks he means her, but then she realizes he means Faith.
They're going to steal the piano. This sentence comes into her head so clearly
and loudly that it's like someone said it to her. Years later, she'll wonder if

maybe Ray or Clarence actually said it out loud, because how else could she be so perfectly certain at that moment?

IN the hospital, Jennie stands beside her father at the foot of the bed holding her motorcycle helmet, so very tired after being up all night, with dirt on her from under the lilac bush and leaves in her chopped-off hair, and she sways and her eyes blur.

Ray says, "Hello, little Mama."

"Where were you?" Faith says. Please, Jennie thinks, please, don't start fighting about Mary again.

Faith wears a plastic bracelet and a cotton flowered nightgown. Where did that come from? Did they bring her to the hospital naked? Did they load her into the ambulance with just a blanket? Did everyone see her *down there*? Faith holds Sunny Boy Blue in her arms. Jennie wants to look at him.

Ray stares at Faith and she stares back. They stare for the longest time. "Faith," Ray says, and to Jennie he sounds like he's saying, Forgive me. Faith, please, this is not the way I meant to be.

"No," she says fiercely. "It's mine."

Now he's mad. "Our house—"

Faith says, "No," and that's all. She says, "No," softly, dangerously, and the baby whimpers.

Ray says, "The crack—"

Faith says, "I don't care."

He says, "Think what we could do—"

"No."

He turns. Jennie calls, "Daddy," but he walks away, his shoes squeaking on the shiny white floor. Sunny sighs against Faith's breast and Jennie calls again, "Daddy, don't you want to hold the baby?," but he doesn't turn; he doesn't answer and then Ray is gone. All around them, the hospital hums and hums.

"Mom?" Jennie says. Faith studies the color of the pale blue hospital blanket covering her empty womb, and tears flow from her eyes as if a glacier were melting, flowing down her cheeks, dripping from her chin, splashing on her full, aching breasts. "Mom?" Jennie whispers. "The baby's here. Sunny Boy Blue is here."

Sunny Boy Blue's tiny rice-paper fingernails press into Faith's breast, and Sunny Boy Blue sucks hard, with all his might, eyes squeezed shut, face bruised and misshapen by his difficult birth. Jennie asks, "Mom, why are you crying?" The answer is, it's Jennie's fault. Faith cries because of the lies Ray told about Mary. If only Jennie had been braver. If only she hadn't been so sleepy. Then she could have said, I was there, and nothing happened. Then Faith wouldn't be crying. Jennie, sick to her stomach, wishes she could sit down or run away or do something to make her mother stop crying.

Faith closes her eyes. She whispers, "Do you think Clarence will come?"

Jennie, so relieved, wonders if this is fainting, this feeling dizzy and alive and light all at once. Then she remembers what Ray and Clarence are doing while Faith lies here crying, on Sunny Boy Blue's first day when everything should be happy, and Jennie is so mad she hates her father.

Faith says, her voice breaking, catching, "I think he'll come."

Jennie knows what to do. She takes a deep breath, and she says, "Daddy's stealing the piano right now." She leaves out Clarence to make up for the other time when she should have called Ray a liar.

Faith strokes Sunny's head and touches his cheeks and then she smiles. Her tears have stopped. "He's so beautiful," she says. "Sunny Boy Blue," she whispers to him, and maybe Faith is thinking about God, who is a liar and a thief, how even the water he gives for life can freeze you, drown you, steal your loved ones away. God saw precious Sunny Boy Blue and made him backwards, tried to take him away before Faith got even the smallest part of him for herself, the way God stole her mother, the way he stole her father and now Ray, too, the way Juniper was born to hate her mother. Faith holds Sunny Boy Blue's warm body against her skin to thaw her fear. She swears to God, You'll not get this one. This one is mine; you promised. At least give me this one small thing. And Ray can go away and I will have Clarence, too.

I give her these thoughts because I'm certain she believed me. Surely she knew the piano would be gone when she brought Sunny home. Maybe it seemed like a fair exchange, her piano for Clarence. But she bought an imperfect, angry love, the wrong bargain with God. She should have used the piano to pay for her baby, not Clarence. In choosing Clarence, she cheated herself out of Sunny Boy Blue. He went to his sister instead.

JENNIE comes closer. Her brother is awake. His fingers open and close, as if he's testing them out. Jennie whispers, scared that Faith will get mad. "Can I hold him?"

"Be careful," Faith says, but she offers him, and Jennie slides her arms under him and for a moment they're both holding him. Faith pulls out her arms and leans back, closes her eyes.

His hair is black as velvet and his face is red, and he gazes up at Jennie with slitted eyes. His fingers are long and pink and speckled with tiny white dots.

He studies his big sister as if he's making up his mind. She whispers, "You didn't want to come out, did you?"

He stares up at her for a very long time. Then he falls asleep. He sleeps forever, and her arms ache, but she cannot put him down. He trusts her. He knows she could puncture his head with her thumb, or that she could so easily drop him, but he sleeps on in her arms. She looks up to ask Faith what she should do, but Faith is crying again. The tears run silently out of her closed eyes and down her cheeks. Sunny sleeps. Jennie hums her father's song to him, softly. "Good-bye, Old Paint. I'm leaving Cheyenne."

When they get home, the driveway is empty: no motorcycle, no Dodge, no Ray, and no piano. "He stole it," Faith whispers, standing in the place where she played the music of queens. "He took it away." And no Clarence. Faith moans, a soft quiet sound that could open a path in the ocean.

Behind the house, Jennie gathers apricots for Faith. She pulls a bucket of water. She eats an apricot. The flesh is warm, sweet. The water is cold and also sweet. When she bites into an apricot, the juice bursts out, over her chin and hands, thick and warm, almost like blood, almost like something no one should eat.

Here is all I know for sure: once, there was a little girl named Faith Lipa Chatwin. She had a mother who loved her, but then her mother caught a cold and died. That much is true. That is the end of one story, and maybe the beginning of the rest. As for blame, I think it resides with the accuser. I know who Sunny Boy Blue would blame. It doesn't matter who came before me.

$\mathcal{T}$HE OCEAN

Early Last Wednesday Morning, Albuquerque

O R begin in August at two in the morning. Begin with the bathroom, and me in it, sweating, freckled with green paint. For the length of our marriage, all eight months of it, I'd been painting at night, avoiding our bed. I can trace the progress of my loathing for my husband by the colors of our walls. Painting, studying, gardening: there are fifty ways to avoid the wedding bed. I had turned out to be a Very Bad Wife.

It was sweltering, August in Albuquerque, and I'd stripped down to my undies. The Bad Wife, on her knees, trying to reach the corner behind the toilet, smelling the urine stink even clean toilets exude when you get close enough. Chris's cat was sitting on the toilet seat, watching me. Bob. The Cat, I preferred to call him. Or Your Cat. Your Fucking Cat. He was always following me around, an imitation of liking me, but I knew from hard experience that if I tried to pet him, he'd rip open some part of my body. He was keeping an eye on me, waiting for the moment when I'd finally commit the crime I had come here to inflict on my victim, his master, his Chris.

Speak of the husband. "What are you doing?" Chris said.

I nearly swallowed my tongue. "You scared the hell out of me."

Bob leapt from the toilet and wound his way through Chris's legs, purring. "It's two in the morning," Chris said, not angry or sad, just tired. The exhaustion in his voice drove me to sarcasm.

"Well, no kidding, Copernicus." Not my best, but it would do.

He leaned against the doorjamb and rubbed his palms over his face. Again he asked, "What are you doing?" Only it wasn't a question. "Jennie?"

I looked regretfully at the paintbrush I held. If I wasn't going to paint, I'd have to wash it, and it seemed such a waste to stop now only to begin again tomorrow. Sighing, I stood. "Go to bed," I told him. I wanted to finish. I wanted to paint the woodwork a glossy white enamel. I wanted it very much.

He said, "Normal people don't paint bathrooms at two in the morning." He reached for my hand. "Give it to me," he said gently, tugging at the brush. "Let it go."

"Stop it," I said. "Leave me alone."

One by one, he tried to force my fingers open. One by one, I closed them. It was comical, really. But I wasn't smiling. Rage built in me. Who did he think he was? I'd been peaceful, even happy, before he showed up to interrupt my beautiful deep green and the soft tick of my brush covering the wall. Now I was watching him attempt to pry my brush from my hand. "Enough," he said. "That's enough."

Then the bell. The phone. The shrill ring at two-oh-five in the A.M., breaking into our little fight the way a phone would interrupt any other couple's fight in the early-morning hours. I was so relieved I didn't even ask myself the usual question: who could it be, at this hour?

Yes, begin with the phone call. Begin with the squeeze past my husband, out of that tight, sweaty, half-painted room, my rush to the phone. Begin, as one usually does, with hello.

Silence replied. Again I said, *"Hello?"* Someone cleared his throat. "Who is this?" I said sharply.

The poor Seattle cop, calling me, asked if I knew a short, black-haired boy who would write something like *Juniper Tree Burning* on a wall. "Juniper Tree Burning," he said. "I don't know if this is a name, or what."

"Goddamn him," I said.

"Him," the cop said. "The black-haired boy?"

"My brother," I said. "That little prick."

And how did the poor cop manage, in the face of my anger, to deliver the news that the dark-haired boy, the little prick, goddamn him, had drowned? Well, the poor cop, he just cleared his throat and tried it from another angle, because he couldn't quite bring himself to say it just yet. At that moment, he knew my future before I did.

"Juniper Tree Burning?" he said. "Is it a name? What does it mean?"

I was forced to say, "It means me." And so I was hating my brother at the moment the man told me Sunny was dead.

"There was an accident," the cop is telling Jennifer Braverman, and he, the cop, would never guess this woman is standing in her panties to hear the news. "An accident," he says. "Or maybe not. I mean, it appears to be suicide, a boy, a man, I mean. Maybe five-seven. Dark hair. Green eyes. He jumped. He drowned."

"Drowned," Jennifer Braverman, call her Jennie, says evenly, carefully, as if practicing a foreign word. She stands, paintbrush in hand, in the living room, in the dark, in her underwear. She has freckles of deep green paint on her chest, her forearms, her thighs. She turns her back on her hovering husband.

"Drowned," the policeman says, making it official. "I'm sorry."

"Don't be," I said. "It's not your fault."

Yes, begin with the phone call and say it's the start of everything. But no. It won't do, because to understand you must know about the wedding, and to understand the wedding, you have to know there once was a boy named Sunny Boy Blue who was born backwards, whose sister baked him apricot birthday cakes and told him imaginary stories about pictures of people they had never met. So begin anywhere. Just begin.

AFTER the phone call, Chris pounced, heaping on platitudes, seizing the moment, opening his arms—talk to me, talk to me, poor Jennie, please talk to me. Jesus. I saw the next several months in a flash; I saw my future, and it was nothing I wanted. God save me from my mother, from a Funeral Meeting, from sunflower wreaths and whole wheat funeral pies; protect me from my mother, red-eyed, copper bracelets clanking, sobbing, "Not Sunny Boy Blue." I'll answer, "Who then, me?" and she'll trundle off to find someone, anyone, to tell about that awful girl, that Capricorn—whispering, "It's the goat in her that makes her so mean, you know. Sunny, now, *he* was a Leo, a lion, a lead— leader . . ." Her voice disintegrating into a high, heartbreaker keening. And my father, wilted, drooping in corners of rooms, his marigold hair gone gray, will mumble, "My fault. I was a terrible, terrible father." And please God, do me this one favor: deliver me from my husband holding out his arms and nagging me to cry.

I poured myself a whiskey, pressed the cool glass to my forehead.

"Cinderella," Chris whispered, reaching for me. The Concerned Husband. "Jennifer Lipishka." He breathed against my neck. He whispered, "Here I am."

I twisted out of his grasp. "No," I said. "Don't. You. Dare." I managed to stop myself there. His hand fell. Because he's a Good Man, I prayed to him: Please, don't say it; say nothing more, for once in your life, Concerned Husband, Chris, get it right.

"I'm so sorry," he said. Goddammit.

Off to the pearly-gray bedroom I went, Chris on my heels, haranguing me to grieve, and behind him the fucking cat. I began dressing. My Concerned Husband was a modern self-help fishwife, telling me I had to grieve, and just where did I think I was going?

"Three guesses, Sparky," I said, pulling my laces tight.

Off we trooped, through the mustard living room, to the front door. I opened it, and the cool night air, freshly bathed by a quick summer thunderstorm, invited me out. The cat bolted through my legs and into the lacy shadows of my flowers. "I won't let you go," Chris said.

For a long moment, we looked at each other. "Oh really," I said. "What will you do to stop me?"

His lips parted as if he had a reply, but then he closed his mouth. I turned and ran into the night.

W e live off Central in nowhere near a safe neighborhood, but I took to the streets, running past gas stations, bars, quiet houses on street after dark, unfamiliar street. When I run, I try to concentrate on one aspect of form at a time, and that night I tried to keep my hands loose, not clenched or splayed, even though I happened to know it couldn't take so very much energy to curl your hands into fists, and I was thinking about this—that clenched hands must make clenched arms and neck and back and legs and therefore lousy running—when I spotted two boys playing on their porch steps, wide awake far past any reasonable person's idea of bedtime.

They made me furious, children younger than six or seven scooting their cars around this late at night. Where were their parents? I thought, I should stop. I imagined the boys rising to their feet under the yellow porch light, their little Matchbox cars tight in their fists, their black straight bangs trembling as they blinked. What would I say? Would I say, "Where are your parents?" Would I ask, "What are your names?" and then, "Where is your mother?" The children would shrug. Perhaps the younger would go and fetch the father. Maybe the parents were sleeping. Maybe the children woke to the patter of rain and they crept past their parents' room and took their toys outside, where they could make soft burping noises and drive their cars fast up the steps—so that the father, roused from sleep, with his broad shoulders, his heavy arms, his gut hanging over hastily pulled-on pants, would glare, would say, "Get inside," and what would I say then?

I tried it on for size: My brother has gone into the sea. My brother is dead. I waited for grief, but I felt only this tight coiled rage that kept me running, and of course it hurt, and my throat was raw and salt stung my eyes, and the streets lay empty and still. The night was so quiet, I could hear the sidewalks hiss as air in the concrete rose through water left by the earlier rain.

I spotted a truck coming toward me. It slowed, then stopped. I didn't falter. I ran straight for its headlights, thinking, Go ahead, just try something, you cocksucker, please, try anything at all, because I know how to make a fist, and I feel like punching somebody tonight. When I passed, he turned on his dome light and I could see him inside. He wore a red shirt. He looked up from his map. I saw his eyes. I sprinted up that hill, not because I was afraid, although yes, I was afraid, but mostly because I would not let this man see me flagging.

I leapt a gutter stream fed by wayward sprinklers, and I concentrated on the slap of my feet, the gasp of my breath, the treacherous terrain of concrete buckling over tree roots. The streetlights reflected deep into the wet pavement. What good were streetlights against rapists and murderers and thieves? What good is anything we do to keep ourselves safe? The weak puddles of light in the dark only make it harder to see what's out there. Sarah was sleeping on her back under the tenderly cared for plants of her violent lover. How was she any safer than me, a foolish woman running down a street at three o'clock in the morning, or safer than those kids sitting on their own porch steps? Anything can happen anywhere, so why bother and who cares?

I sprinted, and even when I rounded a curve and was sure the man in the truck couldn't see, I kept on sprinting, because someone might have spotted me. I sprinted beyond my strength, and I ran until I couldn't run anymore, until I failed. I bent over my knees, huffing and puffing in a way that could sound like sobbing to the uninitiated, and I tried it on again. My brother is dead. I felt myself becoming a role: the Bereaved. See how she runs to work out her grief. Now she will cry, go home, fling herself into the arms of her waiting husband.

J E N N I E walks home. She tastes salt on her lips, and she pictures the cracked white crust of the Dead Sea. Inside, still gasping, she heads straight for the shower, relieved to see Chris asleep, his arms around a pillow, the way he might comfort a child.

She comes to bed damp, her hair wet and braided. The swamp cooler clicks on and blows across her scalp, forcing her to curl around Chris's back. She doesn't want to wake him. She knows he'll turn to face her, sandwiching the pillow between them. His breath on her cheek, he'll whisper, "How was your run?" and he'll whisper, "I was worried."

"Yes," she'll say, "I know," she'll say, "I'm sorry."

All these things happen after the cooler clicks on. She thinks, Everything in our lives together comes in this easily predictable way.

She whispers, "It was a good run. I ran hard." Her throat catches each time she takes a breath, so much like crying, but not. Against Chris's pillow, she clenches and unclenches her fist, wondering how much energy this simple movement can possibly take. She thinks, I will not let this happen to me. I will not, not, not let it happen to me.

"Cinderella," Chris whispers. "Jennifer." Though he must know better, his palm creeps near her shoulder. She feels it close to her skin. She holds herself tense, thinking, If I keep my body like this, my arms like this, he won't.

But he does; of course he does. He's a husband, for God's sake. He squeezes her shoulder lightly. He kisses her neck. He whispers, "I was worried."

She rolls away. His hand falls to the pillow between them.

She says, into the dark, "I ran hard." She says, to the dark, her cheek against the sheet, and she's cold with the swamp cooler blowing on her wet hair, "I ran too hard."

"I know," he says. "You should be careful."

"I am." She can feel the burn all the way to her lungs. She can feel it in the backs of her eyes. The Bad Wife reaches behind her and touches the Concerned Husband's hand. "James," she says, and the nickname sounds silly on her lips. "It has nothing to do with you." A cruel thing to say, she realizes too late. It always, always comes down to one thing: this is the way she was born, the one who charges ahead, stubborn, thoughtless goat, the fool.

He's silent for a long time. At last, he says, "Can't I do anything for you?"

She is the Bad Wife. She should answer, but she can't say anything, because she knows herself for a fool and she knows the next thing she says will be wrong.

"If that's what you want," he says, his voice abrupt and bitter.

"I just want to sleep," she says. "That's all." She longs for a year ago, an empty apartment, a hot green filtered light, the safety and comfort, the effortless, sweaty release. All of it gone, irretrievably vanished, like that apartment whose address she'll never know.

"Okay," the husband says, more softly now. "I understand. You should sleep." And so I did. I let sleep come over me in waves, let it pull me in increments away from that bed, that dark cold blowing air, and into the milky stillness of dreams. From that distance, I heard only dimly, so it mattered not at all, my husband's whisper: *I wish I knew how to bring you back to me.*

4·
SEARCH FOR CURES

Ｔｈｅ Ｕｇｌｙ Ｃｈｉｃｋ Ｒｉｄｅｓ Ａｇａｉｎ

Ｈｅｒｅ'ｓ Jennie in the morning, lying in bed, watching the light creep into the room. She's staring at the ceiling, thinking, This is the first day that I am a sister whose brother is dead. Actually, that's a lie. To be honest, she knows she ought to think something poignant, but she's just trying to remember what she dreamt, because she feels that weird kind of nauseating dread that comes when you wake from a dream and you can't remember it, but you still feel the way it made you feel. More than sad. Wider and deeper than sad. A dream too well dreamt. There's a phrase.

Here is Jennie's husband, Christian Braverman, sleeping, quiet and still as death. You see? Already the most commonplace terms have been hijacked. Bob the Cat jumps on her chest and peers into her face with his evil yellow eyes. Everything in its place. Here is Jennie and here is the cat and sleeping beside her, here is her husband. He is long and slender and she loves him.

I had forgotten to wash the paintbrush. I found it beside the phone, in the kitchen. Already it had stiffened, dark green, useless flotsam. An artifact. Proof.

Ｉ stood in the shower a long time, my hand braced on the wall, the water streaming off the ends of my hair. I finally remembered my dream. Sunday in Arroyo al Fin, the house cracking open, spiders in the walls. Standard stuff, all very Freud. The unconscious is a rudimentary, unimaginative organ, if you ask me. I watched the Coriolis effect take the water clockwise down the drain. I scrubbed green freckles from my thighs.

My brother is dead.

I turned off the faucet and listened to it drip. Well, okay. How can you get your mind around a fact like that? Fact is, you can't. You can only say it to yourself over and over until you hypnotize yourself into believing it's true. Why should I do that? Even thinking it made me feel silly. My brother has drowned. It sounded so melodramatic. Watch her try to force the audience to tears. It was starting to annoy me, the impossibility of doing anything outside the role: the Bereaved. See her mourn.

Out of the shower she goes. There is the cat, sitting on the toilet, staring with his yellow eyes. She loathes the cat. Fuck you, cat. She hates the half-painted bathroom, the smell of latex, the newspapered floor.

On to the bedroom, with the sleeping husband and the closet and wait, what's she after? A PHOTO ALBUM. Aha! What's in the album? She doesn't even glance at the pictures, just finds a postcard tucked between its pages. From her (NEWLY DEAD) brother.

The Bereaved is looking at the postcard. This is the last one he sent, when she was merely the Angry Big Sister and not yet the Bereaved. The little shit, a.k.a. the Drowned Brother, designed the postcard just to piss her off. It's addressed to Juniper Tree Burning, for one thing. It's in Russian, for another. Yes, he spoke Russian. The message is in Russian. She doesn't know the translation. The Bereaved holds the postcard so the audience glimpses the funny backwards letters: how tragic, all that learning down the tubes, or into the sea, and doubly tragic, that she doesn't know his last words. The card's picture is an old black-and-white photograph of those Russian buildings with onion-shaped roofs. The Bereaved's grandmother was Russian, and all of this is calculated to remind her that the Little Prick was family.

At the moment, I was again angry, which is to say, I felt much better. I folded the postcard and tossed it into the closet. Light seeped into the room. I chose an outfit for work. Why not? Should I have stayed home to play the part? On went the stockings, the cool green linen suit.

The sun had risen, and it was not such a marvelous trick. I thought, Well. This isn't so bad. The cat still hates me, my husband still sleeps, and I am dressed. Things proceed. I didn't miss my brother. What's to miss? As he himself pointed out, we had only seen each other five times in the past fourteen years.

Onward, then. I rolled my hair into a French twist and put on the red lips. The cat on the dresser glared at me. And in the mirror I saw Chris sit up, the dead rising. He said, "I'm so sorry about your brother."

"Don't be sorry," the Bereaved said. "It's not your fault." She picked up her purse.

"You're not going to work," Concerned Husband said.

Chris, I'm not trying to blame you, really I'm not, only why did you choose exactly the wrong thing to say? "I have to go," the Bereaved said.

"I love you," Concerned Husband said.

She sighed. "Please don't fuss over me," she said. "Please don't hover."

"Well." He looked at her a long time. "Call me if you need me. It has to hit you sometime."

She smiled. "Is that a prophecy, Mr. Braverman?"

He returned her smile, his face slack with relief. "A medical diagnosis," he said. "You have a case of human nature."

The Bereaved leaned over her Concerned Husband and kissed him good-bye. "I love you, James," she said, while Jennie stood at the door, tapping her foot and checking her watch. Come on now, let's hit the road. Places to go. People to see. Lots and lots of things to do. Her husband caught her arm. "Wait," he said. He knelt on the bed and cupped her face in his palms. "I love you, too," he said. "Remember that."

JIGGITY-JIG. On to my favorite gas station, called GAS, off I-25. Across the street, a car lot sells used pickups. TRUCKS, the place is called. The TRUCKS office is a trailer, and the same salesman always sits on the steps, smoking a cigarette, wearing a brown polyester suit. All summer long, I'd filled the tank, checking out the trucks across the street to the tune of the Polyester Truck Man's stare. It was a fair exchange. Ogling for coveting. I coveted a truck, a nice big mean-looking hunk of a pickup.

I knew Polyester Truck Man couldn't figure me out. This salesman, standing in the door of his office trailer, was thinking how he'd try to explain it to his friends later. This Ugly Chick, drives a Rolls-Royce, always wears a suit, puts her blond hair in a bun. But every time I look at her, alls I'm thinking is, I want to fuck this Ugly Chick.

I pumped gas, blinking against the sunlight refracting off the trucks. Polyester Truck Man nodded at me.

All summer, I'd had my eye on a 1976 F-150, your basic dun-colored Ford, a long rusty scar down one side, a traditional Ray Davis clunker. I loved that truck. It had been there for a year, and I had lots of ideas about it. I'd even looked it over and it was in great shape; some rancher had babied its engine and ignored its looks. Almost eighty thousand miles and I could get it for a song because my father had taught me well, my daddy the bargainer. Every day it was there was a small guarantee of something, perhaps that I could have that truck which had no place in the rest of my life. Today, the truck remained. Things were right in the world.

The GAS Boy, presumably the son of Polyester Truck Man, had a crush on me, or at least on the Rolls—he was always making conversation about the weather and his family, his sister up north in Denver who had packed her clothes in a garbage bag and left in the middle of the night. He loved to talk about the Rolls, though he knew about cars and knew it wasn't quite as special as it looked.

He was tall and skinny and pimply in a sad sixteen-year-old way, and usually I wanted to get the hell out of there, but I lingered that morning. The signs scattered around the shop were emphatically hand-lettered: ONLY TWO (2) TEENAGERS AT A TIME!!! NO BACKPACKS!!!

The boy said, "It's hot again." Well, there's something the Bereaved can't answer. The normality of small talk. What's she going to say, Yes, sigh, and my brother is dead, sigh.

"It'll rain later," I said. "Up north anyway."

"How's that Rolls?" he said.

"I'd rather have a truck."

"You should get one." He nodded in the general direction of the TRUCKS lot. "You can get one cheap."

They had a candy box filled with home-sewn hair ties for $2.99. There were also road maps. I bought one, and six doughnuts and a cup of coffee. "Taking a trip?" he said, putting my map in the bag with the doughnuts.

I shrugged. "Just to work. But you never know when you'll need one of these."

He nodded like that made sense. When I left, he called after me, "Have a good one!" He became my favorite person of the day. Blessed are the oblivious for they shall give me no trouble.

Instead of getting back in the car, I walked across the street to TRUCKS. I strolled through the lot, under the plastic triangles hanging limply in the sun. Polyester Truck Man watched me, trying to figure out what he'd tell his friends. That Ugly Chick was there today, walking through the lot like she knew what's up, and damn if she doesn't go to this heap that's been sitting for almost a year now, a 1976 Ford, in some places the dash is split open so wide you can slide four fingers in the crack, and the upholstery's ripped and the ceiling liner's torn out. But the engine's good, so the truck's a steal, and damn if that isn't where she stops.

I took his card, and before Ramses Smith, a man named for a condom or a pharaoh, could say anything, I told him I'd pay seven hundred dollars, cash. Half the asking price, but hey, it had been sitting there a year taking up space, so what did he care? Slowly, he drew his fingertip up and down the center of his long pointy nose. Once, twice. Up. Down. It came to me that he was scratching. "It's a ranch vee-hickle," he said. "Low miles. Twenty years old and seventy-seven thousand miles—that don't happen too often." His sweat showed through the comb rows in his hair and his shirt was yellow around the collar. He smelled like his cigarettes came from a white box labeled CIGA-RETTES. No wonder GAS Boy's sister ran away from home.

"I don't want to bargain," I said.

He muttered something about paperwork and led me to his shower stall of an office, where he left me to stew behind a closed door. I got up and went outside, where I leaned against the fender of my truck and started on another doughnut. I considered the Rolls beside the GAS pumps. I could see the boy inside washing the glass door. I saw myself over there every morning, and it occurred to me that all summer, Polyester Truck Man thought I was staring at him, and not at his trucks.

Speak of the devil. Here came Polyester Truck Man, huffing across the parking lot. "There you are!" he cried, waving his paperwork. "Thought I'd lost you!"

I chewed. I swallowed. "How awful for you," I said, and took a sip of coffee.

I signed on the hood of the Ford. I told him to wash the price off the windshield for me. I told him I'd be back within an hour.

I hated driving the Rolls home. Never had it felt so foreign, so ridiculous and garish and useless. It was not my car. I had my own vee-hickle now.

I knew Chris was at work by then, but as I opened the door, I called hello. If he'd answered, I'd have bolted; there's only so much sympathy a girl can take. The cat trotted out of the bathroom, meowing. The house was incredibly hot. Chris left the cooler off to save money, and the cat mostly spent the day lolling in the porcelain bathtub. I turned the cooler back on.

The plot, thickening: a wayward wife comes home in the middle of the morning and undresses. Her suit on the unmade bed looks like evidence of a tryst, so she makes the bed and hangs up her suit. Here is the cat, staring. *I knew it,* the cat's eyes say. The wife, now wearing jeans and a T-shirt and a ponytail, shoves running shorts and shoes into her backpack. She's in a hurry. Is this why she scoops the Drowned Brother's postcard into the bag?

In the kitchen I decided to take whiskey. Some perversity, maybe pleasure in my role, made me use the flask Sunny gave me last Christmas. It was engraved with the letters *JTB*. The Little Prick had left a trail of fuck-yous for me. I spilled whiskey on the floor and left it. I had to get out of there. I'd been in the apartment maybe five minutes, and I had a nagging feeling there was something I'd forgotten and would remember when I was too far away, but I couldn't stand still. I called a cab company. I scribbled a note. *I went,* I wrote, and paused. Where? *To Grandmother's house I go.* Does this mean I'm hysterical? Where? Not to Faith's, to break the news about her dead son. Not to my father's, Florida and sadness and cockroaches in his pissy bathroom. To Seattle? Where, the cop said, there would probably never be a body. Almost certainly drowned, he said, and I wondered, why soften it with "almost," when we both know which part of it is true?

I wrote *because.* Ha. You think the first question was hard. I scribbled a few more lines. I crumpled the note and began another. *I have to go,* I wrote. *I'm sorry. I'm fine.* I put it in an envelope. I stepped outside, locked the deadbolt, and taped the envelope over the door's gated window.

The two neighbor girls, maybe six and nine, were chalking rainbows on the sidewalk. The older one said, "I know you."

"No you don't," I said.

"You're that lady."

"No I'm not."

"You're ugly," the younger one said, and ran away, shrieking with laughter, to her house across the street. The older one stayed, her arms crossed, her legs spread, a defiant little soldier covering her sister's tail. She stared up at me, and I looked down at her. Her face and arms were very brown, and like her sister, her hair was brown and straight. They were two little brown berries. "Are you mad?" she asked.

"No."

The younger girl stuck her head out. "Ugly!" she screamed, and slammed the door.

"*Now* are you mad?"

I said, "Tell your sister I have a brain tumor and I'm dying tomorrow at eight-oh-five A.M. Tell her she's invited." Now, *that* was satisfying, a thing that felt more like myself than anything else that morning. The Ugly Chick gets mean.

I T wasn't betrayal and it wasn't a divorce; it was just a truck, like all the other battered used-up vee-hickles on the highways and back roads, a fine old pickup with lots of life left in it, hard-used for twenty years, used and traded and sold and used again, finally waiting for me on a lot in Albuquerque under the gently flapping red yellow and blue triangles. It was only a truck. It meant nothing, that I didn't put the Ford's key on my key chain, to clink against the rest of my life: house, work, bike. Some things are just what they seem to be: I was only in a rush to get the key in the truck's ignition.

I filled it up at GAS. "You bought a truck," GAS Boy said.

"You win the prize," I said.

"You going on vacation?"

I gave him the look. Slack features, hard eyes. It's a scary one. Essie taught me when I was fifteen. She stood behind me and watched me practice in the mirror.

"I mean, you know, the, uh, map, you, uh, bought," he said.

"I'm going to California," I said. "I have a brain tumor."

"Oh," he said. He looked down at the counter, at his hands, which were covered with doodles in ballpoint pen. His eyes, when he glanced up, were a lovely, wet brown, those horrible teenager eyes. They brimmed with the naked misery of a virgin whose cystic pimples are undisguisable evidence of his own hormones. "Oh," he said. "God."

"Don't worry," I said.

"Okay," he said. "I'm sorry."

"I have to go," I said.

"Okay."

"I have to go *now*," I said, backing away. I felt like a complete turd. "I'm sorry," I said, and then I left.

The truck roared along. I forced myself to eat. The doughnut made me sick, but I chewed and swallowed and wiped my fingers on the passenger seat. In the rearview, the Sandia Mountains, curved and broad, looked like the last glimpse of a whale's hump before it vanishes into the sea. Ahead lay Santa Fe and all points north, and it came to me that I could just keep going. I had a truck. I had doughnuts and a cup of coffee and a Road Map of the Western States, and what the hell, it's the open road, the highway that's my way, and what's better than a drive? The Ugly Chick Rides Again. Toss the Bereaved out the window. If she survives the impact, let her walk home, hook up with Concerned Husband. They can have a pity party, invite the paparazzi, entertain the neighborhood, weep into their cups, as long as it's without me.

$\mathcal{S}$ A f E T Y

T H E Y said the first snow would fall early this year, but here it is, two days before Christmas, and still no snow. It's freezing outside, though, and Faith keeps the fire roaring in both the cookstove and the fireplace. Ray has been gone four whole months, since Sunny was born. Tomorrow, Christmas Eve, they're having a Meeting so he'll come back. Faith and Joy and Jennie sit in the Middle Room, cleaning Medicine for the Meeting, and its tart earth smell fills the hot room. Joy and Faith cut the Medicine buttons into long strips they hang over twine strung between the vigas. Sunny Boy Blue sleeps snugly in his cradleboard.

Jennie, sitting beside the fireplace, pulls the white tufts from the centers of the buttons, and the fuzzy pile looks like dandelion seeds. She throws them into the fire, which breathes on her like a dragon's wide-open mouth. Thank you for the dandelion seeds, and now I will eat you, Little Girl.

Faith stands on a chair to hang a strip of Medicine. She says, "I wish Clarence could Run the Meeting," and now she's crying again. Jennie is so sick of her crying. Half the time she cries because Clarence hasn't shown up, and half the time because Ray hasn't. It's so stupid. Faith should be thinking about more important things, like who will fix the house. Instead, Faith's big plan is the Meeting, which makes Jennie mad. Faith says, "I don't know why I can't find him."

Jennie hates Meetings, especially on Christmas. A Christmas Meeting is about a bunch of kids sleeping on her bedroom floor, taking her things. Last year, she wore her only nice sweater, a pretty grass-green with little yellow flowers on it. But a girl liked it, and Faith made Jennie give it to her. If a person admires anything, you're supposed to give it to them. Faith always says, "You'll get back tenfold what you give away." Jennie still doesn't have a nice sweater, so Faith is wrong.

Jennie doesn't want to give away the feeling of hate that needles inside her and sews up her heart. Hate makes her feel better. She hates Joy, and Meetings. She hates Medicine, which tastes horrible, bitter, and gives you a stomachache, and she hates the Church for saying Medicine is God, which is impossible, and she hates Faith for crying all the time. But she doesn't hate Sunny, strapped to his cradleboard, sleeping in front of the fireplace. She loves him so. She hates that his first Christmas will be all wrong. If only it were just Jennie and Sunny, Jack Frost and jingle bells, chestnuts roasting on an open fire, and stockings hung with care. They have the fireplace, but they don't even have a Christmas tree yet. Jennie and Ray always got one, but now Ray is gone and Jennie will have to get it herself.

"You know what I think?" Faith says. "I think Ray was my punishment for things I've done."

"Men are always punishment," Joy says. "They screw you and then they leave town."

Faith says, "He wasn't normal, that way. He had to do it all the time. Two, three times a day sometimes. I was never safe." Faith stares into the fire. "Better he's jumping on that Mary than on me."

They think Jennie doesn't know what they're talking about, but she does. They're talking about sex, and nine-year-old children are not supposed to hear about such things. But she wants to pretend she never heard, and if she says anything, then she can't pretend. She tries to block out their voices with thoughts of Paul, and Lipa, and the house on the highest hill.

"I'm all alone," Faith whispers. "He said he'd come and he didn't."

She means Clarence. Jennie, yanking Medicine tufts and throwing them in the fire, feels guilty, a little. She knows Ray isn't with Mary, and she knows that if she could only call her father a liar, Faith would maybe feel better. But instead, Jennie lets the mad fill her up. Faith doesn't really want Ray to come back. She wants Clarence. So Faith is a traitor, and if she prays for Ray to come back, then she's lying to God. Ray was right to sell the piano because it's worth a lot of money and they need money. If it weren't for Joy, Faith would understand that and everything would be fine.

Joy sprinkles dried cedar on the coals. She prays, "Heavenly Father, thank you for this Medicine." The cedar smolders, and Joy uses a fan of red-tailed hawk feathers to wave the smoke at Faith. "Bless Faith, Heavenly Father, who needs your help, Heavenly Father." Faith starts crying again. Joy fans smoke at Jennie. "Bless, Juniper, Heavenly Father, in her time of need, Heavenly Father."

The fire crackles and the cedar smoke clouds the air. Children can't breathe if the whole house is filled with smoke. Joy should realize this. What about Sunny? The blue fumes settle into their clothes and hair; they eat up the oxygen and every breath lets a little more smoke into Sunny's lungs; he'll suffocate. Nobody cares. Joy is in charge now. Faith prays when Joy says pray, and peels Medicine when Joy says peel. Joy is Faith's sister, Meeting Way, and Faith says she's Jennie's aunt. Joy is short and fat and smells bad. Jennie cups her hands over her nose and mouth so she doesn't choke on Joy's stink and cedar fumes. Joy says, "Put out your hands." Jennie glares at Joy, thinking, I hate you. You are not in charge of me. She does not hold out her hands.

"Juniper Tree Burning," her mother says. "If you keep acting like a brat, you know what will happen."

"Dad's not here anymore," Jennie says. "Remember?"

But Faith doesn't start crying. "God will punish you," she says. "Bad things happen to people who don't stay on the Meeting Way." She tells the story of a friend of a friend who fell off the Meeting Way and drank all the time and one time he even hit his mother, and then he got bitten by a brown recluse, a terrible spider whose poison makes your skin swell and then rot.

Jennie looks at Sunny, sleeping in his cradleboard, and she imagines a brown recluse in the ceiling, dropping down on its invisible web to bite Sunny's face, which would swell up and rot away, and he'd be dead before morning. Who will watch over Sunny when he's sleeping? Jennie doesn't think she's brave enough to do it. "Stop talking about these things," she says.

Faith says, "This man had this crater in his thigh that just kept rotting and rotting until you could see all the way to the bone. They almost cut off his leg. But then they had a Meeting for him, and prayed hard, and he ate a lot of Medicine, and he got better. Put out your hands, Juniper."

Jennie holds her palms out, and Joy pats her down with the fan, waving smoke all over her. Jennie closes her eyes and pretends to pray. She wonders if God will be mad at her for faking it, and this scares her, so she starts a prayer for real. Heavenly Father, thank you for Sunny. You're supposed to start with gratitude before you ask for things.

"Heavenly Father," Joy prays. "Show Ray that he is on the wrong road, Heavenly Father, and put him on the True Road, Heavenly Father." That doesn't make sense. Why is Joy praying to bring back Ray when they think he's Faith's punishment? They are the two stupidest people in the world, Joy and Faith.

On and on Joy goes. Church Prayers go on forever. Faith cries and Joy prays until she cries, too, and the room fills with stinking cedar smoke. Sunny Boy Blue fusses, probably because he can't breathe, and Jennie picks him up, cradleboard and all. He quiets down in her arms, and his lip pouts out and he sucks it back in, his cheeks moving. He's dreaming about nursing.

When the prayer finally ends, Faith feeds the fire, crying. "The thing that kills me," she says, "is that my—" Her voice cracks, and she whispers, "My father, I was his only child, and he couldn't even say good-bye. He couldn't even send something, a note, a letter, anything with the piano."

Sadness fills Jennie up and drives out the hate and suddenly she's saying, "I found something."

Faith says, "What did you say?"

"In the piano," Jennie whispers. Why, why does she say it? It just popped out. She saw her mother crying and out it came. "It was an accident."

"Accident?" Faith says softly. "You go get it. Whatever you found, you give it to me." The fireplace makes Faith sweat, and wisps of hair stick to her cheeks and neck. She's beautiful, Jennie thinks, confused. Faith says, "I'm talking to you. You go. Get. It. *Now.*"

In her room, Jennie digs under the pile of freebox clothes. She leaves Treasured Memories behind and takes only the rules to Faith. Like a test.

Faith snatches the papers and glances at them, a greedy, quick once-over, and then her face crumbles. "God," she whispers. "Daddy."

"What is it?" Joy asks.

Faith shakes her head. "Nothing," she says, "nothing at all," and then she throws the pages into the fire, and Jennie grabs her mom's arm, but Faith pushes her away, saying, "Don't touch me!" and she stirs the flames with the poker and the smell of burning paper mixes with the smell of piñon smoke and cedar needles, and Jennie hates her mother so much and she almost cries because her mother just burned something written in Jennie's own grandfather's hand. "Why did you burn them?" she whispers. "They were mine, too. He was *my* grandpa—"

"You shut up! Shut up! It's none of your business and you don't know anything about it, and you are just like your father—" Faith, the poker raised, gives herself away with her face. She *hates* Jennie, and Jennie hates her back, and hate makes her say, "Clarence won't come, and you can have every Meeting in the world but he isn't coming and you should be glad because he's the one who helped Daddy steal the piano, and no wonder Daddy's with Mary—"

Faith slaps her so hard that Jennie's eyes water, only not because of the slap, but for the rules Faith burned, for Grandpa Paul. Don't cry, she tells herself. Don't you dare cry. Sunny whimpers. There is nothing she can do, and she is going to cry and so she leaves, slamming the kitchen door behind her as hard as she can, and she runs. She runs down the dirt road, into the stumbling black night, and she runs until she's so tired she just sits on the side of the road and she will not, will not cry, but now she is crying.

She looks up at the sky, black and big with stars which she tries to count until she catches her breath and forces her tears to stop. She gives up counting. Too many, and why bother? Nothing matters. She tries to remember how the road looks in daytime. She rubs her shoe through the dust and closes her eyes to make everything colored again. Why do things go black and white in the dark? There are piñons and junipers growing all over the hillsides, and even though they aren't triangle trees, this is where she'll get a Christmas tree tomorrow. She doesn't care about Christmas anymore, but she'll get the tree for Sunny. She's teeth-chattering freezing, but even that doesn't matter. In the valley, Christmas lights blink, and she can see Randall's house, with the glowing plastic Santa and his reindeer and his sleigh. Normal people are down there, snug and safe in their normal houses.

Then she remembers where she is, with the sagebrush all around her, and the dark little nooks and crannies, and she feels the crawling of spiders, and she leaps up and thrashes at her neck and her body and she slaps her hands up and down her legs, and she runs toward home, feeling every whisper of wind, dust; anything that touches her skin could be a spider.

She stops in the driveway because she's afraid of the spiders inside the house. Through the window, she watches Joy and her mother in the golden warm kitchen, playing with Sunny. Jennie, shaking, hugs herself. They look happy in there, laughing, talking, safe. But there's no safe place. In the next six years, she'll have many brushes with spiders; a black widow will dangle before her eyes as she stands washing dishes. None will be worse than the night she finds a spider spinning a canopy over the sleeping Sunny Boy Blue, the skeins fastened to the four sides of his crib. But she doesn't have to know the future to understand the truth. She wills her mother to hold Sunny Boy Blue tighter and pray for help from God. Pray, she thinks. Because there's nowhere to go. Everywhere, spiders are waiting to get her family, and there's nothing she can do, put over their heads, wrap up in, to escape.

I N the morning, which is Christmas Eve, Jennie hikes through the hills, looking for a tree. The best one she finds is small and scraggly, but she can put the bare scraggly side to the wall. She drags it home and sets it up in the Middle Room. "Here's your first Christmas tree," she whispers to Sunny. She's afraid to touch him, because her hands are black with pitch, but she props him up in his cradlcboard so he can watch while she nails two boards to the trunk, like her father always does. As much as she can, she'll make Christmas right for him. This, she thinks, this I can do.

Faith thinks the tree is Jennie's peace offering. She says, "You can't just bring a tree and make it all better." Faith cooks all day, getting ready for the Meeting, and she makes Jennie wash the dishes. Faith makes bread, and cookies, and pumpkin pie without measuring the ingredients, and Jennie licks the bowl before she washes it. If she didn't hate her mom, she'd be proud because it's so delicious. But, she thinks, dipping the mixing bowl into the rinse water, I hate her. So I'm not proud.

Faith, fluting the edge of a pie crust, stops in her tracks and stares out the window. A car is pulling into their driveway, a white car that looks like a police cruiser on a TV show. Jennie thinks two things. First, that the police will arrest them for having Medicine. Then, My daddy died.

But it isn't a policeman; it's Ray, her father, her daddy, her dad. He gets out of the car, as alive as ever. He has grown a shaggy red beard. Faith gasps. "That motherfucker," she says. "I don't fucking believe this." It makes Jennie's stomach clench to hear Faith says *those words*, which God forbids, and which Jennie has never, ever heard Faith say. Faith says, "Will you look at this? Can you believe this?" She goes outside, and Ray smiles his beautiful smile. Faith yells.

Jennie watches them fighting. She picks up Sunny Boy Blue in his cradle-board and watches. Her father, fighting, sees her and waves. I'm not happy to see you, Jennie tells him in her head. You have been gone four months and you can't just drive up happy. I'm going to throw up.

Her father's voice. Her mother's crying. Ray comes into the kitchen, the door slamming behind him. He says, cheerfully, like any old day, "Ho ho ho, Juniper Tree Burning! Guess what Santa brought?" He stands there with his messy beard and his long red hair and his belly hanging over his jeans. She isn't happy to see him. "A car, that's what!" She wants him to be a principal or a teacher with a tie, bald, a person who knows how to be normal. He says, "Juniper, you and me, we're going for a drive in Santa's new white car." Jennie knows it will be worse than ever before, that things are going to fall like rain around their heads, or like the house which crumbles where the walls are cracked and splitting apart.

FAITH comes with them like she doesn't want to get left behind where she can't yell at Ray, who has grown a beard like a fire on his chin, red and thick. "Listen to that engine," he says. "Isn't it smooth?"

Sitting between her parents, Jennie listens. Leaning against Ray, she waits for the first screwup, misstep, backfire in the smooth-running engine. But Faith says, "Ray, I don't care. I don't care if you brought a fucking Rolls-Royce home." That word again, coming from her mother's mouth. It makes Ray go fast, the car close to the edge. Rocks bounce down the black canyon walls. Why is Faith so mad? Hasn't God answered her prayers? But Jennie reminds herself of the truth: Faith wanted Clarence, not Ray. That's what Faith gets for lying to God.

Ray tells Jennie, "Its engine is huge, like a cop car, because it *is* a cop car, and that's irony for you. Do you know what irony is, kid? It's a rat chewing on your tired ass. Listen to that engine. Smooth engine, don't you think? It's a V-8, Juniper." He slaps the steering wheel and hums "I Shot the Sheriff." The car's black dashboard has holes where the police radio used to be. Clean and shiny, it comes from a world where people eat breakfast cereal from Safeway and TV. The black vinyl seats are cold and crunchy, but then the heater warms them up.

"Isn't it nice, Mom?" Jennie tells Faith. "It's practically new."

"Don't bug me," Faith says. She holds Sunny, who's half asleep on Faith's lap. "I need to get back. I have bread baking." She rolls down the window and curves her hand into the airstream. It's too cold, and Jennie worries she'll get sick, and she tugs on Faith's belt loop, but her mother pushes her away. "Stop hanging on me," she says. "Why do you always hang on me?" Faith bounces Sunny on her knee.

Ray turns onto the bumpy narrow road that descends to the river. He says, "It has good brakes. It's got low miles. Come on, Faith. Be happy."

"Where did you get it? From that Mary? Or did you use my money? From *my* piano?"

"Don't start again, Faith. Please don't start."

"Then this car is mine," Faith says. "Bought with *my*—"

Ray slams on the brakes, the car sliding close to the canyon cliff. The car stalls. He asks Jennie, "You want to steer?" He lifts her onto his lap and starts the car again. "You better steer," he says. The car drifts toward the edge, and Jennie grabs the wheel.

Her mother says, "Don't kill us." Sunny coos, happy now. Stupid baby. Jennie can't look at him or they'll all be dead. The car will bounce down the side of the canyon, splattering them into pieces of blood and bone. Her eyes must stay on the road and her hands on the steering wheel. All of her muscles strain to reach the pedals, even though she'll never reach them.

Ray speaks in a voice stretched tight as Jennie's muscles. "There was an auction in Santa Fe. Government cars. Clarence went with me." The trick is, you have to get everybody else in the room to think you don't really care, and then you come in and raise the price while nobody's thinking about it."

"You're an Aries," her mother says. "You just ram right ahead. You don't think. Think about this: you've been gone four months. You have a four-month-old son. My bread is burning."

"So there's this fat redneck guy who wants the car, I guess because it looks like a cop car. But I just look over at him. I know he's thinking, This guy's on some kind of illegal drug. I just keep staring at him while Clarence bids. Scared the shit out of the guy."

Faith says softly, "You'll never grow up. You're a man who's so smart but you can't even make a fireplace that works. What good are all those brains? What good is reading all those facts, when you can't even remember that we're too poor for a new car? You don't think about that. You're like a little boy. You only want to play let's pretend."

"Faith," Ray says. "Faith, please."

Jennie says, "I like the car," because Ray sounds so whale-sad. She says it again, more firmly. "I love the new car."

Then silence. No one talks.

But on the way home, Faith sits on Ray's lap and steers, and they giggle and grope, and Ray drives crazy fast, fifty miles an hour, so they careen around curves and throw up gravel like confetti. Jennie sits by the window, holding Sunny, keeping her eyes closed. It's not so bad if she keeps her eyes closed.

When they get home, her parents leave the car doors hanging open, and Ray growls like a bear and chases Faith up to their bedroom. "Wait till I get you," he roars. "I'll eat you up!"

"Help!" Faith cries, laughing. "Help, he's got me!"

Upstairs, her parents make all kinds of noises that children shouldn't hear. "God," her father shouts. "GodGodGod." Sunny looks up at her, so calm, so serious, so trusting, a happy old-man baby. "Tonight is Christmas Eve," she tells him. "They shouldn't be acting this way." Jennie takes the fresh loaves of bread out of the oven. In the Middle Room, she stokes the fireplace fire nice and hot, and she throws the bread into the flames. Then she gets her fairy-tale book that her father gave her and she throws that in the fire too. These are signs to them. See what happens when you don't pay attention?

Jennie carries Sunny outside to sit in the car. Sunny tugs at her hair and she kisses him absently. All of a sudden, she hates this car. She wishes for a flood to wash the car away, down the road and back to whatever police station it came from, where the cops sit chewing cigars and plotting to take all the pot-smoking, Medicine-eating hippies to jail. Or better, she wishes the water would dump the car in the Rio Alfin, and the Rio Alfin would take it to the Rio Grande, and it would float out to the middle of the Gulf of Mexico, and they'd never see it again.

She's freezing. She holds Sunny in her lap and braces her soles against the windshield. She pushes hard. Under her sneakers, a crack forms on the windshield, spreading like a silver snake across the glass, and she smiles.

The loaves and the book didn't burn. They're only scorched, and their weight put out the fire. Upstairs, her parents are quiet. Jennie throws water into the fireplace and then takes the bread and the book and throws them down the outhouse hole. When Faith asks about the bread, Jennie says, "It was burned up. I threw it away." Ray never asks about the fairy-tale book. What good is revenge if he doesn't notice it? When he finds the crack in the windshield, he blames himself, his crazy speeding, gravel flying in the air.

For years, Faith will use Ray's return for proof of God's Power. She'll say, "God brought your father back to us."

"It was Christmas," Jennie will say. "He came for my birthday. And for Christmas."

"Which is the same thing," Faith will say.

I n the afternoon, people start arriving for the Meeting. Into the tipi they go, carrying pillows for kneeling, and Medicine boxes filled with their holy things, and back to the house they come, to eat standing up, gulping coffee before a long sleepless night. They let out the heat, track in the mud.

The Church doesn't know what it is. It's Christian and Indian mixed together, and the people are whites and different tribes, Pueblo and Navajo and others, all mixed together. The women of the Church wear their long hair in braids or bound in ponytails, and beaded earrings, and when there's a Meeting, they wear moccasins and shawls. They're quiet around men but noisy in the kitchen, working, laughing. When they have their periods they aren't allowed to go into the tipi, but even when they go in, and stay up all night, they still cook a huge Second-Day Feast. It makes Jennie sick, the way they peel and slice and stir and pretend they aren't mad, even though the men sit in the Middle Room telling boring stories and napping. That's how to be a woman. You cook for a hundred people on Christmas Day.

The men wear Levi's and boots and sometimes cowboy hats or baseball caps. For Meetings they wear cowboy shirts decorated with thin satin ribbons. They barely speak and they seem like they know a secret. They hold their lips together tight and they have serious eyes, and they always look like they're thinking something important. They look like they might be thinking, I won't tell. I won't. Or else they look mad.

Finally, it's time. They'll sit up all night, praying and singing.

Jennie has to baby-sit. It's harder to take care of the kids with Sunny Boy Blue in her arms, but when the drumming starts in the tipi, they fall asleep in a carpet of blankets and bags and heads and thumbs. Jennie rocks Sunny and listens to the drums and wonders if praying made Ray come home. She studies the crack, which seems to grow as she stares at it. She imagines the house moaning, the crack like a wound splitting apart. She pictures baby black widows swarming out of the crack like blood, and her scalp crawls. Outside they drum and sing Indian songs. Jennie thinks, Yes. Pray. Pray hard. Pray for all of us. See if it does any good.

The Christmas lights blink in the Middle Room. Jennie hangs up their stockings and goes outside. She climbs the hill and stands under the pear tree. The tipi glows from the fire, which makes shadows of the people praying inside. In the valley, the Christmas lights of the Alfin homes wink at her. The people pray and sing and then, when the songs end, silence. They cough, adjust how they kneel, eat Medicine, and the fire fills the tipi with warmth and light. Outside, Jennie shivers, and wants to sing, wants to pray, forgive me oh please forgive me, Heavenly Father, come into my heart and make me warm again.

I N the early, dark morning, just before dawn, the mothers wake their children to go in the tipi for Morning Water. When Faith comes this time, smelling like cedar, like smoke and the cold snowy air, she whispers, "You have to bring in Morning Water."

Jennie's heart squeezes. "Me? Why? I can't. I don't know how."

Faith says that her period came and she can't go back in the tipi, and Ray wants Jennie. "Your father *asked* for you," Faith says. "It's a great honor. It means you're becoming a woman." She says if Jennie wants everything to be right again, if she wants Ray to stay and the house to get fixed and the piano returned, then she has to bring in Morning Water.

Jennie puts on a dress and moccasins and Faith wraps her embroidered shawl around her, whispering that she should thank God first, for Ray's return, for Sunny, and then ask for things. Pray for Joy's dad, who's sick, and don't forget the Pedros, and Sequoia who has German measles.

The children, half dreaming, stumble to the tipi with their mothers. Jennie goes to the well to draw Morning Water. The Drum starts, a quick beat, light and strong at the same time, and then Ray sings, his voice deep, round like the velvet purple of the sky. Jennie carries the bucket up the hill. She's supposed to stand outside the tipi door, and she's supposed to look hard at the morning star in the deep purple sky, and she's supposed to pray. She has the four Morning Water Songs to pray, and then she has to go inside the tipi.

"Heavenly Father God, thank you," she whispers, "for my mother and my Sunny Boy Blue, and Daddy and Heavenly Father God—" She's supposed to be grateful. Does she have to thank Him for the house? For spiders? Can God tell when she doesn't mean it?

She prays. She prays as she has heard her mother pray so many times, the words falling from her lips; she prays and prays, wanting to feel God, the way Faith says God will come if Jennie only tells Him, "God, I've made a place for you in my heart." Jennie's voice catches and a tear rolls down her cheek and she's so proud of her tear. Faith always cries when she prays. The Drum matches Jennie's heartbeat, and Ray's voice is like breath, rising and falling, rising again.

The wire handle of the water bucket digs into her palm and pulls on her arm, her shoulder. She shivers and pulls her shawl tighter. Even though she cries that one tear, and even though she prays, and even though she looks as hard as she can at the morning star, she doesn't feel Him; God stays away, and maybe this is why Jennie cries. Because though she prays, "Please keep my daddy home," she can't believe that God brought Ray back, or that God even cares.

After the Morning Water songs, the Fireman opens the tipi door. All the people kneel in a circle, around the altar made of packed sand shaped into a crescent moon. The ashes of the whole night are spread inside the crescent, like the old moon in the new moon's arms.

She kneels Meeting Way, sitting on her feet, between the door and the flames. All the people look at her with their tired, up-all-night eyes. The fire crackles and pops, and sparks fly up to heaven, carrying their prayers to God. The Cedar Man throws cedar on the coals and Jennie holds her palms up and he blesses her with his Fan. He sits. Everyone is quiet. Someone coughs and clears his throat.

Jennie says, "I brought water in for you, Daddy."

His face glows with firelight. She can feel him love her. He says, "Thank you, Juniper Tree Burning."

She says, "Thank you for asking me to bring it." The Fireman holds out the stick he's been using to tend the Fire, and with its coal-tipped end she lights the Prayer Smoke of tobacco rolled in a corn husk. The butts from people's prayers are lined around the Moon; just before the Meeting ends, the Fireman will put them on the coals so the smoke can take the rest of their prayers to God.

She takes four puffs and blows it out and says, "Heavenly Father God." She prays, and she stares hard into the flames. She doesn't cry. They listen and she feels their eyes as she asks for all Faith told her to request—heal our friends guard our hopes, thank you for food and water and this fire, for everything, thank you God. She tries to pray for all the men and women sitting in this circle. Don't let me forget anyone. Her back is cold and her face burning and the fire crackles, the wood pops. She is half dark, half light, she is Morning Water Woman, not yet ten, and she cannot feel God inside her.

Then, through the flames, Jennie sees Sunny Boy Blue wide awake in Joy's arms, with Joy's fingers in his black silky hair, looking through the fire, straight into Jennie's eyes, and he sees into her heart; he sees that God never got in. She prays. "Heavenly Father God, thank you for Sunny's life, he almost died, Heavenly Father, when he was born, Heavenly Father, thank you," and she cannot feel the hand of God, but the rooms of her heart are filled with love for Sunny Boy Blue, for his sweet baby eyes on the other side of the fire. She is weeping, they will think for God, but it isn't God at all. It isn't even her father. It is Sunny Boy Blue that she's grateful for, that she mourns for, prays to, loves.

GRUDGE BET

I'v e never liked Santa Fe. Albuquerque is more honest—plain old brown desert. In Santa Fe, everything seems prettified for the tourists: the theme-park New Mexico, with fancy colors, red dirt, intensely blue sky, even pink blacktop, stained by the salt they use after snowstorms. The round, low bushes dotting the hillside are too regularly spaced, too round, like a child's misunderstanding of trees. But that morning, in my new truck, the rose-brown hills dotted with piñons and junipers were beautiful. I couldn't get over how cheerful I felt. I decided to shoot up around the Sangre de Cristos and over the border into Colorado. I'd just go until I didn't feel like going anymore. It's the Jennie way.

She left home when she was the ripe age of fourteen, our Jennie, to live with Essie, the aforementioned fairy godmother of the running water and cheese blintzes. Some people might say, But how could your mother let you go? She was your *mother*, they might say, as if that word had a given, singular definition, and not as many definitions as there are daughters in the world. You were only *fourteen*, they might say, thinking of the fifties, of poodle skirts and sock hops and boys carrying books home. These people, members of the ordinary world—Saturday morning cartoons, Sunday morning breakfast—see a mother in an apron, with a spatula in her hand, casting out her only daughter. That's why they ask the final question, with all its pancake breakfast underpinnings: *How could she?*

This is what I see, my definition of mother, of fourteen:

I see the two of them, Faith and her daughter, standing in the driveway on Christmas Day. Faith holds a knife in her hand. It could be a butcher knife; I have always let people believe a butcher knife. But I remember she had been slicing pumpkin bread. So it could also be a bread knife. I see Faith standing with a knife in the driveway, and I imagine she is thinking, My life adds up to this. This is the sum of its parts and years.

Faith says, "I never made peace with my father and now he's dead."

"So?" Juniper says. "So? You won't make me feel sorry for you." Then she leaves, to Essie Leeman's, the fairy godmother, the rich woman. Faith imagines this Esther Leeman, with her bubble baths and fine china, and she, Faith, closes her eyes, and she sees everything she longs for: Goody hair curlers. Stockings and razor blades. Tweezers and glue, and false eyelashes like captive spiders. Deodorant. Talc. Perfume. Easing into a bath run straight hot. A gray, close sky blocking off distance and light; radiators, smoked salmon, red brick. Girdles and bras.

Snap out of it, she tells herself. You do not miss your father's house, the Steinway. You hated playing it, remember? You do not miss the rain. Not the beautiful locks, the rise and fall of boats traveling between Lake Washington and Puget Sound, the elegant simplicity of a mechanism even you can understand.

The following day, her daughter returns. Faith, polishing a bracelet made by Clarence, takes some comfort in the solid, linear beauty of the thing, but she can't catch her breath. She is, in fact, holding her breath. This is why, when her daughter says, "It's time for me to go," Faith can only let out a long, shuddering sigh. She thinks, Better this way. Better this way, out the door, than through a window in the night. A daughter can always come back, through the door. Let her go. Let her take what Essie Leeman offers. Because an open hand, unlike a fist, can wave hello as well as good-bye.

She says to her daughter, "I think you're right." And it wasn't a failure of motherhood. I am her daughter. Driving toward Santa Fe on my first day of being a Sister Whose Brother Is Dead, I finally know this: letting her daughter go was a gift. It was my mother's finest moment, her best act of love.

JENNIE is nearing the Saint Francis exit, her last chance. Pass it and she's on the road out of this messed-up life. But she hasn't passed it; she has lost her nerve and she's off the highway, headed into Santa Fe. She passes the street where her mother lives. She turns into the driveway. Decisions about leaving are not so easily hers to make. The cops called Jennie. So it falls to Jennie to tell Faith that her son is dead.

"Oh," my mother said when she opened the door, "it's you." She always calls me You. But it's the same with everyone. She calls Ray Your Father and Chris is always Him, as in, "Ask Him if he wants breakfast." Sunny is the only exception. He's never Your Brother or Your Son. He is always Sunny Boy Blue, her darling baby boy.

Was, the Bereaved whispers, hisses, cackles. Was. It's these little slipups that give you away, Jennie my dear, my own little darling.

Even on the front step, I could smell the sulfur reek of Faith's workroom. I

could see her walls, covered with photographs of herself, as if she were still trying to understand who she is. My favorite hangs in the living room, a picture
of her wearing gold hoop earrings and a peasant dress. She's holding a baby,
me. My face is a clenched fist (You were a terrible baby, she always said, always screaming). Faith in the picture is a small, buxom girl, pretty, laughing,
her dark hair in pigtails. Chris says he likes my mother. I tell him, "That only
proves you don't know her very well." Once I had a dream and woke up
yelling at Chris: *You took her side!*

Faith asked, "Why are you here?" Not out of hostility but curiosity.

"Good question," I said. I stood on the front step, not invited in. It had
never been my home, this rented house of hers. She moved here with Sunny
and Clarence. And then Sunny went to live with my father, and then Clarence left her alone with her flowers and her photographs. Lush flower beds
lined the walk. Bleeding hearts under a weeping willow. Nasturtiums, phlox,
hollyhocks—my eyes watered, and the colors blurred. I made a bet with myself. Ten bucks says she'll tell her friends that I stopped by, and I was a little
grumpy, maybe, but you know Juniper. Always a little grumpy. Capricorn, you
know. She seemed just fine.

God, how would I do it? How would I say, Your son, your beloved darling
Sunny Boy Blue—the answer was, I would not do it.

"I was a little early for work," I said.

"I'm already working. I have to finish an order."

"I'm just here a second. To say hello."

"You work in those clothes?"

Surprised, I looked down at my jeans. I'd forgotten. And Faith, she always
makes me fight back. "I'm the boss," I said. "I can wear whatever the fuck I
want."

She flinched. "I have to finish this order," she said again. "I've got the silver
ready, but—" She glanced over her shoulder. She's always working. She always seems to be teetering on the precipice of hysteria, having taken on just
more than she can do.

"I'll stop by another time," I said, desperate to get away. "I'm sorry I interrupted you."

Now she looked wounded. "You're leaving?"

"I have to get to work."

"Well," Faith said uncertainly. "I guess you can come back after work, if
you want."

"Maybe," I said, lamely, ridiculously. We both knew I wouldn't stop by. I
held out my arms. "I just wanted to say hi," I said. "I've been busy. I haven't
seen you." Hadn't, in fact, since my wedding.

She's so small, this Faith, this particular mother. Jennie takes her mother into her arms, this tiny woman who gave birth to a behemoth. If I straightened, Jennie thinks, Faith's feet wouldn't touch the ground. Mommy. My mother. Mom. It must have been such a relief when her son came along, a short boy, his height closer to her eye level, easier to embrace and understand. A Leo, a lion. A leader of men, with hair the color of hers.

He was mine, too. He was my brother. He was her son. He stood between us, joining us and separating us. I want to think, How could she? How could she love him more? How could she keep him close and send me away? But the truth is, I understand.

Faith. I see back to the younger woman you were, weeping, holding your baby boy in your arms. This one is mine, that young Faith thinks. We will love each other best, she thinks. Poor Faith. You cannot possibly know the future. You shouldn't even try to guess.

THE Ford started right away, to my satisfaction. Holding tight to the wheel, I admired its chugging, deep-throated idle. I summoned up my mother's crimes. How she asked, *Are you okay?* On *my* wedding, not his. I summoned her indifference to my tears, the time she raised a frying pan and told me I was so worthless I might as well be dead. I hypnotized myself into believing I was ordinary, and then I hated her for letting me leave at fourteen. I tallied the times she called me when I was in New Hampshire at John Paul Robinson School for Girls (zero). I remembered how, when Sunny was in Germany and then in Russia, she recorded all their (many) phone calls on her answering machine: first love, first hangover, first Russian swear words. His voice wavering and stretching on the overplayed tape. Sunny. "I got drunk for the first time, Mom. On vodka. They won't let me drink the water here." Which he had written on a postcard to me as well, so that I felt a twinge of jealousy and disappointment when I heard it. And how, days before my wedding, Faith said, "Be nice to Sunny, for once, when he gets here." Leaning confidentially into my groom. "She was always a little mean to Sunny. Once she locked him in a car on the hottest day of August. Tell him about it, Juniper."

He's dead. If I actually said the words, this woman would fall to her knees, howling. *Not Sunny Boy Blue, not my baby boy!* and we'd both know she'd give anything to lose me instead. I'm not whining about it; this is simply a fact of her nature. Call it astrology, as she would.

Once I had a nice head of anger going, I pulled away from the curb. Full steam ahead, onward to the plaza, off to greet the people! Off to work we go, whistle, whistle, all the livelong day.

THE HAPPY ENDING

ɪ f. If the piano had never come. If Ray had never built a fireplace which caused a crack which made him steal the piano. If I had never stolen the album; if I hadn't told Sunny all those stories and if Faith hadn't found us, if we hadn't stood in the driveway, with the album burned, and Sunny's birthday tomorrow, and Faith and Ray fighting upstairs.

Faith screams, "You fucking thief! Is everyone in this family a thief?"

"Stop them," Sunny whispers. "Jennie, make them stop."

Thief, meaning me, Jennie thinks. I am the thief.

"Please," Sunny says. Jennie doesn't want to go up there, to crashing, to the unmistakable sound of glass breaking. She's afraid. But she can't tell Sunny.

Ray comes out of the house with the blue wrought-iron headboard on his back. Where is he taking it? Sunny was born on that bed. "Daddy?" He ignores her. He leans the headboard against the cottonwood trunk and goes inside. He returns with the footboard, and then with the mattress, and this time Faith comes, too. She stops in front of Jennie. "You're just like your father," she says. "I could kill you."

Ray piles the frame and the mattress on the roof of the white car, which isn't new anymore. He ties it down with rope. Jennie and Sunny stay very quiet. Faith screams at Ray, "I want a divorce! I want a divorce!"

Ray says, "Don't be an idiot, Faith. Divorce isn't a potato. You can't just waltz in and buy one."

She yells, "Now! We're going now!"

Jennie and Sunny go into the kitchen, where the cake has burned, and on top of the stove the chiles are also burned. Faith follows them. She says, "You're coming with us. We're filing for divorce."

"It's Sunny's birthday," Jennie says.

"What's a divorce?" Sunny asks.

"His birthday's tomorrow. Today we're getting a divorce."

"Can we go swimming?" Sunny asks. He's just a little boy, Jennie thinks. None of this should happen to a little boy. Kids are supposed to have balloons and cake. "You better take us swimming," Jennie says, and to her amazement, Faith agrees. So Jennie and Sunny sit in the backseat in bare feet and swimsuits with their towels rolled in their hands. Sunny still wants to know what "divorce" means.

"We're splitting up," Faith tells him.

"*You* are, anyway," Ray says. "Cracking up."

"You always have to say something, don't you?" Faith says.

Sunny looks so scared. Jennie rolls down her window, but the wind can't drown out the sound of the two of them fighting. "He's got all kinds of ideas," Faith says, "but he's no good at loving people." She won't say his name.

Ray drives with one finger at the bottom of the steering wheel. The anger shimmers off him like the hot wavering air that rises from the highway. On the asphalt ahead, puddles form, reflect the sky, and disappear.

Jennie thinks about Cortez. She thinks about explorers everywhere, and how when they crossed the desert or sea, for days and maybe years, they would see nothing at all, until somebody spotted a lake or an oasis or a pueblo. And they would figure it was a mirage, and they would wait for it to vanish. They learned their lesson from the Seven Cities of Gold. She whispers to Sunny about the meaning of mirage, and shows him the highway, how it looks wet.

"Your father never loved me," Faith says. "He called me stupid." She says "Your father," and she means, *He belongs to you, and it's your fault he's so bad.* Like a sheep-killing dog that has to be shot. "Your father never listens. He always has to be right. He fucked that Mary woman right in front of you, Juniper."

Sunny buries his face in Jennie's lap. The approaching mountains turn from blue to green to tree-covered. With her fingers, Jennie combs Sunny's hair while she floats across the mesa, over the pale silver sagebrush, and now she's cool and happy on top of Wheeler Peak, barefoot in the clouds. Down below, Taos looks like a city of gold. She holds out her hand and the cloud condenses in her palm. She bends close to Sunny's ear. "Condensation," she says. "Do you know what that means?"

"Wet," he says against her thigh.

Faith's voice grows shrill. She says, "Your father screwed that Mary, and then he gave that woman my piano. *My* Steinway. My *mother's* piano." Her voice splinters like ice when she says "piano."

"No I didn't," Ray says.

"Yes you did," Faith said. "Don't try to lie. You stole from me."

"You want to talk truth?" Ray says. "Fine. Here's a scoop: I never fucked 'that Mary.' It was just a little fairy tale, to make you happy—"

"*LIAR*," Faith wails, and twists to look at Jennie. "You were there. You saw. You know—"

"Because I knew it would get to you," Ray says. "Because I knew you wanted to hear it. I made it all up, for you, Little Faith. You were never happy unless I was a cocksucking criminal."

Sunny plugs his ears. Jennie says, "Stop talking this way! Sunny's just a kid." She pulls out his fingers. "There's a place called Seattle," she whispers. "It's the end of the world, where the land meets the sea, and there's fog and when it touches the trees it turns into water, and that's condensation."

"I already know about Seattle," Sunny says.

Ray's anger rolls off him in hot waves. He doesn't speak. They pass the blinking yellow light near El Prado. Faith twists again. "What are you whispering about? Stop whispering. That Steinway was the piano my father gave me." Faith's eyes are exactly the color of Jennie's.

Jennie looks back, thinking, Have you looked at me enough? Then look away and leave me alone. I hate you. Stop looking at me. "We're not saying anything about you," Jennie says.

Faith turns away. And then, even though Faith doesn't sniffle or sob or whimper, Jennie can almost hear the tears rolling down Faith's cheeks. Jennie reaches between the seat and door, and through that crack, she can just touch her mother's shoulder. She isn't sure Faith can even feel it. No one says anything.

For the rest of the drive to town, Sunny keeps his head in Jennie's lap. She likes the heavy weight. It proves he trusts her. She leans her cheek against the door and listens to the wind. She works on forgetting that Faith burned Treasured Memories. She thinks about mist, rain, condensation, water, mirage.

THEY stop at the Taos County Courthouse. Ray gets out without a word, slamming the door hard behind him, waking Sunny. "Where are we?" he asks, his cheek red and wrinkled.

"Wait here," Faith says. Her eyes spill tears and her chin crumples, her mouth twisting in a strange, broken way. Jennie can't look anymore. She hears her mother's quivering gasp and then her footfalls as she walks away.

Before Jennie can stop him, Sunny runs after Faith, calling, "Mom!" Calling, "Why are you crying?"

Faith stops and she says, "Don't you follow me." Her voice freezes Sunny on the spot. "I don't want you in there," she says.

It's August and black asphalt around the car oozes heat, like lava. In his swimsuit and bare feet, Sunny watches his mother climb the steps. She disappears into the building. The windows are like mirrors. "I want to come!" he yells. He looks around for help. Here, at the Taos County Courthouse, which is made of cinder block and plastered to look like something between an adobe fort and a prison, the cops are everywhere, behind mirrors, spying.

Sunny yells, "I want to go inside!" He hops from foot to foot; they must be burning. "It's my birthday!"

Jennie runs across the parking lot and scoops him up and then she can't step lightly and her bare feet are scorched. Sunny tries to wriggle free, calling, "Mom!" People will hear. "I want to go!"

She drops him in the car's front seat. "Mom said she'd buy us a watermelon," she lies. "For the river."

"Watermelon?" He loves to shove his face into a big piece, smearing red juice and seeds over his cheeks, his belly. Disgusting. He squints suspiciously. "When did she say we could have watermelon?"

"She feels guilty," Jennie says. "Since they're splitting up, and it's your birthday. So when you were sleeping, she said she would get a watermelon, and we could go to the river."

"I'm hot," he says.

"I know. Me, too." Sitting beside him, she considers revenge. They shouldn't leave their children out here like this. If you leave a little kid like Sunny in a car, his brain will fry. How long does that take? Divorce. Jennie thinks about telling Sunny what it means, but she stops herself in time.

She gets out of the car and, hopping from foot to foot, opens the doors, unrolls the windows. Sunny lies on his back, an arm and a leg hanging off the seat. Jennie sits in the rear and rests her cheek on her arms on the seat back. "I'm a roasting turkey," she says.

"I'm a cooked chicken," he says.

"I'm a dead duck."

Sunny opens his eyes. They are light green and they see straight through her. "She was crying."

Jennie feels like grabbing somebody's arm and biting. Hard. She wants to feel her teeth sink in, and the blood ooze up around her canines. Incisors. Do you know that word, Sunny? She feels like smashing every cop's windshield. She feels like running, kicking and screaming, or something worse. Something terrible. She jumps out of the car and slams the door and leans in the open window. "I know a story." Her feet burn.

"What story?"

"I'll tell you. Roll up the windows, okay?" When they're all rolled up, she sits behind the wheel and locks all four locks. She puts her arm around Sunny. "It's called Cinderella and Her Brother."

Sunny shrugs off her arm. "I know Cinderella."

Sweat trickles down the back of her neck. "This is a different version, the real Cinderella. A secret version." She puts her arm around him again. "And whoever opens the door ruins the story."

"*Hace calor,*" Sunny says. "That means, It's hot. Your arm is hot."

"Be logical. Think. If we get hot in here, then when we open the doors it will seem cold outside."

"I want to go swimming."

"Please listen to my story? Please?" She digs just a little harder into his shoulders, then pushes him away. "You stink like pee."

He stares out the window. Now he won't talk to her, but that's okay, since now he won't move. The air feels like there's a fire on the floor of the car, under the dashboard. "Two minutes," she says, guessing. "Almost a world record for staying in a car." She grips the steering wheel and remembers the time Ray made her steer. That was when he came back after the piano, after she found Treasured Memories. Why did Faith have to burn the album? Now Jennie has thought the terrible thought. Forgetting is so hard.

Sunny rolls off the seat and onto the floor. A cop exits the building, tall and mean. If he sees them, he'll try to rescue them, and they must not be rescued. Everything depends on staying here, where it's hot. In her mind she chants, Don't look over here don't don't don't. The cop gets in his car and drives away.

Sweat shines on Sunny's face. He crouches, trying to disappear by holding still, like a prairie dog. She can hear the wind in the trees. It will rain soon. "I don't like this story," Sunny says. "I'm too hot."

"I haven't even started yet." She won't open the door. Ray or Faith will have to save them. Who will do it? Ray loves this white car; he won't break the window. Why can't she make herself move to open the door? They'll come out of the courthouse and they'll know she's really mad. Sunny looks more like a troll down there, all red and sweaty, waiting under a bridge to catch unsuspecting travelers. "Guess what? I have leftover candy." She gives him everything she has, and he starts unwrapping, greedy, stuffing his face. She closes her eyes and finds the place and starts her story. "Not very many people know that Cinderella had a little brother named Sunny Boy Blue."

Sunny asks, "Are Mom and Dad arrested?"

Jennie keeps her eyes closed. "Cinderella and her brother were supposed to live in a castle on a hill at the Edge of the World, but they were kidnapped when they were small and taken away to the dry hot land of New Mexico—"

"Are Mom and Dad going to jail?"

Jennie sighs and opens her eyes. "No. They're fine."

A smear of chocolate on his chin, Sunny climbs out of the troll den and onto the seat. "Why was she crying?"

"She was just laughing. Sometimes laughing sounds like crying."

"That's not true. That's a lie. A mirage."

It's so hot it feels like there isn't any air left. Jennie closes her eyes and thinks about Paul's cool green hill. "They lived in New Mexico with a poor hunter and his wife—"

"Are they still fighting?"

"Do you want to hear the story or not?"

"Only if it has a happy ending."

"All fairy tales have happy endings."

"Not yours."

"Yes they do."

He flops on his back and closes his eyes. "Liar, liar." He has already eaten all the candy.

Quietly, as if from a very great distance, an engine starts, a siren sounds, and the wind stirs the trees. Maybe it will rain. When there's wind, usually it means clouds will blow over the mountains and the rain will make everything wet and cool. It will rain soon. "Just listen," she tells him. "Wait and see. You never know. Cinderella and her brother had forgotten where they were from until one day, they found a secret book, a talking book, that told them they belonged at the Edge of the World, where ferns grow wild and there's water everywhere."

Sunny sighs. "Can I open the doors now? I can't breathe."

Jennie feels like her eyeballs are evaporating. But she can't open the doors. "Listen," she says. "A storm is coming. I have to finish before it rains. Do you want me to finish?"

Sunny says, "I'm too hot for stories."

It isn't working. She thought her story would make him feel better, but he doesn't care. She blows on his belly, lightly, like a breeze. Yes, it will rain. Already there's lightning by the mountains. Listen, God, you will save us. "Cinderella and Sunny," she begins.

"I don't feel good," Sunny says. "I'm *sick*. No more stories!"

"But listen," Jennie tells him. "Here's the best part. The story is true. It's a prophecy, which means the future."

Sunny looks down at his candy wrappers with surprise. "My candy's gone," he says.

"Maybe fairies stole it when you weren't looking."

"I'm sad," he says suddenly. "Everything's gone."

Jennie squeezes him tightly. Poor baby boy. She feels sad, too, hearing his sad voice. She says, "There is a happy ending to Paul's story that you might not know about. Want to hear it?"

"I don't believe you."

"Lipa's daughter, Faith, grew up and she had children—"

"That's us." He sounds tired, and sad in the smallest rooms of his heart. She thinks of her father's eyes, the deer. "Why did Mom burn up Paul and Lipa?"

"The sister never left her brother's side. Know why?" He doesn't answer. Fear grows alongside her sadness. "Because she knew she had to stay around and make sure Sunny got to the land of ferns and sea and fish. To Seattle. Know why? Because it was destiny, which means the way things are supposed to be. And one day, she and Sunny set forth into the world. Cinderella put Sunny on her shoulders and carried him across the land and they jumped in the water and swam all the way to Seattle, where they lived in the house on the Highest Hill, in green land by the sea, where ferns grew wild, and they learned to speak in the language of bees."

Sunny says, "That's Russian."

"Right," she says. "Russian." Sunny snuggles into Jennie, his head in her lap, and she loves him so very much. "When Sunny grew up, he went off to college, and his sister did too, only she had a new name."

"Jennie."

"Yes, Jennie, and she went off to college and got married to a handsome prince, and Sunny married a princess—"

"And their mom and dad?"

"Their dad came with them."

"But what about the mom?" Sunny twists to look at Jennie. "Why can't she go with them?" His voice wobbles, and he tries to get away, but she holds him tight.

She says, "The mother followed them, but she was afraid to get in the water. She asked, 'Children! What if I drown?'"

Again, Sunny tries to break free of her arms. He cries, "I'll save her!"

She's so hot. "Sunny. Are you trying to ruin my story?" She's sick to her stomach with heat. "Their mom fell in the river and drowned."

Sunny sits up and again he yells, "I'll save her!"

"Okay. Jeez. So the mother jumped into the river with them, and the four of them floated downstream to the ocean, and they floated to the Edge of the World, and they became very happy. They all lived together in their house on the Highest Hill by the beautiful blue sea, and they had a room completely filled with Bit-O-Honey and chocolate, and each room was vacuumed twice a week by a nice old lady in a pink ruffled apron, and they sat all day eating chocolates, listening to piano music and laughing and laughing—are you awake?" He lies in her arms, sleepy, eyes closed, face flushed. "What did I just say?"

"Laughing and laughing."

"They all laughed and laughed. They lived happily ever after. The End. So you see? There's a happy ending for you, and that's your birthday present."

But now is the time for a different gift. The tops of the trees are tossing and whipping about, and last year's tumbleweeds are blowing through the parking lot, bits of trash. She says, "Close your eyes," and Sunny does, as if she will tell him another story. She studies his face, his black lashes, his cheeks flushed from coming that close to being killed by his own big sister. If he's sick, it's her fault. She pulls up the lock. "Are you opening the door?" he asks, and she shushes him. Keep quiet. Keep your eyes closed. Listen.

In the building Ray and Faith are standing in a long, long hallway, and they are yelling, splitting apart, and there is nothing in the world Jennie can do, except to whisper, "Close your eyes, Sunny."

Listen, Sunny, to the wind, the tops of the trees tossing about, the air slapping this car and moving on, the sun gentled by thunderheads; feel the wind dry the sweat on your cheeks, the way my breath cools your belly. Here for you is the green and wonderful world, piano music and blueberries. Here are the ferns, and here is the rain. Here is the wind. All of these things for you.

And still it isn't raining. She opens the car door, and the wind blows, and still it hasn't rained, but she has saved him just the same.

$\mathcal{N}$ORTH

I am not myself. I am watching myself, Jennie—the Bereaved—as she drives to the plaza. It's August, and the tourists are out in force, be-silvered, be-cowboy-hatted, the beans and rice of New Mexico, camera straps encircling their necks like leashes, like nooses. The teenage locals stand in clots at the bases of trees, their faces simultaneously familiar and strange. What is it about teenagers that makes them seem so dangerous? She—meaning me, meaning Jennie, this woman whose brother is dead—she's twenty-eight years old. What can these big fearless fifteen-year-olds do to her? They sit at the foot of the monument for the martyrs of the Indian uprising, smoking. Cocky, fearless, barely out of diapers, if you think about it. What's ten years, in the scheme of things?

Sunny was still a teenager, the Bereaved reminds her. Nineteen already. A growing boy, a lover, a drinker of vodka, a speaker of languages—

This chick, this Jennie, she's a heartless broad. Today, the first day she is a Sister Whose Brother Is Dead, she didn't stay home to weep in her cups. She went off to work. On impulse, she stopped to blow her summer savings on a junker of a pickup—a story for later, for telling friends in bars, laughing over a pool table. She gassed up the Ford and bought a map and a half-dozen dough-nuts. With behavior like this, it's only right to call her heartless. There are ad-ditional, more appropriate terms, involving other organs. Gutless. Gutsy. Yellow-livered. The rest are nasty. Let's just call her the Ugly Chick, which covers just about everything. But you see, this self-pity is just the sort of thing to transform a person into the Bereaved.

She circles the plaza, looking for a parking spot. If she were a tourist here, she supposes she'd find Santa Fe lovely, picturesque, mysteriously foreign, smack-dab in the middle of the US of A. But she's not a tourist; she's just late for work. She has circled three times. She pulls onto a side street and parks. Walking to Las Novias, she sets to work on another doughnut. A teenager swoops past her on a skateboard.

First the truck and now this. She's very late to work, naughty girl, yet she's standing on the plaza, eating a doughnut and staring in a gallery window. Anyone watching would think, This here's a lady on vacation.

The tourists snap picture after picture. Jennie will be in many of them. Will that tourist, in her broomstick-pleated skirt, notice Jennie in her travel album? Will she see a look on Jennie's face? Will she wish she had done something to help? I certainly don't think so. I'm too sneaky for that. My face is a mask I hide behind.

I just happened to be staring into SARAH's gallery window. I'd gotten into the habit of pausing there every morning. Why? To nurse my grudge, I suppose. To make my point by ignoring her. The display window, filled with concha belts and bronze statuettes of cowboys, was backed with a mural of three Indians on Appaloosas, a gorgeous sunset behind them, their feathers and long hair blowing forward over their cheeks. Inside, the saleswomen, including Sarah, moved around, setting out jewelry in cases. Maybe I was checking to be sure she was alive.

I didn't hate her, I realized, chewing. I just hated the whole idea of. Of what? This question had troubled me. More than once, I'd seen Sarah stop outside Las Novias, and I knew it would be so easy to stand in the doorway, offer a casual hello, and proceed. "You still can't have it," I might have said. She would have laughed, said, "Then why's it still in the window? To keep on torturing me?"

But I could not forgive her for loving a man who squeezed bruises into her skin. A girl—a woman, a beauty—like her could have anything and anyone. To choose unhappiness when happiness is available on a platter—now *there's* a crime. Plus, she had made me the fool.

Sarah dipped into the display window to lay out a squash blossom necklace. She looked up, directly into my face. I nearly choked on my last bite. Her elegant eyebrows drew together, and she gave me a searching, quizzical look. *Where have you been?* her look asked. She smiled. I hurried away as fast as I could.

BEYOND the vintage wedding gowns, Las Novias carries a large array of vintage clothes, mostly mid-twentieth century, for members of the wedding. I borrowed a silk forget-me-not blue Grace Kelly suit, with a kick pleat and a peplum, and seamed stockings and a pair of alligator pumps. Behind the embroidered unicorn curtains, I took off my jeans and shirt and rolled my hair back into its French twist and dressed for the third time that morning. I hated those curtains. I hated fringe. I hated velvet. I had a consultation at twelve. It was eleven-thirty. Oriental carpets—I hated them, too. Did I mention unicorns?

I spread out the map on the coffee table and traced the route of my father's whole life: Seattle to Oregon, Nevada, Colorado, New Mexico, Florida. And Sunny's, start to finish, now that he was dead: New Mexico, Berkeley (Russia and Germany were off the map), Oregon, Seattle. Even my grandfather Swifty's: Oregon, Seattle. Not much for a life.

There I am, Jennie, this woman who is not herself. I am sitting on the red velvet settee, trying to stay put. Let's not feel sorry for me, for her, Jennie. She isn't Bereaved, just nauseated and, let's not forget, heartless. Chewed pastry sits in her belly like a fist, and her tongue and teeth and roof of her mouth taste of sour coffee. She crosses her legs. The shop stinks of her breath, of old silk and the endless dust, and the morning sun slants through the windows and catches the falling motes. Look at her. She can't even sit still.

Outside, the flags stirred, New Mexico yellow, the red white and blue. A storm was gathering to the northeast, great black thunderheads rising over the gallery roofs. In New Mexico, it rains every afternoon of July and August, what the natives laughably call the monsoon season. I popped a breath mint from the spittoon. I touched my hair and smoothed my skirt and still I couldn't keep the words from coming: *I have to go.* I uncrossed my legs and folded my map and put it in my backpack. I stood, ready to leave. Only I finally saw it clearly, the pathetic foolishness of buying a truck. Ashamed, humiliated, I realized: I had been asleep all morning. *Wake up. Nothing is the same. Your brother is dead.* Like scales, like shades or shutters or the folding wings of an insect, say a dragonfly or a cockroach, a sadness came over me, a heavy, slow fragility, and I truly stopped dreaming for the first time that morning. I sat.

And, as if it had been waiting for me to sit, the phone instantly rang. It was Sarah. "Listen, I know you hate me and everything," she said, "but I saw you there, and since I know you probably stay mad longer than God, I thought I better make the first move here, and I wanted to tell you that—"

"Okay," I said. Okay. Okay, absolutely.

The doorbell sounded, and here was my eleven-thirty bride, a quiet, black-haired teenager with a speck of a diamond and a bossy, square-bodied best friend.

"I have news," Sarah said.

I thought, My God, she's pregnant. "I have a customer," I said.

"Like I'm supposed to believe that. You better watch how you hold a grudge, or you'll end up a lonely old lady." She hung up before I could make it clear that I really did, truly, have a customer.

I sized up the bride in a second. Selling a dress is about matchmaking, and I was great at making customers fall in love. I could always read what style they'd like. I knew the stories they'd want to hear—a tragedy or a happy ending.

I can't remember the bride's name, but suppose it was Felicia. She was another ruffled and swagged bride, pre-1880s, like Sarah. I took them to the settee, Felicia and her annoying bridesmaid, call her Eunice. I showed the pictures and told the stories and politely bullied poor Felicia and thereby earned my commission, but it was just my lips moving and breath making sound, because I was back on that trip over the mountains, north to Colorado and beyond, and those words were marching around, as undeniable as any signal of my body, rumbling stomach, aching bladder, tired feet. *I have to go.* As fundamentally true as thinking I need to pee, or I'm going to be sick if I don't get something to eat.

I had my own truck now. I had never had my own vehicle before, tightwad that I am. Carpools, buses. This summer, a Rolls-Royce. The lap of luxury, yes, but not mine—my husband's. I have a truck now, and I have to go. Only now I saw Sarah in my ranch vee-hickle with me, her knees drawn to her chest, sucking on an enormous diet soda, going on and on about her Theory of Something.

"Ma'am? *Ma'am?*" It was Eunice the bridesmaid, braying in my ear. "Do you think you could find her something more modern, with less ruffles, maybe?"

"I like these," Felicia said timidly, peeking at me.

I sent them to the fitting room while I fetched the gowns. When I came through the curtains, Felicia squealed and threw her hands over her crotch. "She's *naked,*" the bridesmaid said. "Don't you knock?"

I looked long and hard at Eunice. Helga, I should call her. "What a shock," I said. "And me, thinking she was here to try on clothes."

"But I *am,*" Felicia said.

"Felicia," I said. "Honey. Maybe you can explain to Helga here about our company policy. I'm *sure* you wouldn't want to be *buy*ing an antique, one-of-a-kind, hundred-year-old gown because Helga, your dear maid of honor, planted her big clumsy foot on the train and ripped the *shit* out of the lace. Now would you?"

Oh dear. Did I say that? What was I thinking? I looked into Felicia's big black eyes and hated her and I hoped I could make her cry. I hate you, I thought, and meanwhile the little Nazis goose-stepped around my brain. I. HAVE. TO. GO. "Understand?" I said. Neither of them answered. "Good," I said. "Raise your arms." Mean old Goat. I had a new truck and a new map. In this shop was a dress no one was allowed to wear, and the Bereaved, who had taken over my life. God Almighty, I have to go.

. . .

F E L I C I A and Helga left. I stood in the middle of the room, watching the dust motes, the tourists outside, the tricky flight of a boy on a skateboard. Clouds were gathering. Fuck it, I said to myself. I went to the dressmaker's dummy and unbuttoned Governor Bent's daughter's dress's 130 buttons. Draped over my outstretched arms, the gown was about as big as a bride. It must have weighed fifteen pounds, though I'm not good at judging such things. Suffice it to say, it was a very heavy dress. Satin, taffeta, velvet, netting, pearls, swags, lace, orange blossoms. I stepped out of the window. I stole my boss's favorite antique dress and left the shop locked up tight in the middle of the day in the middle of the tourist season, and that is how I quit my job.

I walked into SARAH'S. She sat behind the counter, reading a magazine. Under the glass my mother's flowers were laid out on black velvet. Sarah looked at me; she looked at the dress. "There you are," she said happily. "I knew you'd be back. You can't resist me, can you?"

I held out the dress. "You can have it," I said.

She came around the counter and took it from my arms. She held it reverently, stroking the lacy folds. She said, "Do you believe in God? Do you believe in magic?" Her eyes, predictably, filled with tears. "Because I believe in everything, and I believe that things work out the way they're supposed to, and I believe that you and I were meant to be friends."

I realized, then: I had missed her terribly. "The joke's on you," I said. "Somewhere, God is laughing."

"Yeah, like you and Him are on such first-name terms. So now we have to make up, my long-lost friend, and you have to tell me what's new with you and act like a normal human, starting now. I command you to tell me everything."

It was maybe one o'clock, but the clouds made it dark outside; the day seemed finished, in fact. Rolling inside me was this twilight dread, which made me want to go running. I thought, I have nothing to tell. But in truth I had plenty, just nothing I wanted to tell.

I took her arm. "I bought a truck," I said. "Blew my summer savings. Let's go for a drive. You can tell me your news." She must have missed me, too. She snatched up her bag and, trusting me, or fate, or the big giant joke of August, let me lead her out of that place and into the gathering storm.

I N the hot still afternoon of August in New Mexico, the clouds come over the mountains and grow black and heavy with water and then it rains. The afternoon I took Sarah away was an afternoon like that, with the wind kicking the tourists around, along with ice cream cups and weeds, puffs of dust.

The first fat drops pelted the sidewalks and pinged on the tin roofs. I pulled Sarah by the wrist, and she followed in big stumbling steps, carrying her enormous black shoulder bag and the wedding dress I had just stolen for her. When she saw the truck, she laughed. "You spent your savings on *that?*"

The clouds broke open hard. I ran around to the driver's side and flung myself in, slammed the door and pushed my wet bangs out of my eyes and started the truck, which roared, so big, higher than all the Volvos around us. Mean-looking, too. I was silly with pride for my hulking ranch vee-hickle.

"You had a Rolls-*Royce*," she said. She waited. I was supposed to say, "It's not mine."

The Bereaved had other ideas. *Say, "My brother is dead." Say, "He jumped off a ferry and drowned."*

"Even if it was your husband's Rolls," Sarah said. *Throw your arms around her neck and weep against her shoulder. Say, "Help me."* No. Fuck no.

"Don't be a snob," I snapped. "My father always had trucks." Which meant—and she knew it—*You'd do a lot better just to huddle in your corner with your lipsticked mouth shut, little girl.* Sarah did, for about fifteen minutes, a real feat.

Eventually, Sarah realized we weren't stopping. She protested, and screamed, and threatened to leap from the truck. She called me names; she said I was no better than the rapist, *or your brother*, she howled, and I, like my brother, did not listen. I drove on and on.

I drove through a rain so heavy that even with the wipers going full steam the cars ahead were smudges of taillight. I-25 wound through a few mountain villages, and then the mountains opened up and we were on their broad undulating back. The piñon trees rolled away from the highway like scattered pearls, and the rain fell.

The downpour stopped as abruptly as it had started. One moment, the blinding water, the thunder, lightning, then nothing. I rolled down my window. The air smelled sweetly of damp sagebrush. The silence was tremendous.

Yes. Deliver me from a Funeral Meeting. Lead me into my truck, to California, to drunken volleyball players I can fuck in the sand; let me abandon them naked to bake in sun and their own afterglow; thank you for this new friend who might need me; thank you for this Ford and this map and this highway, but take us into temptation, where we'll sleep in the bed of my new pickup truck; if you'll give me my friend and let us eat hamburgers at three A.M. and drink whiskey for breakfast, then I promise we'll shoplift and smoke and God if you're willing we'll stay up through the night laughing about kingdoms and glory, and amen to all that.

Exactly, I thought. Exactly. Now I know: this is how it was for my grand-father, my father, and then for my brother and now for me. That's where I'm going, to where it all started: north. Toward black clouds swollen with rain, spitting lightning, heavy with the too-early dark of a summer storm, and I am waiting for this dream to stop, stunned, and it doesn't rain anymore, and I wait for my heart to wake up, any moment now, and still each moment I am not dreaming; still I am driving north, still north, still north.

$\mathcal{T}$HE OTHER SIDE
OF THE MOUNTAIN

Wednesday Afternoon, I-25, New Mexico

I N the fall in northern New Mexico, wild sunflowers crowd the sides of roads, as if they thrive on car exhaust, and they were in full bloom along I-25. The high plains, broad low hills covered in tinder-yellow grass, rolled west to the Sangre de Cristos. On the other side of those mountains were Santa Fe, Taos, Arroyo al Fin, places I know so well.

"Why are you doing this?" Sarah whispered.

"Because," I said. Which was a fair answer, a true word. Because means "I have reasons." It means "Trust me." It stands in place of *My brother is dead*.

When I was a kid, this side of the mountains seemed like a faraway country, one I'd never visit. "Where is Russia?" Sunny would ask me. Over there, I'd tell him, waving my hand vaguely toward the eastern mountains. When my father sang "The Bear Went over the Mountains," this was the other side I pictured.

Only last November, Chris and I were on our way to Denver—two happy lovers off to the big parental introduction. Eight months later, less than a school year, less than a gestation later, the bride's on the lam. What a bitch, that Jennie. Imagine what Mrs. Braverman would say, raising her black eyebrows and shaking a blue-veined finger at me. *Brave* Jennie. *Mrs.* Braverman.

Sarah, lighting a cigarette, said, "Excuse me, kidnapper? This is an emergency. I have three cigarettes left, so I'll need to stop and buy a pack soon, if you can interrupt my kidnapping for a second."

"You're not kidnapped."

"Oh really? Well call me Amnesia Woman, but I don't remember any kind of consultation, any kind of thing where you go, 'Hey Sarah do you want to take a trip?' and I go, well, sure, let me pack some stuff including *cigarettes*, and you go, 'Jesus that suitcase weighs a fucking ton, what do you have in there, three cases of *cigarettes*?' You've probably been planning this whole thing since your wedding. You probably have some kind of file on me. And as a kidnap victim, I expect to be treated decently, which does not include depriving me of *cigarettes*."

I said, "You didn't have to come."

"Because I'm so much stronger than you, and you aren't fifty feet tall. *That* was sarcasm."

Thunderheads loomed straight ahead, over the ridge of the northern mountains, as if the storm waited in ambush. "We'll have to get windshield wipers in Colorado," I said, surprising myself. It seemed my brain had been working out the details. This made me happy. I was glad to have a plan, at least up to Colorado, at least to windshield wipers. It's a fine thing, to have a goal or two. "You shouldn't be smoking anyway."

"I am going to kill somebody if I don't get a pack of Camels, and I hate to break it to you, but you're the only other person in this heap." Sarah made a big production of digging around in her big black bag, which was apparently bottomless. From it she produced a small pair of scissors, a lollipop, nail polish, and cotton balls, which she spread out on the seat. She announced, "I'm not talking to you until I get some cigarettes."

"Now that," I said, "I don't believe."

She unwrapped the sucker with much crackling of cellophane and slurping of candy. She fiddled with the radio, and twice she found the same fuzzy country station. She turned it off. "And I have to pee," she said. "Don't forget I'm a person who needs to pee a lot." She braced her feet on the dashboard and leaned over her knees. She spoke casually. "Why are you doing this to me?"

"You have bruises all over your body."

"So the punishment for bruises is getting kidnapped? What, you're getting rid of an eyesore, improving the sights for the tourists?"

"You need to get away," I said. "Especially now."

"Oh really. Well, I have news for you. You're in for a big shock, lady. I never asked to be rescued."

I rolled my window down all the way, and the air roared in, loosening one corner of the temporary license, sending it chattering frantically in the wind. My hair whipped around my face, stinging my cheeks and getting in my eyes. I rolled the window up and then I was too hot. The center stripe ticked away. We drove in silence until Sarah said, "This isn't for real, right?" Her growing fear was like smoke clouding up the cab. I felt guilt creep over me, the ugly cousin of grief and anger. "I hate you," she whispered.

"You're like an addict," I said. "You're addicted to Jake. Call this an intervention."

"Oh, I'm so impressed. How psychological. Thank you very much, Dr. Jennie. I saw this thing on TV about the Salem witches? These girls lied and called people witches, and then they didn't want to get caught, so they convinced themselves it was true, and pretty soon it wasn't like they were faking, and they threw up, so it wasn't lying, really. Because *they* believed it." She paused, drew in smoke for emphasis. She said, "I know what you're thinking. You think you're this big-time hero, rescuing me from Jake. But you don't know everything. *I'm* the one who lied—"

"And every liar should get smacked around."

"Stop it," she said. "Stop laughing at me. I'm sick of you making fun of me. Could you please just be normal for a little while, because a person can only take so much condescension and yes, surprise, I know big words. Just because someone is small doesn't mean she's a baby—" She paused. Bent over her knees, her hair falling around her face, she said, "It's so hard to like you sometimes." She opened her nail polish and with great deliberation painted borders around two of the cracks on the dashboard. Then, suddenly, she was crying. Loud, heaving sobs against her kneecaps. "Why won't you listen to me? *I* lied to *him.* He was so mad . . ." Her voice caught. "Fuck," she whispered. "I don't want to talk about this."

"I thought I was the one who changed the subject all the time."

"What I'm trying to say is that a person can convince herself something is true when it's not."

I imagined Jake grabbing Sarah from behind, his hands spanning her waist and convulsing, because he knows it hurts, but she doesn't even whimper. He hates her for it. He pinches her cheeks hard against her teeth and shoves her nose to the mirror, *There,* he whispers. *You see. You're beautiful. Say it.* The white line dashed along. I felt it leading me straight to the end of the world, with the mountains on my left and my right, and the sun setting and Sarah's red nail polish sparkling on the dashboard. And then he tells himself, *She likes it. I know she does.* "I know this much is true," I said. "You're living with an asshole, no matter how many nice plants he has, and you need to move out with no forwarding address, especially with that baby inside you."

Sarah's hands went to her mouth. "Oh my God." She looked undecided on laughing or crying. She decided to laugh. She doubled over with it, clutching her stomach, gasping. "You think you know what you're doing; you think you know everything; you think you're so smart." She laughed and laughed, and then, she fell silent and stared glumly out the window.

WE passed the sign for Las Vegas. "I lived there once," I said, and I felt nothing of the fear and confusion I'd felt the year before when I recollected this forgotten fact. Now it was just something I knew.

"Excuse me?" Sarah said. "Are you trying to chitchat with me? I have news for you, lady. I don't *make* conversation with kidnappers."

We passed the signs for Watrous, Wagon Mound. I wanted to speak but found that I couldn't. I was a distant observer, watching a truck move down a highway in the middle of nowhere. Nothing special. Just a truck, like any other truck. Once it was new and lined up beside others, tens of them, perhaps hundreds, ready, in their shininess and new plastic smell, to be loaded onto a tractor trailer. The driver signed his papers and warmed his engine and started west, to Montana or the states below it, all of them split by the spine of the Rockies, the peaks vertebrae. Flying over in a plane, a man looking down would see those peaks as a rough sea capped with foam, and a man driving might wonder how he'd ever get over them, but not our semi driver with his load of twelve shiny new Fords, climbing slowly, his many-geared engine groaning.

Sarah screamed, in a voice surprisingly loud for such a little thing, "LISTEN TO ME ! I WANT TO GO HOME!"

A truck driver was, in so many ways, like a wagoneer. Or even better, a conquistador, call him Reymundo, riding over this broad empty space, his head clanking around inside his metal helmet, days or weeks from the nearest person, over the mountains in Taos, a world away. What does he think about? His wife's tortillas, his son playing in the water. What stories does he tell himself? On Reymundo rides, into nothing, thinking of ghosts, of his poor lonely Teresita, until he shouts, just to hear the sound of something. If this were my father's story, Reymundo would have sung "The Bear Went over the Mountain." In my story, he sings "Alla en Rancho Grande."

Sarah said quietly, "If you don't talk to me, I'm letting go." I'd missed the exact moment when she'd shoved the wedding dress out the window, but out there it was, held in one hand, the satin catching the wind, the train billowing, a long and glorious banner. Sarah, I thought, what sort of hostage is that? When I've done everything to show you how little I care about it?

"Fine," Sarah said, and let the dress slip away. In the rearview I watched it arc gracefully through the air. Maybe it was all those skirts catching the wind—it seemed to linger for a moment, like the ghost of a bride, before it settled to the dusty shoulder.

She said, "Aren't you going to stop?"

I pulled over without any sense of urgency or, I realized, much feeling at all. Call it the Numb Zone, a state where things don't matter much. Nice. I quite liked it there. "So go get it," I said.

Sarah glared at me. "Can't you at least back up? It's like a million miles behind us."

"Guess you learn something about poor planning."

Sarah slammed the door hard. I twisted to watch her shrink. To a boy in a plane, the truck would be as small as a Matchbox car parked beside the high-way, and Sarah would be a bright dot moving away, and then he could hold his hand to the window and make everything disappear.

This girl, this Sarah, this Pea Princess, had hair that could flag down a semi truck. I could drive off and leave her behind. She'd get a ride, easy. I'd just drive and then drive some more, until I collided with something. God, it would be so easy to drive this truck away. As easy as driving it over a side of a bridge, or against a brick wall, or into the ocean. It would be as easy as turning the steering wheel. Easy as that.

Sarah scooped up the dress. She stood for a moment, then moved into the middle of the highway, right on the dotted line, waiting for a semi to come barreling down on her.

I backed the truck along the shoulder. I leaned out the window. "Get out of the road."

"Fuck you." She glared at the highway ahead, squinting against the sun. "You have to listen to me." She clutched her bangs between her fingers and made a fist. "You can't just jerk me around." Her voice wobbled, and she made a show of trying to fold the dress into a little more order. "You're scaring me," she said so softly I had to strain to hear. "I'm scared." The dress was im-possible, dirty, tangled, damaged, and torn. "Fuck," she whispered. She was not the Sarah I knew, who was loud and fluent and careless. For once, she was fighting instead of cultivating tears.

I got out of the truck and walked over to her. I said, "Sarah, please get out of the road."

"Some things are true, and some things aren't." She took a deep breath. "Jake never hit me."

"Really."

"God," she said, and pressed the heel of her hand to her forehead. "Okay. I want to show you something. Hold this." I took the dress from her.

She began unbuttoning her tuxedo shirt. "Sarah," I said.

"Just shut up," she said. "For once in your life." She took off her shirt and let it fall to the pavement. I was relieved to see she wore a bra, but of course she also wore bruises, over her belly, across her shoulders. Around her neck, for Christ's sake. "Look," she said, holding out her arm. There were bruises circling her biceps, exactly like someone had grabbed her there. "I've seen them," I said.

"Not these. These are brand-new. Fresh today in Santa Fe."

Then I understood. They were my fingerprints. My fingerprints marking where I'd pulled her to the truck. I hadn't been rough; I didn't remember be-ing rough. She'd come willingly. Yet I'd given her a bracelet of bruises.

"Diagnosis, ITP," she said. "Ideopathic thrombocytopeniz." She wrenched the dress from my arms and stuffed it through the truck window, pulled out her bag, and found a cigarette. She lit it, inhaled ravenously, exhaled hard. "Sounds sexy, doesn't it?" Her bra was blue velvet, almost a bathing suit.

"But you have bruises all over you. Someone makes them."

"Jesus, Sherlock Holmes." She looked me with a set jaw, her eyes, for once, not filled with tears. "I can't believe you still don't get it. I've been trying to tell you. I do it to myself. I can do it as easy as this." She pinched her arm viciously, and a red mark appeared. "It's self-inflicted, okay?" She gave me a shaky smile. "It's great for the sympathy vote. Jake thought my mom did it." She took a deep drag, then, with quick violence, smashed her cigarette under her heel, and I longed for the vocabulary, the magic incantation of a smoker. *Forget this,* her heel said. *I grind uncertainty into the ground.*

She said, "Let's get out of here before someone sees me half naked." She seemed to have come back to the Sarah I knew, arrogant, careless, and I was relieved. The sunlight set her aglow in a fantastical way, a fairy tale come to life, standing shirtless on the highway. She looked as if she had been dipped headfirst in honey. I thought, Not the Pea Princess. She's the Bee Princess.

She fetched her shirt from the middle of the road and waved it in a grand gesture, a surrender, a salute to her imaginary public. "Can you imagine if some guy had come along?" She flopped into the truck. "What would I say to him? Hey there, baby, I'm just getting some sun?"

I stared at my fingerprints on her arms. Not fingerprints, really, but smudges that matched my hand. "I did that to you?"

She rolled her eyes. She pulled on her shirt. "Please. Don't get all melodramatic on me, do you mind? Anyway, call yourself lucky. I've only ever told Jake about this, besides you. And now Jake thinks I'm a big fat liar."

"I don't get it," I said. "What did you lie about?"

Her eyes brimmed. "Jennie," she whispered. "It's only a skin condition." She let out a shuddering breath.

I touched her arm gently. "Sarah," I said. "Listen. I could send you home. I bet there's a bus out of Raton—"

Her tears fell. "I'm sorry," she whispered. "I'm sorry I lied." Her pink nostrils flared almost imperceptibly as she took a quavering breath.

"Or you can come with me, if you want to come with me—"

"I *do,*" she said. Her tears got rolling again.

"Then could you just do me this one favor? Just have fun with me. We'll go see my brother. We'll go to San Francisco; we'll get drunk and stay up all night laughing, pick up guys on the beach—"

She burrowed into my lap, sobbing, shoulders heaving, tears dampening my leg. "I love him," she said. "I really, really love him." I hushed her gently, but I didn't say it would be fine. In the absence of any other certain thing, I stroked her hair, I patted her back, I put my hand on the nape of her neck, like a mother or a sister, like Big Paul to Little Paul, like every time anyone has ever soothed a loved one, and I wondered if even this gentle pressure would leave its mark on Sarah's skin.

THE truck wouldn't start. It gave me the slow, complaining slur of a truck turning over and never catching. I heard Ray, so clearly he might as well have been sitting beside me: *Don't flood it, or you'll really be fucked.* When I raised the hood and looked at the guts of the thing, he was beside me in his flannel shirt and work boots, his marigold-orange hair and his leather cowboy hat, leaning in, up to his elbows in grease.

It wasn't the plugs, or the battery, or the fuel lines. Not the radiator, not the filter. I tinkered and Sarah tried the engine and I was reaching the end of my knowledge. I got on my back in the blue silk mother-of-the-bride suit and scooted beneath to inspect the Ford's underbelly, the muffler strung up with baling wire, the Adam's apple of the axle. *Cocksucking piece of shit. Could be anything. Starter. Battery. Try the battery first, Juniper, then the plugs, because you can waste a lot of time forgetting about sparks. You got to have sparks to make combustion. Vengaquí.* I felt that queasy, nervous shrinking in me, twenty-eight years old and even the memory of my father's inevitable failure was enough to make me shiver in my alligator shoes. After a couple of hours, he'd have bloody knuckles from punching the truck door (another reason to buy a clunker; you can abuse it with impunity), screaming obscenities, and God help me if I said anything then. On my back, under the truck, I couldn't breathe. I panted, and my hands were curled in fists. I lay there thinking, Oh God oh God oh God. Fuck. *You don't ever buy one of these pieces of shit without a test drive and a mechanic's seal of approval, that's for goddamn sure.* Daddy, what have I done? Faith would say, *You don't think. You just barge ahead.*

Sarah's face appeared. "Did you fix it?"

"Obviously not," I said.

"You better hurry or some rapist Good Samaritan is going to come along and try to help us."

I slithered out from under the truck. The blue shantung suit was filthy and snagged. So far, I had stolen two dresses, ruined both, quit my job, and blown my savings on a piece-of-shit ranch vee-hickle. With my luck, Sarah's mother would go to the cops, who would blame me for the bruises. I slammed the hood and stumbled back into the highway and shouted out a good long FUCK into the wide-open plains, the enormously blue sky. Fuck. *Fuck.* Fuck.

J E N N I E gets in the truck and Sarah climbs in after her. "Well," Sarah says, "I hate to say I told you so, but I told you so. If you'd only gotten a *real* truck, this wouldn't have happened." Jennie looks at her hands, blunt-nailed and thick-knuckled, a man's hands, strong and capable of anything except reaching for the key and turning it and starting this engine. "Anyway, I don't understand why somebody who drives a Rolls-*Royce* would pick out a piece of shit like this."

Jennie curls her toes in her shoes until they ache. "Shut up, Sarah."

"Shut up? Nice manners, lady. You think you can order people around and expect them to do what you want without thinking maybe some people would just like to stay in Santa Fe and maybe *some* people have better ideas about things than you do—"

"Goddammit," Jennie says, and hears her father's voice, the slow-building violence. Her hands shake. She holds tight to the steering wheel. The shaking will spread to her entire body if she doesn't anchor herself. The diamond on her finger shatters the light into a constellation on the truck visor, a private galaxy called Failed Marriage. She focuses on that, but it does not keep her from saying the second thing: "I am going to rip out your heart if you don't shut your fucking mouth."

Sarah gropes the split dash with her toes. After a moment, she laughs shakily. "Talk about overreacting," she says. "All we have to do is calm down and somebody will come along and help. Everything will be fine."

Jennie turns the key. It starts. Roars, God bless it, to life, loud, hulking, my ranch vee-hickle back in business, yeeeee-*haw! I'm leaving Cheyenne.* "See?" Sarah says. "Would I lie?"

I pulled onto the highway and we drove on without any discussion of turning back. Sarah lit a cigarette. "This is my last one, by the way. We're stopping at the next exit."

"Sarah."

"As soon as you say my name like that, I know you're going to pretend you're a doctor. Sarah, you shouldn't be smoking. Sarah, you shouldn't be drinking. Sarah, you should be a nun." She began rummaging through her bag, as if she couldn't be bothered with me anymore.

"I thought you were pregnant," I said. A pause lengthened into a bona fide silence. She searched that bag like it held gold somewhere in its nether reaches. I said, "Or did you lie about that, too?"

She threw a wadded receipt at me. She said, "You are so dense, I swear to God. I didn't *lie*, I told you. I just didn't correct your stupid assumption. You'd be a lot happier if you figured out how to let go of a grudge, like *some* people do, which is basically what being a friend is about."

This in a nutshell is how I worked to let go of my grudge: I kept my mouth shut. Sarah, sitting with her back to the passenger door, busied herself with projects. She trimmed split ends from her hair with tiny scissors. She smoked. She sucked lollipops, chewed gum. She said, "Why don't you just say it straight out."

"Straight out, I wish you'd shut your mouth for longer than the time it takes to smoke a cigarette."

"People like you have to say things like that." She let her cigarette fly back in the slipstream. "You'd be sorry if I wasn't here. Might as well admit it." I admitted nothing. I drove without speaking, feeling oddly light, as if suspended in air, flying or falling. Sarah extended her leg across the seat and poked my thigh with her toe. "You're so funny. You're just like a man."

I realized what I was feeling. Pleased. I was pleased and proud. I'm the tough nut, the big puzzle, the human jigsaw. I am nothing you can understand. The closer you get, the farther away you are.

$\mathcal{T}$HUNDERSTORM

1982, Arroyo al Fin

STILL, it doesn't rain. Driving away from the courthouse, Jennie studies the black clouds, the trees bending in the wind. *My parents are getting a divorce.* Jennie tries this sentence out in her head and it sounds sensible, which is a word she likes. Ray and Faith are silent, not fighting like before, as if they really did split open and all the mad drained out of them. Which is sensible. Jennie wonders—almost dreaming, her mind turning in lazy half circles— what will happen to Faith; what will happen to Ray. It all seems good. Maybe, split apart, they'll be happy. Maybe Faith will meet a nice rich man and they will live happily ever after. But what will happen to Ray?

And, under all this, Jennie's sad about what really matters. Faith burned the Treasured Memories. That is more terrible than divorce.

Sunny, his cheeks flushed, his eyes shiny, asks, "*Now* can we swim?"

"It's going to rain," Jennie says.

"You promised!" he says. "I want my watermelon!" No one answers him. He glares at Jennie. "Liar," he whispers.

Ray stops at a little white house and gets out of the car, slamming the door hard behind him. The little house is nice, with a porch and a pointy roof. Is this where he'll live? Jennie can stay here in town, and Ray never cares about things like mullein or mixing your proteins. He'll buy cold cereal and he'll get a TV. Raisin Bran. Hot dogs. He'll have a toilet. He unties the bed from the car and takes it into the house. He doesn't come back.

Faith gets out of the car and puts a palm on the hood, as if the car is a horse and she's calming it down. She'll have to drive now. She's not a very good driver. She learned only a few years ago, and she's short, so she can barely see over the steering wheel. A gust of wind stirs her hair around her face, and even on this sad day, she looks almost beautiful. She gets in, sitting behind the wheel. She stretches one arm along the back of the seat to see behind her and steers out of the driveway. Her eyes are mean and hard and far away. She's a different person, a new mother who doesn't cry. She says, "Well, Juniper Tree Burning, you're going to have to figure out which one of us you want."

"No," Sunny says. "I want to go swimming."

For a second, Jennie thinks she has to pick a mom—the one who cried without making a sound, or this one, who doesn't even say good-bye to Ray. But then Jennie gets it. She'll have to decide if she wants a mother or a father.

AT the blinking light, instead of heading north for Alfin, Faith turns toward Arroyo Seco. Sunny says, "Where are we? This isn't the way."

"We're going to get Clarence," Faith says.

"Why do you want to do *that?*" Jennie says.

Faith slows the car. "Do you want to get out?" she says. "Do you want to walk?"

They drive to Valdez. From the road skirting its rim, the Valdez valley looks like a picture book, with its little houses and square green fields. This close to the mountains, everything gets more water. Faith takes the winding road down into the picture, to Clarence's. She goes into the house. It has a low roof. It's very small.

Sunny says, "Why are we here? Why did we stop?"

Jennie hushes him. She should tell him a story. This is where the soldiers live, the ranchers, the ghosts. But she can't think of anything that makes a good reason for them to stop here. So they sit in the car, waiting. This car, Jennie thinks. This car was once a piano. Now it is a car that gets rid of our father and picks up Clarence. This car is the beginning and end of everything.

After a while, Faith comes out with Clarence, the one Faith loves. Clarence doesn't say anything. He just gets into the car.

"Sunny," Faith says, "do you know who this is?"

Sunny kneels on the seat to get a better look at the neck of the man who doesn't even pretend to be nice, doesn't even try to turn around. Sunny asks, "Is he coming swimming?" Clarence looks at them. His eyes are brown and unreadable. "I don't know you," Sunny says.

"Yes you do," Faith says. "Clarence is your godfather. He named you." Faith starts the car and heads toward Alfin.

Later, Jennie will wonder why—in that first moment of Clarence getting into the car and Faith gently latching his door—why, in one glance, Jennie knew that Clarence was dangerous. Maybe it was Faith's eyes. The way she looked at Clarence, the way a person might look at God, or how Cinderella might have looked when her fairy godmother made everything beautiful. Maybe Jennie could see how mad he was, that Clarence was PISSED OFF.

"This isn't the way to swimming," Sunny says.

No, Sunny, she thinks, this isn't the way. But it's okay. I know how to get there, and I'll show you. She bends over, closer to his ear, and in the softest whisper, she tells him to be good and quiet, and one day they'll be in Seattle where the ferns grow wild.

"Hear her whispering?" Faith tells Clarence. "She's just like her father. Her father doesn't think about anybody but himself, either."

"Stop it," Jennie says. "Stop talking about him like that. He's my *father*."

Faith slams on the brakes, and they all fall forward, then back again. The quiet sits down between them all, there on the mesa. There are no cars, no houses. Just the clouds, and in the distance, the mountains. The clouds are so black. When will it rain? "If you think he's so great, then you can pack your bags and go live with him," Faith says. "Get out of the car."

Jennie watches Faith's eyes in the rearview mirror. She studies Clarence's neck, the black hair cut close to his skin. "I didn't *do* anything," Jennie says.

"Didn't *do* anything? You stole my inheritance and you say you didn't do anything? I'm sick of this," Faith yells. "I deserve a little bit of something good now!"

"Mom—"

"Shut up! Shut up!" She twists to look at Jennie. "Get out of my car," she says. "This is my car, that my piano bought, and you can get out of it."

Jennie opens her mouth but then closes it without speaking. Fine. Have it that way. She gets out. She has lived here all her life, but her feet have never touched this pavement. This is what she keeps in mind as she walks away from the car, toward Arroyo al Fin, without looking back. I am in new territory. I am the conquistador. She watches her feet move over the undiscovered pavement, the New World.

Now lightning cracks the horizon, and a second later, the thunder, the first plump drops of rain. Her feet on her new territory are met with circles of water. Behind her, someone is calling her name: "Junie! Junie!" Only Sunny calls her this, and yes, here is Sunny, running after her, crying, "Wait, Wait!"

So he will come with her, and she's glad. She waits, and by the time he reaches her, the rain is pouring down on them, like the sky is a balloon that has burst, a bucket that has lost its bottom, like heavy, heavy rain. He shouts, "We have to go swimming! You can't leave! You *promised!*" She remembers: he's just a kid, a little boy. Behind him, the white car is only a smudge, an erased car, and the two shadows inside are just part of the rain.

Sunny shivers, his hair shaped to his skull, his see-through eyes big and pale in his wet face, his wet eyelashes. If he's crying, she can't tell, because the water drips down his cheeks. He's right. She can't leave.

She isn't afraid of Clarence, or her mother, but she's afraid for Sunny. Sunny, who shouts, "Don't leave me!" Behind him, like a signal, the car lights come on. The windshield wipers start up. The white car, what's left of the piano, moves toward them, slowly inching ahead, searching for them, and they climb in, Sunny first, shivering, wet.

HEARTBROKEN HENRY

Wednesday Evening, Raton, New Mexico

I pulled into the first gas station off the Raton exit, killed the engine, and for a moment I didn't know what to do next. Sarah knew, though. "God," she said, "I have to pee so bad, and thanks to you, I'm probably going to be an old lady peeing in diapers." She angled the rearview mirror to inspect her face. "You better buy me cigarettes," she said, and slung her bag over her shoulder and went inside the cashier's office. I watched all of this in a strange sort of stasis, Jennie frozen on the spot by astonishment or numbness or both. How had I come to be sitting in a truck in Raton? I felt as if I'd kidnapped myself, to tell the truth. I felt as if, kidnapped, I could only watch helplessly while Sarah's charming comedy of manners unfolded: the ingenue emerging from the office with an old bleach bottle, which she holds up as she makes a pretty face to the audience, the unfull house of Jennie, and there the starlet goes, around the side of the building, hurrying offstage to pee.

The black mouth of a garage was decades thick with grease, but the pumps and the Exxon sign were incongruously new, as if the corporation made damn sure of a spiffy logo. In the cashier's office, I found a man with a belly too big for his arms to encircle, brushing a little girl's hair. "Howdy!" he cried. "New truck?" I should have headed east. You'll never find a stranger in New Hampshire trying to be your best pal.

The clerk's smile spread across his fat face. He wore a gas station attendant's shirt, with the white sewn-on badge. HENRY, it said. The little girl, maybe six, gazed at the ceiling with a bored, pained expression, like a put-upon queen. She was exceptionally pretty, with enormous blue eyes and black lashes and pale, pale skin. "My dad pulls too tight," she announced to the ceiling.

"Amanda, that is not the truth," her father said, drawing the girl's hair into a ponytail. "Say it."

"That is not the truth," she said dully. Part of her prettiness was her astonishing skin, so pale it was tinged blue, an oddly delicate, beautiful look. Even her lips looked slightly lavender.

"Henry—" I began, only to be interrupted by Her Royal Highness.

"Henry?" Amanda said, glaring at me. "My daddy's name is Vincent. He just wears those shirts. You shouldn't assume things, you know."

Henry, finishing Amanda's ponytail, patted her head. "I buy them second-hand," he said. "It's like being a new person every day!" He actually laughed at his own joke. "But I'm always Amanda's daddy," he said tenderly, or sadly, or both.

I picked out two lollipops and four candy bars and gum and chips and asked for a carton of Camels.

"Are you going to eat *all* of that?" Amanda asked. "You'll get fat, you know. Anyway, cigarette smoking will kill you. My daddy smokes. I worry about him *all* the time."

"It's for my friend," I told her. "Why do you care about my health?"

"What friend?" She scowled at me, a miniature convenience store clerk, ready for the robbers with a shotgun under the counter. "You're too tall."

"All the better to eat you with."

"That doesn't make any sense."

"Amanda, you aren't being nice," Henry said. "This lady's a *customer*."

Amanda rose majestically and marched to the farthest corner of the little room, where she dramatically pouted, fiddled with the candy display, and made a bigger display of ignoring us. I told Henry about the truck's recent difficulties, praying he wouldn't shake his head mournfully. Instead, he stared at Amanda's back, her tense little shoulders. "I'm going outside, cupcake," he said. She didn't answer. He said, "You can have some candy, sugar-pie. Do you want some candy?" She ignored him. "You'll be okay in here, right, honey?" She shrugged. "She eats a lot of candy," he told me. "She loves sweets."

"So she won't starve to death if we take a look at my truck," I said, sick of the fatherly display. I wondered how long it would take for him to fatten her up, too.

Without turning, Amanda said, "Why should I be nice to her when she's mean to me?" Good question, little girl. My philosophy in a nutshell.

HENRY lumbered out the door behind the Ugly Chick. He asked a couple of questions, said, "Sounds fixable," with such cheerful authority that I felt optimistic myself. He squinted at the truck, lifted the hood. "So it's a new truck, am I right? I knew because of the temporary license. I notice things."

"Actually," I said, "it's a getaway truck. We're running away from home. Her fiancé beats her; my husband, unfortunately, doesn't beat me. I wish he would, since at least it would inject a little excitement into things. Ironic, don't you think?"

Henry gave me his wide, fixed grin and glanced back at the store and Amanda standing in the doorway. "Just kidding," I said. "I'm sorry. I've been in a bad mood all day."

"That's all right," Henry said. "Everybody has bad days." He took out a cigarette and gazed at it. "I'm a sick man," he said. "It's an addiction. My daughter wants me to quit, but I just can't seem to manage." He had nice eyes under all that padding. They were just like Amanda's, bright blue, with thick straight lashes. I wondered why he was so fat. Maybe he was divorced. Maybe these few after-school hours were the only time he got to spend with his daughter. Did he stock up at the end of his day, Cokes and candy bars, a pack of cigarettes and two pounds of potato chips for the long night on the couch? I saw him ladling small comfort down his throat, the flickering TV light outlining his body's furrows. God, I hoped not. Give him a girlfriend. A best friend. A wonderful sense of humor. He doesn't wear a wedding ring, but give him a wife who loves him.

Ever so carefully, he laid the unlit cigarette on the Ford's fender and leaned in, breathing heavily as he poked around, his big belly getting in the way. "I'll tell you the trick to life, to bad days." He spoke with such certainty that for a moment I hoped he would going to say something astonishingly wise and accurate, as if his knowledge about truck engines extended to life in general. But he only said, "Pay attention. Notice the good things. They're all around us. Even bad things have good things attached."

Silly me; I was disappointed. I unwrapped my candy bar and let chocolate puddle on my tongue. From this vantage point, I could see far across the plains, miles of distance Sarah and I had just driven, which gave me some satisfaction. Okay, Henry. There's your good thing. I am the Sister Whose Brother Is Dead, but at least I've covered a couple hundred miles.

Henry ducked out from under the hood. "My theory is, it's the thermostat. Overheated. Then it cooled down, so you could start it again. Should be easy to put a new one in, just a couple of hours work. That's a good thing for you, am I right?"

Sarah was still in the bathroom, doing God knows what—rolling her hair, plucking her eyebrows—or, I thought, and panic fluttered to life in me, she might be on the road, her thumb out, the bag over her shoulder. I gave Henry the keys and told him to have his way with the Ford, and I trotted around the rest of the building, no easy feat in alligator heels, and she didn't open the locked bathroom door, though I pounded and I yelled, so I scurried to the office, and asked Amanda if she'd seen my friend.

Amanda was tremendously busy sucking on a lollipop. She sucked thoughtfully before speaking around it. "She's in the bathroom."

"No she isn't."

"She took the key."

"Aren't you clever," I said. "That proves everything."

"You're mean," she said. "I don't like you."

"What are you, two years old?" There's a zinger, coming from a lady acting like a two-year-old herself: the toddler, rushing outside, spinning, searching, comically hysterical, as if Sarah and her charming ingenue act were the only thing keeping me alive in this world, my heart racing, God oh God where is she—and there she was, next door at McDonald's. She stood at the pay phone juggling the bleach bottle, a big soda, and the receiver, into which she was talking. Is this how parents feel when they find the kid who has toddled into the street? Jennie, losing her cookies, bounds down the hill, plows to a stop, shoves Sarah aside, and hangs up the phone.

"I was *calling* someone," the Pea Princess says loudly. "Or is that against Jennie's kidnapping rules?"

"Shut up," the Ugly Chick hisses. "Goddamn you, just shut the fuck up."

"You are so *tense*. Relax. What's wrong with you, anyway?"

"You have a big mouth," the Ugly Chick says.

The Pea Princess, dignified like a princess should be, offers a cool, haughty smile, which says, *Put another mattress on that pile so I can sleep.* "And you *used* to be cool," the Pea Princess says.

The Ugly Chick drops her crushed chocolate bar, adding litterbug to her long list of crimes. She takes the Pea Princess by the hand and marches her off. If the exhausted vacationers, staggering out of their overloaded station wagons, notice them, they see a tall, mean woman in a raggedy old suit dragging along a pretty little girl in her Indian getup. Later, they will be Eyewitnesses. "That red-haired girl, I noticed her because of her hair, and she didn't look too happy about being manhandled by that ugly chick."

Dragged along, nearly stumbling, the red-haired girl says, "I called the state troopers. You're in big trouble, lady."

"Really."

"My mother. She says I'm safe with a medical student."

"Really."

"Okay. Jake. I called Jake. All that stuff about bruising myself? I lied. Actually, Jake's a homicidal maniac, and he's going to kill us both. That's what you want to hear, right? You're so predictable. Don't you hate being boring?" Now they are back at the garage, hands smeared with chocolate like children, face-to-face with the fat man and his pretty little daughter.

"I need to go to the bathroom, but you stole the key," Amanda said.

"I didn't steal it," Sarah said. "I *used* it."

Amanda's lavender lips twisted into a suspicious frown. "You weren't in the bathroom," she said. "And look at your hands. You're all dirty. You're supposed to wash your hands after you go to the bathroom."

"Aren't you a genius," I said.

"Don't listen to Jennie," Sarah said. "She's a big fat bitch."

"You shouldn't swear around kids," Amanda said.

"How about we all just head inside and stop bickering," Henry said.

In the office we cleaned our hands, ate chocolate, and Sarah and Amanda chatted it up, gossiping girls, catty, knowing, pretty girls. Already, Amanda knew why Sarah wore the orange skirt, the moccasins, and Sarah knew that Amanda lived in Denver with her mother, that Raton was the most boring place on earth, and that she was ten, not the six years old she looked. Sarah told Amanda about Jake, her *ex*-fiancé, looking pointedly at me, and she told her about the dress, which was old, and our trip away from her broken heart.

I knew the exact dimensions of the interior of the garage, and the exact number of bicycle inner tubes mysteriously hanging on one wall. Nine.

"You have nice hair," Amanda told Sarah. "Is it fake?"

"Natural. Isn't it awful?" Sarah said. "Why are your lips blue?"

"Candy," Amanda said. "Blue suckers."

Henry called out from beneath the truck, the ever-vigilant mechanic father. "Amanda," he said. "Is that the truth?"

Amanda sighed loudly. "My heart is broken, too," she recited woodenly. "I had a hole in it. I've had four surgeries. Do you want to see my scars?"

I turned, stunned, and took a good look at Amanda. Well. *Obviously.* The symptoms were written all over her.

"That sucks," Sarah said.

"Don't say that," Amanda said. "It's fine."

"No it's not," I said. "I mean—"

"*See?*" Amanda said to her father's boots. "He always makes me say it. Then everybody acts stupid."

"Nobody's making a fuss," Henry said, sliding out from beneath the truck.

"I'm ready to go pee now," Amanda said. Henry rose to escort her, but she sidled away from him. "I can do it by myself," she said. "You two should go smoke so you can kill yourselves." Henry fondled his cigarette. I stood awkwardly beside him, scrambling for a simple sentence, which came out, "I'm sorry she's sick."

He shrugged. "Things are what they are. Like I said, you've got to shoot for the positive attitude. At least she's here, I mean."

Amanda glared at her father. "I'll be dead of a heart attack by the time I'm twelve. But dogs only live twelve years, so it's not that sad, right, Daddy?" His face stricken, he looked away. Poor Henry. A sickly sadist for a daughter.

"Sugar," Henry began, but Amanda grandly exited, leaving a trail of disapproval behind her.

Sarah saved me from the next wrong thing I might say. Sarah, my gorgeous red-haired social superhero. She dumped the dress on the counter and took Henry outside to smoke a cigarette, her hair lighting up gold in the sun.

HENRY worked on the truck, and I bought us all lunch from McDonald's. I started unpacking the food as soon as I got back to the garage. Other than chocolate and doughnuts, I hadn't eaten all day, and the greasy smell of fries was intoxicating.

Amanda, bare feet propped on the counter, was getting a pedicure from Sarah. "Do you know how *hot* velvet is?" Sarah asked, wedging tufts of paper towel between Amanda's toes. "I feel like I'm in prison, and my mother makes me wear it just because she *wants* me to suffer, I swear to God—"

"I want to try it," Amanda said. "I like that color."

"Fine," Sarah said. "Your wish is my command." Using nail scissors from her black bag, Sarah cut a few stitches in her skirt, and then, with expertise, she ripped the seam, efficiently doing away with the lower tiers. Dressed in a miniskirt, she offered the leftover velvet to Amanda. Sarah said, "I swear, if I could get naked right now, I would." She knotted her tuxedo shirt under her breasts, exposing her belly, an accident or calculation. "If this skirt's so hot, imagine how many yards went into the wedding dress, and can you imagine how hot it would be, with no air-conditioning—"

Amanda said, "Why do you have all those *bruises?*" Which Sarah tried or pretended to ignore: "I mean, what was a bride supposed to do, make sheets for the wedding bed with her train?"

Amanda said, "I just want to know if you're sick, too, or something."

"My father died of a heart attack," Sarah said.

"Oh," Amanda said. She stroked the velvet. I had to admire Sarah's timing, the tone, the cheerful recitation that underlined her devastation. Sarah leaned over Amanda's stick legs, her hair brushing Amanda's bony knees, and she painted a glimmering ruby streak on Amanda's toe and told her the story.

Listening to Sarah, Amanda looked different, and it took me a while to figure it out: she had relaxed. She looked not angry or breathless but tired, with purple shadows under her eyes, her shoulders sagging, her hands resting, loosely curled, on the orange velvet in her lap. How did Sarah know exactly what Amanda needed? Sarah would be a better doctor than I ever could be.

Dr. Sarah ate a fry. This was her rhythm, talking, painting, eating a fry.

Like her eating, like her storytelling, she was methodical with the polish, a real pro. She never spilled. She let it dry between each of three coats. This Sarah, simultaneously meticulous and chaotic, tender and careless. Under her ministrations, Amanda grew sleepier, happier, sweeter. And sicker, as if only bratty selfishness could get her the extra oxygen she needed. In the afternoon sun, Amanda's red toes shimmered magnificently, wetly red.

Sunny would like Sarah. The idea came into my head so clearly, with such certainty, that I didn't doubt it, or even stop to question why. Of course, I thought. Of course. I should have seen it sooner.

The afternoon stretched toward evening. Occasionally, customers came in to pay, but otherwise this tableau of Sarah and Amanda and the ruby-red nail polish went uninterrupted. The idea of Sunny loving Sarah had time to rage through me, an infection of fantasy so strong that it was more like a memory than a wish.

H E R E ' S a typically cryptic postcard from Sunny's freshman year at Berkeley: *We live in barracks—landlord got green paint cheap. Horseshoes, cold beer.*

Here is the house, and here is the porch, both ugly army green. Here is the student neighborhood, filled with students lolling on dilapidated porches, Sunny's house no different, two stories and a pitched roof and sagging steps littered with beer cans and plastic cups.

Sarah's hair shines in the last of the day's light. They're both smoking. She wears an orange velvet miniskirt, its hem unraveling, a tuxedo shirt knotted at the waist. Sunny, in jeans and a T-shirt with a cartoon of a naked woman wrapped in a Communist flag, looks handsome, interesting, and, dare I say it, sexy. Sarah drips polish on the porch, then swears, but Sunny, blowing a lungful of smoke, says, "It's an improvement."

"Say something in Russian," Sarah says. "Your sister has been going on and on about how you speak it, so I'm all primed and everything." He obliges her, and it sounds like the language of a country where people love one another like bears, furry and greedy, honey smeared on their faces, vodka to wash it down. It sounds wonderful. He translates: *In Russia, hope is the last thing to die.*

On the lawn across the street, college boys play horseshoes. The sun slips past the roof. Sarah shudders in the sudden chill. Watching her, Sunny is flooded with a heady sense of certainty.

Sarah capped the polish and blew on Amanda's nails. "Jennie," she said to the ruby toes. "I didn't call Jake. I called Chris."

"Chris?"

"You know, Chris? Your *husband*?"

I took a deep breath. "What did he say?"

"Nothing. You hung up for me, remember? Nobody answered."

"Now I'll do you," Amanda said. "Give me the polish. And finish your story, please."

"Please?" Sarah said. "That's progress." And she picked up her story, her mother and breakfast, the eggs Sarah vomited on the floor of the classroom.

But I didn't listen. I didn't even care that she had called Chris. I was infected with the idea of Sunny Boy Blue saying to Sarah, "Let me try."

Sarah gives him the polish and, drawing all of his rattling energy into the effort, he paints her toe. She laughs at the mess he makes. "It isn't easy," he says. "You make it look like nothing, but it isn't." Across the street, the boys throw their horseshoes. Sarah says nothing, and Sunny's silent, too, and they aren't waiting or nervous because they know the answer already. It has fallen between them, a perfect circle, like the red polish on the porch step, so lovely against the ugly green that it looks intentional.

Sunny fixes dinner, and they eat outside on the porch, beside the red circle. Two people meet, and everything becomes more than yesterday; no food, for instance, could taste better than this pile of bow-tie noodles, slick with butter and pepper, slipping into her lap. They laugh and scoop up the pasta with their fingers. The beer slides cold and sharp down their throats. They sit with an inch of air between them, and in the same way the pasta tastes finer and the beer colder, this air between them is more than what it would have been yesterday. They watch the neighbors playing the endless game of horseshoes, listen to the clink and thump of the game.

SARAH tells Amanda about Mrs. Lucero with the mole on her eyelid. Amanda makes a mess of Sarah's toes, but Sarah doesn't even notice, or at least pretends she doesn't; she just babbles on happily. In my infected mind, though, Sarah falls miraculously speechless, silenced by what is happening with Sunny out on the green porch.

Sarah's ten red toes sparkle in the porch light. They sit for hours, talking softly or not at all, smoking, lighting two more, and even this simple act seems to acquire the solemnity of ceremony. The night deepens. The horseshoe game goes on and on. At last he presses her hands between his palms and says, "Let's go for a drive." Across the way, under the yellow streetlights, the horseshoes still clink, one after the other, solid around the stake in the ground.

On the Golden Gate Bridge, he pours gas into a bucket of tennis balls, and one by one, he lights them and drops them flaming into the ocean. She claps her hands over her mouth at the beauty and ferocity and wild woolly craziness of it. There, smelling of gas and smoke, of buttered noodles and beer, he shelters her inside his coat and whispers Russian, and she knows what he means without translation. Pressed against his fog-dampened shirt, knowing swells in her heart. My God, she thinks. I love him. And at this moment he says it out loud. I love you, he says. Isn't that crazy? No, she says, it isn't crazy at all. Sometimes you just know. And they live. Happily ever after, they live.

SARAH finished explaining ideopathic thrombocytopeniz, and Amanda turned to me, brush poised in midair. "Is it the truth? Is she telling me the truth?"

Henry appeared, loudly announcing, "Your truck is fixed," looking desperate to interrupt any way he could. If I'd been paying attention, I would have stopped Sarah's story myself, for his sake. Just look at the grief in his eyes, the panic, despair, rage. Jesus, Jennie, you fucking idiot. The man doesn't want to hear stories about death by heart attack. I started babbling about how we'd better hit the road, late as we were.

Amanda said, "Late for what?"

"We're visiting my brother. He's waiting for us."

"Oh really," Sarah said. "Is that a fact?"

Henry began adding the bill. Staring straight at Sarah, I said, "I really want to see him." I faltered, then began again. "I don't want to go alone." To my astonishment, it seemed I'd used exactly the right tone.

Sarah squeezed my arm as if she understood completely, and for an instant I was so glad that I forgot I was lying. "Your brother," she said. "It's good to give up a grudge."

It hit me then. I was going to tell one great big whopper, nurse it along; we'd be on the road for as long as I could keep up the Big Lie: Sunny is waiting for us.

"Thanks for fixing our truck," I said.

"Her truck," Sarah said. "I'm along for the ride. I didn't even know where we were going until now, thank you very much."

"I notice a lot about people by their cars," Henry said, and it sounded like an accusation, a threat, or some other terrible thing. A warning.

"We need to hit the road," I said, repeating myself, idiot that I am, trying to figure out how to say good-bye, which is harder when life intersects with a stranger's—too brief to swear friendship, but long enough to know important, indelible facts, to guess at the intricate miseries of their lives. "We've kept you too long," I said.

Henry didn't answer. Clearly, he was furious. Smiling grimly, he handed me the bill. Our Henry didn't come cheap. "I guess the good side is, it's running now," I said as I paid, but he barely smiled.

"Why don't the two of you come for a ride, see what I did," he said. "Insurance reasons, I got to drive it out of the garage anyway." Amanda wanted to come. He said, "Amanda, honey, there's no room in that truck for my big ol' butt and you and these two. Why don't you stay here, get ready to head home?" She protested, but he said, "I'm not kidding around here." He gave Sarah back the velvet she'd given to Amanda, who folded her arms and pouted, dramatically indignant. Henry said, "You can't just take things from strangers." I wanted to bolt, but Sarah knew how to leave. She gave Amanda a long, loving hug, while Henry stood by, oozing impatience.

He pulled the Ford out of the garage so fast it's a wonder he didn't do damage. I'm sorry, I wanted to say. He drove a few blocks, past McDonald's, past another gas station. Abruptly, he pulled to the shoulder, killed the engine, and turned to me. "Like I said, I notice things," he said tightly. "I didn't want to say anything in front of my girl, but I can put two and two together, and what with the bruises, the truck which you bought just today, by the temporary, what with the ring and the story about the boyfriend, I figure what you said about the getaway truck, about running off, it was probably true. And I don't care for it. I don't care for you inflicting this kind of ugliness on my little girl in there, who's sick enough, who's probably dying without having some, some, *bitch* lie to her about people dying of heart attacks—" His voice broke. He laid his head on the steering wheel and wept, his vast shoulders shaking, a horrible, pathetic sight.

"But it was true," Sarah said. "I told the truth about my father, I swear it, I didn't make it up—" And her voice broke too, which sent me completely over the edge into the Ugliest of Uglies, rage, strong and pure and undeniable.

"Look, Henry," I said, "or Vincent, or whatever the fuck your name is, I can't feel sorry for you. Clean up the place. Shovel out some of the grease. Go on a diet; stop smoking so much; stop being pathetic and move on out of that wallowing pit."

"Jennie, stop it," Sarah said.

"Make your bratty daughter behave herself, even if she does have a hole in her heart. Then we'll see if you deserve some sympathy. But in the meantime, don't start deciding who we are just because your own life is a mess."

Sarah cried, "Jennie, shut the fuck up!"

After that little detonation, none of us spoke. Henry lifted his head and, with a slow, deliberate dignity, he opened the door and got out. Henry, I wanted to call. Vincent. I'm sorry. You have my sympathy. The truth is, I feel sick to my stomach with sympathy. Instead, I started the truck, turned it around, and drove. We passed him, walking with a lumbering grace, his head high. He didn't glance our way. I took the on-ramp as fast as the useless, farting old truck could go.

I headed up the pass, toward Colorado. The signs warned of fire hazards, and no wonder, with the tinder-dry grass alongside the highway. The truck struggled along like a middle-aged man, maybe even Henry, who used to run fast when he was in high school, before he was ruined, not by age, but by a beautiful daughter counting her life in dog years.

Sarah chewed gum that stank of artificial grape; she blew and popped enormous bubbles, spit her gum into a piece of velvet, lit a cigarette, cartwheeled her lighter along the dashboard, clicked it on and off. She stubbed out the cigarette. She said, "When I called Chris, I got an answering machine. On the message, Chris says, 'Jennie is not okay.' I'm like, well, there's a news flash."

"You said nobody answered. You lied again."

She sighed. "I did not lie. I told you, he didn't *say* anything, and that's the truth, because I got a machine, which said, quote, If anyone knows where Jennie is, please leave a message. She is not okay. Unquote. So what the hell's wrong with you? You aren't having some kind of psychotic break, are you? Because if you are, I need to make some escape plans, thank you very much."

I knew how it went. Chris said, "She . . ." and there was a long pause while he considered whether to broadcast my Big Secret or to avoid my anger and salvage what might be left between us, and then he ended the long pause with "is not okay." I wanted to scream at Sarah. I breathed. I said, "Remember at my wedding? How my brother took me away?" But I couldn't seem to muster the anger that partnered this fact.

"Didn't like it, did you? Sucks, don't it?"

"Did you leave a message?"

She folded orange velvet and spread it across the cracked dashboard. "Decoration," she said. "Which, if I haven't mentioned it, is what this truck needs. See, you need to be more grateful for what people do for you. And you need to stop holding a grudge. And you can slow down now. I only told him we're in Raton, and that doesn't matter, since we're not there anymore." She lit a cigarette. And then she began to cry.

"Goddammit, Sarah," I said. "Turn off the spigots, will you?"

"Do you think it was Vincent's smoking that made Amanda like that? I mean, secondhand smoke can cause all kinds of birth defects, right?"

I glanced at her. She was staring at the end of her cigarette as if it would answer her question. She said she wasn't, but was this a sign she was pregnant? And with that, she had me. She won, like always. "So put it out," I said gently.

"What's the point?" she whispered. She took a deep lungful. But she dropped the cigarette out the window.

"That's how forest fires get started," I said.

"Who are you, my tía Maria?" She dried her tears. She produced a bottle of acetone, which smelled delicious, sharp and clean. She cleaned off Amanda's sloppy polish job until she had a pile of red-stained velvet squares. "My thighs are sticking to this plastic," she said, and made herself a velvet seat cover. "Too bad I don't have more. I'd cover the ceiling, the floor, the whole truck, or better yet for the price of that much velvet I could probably get a nicer car than this piece of junk. Why'd you buy this thing, anyway? It goes twenty-five miles per hour and looks like a rapist's truck."

"You're the expert on rapists."

"That's a shitty thing to say. Some things are not jokable, thank you very much." She spoke softly. "You shouldn't have said that to Vincent."

"I know." But there was no way to fix it. I rolled down my window, so my hair stormed around my face, and one corner of the temporary license came loose and chattered frantically, and these sounds made up a kind of silence, until Sarah announced, "We just left New Mexico." In the mirror I caught a glimpse of the back of the metal sign. Good, I thought. Good riddance.

5.

fAILURES

$\mathscr{M}$Y BABY BROTHER,
THE GENIUS

Wednesday Evening and Night, I-25, U.S. 40, Colorado
THE road took us in broad sweeping curves down the other side of the mountain, into Colorado. I told myself, I am in Colorado now. A fresh state. I tried to keep myself in that solid Ford by clinging to the steering wheel, but I could not fend off this thought: Sunny could be alive. Maybe Sunny wasn't the boy on the ferry. The police could have gotten it wrong. Maybe he called me from Seattle but returned to Berkeley where he'll greet us and laugh at the terrible mistake of anyone thinking he's dead. It was all the cops' misguided inference. A leap of assumptions instead of a leap into the sea.

No, I told that bitch, the Bereaved, peddler of false hope, I will not allow you into my ranch vee-hickle. In a desperate play to keep myself in Colorado, in the Ford, in this here and now, I cataloged every smell—Sarah's cigarette, my sweat, the grape gum, the light lemony smell of Sarah's hair. Sarah, who takes off her ring and jams it through the velvet, into a crack in the dash, so only the diamond shows. "There, she says, "I'm officially disengaged, and you can stop dragging me around every time I pick up a phone, because there's nobody we need to hide from."

But to no avail; Jennie, this woman who can't keep herself in the here and now, slides into What If. What if Sunny were waiting for us in Berkeley? What if Sarah loved him? What if Sarah married him in that aged and ridiculously opulent dress?

Pay attention, Jennie, to Sarah's diamond, how it breaks sunlight into color; pay attention to the rise and fall, the stream of Sarah's words—alas, too late. Nothing keeps the bell from tolling; five times, five times, five times. Count them on one hand, unfold your fist, consider the palm, which people always say they know so well, which is supposed to hold your future. Five times. He is a newborn and his head fits in the palm of my hand. He is Sunny Boy Blue, a small, dark-haired boy, who doesn't remember being born breech in August, or the piano, or the new white car. He remembers his sister, always there, watching him, protecting him, explaining things. She buys him candy. She combs his hair and gives him baths and takes him to cut down Christmas trees. She makes him a birthday cake, and he licks the sweet batter from the bowl. Flat on her back, she balances him on the soles of her feet, laughing and calling to him, "You're an airplane, Sunny! You're flying!" His sister's real name is Jennie. She teaches him about important things, about manners and Treasured Memories. He loves his sister's stories and the pictures that go with them. He loves his sister most of all, and she loves him, and this is all good—

This, goddammit, is the Bereaved whispering in my ear, and I will silence her. I yanked myself back to the Ford, to Sarah's voice, to how I ached from running too much the night before: in my butt, my groin, my calves and the nape of my neck and the backs of my knees. Quadriceps, femur, clavicle, scapula. Everyone knows these. But I am part of the club who knows that even the places where muscles attach to bone have names. That the geography of your interior has been mapped. Ischial tuberosity. Naviculum. Useless, irrelevant information.

Here. This is relevant. This highway. The sky is blue and the mountains are distant and the road stretches away from us. This is all there is. A deeply split dashboard. A passenger blowing cigarette smoke into the airstream curving around us. Two phrases turning over and over in my head—*I have to go, I want to see him*—until I know them well, like the back of my hand, the palm. With its five fingers, five times, five times.

When Sunny is six, Jennie moves in with a rich woman who lives in Upper Alfin. Jennie's new house is clean and fancy, and when Sunny visits, she gives him little chocolate cakes, or ice cream, or white bread with jam. Going home isn't fun. It's cold there, and sometimes Clarence and Faith are in town all night. One night, he starts a fire in the fireplace, and it catches the house on fire. He runs all the way to Jennie's, but the house burns down.

Then Clarence and Faith and Sunny live in Santa Fe. They have a phone and a toilet. One day, Jennie visits him to explain that she's going away to a school in New Hampshire. He doesn't want her to go. She says he has to understand; the only way they'll ever get to the house on the hill in Seattle is if she gets this education, if she does this important thing. "Is it near Russia?" he asks her, and she laughs. "No," she says. "It's only a state." Seattle, then. But no, it's not near Seattle, either. "You can write," she says. "You can call." She tells him, "I'll see you soon, I promise." She buys him a stack of prestamped postcards, and together they write the address of her new home again and again. "You can write to me every day, if you want."

He sends postcards back with messages about nothing: *My furry yellow kitten Paul. Yellow eyes and farts.* Or: *Pregnant=embarasada. Mom has warts.*

When he calls her in New Hampshire, he asks for Jennie, not for Juniper.

He sits with Paul purring on his knees, the phone tucked under his chin. Jennie asks if he's all alone. He tells her he's fine.

"I'll see you soon," she says. "I'll bring you here. I promise." But she graduates and goes to a different school for college before she sends him money to come see her. His father sends money, too, so there's enough for him to fly. He watches New Mexico get smaller and smaller.

On the plane he drinks three sodas and eats a lunch. There is a cookie. There is nothing but sky. The stewardess tells him he's handsome. He carries his mother's gift to Jennie: earrings with coral in them. The plane begins to drop back to land, which rushes up, green and strange, and he's frightened.

His sister is waiting, and his father, tall with frizzy hair and wild eyes. Then they're all together in New Hampshire. Jennie and Sunny walk across the school grounds, the grass rolling like carpet from building to building. They hike to the hills, to unmowed fields, where thousands of daisies grow.

His sister is beautiful, with her hair pinned up, and around them the summer insects hover. He's nine, but he holds her hand anyway. He looks up at Jennie in the meadow with the sun behind her, and it's hard to see her face.

In his head, he's writing the postcard he'll send her when he's home again. *You and Lipa. Beautiful queens of the world. Russian.* They walk and talk and pick daisies. He gives her the earrings he brought. "Mom made them," he says. "But they're from me."

"That's good," she says, and kisses him. They walk some more, and his father and his sister ask him questions about Clarence, about his mother, about fighting and what it's like in the middle of the night.

And then they tell him that he's rescued. They have a plan. He'll go home with Ray. So Sunny flies to Florida to live with his father, instead of back to New Mexico. He sends his mother postcards from Disney World, and Sea World, and Circus World, all the worlds. And one day he calls and Faith is crying. "Clarence left me alone," Faith says. "I'm all alone now." Sunny knows she's crying, though she doesn't make the slightest crying noise. He has a new cat, Paul the Second. He calls him Second, or later, *Dos,* and *Segundo.* His postcards to Jennie say, *Cockroaches, bad. Mice, good—big bucks.*

SHUT up, shut up, I tell this insidious Bitch, this Bereaved, who hisses, *So you thought you saved him,* and thank God for Sarah who pulls me back, anchors me, uses my thigh for a pillow, the wedding dress for a blanket, who smells of smoke and, faintly, of lemons, who says, "Play with my hair so I can sleep."

The rhythm, the silky texture, soothes me. "My rabbit's foot," I say.

"You can trust me," she murmurs. "I'm your friend."

"That's good," I say.

I really had run too far last night. I ached all over, butt, groin, calves, ankles, the soles of my feet, which made me think of Chris and me, studying on the couch, our backs against the armrests, our feet in each other's lap. Chris held my foot as if it were a talisman. My rabbit's foot, he said. I laughed. Jackrabbit, I said. Kangaroo rabbit. The steady warmth, the sturdy muscles of his palm curled around my instep, his fingers, all five of them. Five times.

IN the ninth grade, Sunny wins another award, this time for German. He spends his sophomore year in Berlin, where he loses his virginity to a girl named Ute and postcards his sister: *I love Ute. Send condoms.* Jennie does, with a letter about the fungus that grows in the mouths of people whose immune systems have failed. He replies with a picture of Ute. On the back he writes a sentence in German, which she takes to a professor who tells her it says, *Breasts like fresh bread, lips like Hatch chiles.* Apologizing, Jennie stumbles out of the teacher's office. She writes her brother a postcard with four words on it: *Thanks a bushel, Sunny.*

By his senior year it's Russian he rattles off to his amazed teacher. His postcard reads, *Russians say bird, and it sounds like a terrible wet burp.*

When he graduates from high school, Jennie flies to Florida. She takes him out alone, without Ray, for a dinner of filet mignon at a restaurant where waiters unfold their napkins for them. Jennie shows him how to hold his knife and fork. Later, he sends a postcard: *Fancy girls like me now.*

Sunny at eighteen flies to Moscow, birthplace of their grandmother, on a scholarship won with perfect Russian and a way of charming anyone who meets him. On a postcard: *Frostbite. Send gloves. Love Sunny.* She writes to beware loose Russian women, to look for sunshine, that the Russian Mafia is delighted to take the money of young American boys. He replies with a postcard of a naked woman, and on the back: *No money. Send condoms. Nicotine=good. No water; only vodka.*

He walks through a museum that once was a Russian castle, his hard-heeled boots echoing on marble as he tries to surprise his love of the moment, a student with flaxen hair and long sly eyes, Slavic bones and a mouth whose corners he kisses, whose full lower lip he takes between his teeth to make her laugh. He sends a photograph of himself on the steps of some building; he is in his army coat and his cap. He likes this picture; he writes in Russian (which Jennie translates by dictionary), *All the chicks say, send condoms.*

. . .

SARAH jerked just before she fell into sleep, a last spasm of consciousness. I tried to remember the name of that jerk, which signified the paralysis of muscles, something about the brain letting go. That's the thing about my studies: the details drain away, leaving a residue of *I know there's a name for that.* Sometimes I think medical school is training in vague recollections. But then I've only been at it for one year, and it was a distracted year at best.

There's nobody we need to hide from. Sarah slept, clutching the wedding gown like a child's toy, her hair shining golden red in the last of the sun, stirring in the wind of the open window. A sharp pain came into my chest, a swelling ache in my throat. Half blind from my own hair whipping around my face, the wind drying out my eyes, I thought, Nobody at all, but I was not reassured.

WHEN he's nineteen he comes home for his sister's wedding, and they have a grand, glorious celebration. After that, Sunny returns to Russia and dallies with a Turkish girl named Yasmin, a French girl named Collette, an English girl named Eileen. He returns to Berkeley.

And one August, on his birthday, his sister drives all the way to California. The battered old Ford creaks to a stop, and Sunny, leaning out of his attic window, sees the lovely red-haired Sarah peering up at him, her hand raised to shield her eyes from the sun, so that she seems to be waving, or saluting. And they fall in love, madly, and he teaches her the Russian word for "fucking." He learns Arabic, Swedish, Japanese, and Finnish. They marry, and they have a grand, glorious celebration.

He graduates, pursues his advanced degrees, and he and Sarah travel across Europe. He translates for money and sends home postcards of one or two sentences: *Have you ever eaten gefilte fish?* and *Risotto! Linguini! Sistina Chapelini!* He takes up horses, and once, in a smallish, backwards state whose totalitarian government may have spirited off a warhead or two, he's arrested by police who see him in his riding boots and pants and mistake him for a fascist. *Greece! Fornication of the gods! Marble!* Sarah bails him out; Sarah makes sure he's fed, Sarah leads him, laughing, through life, her whiskey eyes merry, her good cheer indomitable.

In his early thirties, Sunny settles with Sarah in a country whose language he speaks, where he teaches linguistics at a university and calls his sister from time to time with stories of the locals, mails her pictures of their red-haired son on his knees. *No eyebrows, one soft spot, two ears.* Later, *Paul's potty wars,* or *No beets for Paul.* Jennie copies these sentences onto labels and glues the pictures to the pages of a book with "Sunny Boy Blue" written on its spine.

He grows old; Sarah grows old with him. They visit the States; they visit Seattle, where his sister, a doctor by now, lives in the house on the Highest Hill. It's just as she always said it would be, the rooms light-filled, wooden-floored, with special nooks for special objects. From one of these, his sister the doctor takes out an album. She opens it, and inside are all of his post-cards, all of his women and all of his countries and all of his family. She says, "I've been keeping this for you." All of his sentences, one after the other, and he reads them and finds that, strung together, they make a complete story. His eyes fill and he looks to his sister and understands that she has always been following his fairy tale and then they are both finally crying together.

N I G H T fell, hard and black. I stopped in Denver for gas, Sarah drowsy and pouty, like a toddler. She went right back to sleep and I drove on, alone, past Denver. I started over the mountains on U.S. 40. The highway ascended in a long series of switchbacks, making the taillights of the car ahead flash as they slipped in and out of curves. I felt as if I weren't moving at all, as if the trees leapt out of the dark and into the puddle of light where I sat waiting, then leapt away again. The rhythm of their appearance and disappearance was hypnotizing. *You can go forever*, it said. *You will get there*, it said. I fell into a late-night driving trance, everything coming and arriving and going at once. The taillights flashing: *This way*, they said. *This way*.

I was alone. Outside, I saw only the occasional eyes of an animal, a jack-rabbit bounding away, or the deer which were everywhere. There was nothing in the world but my truck, nothing but those taillights and the French fries on the floor, soda sloshing through its straw, Sarah's lemon smell, the metal door under my left arm, and the Bereaved, whispering vicious, bitter nothings in my ear.

There is a second version of Sunny's story. That version ends when Sunny kidnaps Jennie away from her wedding reception, so that brother and sister part angry, Jennie to honeymoon in the warm sea, and Sunny not to Russia as planned, but to hitchhike up the coast in his old army coat, drinking coffee in diners, keeping himself drunk or stoned. He scrawls a Russian message on a postcard and sends it to his sister.

In August, in Seattle, birthplace of his parents, Sunny arrives at a pay phone in the back of a bar. There, he writes *Juniper Tree Burning* on the wall, and he calls Jennie to say he's sorry, but he makes the mistake of calling her Juniper, so nothing is settled between them. He boards a ferry. Laughing, al-most twenty years after he backed unwilling into the world, he climbs the railing of the ferry and he waves, and then he jumps into the sea and he drowns.

That is one version of the end, filled with everything terrible and irreversible, one his sister never imagined, never predicted, never told herself, one with no possibility of happily ever after.

But I am dreaming of the other version.

$\mathcal{B}$LIND

Early Morning, Thursday, Colorado

T H E N there was the deer, the flash of its startled eyes, a reflected green flash. I had time to think, Don't swerve, and to think of all the people who die swerving, and then I did swerve, but couldn't avoid the sickening and unmistakable sound of metal colliding with flesh. I slammed on the brakes just in time to keep us from slamming into the side of the mountain. Sarah rolled off the seat and onto the floor, and she cried, "Hey! I was *sleeping!*"

I ran back to the deer lying in the road. I felt for wounds in the bristly coat, up the limbs, over the rise of its belly, up its neck, past the tapering jaw, the eyes, the soft whiskered muzzle. I felt for his beating heart and I remembered the feel of a newly dead deer heart in my six-year-old hands.

It was a bad time for nostalgia; the deer came to and kicked me smack in the stomach. I fell backwards with a grunt as the air rushed out of me. For a moment I couldn't breathe, and then the pain arrived. I gasped, moaned. My world narrowed to my belly, my hands, and my pain. The deer struggled to rise. I thought of him wandering through the trees: infection, gangrene, pus, agony. I screamed for Sarah and threw myself on him. He resisted feebly this time, as if that last kick was all he had left. His breath chuffed out of him, desperate, terrified.

Sarah cried, "God, oh God, did you *kill* it?"

I rolled away and lay beside him, wondering how much damage I'd done by falling on him like that. I borrowed Sarah's lighter to see. I put my ear close to his nose and he wasn't breathing. I knew there was a way to give CPR to a dying animal. I didn't think of rabies or anything else that I should have considered; I saw the white hairs around the fine bridge of his nose; I thought that his face was much more slender than I expected. I let the lighter go out. I took his muzzle into my mouth and I breathed for him, and he must have just left his mother, these were probably his first headlights; I was his first human, puffing into him, sharing breath, and I am trying but there is nothing to do he's dead I've killed him.

I sat back on my heels. His flank was covered with the coarse wiry hair of a grown deer, but, I imagined, a certain degree softer. I thought, I have killed this deer. If we wanted, we could butcher him and eat him. Have a barbecue. Young venison is mighty tasty. Beneath his fur, the warm muscle poised to kick or spring up a mountain—

"Jennie," Sarah whispered. "Jennie? Are you crying?"

He moved, a nearly imperceptible quiver.

"He's alive," I said. He was the size of a dog, smaller than any deer I'd ever seen. The truck would terrify him, but it was warm. I needed to get him to a real doctor. I lifted him easily and carried him to the truck.

I used Sarah's lighter to examine him. His legs were delicate-boned, his hooves dainty, and one front leg was crushed, a mess of white bone, cartilage. I looked away. He was going to die. I was not going to cry over a deer, goddammit. Why did I keep coming smack up against the world and all its ludicrous coincidences? Okay, it was dark, it was the mountains, it was peak season for young and stupid deer. Or I could say, the world is a clever joke thought up by God.

"He isn't bleeding," Sarah said. "That's good, right?"

"Or else it's all internal." I felt like a fraud for saying it. Next I'd be saying, get me a crash cart and ten ccs of adrenaline, *STAT!*

We laid Sarah's dress over him. He struggled against the heavy fabric, the human scent. I smelled the acrid urine of panic or near-death, and I thought, Well, it's settled. I owe my boss, my ex-boss, ten thousand dollars, or however much that dress is worth to her.

Sarah climbed in the back of the truck. I turned the key and got nothing. Not even a click. I tried again, and still nothing. Sarah rapped on the window. I rolled it down. "What happened?" she asked. "Did he die?"

"The truck," I said. "It died." I went around to look under the hood. By the flame of Sarah's lighter, I recognized carburetor, battery, air filter, radiator cap—and didn't have a clue. I dropped the hood and walked around the truck, but I couldn't leave and I couldn't stay. I slammed my fist into the fender, then stumbled to the lip of the highway, a gush of pain in my knuckles. I closed my eyes and fought off the tears. I took in my deepest breath and shouted into the canyon: *FUCK.* And then over and over again, softly. Fuck. As my father taught me. Cocksucking motherfucking fuck. The pain in my hand was exquisite.

Sarah touched my arm. "Jennie. You're scaring me."

"I should have known better. You pick it out, you take it to a mechanic, and you don't *buy* it"—my voice rose and broke, and I pulled it back into control—"until you do. Not me. I just barged ahead." I could walk over the edge of the highway and tumble for a very long time. It was so dark, I wouldn't even know which step would take me over the edge. "I brought us here, to the middle of nowhere, in a piece of shit."

"It's not the end of the world. We'll fix it."

FUCK. I howled it out, damning god and the world and every person in it, and then I choked on my own yelling; my throat closed off and in the place of my voice was a swollen ache.

"Jennie," Sarah said, gripping my arm. "We have to take care of the deer, right? Right? Right?"

I turned toward the truck. "Right," I said softly.

"And we have to get out of the middle of the road before someone runs us over, right?"

"Right," I said, and let her lead me to the shoulder.

"Can we look at your hand?"

I held the lighter for Dr. Sarah, who opened and closed my fingers, prodded my tender knuckles. No broken skin. No broken bones, from what I could tell. "I hit like a girl," I said.

Sarah said, "You're not going to go ballistic on me again, are you?"

"I don't think so."

"Well, that's a big relief, let me tell you. So what should we do?"

T H E deer was trembling, from fear, surely, but also from shock. I needed to get all of us warm. I decided to build a fire. "Wait here," I said.

"You're leaving me? You can't leave me."

"I'm getting firewood," I said. "I'll be back."

I climbed up the hill by feel, groping with my feet and hands for wood. When I reached the trees, I paused. My stomach throbbed where the deer had kicked me, and my hand hurt with a louder kind of ache. I couldn't hear anything but my own breath. I threw back my head until all I saw was the dizzying, extravagant stars. I staggered a step. There were so many, foreground, background: they gave the sky depth and body and reminded me I was looking at something limitless. I squatted, trying, I suppose, to come to earth. I listened for anything. There was my breath. In the distance a wind stirred; it grew louder as it approached, and then it arrived, chilling me and populating the air with its whispering. It moved on, growing smaller, quieter, vanishing. In time, a new wind arrived. For what must have been minutes but felt like hours, I listened to the wind ebb and flow, like the sound a child hears in a seashell and calls the ocean. I almost believed, for a moment, that I could stay there forever on that thick pad of needles. I remembered that when I was a child I thought the trees made the wind. It occurred to me that I should pray. I thought, Please. It was all I had in me. *Please.*

Sarah's nervous voice came from below. "Jennie? Where are you?"

"Here I am." I rose and moved on. By now, I could make out the shadows which were trees and the other shadows which were the spaces between trees.

"Again," she called. "Keep doing it."

"Here."

I moved up the hill, calling *here*, and *here*, as if I were inventing my location by naming it. Eventually, I stumbled against a fallen tree and broke off a limb with a loud crack.

"Jennie? Are you okay?"

"Still here." I picked myself up and decided to take as much of it as I could.

"What happened?"

"I tripped over a tree," I said.

Her laughter rang out. "You can't trip over a tree."

"A dead tree," I said. I started back down, dragging it behind me.

After the dark of the woods, the world was almost bright. I could see Sarah's shadow in the moonlight. She was squatting beside the truck with her skirt lifted. She said, "I had to pee so bad. Can you imagine me in labor? I'll be in the middle of a contraction, and I'll be like, Wait, I gotta pee."

"Sarah," I said. I opened the truck door, thinking, What if she really is pregnant? But she's so small, she can't be—"How . . ." How can you be sure you aren't, I meant to ask, only the deer's dark eyes stared without blinking. He was dead. Strange, the way you can tell. The shift from animate to inanimate is as real as anything. How did I recognize the alchemy of it, the transformation from life to thing? I felt his neck where I thought there should be a pulse or some other sign of life. There was none. I confirmed it by holding my cheek near his nose. No breeze of exhalation. I didn't want to tell Sarah.

"How?" she said. "What do you mean, how?"

And I am a fool, so I tried again. "Are you? Pregnant, I mean."

She looked at me and she said, "No, for the last time. You'll just have to believe a liar like me, at least until I get my period and then I'll have some proof."

Ashamed for asking, I gave up searching for fireplace rocks and kicked an indentation in the dirt. Let them cite us for fire building in fire season, if we were lucky enough to have some ranger happen along. I began breaking the branches into twigs and kindling and larger pieces, using my feet and weight when I needed them. The wood broke with satisfying reports that echoed through the clear air. Most birds sing love songs in the early morning, when the air is cold and the moisture has precipitated out of it, because these are the qualities that let sound travel the farthest. Although of course they don't know that. They know only the urge.

"It must have been like being blind," Sarah said. "In the woods, I mean.

I've always wondered if blind people see better with their hands. Do they?"

"Maybe," I said. I was having trouble with a branch. I jumped on the tree with all my weight. It didn't give. I jumped on it again.

She was looking at the sky. "God," she whispered. "It makes me feel like there's no up or down." She lit a cigarette and in her lighter's small flame, the stars faded. She exhaled in a long, melodramatic sigh. On the third jump, the branch snapped with a crack like a gunshot. Sarah said, "You know what I noticed about the deer? It's a girl. It has little nipples."

I didn't want to look at it ever again. I busied myself with crumpling McDonald's wrappers and tenting twigs. My hand pain had diminished to a bland ache, background noise, a reminder. "Lighter," I said.

"Yes, Doctor."

I lit the paper. In the crisp piney air, the cigarette smoke and French fry grease were noxiously foreign. The fire started nicely, sparking and snapping because dead pine burns hot. We moved closer and huddled together. The flames caught the larger pieces. I knew how to start fires; that was one thing my parents taught me. I watched it crackle and flame up, but I saw the pink marrow of that leg bone, the white cartilage, the deer's flaring nostrils, its large dark eyes, its soft underbelly. I cradled my damaged hand. Daddy, you taught me well. He always had some wound brought on by his own temper—skinned knuckles, gouged palms. That caved-in spot on his shin.

"My dad used to hunt deer," I said. "He was a poacher. He hunted off-season."

"I know what poacher means."

I found myself telling her what I had never said out loud, that I wondered if he used his headlights to freeze the deer and make them easy pickings, and I had to undercut this traitorous speculation by telling her about Ray butchering deer, which led us, inevitably, to Sarah wondering if that's why I was a doctor, and I told her I was a doctor as antidote to a life of Signs and Prayer, which made me feel like a more dangerous traitor, this time against God and the Church. I was circling a block that led me to the same place, the intersection of the Fool and her Big Mouth.

The fire obliterated everything; I couldn't see the trees or the sky or the edge of the road anymore. I looked into the flames, and my back was cold and my face uncomfortably hot. "It's complicated," I said guiltily, brown-nosing God. "Believing things seems to help some people."

Sarah looked up at the sparks rising into the sky. "I can't even see the stars," she said. "Isn't that weird? I have this theory about God. You know he's there, like the stars? But you can't always see him. You just have to assume."

The wind moaned through the trees. The wood cracked and popped, and I moved the big trunk in closer. Sarah said, "Do you love your husband?"

"Of course."

"Really?"

Ah, guilt. There it was, tapping me on the shoulder, but luckily, I was saved by the whine of a car coming fast up the mountain. We looked at each other, listening.

"Who drives this late at night?" Sarah said. "Rapists, that's who."

"Milkmen," I said, and the car grew louder and louder; we could see its headlights flashing on trees as it rounded curves. "Let's get out of here," I said. We ran up the hill into the woods. We crouched, panting. The engine grew louder. Down below, our little campsite looked warm and mysterious, the flickering fire, the mound in the truck that was a deer under a wedding dress. "We should have put out the fire," I said.

"Here it comes," Sarah whispered. The engine sounded powerful. My heart raced. How could he not stop? How long would we have to wait for him to leave? I was working myself into the panicked state of a child who believes the boogeyman is on her heels. Sarah squeezed my arm.

Here he was: the bad guy in a sleek silver sportscar, roaring past, not stopping or even slowing, and as suddenly as he arrived, he was gone.

"Man," Sarah said, "that scared the shit out of me."

"Me too," I said. Breathless, laughing at ourselves, we climbed down the hill. The fire had dwindled; we fed it twigs, watched the flames for a few minutes. "Sarah," I said finally, "the deer died."

"I know," she said. "I already knew." She stirred the fire. "Jennie," she said. "You know what it's like to lose your father?"

I considered this question, the yes answer, the no. My father, who left and came back so many times before he left for good, off to the Edge of the World, to Florida. "No," I said. "I guess not."

"I'll tell you what it's like," Sarah said. "One day you have a daddy who loves you, and then he's dead and your mom blames you for it, and you're this little six-year-old and it's your first day of school in Santa Fe, and you're standing in front of a classroom, and you're all alone. You know what I mean?"

I stirred the fire and yes, exactly, yes, I knew the loneliness. Sarah was holding up a mirror to me, and dazzled by the fire, by her accuracy, I listened, nodding.

"It's like there's fifty thousand kids looking at you, laughing, and it's not a lot of fun, I can tell you that, and I was positive they all hated me and I was ready to cry, and I stared out the window, and I remember exactly what I thought: The sky is so blue. I just kept saying that to myself, over and over, *The sky is so blue*, and then the teacher's asking do I want to talk about myself, and I'm shaking my head, like, No way, lady, I'm not doing anything but looking outside at the sky, which is blue, bluer than Las Cruces. The teacher's talking and the kids are waving their hands and getting the answers, and all I can think about is how if only I could squeeze my neck tight enough I could make everything go away. Then outside on the playground, with this big mural of Aztecs and Spaniards and Indians on the wall, the girls are all whispering and giggling and being brats like kids are, staring at me and not even trying to pretend they aren't talking about me. So I climb the monkey bars, and I hang upside down and my skirt falls down and my panties show and I don't even care, and my hair's falling over my face, and I'm thinking, I turned you all upside down. I'm the girl who lives in the sky. And they're all staring at me and I'm thinking, Maybe I'll just fall on my head and then they'll be sorry. So then one girl with curly black hair comes over, and her name is Margo DelaCruz and she turns out to be my best friend. Anyway, Margo goes, 'Eee, Chingao. What happened to you? Were you in an accident?' Because I forgot about the bruises all over my belly, so I'm hanging there, thinking, I can make all these girls be nice to me. But I want to tell the truth, so I go, 'I have a skin condition,' which makes me think of my dad, and then I start crying, and all of a sudden Margo lies for me. She decides my mom is beating me, and she starts getting all mad about my mom, because that's how she is, and that's when I figured out that you can lie without lying. I think about my dad and I cry, and people see my bruises, they just put two and two together, and they jump to conclusions and decide I'm getting beat up, and they decide they'll save me."

Just as I did, I thought. What a fool I am. I stirred the fire, blinded to the mountains outside our circle of light. Sarah had told me the truth all along; I had just assumed. What I wouldn't have given for such a trick when I was little: Jennie, bruised, weeping. Everyone so nice. Poor Jennie. But she was no graceful, gorgeous redhead. Tears and bruises wouldn't have saved our little Jennie. "And Jake wanted to save you," I said.

Sarah said that when Jake first saw her bruises, she told him about the skin condition, about her father, about Mrs. Lucero, the social service people, the diagnosis, and she started to cry, which clinched it. Sarah told him, "It's just a skin condition," but the more she told the truth, the more Jake believed her mother was hitting her. That bitch, he called Helen. And she let him hate her mother, just to be sure of him. Only, when she moved in with him last spring, he started looking at her bruises strangely. How did they keep appearing, now that she was away from Helen? Finally, he figured out the skin condition was the truth. "He was so mad," Sarah said, tossing pine needles into the fire. "He called me a liar, which I don't think was fair, considering I tried to tell him the truth."

"But you never corrected him," I said. "You let him be a fool."

Sarah rested her cheek on her knee and watched the fire. She took so long to speak. I thought she would cry, but she didn't. I thought she wouldn't go on, but she did. "I'm sorry," she said in a voice so soft, so quiet and ashamed that it required a mountain's silence to be audible. "I was afraid."

"I know," I said, and I laid my hand on her arm, because more than anything I wanted to taste the unfamiliar flavor of cutting someone some slack.

She begged him to stay with her, that day on the plaza. He said Sarah was selfish, manipulative, that he didn't even know if she was really raped, or if she made that up, too.

"He felt like a fool," I said.

"I know." That day on the plaza, Sarah realized he wouldn't forgive her. She fell to her knees, and he stood her up and he said, "Tell me when you understand the concept of honesty. Maybe I'll believe you."

"That was six and a half weeks ago," Sarah said. "Forty-five days, and I haven't seen him since. So there's another lie. I let you believe I went back to him, when I only wished I had." She stared into the fire, her shoulders hunched, as if she were braced for a blow. "And if you do the math, how could I be pregnant?"

"I'm sorry," I said, as gently as I knew how.

Then tears welled in her eyes and slid down her cheeks. "I'm not," she said. She glared at me. "I hate him. I *hate* him."

"I believe you," I said.

"Why should you believe me? I'm just a pathological liar." She stared into the flames. "You don't know me. You don't know anything about me."

"You can't fool me," I said. "I've used that same line myself." I put my arm around her and looked into the fire and we sat that way for a long time, Sarah weeping silently, her head resting on my shoulder. She stopped crying at last and lit a new cigarette.

"I know you," I said. "I know you smoke too much, for instance."

"Hello? You think that's news to me?" We smiled happily at each other. We were safe together, in the flickering circle of campfire light.

If I tried to explain it to Chris, would he comprehend the fierce, passionate love that comes over two women doing women things? There's a certain joy to knowing that she's like me, her breasts and hips and toenails, love and the possibility of pregnancy and the endless search for a bathroom. The comfortable safety of our arms around each other's waists. This is not sexual; this isn't anything like sex, but the fiercest, giddiest infatuation for a new and first, unprecedented, precious and most mundane best friend.

• • •

I got out my whiskey and we drank a toast to the deer. We drank a toast to the dead Ford (which I tried again for luck, but there was no hope in Mudville).

Then we talked. Here's a puzzle: time can simultaneously be shortened and elongated. I'm sure Einstein could explain why those three hours we spent on that mountain were as short as three seconds and as long as a lifetime. Which is to say, the hours rushed by, and in the end, I felt closer to her than to anyone, though I told her the same old set pieces, like the Girl With Piojos, Weeping Willow, tortured by Mr. Moletinez. I made it funny, and the more she laughed the more she egged me on, until we were giggling over all the names we could conjure, Smoldering Sequoia, Burning Banyon Tree, and My God, never in my life had I made such jokes.

Here is my little friend. Here is my little friend and we have come out on this trip together. It felt like a slumber party, or better, a campout. The uncomplicated fun of nine-year-olds. Look at me, delighted by something as commonplace as a friend, a feeling like a poor girl's awe over a toilet, a sugar bowl, kitchen cupboards filled with cold cereal. I was the hippie kid who found Essie's bathroom faucets beautiful, her glazed doughnuts exotic. Essie's blintzes: what a miracle!

Thinking this brought on a hot flush of shame, only Shame wasn't invited, and it slithered off into the woods while we passed the flask, and we laughed when Piojo Juniper hacked off her hair, when my mother's piano was stolen, when my father made me drive the new white car; we laughed at Juniper in catechism class, having learned of wine that becomes blood—hands on her hips and a belly full of cookies, announcing, That's impossible. Sarah howled: *Impossible*, and I howled, *Blood of Christ!*, raising the flask, and it was the funniest thing in the world, echoing off that mountainside, and the night seemed big enough to take anything we might admit or confess or blaspheme, so we leaned against each other and laughed some more.

We bring this out in each other, I thought, stirring the fire, sending a prayer up with the rising sparks: Thank you for this, God or whatever the hell you are, fate or circumstance or coincidence. Thank you for Sarah, here. Thank you for this magnificent, commonplace gift, this friend, this New Best Friend. I believed, for a precious moment, that there was a God to thank, and I laughed a hallelujah of gratitude to Him.

I'm not sure if she asked or I took it upon myself, but I told her about Sunny. I began with what I told everyone. That he was a backwards boy. That the night he was born, I had to run to call an ambulance. That he had black hair and light green see-through eyes. That he grew and learned languages and, brilliant boy, went to Russia. Familiar story, it came out of me the way my mother prayed at Meetings, effortlessly, seamlessly, while we waited for sunrise not impatiently or patiently—we forgot we were waiting at all. It was just Sarah and me, huddled together beside the fire. So this is prayer, I thought, talking, and for once I understood the comfort of it, and why Meeting prayers go on all night. I told her how Sunny and I stole a Christmas tree, how he never cried, how we locked ourselves in a hot car one blistering August. I wove those tired old stories into a tale of the closest siblings in the world, and Sarah, listening, ate it up like French fries, her whiskey eyes sparkling in the firelight.

I thought, I will do anything to keep her with me. I'll say anything at all. Then I understood why Sarah lied about her bruises, because I found myself lying about Sunny: He really is waiting for us in Berkeley and oh yes, he'll love you my dear; I know him, remember? He even mentioned you when he kidnapped me—that redheaded girl, he called you—and he hasn't stopped talking about you. He told me to come visit him and to bring you along.

You'd think I'd be choking on such poison, but I reeled out the lies that made the corpse into bait—a terrible pun, I know—and I gave her Sunny, the fabulous Prince Charming in Berkeley, pining for her. She ate it up, too, and her belief made it easier to enchant myself, and Sunny is alive, and there goes the Bereaved, slinking after Shame into the forest. "He sounds so perfect," Sarah said, sighing, and I felt a giddy kind of power, a feeling that as long as I spoke of him the way I always had, there would be no discernible difference between his living in Russia and lying on the bottom of the sea.

Of course it couldn't last. Somewhere in there, I made a mistake and told her a truth. I said that Sunny and I had seen each other five times since I was fourteen, and then I told her about Sunny riding his bicycle all the way from Santa Fe to see me, and then our happy party came to an end.

IT's so difficult to trace the escalation of an argument. We sit side by side, the wedding dress over our shoulders to keep the chill off our backs. I'm telling her about Sunny, making the bridge and the tennis balls and the gas into a charming frolic, and she's listening, her cheek against her knees, dreamy, smiling, when she turns on me. She says, "No wonder he was so awful at your wedding. You left him behind, and then when he visited, you told him to go home."

A person has this conversation with herself. Be calm. This time, just keep it together. But anger is a charging bull and you have to rope it fast. "You don't know what you're saying," Jennie says, hoping for a lasso.

But our Sarah never stops, does she? "It's so sad, I mean, even though you were his sister, you were more like his mom—"

"Shut up," Jennie says, and there is no lasso and God help her, our Sarah spills tears as she says, "You were only worried about the way things look."

There is no lasso only anger charging and Jennie must shut this Sarah up so she shoves her and sends this girl sprawling. "You *pushed* me," the Pea Princess says.

"Don't judge what you're too stupid to understand," the Ugly Chick says.

"Don't tell me to shut up."

The Ugly Chick stands over her, a looming monster. "He got his revenge."

"What, because he took you to a bridge? At least nobody ever left *you* behind. You don't have any loyalty; I swear to God you'd stab anyone in the back. You probably treat your husband like a dog, snapping at him all the time, and it's a miracle you ever got married—and if Sunny's anything like you, then fuck it, I'm out of here, because I don't need this shit, even though I'll probably have to walk because you couldn't get a *nor*mal truck—"

Rage is so close to panic; they come in tandem, amplifying each other with their lockstep charge. When this Ugly Chick was an Ugly Girl, she felt a crawling in her scalp, lice, which felt like spiders, and both rage and panic drove her to claw at herself, to scrape her own flesh and blood under her fingernails, to hack off her own hair. When she feels their relentless march, there's no telling what she might do. If you see her enraged, there is only one chance to save yourself. *Run.*

So that's what Jennie does. She turns and walks away. And I want to stay outside this moment, but I'm there again and I am Jennie I am the person walking away from Sarah, whose voice, panicked, desperate, will not let me go. I am the person who does not listen or think when she, this red-haired girl who has been raped, says, "Where are you going? You can't just *leave* me here. Don't you dare leave me here."

I am stopping. I am the person who says, "Listen closely. I'm going to rip your head off if you don't shut your fucking mouth."

"I knew it," she says. "I knew you'd leave me. Sunny was right. You left your brother, you left your husband, you—"

The Ugly Chick, Jennie, me, I'm the one who slaps her. I slapped her. Pain shot through my injured knuckles. We stood stock-still for a moment. The wind sighed through the pines. She whispered, "What's *wrong* with you?" Then I began to run.

I ran, though I knew I couldn't keep it up for long. What's wrong with me, she wanted to know. You, Sarah. You're wrong. I stumbled up the center of the highway, away from the unprotected edge. Maybe it was all that crying: it pissed me off. It was so cheap, the way she turned on the tears. If she could weep on command, then it was a trivial thing to weep, and worse, to trivially bawl over my *brother*. If I cried, I'd be abetting the crime. Anyway, he was *my* brother. I'd nearly cried over a stupid animal, and I had taken its muzzle into my mouth—absurd, futile—but had not cried over my brother. How could she cry for him? She had no right. What was wrong with me? You, Sarah. You're wrong with me.

My hand throbbed in time with my footfalls. And what about the truck, anyway? It was fine before. Maybe she did something while I was paying for gas in Denver. Loosened a wire, sugared the tank—who knew how far she'd go?

And who did she think she was, going on about Sunny as if she knew what it was like to have him standing in the Taos Inn with his knobby shoulders and his stinking sweat? His sunburned nose. His naked, bony chest. His eyes. Raising his champagne bottle to toast me: Five times, Juniper. I confess this truth and she turns it against me. I concentrated on my heels and toes and heels again, on my screaming knees and cramping thighs, on my breath which was not a simple involuntary rise and fall of lungs, but a decision to move my body up that highway built into the hips of that mountain—only, despite my efforts, with every step I remembered that I had hit her, hit her, hit her, and I remembered not Sunny's see-through eyes but Sarah's whiskey eyes shining in the firelight.

I do not know how long I ran before a car rounded the bend, coming down the mountain fast, a stealthy low-slung car, and I leapt back. It slowed, its brake lights like eyes, and then it was gone. I tried to run on, but then I stopped in my tracks. What about that car? It had slowed as it passed. By now it would have reached Sarah, easier pickings, choicer fare than an Ugly Lumberjack Chick. I looked over the edge of the highway and below I could see the car had stopped beside the truck. I imagined the men in the car nabbing the pretty little redhead, holding a gun to her pretty hair.

I turned back, and just as I did, the car pulled away, disappearing around a curve, and I was running, because I believed for a terrifying moment that they had Sarah in their backseat, bound and gagged, like a woman I once heard about, raped, hog-tied, taken across three state lines—run, Jennie, save her—dizzy, my throat raw my hands shaking, I thought of three calfskin pairs of shoes lying forlorn in a parking lot while a man raped Sarah on a night as dark as this. How did she survive? Did she stare past his shoulders into the sky, or did she close her eyes? Did she pray?

So this is how it was for you, Ray, my daddy, my dad. You commit a crime and leave behind the evidence. Then you go back, because you can't tell which is the greater sin: the reason you left, or the staying away.

$\mathscr{W}$HITE KNIGHT

Early Morning, Thursday, Colorado

BRIGHT light shone around a curve, then headlights came at me. I leapt for the shoulder. The driver swerved; brakes shrieked, and there I was, on the ground, dangerously close to the drop-off, my palms skinned, my injured hand throbbing. I smelled rubber. Red and blue lights began flashing. Of all the cars and all the trucks on all the roads, why did a cop car have to show up here, Sam? Rather, a police Bronco, I saw as I hauled myself upright.

It was a boxy eighties model with old-fashioned Mickey Mouse cop lights on top and a logo painted on the door: BLUE SKY SHERIFF'S DEPT. The fact that I could make out the painted eagle circling the stylized mountain made me realize the sun was rising. It was dawn, that confusing time of day, not light and not dark. Stars sprinkled the pink sky, and the cop's headlights were on, wan and useless.

He rolled down his window. "Morning," he said mildly. "Do you have a death wish?"

"I got out of the way, didn't I?"

"Where you headed?"

"Nowhere," I said. "And not too fast, either."

He had broad, even teeth, a killer of a smile. "I nearly ran into you."

No shit, Sherlock. I took a deep breath, gave him my best Essie grin. "I know. I'm sorry. My truck broke down."

"That one down the hill about a mile?"

"That's it," I said.

"So you're running back to it? Did you forget something? To put out your fire maybe? It's fire season," he said amiably.

"Sorry about that. It gets cold."

"And your deer? Not a Satanist, are you?" His smile was infectious. His eyes vanished into merriment and his face opened to all those white teeth, such a grand smile. "Not into weird animal sacrifices? Poaching?"

I stiffened. "I hit the deer. We tried to save it. It died." Unaccountably, my voice wobbled. "Anyway, the truck wouldn't start. And I left my friend there." He seemed to be waiting for more. "We had a disagreement."

"Well," he said as he started his engine. "Hop in. We'll go take a look. Straighten things out."

I got in, just like that, as if I were prone to such malleability. "Can you hurry?" I whispered. "I'm worried about her."

"That's what police cars are for," he said. The Bronco set off, its tires smooth on the blacktop. The radio crackled and a woman's voice said something coded and mysterious and then the noise receded like a voice calling from a rowboat drifting out to sea. It was probably only thirty seconds later when the cop's voice woke me. "What's wrong?" he asked.

"God hates me," I said. "For good reason, too." It felt as if I'd slept for hours. I rubbed my face and looked at him. "Or maybe I'm just tired. I don't know."

"I was talking about the truck."

"Jesus." To my horror, tears welled in my eyes. "So was I."

He pulled to the shoulder and killed the engine. There was my battered old truck, its door open, the deer's legs poking out. I closed my eyes again. I heard the ratcheting of his emergency brake. His voice was horrible, gentle. He put his hand on my arm. He said, "Let's go look for your friend."

Nothing like a jolt of adrenaline to wake a girl up. "My friend," I said, and left the Bronco to look for her. "Sarah," I called. She wasn't in the truck. "Sarah, this isn't funny!" She wasn't under the truck, over the cliff. I could hear the hysteria rising in my voice. "*Sarah!*" I looked for signs of a struggle, a tire mark, blood—

"You *bitch!*" Her voice came from up the hill in the trees, and there she was, picking her way toward us. I sagged against the fender and watched her stumble down the embankment onto the highway. I was crying. I turned my back and wiped my face.

"You *left* me," she said.

The cop, kicking dirt into the fire to smother it, nodded at her. "You must be the friend."

"Friend? Officer, be my hero. Help. This woman is psychotic."

He was a compact man, maybe an inch shorter than me, nothing threatening, but I still felt defensive. Cops make me feel guilty, regardless of the circumstances, and these were not the best of them. "I'm not psychotic," I said. He was regulation everything. Thick crewcut hair, long narrow eyes, high sharp bones. I decided he was some kind of Indian. He caught my eye and, astonishingly, winked at me.

He turned to Sarah. "What makes you say that?"

"She only left me in the middle of *nowhere* by myself," she said. She wouldn't look at me. It wasn't yet light enough to make out the bruises I knew I'd slapped on her cheek. Shame made me think, Confess. Liar, kidnapper, assaulter. Bereaved.

"We had a . . . fight," I said.

"No kidding," Sarah said. "Are you going to arrest her?"

He squatted to take a look under the truck. "Mind if I lift the hood?"

I shrugged. "Be my guest," I said.

"What kind of cop are you?" Sarah said. "A mechanic cop? Don't you need to book her?"

"Sarah," I said. "Now you sound like a movie."

She faced me, arms akimbo. "Do you have something to say to me?"

I considered. But everything seemed inadequate. What should I say? I'm sorry? I'm a shit, a fool, a jerk? What good would it do?

"Where are you two headed?" the cop asked, raising the hood. "Utah? Wyoming?"

"California," I answered. "I'm really sorry," I said, meaning to say it to Sarah, only I had joined the cop in staring at the greasy engine.

"I'd be sorry about that, too," he said, poking around. "California's not my kind of place, no offense." He pulled a clump of dirt from the grille.

"I'm sorry I left Sarah alone," I said.

"Maybe you should tell her that," he said.

"I want to press charges," Sarah said.

He smiled. "Unless you're a two-year-old, it's not against the law to leave you here."

But it was against the law to hit someone, as far as I knew, and the fact that she hadn't mentioned it meant something. I hoped I could apologize in a way that sounded true, because I meant it. I put my hand on her shoulders and looked her in the eyes. "Sarah," I said. "I'm sorry."

"Your friend here was pretty worried about you," the cop told Sarah.

"This is two against one," she said. She lit a cigarette. "Fuck it," she said. "I forgive you. Which, by the way, makes me a better person than *some* people, who hold a grudge until the cows come home. What should we do with that deer?"

"Call the rangers," he said. "Let them deal with it."

"That's sad. I feel like we should bury her."

The cop said, "I admit, I don't know what's going on in here. Battery, maybe?" I thought he meant assault and battery until he said, "Why don't you check, see if the lights are switched on?"

Sure enough. Sarah peered in on the passenger side, but she didn't meet my eyes. I pushed in the headlight knob. The thought, insidious, logical, came to me again: Maybe she did this.

I lifted the deer from the truck and laid her on the ground. She was stiff, and her eyes had clouded over. Burst capillaries rimmed her irises. Her eyelashes were spiky and wet, as if she'd wept in the night. Her black hooves were tiny. A slight breeze stirred her soft belly hair. Between her hind legs, there was a patch of hairless skin, pale pink, nearly white. I bent closer. There. Tiny nipples, barely skin tags, blending with the surrounding skin.

The cop squatted beside me. "I'm Abe Gomez," he said. "Where are you ladies coming from?"

"South." He was wearing hiking boots with his uniform: muddy, well-used hiking boots, and it seemed silly, too personal for a cop outfit.

In daylight, the evidence of our collision was horrible to see. Under the tidy white tail, a shine of blood came from the anus. Brown blood smeared across the highway. And on the fender of my truck, blood. Between the tire rim and the rubber, tufts of her fur. Oh.

"South . . . ?" the cop said.

"Albuquerque," I said.

"Albuquerque," he said.

I'd had about enough of his act. "Look," I said, "did we do something wrong?"

Sarah said, "No kidding, because if we did, I wish you'd just come out with it. And we'll say, Oh no, Officer, have mercy." Traffic had picked up, and even under the risen sun, the cars had their headlights on. It felt like a spread-out funeral procession.

"Just asking a question," Officer Gomez said.

Sarah took a long drag, then snuffed out her cigarette. "My question is, why is it so *fucking* cold when look, the sun's up, so it should be warmer, right? And also I'm ready to get the hell out of here so we can sleep. We'd be sleeping right now, by the way, if *some* people weren't insomniac psychopaths." Now I could see. The bruises on her cheek were so faint they looked like a smudge of dust. Maybe, I thought, grasping at leniency, I had not hit her too hard.

I crossed the highway and stood at its edge. I thought I might throw up, and no wonder—what was in my stomach? Doughnuts, burger, whiskey. I thought again of the dangers of swerving. I could see how long a drop it was. Why didn't they have guardrails on this road? Far below, I caught glimpses of the pavement, a gray stripe winding between trees.

"Fuck," I said. When Ray used to get mad, I would cower with my hands over my face, yet his voice would be soft as he cursed me and the world. "Fuck," I whispered.

The cop came up beside me. Then he did a curious thing. When I think of it, I'm ashamed and angry and I don't know what else. He said, "Look over here." I turned, and he touched my cheek with his thumb. "You have blood," he said.

My hands were shaking, from embarrassment more than anything. I rubbed where he'd touched. "It must have been the deer."

"Or your hand," he said, pointing. I saw that I had, in fact, bled. What the hell? Everything was off-kilter. I had checked for blood. There hadn't been any. But two of my knuckles were split.

He took an old-fashioned white handkerchief from his pocket and handed it to me. "Spit," he said. I was so startled I did. Taking my face in his hand, he wiped my cheek. I closed my eyes. He said, "Way I see it, you did the best you could. It wasn't your fault."

"I tried to save it," I began, but my voice failed me, and I was afraid. I was afraid even to open my eyes. I knew that in the time since the sun had risen, I'd given myself away, let things slip, and I felt that old longing to correct my presentation of myself. To say, No really, Officer. This isn't Bambi. Not a big deal. My grandfather was a lumberjack.

He asked, gently, quietly, as he wiped my face, "I'm going to ask you something. Did you hit Sarah?"

Grateful my eyes were closed, I swallowed the enormous fist lodged in my throat. "I've been getting things wrong," I whispered.

"They're coming out of the woods a lot, the deer. Like they can smell the chance of fire. Everything's dry as paper." He turned my face this way and that. "Okay," he said. "Good as new." I opened my eyes. He folded his handkerchief back into a neat square and put it in his pocket.

"I could cite you," he said with a sideways look. "For the fire."

"Fine," I said. "Do that. Arrest me for battery."

"Nobody's arresting anybody," he said. There it was again: pity.

"I'm sorry," I said. "For swearing, I mean. For the fire. My grandfather was a lumberjack. A woodsman." Suddenly I was babbling about Swifty chasing his hat, about how he married Edna because he wanted to take her to the movies. I caught myself and stopped. Whatever magic this tale usually works was lost on that mountain. Abe Gomez was looking at me with pity and concern. Shame made my eyeballs ache.

He gave me a long, kind stare. "Anyway," he said. "I'm thinking, since you left your truck lights on, you can jump it easy."

"Fine," I said. "Let's do that."

He said, "You shouldn't be driving. How about I just take you to a hotel, let you rest up, and get somebody to drive your truck in for you? Get it all fixed up?"

"Fine," I said. "Fine." I wanted to say it forever: a litany, a chant, a hypnotist's spell. Fine. Fine. Fine, you sonofabitch. Fine.

I sat in back, Sarah in front. "Give me your keys," Officer Gomez said.

I handed it over, and he looked at the solitary key like it was suspicious. Ordinary people don't have one key, his face said. But I just closed my eyes again. I was too tired to take offense. I was too tired, and anyway, I was afraid I'd cry. When had I last slept—more than twenty-four hours ago? More than thirty-six? I saw my former self, lying beside my husband in Albuquerque. Hey, I said to that dreaming Jennie. Rest up. In twenty-four hours you'll be in a police car on a mountainside in Colorado. Surprise!

The cop returned. "I locked it up tight," he said. "Not that it needs it. That truck's not going anywhere."

"Well, duh," Sarah said. "I'm no mechanic, but that's my diagnosis." Floating on the surface of consciousness, I wondered if cops were allowed to be Good Samaritans. I opened my eyes and saw the sun rays breaking through the trees like steam. How does morning air give body to sunlight?

He asked, "What's your name?"

"Jennifer," I said.

"Jennifer . . . ?"

"Burning," I said. Dizzy, I closed my eyes again. I pressed my cheek against the cool window. He started the engine and we pulled onto the highway. I could hear Sarah talking, Officer Gomez responding. She asked him if he was Indian, because he looked Indian. He said he was Chinese. She laughed and said Gomez wasn't a Chinese name. He asked her if she was Irish, because she looked Irish, with all that pretty red hair. She said, "Hello? Is Martinez an Irish name?" He said he was pulling her leg, that he was Navajo. She asked what Blue Sky was. He said it was an itty-bitty town, used to be called Bear Creek, a mining town. But the mine got used up, and then the mining company loaded all its houses onto wagons and moved them down to Steamboat Springs. Now it's just an itty-bitty town. So small there are three cops, one for days and one for nights and one for in between. "Are you nights, days, or in between?" Sarah asked.

"Days," he said. "I was on my way to work." He said that last winter the town pitched in and set up a rope tow, so the citizens could ski for free. It was that kind of town.

I lost track of their conversation, thinking about a parade of houses, like floats, on the backs of wagons. Sarah and the cop chatted on—getting along like gangbusters, weren't they? What was he up to? What did he think he was after? Albuquerque, he said, like that meant something.

Officer Gomez said, "I've got a cousin in Albuquerque who's a mechanic, he says the gangs are getting pretty bad down there. He knew a guy whose sister got stabbed to death in Tesuque, at a watermelon stand. You just don't know what's going to happen." I opened my eyes. He glanced at me in the rearview mirror. "You don't," he said, as if I'd disagreed.

"It's true," Sarah said. "When I got raped, I was just buying shoes. That's all."

"That's terrible," he said. "Did they catch him?"

"Of course not, no offense. There was this shoe sale, at Winrock Center?"

I closed my eyes and listened to the familiar rhythms of Sarah's rape story and the hum of the wheels on the asphalt, felt myself pushed and pulled by the force of the Bronco taking curves in the road. My ears popped. I should tell Officer Gomez, *One grandfather was a lumberjack, and the other was four foot eleven . . . you should see me play pool.* But Essie always said, *If you have to talk about it, you have to talk about it, and you shouldn't have to.*

"The truth is," Sarah said, "I never told the police about it. Because the last thing he did? He handed me a hundred-dollar bill. And I thought, This is proof. I held on to it, you know, but then I realized he could say I was just a hooker or something."

I was very awake, though I kept my eyes closed. I wanted to hear. I didn't want to hear.

"You were scared," the cop said.

Sarah was silent for a long time. "I was scared nobody would believe me," she said. "I didn't even believe myself. I didn't feel sad, or mad, or anything. I'm just scared of the dark, that's all."

"I believe you," he said.

"Do you know what I did? I bought myself shoes with the hundred bucks. I figured he owed me."

"I'm sorry," he said.

"Never mind. They're nice shoes."

I drifted off again. Thank God for the needs of the body, the license to check out for a while when being awake and knowing who you are is enough to make you sick to your stomach.

"She's asleep," Sarah said.

"What about those marks on your face?" Officer Gomez asked. She told him about her boyfriend, Jake, who beat her. She made me into a hero. I rescued her, it seems, and now I was taking her to my brother, Sunny, in Berkeley, whom she met at Christmastime. That night, at my wedding, Sunny took Sarah to the Rio Grande Gorge Bridge, tennis balls, gasoline, love. She spun it all up, like gold from straw. She read my mind. Was this forgiveness?

And then I am in the Ford, but it's my father's Dodge, and he's telling me about the King of the World, only it's Ray's new white car, and they're driving to the courthouse so Jennie's parents can get divorced and Jennie is thinking, This won't be so bad, and the car is humming over the road, and Sunny and Jennie are in the backseat, sleeping in the hot car with the windows rolled up, sweating, panting, dreaming of the ocean where the ferns grow wild, only Sunny is all grown up and he's saying, *Somewhere beyond all this is me.*

• • •

A voice broke the hot still womb of the Bronco. I came instantly alert, dizzy with adrenaline, heart pounding. I didn't know where I was. I saw the black cockpit, the radio, and Officer Gomez leaning into the window, his hand on my shoulder. I asked, "How long have I been sleeping?"

"About twenty minutes."

"Feels like four hours."

"I brought you to this hotel," he said, gesturing with his chin.

It was my kind of place, a little motel with a faded neon sign: BLUE SKY LODGE. I love those signs announcing a fair price for a clean bed. I love the orderly predictability of their spotless bare essentials.

Sarah said, "We're supposed to sleep *here?*"

Outside the office, plastic geraniums grew in brick planters. "Stay," I told her.

"I'm not a dog," she said. "You can't just order me around." But she stayed, just like I told her.

The guy behind the counter was possibly the most nondescript person I'd ever seen, the sort of mushy man people can't quite remember. He wore a short-sleeved button-down. He wore his hair in a cut given by thousands of barbers everywhere for decades. "Hey there, Abe," he said, his voice flat and impersonal. He reminded me of the silhouettes they put on doors of men's rooms. His name tag said he was Mike.

"Mike," Officer Gomez said, nodding. I wondered if he remembered Mike's name without the tag. Maybe Mike wore it to keep the locals from forgetting. "This lady here needs some help," Officer Gomez said. "Her car broke down."

Mike drank some coffee from a Styrofoam cup. "What size room?"

"Single," I said, out of the habitual urge to save money. His cup had lipstick marks around the rim. I hoped there was a girlfriend on her knees behind the counter. Anything to add spark and dimension to him. Outside, Sarah stood under the vacancy sign, lighting a Camel. "She smokes too much," I said softly.

Mike gave me a tired look. "What size room?"

"Double," I said. "Smoking."

"Here she comes," Officer Gomez said.

Smoke on her breath, red in her hair, Sarah gets ogled wherever she goes: she marched across the parking lot, past the dreamy gazes of three children, their noses and palms pressed to a station wagon's backseat window. To them she must have looked glamorous in her orange velvet skirt, her tuxedo shirt, her big silver belt.

She came in with guns firing. "I was *saying* something to you. You think that normal politeness doesn't apply. Sit Sarah. Stay Sarah. What a fucking bitch."

"No smoking in here," Mike said mildly. "If you don't mind."

She read the clerk's tag. "Mike. Sorry about my language." She dropped her cigarette and put it out with her heel. "I'm kind of in a bad mood. Shit. Sorry about the floor."

Mike shrugged. "Standard," he said. "Everybody fights."

"Normally, I'm very cheerful," Sarah said, picking up her butt. "She's rubbing off on me."

He shrugged again. "Traveling. It gets to people."

Sarah said, "I feel sorry for you. Having to put up with people like us."

"Doesn't matter," he said. "I don't have any smoking rooms. Sorry."

"I like your haircut," she said. "I think men look good with traditional haircuts, don't you?"

He smiled uncertainly, as if he suspected she was ridiculing him.

"I mean it," she said. "Jake, my fiancé—my *ex*-fiancé—had really short hair. Sunny, my new fiancé, he has long hair. But I love him anyway."

"Lucky you," Mike said. He paused, as if searching for words. "You have real nice hair, too."

"Yeah," she said. "Well. It's not like it saves the world."

He took my money, and Officer Gomez escorted us to our room. He said something about the truck, about later, about not worrying. I was half asleep by the time we closed the door on him.

I took off my pants and stretched out on the bed. Sarah took off her orange velvet skirt. "I just might burn this," she said. "If I have to wear it one more second." In her tuxedo shirt, she washed her face, lotioned her legs, and performed other apparently essential rituals; it sounded very busy in the bathroom. I studied the ceiling. I couldn't get my eyes to close. Here I am, here's Jennie, gone off her rocker, lying in a hotel room in Colorado. What the hell happened?

Sarah got in bed. She smelled even more like lemons. Someone had shoved a plastic fork into the soft material of the ceiling; it hung there, like a challenge: just try to tell my story. She lit a cigarette and turned off the light. She said, "This is where Jennie says, 'I really am sorry, Sarah.'"

"Some things aren't forgivable."

To my surprise, she laughed. "You really do have a God complex. You think you're perfect, or you're perfectly horrible. You aren't the devil, either, you know."

"I'm sorry, Sarah," I whispered. "Something—something's wrong with me." My eyes burned, and my throat closed off.

"I know *that*," she said softly. "You think I don't know that?"

I cleared my throat. "I'm glad you're still here."

"I know." She took my hand and held it tightly, my wounded hand, and her grip made it throb, but I didn't pull away. "Don't you get it by now? We're the same, you and me. We just want somebody to stay with us, no matter what. So stay and be nice to me. And I'll stay and be nice to you."

I lay there in the dim light, keeping my eyes wide without blinking, waiting for them to dry. Being forgiven felt worse than being condemned. I listened to Sarah smoking, the drawn breath, the hard exhale. She didn't say anything else, but she didn't let go of my hand. Eventually, she finished her cigarette, and eventually, her fingers slipped from mine and I knew she was asleep.

Outside, a semi pulled in with a steamy hiss of brakes and a demanding diesel chug. Heavy footfalls came up the stairs, and behind them the lighter feet of a woman, her voice rising in bitter, squeaky complaint. A key in a lock, and movement next door. Their fight escalated. *You sonofabitch, you sonofabitch*, the woman shouted. Wonderful. Maybe people spend a hundred dollars on hotels for thick walls. Maybe what you get for your money is the peace of silence.

Somewhere down in the parking lot, a family was packing their car, slamming doors, their footsteps on the stairs, children running—Ellie wouldn't come. Her mother called, "Ellie! Ellie, I'm telling you. Ellie!" I wondered why Ellie would answer to such a threat, unnamed and therefore more awful. The father walked by with his son, discussing the day, how they'd drive to the lake and they'd be there by noon and did he bring that yellow floater? The door again, the engine starting and idling, and still the mother yelling, "Ellie! Ellie, I'm calling you. This is a warning!"

I wondered what Officer Gomez was doing in Blue Sky, Colorado, in his non-standard-issue hiking boots, and then I was asleep, and the room was still, and if the policeman had entered the room he would have marveled at the trust it takes to sleep. He would have looked at the key in his hand which he retrieved from Mike at the front desk. He would have been regretting his heavy breakfast, feeling the constriction of his belt, thinking he'd skip lunch because a person needs some kind of discipline, none of that cow-bellied middle age for him, and if he had come he would have been there to guard their sleep, these girls or women.

He looks at their shoes beside their bed, at Jennifer Burning curled around a pillow at the edge of the mattress, the muscles of her calf clenched, as if even in sleep she can't quite let go, while little Sarah Martinez lies completely exposed, on her back, mouth open, legs and arms splayed wide like some supplicant or sacrifice or innocent. He stands there making sure their sleep is safe, studying the bruises on Sarah's cheek, the wounds on Jennie's hand, the rhythm of their breath.

It might have been like that if he had come to the room. But I only dreamed he was there. We slept far into the afternoon, sweat dampening our hair, the hollows and grooves of our bodies, and I only dreamed that Abe Gomez turned on his Bronco's air conditioner and sipped his Coke, that on the highway he found three cars overheated, and that later, sweating in his black uniform, he agreed with Mike the Clerk that it was strange, such a hot, still, miserable afternoon, so close to September, so far up in the Rockies.

FATHERLESS

IN the beginning, Faith and Clarence are happy. He makes the Middle Room his shop, and he works all day, Meeting Music on the tape deck, the thunk-clink of his mallet like a clock. He teases Faith, bounces Sunny on his knee. These are the good days. Jennie thinks she might love him. She thinks he might be a better father than Ray. Which makes her feel like a traitor, and stupid besides, because by September, there are more and more bad days. Clarence stamps like he's killing something, and on really bad days, the stamping stops. The house falls silent, dangerous, and Clarence stares through the walls and past the garden and into his own memory. Then they have to be very careful, or it will be a bad night, when Clarence hurts Faith, and Sunny cries, and they are awake in the middle of the night. Like last night. It took so long to finally sleep.

Jennie's dreaming in swear words: Fuck-shit-fuck-shit-fuck, which become the thunk-clink-thunk of Clarence's mallet pounding her awake. She's so tired. Clink. Thunk. Lying in her bed, Jennie decides to just ignore Clarence. She'll never speak to him, never look at him again. This will be the Fall of Not Talking to him. She won't even say his name. She'll call him the Devil, or Satan, or Beelzebub. She gets up and marches through the Middle Room like a soldier of God. You are nothing, she says to him, but only in her head.

Faith moves around like an old woman, cooking the Devil's breakfast. Clink. Thunk. Clink. Jennie clangs the oatmeal pot down hard on the stove. "What's that," she asks, "his reward for beating you up?"

"You don't understand about Clarence," Faith says. "He's had a hard life." She piles eggs and potatoes and pours coffee, and takes the Devil a whole plate of food.

Meeting Way, you study the Bible. *Thou shall have no other Gods before me*, but Faith worships Clarence. Jennie gets Faith's Bible, which is filled with underlined passages. When Faith comes back to the kitchen, Jennie will use the Bible against Clarence, and Faith will get rid of him, or else she'll make excuses for Beelzebub, how he was eight when the government kidnapped him, boo-hoo, and sent him to a Bureau of Indian Affairs boarding school and cut off his hair, so sad. If he talked Indian, they beat him. If he used sign language, they tied his hands behind his back. Then he was mad all the time and beat up his father and he called his family Dirty Indians, another sin, because God says *Honor thy father and thy mother.* Faith says Clarence was supposed to be a big chief in his tribe, but the BIA made him unfit for the job, so he joined the army. In Vietnam—"Over There," Faith always says—they called him Chief and put him out in front, because they said tracking was in his blood. He killed men Over There. So Clarence sinned, because *Thou shall not kill,* but he did. Faith says that Clarence gets lost in his bad memories until he can't remember himself. Jennie thinks all of this might be a big lie that Faith made up, like she's saying, "Clarence works in Mysterious Ways."

Faith comes back into the kitchen with a bracelet to polish, and it makes Jennie open her mouth and tell the Old Woman Slave, "I won't forgive him, so don't start talking to me all about his sad shitty life," and Jennie can taste the word, like it left a thick slime in her mouth. How did she say it? She has never said a swear word in her whole life.

"I should wash your mouth out with soap for talking like that," Faith says. "You have the Bible in your hands and you're talking like that."

"I hate him," Jennie says. "You should hate him, too."

"Don't you use that word. Hate is a sin against God."

"Everything's a sin except what Clarence does," Jennie says, and his name sounds like a swear word. Then she smells Sunny Boy Blue, a pee-soaked six-year-old with pajamas that snap at the butt, clutching his pissy sheets to his chest. She's so tired. Of giving Sunny baths, of hearing excuses, of hearing Sunny's cough, seeing his nose pink and runny, his black hair tangled. "Blow your nose," she tells him. "Did you pee your bed?"

"No," he says, with the stinking sheets in his own hands. Sunny doesn't understand how to lie. For a tiny second she's disgusted by her baby brother, her Backwards Boy. What will happen to him? He lies and skitters around like a jackrabbit and he smells like pee. How will Sunny survive school when he's such a scared, stinky jackrabbit?

"Don't lie," Jennie tells him. "You stink."

Sunny looks at the floor. "I didn't," he whispers.

"Leave him alone," Faith says.

"Sunny, you come in here, boy!" It's the Devil, calling from the Middle Room, with his mallet in one hand and his blowtorch in the other. Sunny goes, and Jennie's the only one in the house who remembers what happens in the nights. Sunny doesn't, curled on the Devil's lap, hugging the Devil's neck. At least he's getting pee all over Satan, who laughs his wide-mouthed, deep round laugh. "Ahhhh," Clarence moans, which means that Sunny's walking on his back. The Devil, Jennie reminds herself, is an angel who has fallen, who longs to be back with Father God, but she doesn't know what that has to do with anything. Anyway, Clarence will be sorry. Today, Ray is coming over, and she will tell him all about what it's like to have the Devil living in their house, and Ray will cast him out.

EVERY morning, Jennie walks to Flaco's, where she catches the bus for the twelve-mile ride to Taos Junior High. She hates the bus almost as much as she hates Clarence. Being on the bus is like being a cat trapped in a box with a bunch of dogs who yank her hair and say, "What are you staring at, Piojo?" Jennie hunches down in her seat and glares at the green seat in front of her and she thinks, I hate you all. You're all a bunch of dogs.

The Dog Bus goes from Lower Alfin to Upper Alfin to pick up more kids. In Upper, the people have money. The Garduños have a big pink house with a solar panel on its roof like a hat. They're rich. There's also a house that just got bought by a rich Anglo lady. Like a scientist, which is what she wants to be, Jennie has been gathering facts about the Rich Lady. The Rich Lady parked a brand-new trailer in the yard, where she lives because she's fixing her house, which Jennie deduced by all the workers around. Deduction is one kind of reasoning, and induction the other. She gets them confused some-times, but they're important to a scientist. This year, Jennie plans on winning a science fair prize, a regional, a state, a national, even. She needs to decide on a project.

The Rich Lady has two cars—a brand-new silver sportscar, and a black convertible from the sixties. Jennie thinks that she should be friends with this Rich Lady, who's probably very nice, and who would buy Jennie brand-new clothes, and then Randall Sandoval would say, "Hey, who's that pretty girl?" And it would be Jennie. Like when Cinderella's stepsisters don't even recog-nize her at the ball. Is that coveting, God? To want someone to see you're beautiful, to love you? That's not coveting, Jennie decides.

The Dog Bus stops at Our Lady of Delores, the Arroyo al Fin church, and all the Dog Kids cross themselves because they're all Catholic. It's like a secret club. They have their secret signals, and today after school, every one of them will get off the bus in Upper, because that's what they do on Fridays: they have secret meetings.

What if I were Catholic, Jennie wonders. My grandmother was Catholic, so maybe I am. Doodling hearts and crosses, she imagines her Fairy Godmother, who is part Lipa and part the Rich Lady, giving Jennie a kiss outside Our Lady of Delores. Jennie, in a fairy princess wedding gown, is about to marry Randall Sandoval. Her stomach flutters, like it does every time she thinks his name, which rhymes, like her father's name. Half asleep, half dreaming, she meets Randall Sandoval's eyes, so beautiful, pale blue, a sharp, pointy blue.

Randall Sandoval says, "What are you staring at, Bush?"

Bush, Piojo, Ugly Juniper who doesn't know the secret signals, she scratches out the hearts. The Dogs whisper and look at her, planning something. *Forbidden,* she writes. Stephanie calls, "Do you believe in God, Piojo?"

Hypocrites, Jennie writes in her notebook. She just learned that word. It applies to all these kids. Jesus said, *Love thy neighbor.* Now her notebook says, *Forbidden hypocrites.*

To turn around and head back to the highway, the Dog Bus circles the church and the cemetery behind it. It must be nice, Jennie thinks, to have a place for your whole life, and for your relative's lives. To know where your grandma was baptized, and where she married your grandpa, and where they are buried, which of course makes Jennie sad all over again about the Treasured Memories. Sometimes the sadness comes out of nowhere and stabs her in the chest and it feels like she really knew her grandparents, and now they're dead, burned alive by Faith.

They pass the Rich Lady's house again. NO TRESPASSING, the signs say. There's a new fence, made of sharpened latillas, the pointy ends poking up. TRESPASSERS WILL BE PROSECUTED. Here is Princess Jennie, who lives in a fortress with her Fairy Godmother.

Suddenly, Stephanie plops down beside Jennie. She says, "What's that, Bush? A picture of yourself?" She bumps Jennie's elbow, and a black line slides across the paper. "Sorry, Hippie," Stephanie says. "It's your boobs. They stick out too far. You should get a bra at the Salvation Army. Or you could pray for one. Or maybe not, since you don't believe in God."

Jennie thinks, I will kill you, Dog. Faith always says, "Just ignore them." She makes her face a mask. An Ugly Mask. And for the third time today, a swear word comes into her head. I will fucking kill you, Dog.

Stephanie says, "My mom said we should pray for you, since you're going to hell."

"I know how to pray," Jennie says. First you say what you're thankful for. Then you ask for help.

Stephanie says, "Pray now, why don't you?" Quick as a snake, she snatches Jennie's backpack and tosses it to Randall. He holds it out an open window, and Eloy the Bus Driver ignores them, because he's on their side.

"Come on," Stephanie hisses, "pray."

"*No!*" Jennie cries, as Randall Sandoval lets the backpack go. The bus speeds along. "You kids sit down," Eloy says wearily. It won't do any good to tell him. They'll beat her up for that.

She hates them, especially Randall Sandoval. She clenches her fists to freeze her tears. How will she pay for her books? How will she do her homework? She'll flunk social studies, and even science. She squeezes her fists tight and reminds herself that God will give back tenfold what you give out. Maybe one day, Stephanie will fall out the window and bounce on the wet road and have tires run over her. That would be tenfold.

A f t e r school, Jennie gets off the Dog Bus in Upper Alfin so she can look for her backpack. Stephanie tells Randall, "Your girlfriend's going to church with us," and so it's Stephanie who puts the idea in Jennie's head. Walking along, Jennie wonders if maybe Catholics really do have a program for poor people. Or maybe, if Jennie went in there, she could say, Your little hypocrites threw my books out a window. What does God think about that? What happened to *Do unto others*? And the priest will be amazed that she knows the Bible.

Jennie passes the Rich Lady, who's sitting in the black convertible, talking to a worker in a cowboy hat. She's a tiny, beautiful woman, and even though she has dark hair, she makes Jennie think of Mary, who was supposed to fix the crack. Mary smelled so good, and had bells on her ankles, and ice cream. Don't hint, Mary said. Jennie remembers this most of all. Hinting makes you pathetic.

Jennie finds her backpack ripped open, and the books are split in half and torn and driven over by cars. She'll have to pay for them for sure. She will not cry. I need help, she thinks. She thinks about the Salvation Army. Salvation means saved, so they're an Army of God. Maybe a priest would be like that, like a knight saying, *I'll save you!* On the other hand, maybe the priest will grab her arm and yell, "Hey! Look what I caught! A hippie!" But Jennie decides to turn back and go to the church, to risk it because God Helps Those Who Help Themselves.

S h e has never been in a real church before. When her eyes adjust, she sees long dark benches, vigas high overhead, and at the front, above the altar, Jesus nailed to his cross. Along the walls are *nichos* with carvings of Mary and other saints praying with halos around their heads. She thinks, This is a church. Not a tipi with people up all night eating Medicine and calling it Father God and singing songs in a strange language they don't understand.

A door opens, and through it comes a gray-haired fat woman, who puts her hand to her large bosom, and says, "*Miha!* You made my heart attack!"

"Sorry," Jennie whispers. "I'm sorry." She starts to leave, but the woman says, "Are you here for Youth Group?" The woman leads her across a court-yard to an adobe house. From the living room a man calls, "*Vengaquí*," lean-ing over, beckoning. "*Sientate*," he tell her. "I'm Father Arturo."

"Why is *she* here?" Stephanie asks. "That's Juniper Bush."

Father Arturo smiles at Jennie. "We're all the children of God, Our Father," he says. This pleases Jennie but also bothers her, because it sounds like some-thing Faith would say. "My name is Juniper," she says, wishing she could lie, but the kids would tell. "My grandmother was Catholic."

The house smells clean, like Pine-Sol and bleach. Our Lady of Guadalupe gazes down from a painting over the sofa, and Jesus hangs next to her with his flaming heart in his hand. There are *biscochitos* and Hawaiian Punch, and Jennie eats cookies fast and drinks three cups of punch while Father Arturo tells a story about a bird moving a beach across the ocean one grain at a time. "We know this already," Stephanie interrupts. Jennie hopes Stephanie will be in trouble. And sure enough, Father Arturo says that it's good to be reminded, and their guest doesn't know, and then he explains, as if he's talking just to Jennie, that when the bird was finished moving the entire American coast, that would be one second of eternity. He tells her about sin, and the cost of dying unforgiven. About burning in hell forever and ever. He pats his Bible each time he says it: For ever. And ever.

The cookies and red punch sit in her stomach like poison. Eternity. Hell. Fire. Father Arturo is nice, with his gentle, worried eyes, and she can't make her face a mask because he sees straight through. He wants her to believe, and he makes her feel safe. Stephanie and Randall can't do anything with him there. He'll help her. He is a Father, and that's what Fathers do—they give you what you need. Even Santa Claus is Father Christmas. Faith says that, Meeting Way, Clarence is her father, which she's pretty sure is inductive reasoning—she has lost track of Father Arturo's eternity story.

When it's over, she leaves fast before any of them can get her. Down the road, the Rich Lady's house is a promise, or a dream. Here is Jennie, the Rich Lady's daughter, walking home, because her mom wants her to pick out wall-paper for her bedroom. Jennie's Rich Mother will call the principal and yell, and then Stephanie Martinez will have to pay for her books, whatever they cost.

When Jennie passes her house, the Rich Lady waves. Jennie waves back. But Jennie doesn't stop at the trailer to talk to the woman, who's a stranger, af-ter all, not a mother or even a fairy godmother, and the signs on the fence say NO TRESPASSING.

S U N N Y and Faith are in the garden. "We're planting flowers," Sunny says.

Jennie says, "The kids threw my books out the bus window."

Faith sighs. "What do you do to make them hate you so much?"

"You always say that." She stares at the big bruise on Faith's arm. "What do you do to make *him* hate *you* so much?"

"He was nice today," Sunny says cheerfully, because he always forgives Clarence. Clarence is the king of darkness and Sunny is a loyalist, sympathizing with the enemy. Jennie's studying the American Revolution in social studies, which she can't read about now, thanks to the Dogs.

"I can't afford to pay for any books," Faith says.

"You can afford tulip bulbs."

"I can't even afford food. If your father gave us money like he's supposed to—"

"You always say that, too," Jennie says. "You need new lines." She feels the fighting starting up between them like an engine turning over, but before it can roar to life, like magic, they're interrupted. Ray pulls up on a motorcycle, his guitar on his back.

"What's *he* doing here?" Faith says.

"It's Daddy," Sunny says, like that's an explanation.

"What about that *motorcycle*? Why don't you ask *him* for money, if he's so rich that he can have a motorcycle?" Jennie flushes with relief. That's what she'll do. She'll get her father to pay for her books, and then he'll take her to the library and help her with the science project. Maybe she'll live with him in town and never have to go back to Alfin again. "You stay and finish planting," Faith says, and hurries off to pick a fight about money.

They hear Ray's voice, low and angry and scary, but not his words. Faith's higher voice is easy to understand. "You have no right!" she yells, "you *sonofabitch*." Jennie throws a bulb across the garden. "Don't do that," Sunny whispers. Jennie tosses another bulb. Sunny says, "Mom will be mad." Faith runs inside the house, Ray behind her, calling all kinds of terrible words, and Sunny whispers, "Make them stop."

"I can't." She means, I can't stop them, and I can't stop myself from throwing these tulip bulbs across the garden. Inside the house, things crash. Sunny doesn't cry. He feels through the dirt and finds a bulb and throws it across the yard. Then they collect all the bulbs and dump them down the outhouse hole. "This is a science project," Jennie says. "Will tulips grow in poop?" Sunny smiles. Jennie feels better, thinking about Faith next spring: *Where are my tulips?* "We'll say we planted them," Jennie tells Sunny. "That's sort of true. We planted them in poop."

AFTER a long time, Ray comes to the garden and tells them, "Okay, offspring. The three of us, we're going for a swim."

"It's too *cold* for a swim," Jennie says. His lips are thin and she doesn't want to go anywhere with him. "Anyway," she says, "there's three of us and all you have is a motorcycle. That's dangerous for little kids."

Ray says, "Who appointed you Madame Mommy?"

Faith's inside, watching them. Faith didn't honor her father and mother. She burned them in the kitchen stove.

"I want to swim," Sunny says. "I love swimming."

They put on their swimsuits and their shorts, and Sunny wears Ray's helmet, and they pile on, Sunny in front of Ray and Jennie behind Ray, a father sandwich, and the bike's clumsy with three passengers. Jennie has to wear the guitar on her back. She thinks, If we crash, my father will be dead because he gave his helmet to Sunny, but we'll be alive, and fatherless. The wind sings through the guitar strings. She keeps her balance very carefully, leaning into every curve.

Ray takes them to the Rio Grande. Sunny jumps right in. Ray and Jennie stay on the big black rock, and Ray rolls a joint. He asks, "So. Does she bitch about me all the time?" No, Jennie tells him, and he says, "Your mother, she gets fixated; she's paranoid, and your paranoids need a bad guy, and that's where I come in—I'm the Monster, whatever I do. You better watch it, because next it'll be you."

Clear and cold this late in the year, the water sparkles like diamonds in the sun. Sunny, splashing, yells, "I'm swimming!"

"I don't want to talk about Mom like this," Jennie says.

"And she needs a good guy, which is where he comes in, ho-ho-ing her into happiness." He licks the paper and twists the ends and his joint is finished. Sunny calls, "Junie! Watch!" He ducks underwater then pops out, gulping air.

Ray lights up and, holding in his smoke, croaks, "I bet they fuck all the time. Does he talk about me?" No, Jennie tells him, and he presses his lips together like he expected as much. "A bargain, that guy gets. My house, my kids, my wife. My money, too, or at least that's what they want." He lets his smoke out in a huge plume. "I don't have a dime thanks to them. The bad guy gets it in the end, Juniper. Hey, Sunny," he calls. "How do you like your new dad?"

Sunny cries, "I'm swimming!" He sounds retarded. "Junie," he shouts, "come swim! Daddy!"

She hates this, hates that Ray can't remember he's talking to his own kids, hates the smell of pot which is against Meeting Way. Hypocrite, she thinks.

Ray picks up his guitar and starts strumming. He sings, "I'm an old cowhand. From the Rio Grande." He plays guitar sweet and slow and almost like he's forgotten he's playing. Then he stops. "So is he a better dad than me?"

Jennie says, "The kids threw my books out the window. I need you to pay for them." This is not how she meant to do it at all. She thinks, Here is Jennie, the Stupid Girl.

He lays his palm over the strings, a tender, final gesture, and he stares at her. "I gave all my money to your mother. I can't pay for any books."

"But you're my *father*," she says, which is the wrong thing to say and she knows it because his face hardens and his lips seal in the tight line, but she can't stop from making it worse: "You have money for a *motorcycle*," she says, and he says, "Don't look at me that way. Don't you stand there judging me, little girl," and she says, "I'm not," and he says, "Then what do you think you're doing?" and she says, "Nothing," and he says, "What do you mean, nothing?" and she says, "I'm just, I just need money," which is exactly the wrong thing to say, because he yells, "You and your cocksucking, adulterous *mother*," and she takes a step backwards and she thinks, He's going to hit me, I'm fourteen and he's going to pull down my pants and beat me, and she says, "Daddy, you're scaring me."

"*Scaring* you? What do you mean, scaring you? What are you trying to say?" He rises to his feet, with his raging red face and his fists, and he roars, "What do you *want* from me?" She backs away from him and turns and runs toward the road, then up the hill, and running, she listens for the sound of the motorcycle, afraid he'll come after her, afraid he won't, so she doesn't even know what she wants except that she wants to stop crying and feel that pure and certain rage again. If there really is a God, she thinks, it's time he gave me something to be thankful for, and in time to her footfalls she makes a list of her demands: to run and run and be in Seattle, to have a clean house and a good father and a nice school and best friends and new clothes and not this life, this mother this father—*and what about Sunny Boy Blue?* This is always the question she can't answer and so God wins again.

She has to go back, of course. Where else can she go? And there's Ray on the black rock, smoking a joint and playing his guitar like nothing ever happened. He says, "Where'd you go?"

Everybody in my family has amnesia, she thinks. We are the Amnesia Davises. "Running."

"Running," he says. "I used to run. Sweaty business, running." Now he's like a guilty dog, crawling on its belly. "I didn't know you were a runner."

"Junie!" Sunny calls. "Come swim with me."

Look at my father, she thinks, so weak, his pot smoke slithering into the air. She says, "You don't know a lot of things." Disgusted, she strips down to her bathing suit and runs into the shocking-cold water.

Ray calls after her, "I know you're turning out purty. Tall, like me, and looking good in a swimsuit. Do you have boyfriends?"

"It's almost Christmas and we're swimming," Sunny says, his teeth chattering between his blue lips.

"It's not almost Christmas," Jennie says. Sunny is so stupid. She dips her head into the current, the water blocking out sound and the sky and Ray and Sunny. She floats in the cold water with weeds and beer cans and slithering garter snakes, so cold she can't feel her skin. Maybe she'll just breathe the water, become a mermaid in the deep blue sea. She comes up gasping. She goes under, into the silence. She scrabbles toward light, toward sound, then sinks again. What if she drowned? Her feet reach for a bottom that isn't there, and she's scared, but then she feels mud underfoot, and she feels Sunny's hand on her arm. She surfaces.

"We have to go warm up," she tells Sunny, her jaw cramped from being so cold. She can barely talk. "You'll get sick."

They get out and lie on the big black rock. Ray says, "There you are. Trying to swim off?" He takes a toke. If she drowned, he probably wouldn't notice. He'd be too stoned. Stoned, he stares at the river, playing guitar. It's too cold to be swimming. She can't stop shivering.

Ray says, "Listen, Juniper. I'm moving to Florida, and you're coming with me."

Sunny cries, "Florida!"

"They have oceans of swimming in Florida," Ray says.

"What about me?" Sunny says. "Can I come?"

"You're staying with your mother," Ray says.

Then Jennie hates her father, a shocking, numbing cold hate, like river water, and she says, "I'm not going anywhere with you," and his eyes say, *But you're mine*, which makes her feel guilty and sad, only somehow, confusingly, she's screaming, "*I hate you I hate you!*" and she finds herself screaming about the blue bed that he stole, and she calls her father an asshole for making her mother sleep on the fucking floor, for buying motorcycles when they can't even afford food or schoolbooks and even while she screams she wonders, When did I ever take my mother's side? Why doesn't he realize that I *lied* for him, or at least let Faith believe that he had sex with Mary, *that* Mary? Which is worse, *Thou shall not lie*, or *Thou shall not commit adultery*? And when did I start being a person who swears?

"*STOP FIGHTING!*" Sunny cries.

"Clarence isn't fucking her in *my* bed," Ray yells, and Jennie watches her father's mouth move, his yellow teeth, his veins bulging on his forehead. Am I ugly like him? How much shouting would it take for a vein to pop? I'm Jennie the scientist, observing his see-through eyes, his furiously moving lips, and my own mouth moves without me, a different person shouting, "You only care about yourself, and you weren't even there when Sunny was born, and you lied to Mom! You cocksucker! You thief!" Shocked, terrified, she backs away. *Honor thy father. Thou shall not steal.* God's rules are useless.

But Ray only laughs. He says, "You need help. You're a sick kid, Juniper. You need a psychiatrist." It's worse than if he'd pulled off his belt and beat her.

"*STOP IT!*" Sunny yells, his hands on his ears.

Please, God, don't let me cry. "But Sunny," she whispers. "Sunny Boy Blue was born in that bed. Don't you care?" Mad is so much easier than tears. Let me be mad.

Ray says, "You're fucked up. You're as loony as your mother." There it is. Faith always says, "You're exactly like your father." With them both crowded inside her, how will she find room for plain old Jennie?

"I'm your father," Ray says. "Look at me."

She won't look. Nothing in the world can make her look at him. Except maybe if he said he was sorry, but then she's the one who should be sorry and she's so confused she can't stop the tears from coming out of her eyes. Everything's tangled up, flipped on its head, twisted, until she can't tell who's right and who's wrong. Please, God, she prays, please, let me be mad again.

"Do you know what it means to be fatherless?" he asks her softly. No, she wants to say. I am not fatherless. You are my father, my daddy, my dad. Ray says, "Let's go for a drive, the three of us."

She doesn't like having her arms around her father's belly, or pressing her chest into his back. But she still loves the speed, the leaning, which makes her forget her books and the bus and everything else, and the world is the bike roaring out of the canyon, swooping fast over the mesa.

HE stops right in the middle of the Rio Grande Gorge Bridge and parks the motorcycle, hops off, squats, and tells them to do the same. He puts his hand on the pavement. "Ever stood in the middle of the road before?"

"This is dangerous," Jennie says. "Sunny, get out of the road."

Sunny, squatting on the center line, asks, "Are you getting me something for Christmas, Daddy?"

"That's my Sunny Boy," Ray says. "Here's a trick. When a car's coming, you can feel it before you see it. A rumble is like a prediction. As soon as we feel a rumble, we'll get out of the way." Sunny puts his hand on the road. Ray says, "Try it, Juniper. Come on."

The pavement feels warm, solid and definite and comforting. Jennie reminds herself that underneath it there's nothing but air. "I need to go back and do my homework," she says. "I have responsibilities." She looks away. But not before she sees Ray's eyes, wavering between fury and disappointment, and his feelings seep into her like cold air, until she, too, is angry; she also despairs.

Ray says, "Okay, kids. Tell me about yourselves."

"I like chocolate," Sunny says. "And Christmas." He sounds so stupid.

Jennie says, "It's too late for telling about myself."

Ray looks down the highway at the setting sun, and the yellow center line meeting with the sides of the road way off in the distance. In the sun, his leg is very white, his scar a horrible, livid pink, dented. "Do you feel it?" he asks. "Do you feel a rumble?"

"I don't feel anything," she says.

"Then we're safe," he says. He squints at the sunset. He says, "I'm moving to Florida next week." Jennie doesn't answer. But she stays there with him, her hand on the pavement. Sunny walks back and forth and back and forth on the yellow line, talking about what he wants for Christmas. The sky bleeds from lavender to blue to black. They wait until dark for the first hint of trembling, but a car never comes.

WHEN Ray drops Jennie and Sunny off, nobody's home. "Clarence is off beating her up somewhere," Jennie tells Sunny. Why didn't she tell Ray about how mean Clarence is? Whose side is she on? She can't stop seeing herself through Ray's eyes, loony, a traitor. She can't figure out why she acted like that, yelling at her own father. Please, please, God, she prays. Please, Heavenly Father, I want my dad. Why am I staying here?

"I don't think they're fighting," Sunny says. "I think they're having a good time. They're dancing somewhere."

Why didn't she tell Ray that Clarence is dangerous, or about Sunny's earaches and conjunctivitis and colds and sore throats? That Sunny, five years old, still pees his bed? Jennie kneels in front of Sunny and looks into his see-through eyes, his dark hair which is too long, his smile curling up at the corners, his beautiful smile. "Give me a hug," Jennie says to her brother. His arms remind her. His warm little neck, his strong body—all of him reminds her who she is. I know who I am, Jennie thinks. I am the sister of Sunny Boy Blue. I am staying here for him. *Thou shall take care of your brother.* There should be a commandment.

Sunny's shivering, but his forehead is hot. He says his ear hurts. I never should have let him go in the water, she thinks. She decides he needs a bath and maybe some tea. She knows all the right teas from Faith. Mullein and chamomile are good for colds. She chops wood. She staggers back with an armload of piñon and dumps it in the woodbox. She knows all about fire. She knows how to hack kindling, load the stove, coax flames, and open the damper, which she does tonight. When the fire's roaring, she hauls water and puts it on to heat, then makes them some beans and rice.

Next to the stove, she sets up the tin tub and undresses him and scrubs his back, and while she does this, she tells him about Paul and Lipa. She tells him that someday, they'll live in Paul's wonderful house on the Highest Hill in Seattle. She squeezes the washcloth and the hot water runs down Sunny's back. She tells him to pay attention because they have to remember by heart, ever since Faith burned the album.

Faith says that Sunny's always sick because of white sugar, because it's an artificial chemical that humans are not meant to eat. Faith says Medicine cures sickness. But lots of people eat sugar all the time, and nobody eats Medicine, so it's the opposite of what Faith says. "I wish we had hot chocolate," Jennie says. Which is hinting. She will have her own commandments from now on. *Thou shall not hint.*

Sunny says, "For Christmas, I want a bunch of candy bars."

"You and Christmas. It's September, Sunny." How she loves him. She carries him, clean and warm but shivering, to his bed, and she gets in with him, and he curls snug in her arms. She remembers his head in the palm of her hand; she remembers changing his diaper and his penis spraying pee on her, and his laughter, like he knew what he'd done. She remembers spinning him around by his hands, thinking, I have to hold tight. If I let go, he'll fly away. He'd laugh and laugh. None of that happens now. He never cries, but he doesn't laugh, either.

After he falls asleep, she gets in her own bed and lies there crying—about the house cracking open, spiders, the Dog Bus, Sunny sick all the time, her books, money, the house—around and around it all goes. She should go to sleep so she can get up for school, but what good is school? School won't fix anything, and neither will praying, or the Church, or Medicine. The police will probably come and arrest them for having Medicine, which is illegal. She remembers the deer her father poached, the heart in her hands, and feels like she'll cry herself to death. *Fatherless,* she hears Ray saying. *Do you know what it's like to be Fatherless?*

IT's the middle of the night, and Jennie's awake because something was touching her, and it might be a spider, but then it's only Sunny, whispering, "Junie, Junie, it's me." He coughs, a painful, hacking sound. She puts her hand on his forehead. He's hot. "It's bad," he whispers. She thinks he means his earache, but then she hears Clarence and Faith upstairs, yelling. Sunny squirms; he wants to go to Faith, but Jennie holds him tight.

Faith cries, "Please, don't do this to me, Clarence, please, please—" and they come downstairs and Sunny breaks free and runs to the Middle Room, and Jennie rushes after him, calling his name. Here is Clarence, holding a black trash bag, and Faith, hanging on his arm, and here is the sound of Clarence's fist hitting Faith's cheek, a crunch or a smack. A pop. Here is the sound of Faith falling. Here is Sunny, seeing everything.

The trash bag is filled with Clarence's things; they're spilling onto the floor, his tools, his silver, a pair of socks. The lightbulb glares. Jennie thinks, This is wrong. Children should not be awake in the middle of the night. Sunny says, "Mommy?"

Faith lets out one great, shuddering, helpless breath. Clarence notices her. "Get up," he says, and when she doesn't, he grabs her and suddenly she's across the room, falling against the workbench and the blowtorch is falling. He must have thrown her. But things seem to be happening out of order. Jennie hasn't even noticed he's throwing Faith before she's thrown.

Sunny yells, "Leave her alone!" Charging Clarence, slugging his thigh, and Clarence shoves him to the floor and kicks his side, a little tap. He says, his voice slow, quiet, almost gentle, "Peed your bed?" He kicks again. "Only little girls pee their beds. Are you a little girl?" He kicks. "Do you make your mama cry?" Kicks. Sunny will not cry. "Are you listening, girl?" Again. "Girl." And again. A tap that probably begins to hurt after the third or fourth time, and with each kick he says softly, "Girl. Girl. Girl." Even this doesn't make Sunny cry. He just lies there, his eyes squeezed shut.

But I am Jennifer Braverman now, and cannot stay inside this moment that has nothing to do with me, with Jennifer Braverman who is tall and strong and comes from lumberjacks, because who can stand this distant melodrama of the lowest kind, who can bear this boy, this pissy Sunny, a shadow-child, a sickly parrot, squawking, "Christmas? Christmas?" Why can't I remember more of him? I never once asked myself, Why is he so obsessed with Christmas? Jennie, you fool, you idiot, you simpleton: he's waiting for the second coming, for Father Christmas, for Heavenly Father God, for Daddy on his motorcycle. If his big sister can't save him, maybe your Heavenly Father will reach down through the clouds with a big box of chocolates and save you both. Maybe he'll come down the chimney or through the window.

I'm worse with Faith. I should apologize to them all, these cartoon memory people, Faith running around weeping and snapping, the parrot brother, the evil stepfather, the luckless sad-sack dad. Who are they, anyway? What were they all fighting about? Money? Sex? Ten commandments broken?

· · ·

CLARENCE kneels in front of Faith and takes her by the shoulders, and his voice is low, urgent, as if trying to convince her. "I don't belong here," he says. "I'm wrong here," and Faith wails, "No, no, no—"

Jennie grabs Sunny, and they're in her room. *Sh sh sh, be quiet Sunny,* and she lifts him through her window and follows him into the night, *Sh sh sh Sunny,* and if they could just sleep through the night, maybe these things wouldn't happen. Jennie carries Sunny to the garden, feeling for the path with her bare feet. She holds Sunny and watches for the house lights to go off. Sunny smells like pee. He's five and he still pees his bed. Clarence was right about that. Sunny pees in his bed, a stinky kid with stick-out ribs who always has an ear infection.

He shivers. "I want to go back," he says. "Is Mom okay?"

"Pretend it's Christmastime," Jennie says.

"Is it Christmas soon? Can we get a tree?" He coughs, a thick, painful cough. "Can we?"

"It's Christmas now," she says. "In just a little while, we'll get a tree."

"I'm too tired for Christmas," Sunny says. "I'm too cold."

"Just pretend," she tells him. And then she tells him to imagine himself warm. To imagine it's the hottest summer ever. Listen to the river, smell the sweet peas, hear the rustling corn, the bees. Taste the apricots.

"I thought it was Christmas," Sunny says.

"It's a special Christmas, a warm Christmas," Jennie says. *Listen, Sunny. Do you hear the crickets, which are good luck, unless you kill them and then terrible things will happen for as long as you can imagine. Shh. Do you hear?*

$\mathcal{A}$ Little Like Prayer

I'd been dreaming and didn't know about what, but I knew I'd been dreaming. My heart pounding, I looked up at the fork in the ceiling. Despite the drapes that hang in motels everywhere—rubber-backed, pleated, and speckled—the light seeped through, fiercely hot. In this way, attending to light and heat and the ceiling, I came awake. I had my first clear thought of the day: I should have cleaned up that whiskey on the kitchen floor. I tried to uncurl my fingers, but the pain stopped me. My knuckles were swollen and bruised. Were they broken? Surely I would have known. My belly ached as I rose; the deer had bruised it nicely.

Beside me, Sarah breathed the thick gurgle of a smoker. I listened to the oddly comforting sound for a time, then pulled the bedspread over her bare shoulder, a silly mother gesture, given the heat. Still asleep, she knocked my hand away. She shrugged off the covers, threw her arms wide, rolled on her side, shifted to her belly. What was it that kept her so restless? Her lashes, long and thick and curling, gave her the vulnerability of a sleeping child. Her hair hung to the carpet and stuck to her damp face. My hand fit neatly over the shadowy bruise on her cheek.

In the bathroom, I took inventory. That woman in the mirror? She's the sort of person who would strike her friend, punch a truck. Pale lips, pale skin, pale lashes. My beady brown eyes bloodshot and the skin under them lavender. I unfastened my braid and spread it out over my shoulders. I used Sarah's brush from her black bag, my left hand making awkward work of the brushing, until my hair crackled with static. I wet the brush and smoothed it down. I ran cold water over my right hand. A lot of good it did. It hurt like hell.

I leaned close to the mirror and looked myself in the eye. You there. Fool. You're hollow where your heart should be. Prancing around bars and drinking whiskey like you're some kind of special. Or maybe you're septic rather than hollow; maybe if they cut you open, they'd smell rotting. But you're blond, so nobody looks past the hair.

What made that cop think he could touch my face? What guilt or innocence? Someone doesn't touch you like that without knowing who you are. Did I look like a liar, a thief, a person in need of comfort? Maybe he just wanted to get into my pants.

This was my second day of knowing that my brother is dead. It felt as imaginary as the first. Your brother is dead, I whispered to the woman in the mirror, but she looked back at me unmoved. Now this, her look said, is some first-class feeling sorry for yourself. The Bereaved makes her move. Next you'll be wailing, tearing at your clothes. My face looked at me, contemptuous, dismissive. Get real. Real, I thought. I don't know what that is.

Here's a fact: no matter what the circumstances, the needs of the body assert themselves eventually. The woman in the mirror was swooning with nauseating hunger, thirsty from a hangover, in need of coffee, and she had foul, foul breath. I needed to get myself a toothbrush. I needed a store.

THERE was Johnny Law himself, smack in the middle of my way, that is, in the hotel parking lot, leaning against his Bronco, arms folded, waiting. It was a dazzling-hot afternoon; circles of sweat showed in the armpits of his dark uniform. He said, "Jennifer. Jennifer Burning."

For a moment I thought he was ridiculing me, but then I remembered how I had lied this morning. "That's my whole name." I tried to settle my face into what felt nonpanicked.

"How'd you sleep?"

"I slept fine." I looked around like I was enjoying the day. "Where's our truck?"

"Bad news," he said. "Looks like you're in for some repairs."

What a nowhere we had come to. We might as well have been in the woods; we were high in the mountains, tall trees poking at the blue sky. Main Street was also the highway. There was a bar, a gas station, a store, a post office in a prefab building, which, the sign said, was also City Hall and the police station. "So this is Blue Sky," I said. "Where are the houses?"

"People live in caves, up yonder," Officer Gomez said, pointing with his chin. "The rich folks got tents."

"You're a regular stand-up comedian."

He cleared his throat. Always a bad sign. "Listen," he said.

"That's what I'm doing."

"Your truck might keep you around here for a few days. I had it towed to a mechanic."

"Really," I said cautiously. I waited. I didn't want to seem rushed or nervous.

"Sorry to disappoint you," he said.

I shrugged. "No disappointment," I said. "I knew it was a piece of shit." I bent to retie my shoes. Sore fingers don't tie good bows. Awkwardly, I used my first finger and thumb, like a priss touching dirty laces.

"Okay," he said. "So when you get back from wherever you're headed just now, I'll take you up to the garage, Mrs."—he paused long enough to make it clear his pause meant something—"Burning."

"Jennifer," I said. "You don't have to be so formal." Really, I had to admire my skill at faking calm. As I trotted away, my heart was pounding like I'd just run miles.

I went into the only store. It was crammed with dusty bare essentials, rows of canned goods and basic white bread, a stack of notebooks in concession to back-to-school, and an entire wall for liquor. I wandered up and down the aisles until I found the nonedibles, dog collars and paper towels and sanitary napkins. Tampons. I thought of how Sarah had offered her next period as proof, and took a box to say, I believe you. A toothbrush, and, lo and behold, hair dye. On the package, a woman peered slyly around a glossy sheaf of red hair, her eyes saying, *Yeah, that's right.* I saw myself as a redhead. Dark red, not the orange of my father's hair. Titian-haired Jennie, leaning against the bar, tipping back a drink. She tosses back that shiny red hair and racks them up, and watch out, boys, because she's got a temper. I wanted that red hair. Why not? I took the box and moved on. At the breakfast cereals, a woman was considering cornflakes. Too tired to make up her mind, I guessed. She gave me a weary, almost puzzled glance. For some reason, this embarrassed me, and I left the dye beside a box of Shredded Wheat.

I bought food, coffee, a toothbrush, more cigarettes for Sarah. On the way back to the motel, I actually felt a little jolly, thinking about volleyball players in California, a trip to be had once the truck was running—thinking if we were at a Holiday Inn, I'd start to believe that prayers could be answered.

SARAH and the cop were leaning against his fender, talking. "You're still here," I said.

"I never managed to leave," he said.

"I captured him," Sarah said. "I came outside to smoke and ambushed him."

He said, "Sarah tells me your name is Jennifer Braverman."

I shifted my bag. "Did she? I guess you should arrest me." I shouldn't have shifted my bag. It felt like a giveaway of some sort.

"Ha," Sarah said nervously. "Don't listen to her. She thinks she's sarcastic."

"Sarah also said she's engaged."

"She's not engaged." I sat on the steps and took a muffin out of my shopping bag. Cool, Calm, Cucumber. I am a woman of C's. "She's disengaged."

"I told him," Sarah said. There was something in her face I didn't like. Her chin lifted, her jaw clenched. Not anger or malicious intent. She took a long drag off her cigarette and put it out under her heel. Determination?

"I brought you a cup of coffee," I said, "and that doesn't make me a hero, either."

"I told the whole truth and nothing but the truth, so don't let her lie to you," Sarah said. She bent over at the waist and flipped her hair forward.

"Hey now," said Officer Gomez. "I'm not calling anybody a liar."

"I bought you tampons," I said. "You might want to dart upstairs."

Sarah glared at me through her hair. "Are you trying to embarrass me? Because guess what, I'm not embarrassed by bodily functions, thank you very much." She gathered her hair in a high ponytail and straightened. "Poor Jennie," she told Officer Gomez. "Believe it or not, she loved that truck. I think she identifies with it." Her voice made it clear that I might as well love an obese rat.

"Doesn't she have nice hair?" I said.

"She does indeed," Officer Gomez said.

"It's dyed," I said. "Good job, don't you think?"

"I told him how you rescued me. And how you've been so worried about me, and that's why you don't seem okay. Why you seem like such a *bitch*."

"So is it Braverman or Burning?" he asked.

I put down the groceries. "I'm a newlywed." I took a huge, dry, stale bite of muffin. I chewed. I shrugged. I took a sip of coffee. "It's hard to get used to Braverman."

Officer Gomez arched his back and sighed and looked up at the bright blue sky. "Hot," he said. "Fires everywhere this summer. If you pay attention, you can catch a whiff of the one over in Steamboat. They finally put it down a few days ago, but you can still smell it."

"What I'm wondering," I said, "is if you ever work."

"What do you think I'm doing?"

"I don't smell any fires," Sarah said, wrinkling her nose, looking up at the sky as if she expected to see flames there, or a trail of smoke pointing the way toward danger.

THE couple next door was fighting again. Two people who probably imagined themselves in love, fighting. Just the sort of fight that happens between travelers at cheap hotel rooms because traveling, it gets to you, as Mike the mushy clerk (what *did* he look like?) knows. On they went. *You sonofabitch* and a door slamming.

We spread the food over the bed. Officer Gomez would be back in an hour. Sarah lit a cigarette. "So how come you're mad at me? I'm supposed to be mad at you, remember?"

"This is a no-smoking room."

"Fuck no smoking," she said, blowing smoke. On the man ranted, a tight quick beat of anger. Sarah smiled, head cocked. "Love is strange," she said.

"Love is about power," I said. "There's always one who loves more and one who loves less, and the one who loves more is fucked."

"Listen to you," she said sadly. "You told me that before, and it still sounds like bullshit."

Embarrassed, I gnawed on the muffin. "At least I know you're paying attention."

She turned the TV to the news channel, to those anchorpeople who look the same everywhere, their oversprayed hair and false chatter about this and that in between teasers about how the most interesting news is still to come.

"We're not in the headlines, anyway," I said.

"Are we in trouble? Because I really just don't want to be in trouble."

"How can we be in trouble? You asked him to arrest me twice, and he didn't listen either time."

"Maybe he has a crush on you."

"Or on you," I said.

"What about the dress? Are we in trouble because we took it?"

"It's worth about eight thousand dollars," which seemed like a good ballpark figure. We had a few perfect specimens at Las Novias that cost that much. "I'd say that puts us pretty solidly in the felony zone." I found some satisfaction in the panic on her face. I don't know why I felt so mean. "But he won't know about it. Oh wait, silly me. You'll tell him."

"Maybe there's an APB out on us. Maybe your boss called the state police and they have some kind of system."

The anchorwoman had thin hair sprayed forward to look like more hair. She was talking about the unprecedented number of forest fires in Colorado this year. "Unprecedented," she said, as if she was proud that she knew how to use the word. "Terrible," her coanchor said, shaking his head solemnly. "Really bad news, Jane. City councilors today . . ." I changed the channel. Our neighbors' fighting worsened. The man's low angry murmur was punctuated by the woman's high refrain: *You sonofabitch! You sonofabitch!*

"I think love is like a prayer," Sarah said.

I laughed. "A hope and a prayer."

"Whatever. I mean, love is something you do even though you don't have proof it will work."

The tone and pace of the fighting changed from shouting to keening. Sarah and I met eyes in the mirror.

"Should we check?" Sarah asked.

The woman was crying now. *You sonofabitch you sonofabitch.* I rose. "Shit," I said. "I don't know." But their noises decided for me; they grew rhythmic, louder and stronger and faster.

"They're having sex," Sarah said, grinning.

The man chanted, *Godohgodohgod* . . .

I banged on the wall, and the noise stopped abruptly. I said, "What's the worst thing about being an atheist?"

"Did Sunny ever teach you Russian?" Sarah asked.

"No one to talk to when you come," I said. "What's Russian got to do with anything?"

"I was just wondering about that word, 'fucking,' and if Russian has a better one. I don't even know what Russian sounds like. The only Russian word I know is Moscow."

"Borscht," I said.

"Vodka."

"Brezhnev."

"Glasnost."

"Kopek," I said. "Matryushka."

"Kremlin," Sarah said. "I knew more than I thought."

"I don't want to play this game anymore," I said.

"Your joke was quasi-funny," she said. "Just so you know I was listening."

I flipped past a channel of football, a soap opera where a woman's eyes were filling with tears, a soap opera where exactly the same thing was happening to another woman. I thought, but did not say, I'm glad you're here to listen.

6.

WELL-LAID PLANS

Hard-Hearted Maggie

Thursday, Blue Sky, Colorado

Officer Gomez drives Jennie and Sarah out of Blue Sky to the truck hospital. Jennie sits in the front seat, watching the trees beat by, a forest interrupted only by the odd, lonely mailbox beside a dirt road heading off into the pines. She wishes she were sprinting, but there will be no running today. She thinks, If you knew how far I could go, you would not dismiss me.

Jennie's making a case for herself: point one, this cop is shorter than her by a couple inches, maybe more. Point two, he lives in the middle of nowhere. But what's Jennie making a case for, anyway? Try this: she must keep herself cool, calm, collected, because this is a cop car and above all because she does not want any more tears and shouting.

The cop says, "Did you sleep okay?"

Jennie is pleased. Point one, he's short. Two, living in Paluka. Three: "You asked me that already."

"So I did."

"What, are you verifying? Checking for consistency?" But Jennie's pretty sure Officer Gomez isn't out to throw them in jail. Why would he care if they lied about their names, anyway? It's not like they're smuggling drugs. She thinks, We've gotten impressed by our own petty crime.

"You see?" Sarah says. "She's trying to be sarcastic again."

He passes mailbox, mailbox, mailbox. Then a blank space between the trees, a grassy bald spot on the mountainside. "There's the rope tow," he says.

"They tore down all those trees for that?" Sarah says. "I don't think that's very environmental, do you?"

"It's free," he says, turning onto a driveway just after the clearing. The Bronco takes the rutted dirt road easily, if slowly. The rope tow flashes in and out of view as the road picks its way up the mountain. The ruts worsen. They jostle and bounce. "Jennie, is this man taking us to a remote location?" Sarah asks.

"I believe he is." Jennie is a cucumber, all right. Cool, crisp. What else? Caustic. That's a good one, she thinks, happy with the way things are going.

The road dead-ends among the pines. A chain-link fence encircles a steep clearing, littered with the bodies of Volvos in various stages of decay. The Ford, parked on a precarious slope, looks in danger of rolling back down the mountainside and into town. God knows its brakes could give out any minute, the useless old hunk of shit.

"Does this guy even know anything about Fords?" Jennie asks. "Looks like a Volvo man to me."

"Woman. Maggie Rodriquez. She likes Volvos, but she can fix anything."

"A lady mechanic," Sarah says. "Is she a lesbian?"

"That's a stupid thing to say," Jennie says. Although, admittedly, she too is surprised.

"What, just because I think lesbians are the only women brave enough to tread where no woman has treaded before? I have this theory they do the interesting jobs because they don't care what men think, while the rest of us girls are worrying whether the boys will want to go on a date with us if our nails are dirty. But I'm stupid to think that way, according to you."

"I'm pretty damn sure she's no lesbian," the cop says, smiling.

"What, have you slept with her?" Sarah says.

"Not exactly," he says. "Isn't that a personal question?"

"Why should you have all the fun?" Sarah says. "Like cops are the only people who get to be nosy?"

Jennie gets out of the Bronco. She looks up at the circle of sky ringed by tall pines. She breathes deeply, to test for the smell of distant forest fires, to take a breath and keep herself firmly in the realm of C. Cocky. That's a good one.

The Lady Mechanic, elbow-deep in a Chevy's engine, straightened and eyed us with a look that could have, as they say, treed a bear. "Abe," she said.

"Mags," he said. His face something like respect and something like complicity, as if they knew something the rest of the world didn't. Sure enough, he'd slept with her.

She wore coveralls. She wiped her hands on a grease rag, just like a real mechanic. "You're the Ford, I'm guessing," she said to me.

"If I am, then I'm a useless piece of shit," I said.

"You said it, not me." She extended her hand, and when I took it, her grip made my bruises throb.

Maggie was a tired, harried-looking woman in her thirties, with long hair carelessly barretted atop her head. Her face held traces of a younger, prettier woman, but she had smoked and worried herself old. Maybe she had a baby or two, a morose man with a liking for vodka cranberries. Maybe she used to be a cheerleader for the Blue Sky High School football team. Maybe she held hands with the quarterback, and things turned out like this. Go figure.

"Maggie here has a special talent with engines," Officer Gomez said. "Isn't that right?"

Maggie smiled at him, and a deep cheerleader's dimple appeared in each cheek. "I'm not the one to say so." She turned to Sarah, and there was no mistaking her hostility. "Is that your wedding dress in the truck?"

"It's not for sale," Sarah said.

"Might be a good idea to rescue it before it gets greasy shit all over it," Maggie said. "I wouldn't want to piss you off."

"Oh really?" Sarah said. "What do you think, Jennie?"

"I think Maggie just might spill something on your dress," I said, the best I could muster, weary as I was. Sarah beelined for the dress, and we trooped after her. I did not recognize myself, this passive Jennie following quietly, watching silently while Maggie lifted the Ford's hood and delivered disaster, pointing to wires and coils and announcing the Ford needed a valve job, and a fuel pump, and probably a water pump, and it was a miracle it had driven at all, and I'd just have to sit tight since she had a whole bunch of jobs ahead of me.

Sarah, gown safe in her arms, asked, "Is the piece of junk dead for good?"

Maggie leaned closer to the dress. "I sew some," she said.

Sarah took a step away from Maggie's greasy fingers. "A seamstress *and* a mechanic?"

"She's handy with everything," Abe said. That annoyingly private look passed between Maggie and him. "She used to have a sewing business," he told me. "On the side."

Maggie said, "This here's a French seam. See how it's all covered up, no raw edges? That's craftsmanship. This dress is old, isn't it? Antique?"

"It was Governor Bent's daughter's dress," Sarah said.

Maggie gave her a narrow look. "Is that a fact," she said flatly.

Sarah, my magnificent, unflappable friend, said, "As a matter of fact, it is a fact. What, you think I'm lying? Ask Jennie. The fact is, it was supposed to be my wedding dress, and the fact is, I got jilted, thank you very much for reminding me. And the fact is, Jennie and I are on a grief trip. Bonding. And you better watch it, because the fact is, redheads have a temper."

Maggie gave me a long once-over. She had a noncommittal face: eyes that were neither blue nor gray, hair a mousy brown that was almost blond. Yet, and I hate to admit it, she intimidated me. So I stared right back. Fake it till you make it, baby. I decided then and there, standing inside a ring of pines and under a blue sky, that I hated Maggie. But I couldn't think of how to put her in her place when I needed her to fix my truck.

"Maybe Jennie's pulling your leg," Maggie said, smiling at me, those deep dimples puncturing her cheeks. "Maybe she bought that dress at a flea market. Maybe you dye your hair."

Sarah said, "And maybe you just want to look at my pubes."

"Hey now, no need for that," Officer Gomez said, and Sarah was charmingly apologetic. But when he turned his back, and when Maggie wasn't looking, Sarah pressed her lips to my ear and said, "What. A. *Bitch*." I agreed, but the fact was, united against this hardhearted, inexplicably hostile woman, I felt as if Sarah and I were friends again. So I was beholden to the enemy, and even grateful for my truck's mechanical collapse, if these hardships were what it took to bring my little friend back to me.

$\mathcal{C}$URES

DAYS pass, a week. Jennie and Sunny are fatherless now. Their father lives
far away, in a land where it's always summer. Fatherless, Jennie tries to decide
on a science project and tries to figure out how to pay for her books. Two
fatherless weeks pass, and three. At night, Clarence and Faith fight. Jennie
doesn't go to Our Lady of Delores again. At night, she dreams of her father's
boots, and the deer's heart, which becomes a bucketful of money, so she can
say to her teachers, I lost my books but I can pay for them.

Clarence and Faith spend the night in Santa Fe all the time now, selling
jewelry. Jennie tells Faith, "You're supposed to stay with us. It's irresponsible
to leave us alone."

"Don't you talk to me like that," Faith says. She says Jennie's old enough to
take care of Sunny, and they need money, and if Jennie's father sent money
things would be different. "Don't you talk to me about responsibility," Faith
says. "You and your father don't know anything about responsibility."

October marches by. Every night, Jennie tries to solve the problem: Where
do I get the money? Who will give me money? Who has money to give?
Around and around in her head the problem goes, and she can't figure out if
she's deducing or inducing, or if there's a scientific way to solve this riddle.
The leaves drop off the trees. Randall's mother puts smiling plastic jack-o'-
lanterns on her roof. She changes them to turkeys in November.

Sunny's earache gets worse and worse. "He needs a doctor," Jennie says.
"He needs penicillin."

Faith, polishing one of Clarence's bracelets, says, "I'm not giving him that
poison. It destroys the immune system." Polishing hard, she says, "You think we
have that kind of money? We'll have a Thanksgiving Meeting."

"That's so stupid," Jennie says. "That's not scientific."

"You think you're so smart? Nothing is more powerful than eating Medicine. You're taking God inside you."

Jennie says, "Then how come Sunny's still sick? Does God hate us?"

Faith stares at her. "It's your father," she says. "Your father makes you this

way. Talk like that gets you punished. Don't forget, a Meeting brought your father back. God helps True Believers."

"That was a coincidence," Jennie says. "He came back for Christmas."

"That's what you think," Faith says, setting aside the bracelet. Jennie's hate
gleams inside her, hard-edged and solid and metallic, a bracelet around her
heart. What happens to a girl who hates her own mother, who dreams in
swear words? She dreams fuck you. She dreams cocksucker and shit. She's a
girl who steals, too.

"You believe in God," Faith says. "You're a True Believer."

"I believe in science," Jennie says.

Faith says, "Science has nothing to do with God. You can't turn your back
on the Church. I gave you four Meetings. You'll always be a Medicine Girl."

Jennie thinks, *Then I am a Medicine Girl who swears and hates and steals.*

AFTER school, Sunny is standing in the driveway, in the dark, a strange
Backwards Boy, with snowflakes in his hair, on his eyelashes, his shoulders.
He coughs, a terrible sound thick and deep in his chest. "I'm waiting for you,"
he says.

"It's too cold," she says. "You shouldn't be out here." She sits him in the
kitchen and makes a fire and goes into the falling snow for water. On the
clothesline, jeans hang like boards, frozen solid.

She heats the water and pours a bath for Sunny and scrubs him clean, worrying about his cough, about her mother driving through the snow. If only,
just for a little while, there was nothing to worry about.

Her science project will prove that none of Faith's remedies can kill bacteria. Goldenseal, Medicine, prayers: Jennie will prove they're all worthless.
Only she isn't quite sure how she'll prove it. She has stolen science project
supplies from school, cotton swabs, petri dishes. In the kitchen, she swabs
Sunny's throat and infects a petri dish.

She takes her own bath, and they sit in front of the fireplace in the Middle
Room, staring into the fire. Food, heat, light. Fire is all of these things.
Clarence's blowtorch, with its big tank of fuel, reminds her that fire is also
work. It's supposed to be hell, too, and Medicine Way, it takes prayers to God.

"Junie," Sunny says, "tell about Paul and Lipa," and the Treasured Memories sadness stabs her right in the heart.

Jennie and Sunny snuggle in her bed, warm and dry, but Jennie can't
sleep. Sunny does, struggling for breath with his mouth open. Jennie worries,
her official job. We're Hansel and Gretel, she decides. Our parents have left
us alone in the dark woods. We'll have to figure out how to take care of ourselves, to make it to morning. At last, she sleeps.

In the middle of the night, Sunny's pee runs warm and wet over Jennie's legs and she leaps out of bed. "WAKE UP!" she shouts. "YOU'RE PEE-ING!" and even half asleep, Sunny lies, mumbling, "No I'm not," and she says, "You *liar*," and she drags him outside, through sparkling blue snow. "No," Sunny says, "no, I didn't—" and she drops the bucket down the well, and he says, softly, desperately, "No," and Jennie, hauling up water, tells him, "You have to stop lying. I'm soaked in pee," and he says, "I didn't," shrinking away, backing into the snow, like he's afraid of her, like she's Clarence, and something in her goes crazy. She dumps the bucket of water over Sunny's head. He doesn't cry. He says, "No." She scoops him up, and he's shivering so hard. She carries him inside and undresses him and puts him in his own bed. She lies with him. She stinks of pee, but that's her punishment. She won't wash. On the Dog Bus, they'll smell her, the Bad Sister who gets what she deserves.

I N the morning Sunny's sicker, and Jennie the Bad Sister makes him promise to stay in bed all day. Outside, everything's hatted with snow except for the white car. This is evidence. Clarence and Faith got home so late that the snowstorm had stopped. That is deduction.

Jennie walks through the absolute quiet, through the padded world where nothing can rattle around. The snow soaks up sound, warmth; the sun shines in a bright blue sky, but it's a cold sun; the hairs in her nose freeze. She pauses now and then to look back at her footprints, the only mark on a clean piece of paper. The sunlight bounces everywhere, blinding.

At Flaco's, Randall Sandoval stamps his feet, talking to his friends. There's a frozen dog lying on the road, legs sticking straight out. Frost dusts its shaggy fur. She squats beside it. What is it like to freeze to death? Maybe the dog just went to sleep, except its filmy blue eyes are open. What does the dog's heart look like, frozen? She wishes she could dissect it, the way a scientist would. That could be her science project.

Randall Sandoval and Peter Vigil come over and poke the dog with their boots. Jennie doesn't move. They talk about throwing it in the trash. "It's a health hazard," Randall says.

"I have a knife," Peter says. "We could cut it up."

Randall Sandoval squats beside Jennie, and by accident, she looks directly into his face, and his eyes are sharp blue. Light, bright, pointy blue.

Randall says, "What are *you* staring at?"

"She's in love," Stephanie Martinez cries. "Piojo loves Randall!"

"Shut up," Randall says.

"Piojo loves Randall!"

"Shut up," Jennie says. Shocked, she tells herself, *You* shut up. But more words come. "You better shut up."

"Make me," Stephanie says, and Jennie wants to laugh. Stephanie is so stupid. All she can say is *Make me*. Jennie hates herself for going inside Flaco's. If she were stronger, braver, not so ugly and pathetic, she'd stay out there and say, *Make me? That's all you can say?*

The dog is a statue. That's rigor mortis, which she learned in science. Through Flaco's window she watches as Randall grabs the dog and swings it by its leg, and Stephanie jumps to her feet, laughing and screaming, and now Peter drops snow down Stephanie's coat, and Randall stands back, watching, still holding the dog.

On the bus, the Dogs won't let her sit down. Every place she tries to sit, they put up their legs. "I'm saving this seat," Randall Sandoval says. Stephanie stacks her books on the seat and says, "What are you staring at?"

Jennie sits on the bus steps, by Eloy the Bus Driver. She watches the road speed by, just a few feet from her. Thinking about her books, she feels like crying. She can use some of them, but not the others, and she's so behind. She doesn't know what she'll do. And she's so sick of being split in half. It seems like there's half of her who could be Jennie, strong and normal and smart. But the other half, this Juniper girl, always shows up and makes her into a helpless crybaby who runs into Flaco's. She wishes she could kill the Juniper part, shove her out of the bus, splatter her head all over the highway. Randall Sandoval would squat beside her dead body, his eyes filled with tears. Even Faith would be sorry.

The bus reaches the paved Upper Alfin road, and everything goes quiet. Anyone in Upper could pay for her books. Anyone could pay for Sunny to be better. If only I were rich. If only I lived in Upper. It would be like living in heaven. Randall would call me his angel. Jennie thinks, If Upper Alfin is heaven, then I live in hell. She remembers Father Arturo: *For ever. And ever.*

I T ' s easier to find sympathy for a child, isn't it? Teenagers are harder to pity. I hate the little shits myself, can't stand them, with their hormonal poisoning, their know-it-all struts giving them a blind man's road map, their clumsy bull-headed charge through the china-shop rooms of a heart. Underneath that oily, acne-treatment veneer lurks their desperate need, their whining, oozing, helpless sniveling: Tell me who I am, love me love me do, like the chorus to a bad song playing over and over until, singing it helplessly, you'd shoot yourself in the head just to get it out of your mind. True, some of them are slick, strutting their newest fashions and newer slang, but it's an oil slick, a sebum-clogged skin-deep slick, and if you're lucky, they put on a good act because worst of all is the kid whose case is so bad, whose oil so black and sludgy, that you take one look and get sucked into the tar pit of their desperation. These belly-slithering outcasts—they're the worst, and if you see one, don't walk. Run. Run as fast as you can, because they'll get you. They are not harmless. They'll lie; they'll cheat and steal and scam their way into a little love, and then they'll slide off into the dark, leaving you covered in their slime. Don't pity them. Hold them completely responsible. Children, they know not what they do, but any kid old enough to get her period, to poke his willy into girls, to leave home, do drugs or any of a thousand decisions teenagers make, any kid that old should be held responsible for the damage done along the way. You can't have it both ways, you teenage monsters. You don't get to act like you know everything, and then cry, *But I didn't know!*

B Y the Thanksgiving Meeting, Sunny Boy Blue can't talk, and his throat has swollen shut, and he can't stand without falling. Mute, hungry, thirsty, whimpering, he lies clutching his ears. Jennie wants to take him to the doctor, but Faith says, "God will heal him." She is so stupid. Even when Meeting kids come, Sunny sleeps through all their playing noise. Hot-faced, sweating, he sleeps. Jennie strokes his hair and maybe she's praying inside. His violent cough shakes him awake. He asks for water, and Jennie gets it, but he can't swallow.

Faith wraps Sunny in her Meeting Shawl with the long silky fringe around its edges, and Clarence carries him to the tipi, and the Meeting starts. The kids go to sleep. The house falls silent. Sunny needs a hospital. Jennie feels a little smug about this. She's almost looking forward to morning, when Sunny's sick, and Faith's wrong. But Grandma Lipa died of a cold, and I dumped water on him, Jennie thinks. If he dies, it's my fault. I am the Bad Sister.

She goes outside and sits close to the tipi. The fire makes the tipi glow like God's lantern. The Meeting Peoples' shadowy silhouettes sway, their Starting Prayers blending into a murmur of bees' wings humming up to God. The fire sends sparks shooting from the tipi's top. The prayers finish. People shift, cough, none louder or harsher than Sunny's hacking. A little boy should not cough like that.

Clarence sings the four Starting Songs, his deep, urgent voice matching the fast shake of the rattle, the racing beat of the drum. Usually, one man sings by himself, but tonight all the men join Clarence, and the women, too, their voices high and sad, and nobody knows the language of the songs, not even the Indians, not even Clarence. But Jennie knows what they're singing: *Oh*

God, feed our sick, save our hearts, fix our houses, heal our hopes, our Sunny Boy Blue is sick, Heavenly Father. Please heal him. Please. And Jennie doesn't sing, but she prays hardest of all because in her heart she knows she is the Bad Sister, and if she believed better, if she hadn't dumped water on him, he wouldn't be so sick. The Meeting Drum fills the cold sky, like Santa's jingle-bell reindeer, God's heartbeat, or a voice saying over and over *YouDidItYouDidItYouYouYou.* Teeth chattering, she stays, and they sing and Sunny coughs, and she stays and stays until she can't stay anymore.

I N the morning Sunny has an enormous bruise on his cheek and glassy, shining eyes. Jennie is so mad she's afraid of herself. She asks Sunny, "Did Clarence hurt you?"

"He's better," Faith says, like nothing, like it's about as important as the pumpkin bread she's slicing. "His fever's down."

"It was a spider," Sunny whispers.

"He has a *bruise,*" Jennie says, her voice rising.

Sunny shrinks away from her. "It was a big spider," he croaks. He doesn't sound like himself. "Clarence sucked a spider out of my cheek and it ran right into the fire and exploded bang like that and then they gave me Medicine and I'm all better now."

How did Clarence do it? Did he put a spider in his mouth? Did he hide it in his hand? "He's really sick, and you kept him up all night, and you let Clarence beat him up. How can you believe in this bullshit?"

"You shut your filthy mouth," Faith says. "He was sick, and now he's better." The pumpkin bread falls away from the knife in thick moist slices.

"You gave drugs to a little kid," Jennie says. "He's really sick!"

"He's *better,*" Faith says, as if repeating herself will make it true. "Sunny doesn't have a problem anymore. I don't have the problem." She points her knife at Jennie and says, "*You* have the problem," and her knife aims right at Jennie's heart, and she says, "If you don't like it here, you can pack your bags and go live with your father."

"Come on," Jennie tells Sunny, taking his hand. "We're leaving."

"Mommy," he whispers, clinging to Faith's leg, his voice sore and choked. Why can't Faith hear how sick he is? And why is he afraid of me, his only sister?

"Leave him alone," Faith says. "Can't you see you're scaring him?"

Jennie says, "Fine. Kill him, for all I care." She dodges through the Meeting People and runs down the road, away from Sunny's bruised face, past the pilgrims in Randall's yard. She stops at Flaco's pay phone, the same one she used when Sunny was born backwards. She has no dime, but she's older now and she knows what to do: she dials zero. "Operator," the woman says, like the voice of God. "I need an ambulance," Jennie says. She's older now. She knows exactly how to give directions.

Jennie runs all the way back to wait for them, and she hides on the hill with the piñons so Faith won't see her, watching the highway across the valley. When the ambulance comes flashing down into Alfin, she times it just right, so she gets down the hill just when the ambulance arrives. It parks in the middle of the road because there's no room in the driveway, with all the Meeting cars.

The men, busily, scientifically, get out and open the back of the ambulance. They have a whole routine; they are efficient and graceful. Jennie wishes she could help. She says, "I called you. My brother's sick."

The driver, bag in hand, turns to the house, ready. "What is this, some kind of party?"

"A Thanksgiving party," Jennie tells him.

"You must have a lot to be thankful for," the driver says, and for a moment Jennie believes that this man with his black hair and black bag will cure everything in her life.

Only here's Faith, running out to meet them, Faith saying, "What did you do? Juniper, what did you do?"

"He needs a hospital," Jennie says.

"Ma'am," says the other ambulance man, holding his medicine bag. You see, Mom? He has real medicine, a real cure. "Ma'am, are you the mother?"

Tears in her eyes, Faith whispers, "Do you know how much this costs? Do you have any idea how much this costs? What will we do?" Faith's tears spill, and uncertainty creeps into Jennie. "How will we pay for this?"

"Ma'am," the ambulance man says. "Can you take me to the boy?"

"He was better," Faith says, wiping her eyes. "Clarence made him better." She smells like wood smoke, like a Meeting. She looks the ambulance man straight in the eyes, and for a moment, confusingly, oddly, Jennie feels proud of Faith. "This way," she says. "I'll take you to him." She turns to Jennie and says, "You'll pay for this," and Jennie knows she has done exactly the wrong thing, even though the ambulance men agree that Sunny needs the emergency room, so Jennie was right. But she hasn't won; it's Faith who rides in the ambulance with Sunny, and Clarence who drives them home, and Faith who gives Sunny his dropperfuls of pink medicine that night. Jennie just stays alone in her room, thinking, How am I going to pay for an ambulance? How much does it cost? Where will I get the money?

$\mathscr{D}$IVE

MR. Officer Gomez, keeper of peace, invited Maggie to meet us for dinner and some pool. "Might as well hang out," he said to me, "given that you'll be here a while." I liked the picture: Maggie's dimples undimpling as I circled the table, winning and winning some more, and so I didn't protest. This, anyway, was how I explained it to myself.

He pulled up to a dump with a neon comet for a sign: LITTLE JOE'S BAR AND CAFÉ, sitting shoulder to shoulder with the few other Blue Sky buildings, and Mr. Officer said he'd be right back—"I have errands," he said to Sarah's fury, and so we stood, deposited like cargo in the parking lot.

To the tune of Sarah's tirade, we marched inside to get out of the heat, and found ourselves in a dive, with a few round tables crowded in the front and three pool tables in the back, with plastic bamboo shades that sliced the afternoon sunlight into stripes of dust. At the Formica bar, the bartender washed glasses, the waitress chatted, and Mike the Motel Clerk stood there, nodding and listening, and what a surprise: our Mike was a giant, long skinny legs up to his neck, and he must have been close to seven feet. Who knew?

Sarah, fuming, dumped her dress on the counter like a challenge, and Mike raised his hand in greeting, but otherwise, everyone ignored us. Cast-off clothes festooned the low ceiling—mostly baseball caps and cowboy hats, but also the odd pair of ladies' panties or beat-up jeans—nailed or stapled in place, inscribed with black marker: dates or names or things like *I fucked Velma, so she fucked me over,* or *Tex-Mex cooks do it on the range.* Pants legs and shirt arms looped down, dusty and uneven bunting. No doubt about it; this here was a dive, like Antonio's Pool House, and I actually sighed in relief because I knew the rules of this place, and I could relax, truck or no truck.

The waitress, a tiny blond sprig, was blathering about this summer's huge outbreak of forest fires. She had a high, piping voice, enormous eyes, and a mouth the size of a butterscotch: the tiniest mouth I'd ever seen, as if the bottom half of her face had stopped growing at birth. "Two times the national average, they said on the news," the waitress said. "They say it'll only get worse, but I'm praying."

Mike the Clerk said, "Jeez, I didn't know." He wore a bright red T-shirt with the words BLUE SKY HOTSHOTS on the back.

Sarah said, "Is this the *rude* town? Because first we get abandoned and now these people don't even notice us, like what the hell, is this the *rude* bar?"

"Well, guy, Mike, you should know *that*," the waitress said. She leaned toward him in a sweet attempt at the coquette.

"It does seem like an unreasonable excess," the bartender said. "Perhaps arson?"

"Global warming," Mike offered.

"Excuse me," Sarah said. "We're sitting here."

The bartender smiled politely. "Greetings," he said. "Are you in need of libations?"

Sarah said, "Greetings? What are you, from *Star Trek*?"

The bartender gave Sarah a soft, friendly sort of smile, as if in her he saw everything he could have been, everything good and clean and easy. "I must concede that is one way of considering things." He was a little old bonbon of a man, gray and thin on top, pink-faced and pink-scalped and pale-eyed.

Sarah smiled back, softening instantly. "Give me a hamburger and a Diet Coke and a bottle of ketchup and about ten thousand French fries, and then we can be friends."

"This is a small request that can be easily arranged," the bartender said. Had he attended some kind of elocution class? Did he get an A?

Maggie arrived in jeans, with her hair down. Otherwise, she was pretty much the same, a woman with black fingernails and an attitude. She marched right behind the bar, kissed the bartender on the cheek, glared at me, and ignored Sarah. "Gus, take a break," she told the bartender, and he promptly did, leaving for the great outdoors.

Maggie turned on us. "I guess you want food, too?" she said, like she owned the place, and I finally clued in that she did. Own the place. How many businesses did this lady have?

Sarah leaned back to study the ceiling. "Who puts that stuff up there, anyway?"

"Maggie," the waitress said.

"I did it *once*," Maggie said. "Lord, Candy, you talk like I do it every weekend."

"Well, guy," the waitress said. "You don't have to swear."

"I didn't swear."

"Don't take the Lord's name in vain."

"'Lord' is not the Lord's name," Maggie said. "It's his title."

"Excuse me," I said, amazed. "Your name is Candy? That's perfect."

Candy looked at me head-on for the first time, her butterscotch mouth pursed. Her blond hair, badly permed, fluffed around her head like dandelion seed. "Thank you," she said uncertainly. She had the big eyes of a cow, sweet but wounded. No doubt about it; this girl had been ruthlessly teased. Liquor is quicker, but Candy is dandy.

Maggie turned her evil eye on Mike. "So you're going?" she said. "You're an idiot."

Poor Mike. He blushed and couldn't even look at her. He should have just worn it on his T-shirt: HOT FOR MAGGIE. "You can make twenty thousand in a summer, fighting fires."

"You can make twenty thousand as a whore, but I don't recommend that, either."

"Gee whiz, Maggie, you have a dirty mouth," Candy said.

"Gee *whiz?*" Sarah said. "Man, this town is weird."

Abe arrived, standing in the doorway for a moment, smiling at them all, a beneficent rooster watching over his chickens. Maggie smiled back at him with dimples and joy. She got busy washing the rest of Gus's glasses, and joined their talk of fires. She raged against weekend hunters and smokers all working to burn down the countryside, but most of all, Maggie blamed nature, which will kick your ass when you turn your back, lightning, spontaneous combustion, you name it. Mike and Candy agreed it made more sense to blame it on human stupidity.

It was like high school bathroom graffiti: *Candy loves Mike but Mike loves Maggie but Maggie loves Abe.* Abe, apparently, loved them all, in a policemanly sort of a way, and hoped he wouldn't hurt anybody. They made me sad, the four of them, working to hide the obvious. There was a certain innocence in their square dance, a person at each corner. Do-si-do and break your heart.

I was so deep in this little fantasy that I jumped when Sarah touched my arm. "It's okay, Jennie."

I looked up at the clothes on the ceiling. Our locals were laughing over some joke. "If you're trying to make a point, I don't get it."

"I forgive you," Sarah said. "That's all."

O U R food arrived, and watching Sarah's ketchup ritual, Maggie said, "Don't get any stains on that dress." She scowled at it. "Hand-sewn seed pearls," she said. "I used to be small enough to fit in this dress."

Mike blurted, "You'd be gorgeous in it, too." Blushing, he glanced around frantically for an exit or the calvary.

Sarah said, "Maggie, you could sew a dress like this for yourself, couldn't you?"

"Goddammit," Maggie snapped. "I'm not having any weddings."

"That's swearing," Candy said. "You can't pretend it's not."

"Well don't get all offended or anything," Sarah said. "I'm only curious if you could make one, considering you're a seamstress and everything."

Maggie leaned closer to Sarah. "You didn't really get jilted," she said. "Did you?"

Sarah blinked. What do you do when your friend needs rescuing? If you're Jennie the Ugly Chick, you tell a big old whopper, a great story of Sunny and Sarah, leaving my wedding for the Rio Grande Gorge, where they lit gas-soaked tennis balls and fell in love, and now the big trip, so she could marry Sunny before her evil ex-boyfriend found out.

"Romantic, isn't it?" Sarah said. "Aren't you jealous?"

But Maggie said, "Not much of a trade, a beater for a firebug. What's a pretty girl like you doing with parasites? Something wrong we can't see?"

Abe put his hand on her arm. "Mags," he said.

"You can start a fire like that. Throwing burning tennis balls around, with all the piñon, juniper. The Rockies are way above the national average in forest fires, you know. People have to fight those fires."

I said, "Back off, Mags. Have a little compassion, why don't you?" What the hell was up with this lady anyway, spitting at us like this?

She said, "I don't like arsonists, and I don't like liars."

Sarah's face flushed. Her eyes filled. "I need to go to the bathroom."

"It's a convictable offense," Maggie said, "lying to a police officer."

"Maggie," Officer Gomez said. "Nobody's convicting anybody here."

"You listen to me," I told the Mechanic Bartender Harpy. "That girl has bruises all over her body. She doesn't need you picking on her." Sarah dropped her face in her palms and she sobbed, a heart-wrenching sound, unbearable, horrible. I said, leaning across the bar so I could get right in Maggie's face, and I was this close to leaping over and grabbing the bitch's throat, "I don't know what your problem is, *Mags*, but if you make my friend cry again, I'll rip your fucking head off."

Well. Goodness. The Ugly Chick may lack originality, but she sure is uppity, running around threatening heads like a movie monster. If a thriller would have the room fall silent and the hero go at it, in real life the Ugly Chick just stands there, feeling the fool.

Maggie knows it, too; she smirks a dimply smirk, one that says, *What a fool you are. I see right through this act into the heart of your foolish, galumphing self.* "Yikes," Maggie says.

So the Ugly Chick, fighting for dignity, scoops up the dress and says, "Come on, Sarah," and off they go, a magnificent procession headed for the door labeled TOILET in a black hand-painted scrawl, an appropriate destination for the foolish likes of foolish me.

In the afterthought of a bathroom, black-walled and tiny, Sarah sat on the toilet and grinned happily. "That was so *cool*," she said, "the way you just played along with me, like we were a team, the two con artists—could this bathroom be any smaller? I could pee and wash my hands at the same time, if you think about it."

The place reeked of strawberryesque deodorizer. There was a window, painted as black as the walls. Various graffiti had been scratched into it. We traded places, and I sat there trying to collect myself, to figure out whether Sarah's tears were an act and I was a sucker, or what. "You make my head spin," I said.

Sarah lit up, tapping her ashes into the sink. "You know what? I feel so sorry for that Maggie, even if she is a bitch."

"*Sorry* for her?"

"Let's put the dress on me, okay?"

I told her to put out her cigarette first, and she rolled her eyes and took a few more deliberate puffs, saying she felt sorry for Maggie because she was so obviously alone, and who would want a bitch like her, anyway, it's a chick and egg thing because, Sarah asked, was she a bitch before or after she was all alone? I said, "If you don't put it out, I can't put the dress on you." So she did, and I dropped the dress over her head and began closing the hundred buttons and saw the fresh bruises on her skin. "What about the cop? Maybe Maggie has him for a somebody."

"Cute, isn't he? Too bad you look like shit, or maybe the cop would go for you. Except you're married, of course, not that you're keeping your vows or anything."

"And not that you've learned to keep your mouth shut."

She grinned over her shoulder. "What are you going to do, hit me?"

"You win."

"I always win."

I touched one of her bruises. "You're still doing it."

She studied her face in the mirror. "You think I have a choice? You think I can stop, just like that?" She looked down at her hands. "I guess you don't believe anything I say."

"Yes I do," I said. I gathered her hair and put it over her shoulder so I could finish buttoning, and the nape of her neck, so white, so little-girl, made me want to cry or scream at her or simply fold her up in my arms. "I'm glad you forgive me, Sarah."

"I know," she said. "You can't help being a bitch, either." I finished the buttons. She climbed on the toilet, craning to see herself in the small mirror. "Do I look great in this dress or what?"

"You look great in that dress." Which was true. It fit like it was made for Sarah, one hundred years in advance. Just as, standing in that tiny bathroom with our bruises and our hangovers and our accuser at the bar, it felt that we were meant to be friends, that everything had led up to this moment of rightness, that even if our lives were in the toilet we could still find some comfort in being there together.

SARAH paused at the threshold of the room, waiting to be noticed. "My gosh," Candy said. "That's the prettiest thing I've ever seen."

Maggie looked up from the pool table. "Did you put it on so everyone would stare at you?"

"No," Sarah said. "I put this on so you could be jealous that I'm such a beautiful bride, and then you could leave me alone."

"I thought you weren't getting married," Maggie said. "Or you are, but it's to someone else? I can't get the story straight."

"As often happens when it's none of your business," I said.

"Don't worry about Maggie," Abe said. "She has complications."

Mike spoke up. "Complications are, she's a bitch."

"Fuck you, Mike," Maggie said pleasantly, and Mike, predictably, blushed and stared at his beer in a nice, uncomplicated way.

Sarah drew on her cigarette, shaking her head. "It's the shadow in her," she said on the exhale. "There's a shadow in everyone, you know. Our dark side. I have this theory that what you love about a person has its exact opposite, and that's the dark side, and it's the price you pay for the good side. That's Jung, by the way. I mean, when I got raped I was thinking how Jung says even a rapist has a good side."

"Jesus," Maggie said. "Here we go again."

Sarah's eyes welled up. "Why are you so mean?"

"You aren't going to cry again," I said. "Sarah."

She shot a long-suffering smile at our company. "My manager here decides everything for me."

"Manager, my ass," I said. "Lady-in-waiting, more like it."

I caught Maggie's gaze, her eyes measuring and calculating, and I wondered, with the indignation of the falsely accused, why this woman had it in for me, and I suddenly wanted Sarah to cry so I could stick it to this Mechanic Harpy, peg her for the criminal she saw in me.

But the moment passed, and Sarah and I finished our burgers and chatted with Mike, and soon the place filled up. Gus the bartender returned, and a band arrived, or rather, two guitarists who plugged in a microphone and began playing the sort of country-western my father liked to play, Hank Williams, Johnny Cash—bluesy, folksy, swinging. Men in cowboy hats, women in jeans. A group of ten men arrived wearing Mike's T-shirt—bright red, with BLUE SKY HOTSHOTS on the back. They oozed confidence, swaggering with their superior understanding of life. Bearded, scraggly, convincing. All but Mike, that is. Candy explained that Mike was going to Idaho in the morning with this team of firefighters. Apparently, he'd been trained last spring and slated to work this summer, but then he chickened out or came to his senses, depending on how you looked at it. Now, a broken foot and a virus later, they were hard up, and he was filling in at the last minute. Candy spoke worshipfully, but when she went off to serve drinks, Gus said that Mike hadn't gone with them this summer because things came up. "More specifically, to be precise about it," Gus said, "in confidence, Maggie arose."

"I see," I said. Indeed, I did. Mike watched Maggie, ate her up with his eyes while she flirted with the customers, lifted their bottles to check for empties, gave them fresh ashtrays. Because he was so tall and so fixated on her, Mike gave the appearance of hovering, even when he was across the room.

I helped Sarah out of the wedding gown after Officer Gomez wrangled us into playing pool, even though I was literally handicapped, by my hand and the many whiskeys I'd swilled. We played teams, Abe and Sarah against Mike and me.

I couldn't shoot straight. My right hand throbbed every time I held the cue. The more I tried, the worse I got. I blew the easiest straight shot, and here was Mikey giving me pointers on some cockeyed technique about aiming for an imaginary ball. I should have cut my losses, walked away, but pride held me in the game. For her part, Sarah was perfectly happy to be the fool, to have her stick move the ball a few wobbly inches. She laughed at herself, waggling her hips as she tried to line up the balls.

"Butt down," I told her. "You're not advertising, you're playing."

"Lay off, Big Mama," she said. "I'm concentrating here. Anyway, you aren't on my team, remember. How do I know you aren't sabotaging me?"

"Jennie's got things on her mind," Abe Gomez said. "Don't be mean to her, now."

"Yes," I said, "like, for instance, at this moment Jennie has whacking both of you over the head on her mind."

Sarah gave Officer Gomez a roll of her eyes. "She's just mad because we're beating her."

"Maybe it's a guilty conscience," Maggie says.

"Maybe it's your ugly face," Jennie says in all her brilliance.

Now Officer Gomez puts his arms around Sarah and sets up her shot, making his move at last, and Jennie's jealous, pathetic girl, jealous and hating him, hating Maggie the Bitchy Proprietor and whiskey and even sweet Mikey with his legs and his bravado, off to war against the devil's fire, and why is she so pissy, our Jennie? Why does she care when Sarah drops the ball neatly in the pocket and sashays around the table?

Jennie tosses back her whiskey, thinking, I know this game. On an ordinary day, I could beat any of you. And here's Candy, bringing another drink, her big cow eyes worried, her butterscotch mouth pursed. She touches Jennie's arm. "You don't look so good," she whispers. "I mean—"

"You mean, maybe I should cut this bitch off."

"Well, dang, you don't have to cuss. I'm just trying to be nice."

Jennie misses another shot and leans against the wall. Time spills on the floor, spreading in a greasy puddle until minutes are hours, marked by a new drink from Candy's magic hand, conversation coming in snatches from a great distance. Sarah, holding court with the firemen, says, "And those shoes were kid leather, so soft. One pair was yellow and one was ivory and one was blue. I bought three pairs."

In the corner, Mike steals a kiss from Candy's butterscotch mouth, and Jennie's furious because this guy loves Maggie and now he's toying with poor little Candy's affections, poor Candy, giggling and slipping away, an annoying little gidget of a girl, irritating in her easily pleased, easily wounded cow-eyed self.

Sarah blows a smoke ring. "The weird thing was, after I got raped, I didn't feel anything."

Above Jennie's head, someone had stapled a pair of the largest boxer shorts in the world. Three men could fit in them, and Jennie's irritated by the person who wore them or the person who put them up or both, and then she's thinking of brokenhearted Henry, his breathless, blue-lipped daughter Amanda.

"You have to understand about Jennie . . ."

Jennie's eyes sting from the smoke, thick as a forest fire, thick as medical students smoking cigars.

"Her brother kidnapped her from her wedding . . ."

The question comes suddenly, violently, in Jennie: was there a Candy for Sunny? A waitress, young and stumbling, her first day on the job, who sloshes hot coffee on his hand and stutters, "Oh god, oh god I'm sorry are you okay?" Please, Heavenly Father God, let him look up at his waitress, his Candy, at her pink face, downy with gold hair, and yes, give her red hair like Sarah's, let her say, "I'm such a klutz, a walking firebrand my mom always says. Please tell me you're okay?"

"So then she tries CPR on it . . ."

Did Sunny have the impulse to reach for this waitress's hand, to say, "No. I'm not okay. Help me please, won't you?" Did she crouch down beside him and wipe his hand clean with her apron, stroke the fingers and finally the palm, and did she whisper, "You're okay, you see?" All he needed was one stranger to ask the right question, to turn it all in a different direction, so that on the verge of boarding the ferry, his burned hand would remind him of the waitress, her lovely hair and klutziness. Maybe he didn't get on the ferry. Maybe he went back to the bar, found his Candy, and went home with her. He could be there still, lying safe in the warm circle of her arms. The whole drowning a terrible case of mistaken identity.

"And then," Sarah says, "she totally forgets I've been raped and she leaves me there in the dark, totally scared. . . ."

In a person's life there are small things which are reasons for the larger things that follow. I could say I met Chris because I like to play pool, or that I married him because of red gloves. Please God, or fate, or the powers that be. Let spilled coffee keep my baby brother out of the sea.

By now the whiskey has taken Jennie completely outside herself, so that the sane and sober part watches this other Jennie drain her glass in one desperate gulp. Candy, magic attendant, brings another. Drunken Jennie says, "Still not cutting me off?"

Candy glances at Officer Gomez, Johnny Law, the Long Arm Of, who drops the eight ball and holds out his hand. "Good game," he says. Before Jennie can dodge him, he palms the nape of her neck and whispers, "Hey now. Don't feel too bad. You didn't lose anything that matters tonight."

Sarah tosses her shimmering hair, her beautiful, exceptional gift. Jennie thinks, How I love my new friend! With her orange velvet miniskirt dropping shreds from its fraying hem, like gold dust in her wake. My beautiful friend. "The truth is, I never cried about the rape. I keep telling myself, You were raped, waiting, you know, for when I'm supposed to cry. It makes it seem imaginary, if you don't cry."

"You didn't cry because you didn't really get raped," Maggie says. "Do you even realize how disgusting it is to lie about something like that?" And now Jennie's whirling and she has her stick in Maggie's face and Jesus, is she going to break this stick over Maggie's head? Who can tell? She's out of her mind with booze and fury and hate and anything could happen and this is why you need a truck and a road and goddammit nothing goes like it should go in this world—Jennie swings the stick and it whistles past Maggie's shoulder and slams against the edge of the table and snaps in half.

The world stops. The bar stares.

"Jennie," Sarah says. "I'm fine. I'm okay."

"You better pay for that," Maggie says.

Jennie drops the pieces of the cue and tries to stalk, but mostly totters, past the men staring at the Ugly Chick and nothing is the way it's supposed to be and the world is down the toilet, but Jennie's getting out of it, out the door, into the pine-scented night.

DID Sunny play pool? Did Sunny play pool did Sunny use drugs did Sunny smoke pot was Sunny the son of his father or the child of his mother? Was Sunny a brooder was Sunny a laugher was Sunny a scholar? Sunny Boy Blue— where have you been, Sunny Boy, Sunny Boy? Where have you been, charming Sunny? Was Sunny a dreamer, a planner, a schemer? Sunny Boy Blue, come blow your horn. Was Sunny a person I knew? I saw him five times in the years after I left home. He unfolded his fist, a finger for each: once for a bicycle ride on his birthday, once for my graduation from high school, once for his, once for my college graduation, once when he kidnapped me away from my own wedding. And this little piggy cried . . . Did Sunny play pool? Was Sunny a lover? Could he span a Russian girl's belly with one hand; did he lap vodka from the bowl of her pelvis, making her laugh? Sunny. He sent a postcard from Russia: *Sex is good. Send condoms.* Did Sunny suffer a broken heart?

I am leaning against the policeman's Bronco and here is the man himself, Officer Gomez, coming toward me with his officer walk. Jennie, you need to make for the hills. But Jennie, that fool, she just props herself against the Blue Sky cop car and waits to get caught.

A Ford pulls up, raising dust in the dirt parking lot. The men who spill from it call out the good cop's name. "Solved any murders lately, Officer?" He laughs, greets them by name. John. Andy. None where you're a suspect.

"So, Officer," I said. "Am I under arrest?" The officer didn't answer. He opened the Bronco's back window and produced a first-aid kit, an Ace bandage. I imitated a laugh. "Good Samaritan, cop, and doctor, too?"

He took my hand and inspected both sides. I winced. He said, "I figured you for tougher, with all those lumberjack genes in you."

I gave him an Essie look. "You aren't flirting with me, are you?"

"Certainly not," he said. "A married woman like you." What a grin he had. From inside, loud music thumped. He sniffed the air. "Smell that?"

I took a deep breath, caught pine, cigarette smoke.

"I can smell the Steamboat fire," he said. "Or else knowing about it makes me think I do." He held my hand in his warm palm and gently palpated my fingers. "Nothing's broken, as far as I can tell," he said.

"Have you ever fought fires?"

"Not me," he said. "I go for the low-risk job. But pretty much everyone around here has, at one time or another. Including Maggie."

I wanted to tell him things. What you see here is not myself. I'm a medical student. I can play wonderful pool. My brother is dead. And here's what I really need to know. Did Sunny play pool? Tell me, because if I just know that one thing I think I can keep it together.

The neon LITTLE JOE'S sign came on with a buzz. The comet tail lit up in stages until it collided with its ball and lit the sign: LITTLE JOE'S, it flashed. LITTLE JOE'S against the high pines, the deep purple-blue sky. How had it gotten so late? Through the bamboo shades, I could see straight inside. Sarah in her orange velvet skirt had climbed onto the bar, the wedding dress in hand. "Great," I said. "Next she'll do a striptease."

Officer Gomez smiled. "She'll be fine. That girl takes care of herself."

Maggie watched, leaning on her cue stick like Moses with his staff, glaring. "And that woman can bitch you out with a look," I said.

"Don't pay attention to Maggie. She's not so bad. That's her car over there, for instance." He nodded toward a low-slung sportscar, an odd specimen alongside all the four-wheel drives.

"Officer Gomez," I began.

"Abe, for God's sake." He held the bandage tail in the center of my palm. It reminded me of the obscene gesture men sometimes use to say they want you. A finger, stroking your palm as you shake hands. Five fingers unfolding from the palm. Five times. The hand outstretched, waving, reaching. Could Sunny play pool? Did he arch his fingers for a bridge?

"Abe," I said. But really, I had nothing to add.

"That car? That's Maggie to a T," he said. "She had a fiancé, Tom, a firefighter." He paused in his winding and looked at the car. "She'd kill me for telling you this. But I hate to see you misjudge her. You two are a lot alike, I think. And anyway, Maggie and me, we go so far back, we have to stick up for each other." I tried to imagine a situation where he'd need a champion. Maggie on the playground, punching a bully's nose.

"So she was engaged to Tom," he said. "Tom was the mechanic. He taught her. Before that she sewed, like I said, though there wasn't much call for that up in Blue Sky. In the summers she had a business called Artemis. She took women hunters on guided trips. It was real popular. People down in Steamboat Springs would send her customers. And of course she always had Little Joe's."

He wound the bandage over the back of my hand, up my fingers. He said, "Tom was the one who loved Volvos. He used to buy junkers, fix the engines, fix the bodies, and sell them for a profit. Especially the P1800s, like that one over there. Late sixties, early seventies models. That one was his baby. Nineteen sixty-six, the best year for chrome."

I felt dizzy with whiskey. I stared at the bandage, at my hand in his. This didn't help to steady me.

"Anyway, in the summers, Tom fought forest fires. And one summer, he burned to death. The sap in trees gets hot in a fire, and sometimes it explodes. One exploded and what was left of the tree fell over and landed on him."

"Shit," I said. His brown fingers were long and graceful, pianist's fingers. Or surgeon's, I thought, with a guilty jolt. Like Chris's.

"Worse than that." He finished my bandage. "He died two weeks before their wedding. When he got the call for the fire, Maggie didn't want him to go. Screamed and carried on, right out here in the parking lot. That just wasn't typical of Maggie. We figured it was with the wedding being so close. Nerves. Anyway, Tom, he left mad." He looked at the racy little Volvo. "Some say she had a premonition, and others say she made it happen. I say accidents happen. Anyway, she wasn't the same after that. She never goes hunting, for instance. Says she can't stand to be around trees. She has a grudge against them, like they killed him on purpose. One day I went up looking for her, and she was in the woods, cutting down trees. I followed the sound of the chain saw. That rope tow? It was Tom's land. Maggie gave it to the town of Blue Sky, on the condition they finish cutting down the trees. She would have axed the trees around her place, too, but then there were Tom's wishes: he loved having a place in the woods. He was particular about keeping the trees up, so she tolerates them around her house for him."

He leaned against the Bronco's fender. Inside the bar, couples were dancing a swingy western two-step. It was like big-band dancing to country music — a low, gliding dance, with intricate twirls and spins. Maggie was dancing with a firefighter, but not Mike. "After Tom died, Maggie broke loose. She inherited everything from him, his house, his garage. She gave up Artemis and took over his business and worked hard, but at night, she went to bed with any taker, which was pretty much everybody. She slept around, did a lot of drinking."

From atop the bar, Sarah said something to the knot of firefighters, their faces turned up to her like acolytes'.

"Then she met Earl, down in Steamboat," Abe said. "Little punk-rocker weasel. He plucked his eyebrows, dyed his hair black. He was always fixin' to do. Fixin' to start a band. Fixin' to go to L.A. We really hated him. We started making fun of his name. Duke, we called him. Or else Hey Kaiser. Hey Prince, any royalty we could think of, but Maggie let him move in with her, and she decided to marry him. She made herself a purple dress for the occasion. But on the wedding day, his royal highness doesn't show. So Maggie gets up on the bar and nails that purple dress to the ceiling. Turned out later that before he took off, the weasel saw fit to take her tools for a souvenir. She's the only person in Blue Sky who locks her door."

"Abe," I said.

"Better?" he asked. "Too tight?"

"Fine," I said. The pressure of the bandage was good. It didn't so much soothe the pain as contain it, something like the embrace of a loved one when you're grieving. "Is there a moral to this story?"

"Maggie doesn't work on Volvos," he said. "Hates them, since Tom died. She let them all rot in the yard, like you saw. But she keeps Tom's P1800 as good as new, and it's all she'll drive. You have to love a woman like that."

I kissed him. I leaned across those few inches of air and kissed him on those full lips. Smack on the mouth; my aim was perfect, although I hadn't talked myself through it beforehand.

He took a step back. He put his palms on the crown of my head and smoothed my hair over my ears. He whispered, "You don't mean that." He tugged the ends of my hair in a gentle, playful way. "Silly mixed-up woman," he said. "I'm going inside now. Let's see what kind of pool you can really shoot."

He was decent, leaving me there to feel that humiliation on my own, the waves of it washing over me, which is the perfect way to put it, since I couldn't catch my breath and felt as if I were drowning in shame.

$\mathcal{T}$HE GINGERBREAD HOUSE

AND the days march on, the same, the same. Sunny gets better. Jennie's worry gets worse. Sunny wants a Christmas tree. He wants presents. Jennie doesn't talk to Faith and she doesn't talk to Clarence and the house stays dangerous, silent. She uses her ruined books to do some of her homework. She hasn't started her science project. The staphylococcus bacteria she took from Sunny's throat grows in fuzzy colonies in the petri dish living in the refrigerator. But she needs more petri dishes, and agar to feed the bacteria. She can't steal all of that; she needs money. She decides to ask for help. On a Friday she goes back to Our Lady of Delores.

Father Arturo says, "I'm glad you came back, Juniper." Jennie eats more cookies, drinks more Hawaiian Punch. How will she get him alone so she can ask about money? She'll say, You have charity, right? Well, I'm charity. My brother is charity. She takes a stack of four cookies, for Sunny Boy Blue. When Father Arturo isn't looking, Stephanie mouths, "*Cuchina.* Pig."

Today, Father Arturo talks about forgiveness and Holy Communion. He tells how the bread and the wine are transformed into the Body and Blood of Christ, so they're taking the Son of God into their own bodies, and then they are forgiven. Which sounds exactly like Faith talking about Medicine. I don't need more Medicine, Jennie thinks. I need dollar bills. He talks about eating God, and Jennie gets madder and madder until her mouth just opens. "Is that what you think it is, that it's like magic—poof, it's Jesus?"

"Through the Grace of God."

"And then you're forgiven, just because you ate bread?"

"When you take the Body and Blood of Christ, you enter a State of Grace."

"So you think you're *eating* Jesus?" Just like Medicine. They pretend this Catholic stuff is so special, but it's the same as the Church. "All somebody has to do is eat a cookie and it's okay that she ruined my social studies book? All I have to do is eat a cookie and like magic, I don't need to pay for an ambulance? That's the dumbest, the most ridiculous"—she is Hating Jennie, Angry Jennie, rising, Sinner Jennie who dreams in swear words—"*that* is im*p*ossible.

That's such a load of shit—" Which is exactly the wrong thing to say and now she's Cast Out, running through the snow with cookies, sweaty, crumbling, in her fist. She passes the Rich Lady's house, and Hating Jennie won't ever be rich, because no God, no Church can help her, and nausea rises in her throat and she vomits a pink chunky mess into the snow.

She thinks, That's cookie barf. If I barfed Communion, would it be Jesus barf? No. Things are what they are. Cookies are cookies, and punch is punch, and bread is bread, and wine is wine, and Medicine is nothing but illegal.

I am so stupid, she thinks. The truth is, I'm Jennie only in my head, to my-self. As soon as I get around people, I'm Hippie Juniper, the Piojo Bush, who everyone wants to drown in kerosene and set on fire.

Snap out of it, Jennie orders herself. She wipes her tears and this is what she decides: she doesn't believe in God so it doesn't matter if he's on her side or not. You have to take care of yourself.

So what do I need? I need money. What will I do? I will get money. My grandmother Lipa needed a little help with Bartók and she got it. My own grandchildren will tell my story. Once there was a poor girl named Jennie, but everybody called her Juniper because she was enchanted. One day, she set out to rid herself of the curse. She marched bravely to the house of a queen. She climbed the steps and knocked on the trailer door.

The door opens and here is the Rich Lady, wearing a crisp white apron that covers her chest and most of her legs. A wonderful smell, the sweet, warm, loving smell of baking cookies, reaches out and welcomes Jennie. "Bloody hell," the Rich Lady says. "You're a proper behemoth, aren't you?"

Jennie takes a deep breath. *Don't hint, just ask.* "My name is Jennie. I came here because I want to be your friend." This, she's certain, is not hint-ing. "And because I want to know if I can have a job. I can garden," she says quickly. "I can clean."

The Rich Lady smiles, a slow wide smile that says, *I see right through you.* "I'm afraid there's not much need for gardening around here."

"I need to pay for schoolbooks," Jennie says. "And a science project. And some other, some other things."

Now the Rich Lady laughs. "Come in, why don't you? Eat some pastries for me. I'm baking. I could use an audience. And a friend. And," she says, "a Little Jennie Friday." Like magic. The Rich Lady says "Jennie" out loud, and Juniper is gone. The queen lifted the spell, and everyone lived happily ever after.

H E R name is Mrs. Leeman, Esther, "Call me Essie," she says. "Esther is such an old-lady name. Of course, now that I'm living in a trailer . . ." She's an old woman but still beautiful, with smooth skin taut over sharp bones, with deep red lipstick and black liner painted on her eyelids. Only her hands look old, and the crepey freckled skin of her arms, which wobbles as she offers a platter of sweets to Jennie. Essie baked them all, even though she doesn't eat them. "It's the scent I love," she says. "The sense of smell is so important. And the recipes. The more complex and impossible, the better. It's like dancing." She points to the platter and names them: petit fours. Bear claw, baklava. Jennie loves the petit fours, tiny cakes decorated with delicate flowers. She couldn't possibly eat something so pretty, so she eats a bear claw instead. If Jesus has to turn into bread, she thinks, he should at least come back tasting this good.

"A starving girl," Essie says. "Consider it an asset. A man enjoys a woman who eats with gusto." But then she says, "Of course, this girl should not eat too terribly fast. You could be mistaken for desperate." The bite in Jennie's mouth turns to stone. She swallows, and it lodges in her throat. Essie says, "You never want to look like you're hungry for anything. You always want to look like you're accustomed to pleasure. Have another." Jennie takes a baklava and eats a bite, slowly, slowly chewing. It tastes of honey and nuts, sweet and sticky and light at the same time. "Good girl," Essie says.

Essie loves to talk about herself. Jennie sits on a high stool in her kitchen, eating sugar, and listens, while Essie rolls out a thin, thin dough she calls filo, and talks. "I was a ballerina. I danced in New York. There's nothing better for keeping the derriere high and tight." She pats her butt. She wears her gray hair pulled back, flat against her skull. "I like your hair," Jennie says.

"Goodness, my dear, don't interrupt," Essie says, and Jennie stares at her hands, because she knew that one, and now Essie will send her away, only Essie says, "It's a French twist," which sounds like another pastry, only she's talking about her hair, Jennie realizes, and by then Essie has gone on with her story like she never stopped. "After that, I moved to Santa Fe," she says. "I have a house down there. We'll go visit it sometime." She's filled with promises like this. She speaks in a cigarette-husky voice, and the sweet kitchen also smells of tobacco smoke. She says that being a ballerina was about lots of men. Lots of flowers. Very glamorous. She leans against the counter and inhales. "Lots of sweat, too, and ugly feet. I never liked it much. I liked riding horses. I liked playing pool. Men, they're drawn to the combination—a ballerina who plays pool. Remember that."

"I don't know how to dance," Jennie says.

Essie stubs out her cigarette. "That's not the point," she says.

A ballerina. How much money does she have? She doesn't work, and she moves around the way some people rearrange furniture. Is she a millionaire?

Essie whips egg whites; she spices and she mixes. She grew up, she tells

Jennie, divided between Arizona and New York. She says "divided" with relish, as if somehow the idea of a child cut in half pleases her. She rode airplanes when flight attendants were stewardesses in uniforms that made them look like WACS. She slices an apple expertly, so it falls apart in perfect little squares. Jennie wonders about WACS, but doesn't ask. Later, she'll try to find the definition.

Her mother, Caroline, created quite a scandal by running off to Tucson in the thirties, where she drew alimony and trust fund checks and worked hard at being an independent woman. She cultivated a cactus garden, with saguaros as tall as her house, and meanwhile Essie—Jennie pictures a graceful girl in toe shoes—learned to play pool and ride horses and dance ballet.

Essie drops a whole stick of butter in a hot pan and says her mother went mad at thirty-two. Mad, she says emphatically. She doesn't say crazy. "After that, she wasn't the same. She was weak. I went to boarding school."

The convertible is an artifact from Caroline, Essie says, rolling out "artifact" in a satisfied way. She calls the Cadillac the Batmobile. "I christened the backseat with a boy named Jasper when I was seventeen," she says. Jasper filled the backseat with flowers and they made love on the petals of six dozen yellow roses.

"Did you marry him?"

Essie laughs. "He was too short."

The sportscar is a brand-new Jaguar. Jag, Essie says. The Jag is for reliability, for long trips. "I'll teach you to drive in the Batmobile," Essie says. "The Jag's too hard to handle."

As Essie tells her stories, Jennie has the uncomfortable feeling that they sound like lies—and yet she wants to believe. She hooks her heels on the rungs of the bar stool and listens, watching Essie in her crisp white apron, reaching for a plate like she's dancing. Jennie decides to believe.

She also decides that she can never bring Sunny here. He'll hint, and interrupt, and worse, eat like a starving boy, smearing food all over his face, and he'll smell of pee. Ashamed for being a traitor, she blurts out, "I like cookies, too." *That* was a hint, made by disgusting Juniper. How did she get in here?

Essie smiles her Essie smile. "I like a girl who knows what she likes. But cookies are so . . . easy, don't you think?" She blows smoke out of the corner of her mouth. "What a ragamuffin you are. Your hair is positively frightful. Did your mother cut it?"

"A haircutter cut it," Jennie says, blushing, and also hating Essie, for just a tiny moment. "My mom gives me money to get all kinds of things done."

Essie laughs. "Silly girl. If you must tell a lie, at least do it with style. Don't appear as if you don't even believe yourself." I knew that, Jennie thinks. Juniper the Ugly Troll hides under the table, waiting for her chance. She is the Enemy.

"In any case, we must get you a proper style." Essie uses words like "proper" and "bloody" because she has traveled to Europe. She says Americans are uncivilized. "Good hair is one of the keys to power. Remember that. We'll make a civilized girl out of you yet."

Jennie asks, "Can I, may I, take some pastries to my brother?"

"A grammarian! Bravo!" Smiling, Essie wraps three pastries in plastic. "Here's what I've decided," she says. "You'll clean house for me, help with the dishes, that kind of thing. I'll pay you for it, but I'll also civilize you. Agreed?"

"Agreed," Jennie says, thinking, Now I can pay for the books, for the ambulance, for a haircut and everything else I ever needed. She washes piles of pots and pans and measuring cups and special tools, but it's easy work, with running water and a dishwasher. Jennie rinses off the stickiest sugar and puts everything in the machine, and Essie gives her five dollars, just like that.

JENNIE has the solution to the Juniper problem. She'll be like Essie. She'll smile Essie's smile and see through Essie's eyes. Walking home, Jennie tries her Essie eyes out on Randall Sandoval's house. His mother has put up an electric plastic Santa and all the reindeer on the roof. It isn't so special. She has Essie eyes, and she sees a little adobe hut with tacky plastic decorations on it. Her new Essie eyes see Randall Sandoval, too, and he's short.

With Essie eyes, she sees Sunny waiting in the driveway, throwing snowballs, and his haircut is frightful, long, past his shoulders. "You're a liar," he says. "You said you'd come home early. You said we could get a tree."

Jennie checks his cool forehead. He's so much better now that there's real medicine. "I got you pastries instead."

"I want a tree!"

"Pastries are *doughnuts*, you dummy," she says, and then he's happy to follow her into the kitchen.

"Can I have a doughnut now?" he asks.

"Medicine first." She measures a dropperful of pink penicillin. "Stick out your tongue." His eyes are pale green, and he sees through Jennie, more than Father Arturo, more than Essie. His eyes see Juniper. "Stop staring at me."

"Mom says this medicine doesn't do any good." But he sticks out his tongue anyway. "She says the Meeting made me better. She says this pink stuff will poison me with sugar."

"Swallow." Jennie shows Sunny her petri dish, where the staphylococcus grows in fuzzy clumps. "This is what made you sick. I should put this in Mom and Clarence's coffee, so they'll be miserable, too, and be punished for torturing you."

"Don't talk that way," Sunny says.

Jennie lights a fire and they sit in front of the fireplace, sharing pastries. Everything looks different now because she has Essie eyes to see through. Same crack, same fireplace, but uglier and sadder, and she smells the wet adobe, the pee on Sunny. *The sense of smell is so important.* This stink belongs to Juniper. Her Essie eyes see the mud under Sunny's fingernails, the crust of filth at his hairline. He eats so fast he spits pastry at her. "Don't eat like you're starving," she says. "Eat like you're used to pastries." But he doesn't understand.

Jennie bunches the plastic wrap and tosses it into the fire. That's her Juniper skin. The plastic melts and then bursts into flame and then vanishes. What if those glowing coals were hell? The fire could leap out like the devil's hand and yank her in. Fire would be the worst way to die. Her flesh would be like the plastic, quickly blackening, melting. Anyway, hell doesn't exist. Neither does Juniper. Jennie practices her Essie smile, slow, knowing, easy. "What's funny?" Sunny asks.

"Let's go get a Christmas tree," Jennie says. They take a flashlight and, bundled against the cold, they tromp through snow painted blue by the moon. They can see their own shadows. Down in the valley, Christmas lights blink on the scattered Alfin houses.

They follow the ditch, searching. Stumbling along, Jennie thinks, I want to be back in Essie's kitchen. All those shiny, matching pots and pans. The smell of baking sugar. From here, high on the side of the valley, she finds Randall Sandoval's house, his Santa and the reindeer glowing on the roof. "Look at Santa," she tells Sunny, thinking, Essie will teach me how to be normal, and Juniper will be banished to hell, and Randall will put six dozen roses in the backseat of the Batmobile for me. That is my plan, and I'm about to tell Sunny, when he opens his mouth and says exactly the wrong thing.

"Junie?" he says. "Why are you mad at Mom?"

Won't he ever get it? How many times do I have to explain? *Again*, she tells him how stupid Faith is. "But there was a spider," Sunny says, and she has to remind him *again* that it was a trick, that only science is true, and her science project will prove it.

Sunny says, "Rudolph's nose is Jesus's star."

"What are you *talking* about? Hold this." She is Jennie with her Essie eyes and she sees so much more than him. She hands him the flashlight, and they consider a tree. "This is the one."

"Rudolph flew over Baby Jesus's head and turned into the star."

"That's stupid. Rudolph goes with Santa, not Jesus. Anyway, Mom only believes in God so she can let you be sick."

"That's wrong. That's not true."

"It's like torture. You didn't have to be that sick. You didn't have to go in the ambulance. You'll see when I finish my science project." Jennie clears the snow away from the trunk and I am Jennie, sawing this tree, and my brother is a normal boy standing behind me, sweet and cute and nice. But it's so hard to be Jennie when Sunny stands there, staring up at the stars, giving me the silent treatment because I told him how the world works. "So tell me a stupid reindeer story," I say. "Quit it, Sunny. I mean it." Jennie slips away and she's the Bad Sister, sawing a tree trunk. "Grandpa Swifty was a lumberjack," she says. "It's in our genes, to cut down trees." He doesn't say a word.

In silence, Sunny and his Bad Sister drag the tree down the hill, along the ditch, to where the white car sits in the driveway, and you see, she tells herself, this is your home, with the outhouse in the corner of the garden and your mother and the Evil Clarence in the house. Say it. I am Juniper.

Jennie thinks, No, no. No, I'm *Jennie*. Jennie drags the tree into the kitchen. Faith is making a pumpkin pie, and the kitchen smells like Christmas, cinnamon and cloves. "Why are you making a pie?"

"Clarence wanted one," Faith says. "Oh. You got a juniper. How funny." On her cheek is a bruise as big as Clarence's fist. Sunny holds his hands over the cookstove, speechless. Faith asks, "Sunny, what's wrong?"

You idiot, Jennie. You'd think you could at least recognize one of the stupid trees when you see them, ugly, stunted and scrawny, the twisted trunk. Besides, what good is a tree when there's no stand? I had a daddy, a father, a dad, and he always made the stand out of boards, but he's gone to Florida. Don't you dare cry. If you cry, you're Juniper again. "I hate this tree."

Faith says gently, sweetly, like a real mother, "Look at all the berries. It's God's decoration. You did a good job," and this mother's arms hug me and out the tears come. Does this mean I'm Juniper?

Sunny stalks off to his bedroom. Fine. I may be brotherless and fatherless, but I have a mother, and I'm making a stand while my mother untangles the lights and sorts through the ornaments. My mother and I are decorating for Christmas together. It's almost peaceful, almost fun, with the fireplace crackling merrily and the pie baking and the tree filling up with ornaments.

But that's all temporary, gone in a puff of smoke when a horrible crash comes from Sunny's room. They find him pushing over his cinder-block-and-board shelves. He picks up a book and heaves it at the wall. "I'M MAD!" he screams.

Faith says, "What did you do to him, Juniper? Why are you always so mean to him?"

"Nothing," Jennie whispers, but Faith won't believe her, because Jennie is the Bad Sister, so she leaves. Running, she has trouble keeping her balance. Beneath the fresh snow, slush has frozen to ribs of ice. But she runs. She runs until she's in front of Randall's house. His Santa waves happily at her. She stares past Santa to the stars. The morning star is Rudolph. How could he be so silly? But why was I so mean to him? Why did he get so mad? *Mad*, Essie said about her own mother. *Went mad*, like it was a country you could visit.

So I am Jennie, walking home, trapped in the Land of Mad, which is outside, in the cold, in the driveway, spying on my family through the kitchen window. This is my family. Clarence and Faith and Sunny Boy Blue, sitting at the table, eating pumpkin pie. They're in the Land of Happy. Past them, in the doorway to the Middle Room, the Christmas tree winks and glows. In the lights, the funny needles look like lace. It's a Christmas-card tree, a fairy-tale tree, a Happy Land tree. The lights blink on and off and on, and I'm the Bad Sister watching, shivering in my sweaty clothes, motherless, fatherless, brotherless. But I have a Fairy Godmother. Her name is Essie and she lives so close I can practically touch her from here.

$\mathscr{W}$IND

Hᴇʀᴇ's Jennie, turned down flat by a small-town cop, stumbling into a small-town bar. Look at her, standing like an idiot, like the fool she is, trying to muster up some cockiness to get her through the night.

In a capsized, upside-down world, it makes sense to see Governor Bent's daughter's wedding dress hanging from the ceiling. Sarah stands on the bar with her head thrust into the folds of the gown; only her legs and feet show, the opposite of a bride, I think, because I have become Crazy Jennie, the chick who thinks in non sequiturs. Unless a bride has gorgeous feet and an ugly face, I think, and then, horror of horrors, my eyes sting. "I thought you loved that dress," Crazy Jennie says.

Sarah squats and meets Crazy Jennie eye to eye. Be careful, Sarah. Watch it. She's nuts, you know. "I do," Sarah says. "But I thought you wanted me to leave my past behind me, become unengaged, et cetera. I thought we were changing together."

"What a load of shit, Sarah," and so much better, this, the Ugly Chick, familiar in her anger and her nasty attitude. "What a stupid thing to say."

"There you go again, being mean. Don't you want to be different?"

Not a lady who sticks around, the Ugly Chick grabs her backpack and books it to the bathroom. Sitting on the toilet, she stares at the floor—old-fashioned linoleum laid down in big squares—and the filthy line where it meets the black wall, and it all intensely irritates her, the black paint, the country music throbbing through the walls. What's she doing in this joke town, in a joke bathroom where people steal quickies, buy a little small-town weed, cake on a little small-town lipstick, aim for the small-town rim and piss on the wall because you're a small-town firefighter drunk out of your mind because tomorrow you go fight the big-ass blaze.

The Ugly Chick, that bitch, she surfs this wave of nasty contempt, and because she's drunk and leaning a cheek against the bathroom wall and studying the dust bunnies, she manages to check out for a second or two, but only a few, before a thought brings me straight back to myself.

Sarah had extricated herself from me. I could see that now. She might say she accepted my apology, but she didn't see me the same way. My eyes still burned. We weren't the friends we'd been on the mountain in the night.

Okay, I said to myself. Okay. Who am I? I'm Jennie, in running shorts and a T-shirt, and my hair is dirty and I am not, as Essie would say, doing it up. No problem. You can pull your world together with a bobby pin. I changed into jeans, cowboy boots. I barretted my hair back, put on red lipstick and an Essie grin. I said to my reflection: You are Jennifer Braverman, tall and strong, not fat but full. You come from lumberjacks. Your grandmother died of a cold. Your father kidnapped your mother and took her to New Mexico. You play a mean game of pool. Go get 'em, Cowgirl. There's a C.

JENNIE, coming out of the bathroom, bumps into Mike. He sways, she sways; they slump against the wall. "Drunk?" she says. "Because I think I am."

"Hey," he says. "Fires make their own wind, you know."

"Is that a fact?"

"A hundred, hundred-fifty miles an hour. And sometimes the fire jumps right ahead of you, so you're surrounded." She looks up at him, an unfamiliar experience for her. He leans closer, so she sees the pores of his mushy indistinct nose. "Hey," he says. "You're a woman."

"Yes, I believe so," she says.

"So, do you think Maggie could love me?"

Why not? "Yes," she tells him. "Yes, absolutely, yes indeedy."

He swallows. "Good," he says, nodding. "Good." He leans his forehead against hers. "Because I could die, you know, out there, in the fires?"

She steps back. "You aren't going to die," she says. "You're going to be a hero, and then you'll marry Maggie and grow old and live happily ever after." The lie leaves a terrible aftertaste in her mouth. Is it the whiskey, or can words have flavor?

"Really?" he says hopefully, plaintively. "Really?"

"Really," she says carefully. "And I. Am. Always. Right."

"That's a relief," he says, his palm against the wall, his eyes on the floor. "That's a real good thing to know."

She heads toward the bar but stops.

There. Over the heads of the drinkers, the pool players and liars and lovers and thieves, she sees her husband sitting at the bar. She thinks, Finally, I've lost my mind; next I'll be seeing Sunny playing pool, because she sees her husband, Christian Braverman, sitting with Officer Gomez, Maggie, and Sarah, all of them talking like the conspirators they apparently are. They watch her coming toward them. They stare hard. She feels conscious of her hands at her sides and the way she is walking.

"There you are," Abe says.

"We thought you made for the hills," Maggie says.

I looked from face to face. "It's called urination. A simple biological process. Involving the bladder and such."

Chris had ordered the two of us drinks. They sat side by side on the bar, the glasses touching, like a subliminal suggestion of how this little meeting should go. He looked at me and didn't say anything.

"James," I said. "I went for a run."

"I noticed," he said.

"It was a long run."

He smiled, but it was a noncommittal twitch of the lips, unreadable. It meant, *I heard that, and I know it was a joke.* Like you'd nod to a stranger who greeted you on the street.

Sarah said, "Chris remembers me, from the wedding? I was just telling him, Don't worry, I took good care of her."

"And I was just asking her, What happened to your face?" Chris said, his eyes on my bandaged hand.

Sarah touched her cheek. "Oh, *that.* Well . . ." She stopped. "It's hard to explain. But it's really just that I have this skin condition."

He drank. He looked at me over the lip of his glass. Did he think I was that much of a monster? But then I remembered that I had, in fact, made the bruises he suspected me of making.

"I thought your boyfriend beat you," Maggie said.

"What's it called, Sarah?" I said.

"Ideopathic thrombocytopeniz," she said. "Doesn't that sound official? You're thinking that Jennie beat me up or something, but it's not that dramatic. She only punched a truck. You're thinking cops, bruises, something bad happened, but it's easy to misinterpret things, you know."

"Chris doesn't jump to conclusions," I said.

Maggie said, "So you're the husband."

"Apparently so," Chris said. He looked so calm, relaxed, leaning against the bar. I thought of the many times in the past year when I'd picked a fight just to see if he would come unruffled. But I knew he wouldn't. I'm right here, I could hear him say calmly. You don't need to shout.

Sarah said, "So, Chris, you poor thing. I keep picturing you coming home, finding out Jennie was gone. I'd be bawling my eyes out, I can tell you that."

I looked up at the ceiling festooned with people's cast-offs. Sarah had taken down the wedding dress. It didn't take much searching to find the ruffled purple dress that was Maggie's second wedding outfit.

"I hit the redial button," Chris said. "To see who she'd called."

"Smart," Abe said.

"I got a cab company. I thought, Well, she didn't go far, if it's a cab. Then I found out the cab took her to a car lot." To my astonishment, he began to regale them with an amusing story of the neighbor girls, of a cabbie named Sky, of Ramses Smith at the car lot, as if the whole thing was an enormous joke. This was not like my husband, not at all. He was not a teller of anecdotes at parties. But there he was, describing his hysterical questioning of the neighbor girls, making Maggie laugh over the stoned-out hippie cabdriver. Ramses Smith, slowly thumbing through a stack of receipts. The point of the joke seemed to be that no matter what Chris found, it told him nothing.

Sarah turned to Abe. "So what else does a guy do if somebody's missing? File a missing-person report?"

"Have a party," Maggie said.

"Depends on who runs off," I said, giving her a nasty look. "Doesn't it?"

"One time I knew this guy," Abe said quickly. "He had a crazy daughter, literally crazy with schizophrenia. They put a rider on her driver's license. 'Call your father,' it said, so that if a cop pulled her over and ran her license, she'd get the message."

"Did it work?" Sarah asked.

"Let me guess," I said. "She didn't drive."

"She drove," Abe said. "They found her." He gave me his trademark Concerned Policeman look. "It's best when things work out."

"Please," I said. "It's best when people mind their own business."

"Or do their jobs," he said.

"So what did you do," I said. "Run an APB on us? Because Sarah was making a fuss?"

Abe shrugged, rolled his beer bottle between his palms. "I went back and poked around a little, found your receipt for the truck. Called the dealer. Gave your husband a call. Got the answering machine the first time."

Sarah said, "She is not okay, unquote."

They chattered on like this for a while, discussing the logistics of Chris's adventure. I was the butt of the joke, but I felt like a distant observer, the way anyone, say a man watching from across the room, might see this clutch of people—a tall man, a cop, a blonde, a redhead, and a lady mechanic—and he might think they were friends, out for a few. "Isn't this a nice little tea party," I said finally. They fell silent. A song ended. "Sorry to interrupt," I said. "I don't mean to ruin your fun."

"Jennie," Chris said. "Your brother jumped off a ferry and drowned."

I stared them all down. "That's nobody's business but mine."

A wail rose into the midst of this charming moment, the sound of a baby dying. It was my old friend Bob the Cat, sitting in his crate on the floor at Chris's feet. "I see you brought your familiar."

"I couldn't leave him," Chris said.

"Is that supposed to have some kind of double meaning?"

"He can't feed himself," he said.

The band returned from their break and began to play. "Maggie," Abe said, once again Doing the Right Thing. "How about dancing with me?" Off they went.

"Don't the rest of you want to go with them?" I said. "Since you're all such good friends and everything."

Sarah, ignoring me, put the crate on the bar and cooed at Bob in his portable jail. "Poor baby," she told him. "Poor little kitty. You don't like it in there, do you?" Bob hissed at her and shrank against the back wall of the crate. Chris watched the dancers and sipped his drink.

"He hates people," I said.

"He's just scared," Sarah said.

"You don't know him," I said.

She stuck her fingers between the bars and he hissed again. Sarah said, "So, Chris, you'll forgive her, right? Circumstances and everything? I mean, everybody reacts to grief differently? I have this theory that you know you really love somebody when you find out the worst thing about them and then you really love them because now you know everything about them?"

"Shut up, Sarah," I said.

She glared at me. "I told you before. Don't tell me to shut up."

The swing dancers swayed and twirled between the tables. There were five couples now. Abe glanced at me as he swung Maggie past, then looked ahead for his next patch of space in the room. Over his shoulder, Maggie smiled, glee or confidence or sarcasm glinting in her eyes. What mattered was that I recognized it; I've worn that look myself at the pool table and in the parking lot buying a truck.

"Are you angry?" I asked Chris. As soon as I said it, I knew: it was completely, precisely, exactly the wrong thing to say.

He shrugged. "What happened to your hand?"

"Like the girl said, I had a fight with my truck."

He turned from me and watched the dancers. Sarah sat beside us, the child who keeps quiet, hoping no one will notice her, waiting to intervene if the fighting gets ugly.

"Aren't you going to say something about my truck?"

"I don't see that it's the issue here," he said.

"It wasn't personal," I said. "This whole thing."

He stood and stretched, hands on his hips. "That's a stupid thing to say. Of course it was personal." His hair was dirty, his eyes fatigued. Everything about him seemed to be limp with exhaustion. "You're my wife," he said. "Or did you forget?"

"I'm sorry," I said.

He turned to face me. "For what? Apologies mean nothing if you don't know what you're sorry about."

I took a drink. The dancers circled, some of them graceful, comfortable in their half-gliding, half-shuffling two-step. Others looked tense and nervous, their eyes fixed sightlessly on the space over their partners' shoulders. "You look beat," I said, as a beginning.

"Jesus, Jennie," Chris said. "No shit. You win."

Something rose inside me that felt exactly like grief, that throat-closing, heavy longing for the irretrievably lost, but it swiftly became anger. "Nobody asked you to come," I said. "I didn't ask you to follow me."

He pressed his fingers into the corners of his eyes. "There wasn't any question about it," he said. When he looked at me his eyes were cold and distant, not quite focused on my face. "Was there?"

"Everywhere that Jennie went, the lamb was sure to go."

"Stop it," he said, looking away. "I'm too tired for this."

I drained my glass. The drinks I'd swallowed over the evening had joined forces, a gang of hoodlums who pounced as a group. I was, as they say, unsteady on my feet. I braced my hand on the bar. "Look at me," I said. He glanced over. His eyes were cold, and he looked right through me. I hated him. "What, were you going to save me? Big man Chris, the Knight in Shining Armor." My voice rose. "Brave Mister Braverman, just like his daddy." Bob must have heard me; he began to howl. There is a certain relief in giving in to what you have guarded against, a giddy carelessness. "You should be a cop, or better yet, a firefighter. There's a crew leaving tonight."

Chris took me by the shoulders. "You *push*," he said. "You push and push." He closed his eyes, and when he opened them, he released me with a little shove. "I can't right now," he said. "I'm going to dance. Dance with me, Sarah."

"Fuck you both," I said. "Fuck all of this."

I walked toward the door. I was shaking, breathless, half expecting him to grab my arm, but pretty sure no one would stop me. I stepped outside, into the sweet, cool air, into the dark, the relative quiet.

Through the bamboo shades, I saw Chris take Sarah in his arms like a pro, his hand in the small of her back, guiding her with authority. He executed a tricky little twirl. Sarah spun under and through his arms, ending up back where she started, and off he went again. She laughed, young and fresh and not at all tired, her hair swinging with her spins. Chris must have known how to dance before this. Surely no one could learn that fast. So there was one thing I didn't know about him. Damn him, I thought. Damn him; damn them all, straight to hell.

$\mathscr{C}$APRICORN

Thursday Night, Blue Sky

I got about two buildings down the road before Chris caught up to me. He spun me around hard, not dancing at all. "No you don't," he said. "I won't have it."

"Won't have it?" I laughed. "You sound like a schoolmarm."

He held both my arms and shook me once, then let me go. "You have no idea, do you? You don't have a clue. Do you know anything about me?"

"I don't need this," I said, but he had me in his clutches again.

"Not this time," he said, squeezing my arms. "This time, you'll stand here and listen to me."

"Let me go."

He obeyed. I crossed my arms over my chest and waited. "All right," I said. "Speak."

He strode to the center of the highway and back, as if he couldn't leave or stay, as if he couldn't figure out what option he might have besides that two-way street. "Why are you like this?" he said. "Why do you want everyone to hate you?"

"If you hate me so much, leave me alone."

"I don't hate you," he said. "Jesus Christ." He reached out, as if to take me in his arms. "Why can't you let me help you?"

I shoved him away. "What do you want from me?" I yelled. "I'm not going to burn fifty-dollar bills, and I'm not going to go sobbing around the house like a little woman; if you want a weakling, she's out there to find. Take a look two doors down. Try Sarah; she's single."

Because he stopped abruptly, stood still in the center of the highway, I heard his sharp intake of breath. "Sometimes," he said bitterly, "I think all we have in common is height." Pacing again, he was silent for a time, but then he spoke in a quick, angry voice, pausing before me, then moving away, then returning. "Do you know what it's like?" he said. "Do you have any idea what it's like, night after night, week after week, month after month, to lie in bed, to love someone, to long to be close to her, but it's two A.M. and she's in the living room—*painting*--and when she comes to bed, you better fake sleep; you better not say anything, and you sure as hell better not touch her, because those few inches of sheet between you, that's the no-man's-land. So you lie there with your mouth shut, even though she's your wife, and you *crave* her. Of course it's sex, but more than that, you just want to be close, to have a wife, a lover, and not a cool roommate who doubles as a housepainter. You are more lonely than you ever imagined, and you crave it, closeness, to have *her* touching *you*—anything, just her fingers on your back, a small sign that she wants you, chooses you. And do you know what's worse than never reaching for your wife? It's this: if you dared to try, she'd slap off your hand, like a gnat, like a fucking spider, less than a spider, a nothing, a breeze, because that's a desert, that sheet between you—it's a wasteland. She's not going to let you have one inch of her. If you touch her shoulder, she'll say, 'Do you want me to pretend?' and she'll say it without guilt, with indifference, not even a recognition of what she's doing to you, this inconvenient gnat that you are, drifting, waiting to be swatted down. 'Do you want me to pretend?' she asks, and the answer is God yes, pretend, please, wake with a sigh and open your arms and in a sleepy voice, ask me in—you *bitch*, I'm starving, and you don't think, you don't care, you have no idea—" Chris, pacing into the road, out of the road, stopped in his tracks. He ran his fingers through his hair; he clutched his bangs in his fist. "I was so stupid," he said in a kind of wonderment. "I thought you were scared and sad, but the fact is, you're just careless. You only think about coming ahead of the pack. How could you give anything away? You might *lose*. Well, guess what? I forfeit the game; I surrender. I give up." He stopped his pacing and spoke very carefully, with pauses, enunciating for a speaker of a foreign language. "I. Give. Up. On. You." He walked away, toward Little Joe's.

My husband's back, receding. I thought he'd return. Hadn't he been returning and leaving and returning throughout all his talking? But he kept walking away. I didn't call to him. What could I say? Wasn't it all true? Two doors down, the music throbbed, firefighters danced and laughed and knocked striped and colored balls down holes in a table, a cat howled on a bar, and a purple wedding dress hung from the ceiling. Like the night of my brother's birth, the sky was prickly with stars, but I could not use the only get-out-of-jail card I had. It would do no good to say, *But my brother is dead.* Even if that obscenity should cross my lips, in truth, Chris was talking about things that were present in this world months ago, when my brother still breathed this air, still spoke my name. So the fact of Sunny's drowning had no bearing on what Chris said, none at all.

Chris went into the bar, music floating out as he disappeared. Each time someone entered or exited, more snatches of guitar and a distant mournful voice escaped.

Dizzy, my limbs weak, I sat on the highway shoulder. Inexplicably, I thought of cows, what I'd read once about how they're slaughtered. Stun them, hook them upside down by the feet, and send them glassy-eyed toward the throat slitters, still alive, but so dazed and docile you can do anything to them. Sometimes they fall and lie on the floor, inches deep in blood, unable to rise. It's what they were born for, the expected end, the interviewed man said. Nothing tragic about it. They're livestock. Deadstock, I thought, amused with myself. That's what I am, I thought. Deadstock. Goats, cows, what's the difference.

Sarah was standing over me. "Hey, you," she said, crouching. "What are you doing, hitchhiking sitting down?" She took my hand.

I tried to tug it free, but I was too weak. "I had to sit down," I said.

"He's a really great guy, you know. I like him a lot."

The perspective was interesting from down there. I slumped on my side and stared at the pink and blue glow of the Little Joe's comet. If I lay here, or better, in the road, like a damsel tied to train tracks . . . the gravel hurt my hip, and the soft skin of my underarm. I studied the trucks in the full parking lot, the overflow of ranch vee-hickles parked up and down the highway. There, in fact, was the Rolls, a ways up. I could see the winged woman poised to leap off the roof of the Greek temple grille. The parking lot must have been filled by the time Chris arrived. I imagined him thinking, Great, my wife ran off to an overcrowded bar with inadequate parking.

Sarah sat beside me. "Don't worry," she said. "He'll forgive you. You did mean things to me, and I forgave you, right?"

"I was thinking about cows," I said.

"Okay." She lit a cigarette. "What about them?"

"They hang them upside down and slit their throats."

"Okay."

"You don't understand," I said. "They deserve it. I mean, it's their job."

"You're drunk."

"No shit, Pea Princess."

"What did you call me?" She drew on her cigarette, and its smell settled over me. "Never mind. I know your tricks, and I'm not going to get mad, so you can just forget it."

I watched the Little Joe's neon comet ignite once, twice. Someone got in a truck and drove past us so that we got a breath of exhaust, the wind. I needed to get up, but my muscles were weak.

"All I know is, Chris is a nice person. He's not going to stay mad at you, I promise."

"You don't understand," I said, moving my tongue carefully around the words, which were too large for my mouth, the way words are for drunks.

"Yes I do," she said. "*I* believe in love, remember?"

"He quit." I remembered I had known he could dance. At our wedding, Chris was a terrific waltzer, although we had just the one dance before I was shanghaied. Nauseated, I became aware of the spinning of the earth. "I need to go," I said. I tried to rise but succeeded only in sitting up.

"Go where?"

"Seattle," I said. But then I laughed. "To the bathroom."

"I'm sorry about your brother. I really am."

"Don't be sorry. It's not your fault."

"Please. Like you don't know what I mean."

"Help me," I said. Now I was on my hands and knees. Maybe I would throw up.

"I'm trying," she said. "That's what I'm trying to do."

"No," I said, holding out my hands, "help me up."

She hauled me to my feet. "Come inside."

I was a little tottery, but not as bad as I'd thought. "I can't go inside. He quit."

She took my hand. "Come on. It's going to be okay. You'll see. Anyway, if you sit out here long enough, some guy wearing Aramis is going to come along."

I laughed. "Look who's giving me boy advice."

She began walking, and docile me, I followed her, a good child. "I told you, I'm not getting mad at you," she said. "So you can just shut up with the wisecracks."

"Not the rape," I mumbled. "I wasn't talking about the rape."

She stopped and patted my arm. "I know that," she said. "Some things even you won't say, no matter what. Even if you're completely messed up."

IN Little Joe's, where my husband was dancing with Maggie, Abe tried to catch my eye, but I avoided his look. Candy thrust a bowl of milk at me. "This is for the kitty," she said. "Can I feed him?"

"His name is Bob," I said. We followed her to his crate. Or rather, Sarah followed, pulling me along.

"Hey, Bob," Candy said. "Hello, pretty boy." She leaned closer. "Is this pretty kitty hungry?" Bob's complaint slid from a high screech to a low, agonized moan.

Candy said, "Can't I hold him?"

Bob's behavior is as predictable as the sun. At the vet's, we keep a leash threaded through the bars of the crate so we can restrain him once the door opens. So I knew exactly what I was doing when I said, "Sure you can." I flipped the latch and swung open the bars and out Bob came. Hissing, claws swiping for anything near, at a full run. He slashed Candy's cheek, and she leapt back, shrieking. He didn't even look for a destination; he crouched on his hind legs and rocketed off the bar with a mighty push. He soared over the heads of the drinkers sitting at tables, while Sarah and Candy shouted, "Get him! Get him!" He landed on a woman's back. The woman screamed, and Bob vaulted for the next safer place, and people began shouting and running about in the useless way people do in such situations.

"I have to go to the bathroom," Jennie says to no one in particular, looking around blindly, thinking she'll leave, just EXIT like the sign says, glowing greenly over the back door, only the door is locked and she can't get out and the sign says ALARM WILL SOUND, so she backs into the black-walled bathroom instead. She isn't stunned anymore; she's angry, furious, she wants to punch another truck. She's learning all kinds of things about her father. What was it that made this man drag his daughter to the chicken coop? Same thing that's in his daughter. And why couldn't her mother forgive? Why did she hold a grudge against Paul all the way past his death, this woman who tallied her daughter's offenses from the moment she kicked in the womb? The Ugly Chick has the same cruel, black heart, the one that can't forgive.

Last week this Ugly Chick took a phone call from her brother. *I'm sorry,* he said. Was it only last week? Last week, then. *I'm sorry, too*—that was what she should have said. Three simple words. What part of her kept her from saying them? It's hate; it's anger. It's the part of her that sent Sunny Boy Blue into the sea.

Then I threw up. I heaved into the toilet, my eyes watering, moaning, and when I finished, I sat on the gritty floor of a bathroom in Colorado and I cried. Finally and at last. The sound was harsh, from deep in my belly, reflexive, convulsive sobs, a close relative of vomiting. I could not possibly stop it. They were waiting out there for me. Soon they'd be banging on the door, and they would find me leaning against the cool porcelain toilet and they would hold out their arms and I would never stop heaving up this horrible sound.

So I took off my shirt, wrapped my hand in it, and smashed open the window that was painted black and scratched with graffiti and just large enough for a grown woman to squeeze through, even a tall woman with lumberjack shoulders, with heavy breasts and hips and a loud coughing sob escaping with every exhalation she makes.

7.

ESCAPE

A Liar and a Thief

Thursday Night, U.S. Highway 40, Colorado

So the Ugly Chick flees Little Joe's Bar and Café: out the bathroom window I went, and down on my hands and knees. When I tried to stand, I fell again, partly because of the whiskey, and partly because the slope behind the bar was so steep it nearly sent me back through the window. I scrabbled up the hill as fast as I could, digging into the dirt, dragging myself.

The hard work calmed me, and in a few minutes, I paused. I unwrapped my shirt and shook it out and put it back on. It was too cold to be running around in a bra, never mind the decency factor. Down below, Little Joe's sign lit the flat roof and the trees with a wash of pink, then blue. I kept expecting to hear them calling. I scooted behind a tree. So here's Jennie, hiding behind trees in the woods. Silly girl left her money in her pack, sitting on the bar. Not much to be said for poor planning, is there? For a moment, she feels hopeless, which tastes like the bile in her mouth. Then she remembers yesterday (only yesterday?), when she bought a truck and put the keys to her other life, house and home and Chris, in her jeans pocket. The jeans she is now wearing, and the keys which are still there. The keys, which can start up the Rolls, which is parked just down the road.

I skirted Little Joe's and cut down the hill. I backtracked up the highway until I found the Rolls. I opened the door, adjusted the seat, started the engine, and drove away, easy as you please, thinking, Well, shit. Aren't they all such clever pals. My truck was probably fine, certainly not catastrophic; Maggie obviously was in on the plan, gleefully concocting a broken vee-hickle just to torture me, or to please Abe, who said something like, *Just keep her here, make it sound bad, that her truck needs days to fix.* Sarah knew, too. All that fuss about playing pool. And Candy bringing drinks. *If all else fails, get her loaded.* "You don't mean that," the cop had said, like he understood me—only he was in on the joke. Of course I didn't mean anything, when he knew my husband was on his way. They were all in there, yucking it up over how easily they fooled ol' Jennie, or worse, tsking and shaking their heads over her, poor little Jennie, the wounded muskrat, the whole lot of them a fucking self-help group—even drunk, even raging, I still found the rope tow's shaved stripe of mountain, and Maggie's driveway right beside it. I drove as fast as I dared over the rutted dirt, jostling and bouncing so hard I nearly lost my hold on the wheel.

I parked nose to nose with the chain-link fence, the gate with a big fat lock on it. Leave it to Maggie. Nobody locks their doors in little towns like this, except for bad-ass chicks with chips on both shoulders. I climbed the Rolls's hood and hauled myself over the fence.

My truck wasn't in the yard, so I figured it was in the garage, which was locked tight. You'd think Maggie lived in the middle of New York City.

I decided to try around back. The fence encircled a long, narrow lot, with just a few inches to spare between the house and the chain link, and I edged forward into this tight corridor. Feeling my way along the stuccoed wall, getting a wee bit claustrophobic, primed for panic, I hit a spiderweb. I knew it instantly, that whispery brush on the skin, and where there's a web, there's a spider— screaming, slapping at herself, Jennie whacks her bad hand on the wall, and like a pig in a chute, she squeals out of there, black widows and brown recluses in her hair, on her cheeks, down her shirt, not a pig, an arachnophobe in a spider-infested tunnel—she bursts, panting, into a backyard.

A tidy garden, corn and lettuce and squash, a lawn, a plastic wading pool. A little stoop, a porch light already on. A door, locked. My scalp crawled; I brushed my face, ran my fingers through my hair, and I had to get inside but there wasn't a key under the welcome mat, so I moved a pot of marigolds with my boot because spiders live under flowerpots, and thank God, a key glinted in the circular stain, and slapping my arm, the back of my neck, I got myself inside, where I stripped off my shirt but still my skin crawled. At one side of the room was a sewing machine, an old-fashioned trundle like my mother had, and I pulled open its drawers and found a pair of scissors, thinking, No, thinking, You'll be sorry, as I gathered a clump of my Blond Chick's hair and whacked off the source of my strength, my clever disguise falling, brushing my naked shoulders, wafting to my feet, and one sobbing Jennie worked the scissors while another said, *I can't believe you're doing this,* and I cut and I cut.

Last week, I answered the phone and someone said, "I love you."

It was a man. I said, "Is that so?" I didn't recognize the voice. I thought he was some old lover, a prank call. The voice was thick, choked; I figured he was drunk, whoever he was. It didn't sound like the crying of anyone I knew.

He said, "It's your brother, Sunny."

I lied. "I knew that."

He said it again, needlessly, as if it meant something other than what I understood it to mean. "It's Sunny."

"Sunny," I said. "Where are you?"

"Russia," he said, and laughed.

In my memory, I hear ferries. But I think I'm only imposing what I now know. In everything he said, I hear the future. I think, There. There. There. Goddammit, Jennie, pay attention—*there*. I remember the moan of a boat, the call of a mother to her child. I remember Sunny crying. But I don't trust even that. He could have been drunk, or his throat thick with the phlegm of smoking.

He said, "I swam across the ocean, and the bees carried me the rest of the way." He laughed again. "I'm crazy, Juniper."

"Sunny—"

He said, "Don't worry. I haven't killed anybody yet. I'm not really in Russia." He said, "I love you."

Sunny, I thought you were toying with me. I resolved myself against you, thought, You little prick, calling me like this, drunk, high, whatever you are. I said, "I don't have time for this. If you have something to say, say it."

"I'm in Seattle. The water's great. Come to Seattle."

"You are crazy," I said.

"I told you." He laughed again. "I knew you wouldn't come."

I sighed. I was pacing the kitchen floor. My white sunny kitchen. The back door open to my own neat rows of squash, corn, lettuce, carrots. I should have said, The sweet peas are so high, Sunny. "Then why did you ask?"

"I love you," he said. He paused. I heard him swallow, or at least I remember he swallowed. He said, "Juniper Tree Burning. Are you my sister? I miss Juniper."

You little prick, I thought, furious, irrationally, insanely furious. God forgive me, but I thought, You cocksucking prick, and I was about to say it when he hung up the phone.

My brother's best, last gift: he hung up. In this act, he gave me a chance to believe that I would have said I loved him if only he'd stayed on the line, and maybe one day I'll even believe that I meant to say, *I'm the one who should be sorry.*

I stood in the middle of Maggie's living room and came back to the world around me. The house smelled good, sugary, fruity, like pies. A braided rug under my feet, an old sofa, covered in the bristly velveteen of the forties. Above it hung a mirror with a faux gold-leaf frame. Opposite the sofa, an upright piano, a doily across its top, sheet music spread out on its shelf, ready to play. Lace curtains on the windows, by the way. Astonishing. I stood for a moment, trying to reconcile Maggie to this house.

I caught sight of myself in the mirror. My hair stuck out in all directions around my face. I was also filthy, and there were pinpricks of blood on the T-shirt from slivers of window glass. I tasted bile. Face it; I was a mess. I felt a sharp pang of regret. Years. It would take years to grow back my hair. Or maybe what I felt was panic. Without my hair, I wasn't even the Blond Chick. I was a tall manly woman with a bad hairdo. Who would look at me twice, except to laugh?

Chris had quit. I didn't blame him. What good is regret, what use apology? Apology doesn't change what you've done. Forgiveness is a sham thought up by polite society. The truth is, if somebody, your brother, let's say, burns down your house, you don't really care how many times he tells you he's sorry. I'm sorry, I'm sorry, I'm sorry. Nothing is different for all of the arsonist's shouting. So how could I have the audacity to ask forgiveness from anyone? It would be like trying to glue the hair back onto my head.

I went to the bathroom, where the ruffled shower curtain was covered in pink roses. I washed my face and picked glass from my chest. I rinsed my mouth.

He spoke Russian. He spoke German. He spoke Spanish and English. He spoke the language of our childhood, the Treasured Memories and Paul and Lipa. Why in God's name, with all those languages, did I refuse to understand?

Squeezing glass from my flesh, I wondered why I was acting so calm. I wondered why I didn't writhe against being inside my own body. If I could rip off my skin, I'd leave it in a bloody, shapeless heap on the floor beside the toilet, like so much dirty laundry. I'd beat my head against the wall until there was nothing left of my face, if it would get me outside of myself.

There are ways. A knife, for instance, a quick, surgical incision—up, not across, the wrist. But the veins are tough little vessels, and the heart pumps on for a while after you've done the cutting. I need something instant. There are trains. There are mountaintops, bridges, the air. There's the center of the highway and all the trucks barreling down. There is always the water.

To go after him, to stand on the rungs of a ship and fall forward with my eyes closed, the water rushing up, the shock of cold, and next, the ocean closing over my head, the water swallowing me as I swallow the water, as I breathe water and gulp water and the ocean fills me and bears me like a wafting leaf to its dark and sandy floor.

I went to Maggie's bedroom. More lace, more roses, an antique dresser with brass handles and a beautiful silvery mirror and, tucked into the mirror's wooden frame, photographs of what looked like every citizen of Blue Sky, Colorado. Abe, Mike, Gus, the whole gang of firefighters. And snapshots of kids. Kids in the snow with the rope tow behind them. Bathing-suited kids squeezed into the plastic wading pool. God help me, tears rose in my eyes. I thought of Sarah, six years old, standing in her bedroom with her hands around her neck. I thought of Maggie, brushing her hair and mourning the children she and her firefighter would never have.

In the dresser, I found lacy bras, matching panties, and in the second drawer down, Maggie's wedding dress. I rocked back on my heels. This was wrong. I shouldn't be seeing this. I didn't touch the folds of white peau de soie. I closed the drawer gently. It was worse than coming in on someone naked. More than anyone ever had a right to see.

In the bottom drawer, I found tops and pants. I took only a T-shirt. I might have taken a pair of jeans, considering that black widows had probably set up housekeeping in my pockets, but Maggie was a lot shorter than me.

I cleaned my hair off the living room rug as well as I could. Months from now, Maggie would find long blond hairs in odd places, between the pages of a magazine or floating in her afternoon cocktail, and she would curse my name.

Such a sweet, pretty house. Even the hallway was lovely, with its runner, roses and vines woven into its surface, with wall sconces. Framed pictures. Everywhere pictures. And in the middle of them all, a picture of Maggie laughing, being held by a laughing man who was clearly Thomas the Dead Firefighter. He was scruffy and ponytailed, handsome in a bony, tall kind of way. He looked straight at the camera, but Maggie gazed up at him, and she was younger and nakedly, desperately, violently in love. It glowed on her face; it filled her dimples to the brim. The afternoon sun lit up the hairs on their arms, and her hands were laced tightly around his waist, her cheek pressed into his rib cage. God, Thomas, don't go fight that fire. Stay here with this woman who loves you, your bride, the mother of the children you will never, ever have.

Again, my tears rose. I tried to mock this gingerbread house for my own sake, to ridicule or at least pity Maggie and her torch carried high for a dead man, but I couldn't, and anyway, I came to the kitchen: brass canisters, a round table with a checkered tablecloth, and two cookstoves—on one side a gleaming gas stove, and on the other a wood cookstove. Jesus. My eyesight blurred. I had to get out of there fast before they found me wailing like a banshee over a wood cookstove in the kitchen.

On a magnetic tablet stuck to the fridge, under *bread, milk, salsa*, I wrote, *Maggie, I'm sorry*. I stopped, considering. Because it seemed only fair, I wanted to add something private about myself, something ugly. Would my apology gain value with a little humiliation attached? *I am a fool.* But she knew that already. And why was her forgiveness so important to me all of a sudden? I underlined "sorry." Forgiveness. Add that to the shopping list.

Someone, the Dead Firefighter probably, had tacked the garage onto the house, a lean-to business. Beside the kitchen door, I found what would have been the porch light switch and flipped it. The office lit up, and through the window over the sink, instead of a front yard view, I saw a desk. On the wall, a pegboard, hung with key chains. One of them to the Ford.

Maggie, who seemed to miss the point of locking things, had left the cash-box key in the pencil drawer. I cleaned out the till and, beneath it, found a thick envelope of more cash. I took that, too, greedy robber. I went to the kitchen and wrote, *There's enough in my savings account to cover what I borrowed. Chris will give it to you.* I paused, then wrote another *I'm sorry.* Such a useless word, but cheap, which was good for me, the Groveler, tossing out apologies like Monopoly money. Every move I made was another reason to feel guilty.

I opened the garage door and my trusty Ford started up just fine, thank you very much. I backed out of the garage, swung it around, and aimed for the gate. Where Chris's car was parked. Shit. I left the Ford idling (who knew when it would start again?) and climbed the hood, jumped the fence, moved the Rolls, and climbed the fence again. I sat in my truck for a second, considering whether I should look for the key to the gate. I'd had enough. So I floored the truck. That old Ford could do zero to sixty in about fifteen minutes. The gate gave a little, but I had to back up for another try. It was tougher than they made it seem in the movies. Behind me, the light from the hidden house blazed up around the garage, giving it the look of a glowing destination for some religious pilgrimage, what the Three Wise Men were looking for one night a while back.

$\mathscr{T}$HE LAND OF MAD

Christmas 1982, Arroyo al Fin

JENNIE presses her forehead to the cold bus window, trying not to listen. Stephanie says, "You're going straight to hell, after what you said to Father Arturo, Juniper Bush." I am not Juniper; I am Jennie, and after school I'll be sitting in Essie's kitchen. Stephanie says, "In hell, you'll be a burning bush for all eternity." It's not even funny, but all of them laugh, including Randall Sandoval. In Essie's kitchen I am Jennie, who will soon have a stack of five-dollar bills to pay for books, for the ambulance. Stephanie can't change me into Juniper. There's no such thing as magic and I am who I want to be.

Today Essie teaches her how to shave her legs. Jennie sits in the bathtub and Essie lathers her calf. Essie says, "Hairless skin makes a man feel like you're truly naked, and a tiny bit like you're a child." She says, sipping her whiskey, shaving Jennie, "Make a man want to sip you, to savor." Essie supervises while Jennie shaves her other leg. She shows her how to rub oil into her skin while it's still damp.

Essie tells Jennie to hang up her towel, but Jennie does it wrong. Essie says, "Do you mean to say you've never hung up a towel?" She folds it in thirds, so the monogram shows, and puts it on a rack.

"I have." Which is almost true; she has hung them on nails.

Essie rolls her eyes. "I wonder when you'll listen to me?" Jennie scowls at her reflection. You Retard. Fool. Ugly Girl. Juniper.

Essie says a good woman can make Levi's look like rare silk. She says Jennie should stop skittering and start thinking about grace. Essie lights a cigarette. She takes Jennie by the hand, and she says, "I have a present."

Seven racks of clothes fill the spare bedroom—garment racks, Essie calls them. "I have a Ritz-Carlton wardrobe and a trailer-park closet," she says gaily. She begins searching through the boxes piled in the corner until she produces a yearbook. "Voilà!" The John Paul Robinson School for Girls, embossed in gold, like Treasured Memories, which stabs Jennie in the heart as usual. Jennie pages through the yearbook while Essie looks through the garment racks for an "Early Xmas present," she says. "You may as well know, I'm no Christian!" Which is fine with Jennie, now that she doesn't believe in God.

Here's a picture of Essie in her prom dress, a flower pinned to the shoulder, Jasper on her arm. If Essie adopted me, maybe one day I could go to this school and be in this yearbook. Here's Essie, wearing a tutu. If only she still had Treasured Memories, she could show Essie. "My grandparents were pianists," Jennie says sadly. "They were from Seattle." Essie will probably think this is a lie.

Essie says, "I was beautiful, wasn't I? All the girls hated me."

They go to the master bedroom, all white and filled with white movie-star furniture. "Mother!" Essie says. "She thought she was bloody Carole Lombard." Essie lounges on the bed, watching Jennie try on a long pink skirt and matching sweater, fuzzy pink, incredibly soft. "That was Mother's," Essie says. "She was a behemoth like you." Essie pats beside her, and Jennie sits, a puppy dog. "Now you're almost presentable," Essie says. "You'll have any boy you choose when I'm through with you. Look at you, the ten-foot-tall blushing schoolgirl. And who is the boy? Never mind. I know all about boys. I'll be your fairy godmother, Cinderella." Then she says, "Christ, your breath could knock over a horse. Didn't your mother teach you to brush your teeth?"

"I forgot today," Jennie lies, horrified. Where else is Juniper lurking, waiting to pounce and give her away?

Essie sighs. "You should learn more about hygiene," she says. "Come. Walk for me." Jennie marches up the hallway with Juniper on her shoulders, her terrible breath, her bad hair, her bad hygiene. Essie, sipping her whiskey, smoking, watches Jennie, until she cries, "Stop! I can't bear it. Look at you, the Hunchback of Alfin. Listen, my dear. Whatever is your greatest weakness, make it into your greatest strength. Being tall, for instance. My mother was tall, like Georgia O'Keeffe, a woman ahead of her time, along the lines of Katharine Hepburn if you get the idea. Maybe being tall had something to do with my mother being so fearless; maybe women aren't afraid of men when they can look them in the eye. Small men are always the worst, Napoleons prancing around with their chests sticking out. But I was making a point, wasn't I?" she says with a laugh. "So you're tall. Lovely. If you present yourself well, people will mistake you for a statuesque, beautiful woman. Cut your hair nicely. Wear the right clothes. Brush your teeth twice a day. Do it up, my dear, and you will rule the world. Now. Walk tall for me."

E s s i e pours two whiskeys and leads Jennie outside, through the snow and to what she calls the Big House, where the cold, gutted living room stretches to the second-story ceiling. There's one table, covered, in the middle of the room, and there's a fireplace, with a pile of wood beside it. Jennie says, "I can make a fire."

"That's my girl!" Essie says. She hands Jennie one of the whiskeys. "Every-one plays better with a drink or two. It stops one from thinking with one's head. You'd be better off if you thought with your body, Little Jennie." She makes Jennie take a slow sip. "Even if all you care about is getting plastered, you don't want to give that away." Essie pulls the cover off the table with a flourish. "Now I'm going to teach you pool, the *real* route to a man's heart."

The whiskey burns a path through her insides. The tiny flame licks up the paper, catches the kindling, growing. Jennie stands and tries to walk tall to the pool table. "I don't know how to play," she says. The fire fills the big room with flickering light.

Essie's face changes. "As I just *said*. I am going to teach you." Essie silently arranges the pool balls into a triangle. "This is racking," she says. Several sticks lean against the wall, and Essie picks one of them. She aims for the triangle. "This is breaking," she says, and with one hit scatters the balls to the four cor-ners of the table. Jennie wonders how to make Essie like her again.

Essie, circling the table, asks, "Why is my Little Jennie so desperate for money?"

Jennie, whiskey-dizzy, folds her arms and secretly strokes her fuzzy pink sweater. She's always saying the wrong thing, and she wants to get this right. If she tells about the books, and Stephanie, she'll really be telling about Juniper Bush, and Essie will be disgusted. So she decides to tell about Sunny. My poor little sick brother is how she'll tell it. She starts with the Church, which she blames on her Indian stepfather—she calls Clarence her stepfather, not her mother's boyfriend, because stepfather is more permanent and dangerous. Sunny is so smart, and Sunny is so cute, and he's probably a genius. Sunny was so sick, and my stepfather, Clarence, would only pray for Sunny, which sounds a lot better than *Clarence sucked a spider out of his cheek. They had a Meeting. I called the hospital.* "Now I have to pay for the ambulance," Jennie says.

"That's outrageous!" Essie cries, and Jennie, triumphant, is ready to learn pool, because now Essie is on her side again.

Jennie's a natural. That's what Essie says. She shows Jennie simple things and Jennie gets them just like that, even the first night, even while Essie, fas-cinated, asks all about the Church, and Jennie answers until she has said too much. No one is supposed to talk about the Church. Bad things happen if you do. Plus, the way Essie talks about it—"This is a cult, plain and simple," she says—makes Jennie think of the Meeting People, awake on their knees for a whole night, praying, weeping, singing, and she feels guilty for making them look crazy. "I'm not supposed to talk about it," Jennie says carefully, because her tongue is a bit stumbly from the whiskey.

"Oh, for Christ's sake," Essie says. "Anyway, I don't believe in God. God is for weaklings who don't want to take charge of their own lives."

"That's what I think," Jennie says. "I'm going to prove praying doesn't do any good." She describes her science project, how she'll use chamomile tea, and mullein tea, and yarrow tea (she'll do Medicine, too, but that's a secret). She'll soak tiny discs of paper in these teas, plus in penicillin. She'll put penicillin discs in one petri dish and chamomile discs in the another, and so on. There will be two petri dishes without any herbs at all. One is to test God. She'll pray over this one. The other is the control. Untreated by anything. It's important to have controls because it's too easy to forget what normal looks like, or to think things have changed when they haven't.

"My little genius," Essie says. "Put a little whiskey in you and you've got the world figured out."

Jennie really loves science, so clear and true and dependable: your body works a certain way. There are always rules. They exist and Jennie will prove it. But another part of Jennie talks about science just to make Essie give her money. Which Essie does, enough for more petri dishes and agar. Essie says she'll buy a microscope so Jennie can count bacteria here, at Essie's house, so Jennie can go to the state science fair and win an extraordinary prize, which Essie says isn't even a question since Jennie is such a clever girl. "I'll bake, you'll challenge God," Essie says, smiling, sipping her whiskey. When Jennie walks home in the dark, she's happy, but also confused. She isn't sure whether or not she lied tonight, and if she did, which part of what she said was the lie.

EVERY day Jennie goes to the trailer and checks her bacteria. Under the microscope, she counts the colonies. The spots of bacteria growing in the chamomile petri dishes are too numerous to count. The same for mullein and yarrow. TNT, she writes, because she likes how it looks, like the ingredients for a bomb against superstition. TNT, TNT, except for penicillin, which has no bacteria, exactly as expected.

Jennie prays over the God Dish: Heavenly Father God, kill this bacteria. She feels guilty, since she doesn't really mean it. But maybe God will answer the prayer anyway, to prove Himself. Although he'll really have to make a miracle, since the bacteria in that dish are thriving.

After Jennie finishes, Essie gives her coffee and a pastry while they have civilizing lessons. Essie teaches her to coil her hair into a French twist, and how to pluck a perfectly arched eyebrow. Jennie learns how to hold her knife, unfold her napkin, spoon soup away from herself.

Then they have lessons to teach Jennie pool, and also to teach Jennie that it all links up, geometry and physics and pool and being attractive to men. You can put your hair in a French twist with fifteen seconds and a bobby pin, and in pool, one shot can decide a whole game, which is like the bobby pin, and all of it is How to Deal with Men. With one move you can get a man exactly where you want him to be, so effortlessly it seems like magic or fate when really it's just skill, the right force in the right direction. When something goes wrong it's because you didn't see, you didn't aim, and you forgot the rules. It's all physics.

Playing pool, Jennie doesn't think about Sunny Boy Blue, sneaking out to hang up pissy sheets, lying if you ask him—fix my shoes, give me candy, tell me a story that goes on forever about nothing.

After Essie wins their pool game, Jennie washes dishes, and then she leaves with a five-dollar bill in her pocket. She walks home in the dark, past Flaco's, past Randall Sandoval's house with its glowing windows, and if he looked out the window he would see her tall, beautiful, with money in her pocket, and he would see the Error of His Ways.

WHAT SANTA BROUGHT

Christmas 1982, Arroyo al Fin

Essie decides to have an Xmas, not Christmas, party. While they play pool, Jennie and Essie make plans. Essie will order three massive trees for the Big House. "Who cares if it's disassembled," she says gaily, waving her hand at the unfinished room. "We'll drape it in finery. Candles work wonders, my dear. Remember that." Jennie thinks, I get to go to a real Christmas party. I am making plans with Essie. We're talking about petit fours and flambé and fondue, pine garlands hung from the rafters, red bows and many, many candles, because flickering light is the best.

The trees arrive a week before Christmas. Essie, smoking, watches Jennie hang strands of white lights. Colored lights are garish. Essie runs her fingers through Jennie's hair. "Here's what I decided," Essie says. "I'll buy you a good haircut—I'll make the appointment—and you'll be the little French maid, help with hors d'oeuvres and such on party night, and you'll sleep over. Fair enough?" Jennie nods, her heart pounding. She thought Essie was looking for piojos. "And," Essie says, chalking her stick. "Your boy could help you."

Jennie thinks of Sunny. "What boy?"

"What boy," Essie squeaks, imitation Jennie. "Don't play stupid. It's bloody unattractive." She breaks with quick, perfect aim. "The one you're sweet on. We'll ask him to be our little waiter boy. It's a glorious opportunity."

"I'm embarrassed. Maybe my brother could help."

"*No,*" Essie says slowly. "You don't *get* embarrassed. You say, 'We've chosen you to work our party,' like it's a prize. He'll fall in love immediately. Make this shot. It's a confidence builder."

Jennie makes it. But her confidence isn't built. You don't know anything, Essie. You don't know about Juniper Tree Burning, that stinky, dirty troll lurking under the table.

"Don't wrinkle your forehead," Essie says. "Always be conscious of wrinkles." She lights a cigarette and lets out the smoke in her elegant way. "We'll see," she says. "There's hope for you yet, Little Jennie."

• • •

O N a bright, clear December morning, the last day of school before vacation, Jennie sits on the Dog Bus, watching Randall Sandoval. His hair falls into his flashing eyes as he laughs. He tosses it back with a flick of his head and her stomach rolls over. How will she explain that he isn't coming? She'll tell Essie that Randall has to go to Mass. That she doesn't like him anymore. That he's stupid.

Stephanie notices Jennie staring and says something. Randall squints at Jennie in his pointy blue way. Jennie feels heavy and sad. It will always be the same. No matter how much pool she plays or how many rules she learns. I am Juniper.

You hold it right there, she tells herself sternly. The balls go where you put them. Stare them down. You wish you were this tall, she lets her eyes say. You wish you were like me. You just wish. Jennie forces herself to keep looking into Randall's eyes. I am tall, she tells herself. Tall, tall, tall. Essie's trick works. Randall looks away. Stephanie looks away. Stephanie cups her hand to Randall's ear and whispers.

Then Stephanie slips into Jennie's seat. "Hello, Piojo," Stephanie says in a friendly sort of way. "Have you learned to pray yet?" She plucks at Jennie's fluffy pink sweater. "Did you pray for this?"

"Leave me alone."

"Are you praying that Randall will love you?"

I am tall and I am grabbing Stephanie's hand and squeezing it hard, hissing, "*Leave me alone, you cocksucking cannibal.*" These are my father's words and they're so powerful that Stephanie can't answer them, and nobody else hears me say, "I'll kill you, I swear to God," and Stephanie believes me; she's afraid, and this is the best feeling in the world, and I drop her hand like she's nothing, like trash, like shit, like everything ugly in the world.

At Essie's, Jennie paces in the muddy yard until she catches her breath. She has to be calm. I'm tall, she tells herself, and goes into the trailer, thinking *tall*, so she's ready when Essie asks, "And how did things go with your boy?"

Jennie shrugs. "He's too short," she says. "I don't think I like him."

Essie smiles. She taps the ash off her cigarette. "Men are often disappointing." She pats beside her. "Sit down, Little Jennie."

Jennie sits. "He's stupid, too. He just sits there saying, Uh, and Hey."

Essie laughs this time. "Alas," she says. "Struck dumb by your beauty." Jennie gets herself a glass and pours herself a whiskey. Essie says, "To all the other men." Jennie clinks glasses with her. "Next!" Essie calls merrily.

P E T I T fours are complicated, not in the baking but in the decorating, their perfectly smooth icing, their intricate flowers: pansies, roses, sprays of forget-

me-nots. For the occasion, Jennie and Essie also make poinsettias and miniature Xmas trees. It takes two days to decorate the little cakes, each one a perfect
work of art. How can anyone bear to eat them?

On Christmas Eve, the florist delivers garlands of pine and racks of poinsettias and piles of red tablecloths. Jennie and Essie decorate all day, and then
they get ready.

Essie, in a towel, sits at her vanity, and Jennie, in a towel, sits beside her,
fixing her own face. Essie says, "Primping isn't just about the makeup." Essie
looks old, like a wicked witch, her scalp showing through her stringy hair
hanging down around her shoulders. Essie says, "It's about deciding who
you'll be tonight." She hair-sprays her palms and smooths the sides of her hair.
"Look in the mirror. Who do you see?" She smiles at Jennie in the mirror.
"Mirror, mirror, tell me right. Who will Jennie be tonight."

Jennie shrugs. "I don't know."

"Be daring," Essie says. "Be brave. Be Catherine the Great. Let it be an experiment. Let yourself be the science project." She French twists her hair and
spritzes her neck with perfume. "For myself, I see a dangerous Annie Oakley,"
she says. She dresses in suede pants and a red velvet blouse, long squash-
blossom earrings and a heavy concha belt, the kind of Indian jewelry Clarence calls Good Boy Tonto. "Perfect," Essie tells her Annie Oakley self. Off
she goes, to light the candles, the Annie Oakley queen.

Jennie stands in the bathroom. The girl in the mirror, who is she? The hair-
dresser cut her hair boy-short so she has a tiny person's head plopped on a giant's body. I am the Jolly Painted Giant, not Catherine the Great at all, Jennie
thinks. I don't know how to be Catherine the Great. I don't even know who she
is. "Jennifer," Essie calls, "come here, please." Essie will say you don't belong
here. "Jennifer, this minute, please," Essie calls. She'll say, How can I live with
a girl who can't even be Catherine the Great?

SUNNY Boy Blue, wearing a filthy white parka, cowers in the kitchen like a
chocolate-smeared ghost. Essie's red lips blow smoke. She says, "I caught this
little mouse in the Big House, eating petit fours. You'd better explain to him
about private property, about stealing. This *is* your brother, correct?"

Sunny, terrified, wide-eyed, cries, "Junie, I didn't!"

I am Juniper and this is my brother in a dirty white coat. "He didn't mean
anything—"

"That," Essie says, "is between you and him." She takes a long puff. "You
come from a sneaky family, Little Jennie."

In Essie's eyes, Jennie sees something worse than anger. Disgust. Jennie thinks, Don't throw me away. If you throw me away, then what will I do? But she also thinks, You don't know anything about him. He's Sunny and I saw him born and didn't you see his eyes? Don't you see how scared he is? The cuffs of his coat are frayed and nearly black with grime. "I'm going to straighten things," Essie says, and leaves for the Big House like she's done with them forever.

"We have to hang our stockings," Sunny says.

His voice, soft, pleading, hungry, makes her feel sick and scared, like she's sinking. She tries to make her voice good and kind. "I can't. I'm working for Essie's party. I told you already."

"We can do it after," Sunny says. His see-through green eyes belong in her father's sad-whale face. Tears prick her own eyes. "Junie?"

"What, Sunny?" He waits so long she says softly, trying to keep herself patient. "Tell me."

"I ate like a starving boy," he whispers. "And I cried. I'm sorry I cried." He wipes his eyes with the sleeve of his filthy white coat.

Kneeling, she brushes his hair from his forehead and gives him a hug. "It's okay, you Backwards Boy. I love you anyway."

He whispers, "Why are you wearing a towel?"

The minutes are slipping away. The guests will be here soon. But she lets him stay while she dresses in her fuzzy pink sweater and the pink skirt. She walks him down the driveway. She says, "I have to go back inside now."

"Okay," he says, smaller still. All through the valley, the Christmas lights blink and luminarias glow, and Randall Sandoval's Santa Claus smiles on the roof. Sunny asks, "Can you walk me home?"

What can I do? I want to walk him home but I want to be with Essie, too. "I'm working, Sunny. I have to go work. I'll be there in the morning, though. I'll be there when you wake up, like a present, okay?" And I will not cry I am Jennie watching my little brother become a white dot and then disappear down the dark road like a Christmas light winking out and I do not cry I am Jennie who does not cry.

She finds Essie smoking in the Big House. "Yes?" Essie says, and for a moment Jennie's scared, but then those irritated eyes soften. "Don't you look pretty."

Jennie studies the floor. "Don't hunch," Essie says. Jennie straightens. Ask for what you want. "I need perfume," she says.

Essie smiles. "Of course you do." She gives Jennie a bottle, and a five-dollar bill to tuck between her breasts. Mad money, she calls it. "Just in case your young man shows up after all and whisks you away!" she says gaily, in the Festive Mood again. In the bathroom, Jennie stares at her reflection. Mirror mirror on the wall, who's the ugliest of all? The answer stares back at her, scowling.

. . .

M O S T of Essie's friends are young artist men, because, she says, it's good for an old lady to have young blood around, and even Georgia O'Keeffe has a young man or two tucked away down in Abiqui. Jennie doesn't like them because they look her up and down and make her feel like Juniper.

Moving through the guests with her tray of petit fours, Jennie hears Essie say, "I've got myself a stray girl. I've taken her on. It's positively Pygmalion." Essie says that she adores her little ward, who really should move in with her. "I'll give her the closet room," she says. "I'll put the clothes racks in the halls." Jennie stares at the pretty flowers on the miniature cakes. I saw my brother in his white coat walk down the road and wink out like a Christmas light, and anyway, Essie doesn't mean it. Jennie might hate Essie. She hides this tray of petit fours behind one of the Christmas trees, for Sunny.

Essie's friends drink three cases of champagne, and they eat all the petit fours, chewing up the little flowers, the leaves. They decide to caravan to Santa Fe, which is Essie's word, caravan. Essie says, "There's big money for you, Little Jennie, if you get this mess clean by the time I come staggering back!"

"I want to come," Jennie says. "You said you'd take me to Santa Fe."

"Did I?" Essie says. She plucks at Jennie's hair. "It's a bit too short, isn't it? Pity."

Here's Ugly Jennie, alone on Christmas Eve, in a gutted house strung with boughs of pine, red bows, and three Xmas trees hung with white lights. Jennie, collecting half-eaten petit fours, teethmarks in the icing, and champagne bottles, thinks, I am nothing but the cleaning girl. I believe Essie's promises like an idiot, and now I'm in the Land of Mad, with an armful of champagne bottles, in a cold unfinished house, and I have to remember that Essie forgets promises on purpose, because she only made them to get a free maid. I am the Cleaning Girl and I have a brother in a dirty white coat and Essie had no right to look at him the way she did, like bacteria fuzz in a petri dish—Essie isn't the Fairy Godmother but the Wicked Witch, like the witch in the gingerbread house. Hansel and Gretel thought they were saved, but they were only dinner. And if I knew how to drive, like that Essie Witch promised, then I could zip over and give him this hidden plate of petit fours, and this five dollars of mad money, and now I am throwing these empty bottles at the wall and watching them explode.

In the trailer, on a mahogany table, is a silver tray for Essie's keys. Jennie gets them and starts the Batmobile. The engine chugs like a satisfied lion. She moves the seat back. I am Jennie and I have longer legs than you and I can drive this car, because I'm smart enough to remember all the times I watched my parents do this, and anyway it's easy to figure out. D means drive. Press the gas slowly, slowly. I turn the car toward Lower Alfin, and I am stronger and meaner and better than you. Sunny would love this! He would hold his hands up into the wind and laugh. Can we go to the river? Can we go to town? I will drive him anywhere he wants to go. I will be there in the morning with this car as a present. Here is Randall's house, the Santa on the roof, waving happily. Fuck you, she thinks, the words like a shout in her brain. Fuck you, Santa Claus, and fuck you, Randall, and fuck you, Essie Leeman.

She hears the Meeting before she sees the cars crowding the driveway. The tipi glows, a different kind of Christmas light. This is Christmas Eve. What about Santa? Does Santa ever feel lonely, sneaking into children's homes, knowing that nobody will leave presents under his tree? Who does Santa believe in?

Stupid. I am Stupid Ugly Hippie Juniper. She presses the gas pedal and the car lurches forward; she brakes and the car slips in the mud and slides, the car which once was filled with six dozen yellow roses and Essie naked in the backseat, and Jennie stomps the brakes but it slides more and there's nothing she can do—it slides right into the fence alongside the road, and the engine dies.

The Meeting Drum throbs. Jennie sits in the dark and prays, "Please God. Please, please, please," and the Drum prays with her. She turns the key. The car starts up fine. She turns its big nose around and carefully, carefully, drives it back to Essie's and all night, asleep on the couch, she dreams about explaining how the car got scratched, and all night she dreams Essie blames it on her drunken friends.

J E N N I E sleeps far into Christmas morning. In the bright sun, she sees that the Batmobile isn't scratched, really, it's just a tiny scuff on the fender, nothing worse than mud. Maybe Essie won't notice. And maybe Sunny won't notice how late she is, the Bad Sister who didn't keep her promise, running home, so late that when she arrives, Faith is already praying over the feast: blah blah blah, Heavenly Father, blah blah blah, Father God, blah blah blah. Tired Meeting People crowd the kitchen, and Sunny, clutching a book to his chest, eyes the food, a starving boy, bobbing on the rise and fall of Faith's voice, until finally, at last, Faith says, *Amen.* The children must wait while the women fill their husbands' plates.

Sunny, waiting, sees Jennie. "You're a liar," he says.

"I'm sorry," she says. "I brought you these." She gives him the package of petit fours. "I slept late," she says. "I'm sorry," and she thinks, If I am not

Sunny Boy Blue's sister, then I don't know who I am. "I'm really sorry," she says, and his face softens and he's back inside his eyes and this is all it takes to make her feel better. "You have a present," Sunny says. They go to the Middle Room, where Jennie's gift is the only one left. It's a shawl. A Meeting Shawl, yellow, with enormous roses embroidered on it and long golden fringe. She says, "It figures Faith would get me something I'll never use. She knows I don't believe in Meetings."

Sunny says, "We got it to match your hair. I helped pick it out."

"I like it," she lies, and drapes it over her shoulders to prove it. She tosses the wrapping paper in the fireplace, and flames shoot up, licking the hand-prints, Jennie's small one beside Ray's huge paw, blackened with soot. The shawl's fringe sways with every move. What if the shawl caught fire? It would melt. It's probably all polyester, which Essie says is the devil's revenge on the poor. It would melt and Faith would come running. My baby! My baby! But she'd be talking about Sunny Boy Blue, who's plucking at her shawl right now, who's saying, "Junie. It's a miracle. Look what Santa brought."

Why didn't I see before? That book, pressed to his bony chest? It's the photo album, Paul's album, Jennie's Treasured Memories, the one Faith burned only she didn't; she lied, and now it's Sunny's and this is Faith's revenge, and I am in the Land of Mad; I'm yelling, "GODDAMN you!" and I said *that word*, which Faith hates most of all, so I run through the kitchen past the women and their plates, and I can't stop from screaming it, almost like a prayer, "*Goddamn* you, goddamn you," but here's Faith following me outside, digging her fingers into my arm, hissing, "What did you say? What did you say?"

This is not my mother. I am fatherless, motherless, brotherless.

Tears stand in Faith's eyes. She says, "I never made peace with my father and then he died."

"You won't make me feel sorry for you. You *lied* to us."

"You were always like this," Faith says. "You were born to be this way. Even inside me, you kicked me; you hated me. You never wanted me to be happy. You even stole my inheritance."

Say it calm, powerful, like a person who can fight. "You're not supposed to say things like that to your own daughter." Then say the meanest thing possible. "It's Clarence you should hate. *Clarence* lied to you; he helped steal the piano. And Dad never cheated on you. *You're* the cheater. *You're* nothing but a cocksucking, adulterous liar."

Faith slaps Jennie hard. "You should be dead for saying that." Sunny barrels out of the house. "Leave her alone!" he screams, clutching the album to his bony chest. "Don't hurt her!" Who's he protecting?

Jennie walks away, so very calm. So very slow. Sunny runs after her. "Wait,

Junie, wait, look, we can share!" Jennie turns. "Traitor," she says. "Do you know what that means, Sunny?" She walks slowly away. Only when she's around the bend does she run, and she runs and she runs.

It's true, she thinks, running toward Essie's empty, half-built house, that Faith never said she burned the pictures. She just let them see it that way. What I need, Jennie thinks, is proof that Faith's a liar, something better than these strange flashes of memory: Faith burning the list of rules; Faith at the stove when they asked about the photo album; Faith with a knife in her hand, even though that was Thanksgiving and not today, and not a bread knife, but a carving knife. It all depends on what you call it. I am independent, not alone, cleaning this big mansion, not house, of its Christmas trappings. She cleans it spotless. She finds every speck of green glass. She waits. She checks her bacteria, which haven't grown in the penicillin. In the Medicine dish, they're thriving. Too numerous to count, she writes in her journal. TNT. TNT is what she should do to Faith, to Clarence, to Sunny, to Juniper's whole life. *Please*, she prays over the God dish. *Please*.

Jennie thinks she hears Essie coming home. She stands very still, holding her breath. She hears only the hum of the refrigerator. A sinking starts in her chest, like there's a boulder in the bottom of her heart, pulling it down into a dark well inside herself, with cold black water at its bottom. She remembers her mother's voice from long ago. *I'm all alone here.*

JENNIE, kneeling, searches for the yearbook in the closet. John Paul Robinson School for Girls. She flips through the black-and-white pictures of smiling teenagers, and if she could snap her fingers she would be inside the pictures, black-and-white and frozen in the Land of Happy. Half of her wants to keep this book for herself. Half of her wants to burn it for revenge on Essie, for leaving her behind.

She tries on more of Caroline's clothes. A suit of orange sherbet wool speckled with pink and white flecks, a red dress with white kick pleats, a deep green suit with a chain sewn into the hem to make it hang properly. They all fit like they're meant to be Jennie's, and why didn't Essie just say, *Have them all, you bloody behemoth.* Maybe wearing them would make her belong in those black-and-white pictures. The closet door is a mirror, and she stares at herself in a black evening gown. *Mirror mirror on the wall, who is the fairest one of all?* Not you, even in that black evening gown, which is Essie's mother's, and *Hey, Essie, can I have your dead mother's clothes?* It's an awful thing to see, the Ugly Girl, Hippie Bush, trying to be normal. Like Sunny in the kitchen, stolen chocolate smeared across his face.

. . .

JENNIE waits calmly in the living room, and late that night, Essie returns. Jennie, tired, limp, says it perfectly: "My mother came after me with a knife in her hand. My mother told me I should be dead." All of this is true, she reminds herself. So stop feeling guilty.

"Poor little ragamuffin," Essie says, stroking Jennie's hair. "Don't you worry; I'll take you in. You'll live with me now." She gives Jennie a twenty-dollar bill for cleaning up after the party, and she gives her the garment-rack room. Lying in her new bed, Jennie folds and unfolds the money and stares at the ceiling. The clothes racks stand over her like guardian angels. The yearbook sits in the back of the closet which is now hers.

In the morning, Essie drives Jennie to her mother's house. Jennie finds Clarence and Faith in the Middle Room. Clarence rests his mallet. She looks directly into his eyes for the first time in as long as she can remember. Beside him, Faith bends over a medallion, polishing it with steel wool. Jennie tells her, "It's time for me to go. I don't belong here." Faith rests her hands, palms up, on the worktable. Her fingers curl tenderly around the pendant of silver and jade and coral. She lets out a long sad breath. She says, "I think you're right." Under the bright work light, the silver gleams. Sunny stands between Clarence and Faith. As she passes, Jennie sees herself through their eyes. There's Juniper, leaving, good riddance. There's my sister, with a bag of her things, leaving. Jennie kneels to see Sunny eye to eye. "I'll see you soon." He doesn't cry, and he doesn't say good-bye. She leaves. But he runs outside after her, scrubbing his eyes. He whispers, "You should stay here." His little hands are balled into fists. "You're my sister," he says. "You're supposed to live here."

"I have to go," she says. "I can't stay. Mom doesn't want me here."

He screams. He shouts STAY. He runs after her, drives his fist into her belly, whacks her hard in the face, before she gets her arms around him and holds him as tight as she can, until he calms down. She says, "I have a present for you." She gives him the twenty-dollar bill, which is the only thing she can think of. Then she gets in Essie's car and she leaves him standing in the driveway, trapped in the Land of Mad.

PRINCE CHARMING

IN early February, Jennie's science project gets first place at the local science fair: *Conclusive evidence that traditional medicines based on superstition and misguided ideas of how the human body functions are completely inadequate, while the efficacy of penicillin is unequivocal.* This is the best sentence she has ever written. Her science teacher suggested the word "efficacy," but the rest is hers. On the Dog Bus, Jennie reads the sentence again. It sounds so—*real.* So true.

It's a beautiful, gorgeous day; a warm, false spring has thawed all the snow and fooled the fruit trees into blooming. Just wait until I tell Essie. I have a blue ribbon. Essie will be so proud.

Only, when she swings open the door, Sunny is in Essie's kitchen, with his hungry eyes, his dirty fingernails. "Look what I brought," he says. "For your birthday present." He has chocolate in the corners of his mouth. Treasured Memories lies open in front of him, pastry crumbs on its pages.

Jennie says, "My birthday was a month ago."

"Sunny's been telling me your family history," Essie says, and in that moment, it hits Jennie. If she is the experiment, then Sunny is the control, which doesn't get the treatment, which shows how things would be if left alone.

"Let's go to the culvert," Sunny says.

"I can't," Jennie says.

His starving eyes fill with tears. "We haven't been in *so* long," he says. "Please? I brought the book."

"I don't care about the stupid book," she says. "I'm way too old for that. Anyway, Mom gave it to *you*, remember? I wish she *had* burned it, I wish *you* would burn it, so you could leave me alone"—now Essie has seen Juniper, ugly and mean—"you smell like pee."

"No."

"Yes, you do. You smell like pee and I don't want you here will you please *go home* and play with your mommy and pee in your bed?"

Crying, he leaves with the album and without closing the door and Essie says, "High drama at the trailer park," and shuts the door.

Tomorrow, Jennie tells herself. I'll talk to Sunny tomorrow. Jennie feels her-self receding, falling into the deep well, to the cold black underwater bottom and from this dark, deep place she hears Essie saying that she's going to spend some time in Santa Fe. "You're leaving?" Jennie says in a small underwater voice.

Essie, tapping ash in her irritated way, says, "Did you just interrupt me?" Now Essie says that while she's gone, the workers will move her furniture, and Jennie, underwater in her dark deep well says, "Move?" and Essie says, "Jesus Christ, did you think I'd sleep in a trailer for the rest of my life?" and Essie says Jennie's job will be to transport Essie's wardrobe to its new home and Essie says, "You'll earn your keep, as we agreed. I'm taking my car." She says *my* car, as if she knew Jennie took it and scuffed it. She means, *You liar. You thief. You ugliest of all.*

S H E ' L L run after Sunny and tell him she loves him and make things okay, and she'll bring the John Paul Robinson yearbook, and they can share two books, two stories in the culvert—Jennie, clutching the yearbook, runs, think-ing that any minute she'll catch him with his short little legs, any minute now, but Sunny has vanished. How could she have abandoned him for the Wicked Witch when he's Sunny Boy Blue, whose diapers she changed, her Backwards Boy with the see-through green eyes, her one and only flesh and blood?

Randall's mother has put up Valentine's Day decorations, big pink plastic hearts with feet and happy faces marching across the roof, and she runs but Sunny isn't anywhere, and then here's Randall Sandoval, driving past in a muddy red Ford. The taillights brighten; the truck stops, backs up. Randall rolls down his window. "Hey," he says. "Want a ride?"

She doesn't want to get into his truck. She thinks of all the Essie reasons she should not want to get into the truck, all the Essie reasons she should hate him now, but look at her, she's getting into the truck and he is driving. "Beer?" he asks, nodding to the six-pack between them.

"Sure," she says. I am Jennie, drinking beer for the first time with Randall Sandoval, my date. Beer is easier than whiskey. "I drink whiskey all the time," she says, and hates herself. Idiot. Fool. Retard.

He says, "Why were you running?" She shrugs. He says, "Exercise?"

She says, "I guess." This is stupid, she tells herself, but also it's wonderful. This is Randall Sandoval. "What's your middle name?" she asks.

He says, "You like me, don't you?" She sees the past in one big mirror, all the times she liked him and let it show. What an Ugly Girl I am. My body, large and knobby, folded in strange places, doesn't belong in this world, and my nose is so big I see its tip in the peripheral vision of my shifty, beady, probably crossed eyes. "Yes," she says, and then she wants to kill herself for saying it. She can't catch her breath.

He says, "So where should we go?"

And, she, Jennifer Davis, who used to be Juniper Tree Burning, tells him where to drive, and when they're almost there she sees Sunny with his Treasured Memories walking away from the culvert toward home and she looks at him and he sees her, and then they have passed him.

W H Y didn't I know? When Sunny came to Essie's house with the Treasured Memories, I should have known something would happen. It was the Sign, the ultimate Sign. That album preceded every disaster that ever befell my family, piojos and theft, divorce and kidnappings and drownings. Dammit, God, why didn't I take it, burn it, give it back to my mother, anything? When my brother kidnapped me from my own wedding, the Little Prick tried to give the album to me and I should have known at that moment: a disaster would be coming. But I was in the midst of disaster, so how could I be expected to worry about what he might do? Damn you, Jennie, why didn't you fret? Why didn't you call in the state troopers when Sunny Boy Blue wrapped up the album and mailed it to you? If there is a God, why didn't he open my eyes to that harbinger, that Only Sign of every calamity? If God can make plagues visit themselves on pharaohs, and burning bushes talk, why could God not let me open my eyes and see the Sign before me? The answer is obvious: God didn't want to help. Let's toss out the drivel about free will, about apples and snakes. Come on, Jennie girl, blame it on yourself; God's an unsatisfying scapegoat. It comes down to this: I didn't look. Still, I remember Sunny with his album, standing on the road, watching me drive past in Randall Sandoval's truck, and I tell myself, as if it will do any good, again and again I tell myself, I should have, should have, should have known.

S H E takes her beer and leads him over the fence and across the field. Randall follows, the six-pack dangling from a fingertip. The field, wet from the early spring thaw, packs mud on the soles of her shoes, and holding her open beer, she struggles against tripping.

When they get to the culvert, Randall laughs. "This isn't secret! Everybody comes here." Jennie imagines Randall and his friends spying on Juniper and her brother, who are telling stories and stuffing candy down their throats. They sit on the cold concrete. Randall asks, "Why did your parents give you that name?"

I want to say, *Because they're stupid*, but I also want to protect them. "My friends call me Jennie," I blurt out. I gulp down my beer and start on the new one. I won't get drunk. I drink whiskey all the time. I stare at the graffiti which I know by heart. *Sangre y sangria.* I say, "What's your middle name?"

"Can I give you a kiss?" Randall says, and a swift and tremendous joy infects every cell in her body. She would do anything to keep feeling this wonderful, wonderful joy. She can't look at him and *yes* seems wrong and *please* seems wrong, and thank God, Randall saves her by taking her chin in his hand and turning her head. She closes her eyes and thinks, I am about to be kissed. I am being kissed. His tongue is large and wet and slides into her mouth, cold, tasting of beer, and I am kissed, okay, okay, okay, I'm kissed.

He stops. I can't look at him. I keep my eyes closed. He pulls my head to his chest and if I open my eyes I'll cry, because surely this means he likes me, this pulling me to his chest, to his heart, and I let myself lean into him, inside his jacket, his T-shirt, and under that, his warm solid muscle, and under that, his ribs, and under that, his heart, his lungs which rise and fall. His arms are around me and I am inside them. I tell myself, Here you are. Your eyes are only closed. You are not dreaming. Feel the cold concrete under your thigh. You are awake.

His hand strokes my hair, warm and gentle. But then he pushes my head downward. For a moment my face grazes the warmth of his belly, which, okay, is nice, but he shoves my face into his crotch, my neck at an awkward angle. "Undo my pants," he says.

I want to; I don't want to; I don't think about wanting. I think about how close we are now. If I get this right, we will be in love, and *he needs me.* An enormous tenderness overcomes me as I unbutton his pants and his fingers wind through my hair. *He needs me.* The warm tip of his penis springs at my face. Only I, Jennie, can give him what he needs, and his need makes him weak, which is why I feel tender.

He whispers, "Suck it."

Jennie thinks, This is Randall Sandoval, and all I want in this world is to have my cheek on his chest again, my head rising and falling with his breath. My eyes are closed, and this penis, it's a warm, firm thing, almost like a nose pushing against my lips, pushing through my parted teeth, not even as bad as his tongue.

He whispers, "You get straight A's and you don't know how to suck cock?"

I do, she thinks. I do! She opens her mouth as wide as she can; it knocks her tonsils and she fights the urge to gag. He sighs, groans, mutters, "Oh God," and a thrill shoots through her, and the tenderness again, so that she thinks, You're safe with me, I love you, you're safe. Her jaw aches, cramps, but she doesn't stop bobbing to the rhythm of his hips. I love you, she thinks. "God," he whispers, groaning. I love you, I do, I love you, and what I want most is to know how it feels to say that out loud. She lets her teeth graze its tip, but he grabs her head and says, "No teeth." She moves her head with his hips. *I love you,* and his penis jerks and bangs the roof of her mouth, and "Oh God, God," he moans, "God," and there it is, ejaculation. Not as much as she imagined. Hot. Tasting exactly like mucus, the consistency and saltiness of anything anyone might blow into a wad of toilet paper or spit into a muddy field.

"Swallow," he says, sighing. "Swallow." And she does. She turns her cheek against his belly. She whispers, "I love you."

Randall says, "Man, that was like, Fly the Friendly Skies."

She sits up and wipes her mouth and drinks some beer, but the taste of what she swallowed clings to the back of her throat, as if it's caught on her tonsils. She imagines gooey strands of it in her esophagus. She thinks of how Faith always says dairy products cause mucus.

"You're pretty good," he says, and this compliment thrills me, and he said *Oh God* like a prayer, and all I want is for you to kiss me again. "I need to get going," he says.

"Don't you want to drink more beer?" She holds up what's left of the six-pack. "Don't you want to do something else?"

"Nah," he says, zipping his pants, buckling his belt. "I've had enough." He looks out toward the fields. The sun is gone. "Bye," he says.

She stands, too. Maybe he'll say it. Maybe he'll turn to her and say, *Juniper, I've loved you for so long.*

Call me Jennie, she'll tell him. *Please stay.* Only she remembers what starving eyes look like, pathetic chocolate-smeared lips saying *please* in the kitchen.

"Bye," she says. Alone in the culvert, she tastes salt, tries to cough away the thickness in her throat, and she's concrete-cold in every cell of her self, her ugly, pathetic, dirty, Juniper self, and that is when she remembers: I left Essie's yearbook in his truck.

She clomps over the muddy field, but of course Randall's truck is gone, so she runs through the sagebrush across two fields, toward the setting sun, bleeding orange and lavender and pink, down the dry acequia, leaping over tumbleweeds and trash, beer cans, down the route she knows by heart, down the hill scattered with fruit trees. The pear. The cherry. The apple. The chokecherries. The trees, fooled into spring, are all blooming, the scent delicate and sweet. *The sense of smell is so important.* Petals lie across the hillside, like snow in this twilight. It's too early and the flowers will freeze, so there won't be much fruit this year. I miss my father, my daddy, my dad, she thinks.

There's the house. Its four windows face east, two on top like eyes, two on the bottom like teeth, the windows glowing warm and happy, not like a house that's breaking in half. She follows the ditch, past the outhouse, through the garden. She stands outside the kitchen windows. Inside, Faith kneads bread.

Clarence sits at the table, polishing a bracelet. He says something that makes Sunny laugh around a mouthful of green chile. Faith turns, flour on her hands and, holding them away, leans over to kiss Clarence.

Jennie runs down the road, around the curve, into the valley, past the Sandovals' hearts marching across their roof, and the dirty red pickup is not in their driveway, and with every breath, she feels Randall caught in the back of her throat. She runs all the way to Flaco's, where she buys three candy bars with her mad money. She eats them fast but the taste stays, a thick salty clog. At the trailer, Jennie pours herself a drink. She gulps burning whiskey, and it washes away the last traces of Randall.

Later, lying in bed, Jennie feels Randall Sandoval's breath again, his heart, his warm skin, his arms around her. *Oh God.* Every time she thinks of how he said it, the same thrill shoots from her head down through the center of her body. She opens her eyes to the clothes racks hovering over her in the dark. She remembers how he walked away. She thinks of Essie's yearbook, sitting in the cold truck. She feels sadder and lonelier than she has ever felt, and the tears slide into her hair.

She dreams of Randall, of his pointy blue eyes gazing into hers as he whispers *God. God, how I love you,* and she is complete, loved. And then, like a ghost or a cobweb, Sunny comes through the window to wake her up and tell her their house is burning down.

O N Monday after school, Stephanie Martinez sits behind Jennie on the bus. She leans over the seat, close to Jennie's ear. Jennie doesn't turn, though she feels Stephanie's warm breath, and Stephanie says, "You smell like smoke, Burning Bush." Maybe Jennie will never get rid of the smells, pee, mud, fire. "Do you know why your house burned?" Stephanie says. "God was punishing you." Stephanie holds a book in front of Jennie's face, and it's Essie's yearbook and Stephanie tosses it to Randall, who throws it out the window while Stephanie whispers softly, triumphantly, like a snake, *"Cocksucker puta."* Jennie sees it all, sees the Sangre de Cristos, the pure white snow high on the mountaintops, the green seat, the open window. *"Cocksuckerrrrr,"* Stephanie says; Jennie sees Randall and all the Dogs laughing as Stephanie says, *"CockSSSSSSucker!"*

I cannot get rid of the smell and my house has burned down and I still taste the salt at the back of my throat but I can do this: I can grab your Stephanie neck and smash your Stephanie cheek against the window and you can't get away from me, the cocksucking Ugly Girl, digging my fingers into your neck and whispering, *"You fucking bitch, I'll kill you."* You can't get away because I'm tall and I'm stronger than you and I know how to make a fist. God, it's so obvious; the most important thing is to know how to fight back as hard as you can.

Jennie gets off the bus but she doesn't run; she crosses her arms and waits for Stephanie. The kids gather around them. Stephanie says, "You think you're so bad, Piojo?" She charges, but Jennie easily traps Stephanie's head in the crook of her elbow. She punches Stephanie in the stomach four times, and then she pushes her face first into the thawed-out, rotting dog, and she says, "I can do anything I want." She stands, and with one boot she presses Stephanie's head into the dog. With the other, she kicks Stephanie's side, softly, in time to her words: "So. Leave. Me. Alone."

Then Jennie makes her heart as blank and white and smooth as sheets of snow. She is tall and strong and she comes from lumberjacks. She knows what to do. Look down at this Stephanie. Smile an Essie smile, and for God's sake don't say anything; just stare at her and think, I see you; I see right through you, until she knows you do, and then spit. I am Jennie, being strong, but I have to hurry away because I just might cry, and I can't breathe, and more than anything I want to go home, and I'm Jennie, running to the burned house, Jennie who can't go fast enough, like a kid with a skinned knee running for Mommy, and she'll be fine if she can just get home, just a little more and then, at last, here it is.

Nothing. Here is nothing. The fire burned it all, the tree, the house, the crack. The blackened adobes, rising jaggedly out of the twisted metal, the blackened cottonwood stump—these are worse than nothing, like skeletons of dead people. And where is Faith? Where is Sunny? She walks through the used-to-be window, through the black mud puddles of used-to-be floor to the used-to-be Middle Room, to the fireplace, still there, still at the black heart of this used-to-be house. She sees herself through her used-to-be family's eyes, running away while the house burns, *That bitch, leaving in our time of need*, and through Essie's eyes, watching from the Big House as Jennie steals the Cadillac, *A thieving stray dog I tried to teach her but she comes from a sneaky family*, and Randall, watching the top of her head bob between his thighs, *Ugly Hippie Bush she'll swallow anything you give her*, and she picks her way through, sees herself through the eyes of God; she sees an ugly teenager squatting in the mud with snot running down her face: *You prayed to me and didn't mean it, and this is what you get, you liar, you thief.* Jennie begins to cry, a terrible noise she can't stop, squatting in the puddles, the water which drowned out the fire and she cries and she cries and every moment she hopes, Maybe they'll be back for me, maybe now, but no white car arrives and so she cries all alone with the shadows and the water, feeling the emptiness behind her, around her, inside her.

$\mathcal{N}$IGHT

Early Friday, U.S. Highway 40, Colorado and Utah

I drove past Little Joe's and kept on going. My head felt strangely weightless without my hair, and the chill curled down my naked neck. I gave my new heater a whirl, and it worked just fine, thank you very much, blasted so hot, in fact, that I had to run it with the windows cracked. I knew when I was close to Steamboat because I smelled the smoke from that fire they'd all talked about in the bar.

I realized I was still drunk. In my panic I hadn't really noticed, but now I was very conscious of keeping my hands at ten and two, my eyes straight ahead. I reminded myself to blink. I turned on the radio but got only static. I prayed I wouldn't kill anyone.

I expected a forest fire. I thought the sky around Steamboat would be glowing, red and eerie, but the sky was black as ever. For a moment, I thought Officer Gomez had lied about that, too. But then I remembered the fire had been, as he said, put down.

I got on Highway 40 and headed north. I needed gas. After an hour or so, I tried singing what my father always did: "Good-bye, Old Paint," I sang. "I'm leaving Cheyenne. I'm leaving Cheyenne; I'm go-in' to Montana." But my voice refused, my mutinous voice. I am not going to Montana. I'm going to Seattle, where the ferns grow wild. It came to me that I was crying, a steady runoff, a bodily function like anything else the body does on its own, a beating heart, a breath, and I tried to get some perspective, to get a grip, and here's Jennie, gripping that steering wheel and telling herself, You better pull your ass over soon. Take a little nap. It's one or two in the morning, and a body requires rest even if it is in motion. The fence posts beat out their rhythm, flashing in and out of my headlights: pull over, Jennie, pull over. At any moment you may drift. But I can't pull over so I roll down the window and drive.

What should I have said to Chris's back, as it receded toward Little Joe's Bar and Café? I could have called his name. Chris, I should have cried, Chris. But what then? Even if he turned, which is doubtful, then what? He would have looked at me and looked at me and looked at me, waiting to see

what I could possibly say for myself. I'm sorry. Such simple words. Even the Seattle cop said it. "There won't be a body, the tides like they are," the cop said. "I'm sorry," he said. "I'm so very sorry." Softly, gently, as if he knew me and the nature of my life, as if he bore the weight of carrying the news to me with grief and longing for it to be otherwise.

"Don't be," I told the cop. "It's not your fault." Which meant, *Shut your mouth*, which meant, *My life is beyond your comprehension so don't you try that empathy shit with me.*

I'll meet Chris at a bar with two whiskeys ready, and I better have some way to explain. Chris, I'll say. It just happened, one two three, the way the holidays roll around every year and kick you in the ass. The way you live your days and come home and eat your dinners and go to bed and then morning comes and the alarm clock starts it off again. It was just morning, Chris. That's all. Blame it on that. Morning, and August, and the same old Jennie, that bitch, that coldhearted thoughtless barge-ahead Billy Goat Gruff. She woke up one day and thought, I cannot stay here anymore. Or maybe I'll just tell the whole thing like a silly story about someone we both barely know. Together we'll sip our whiskey and shake our heads over her antics, that whacked-out Jennie with all of her problems.

Maybe I'll say this: I thought I loved you, but I was mistaken.

But I cannot deny the memory of Chris, chopping onions for guacamole. So dexterous and perfect, the confident rat-a-tat-tat of the knife blazing through those onions, a mundane domestic task he elevated to a dance of risk, where the life he planned was balanced against a sharp blade. Here was a man who wanted to be a surgeon, to use his long supple fingers to operate on babies still in their mothers' bellies. His fingers had to be perfect for the microscopic heroics he planned, yet rat-a-tat-tat, he risked all for guacamole, and though I knew it was silly to find this small task so extraordinary, he was a hero to me, brave and reckless and graceful, even as he wept, the tears salting the onions he chopped. Faster and faster he went, rat-a-tat-tat, an untenable risk for his surgeon's fingers, a drum roll for his magnificent feat.

I could offer my childhood as an excuse. See here, husband, isn't it all such a sad story? Poor, poor Jennie, beat up, spit upon, lice in her hair, spiders lurking in the cracked wall. A cast of a thousand villains, or at least two—here's the big bad runaway daddy and the mean old mommy, here is the church and here is the steeple, or the tipi, as the case may be; here is the house that burns in the night.

I'll say, Yes, Chris, it's true. Before I was Jennifer Braverman, I was Juniper

Tree Burning. Three names, all of them a mistake, all of them so easy to ridicule. Juniper, called Jennie, tall and awkward, living in a trailer in Arroyo al Fin, lying about her name to Essie. A month after she moves in, she has driven Essie to sleep in the Big House and Juniper called Jennifer worries that the other rooms will soon be finished, and room by room, Essie will leave. Juniper—let's call her Jennie—decides to help herself. She dials New Hampshire information and gets the phone number for the John Paul Robinson School for Girls, and she calls for an application, which is easy, the grades, the teacher recommendations. But there's a question to answer. *At John Paul Robinson School for Girls, we believe that education is as much decided by the example of your peers as it is by the quality of your teachers. With this in mind, please explain, in a page or less, what you can offer your classmates in terms of life experiences and goals.* She memorizes it.

Jennie, with short blond hair and a penchant for sugar, likes to run. Running, the words come at her. Example. Life experiences. Goals. At first she despairs. She'll never be like those girls in their prom dresses and ballet shoes. Example. She can only be different. The word seems like a good idea, and she repeats it as she runs. Different, different, different. In the trailer, she writes *Different* on a piece of paper, then crumples it. On a fresh sheet, she begins again. *I am unique*, she writes, swallowing. *My parents are hippies.* She erases the word "hippies" and tries to think of something else. Different? No. She rewrites *hippies.*

But it's still not exactly right. She begins again. *Before I was named Jennifer, I was named Juniper Tree Burning, a fact my mother blames on me.* She's got it now. It rushes out of her, easy, a story she's heard all her life. She tells them how her father kidnapped her mother, how she grew up with hippie parents, an Indian stepfather, Hispanic classmates and historical resentment, an outhouse and no running water and racial strife. She milks it, telling things in just the right way, because you tell the part of the truth that gets you what you need. You make them believe they should be astonished.

Her brother who's always sick, her mother who relies on folk medicine, her abusive stepfather, all this will get the sympathy vote. Esther Leeman, her JPR alumna (she has to look up the word)—what does she call Essie? Fairy Godmother. Benefactress. Foster Mother. She chooses this last label for the way it makes her a relative. *Esther Leeman, my JPR alumna foster mother, gave me a way out.*

She works the bootstrap-nightingale angle: *I want to make my own way, give back to the world. I want to cure people with real medicine.* She tells them about her science project, award-winning (which is true, at least at the local fair), and that she wants to learn from her past but write her own future. *I need*

a full scholarship: room and board, tuition. Help me. Help me become what I have chosen to be.

What she doesn't tell them could fill a book. That she has to search for them. That her father, off in Florida, laughs when she tells him that their house burned down. "God is the fucking court jester," he says. "Good thing you have a sugar mommy." That she goes to her mother's friend Joy, who says that Faith and Clarence and Sunny moved to Santa Fe. That she, the escapee daughter or the abandoned culprit, doesn't try to call them or write because it's so much better this way, to pretend they have vanished. That one night, her baby brother, her Sunny Boy Blue, calls and she almost hangs up when she hears his voice. "Junie?" he says. "Junie?"

That she finally answers, and that, hearing his voice, she wants to escape and wants to cry and wishes he would leave her alone so she can go back to pretending her family has vanished. "We have a phone now," he says. "We have a toilet, and a shower, and Clarence sells his jewelry on the plaza, and Mom is learning, too, and everything is good and you should come visit." She laughs. And then he falls silent, as if the speech was all he had in him, and she says, "Are you okay?"

"Yes," he says in an odd, tiny voice, which she recognizes. Later, running, she knows the voice because she feels it, the bottom-of-the-well, underwater feeling, and if she spoke, it would be like that.

She doesn't tell the John Paul Robinson School for Girls that at the state science fair she doesn't win a thing, and that one judge tells her, "Proving the efficacy of penicillin is not a great discovery, my dear, especially not with a flawed experimental design." That when she returns, she finds that Essie has removed her perfumes and makeup, her towels, her shampoo, her special brushes and ceramic tray for earrings: Essie's primping self, all gone. That in April, Essie moves the kitchen, taking away her baking self, and shortly thereafter, Essie has removed herself completely from the trailer she shared with poor little ragamuffin up-by-her-bootstraps budding altruist Jennie.

None of this matters. Jennie has her interview with a JPR woman. She carries the orange sherbet suit to school in a bag and dresses in the Taos Inn bathroom. She meets the woman in the lobby. She sees herself through the woman's eyes. So brave, so strong, so independent and resourceful. So very smart. So . . . *unique.*

They send a letter offering room and board, tuition. They write, *Indeed, you are unique, and in keeping with the John Paul Robinson School for Girls philosophy of social and economic diversity. We are very excited . . .* Jennie doesn't tell Essie, although later she wonders if they told her themselves, and if that made Essie look for her yearbook, because soon after the letter comes,

Jennie looks out the trailer window and sees one of Essie's artist boys carrying Essie's suitcase. Essie, waiting in the Jaguar, starts the engine, and off they go.

Essie calls to say that Jennie can use the Batmobile to work on the landscaping. "You do know how to drive it, don't you?" she asks. She says there's an account for purchases at the Lilac Shoppe in town. That she'll send checks from time to time, but that she needs to stay in Santa Fe for a while. "It's better this way," she says. "Don't you think?" So this is Essie's final lesson: when you sink the eight ball, leave without a backward glance.

B U T years later, names later, states later, she'll be driving U.S. 40, our Jennie, half drunk, bawling like an idiot, checking her rearview, hoping her husband and Sarah will catch her, fearing they will.

Maybe, our Bereaved thinks, maybe the truck will break down and I'll die on the side of the road. Why did pioneers venture out into the wilderness? I'm betting a lot of them just wanted to disappear, never to be found. And so many got what they wanted, dropping dead of thirst, their cadavers rotting, ribs poking out like the remnants of some strange architecture—these are the morbid ramblings of the Bereaved Ugly Chick who thinks Ugly Thoughts as she hightails it out of Colorado, which, by the way, isn't all mountains and pine; even in the middle of the night, she can tell that the scenery is more of the same, miles of sagebrush, just like New Mexico. The Ugly Chick's either hallucinating, or she sees in the dark, or, in a really bad school play, she's declaring: Ah'll never be free of this dry, dead land (clutch at the earth and cry it out in a phony Texas accent, sand running through your fingers).

It's easier to think about what was or what will be next. To think of strategies and angles, to ask, should I tell Chris about Jennie, abandoned by Essie, alone in her trailer in Arroyo al Fin? Can I possibly make him feel sorry for poor little Jennie, this five-foot-ten lumberjack girl who decides, I am the sort of person who gets revenge?

What better revenge, Jennie decides, than to suck every possible drop of money out of Essie? On grid paper, she draws complicated, expensive garden plans, consulting library books and her own memory. She gives workers tasks that will cost Essie buckets of money—she has them build terraces, raised beds, a sprinkler system, a complicated rock wall leading to a rock pool. She rents a rototiller, orders manure, plows it under; she chooses flagstone for the walk, which the men install.

From time to time, Sunny calls, and Jennie listens to his faraway voice, and after these phone calls, she runs up the steep hill, away from Lower Alfin and never, ever, to the skeleton of a house. She runs out of Arroyo al Fin entirely, across the mesa, through the sagebrush, under the hot sun. She gets so tired she has to walk home, but she doesn't think about her brother on the walk back.

Sometimes, in the evenings, Jennie drives the Cadillac to the Rio Grande and watches the place just south of the bridge where the seamless black water breaks over rocks, and she doesn't think of her brother born backwards; she just listens to the sound of the rapids and waits for the night, the month, the summer to end.

August arrives, and the rains come every afternoon. She likes to run in the rain that comes down so hard she can barely open her eyes against the downpour. She runs through this blurry world, and running, she's already a student of the John Paul Robinson School for Girls. She's Jennifer Davis, and everyone loves her hair, and the vintage clothes she wears, and her red lipstick, and her cocky attitude with boys.

Sometimes, transplanting flowers into freshly tilled soil, her nails packed with dirt, Jennie thinks of her mother, kneeling in the garden, under a forever blue sky. She thinks, My mother showed me how to pull this weed and shake the roots clean. To turn manure into the earth. To guide the ditchwater. She transplanted flowers whose roots she loosened before pressing fresh earth gently around their stems. She showed me the bleeding hearts underneath the chokecherry trees. She grew sunflowers, sweet peas, marigolds, nasturtiums whose bright orange flowers and spicy leaves she put in salads; she grew pansies and carnations that smelled like cinnamon; geraniums, cosmos, foxgloves, morning glories. She taught me to thin the shoots, make the salad, wash the dishes, cook the rice, stir the chile, tend the fire, paint the walls, sweep the floors. To slice apricots and can them in jars we stored in the pantry where the drying herbs sifted into my hair. My mother taught me to swim, to find watercress growing in the icy water of a spring. She grew mint along the shady backside of the house. When the herbs had dried, she made them into teas: mint for a stomachache, chamomile for a cold. Or was it mullein for a cold?

Jennie catches herself thinking this way, a whole bed of flowers planted. Then she runs until she doesn't think about her mother, until she cannot possibly think, Why has my mother left me alone here?

Just before she leaves New Mexico altogether, she drives to Santa Fe to visit Sunny. She takes him for a ride in the Batmobile, and he raises his hand in the wind and laughs, just as she knew he would. She tells him she'll be going away to school in New Hampshire.

"Is it near Russia?" he asks.

"The other end of the world," she says.

"You're never coming back," he says.

"I'll come back," she says. "Maybe not in a week, but sometime."

"You're never coming back," he says.

"Stop saying that. You sound like a tape recorder."

"I miss you," he says.

"I'm not even gone yet."

She pulls the long nose of the Batmobile into the post office parking lot. She turns to him and says, "I'm right here," and in the sun, with his see-through green eyes glowing, he says, stubborn boy, "I miss you." They wait in line, and she buys him a stack of prestamped postcards. She takes him to McDonald's and buys him everything forbidden, French fries, Coke, a choco-late shake, a gooey cheeseburger. While they eat, she writes her address over and over, on every card, so he can contact her whenever he wants, and she doesn't think about what was—the culvert, and Sunny in it, telling stories, laughing—she thinks about what will be, how on the day she leaves, she'll write Essie a note, explaining how to water the flowers. It will say, *I have to go. Thank you for everything.—J.*

Jennifer Davis, she writes, *John Paul Robinson School for Girls,* and writing her address, she sees how the JPR girls will love her, will love to take pool les-sons from her, and they'll find her mysterious because she won't talk except to tell certain stories, like how Swifty Davis kidnapped Edna, how Lipa and Paul fell in love, how her father used mud to patch the tin roof of a Casita on the Mesa. Something about these tales will always seems a tiny bit invented, but the JPR girls won't believe Jennie is lying, which she won't be; she'll be telling a particular kind of truth. She'll say she comes from lumberjacks, and it will be an exotic genetic fact to explain her broad shoulders.

Then Jennifer Davis will go college to be a scientist, a doctor. She'll be popular with the boys, and she'll date preppy boys and cowboys and football players and artists. She'll always drop them with a happy wave of her hand, tralala, good-bye, Old Paint, I'm leaving Cheyenne. One boy, the business-school boy or the preppy boy, won't leave quietly. He'll follow her to class. He'll try to drag her to his car, having forgotten that she's Jennifer Davis, five foot ten and strong, descended from lumberjacks, a woman who knows how to make a fist. She'll fight back, knee his groin, slug his belly, and when he's good and doubled over, sobbing in the hallway, she'll tell her astounded pro-fessor to call the cops.

She'll finish college and go to medical school where she'll meet a man who's handsome and rich and charming. They'll marry by candlelight, in a church with a steeple, with garlands of pine strung between the pews. Chil-dren, seeing her walk down the aisle in her heavy satin gown, will whisper, "Is she a princess?" At the altar, her groom will wait, tall in his black tails. The children will think, *She has rings on her fingers and bells on her toes. She shall have music wherever she goes.* The Bride and the Groom will have two children who will grow up strong and smart and happy, who love to look at the Wedding Album while they hear the story of their parents' meeting. They'll all live happily ever after, for ever. And ever. Amen.

Is that the excuse? A sad-sack story of teenage woe? Shall I make it a romance novel, tell Chris, You are the happy ending, my love? No. All that crap has nothing to do with me now. It's phony and cute, and Chris is too smart to swallow it whole; he'll see right through me. What else? Should I plead the insanity of grief? My brother, I'll say. My brother is dead. But it still doesn't seem true, and anyway, marching it out as an alibi nauseates me. It would be obscenity, blasphemy, to turn my brother's death into a neatly packaged story guaranteed to get me what I want, and it probably wouldn't, because he made it so clear, after all: I. Give. Up. On. You.

Pull over, Jennie. There's such a thing as road hypnosis, you know; there's such a thing as feeling sorry for yourself, too, and being a weepy weakling, and let's talk about the dangers of swerving. But the Ugly Chick, she just keeps on driving and checking her rearview for anything coming out of the dark, husbands or goblins or ghosts of dead pioneers, looming large in the mirror, hidden in the back of the truck. *We'll eat you up, we love you so.* Fuck 'em. Fuck God and Chris and Sarah and Abe and Faith and Ray and most of all, fuck you, Sunny Boy Blue of the see-through eyes, you Backwards Boy whose head once fit in the palm of my hand, fuck you for taking the coward's way out, for one last fuck-you to me, for this mean, petty, hateful thing you've done and how will I tell our mother and how will I survive when she tells me, *It's your fault. It was always you.*

And then, a Sign. Look, try to ignore God, to be a scientist, to curse Him, to deny Him, but the fact is, if you were raised on Signs, then you call it a Sign when the Fist of God comes out of the dark and smashes you in the kisser. He's a mean and petty God, and worse, He's a thief, and He has a Nasty Sense of Humor. Which is to say, the truck, it died. Just up and died. The engine simply cut out, a sudden silence where there had been a roar, a drift where there had been momentum. God ran his finger across his throat and I was left with nothing.

When a truck dies in motion, at first you can't believe it. You press harder on the gas, but the old tricks don't work. The truck slows, and slows, and, hardly believing it, you guide it to the shoulder where it finally stops. So there I sat on the side of the road, in absolutely nowhere in complete silence and darkness. The vomitous sobbing rose to my lips, but I choked it down and turned the key. A click was all I got from the useless piece of shit, the biggest mistake of my life, the fucking Ford. That was it for me. Oh baby, you're in big trouble now, little girl, Ugly Chick—what will you do, in your dead truck with nothing to tide you over? You know only one thing: *run*. Pack up the valuables, which consist of Sarah's ring on your pinkie, and get out of Dodge, or Ford, as the case may be. But there's nowhere to run, you fool, you fucking goat: the joke's on you, and anyway, you got yourself into this mess, buying a truck on impulse, barging ahead despite not one but two breakdowns—your luck has run out, and look at you now, stranded in the wilderness with the coyotes, all alone waiting for the roadrunner to drop an anvil on your head, under the stars, all alone because look at everything you've done to make the world hate you. Go eat them worms, kiddo. There's no food out here for the likes of you. Look, maybe it's God, or maybe it's self-destruction; does it matter? You always held your parents in contempt for running headlong off the cliff, but you're just like them, Jennie Girl, a cartoon character who hovers in the air for a second, realizing her fate, then drops like a rock. You're all the same, little Jennie. The Davises. A family of fools.

Look what you've done to Chris. Take a look through his eyes, and if I were him, I'd hate this Bad Wife, Jennie. I'd hate her for all the nights I lay awake, listening to her paintbrush moving across the walls, the water running, the click of the light switch, her stealthy entrance into our marriage bed: I'd hate her for not even guessing I couldn't sleep. If I were Chris, I'd hate Jennie for making me afraid to touch my own wife. Lying awake, starved by loneliness, Chris lay with a dry, unpopulated desert between them, a prairie of sheet miles wide, months long. If I were him, I'd hate this Jennie bitch for asking, "Do you want me to pretend?" For making me want to beg. Please, wake with a sigh and open your arms and ask me in, bridge this universe of five sheeted inches between us. Lie.

I'm starving, he whispered, letting his lips move but making no sound.

I'd hate Jennie already, if I were Chris. I'd hate her the day I came home to find a note taped over the little window in the front door. I'd have given up on her already, already seen her for the Ugly Chick she is—if I were Chris, I'd have already hit the road, scratching my head over why the hell I thought I could stand her for the Rest of My Life. Just leave me alone, Jennie always told him, and if I were him, I would have granted her wish.

A N D her wish is granted anyway: there she is, alone as can be in the middle of the night in the middle of U.S. 40, even her Ford gone, left behind like so many dead oxen. Oh pioneer. Into the stars, the darkness, the impenetrable, unpopulated silence. I walked down the highway center line, stumbling over my own feet. I headed north even then, and I think that in my deepest heart I still expected Chris would arrive, would skid to a stop beside me, only it wasn't the Rolls that came along but a truck.

I heard it behind me, a grinding, roaring semi. I turned. I did not move. I faced it down. Tiny pinpoints of light grew and grew, the orange row marking its cab, the headlights. I stood like a deer, like a tired woman. Come on, run me over. Make me roadkill. Me and the coyotes. Or pick me up: see, my thumb's out; I'm hitchhiking like a bona fide hippie with her hair all whacked, a nutcase, probably on drugs, too. I raised my hands against the glare and waited for Sarah's rapist who smelled of toothpaste and cologne. Fine then, I thought. It's only fitting.

But I was the chicken and at the last moment I crossed the road, and the truck roared past, its horn blaring contempt and dismissal, its wind taking a last spit at me before I was again alone in silence.

I could not keep going. I walked back to my truck and lay across the seat and curled up as small as I could get and I cried, a great heaving self-pitying sobfest to the universe smeared across the velvety sky, to the vast silence and the utter emptiness inside this dead truck. Then, unbelievably, I slept, or passed out, or simply shut down, like the Ford.

THE WOODSMAN

SHE sits with her brother in the culvert, and outside, the sun is hot. Over them, great trucks hum along, carrying food, carrying dolls with long-lashed lids that slowly close over great blue eyes, carrying apricots and honey, carrying candy balls of fiery cinnamon and melting chocolate, carrying all that's pure and true in the world, sweet pink medicine in bottles with droppers and film in cameras and books for photographs, carrying chamomile and lemons for hot soothing tea, carrying wedding dresses and ferns and great black pianos and houses on hills and velvet dresses and pink foam curlers, guitars and legions of cowboys singing "Good-bye, Old Paint" to watercolor Indians on Appaloosas, carrying all the magic of the world to the end of things, to the place where a great crowd stands in the water with their hands outstretched.

Juniper Tree Burning sits between Sunny Boy Blue's knees, her warm brown baby brother with hair as silky and black as cat's fur, and she leans back against his frail ribs and bony chest. Candies spread around them in a great colorful carpet, chocolates wrapped in red tinfoil and bright orange drops and green-apple Jolly Ranchers, and propped across their knees is a photo album filled with every person who ever lived. She's fourteen, much too big to be sitting in his arms, but he wants to be the big brother and she lets him. She leans against his bony little chest and she smells the faintest tinge of urine, but it's sweet somehow, a good smell like lemons or apricots. Still the trucks come, thumping and roaring, and the culvert shakes and the yellow crackling weeds outside quiver in the wind of this great caravan.

Sunny's toes curl and he says, "I know where they're going."

She twists, straining to see his eyes, glowing light green.

He says, "They're going to Russia."

He turns the pages of the book, past Paul and Lipa laughing in their wedding clothes, past little-girl Faith in her straw hat and shiny black shoes with her pail of blueberries slung over her arm, and there at the end is the postcard of onion-topped castles. She tries to turn it over, though she knows the message is in a foreign language with backwards letters, but it's glued down. She again cranes her neck to see his face. "Tell me what it says. Tell me what it means." He pops a chocolate in his mouth and his eyes are merry. "Tell me," she cries. "Tell me. Please?"

"It's a secret," he says, sucking on his candy. "Try to guess."

She leaps to her feet. "It's not fair. You're supposed to tell!" But he shakes his head and waits and wins the waiting game. She sits with a sigh. The trucks barrel down the highway into the valley with the steamy desperate hissings of their brakes, and the weeds outside tremble in their wind.

He asks, "Want a lemon drop?" She shakes her head. He says, "Please don't be mad. Play with me instead."

The candy has called in the bees. They swarm and dive and tickle her shoulders, but because of the trucks, she can't hear the buzz of their tiny wings. "Does it say, *Where were you?*"

"That's a good guess. But it's wrong." She squirms, but he holds her tight and he whispers close to her ear and his breath is sweet with chocolate, "Silly Jennie. You have three guesses. Why don't you try again?"

She stops struggling and the bees crawl through her hair but she isn't afraid. She asks, "Does it say, *Why did you leave me?*"

Again he shakes his head. The semis pass and she thinks that he's such a foolish backwards boy to believe these trucks could go all the way to Russia, that they could drive across the sea and over the walls of China to get to the land of onion-topped castles. She smiles. "Does it say, *Why didn't you come to Russia?*"

"So close, little Jennie. Very very warm." Over them the trucks carry their loads and her eyes fill with tears because she has no guesses left. He says, "Don't be sad. I'll tell you a story. Do you want to hear a story?"

She says, "I want to know what it means. It isn't fair—"

But he shushes her and he whispers, "Listen. Listen."

She sighs. "I don't hear anything."

"Listen harder."

So she holds her breath and listens with her everything—her eyelashes, her fingers and toes and skin and tongue—and the trucks' roar recedes and she hears the bees, the beating of their tiny wings. He whispers, "Not that. Listen harder." So she does and the bees recede and she hears the rushing laughter of the Rio Arroyo al Fin, but he says, "Listen harder." Then she hears it, a steady throbbing, a beat as regular and perfect as the sound of her own blood or God's heartbeat, and she knows it's the Meeting Drum. "I hear it," she says.

Sunny whispers in her ear with chocolate breath, "It's Juniper Tree Burning. The woodsman, he's chasing her. When he catches her, he'll cut out her heart."

"Is that what it says?"

He hugs her and he kisses her cheek and opens his palm and there, pow-dery yellow in his hand, is a lemon drop. She takes it and it's sweet and sour and good.

"But who is the woodsman?"

"Silly girl. The woodsman is you."

The sun is setting. The trucks have passed and the bees have gone and all she hears is the sound of Sunny breathing, or maybe it's her own breath echo-ing in this cool damp shelter. The lemon drop on her tongue has melted to nothing. Juniper shivers. In the darkness she can't see him. "It doesn't make sense," she says. "Tell me what it means!" She runs to the twilight mouth of the culvert. The passing trucks blow back her hair and breathe warm exhaust into her face.

They are not in the culvert anymore; they're in a truck, and there are beer bottles on the floor, which roll and clink with every turn. "But the postcard," Juniper whispers. "Does it say, *Why didn't you come?*"

"No," he says sadly. His bony thigh tenses as he shifts. "Even after all that, you still don't understand?" He whispers in her ear with warm chocolate breath. "It says, *I'll meet you where the ferns grow wild. You go by land. I'll go by sea.*"

I was awake. It was morning.

8.

THE DREAMER, WAKING

$\mathcal{E}$ M P A T H Y

T H E Ford, true to form, started right up. So I drove. I drove into the sunrise and out of Colorado, waiting for the first town with a bus station, because I was done with this unreliable truck and I wanted to be sure of getting to my destination.

Into Utah. First with hills dotted with junipers, and elephantine mesas in strata of purple and cream. And then the hills became cliffs as red and singular as Sarah's hair. I never thought Utah would be so beautiful, its rolling red hills unfurling to mountains in the distance. All I'd ever known of Utah was that Mormons lived there, and I had a vague notion that they were obsessed with genealogy. I pictured people in library carrels, bent over obscure texts, their necks exposed to fluorescent lights, or else in a temple the rest of us cannot enter. How I envied them, knowing exactly where they came from and exactly where they were going.

I stopped in Vernal, Utah, and left my truck there, useless flotsam, discarded junk. For all I know, it's sitting there still. Or maybe not. I left the key in the ignition and maybe some other fool found it, and thought, *Lucky Lucky me.* I caught a Greyhound to Salt Lake City.

It's true that I'm prone to hyperbolic storytelling, but I believe I'm being accurate when I say I've never felt so alone as I did on that bus. Seventy-odd people in close quarters, moving across Utah to our various destinations, everything quiet except the engine and the gentle hiss of air from the window sill vents. Who would travel in such circumstances by choice? Trying to find a comfortable way to sleep, breathing one another's exhalations, knowing every minute that our bodily wastes were sloshing around in the outhouse at the back of the bus. It was poverty, or fear of flying, or urgent circumstance that put us on that bus, always something shameful, or terrible, or worse, simply pathetic—a reason we would not want to reveal to the strangers sitting around us. So we kept our silence in that space no bigger than some living rooms.

I took out the envelope I'd taken from Maggie's garage. I had stolen nearly a thousand dollars and I hadn't finished counting when I began to cry. I cried and cried, trying to keep it quiet, feeling unspeakably sad for us all, though I also kept telling myself, Who are you to presume to grieve over the lives of strangers? Still the tears came, the thought coming over and over: *My brother is dead and I am alone.* Eventually, I understood that I was also crying out of shame over all the times I'd inflicted my ugliness, my selfish, petty cruelty, on the citizens of the world, on strangers in gas stations and my own mother, my own husband, my friend, my brother. How I'd hate me if I were them.

Chris. I know your ways. I know, for instance, that you open envelopes by tearing off the stamped end, because that way you won't lose the return address. I know your capacity for stillness, how you study even the simplest problem before attempting a solution. So you would have dropped the sheet of paper into your hand and held it for a moment before you unfolded it.

He's been waiting for this. It's a relief, in a way. The sun is very hot. The neighbor girls are racing; one girl sashays a victory dance, then bends backwards, her belly to the sun. Her hands and hair touch the ground.

Chris unfolds the note.

I had to go. I'm sorry.

—J

This is the way she finishes all her notes, with a dash, as if to say, *You know the rest.*

Does he panic? Does he run from room to room, calling her name? Does he phone the police or her mother? Not Chris. He picks up his cat and walks to the bedroom, where he finds the bed made, her suit neatly hung. Her running shoes aren't in the closet; her cowboy boots are gone, too, and her backpack. Boots for the bars and shoes for the road. She has everything she needs. Her Cinderella slippers march across their shelf, the unpaired shoes like a prediction. What a bad idea, to have such a split-in-half symbol hanging over the marriage bed.

A sudden thought sends him to the whiskey-reeking kitchen, to the trash can under the sink. He pulls it out and dumps it on the floor, and on his hands and knees he sorts out the eggshells and coffee grounds, the paintbrush stiff with dry green paint. Anything to tell him where she is. He sits back on his heels. Stupid. It would have been on top, whatever it was. Bob daintily picks his way through the mess, sniffing. Chris spots the balled-up paper and spreads it out on the floor.

I went . . . the draft says. Beneath it, *because . . .* and *Please.*

At least she had to struggle a little. At least it wasn't as easy as it looked. He scoops the trash back into the can and washes his hands and sits back at the table with the paintbrush and the wrinkled, dirty draft of the note for him. A gentle man, his floppy brown hair falling into his eyes, his long-fingered hands stroking his purring cat. A tall, carelessly graceful man. He stares at the

paintbrush. All those times he woke alone and lay in bed listening to the whick of the paintbrush on the walls.

•

AT a bus stop, under a wan and jaundiced fluorescent light, Jennie calls her home number and listens to a series of beeps. But what message will she leave? Will she ask, Do you think we could glue Humpty-Dumpty together again? She hangs up. The lonely, sour bus riders stagger around, dazed, wondering, How did I come to be here? Where is my real world? Three children wander past, their eyes half closed. Where is their mother? Why are they standing in the middle of the bus stop in their footed pajamas, hugging their pillows? Why aren't they sleeping on the bus?

Jennie dials again, and again hangs up. She calls three times, the series of beeps growing longer and longer. The mother of the three children hurries into the bus stop, and if she had three arms, clearly she'd slap all three of them, but she can only hold one and slap the other while the third sidles away, a little tangle-haired rabbit with nothing to redeem her features, a beige child who will become a beige woman, shrieking like her mother, who says, "You get over here this minute, Missy." Dragging Missy by the arm across the bus station, saying, "You idiot. You fucking, fucking idiot."

Jennie dials again, but now it's time to go. She climbs on the bus and the driver pulls away, and she sways backwards, forward, with the shifting gears. It would be so clean, to have a knife sink through skin and muscle, tendon and bone. To have this bus run me down.

I am Jennie. I can't pretend I am not this woman, alone on a bus with all these people who are also alone, trying to get where we need to go, although most likely, it's already too late for us all. Too late for Missy, blocking the aisle, staring at me, her face smeared like her dirty pillow, watching me. "It's okay," I whisper, and she stares until her mother shoves her along.

CHRIS crosses the street to talk to the two neighbor girls. He squats and says hello. "You're that man," the older girl says. "I know you." The younger hides behind her sister. Jennie calls them the Flower Thieves.

Chris asks, "What's your name?"

"Katie," the elder says. "This is my baby sister, Annie."

"I'm not a baby," Annie says.

"I'm Chris. I need to ask you something very important, okay?" They both nod solemnly. "Do you know my wife?"

"That tall lady?" Katie asks.

"Did you see her this morning?"

Behind Katie, Annie stares at the sky. "She isn't pretty," Annie says suddenly. She glares at her older sister.

"Yes she is," Katie says pompously, crossing her arms.

"No she isn't."

"Yes."

"No."

Katie sighs a long, loud sigh. "My sister's so *little*," she tells Chris.

"I'll show you something." He fumbles for his wallet and flips it open, and between his credit cards, he finds a wedding snapshot. Jennie's mother took it of the Bride and Groom just after they swallowed several shots of whiskey. His arm is around her. She's staring into the camera with the look of a person poised between joy and panic. He shows it to the girls. "Her. Did you see her?"

"She's pretty," Katie whispers softly, taking the picture in her brown fingers. "See?"

"I saw her this morning," Annie says, stepping in front of her big sister. "She was mad. She's always mad."

"She is not," Katie says.

Chris looks into Annie's grave face. "This is very important," he says. "Was anybody with her? Was anybody bad or mean, a—a man, a bad man, or anybody—"

"I don't know," Annie whispers.

Chris seizes Annie by the shoulders. "Was she in jeans? Was it after lunch or before lunch?" He imagines Jennie with a lover, his arm along the backseat, her head tucked neatly into his shoulder. He asks, "Was she alone?"

"I don't know," Annie whispers, barely audible.

"You're scaring her," Katie says. She takes her sister by the hand. "Come on, Annie. Let's go inside."

"She isn't pretty," Annie shouts over her shoulder, just before they escape into their house. "She has a brain tumor!"

I woke to the sound of the bus's brakes hissing and squealing. It was late in the day, and I was in a city, presumably Salt Lake by the size of it. We were pulling up to a bus station. I got up and got off the bus and tried to orient myself. My eyelids, swollen from crying, stung each time I blinked. My breath smelled like a hangover. My belly ached where the deer had kicked it, and my hand throbbed.

People slept on the floor, on the plastic bucket chairs, their heads fallen to the side, their mouths gaping open. The three children slept draped over an

enormous duffel bag like coats on a bed. My head throbbed. There was a pay phone. I picked up the receiver. Should I call information for the telephone number of Little Joe's? Call home, to get Chris's message again, to say—what? Come get me? Not this time, little lady, he'd say. I give up on you.

I called a cab instead. Come get me, I told them, and come they did. The beauty of a commercial relationship.

God, the logistics of it, the sheer will it took for Chris to find me. I know he found his way to TRUCKS. I know Chris. I know how, waiting for Ramses Smith to dig up the receipt, Chris would go to the window, and I know he'd see the high thunderheads receding north, and he'd probably try to imagine what I was doing.

Here is Christian Braverman, pretending to be his wife in a truck, under that rain in the north, steering toward her brother, but he can't get beyond her hands on the wheel. During their courtship, he studied the smallest parts of her. The hair on her arms. The dimple where her buttocks rose away from her spine. Stop *staring*, she'd say, but she did the same, studying his elbow, the webbing between his finger and thumb. Where did they find the time? In memory, the slowest, finest minutes are stretched and exaggerated into months. The mind enlarges what matters.

"Here it is," Ramses Smith says. "That woman could tree a coon with one look, if you don't mind my saying so."

Chris studies the receipt. A Ford. 1976 F-150. The price, cheap. He knows her bargaining face. Cold. Flat-eyed. Nothing given, nothing yielded. The receipt tells him his own address. His own phone number. His wife's name. The clues he finds are like junk mail, a bulky accumulation of nothing.

I T ' s a five-hour flight to Seattle. I sat between a man and his son. The father kept trying to show his son articles in a hunting magazine. The boy, hunched against the window, pretended to go on reading his novel. I could infer their story. I could even strike up a conversation with them. Or with the couple across the aisle, nuzzling, holding hands, the stewardess with her giant diamond and her oversprayed hair and her button which read MY NAME IS NOT "MA'AM." But I didn't want any more company with strangers. They're like the three bears. Goldilocks trips into their house, thinking she'll lie down and sleep for a while, and eventually they wake her up with a *there she is* and off she runs, no more rested than before. There is no escape, no rest, with strangers.

Sitting between this father and son, I cried. It seemed I was going public whether I liked it or not. The tears ran out of me, like the symptom of an illness. I needed a complete medicine, a running-eyes, stuffy-nose, sore-throat medicine. Don't mind me; I've caught the common grief virus. I have tried to fight it off, but it's a persistent little bug. My brother gave it to me.

A N D the GAS Boy tells Chris, "She comes every morning. Doughnuts and gas and a cup of coffee. She's always dressed up, too, that chick, sorry, your wife, but then, later, this morning, I mean, she came back, only in jeans, and she bought a truck, you know, and I thought, that's weird, is she like, on vacation? And when you've got a car like that, what do you want with a pickup truck—" Chris interrupts this nervous monologue to ask which on-ramp she took.

The boy shrugs. "I'm guessing north," he says. "She always goes north. But I could be wrong. It's a fifty-fifty thing. Or maybe one in four. I suck at math."

Chris thinks, Do I know my wife at all? Every morning this summer, as I slept, she bought doughnuts and gas and a cup of coffee at this counter. This pimply boy knows that. Why this gas station? Why this coffee, this boy?

"She bought a map of the western states," the boy says.

Chris says, "Her brother died."

The boy nods, as if he knew it all along. Chris wants to demand the answers to everything: *Will I save her? Does she love me? Will she be okay?* Ah, Chris. You ask the impossible questions.

What did Chris do next? What could he do?

Lacking options, he gets the cat and he drives north. How well I know that urge, that impulse: *Do something. Do what? Drive.* He drives to Raton and stops at Henry's gas station, the first off the highway. He learns of Sarah, more useless information. He drives north. He stops at his parents' house. "I have to lie down," he tells them, and he does not wear a pancake happy face. In his room, he dials home, gets his own desperate voice, begging for a message. *She is not okay.* There's one hang-up, which we know is Sarah's.

Revolted at himself, angry, Chris presses the code to record a new greeting. He says, "If anyone knows where my wife is, leave a phone number and an exact location. She is not okay. Her brother is dead." His hands tremble with fury, with the adrenal satisfaction of exacting revenge. He has said it outright. It will make her livid.

He tells his parents he's going for a walk. He walks faster and faster until he falls into a run, just as she would run. He runs past houses he has known all his life but never entered. His breath comes hard, and his shoulders ache. He puts himself behind her eyes; he sees what she sees. *Who is chasing me? My brother is dead. Where am I running? My brother is dead.* He stops cold. She's not running from her brother. She's running from herself. She'll keep running until she runs right over the Edge of the World. Let me say this straight. She just might kill herself.

Chris heads back the way he came. Why this red-haired girl and not me? Who does she think she is? That bitch. The solipsism and anger and selfishness of her action, the ridiculous extravagance of it. He walks faster and faster. She just might kill herself, that coldhearted, selfish bitch, whom he married despite her chilly heart, despite her brother who is now dead. Walking so fast he's nearly running again, he says it aloud: "Her brother has drowned." But he doesn't feel pity; he feels rage, that she would inflict on him this fear and grief and why has he spent all these months cooing like a pigeon, waiting for her crumbs? He's starving. He's tired of starving.

His parents are sleeping. He collects his cat and writes his parents a note. Then he gets in his car, starts the engine, and steers it south, all the way back to Albuquerque. Dawn breaks as he approaches the city. He thinks, There's nothing I can do for her. The sky glows pink behind the massive hump of the Sandias.

I know the whole plot now, folks: meanwhile, back in Colorado, Officer Gomez drops Sarah and Jennie off at the motel, where they collapse into bed. The Good Samaritan Cop goes back up the mountain to the broken-down Ford. Abe: a kind man, a college graduate who lives in his hometown because it's the best place to live. He rifles through the glove compartment and finds the bill of sale. This woman, this Jennifer Braverman, a.k.a. Burning, got a good deal on the truck. That is, if it's not completely mechanically shot. He returns to the police station–cum–city hall. He phones Ramses Smith, who says, "That bitch? Everybody's looking for her." Ramses gives him Chris's number. Officer Gomez, that meddling Good Samaritan, listens to Chris's message. *Her brother is dead.* A flat, cold, unkind message. He thinks of how, when she realized she'd left her lights on, she completely lost it. He resolves to help her. He decides not to leave a message just yet. Who knows what, exactly, she's running from.

He orders a tow, supervises the transport of the Ford. He cooks up a plan with Maggie. *Tell her the truck needs everything. Keep her here while we figure out what's going on.* Maggie doesn't like it. Maggie thinks Abe Gomez goes too easy on people; he's a born sucker. But there's not much she wouldn't do for Abe Gomez. From Maggie's, he dials Jennie's home number.

So that Chris, half asleep, is now listening to the phone ring. Bob winds through his legs, meowing. Chris sits in a kitchen chair, holding the black phone, sleek and compact as a cockroach. The kitchen reeks of whiskey. The phone rings and rings, but he cannot bring himself to answer.

Do I have the audacity to ask my husband's forgiveness? I've always said anything can be made beautiful. I should have also said the opposite. It takes much less time and effort to be destructive, minutes instead of days. In seconds, anything, even a husband's love, can be ruined. Look at what I did to Chris: all his beautiful calm excised as, hands trembling like his own mother's, he lifts the receiver for news of me. A crumb of information. Or worse, what if his hands aren't trembling? What if I've damaged his open, fearless heart? What if it's sewn up with hate, like mine? Wouldn't that be an uglier crime?

This is confusing; I can't tell what it says about anything. And what good does it do to imagine the bystanders talking about the Jennifer who stomped through their Wednesday? I can pretend I'm the world, hating myself, and it doesn't change what I've done.

Underneath the wedding picture in Chris's wallet, there's another. In that one, the Bride's and Groom's foreheads lightly touch as they look each other in the eyes. They have frosting on their fingers. A snapshot between formal poses, taken just after they've fed each other cake. It's a portrait of an utterly private moment. It's his favorite picture, though it's not much of a likeness. Laughter and bad focus blur their features. It's certainly too private to show the girls, or Ramses Smith, or Henry. And in truth, Chris can't bear to look at it. He'd be dizzy with grief for everything promised and possibly lost.

But let's be honest here, Jennie Girl. I'm the one who wouldn't be able to look at it. Empathy is just another way to talk about yourself.

ℛ U S S I A

M Y plane landed in Seattle at two-thirty in the morning. I sat on the airport chairs designed to keep travelers from stretching out and sleeping. It was exactly the wrong hour to do anything at all. Bars were closed. Even coffee shops were closed. I called Albuquerque again, listened to the long series of beeps, and hung up. Then I claimed a corner of carpet, near a gate, and slept for a while.

When I woke, I went outside and hailed a cab. I didn't know what destination to give. The cabbie asked me, and I said, "The city."

He laughed. "Can you be more specific than that?"

"Ferries," I said. "Where the ferries are."

"Oh—kaay," he said. "Can you narrow that down just a teensy bit?"

It's raining but not pouring. Jennie has flown to the land where ferns grow wild and the rain falls in a steady drizzle, the raindrops so small you might not notice them if not for the fact that you got wet. "Bainbridge Island," Jennie says. *Lipa on Bainbridge Island.* "That ferry."

The cab pulls into traffic. Water blows back on the car windows. She watches the smudged, shadowed landscape pass by: leaves. Even in the dark she can make out the vegetation, lush, dense, green. Everywhere green. Here, there is no horizon or distance, only the trees and underbrush, closing in.

I was surprised by how long it took to get to the city. I had no sense of the direction we traveled, with one hill on my left looking the same as the next hill on my right. In Taos, there are the mountains to the east, the broad mesas to the west, and beyond them, the distant, smaller mountains skimming the sunset's edge, like a border framing the sky. You always know just where you are with such markers, even at night, when the the lavish stars abruptly end far in the distance, at the mountaintops.

We came out of the hills and I saw the black expanse of water. Mostly, I saw the rain, the cars passing, the sweeps of this highway, that highway, that bridge, this bridge. Then, the city. Skyscrapers, the Space Needle. Traffic. The city light made a strange sort of dawn. A confusion of underbridges, overpasses. Now and then a glimpse of water. Where, I wondered, was Mount Rainier? The house my great-grandfather built? Enormous cranes crouched at the water's edge like red praying mantises. My mother used to buy boxes of mantis eggs, which hatched into insects that ate the aphids in her garden. The mantises were pale green, spindly-legged, poised. They were efficient killers.

The cab stopped. "You just go in that building," he said. I paid him and stood on the curb, waiting to cross the street. An overpass ran directly above me. There was a little yellow trolley running parallel to the water. I was cold in my T-shirt, my jeans, my cowboy boots. I wrapped my arms around myself. The rain fell. Now and then a car arrived, releasing passengers who hurried into the ferry building, gray silhouettes darting through the rain. I ran across the street.

Where was I? A wharf? A dock? There was a whole commonplace language I didn't know. Honey, I'll meet you at the dock and we'll take the ten-oh-five to Bainbridge. The language of a people raised on water and green. Shore. Tides like they are. Bow, prow, sail, tack, buoy. Boat, ship, catamaran, schooner. Ferry. My mother knew this language.

The water rocks gently against the foundation of whatever it is Jennie's standing on. A pier? Ducks bob with trash on the water's surface, rainbowed with oil. Or are they geese? Boat horns moan. She feels the city awaken; the traffic noises growing, people bustling off to starting time. Gulls dip and rise in the air, calling out, landing. The sun rising. Dawn again.

God, I was sick of being outside myself. I was sick of being.

Here is a man, eating an apple. He throws the core into the water. The gulls bicker over it. The strongest wins and wheels into the air, his breakfast in his beak. Here are workers, untying a rope which is all that tethers an entire red and white ferry to shore. The passengers hurry to board. A horn sounds. The ferry backs away.

There is a pub nearby. This she knows because the policeman told her. Across the street, the cop said. There probably won't be a body, he said, the tides like they are. She turns away from the water and crosses the street again, back under the overpass, through a parking lot. There it is. Murphy's. She wants to go inside, but this early in the morning, the door is locked. It must have been afternoon when Sunny came here. Night? Surely he didn't wait all day to decide. Day then, she selects. So he could see the water.

Again she crosses the street, I cross the street, Jennie crossed the street, all of these things together for I am the watcher and the watched, the detective and the criminal, the event and the remembering. I am the woman buying this ticket as the poor unfortunate prick, my brother, Sunny Boy Blue, the Backwards Boy, once bought a ticket not so long ago. There are no signs, no half-masted flags, no posters to mark his passing. A boy drowning is merely gossip for this ticket seller, with her prim mouth, her curled, grandmotherly hair, her plump fingers counting money—gossip: You won't believe it . . . could have been me that sold him his ticket . . . they say there won't be a body, the tides like they are—it's gossip and a headline in the stack of newspapers on her back porch.

I thank her. She thanks me. I am the thanker and the thanked. I am the Bereaved.

I waited for my ferry, but at the last moment, I couldn't get on. Embark? I sat there. I watched it pull away, sounding its horn. It moved slowly, as if reluctant to leave.

There's so much I left out. So much I treated like backyard gossip—Grandmother Dies of Cold; Hippie Mother Follows Signs—as if the truth could be captured by the headlines' bare facts. But now, unanswerable questions plagued me. Jennie, watching the water: think of your mother, who was born here, had a mother who died here, played piano. What do you know about her? How much have you really considered? I always longed for green, for the land where the ferns grow wild. I paint my childhood as dusty, dry, but my mother filled it with flowers. My mother taught me the names of herbs and the places where they grew. The furry tongues of mullein growing along the ditch bank, the musty yarrow with its tight umbrellas of tiny white flowers. She showed me the rosehips on the thorny wild rosebushes twining along the fences. She hung herbs on nails in the pantry. She grew rows of lettuce, rows of corn, carrots, and beans. She showed me the white aphids crawling in a crook of the apricot tree, and she let loose boxes of ladybugs, praying mantises. She was on intimate terms with God. He lived in the rooms of her heart, right next to Sunny. *All I ever wanted was to make something beautiful.* Faith. You made Sunny Boy Blue. You made me. Doesn't that count for anything at all?

I am reduced to a sniveling child. I want my mother, my mommy, my mom, to stand beside me on the shore and tell me about the water, about my grandmother, about the language of this world. I just want that rock-me-to-sleep safety, to be told it will be okay with the magic certainty only a mother possesses, the kiss-it-better power, and I know because I am your mommy and we know, we mothers—we sit at the right hand of God and the left hand of Santa Claus; we are the Tooth Fairy, the Easter Bunny, and your Fairy Godmother. Faith, I was your baby your daughter your little girl. Why did you give up on me so easily?

At last, I understand something I should have realized long ago: my mother has suffered all her life over the death of her own mother. One day she called for her mommy and no one answered, and she was infected with the incurable disease of grief, and now I will add to its symptoms. You. Jennie. Remember that howl that came from Faith when Sunny was born backwards? Deep from the belly, agony to hear. The sound she'll make when she knows he's dead. How will she survive?

I, Jennie, this Ugly Chick, this mournful daughter, the Bereaved, watched the ferries come and go while the sun rose. The water changed color, lighter and lighter, along with the sky. The ocean had this in common with New Mexico mountains. Day had fully broken, and I saw that—my God—it wasn't green here at all. I could see now. The deep gray water, and gray-lavender sky, and gray land in the distance. The clouds are low. They are sitting right on people's shoulders, gray, looming.

Dawn. As a young girl, Faith swims while the world comes awake, birdsong and engines, foghorns groaning. Juniper stands outside the tipi, head tipped to the morning star, praying, the water bucket's wire handle digging into her palm. She sits in the kitchen, thinking, I have a brother now. I stayed up all night. The sun is rising. Oh, Mama. We are the same, you and me. We aren't opposites at all.

WRITING ON THE WALL

MURPHY'S Pub was a house of Official Irish Theme: four-leaf clovers, an Irish flag, green and orange everywhere. I ordered vodka. I sat at a wooden table in a wooden pew. The wood was carved with names. The vodka was like Sarah's nail polish remover, sharp and pungent and not altogether unpleasant.

The Seattle policeman, proud of his sleuthing, had said, "It only took us a few minutes to find the pub, since it's right across the street. The bartender said that he, your brother I mean, had a drink, used the phone. Under your name, there was Russian, on the wall? The witnesses on the ferry said he spoke Russian?"

"He did," I said. "But that's not my name."

Jennie goes to find the phone. A leprechaun in a skirt: LASSIES, the women's room sign says. A leprechaun holding a pot of gold: LADS. Between them a pay phone, and messages scribbled across the wall, numbers, invitations, partial records of conversations. Drawings of eyes, penises, hands, the Space Needle, and there. There, in the same handwriting that's on the postcard with the onion-topped buildings, the handwriting with the funny European eccentricities, her name: *Juniper Tree Burning*. Below it her phone number, and then the Russian message. He has drawn a box around the message. She touches it.

There's a change machine next to the jukebox. She slides in a twenty and catches the cascade of coins in her hands. Maggie's money. She returns to the phone with a pocketful of quarters. She dials and inserts them, one after the other, an orderly, methodical series of events leading to this:

"Hello," Chris says.

"Hello." She waits, but he doesn't respond. "It's Jennie," she says.

"I know."

She sucks in her breath and leans against the wall. "I've been calling," she says. "You weren't home."

"I had to *get* home first," he says.

She puts her hand over the mouthpiece and takes a deep breath. On

Chris's end, water runs, porcelain clinks. Her breath shudders out of her, like a child's who has been crying too long. I am weak, she thinks. I am weak.

I remembered how it felt when Chris cradled my blistered foot in his palm. The rat-a-tat of his knife as he chopped onions. My Cinderella slippers in the bedroom. The particulars of intimacy, tabulated only after they are lost. The way, after a fire, people must remember all the sundries of their lives, which suddenly seem as vital as air or water. That's the moment when you under-stand how weak you are, that you need everything, cinder-block shelves, black widows, cracked adobe. An unwashed brush, ruined by green paint. An evil, yellow-eyed cat named Bob.

She squeezes her eyes shut, but the tears escape. She presses her forehead into her palm. She takes her hand away and speaks evenly. "Are you doing dishes?"

"They have to be done," he says. "The world didn't stop because you got off." Someone asks a question. "It's her," Chris tells the someone.

"Is that Sarah?"

"Yes," he says.

"What's she doing there?"

He sighs. Porcelain clinks. "We drove all night. We were both exhausted. She wanted to come home with me, in case you were there. I told her you wouldn't be, but she insisted. We slept. She's feeding the cat."

Exactly, I thought. Exactly. Here's what he needs, a gorgeous little girl, full of all the love he craves. Exactly. She'll cry at the drop of his hat, her need for him corporeal as salt water. "What a cozy domestic adventure for you both." *No, no, no*—damn you, Jennie, damn you for picking exactly the wrong thing to say. Say, *Forgive me*. Say, *I was wrong*.

He turns off the water. "I'm hanging up now." But in the background, Sarah is screaming, *"Don't you fucking dare hang up."*

Let him have Sarah, who will slip into that cold, lonely bed and curl around him, warm him with softness and beauty. What are best friends for?

"What the *fuck*?" Sarah says to Jennie. "Where the *hell* are you?"

"Seattle."

Abruptly, her voice gentles, devastating. "Are you okay? Jennie, arc you okay?"

My face convulsed, seized, and I held it together with my hand and kept the phone away from me so she wouldn't hear the wretched sounds I made. Her tinny, distant voice called my name. At last, I controlled myself and re-turned the phone to my ear. "I'm in Seattle. In the pub. Where Sunny was."

Sarah, my Pea Princess, my unprecedented best friend, she whispers, "Oh my God." A muffled conversation with Chris, and now he's back on the phone. "What's the name of the bar?" Crisp, all business.

"I'm sorry," Jennie whispers, but you bitch, you've ruined things already.

"Sorry for what?" The pause stretches over these wires and miles. "What are you sorry about?"

"Everything," she says. I said. I say. I said *everything* and I came back to myself, understood what I wanted, saw the bartender across the room, watching daytime television.

"I want . . ." I said, and my voice caught. "I made a mistake."

"Yes," Chris said. "You did." And then, offering hope, a reason to stay put and not go do anything crazy: "Try not to make any more."

I whispered, "Do you think . . ." and my throat closed and I pressed my head against the wall and found my voice, and it took everything left in me to continue speaking: "Do you think you could come here?"

"We'll catch the next flight."

A sob rising in my throat. The bartender, a dancer, perhaps, is stretching with one foot up on the bar. He sees me watching him and hastily removes his foot. On TV an old comedy plays, simultaneously foreign and familiar. "It's raining," I whisper.

"Stay right where you are. We'll be there soon."

"Can I talk to Sarah?"

The phone, muffled. Whispers. Here she is, little friend.

"I don't know how to be without him," I said, my throat closing.

"Him," she said. "Him, Sunny? Him, Chris?"

I laughed. "You sound like a bad TV Western."

"Or Tarzan," she said, and she sounded so relieved to be joking. "Me, Jane. You're going to be okay, right?"

I asked for my backpack, a sweater. "It's fucking freezing here," I said. Smiles, laughter, an illusion of normalcy, banter: all this made it possible to close down the conversation without melodrama, as if we were all just fine. I played along. I owed them a little peace of mind, didn't I?

HERE is a woman on a day in August, sitting in a nearly empty bar. She does not look so good. Dirty, chopped-off hair, dark circles, red eyes, trembling hands. A drug addict? She slumps in her booth, crying silently, steadily, a leaking from her eyes. If you are the bartender, watching, you doubt she needs any more alcohol, and so you presume to take her a cup of coffee. You put it down and she looks up, the misery on her face so open and naked that it turns your stomach a little, as it always does to see a raw wound bleeding, to hear a person whimper. She says, "A while ago, a few days ago, I guess, there was a boy, a young man, who jumped off a ferry?"

"Yes," he says.

She says, so softly he almost doesn't hear, "He was my brother."

What is there to add, to say? He is dead, and nothing the bartender says or does will undrown him. The bartender, though, does not speak. He puts his hand on her shoulder, and keeps it there.

"I'm waiting for my husband," the woman says, looking down at her trembling fingers, as if to direct the bartender's attention to her marriage rings. "He has to come from New Mexico," she says. "It might take a while. Is that okay?"

And if you are the woman, you are ashamed to be asking for help. You're also relieved, because the bartender is kind. If you are the woman, you wonder if this day marks the end of your strength and the opening of the great yawning weakness inside you. You think of your mother and all her weeping need. But really, you ask yourself, is it really so much more honorable to refuse to lean on those who love you? Is it truly a sign of strength to go it alone?

The bartender set down a slice of pizza. "Just watch this," he said, pointing to the TV, "and try to eat."

I obeyed, swallowing and chewing, swallowing and chewing, watching the antics of TV people who were like neighbors: I knew them, but not really. From time to time, I'd realize that I was crying. This realization momentarily surprised me. But then my mind wandered back to the television, to the chill that blew in when the door occasionally opened, and I'd forget the tears.

The people moved on the television screen. The laughter swelled in a wave, and then fell away. I was warm and clean and my belly was full. I was crying in public.

Sunny came into this pub, and he charmed someone, a waitress. Or, if not a waitress, then maybe a friend. Maybe a boy on the ferry, a college boy with a crewcut who shared cigarettes with Sunny, took a pull from that flask he kept full of vodka. No, a group of boys, college boys, whom the policeman would later call witnesses.

How they loved their new friend! Of course they did; it was Sunny, handsome Sunny, laughing, spouting Russian as he climbed the rungs of the railing, as he balanced there, his black curls glossy for it wasn't raining that day, his eyes bright, light green, see-through. His wide, curling smile, and the little curves, like crescent moons, framing the corners. His face that if they weren't boys they'd call beautiful.

And there was a time when his head fit into the palm of my hand.

"Listen," I said to the bartender, "my husband will be coming, with a little red-haired woman. You can't miss her. Will you tell them I went—" He looked at me with gentle, attentive eyes, and I couldn't decide how to put it. "Tell them I'll be back," I said.

"Are you okay?"

"I have to go," I said, my own personal cliché.

I went to my ticket seller, the same woman with ruffles at her throat, and bought another ticket. This time I boarded the ferry. I joined the commuters inside under yellow heat lamps. We looked out through a badly scratched plastic window toward our various destinations.

The ferry moaned and crept away from shore. Its interior was much like a bus station: cold, the floor filmed with muddy water from the people's boots. Traveling is a series of the same. Dirty floors, molded plastic seats, sunrises, and bad coffee. This shivering woman, people—standing beside you in a T-shirt which is too cold for this weather—is sick of traveling. She's tired of the stubborn, redundant sun, rising and setting, endless revolutions and orbits. But don't be too troubled; she's going outside anyway.

The ferry had picked up speed. I stood on the deck and faced the brisk wind head-on. A man in shorts and a T-shirt was running the perimeter of the boat. He passed me twice.

Rain flew at me. I found the tip of the boat. The prow, if that's what it's called. A long stick extended over the waves, like a unicorn's horn. The water looked heavy, almost solid, blue-gray stone that moved. It spun out around the prow, then folded under the ferry.

The railing didn't have rungs, as I'd expected. It was a fence of waist-high wire mesh, topped by a handrail. Which meant that once Sunny got up there, he was committed. He could hold his balance only for a moment. But couldn't he have fallen backward as easily as forward? Returned by our savior, gravity, to the deck? Why not? He was the Backwards Boy.

Because, I answer myself. He wanted to go forward, into the sea. He chose it.

I put one foot up on that small space between the mesh and the railing, as if I were stretching a hamstring.

The running man trotted by. He would be my witness. He would say, I swear, Officer, I swear she only put her foot up, like she was stretching or tying a shoe, and I swear if I'd thought she was going to jump, I would've gone over and stopped her.

I put my foot back on deck. I leaned over the waist-high railing, and let my hands dangle over the side. I looked down into all that water. It was everywhere around me, in my cells and bones. All my life, I have believed I belonged with the ocean, as if it called me, as if, when I held a seashell to my ear, I heard not waves but a voice whispering, Come. Maybe we'd go one by one into the sea, the Lemming Family Davis.

I wanted to finish it. To stand on the rail as he had, waving. I lifted my feet off the deck, so that I balanced on my waist. Instantly, reflexively, my hands grabbed the railing. "Goddamn you!" I cried out to my disobedient hands, to

Sunny, to God Himself. God, *damn* You. Give me back my father, my mother, my home, my self. Give me back my brother. Please, please, God. Damn You. Please.

The wind blew my tears back with the rain and the sea spray and the three forms of water were indistinguishable. *Come,* the water called. I wanted to. I wanted to lie beside his body on the sand, under a blanket of sea.

I stood shivering: the best I could do. Soaked, teeth chattering, I thought, Maybe I'll catch pneumonia. Then I laughed. What was this supposed to be, penance? Would I ever have a pure moment of unself-conscious grief for my brother, or would it always feel like playacting? Would I ever just be, without watching myself, knowing that others were watching?

I joined the commuters inside, under heat lamps, and I sipped coffee along with them. The runner ran past periodically. We reached Bainbridge Island. More of the same. Green and gray and wet. I stayed on board and rode back to Seattle. I got off long enough to buy another ticket. The ticket lady with her prim mouth and ruffled collar didn't recognize me.

This time, on the way to Bainbridge Island, I thought about my grandmother Edna. Eighteen, on the water for the first time, just like me. Her beau digging his fingers into her neck and crying, *If you don't marry me I'll drown you.* Guess what, boys? Edna's grandson, my brother? Fifty years later, he took this same ferry and he jumped into the sea and he drowned. How's that for funny? How's that for ironic?

The next time I bought a ticket, the ruffled woman eyed me suspiciously. I smiled broadly at her, a strange and unpleasant stretching of my lips. I bought the third ticket at a different window. I took the trip again and again. Back and forth I went, until I lost track of how many times I crossed the water. I found that the longer I stood huddled in the brisk wind, the more numb I grew. My tears stopped. The sun came out for a while, and I was a little warmer. I felt a nice, steady, dull anesthetic take hold.

$\mathscr{T}$HERE WILL NEVER BE SIX

T H E ferry docked and I got off. There was a new shift of ticket sellers. I was in the act of handing over my money when Sarah, crying my name, flung her arms around me. "Jennie," she said, and she was crying. "Jennie, it's you."

I said, "Did you bring my backpack?"

"Nice to see you, too," she said.

"I'm sorry."

Chris, his hair and shoulders wet, stood at a distance. I tried to catch his eye, but he looked straight through me, as if I were transparent.

"You better be sorry," Sarah said. "You fucking well better be really fucking sorry." She did not let go of me.

"You're here," I said to Chris over her shoulder.

"We've been waiting for you," Chris said. "We figured you were on the ferry."

"I didn't jump," I said.

Sarah pulled away from me. "You *bitch*," she said. "You think that's funny? Don't you know you scared the *shit* out of me? Did you stop even for a second to consider that it would fuck me up for the rest of my life if you died, or didn't you remember that I'm a person whose father died in front of her eyes and whose fiancé recently dumped her? There's not a lot more I can take, you know." She threw her arms around me again. "God, you should have seen Maggie's face. It was worth it, almost, to see her face."

"Ma'am?" the seller said. "Ma'am?"

"One," I said.

"Three," Sarah said. "Like we're letting you on there alone."

"Did you bring my backpack?"

She shoved it at me. "Are you trying to hurt my feelings on purpose?"

I took the pack and held it against my chest. The nice, chilly numbness of the ferry riding was obliterated. My eyes burned. "I can't help it," I said, and the tears rolled. "I always say the wrong thing." To my ears, I sounded pathetic, whiny, selfish, and insufferable.

"Nice haircut," Sarah said. "You look like a refugee."

I wiped my eyes. "Like it? I'm thinking about getting a tattoo next." Banter. Evidence that one day, normalcy will prevail. But then an awkward silence descended between us. I searched my pack, sorting through clothes and papers which reeked of whiskey, cigarettes, sweat. I found the rumpled postcard with its sepia photograph. We always did like things old-fashioned, Sunny and me.

In Red Square, Sunny spins a rack of postcards, choosing this one, paying. Those onion-topped buildings are something out of a fairy tale. Jennie will love this, he thinks. Or, he thinks, Juniper will.

Sunny Boy Blue, come blow your horn. Where have you been, Charming Sunny? I've been to Russia, to visit the Bee Queen. He went in a wide-bodied jet, and when the stewardess in her smart blue uniform offered him lunch, he replied in Russian so perfect she asked him if he knew her sister in Siberia. What happened to you, Charming Sunny? Sunny Boy Blue, he drowned. This postcard, with its onion-topped castles, did not come from Russia. There's a U.S. copyright on it, and its caption is in English. So Sunny bought it somewhere on the West Coast. He mailed it last May. The postmark says Seattle. Did he even go to Berkeley? Or, after the wedding, did he skip school and hitchhike up the coast? Did it take him three months to get to Seattle? I could advertise, locate those who'd picked him up, truck drivers and loggers and ski bums. Or did he fly, arrive quickly, spend months here at the Edge of the World? Where did he sleep? I could track this down. Discover things. Maybe I could do what he did, look for Paul's house on the hill, get tired of ferns and rain.

And one day, on some nearby street, in some funky bookstore, I'd find a postcard like this one; I'd spin the very rack he touched, and I could even buy a duplicate and mail it to the husband who isn't speaking to me.

Sarah held fast to my hand, as if I might reboard the ferry alone and ride it back and forth forever, unable to jump into the water, unable to stay on land.

THEY followed me across the street, to Murphy's. I went to Sunny's message on the wall, and I found what I'd suspected: the Russian letters he'd scribbled there were exactly the same as those on the postcard. Relief surged through me. I could still understand. There was more to know. I could search out the clues. I could surmise, for instance, this: these messages were written three months apart, yet were identical. So they were probably memorized, a line of poetry, a song lyric, maybe. Or, more logically, more neatly, he might have written what he kept saying on the Rio Grande bridge, that proverb: *In Russia, hope is the last thing to die.* Better yet, I could translate it. Learn Russian. Go to Moscow. So long as I had something left to learn, he would continue to be alive for me. There would be no body, the tides like they are. I could tell myself, as I always had, Sunny is someplace in the world, living an adventure. Alive.

"You're shivering," Chris said. "You're soaked."

False relief is fleeting as rain. My shoulders were shaking because I was crying. It seemed to me, as I searched Chris's face for some softening, that he was thinking the question I always asked of Sarah. To what end these tears? I thought, To no end. They will go on and on, for no reason at all except for a stupor of grief. It sounded like a food. "Tonight I'll have the stupor of grief," I said. "With a side of self-pity."

"Don't make fun of yourself," Sarah said. "Shame on you." She handed me a sweater. "Put this on."

I obeyed. The thing was, it didn't matter at all, making neat associations, constructing hypotheticals and landing on likely answers. Sunny was gone. There would be no sixth chance to see him.

THE BEGINNING OF THE WORLD

Night, Saturday, Seattle

FROM the ferry, Sarah and I watched night fall over Seattle. The lights blinked on, brightly rimming the shore, an abrupt end to the water's dark simplicity. The cranes hung over the water's edge, their spindly limbs adorned with light. I looked behind me, toward Bainbridge and whatever lay beyond. Ferns and fog and mountains. The ocean and the islands in it. The wind blew down the nape of my neck.

The shore seemed to pull away from us. Chris was inside, buying coffee. Sarah clutched my hand and babbled frantically. Officer Gomez put out an APB on my truck, that piece of junk. Maggie wanted me arrested. They all fought and worried and then Chris said, "Let her be." Let her be, he said, like that, and then he took Sarah back to Albuquerque.

I knew what that was. It was Chris accepting what I'd given him. All right then, he thought, if that's how she wants it. Let her be alone.

He returned with our coffee. We huddled together at the railing, shrugged over our hot paper cups. I felt the heat travel all the way to my belly. "Thank you," I said. "That feels really good."

"You're welcome," he said. His formality frightened me.

"I'll tell you one thing, that Bob is one neurotic cat," Sarah said. "I think he secretly misses you." She tucked her hair inside her jacket and tried to light a cigarette. The wind blew out her lighter. Finally, she succeeded, although the smoke blew straight back and the cigarette quickly went out. "Fuck this," she said. "There's a reason nobody else is out here."

She went inside. I thought she was leaving us alone on purpose, and I was panicky at the thought. What would we say to each other?

Nothing, apparently. We stood side by side, not touching, not speaking. In the night, the water seemed a flat, calm, black. Bainbridge Island stood out as a darker line, sprinkled with lights. Toward Seattle, the sky was pink, though we could no longer see the city.

"Are you planning to stay in Seattle for a while?" Chris asked.

"What I want—" I said, and then I was afraid to continue. He was so polite.

Excruciatingly solicitous. I realized I had no desire to stay in this place. Yes, this was the city. Our Russia, Sunny's and mine, the land at the Edge of the World, home of Lipa and Paul. Seattle. Most likely on some hill around here, there was a house that I would recognize from pictures. I could call my mother, narrow down the location, climb some steps, if any were left. I could stand outside the remodeled, repainted house and stare. A woman would emerge, wiping her hands on her apron: Can I help you with something, dearie?

Did Sunny find the house? Sunny, climbing the steps, standing on the walk, waiting. For what? For everything I'd promised him—love and peace and candy bars—to come out the front door. Hands shoved deep in his army-jacket pockets, he waits for happiness in an apron, which looks like violets and tastes like blueberries and sounds like a piano. He stands, listening to the distant boats, shivering in the damp evening, staring at this familiar, unfamiliar house. Not his home. Just a structure, made slightly recognizable by a few stolen photographs. He sees a girl pull aside a lace curtain and then duck out of sight. He knows he's waiting for the impossible, but he can't quite make himself turn away. In his pocket, he finds the silver flask. The smooth weight of it fits neatly into his palm.

He turns to leave, and he cannot see Mount Rainier because of clouds. Even that isn't how they dreamt it.

I unwound the bandage on my hand and felt the cold air hit my bare skin. I opened and closed my fingers, and the bandage caught the wind and blew back like a scarf. I let it go. Released, my skin tingled. "Where's Bob?" I asked timidly.

"I left him with the neighbor girls," Chris answered. Politely.

Sunny Boy Blue's soft spot pulses. Ray's shoes squeak on the hospital floor. Sunny helps Juniper carry a Christmas tree. Resplendent, tuxedoed, Sunny holds up his hand, fingers spread, palm out, like a demand for me to stop: *Five times, Juniper. Five times.* My brother is gone. He is sitting in the culvert, between my knees, laughing. Yet he is gone.

Those memories coming at me were prayer.

Not spoken prayer, not in words, but if prayer is begging for what you don't have, then I prayed.

"Chris," I said. He didn't shift his gaze. "Chris," I said again. "I'm sorry." He didn't answer. I took a deep breath. "You *should* be angry." Sorry is such a worthless word.

"You don't owe me anything."

"Yes, I do." I could just make him out, a dim shadow beside me. My coffee was gone. I moved to the trash can and Chris spoke to me from a distance. "You can't fix things just like that."

I stood beside him and I felt that spread of railing between us as he must have felt the space between us for these many months past. An endless expanse of a few inches. "I know," I said. I took a deep breath. I turned to the darkness that was the water and shivered, folding my arms around myself, and when I spoke, what I said came out of me whole, and fierce, a monster that had waited all these years to escape its cage.

When I was thirteen, I said, I tried to enroll myself in catechism, and I know I told you about it, and ho ho ho, isn't it a poignant funny story. Let's all pat Jennie on the back. And it's true that I rode the bus to Upper Alfin, and it's true that I watched my classmates cross themselves, envying their signal to God that they belonged to his Club. But what I don't say is this lovely fact: when I hunched down in that green vinyl seat, watching them step off the bus, I stuck my thumb into my mouth and sucked hard, my tongue pressing against the familiar lump of the knuckle, the hard nail, and I stroked my soft, silky, cool nose. This was comfort. Yeah, suck hard, little Juniper. Listen to the children whispering and giggling; feel them yank your hair and do what your mommy told you to do: ignore them. Look out the window at the church, at the Garduños' pink house with its real toilet, and suck hard, child, suck hard for the polluted nutrition of your thumb fitting neatly to the top of your mouth, your spit making a nice soup with the grime on your skin, the filth under your nail; smell your rancid breath wafting into your palm, because these things are yours; they if nothing else are yours.

And let's be careful here, I said—clutching the cold metal bar that stood between me and the ocean—before I glamorize this isolated child sucking her thumb, consider her fourth-grade picture: she's an ugly kid. Her nose is big and her eyes are beady and she grimaces instead of smiling. Her dress is too small. Where did she get such a stupid dress, tight against her flat chest? Her blond hair is tucked like straw behind her big ears, and her fingernails are filthy with black dirt that shows up even in this cheap school picture. Because when you don't have running water, there are a few things your parents might forget to teach you. Washing your hands. Brushing your teeth.

Let's be objective. Let us try to see this girl for what she is, a dirty little girl, Juniper Tree Burning in her clothes that her mother found by fishing through the discards of others, the triumphant lifting of the dress still in its cellophane wrapper, and this girl, this Juniper, she doesn't even have the good sense to know that the brand-new dress, of which she is so proud, is also two sizes too small.

All she knows is that this dress is hers, and that modicum of acquisition fools no one but her; should we judge her for this? Yes, let's call her foolish and an idiot, and let's call her pathetic, with her messy hair and smile that says, *Please for a moment can't I be a beautiful, normal kid?*

Let's not, not glamorize this. The loneliness of a lonely, socially inept child is a disgusting thing to see. It's vile and embarrassing, like seeing an old woman shit her pants in church. Of course you pity her. Of course you don't turn when you smell it—you just go on praying and singing—and of course you don't turn when she shuffles out of church, trying to pretend she's not stinking up this house of God—of course you stay face-to-face with Jesus, praying you won't be like that someday, never you—why couldn't she hold it? Why did she have to shit her pants in church, during Mass, when we all had to look?

A lonely child is like this, the weakest outcast girl with her wrong hair, wrong smile, wrong dirty fingernails: pathetic, pathetic girl. You want to say, What makes her so clumsy, so desperate, so hungry? So *wrong*? What makes her, regardless of her family, so incapable of simple friendship? Why can't she teach herself to brush her hair, to clean her nails, to wear clothes that fit and talk to the children around her, and what *is* it that she does, to make them hate her so? Who cares. Let her eat worms. Don't you *dare* pity her; hate her for what she is; hate her for being the one who lets herself be ridiculed, who lowers her head and inserts a thumb into her mouth and who never turns to ask, Do you want to come over to my house? because how they would laugh at this small request that trips so easily from the lips of children less contemptible than she.

If she could, she would go to the Catholic church and pray for the girl in the picture, who is herself. Maybe that's why we hate her, pathetic child. She can't pray for herself, and who in the church will stand to announce, *That woman over there has soiled herself. Let us pray for her wounded pride, for her shattered dignity, and for God's sake, let us address the small brown gush on her pew bench; let us pray it never happens again, or at least not where we can see it.* No one will stand in the church. Better to keep the old lady out. Better to keep the church doors closed, to block the entrance and say, Old Woman, your bowels have failed you, and Old Woman, stay home. Stay home. The world is a church and the outcasts aren't welcome, so here's the lesson, the moral of my little tale: to change your name, sneak inside the world, lock the door and shout at her, *You, Girl Who Sucks Her Thumb, go home.* Go huddle in a cracked-open house. There is no place for you here in the world, on this bus, in this church, in Upper Alfin, you with your bad hair and dirty thumbnail stuck into your dirty mouth. Go home, Weeping Willow, Burning Bush Bush Bush, and your mother will say—

I couldn't speak; my face convulsed and I covered this ugliness with my hands—and your mother—

"Jennie," Chris said softly, but I shook off his hand when he reached for me—"And your mother," I said, but my voice failed again.

"Jennie," he said.

"Your mother, she says 'What do you do to make them hate you?' You want to say, *God, don't you think if I knew I would stop? Don't you think I've spent my whole life trying to stop?* Because you hate her, too, that ugly pathetic child Juniper, you *hate*—"

He had me in his arms. I fought him. Sobbing, I struggled, but he held me fast and he didn't say anything except, "Cry, cry, oh my poor beautiful Jennie, go ahead and cry." I cried and choked on my crying and still beneath it was this: Juniper. She is always there, crouched inside me, twisting me until I don't know who I am, and I am running but she's still on my heels, always ugly, always doing it wrong, always hated, always crying, always waiting to drive them away. And now, Sunny Boy Blue, the only one who loved her purely and who made her feel for a time as if she could get it right: now he has gone into the sea, and all the crying in the world cannot undrown him, and you are crying after him, too late, *I'm ashamed, I'm ashamed, God forgive me, I'm ashamed of what I've done.*

I stopped, eventually. I looked up at my husband. I touched his lips, his high cheekbones, his slanted eyes. "Be angry," I said. "Be furious. I ran away. I left you alone."

His tears trembled in his eyes.

"I don't want you to hate me," I said. "You're—" I took a shuddering breath. "You're my husband," I whispered. "You're my family." I put my arms around him, and his arms came around me, and his nose pressed into my hair. I smelled the wet wool of his sweater. I welcomed the texture, the rise and fall of his breath, the beat of his heart. I'd misjudged him completely. He wasn't weak at all. This was a man who kept his parents' gift, the Rolls, though he winced every time he drove it. A man who declared his unfolding love in grocery stores, who gave me shoes, and gloves, and, so easily and generously and with such conviction, his heart. This was the most astonishing thing about him, his bravery, in loving as he did. Loving, of all people, me. *My God,* I thought. *My God, I love him.* Not despite his bending and swaying. Because of it.

He said, "If you insist, then I'm still mad."

I smiled and wiped my eyes. Inside his arms, with the world narrowed to his warm shelter, I could say the truth. "I left Sunny behind."

"You were just a little girl."

"No. I was a grown woman. I should have done something."

"You're one person."

"He needed me, and I didn't do anything."

All right then. There it is. The terrible power of *What If*, the new and permanent member of my family. What If's lover, *If Only*. And their infant offspring, *What Is*. I held on to my husband with all of my strength. "I'm sorry," I said. "I wish I hadn't hurt you."

"Maybe it was necessary."

Flooded with gratitude, drowning in it, I was frightened "I'm pathetic," I said. "I'm weak. Look at me."

He laughed. "Jennifer, everyone needs to rest now and then. Even God Himself took Sunday off."

"Do you think you'll forgive me?"

"I can't tell the future." Then he relented. "You're my wife," he said gently. "It's part of the bargain."

"I'm a lot of trouble."

"Serves me right. I knew you were difficult when I married you."

Miracles. The kindness returned to my husband's eyes. The joy I feel at seeing it. To relax for a moment against his collarbone, inside his arms. Such a feat, to allow myself this rest. Please God. Let me be brave enough for this. Let me be careful and brave with what he offers me.

W E went inside and found Sarah sitting under the heat lamps. "Are you guys made up now?" she asked. "Because I really can't take more than one major breakup per year."

We looked at each other. "For now," I said. "I guess so," he said, both of us cautious, both of us knowing that forgiveness can't be made in a moment; it can only begin with one.

I sat between them. We couldn't see anything of our progress through the scratched Plexiglas, with the dark outside. Well, I thought. What next? I closed my eyes. They returned to me, my brown-eyed children, tucked inside my arms, eager to hear their parents' love story. So they were still possible.

"You're tired," Chris said. "Why don't you sleep?"

"What next? Will we live happily ever after?"

"Why don't we just live?" Chris said. "See how it goes?"

What should I tell my children? Where should I begin? If Chris and I remain together, if we ever have even one child, a daughter, I'll have to tell her that once I left her father, just like Grandpa left Grandma. What kind of love will my daughter salvage out of what I tell her? What stories will she choose for my mother, my father, and, I hope, for me?

I will tell my daughter, *I had a brother. His name was Sunny Boy Blue.*

I leaned on Chris and his arms encircled me. Days without sleep or much food and far too much running caught up with me. I lay on the line between sleeping and waking. The memories rushed at me. My father offering the heart of a deer. Flickering candles, my mother's screams, the piano's keys, music. Sunny dancing in my mother's belly.

I will tell my daughter, *He had see-through eyes and he was born backwards.*

The heat lamps are hot sunshine on my eyelids. Freshly washed diapers cling to my face, and the sun through the muslin is church light. The damp cloth sucks into my nose and mouth with every breath. My brother is heavy and solid in my arms. My husband's chest rises and falls.

Beneath me, the ferry's engine throbbed, a heartbeat, a drum, the footfalls of someone running. She has always been hot on my heels, that little girl, Juniper. Here she is now, with her tangled hair. The lice crawl in; the lice crawl out. Hinting, begging, needing, stealing what she can. Acting as if she doesn't care. Hiding inside her own face. Oh, Juniper. We are the same, you and me.

I opened my eyes. "I'm still here," Chris said. "So far so good."

Prayer, I remembered, is not only for making demands; it's also for gratitude. Heavenly Father God, thank you for Chris's sure hands, for Sarah's bright hair. I closed my eyes.

Sunny's laughter spirals down the concrete culvert and flies into the hot summer air. Little Faith, dressed in her Sunday best, swings a pail of blueberries. The tin roof screams as it twists in the fire. *Go home, Sunny,* I say to him, as he stands, sweating and sunburned in the hotel lobby. His eyes, pale, see-through green. His bony shoulders. *Sunny, go home.* I am lifting my wedding skirts and running away, and he is laughing, calling, *Juniper Tree Burning! You get your ass back here! Come back or I'll jump!*

I opened my eyes. "Still here," Chris said. He laid his palm over my forehead. I closed my eyes and the past rushed at me, alive and as present as the present.

"Sleep," Sarah said.

Here. Rest, drifting between sleep and waking, between Sarah and Chris. *I don't deserve them.* I shivered, but then I sighed, and my shoulders released, and I was warm. *Yet they are here.*

I wanted to go home. To the wide-open sky, to dry air and fierce sun, where water is scarce and thirst is common, where apricots rot beside wishing wells and small stubborn trees grow on hot, dusty hills. Take me to the place where the piano doesn't play but the drums always do, where babies come backwards in cracked-open houses. Hurry, hurry me there, to a place where history is fluid but truth remains rooted, oh, hurry me home in your arms, inside what comfort you can offer. Tell me what I can give to you. Take me to what is and not what might have been.

I am Jennifer Braverman who is also Juniper Tree Burning. I am a sister whose brother is dead. I can't know the future, but I believe there will be days of grief, nights of mourning. If people don't say, *Not Sunny Boy Blue,* then I'll say it myself. There will be a Funeral Meeting in Arroyo al Fin, where he came backwards into the world. There will be apricot pies and watermelon and Bit-O-Honey. We, meaning my father, my mother, and I, will kneel through the night, each of us remembering the many ways we failed him, and the many ways we didn't. We'll pray, offer gratitude and hope for us all. In the morning, we'll be dazzled by the sunshine and the sky which is blue like forever, and my husband and my friend will be there. I'll say to them, to all of my family, Let us begin again here. I will say, I'm sorry. I will say to my father and mother, I think I understand. You did your best. You loved this valley, nestled into the mesa. Though it cracked and burned and ached with grief, it was my brother's home, and mine as well. Arroyo al Fin, that place with a river through its heart, where all that I am begins and ends and begins again.

Acknowledgments

A Litany of Heartfelt Gratitude:

To the following institutions, for supporting me while I wrote this book: The Iowa Writers' Workshop, The Creative Writing Program at Stanford University, The Ucross Foundation, The Virginia Center for the Creative Arts, the Cottages at Hedgebrook, the Michener-Copernicus Society, and the Hackney Literary Award for the Novel. To Robert Boswell, a wonderful teacher and writer, who was there when I first wrote about these characters. To my exceptional teachers Antonya Nelson, Kevin McIlvoy, Anne Rohovec, Frank Conroy, Marilynne Robinson, Elizabeth Benedict, Nancy Packer, and Jim McPherson. To Thom Jones. To Deb West and Gay Pierce. To the fabulous and gifted René Todd, magnificent reader, writer, and friend. To Michael Byers, who read multiple drafts; to Bay Anapol; to Ann Williams and Andrea Bewick; to the many other talented writers and readers along the way, especially Nan Cohen, who gave exactly the right feedback at exactly the right moment. To my sister, Keja, who was the first of my family to read this book. To Detective Allen James and Dan the Alpha Omega Man, for technical advice. To Dr. Paul Cutler, for Sarah's diagnosis. To those who housed, fed, and tolerated me, especially The Four Blairs, Martin and Cathy, Pudding House, and Solveig and Jake Sedlet. To Grandma Norma Darrah; this book is for her, too. To the wonderful Harriet, an artist in her own craft. To Margaret Locatelli. To Kyung Cho. To Jane Dystel and Jo Fagan. To the staff of Simon & Schuster, particularly Suzanne, Nicole, and Tara. And to the indefatigable, extraordinary, brilliant, beautiful gift from God: Marysue Rucci, my fabulous editor. And to Sean, of course, and always. He knows why.

I am on my knees to you all.

ABOUT THE AUTHOR

GOLDBERRY LONG is a graduate of the Iowa Writers' Workshop. She has received various awards and fellowships, including a Wallace Stegner Fellowship, a James Michener Fellowship, and a Hackney Literary Award for the Novel. She has held residencies at the Cottages at Hedgebrook, Ucross, and the Virginia Center for the Creative Arts. A native New Mexican, she lives in northern California with her husband, a Canadian molecular biologist, where she runs, teaches writing, and walks her dog.